A PROMISE OF POWER

For Dan.

THRANE
ARGAL
Westwatche
Obsidian Mountains
Necrium
Nighhelm
ICENA
Caern
Seahenge
Eastwatche
Godsreach
Croydyn
Highclere
Aremore
VIKANDAL
River Steyr
STRAETH
Iren Mountains
IRE
Evoire
Ealdtown
Yalstad
Hartford
Iren River
ANDAR
Kilney
Kingsport
King's River
LOCHLAND
Parsielle
King's Cross
Isle Cassia
Port Lethney
PARTHE
OSTALLA
Merida

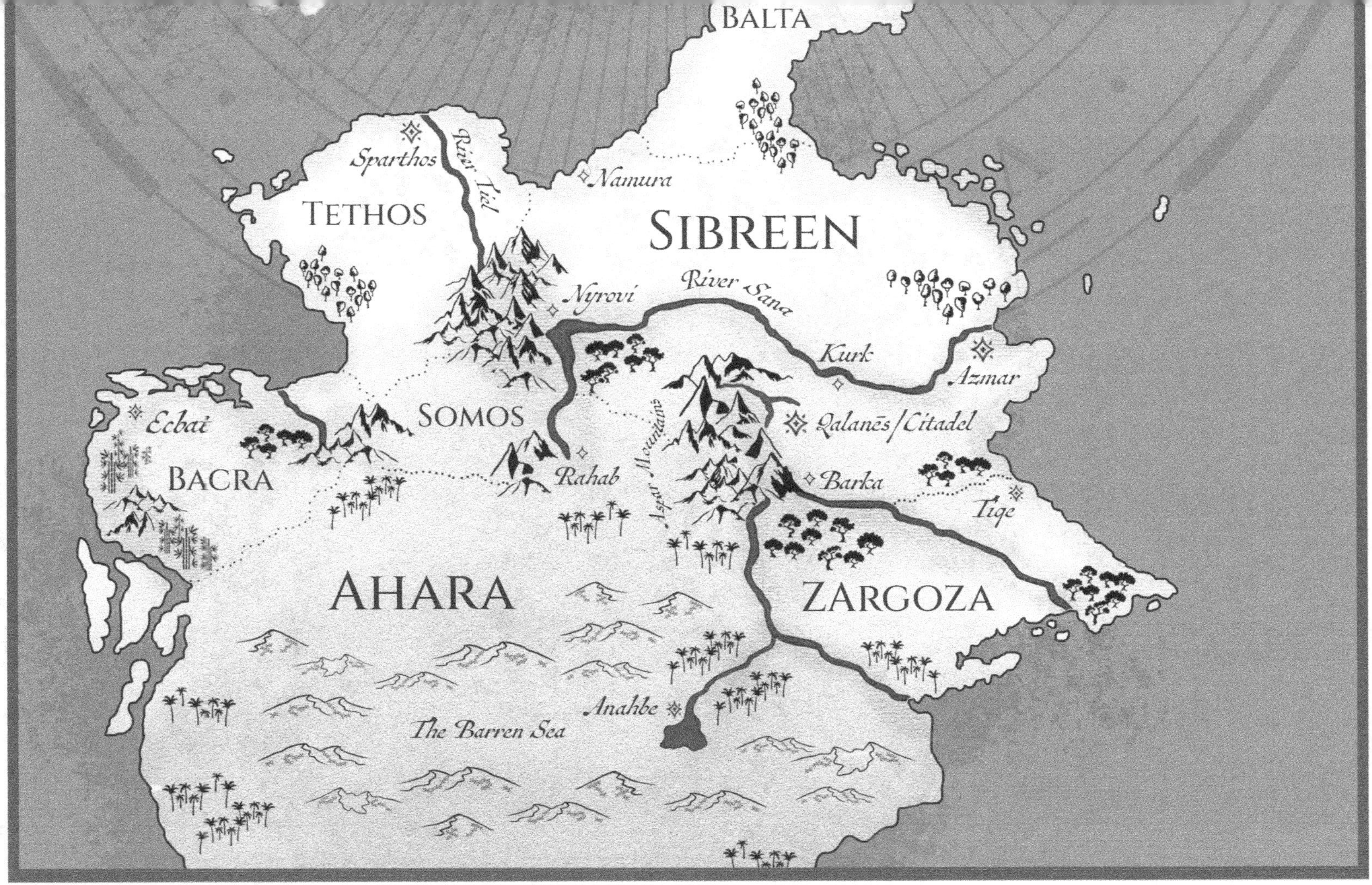

BALTA
SIBREEN
TETHOS
Sparthos
River Tiel
Namura
Nyrovi
River Sana
Kurk
Azmar
Somos
Qalanēs/Citadel
Ecbat
Bacra
Rahab
Aspar Mountains
Barka
Tige
Ahara
Zargoza
Anahbe
The Barren Sea

AUTHOR'S NOTE

This story contains subject matter that may be difficult for some readers. For a list of advisories, please visit rachelenriquez.com/contentwarnings.

PRONUNCIATION GUIDE

PLACES
Ire: I-er
Thrane: Thrayn
Straeth: Strayth
Parthe: Parth
Sibreen: Si-breen
Qalanēs: Kal-a-nees

OTHER
Elah Esērii: El-ah Eh-sear-ee
Hais z'Nosiš: Hise za-No-seesh

CHARACTERS
Neith: Neeth
Calithea: Cal-a-thee-a
Nara: Nar-ah
Catrianna: Cat-ree-on-a
Cerys: Care-iss

SURNAMES
Ironne: I-urn
Dracos: Dray-kohs
Nyanthi: Nigh-ann-thee
Turan: Tur-uhn

1

Neith

"For their misdeeds and transgressions, the Gods struck Etherborn from our world, declaring never again shall mankind wield."

HEXADIC PRECEPTS
ZATHRIAN BYGRAVE, 719 AQ

The village burned. Bright, beneath the shroud of night. At such a distance, it appeared to breathe. Gentle inhales and exhales, swelling and subsiding. Distant screams united in choir, echoing up the mountainside. She found it a mesmerizing, yet foreboding, sight.

Neith Dracos sat atop her horse, flanked by her father and brother, overlooking the village of Godsreach. Or better, what had been. By her estimation of the moon's progression, it had taken one hundred of her father's men less than one hour to raze it.

A wisp of her black hair caught in the wind. The dry, bitter air blew harsh on her cheeks. Neith reached for the hood of her cloak, pulling it closer around her face. Time had long turned winter to spring, but the season's last snow still clung to the earth as it did every year in the far north. *How odd it is*, she thought. *Too hot and it burns, too cold and it burns.*

Her father's horse stepped forward. Moonlight blanketed the cliff, reflecting shades of azure on its onyx coat. Neither horse nor man feared the edge.

"This is where it begins," he said. "It is time for us to take our rightful place. Far too long we've lingered in the shadows of this world." His horse pawed at the rocky earth, in beat with his words, as though his restless spirit was shared between them. "For over twenty years, we've prepared. We've sacrificed," he continued. "A new age of wielding is born this night. Etherborn will reign again."

Lorcan Dracos was not a man prone to exhibition, but Neith felt the appetite in his manner. In the quick darting of his gaze. In his grip on the reins. It smoldered around him, quiet but palpable, as if she could reach out and be singed by it. All he had worked for was finally in motion.

Dread blossomed in her belly. She clenched her hands to fists to still their tremble. Neith had not borne witness to a battle in her nineteen winters—not a true one. Her entire life had been a preparation for this day. The training was supposed to prepare her. She felt anything but.

Her father held out his right hand, palm open to the night. Neith felt his call to his power as a small, silver flame ignited, hovering above his skin. He cradled it between his fingers, kindling the etherfire, feeding it until the metallic glow grew the size of his fist. He released it before them, illuminating their path down the mountain.

Neith knew she would be forever altered, changed by what she would see, what she might do. But there was no going back. The war had begun.

"Come," he said, bidding his horse forward.

Roman encouraged her to follow with a flick of his chin, moonlight intensifying the sharp angles of his face. It was resolute, but lacked the quiet frenzy of their father's. Neith was often told she'd inherited her softness, roundness of cheek from their mother. No matter their differences, there was no mistaking Neith nor Roman as the children of Lorcan. Every Dracos in her father's line shared the same pale blue eyes, alabaster skin, and midnight-black hair.

Roman's long, lean body was upright, but his shoulders eased. He was not gathering his courage as she was. It made her feel clumsy and ill-prepared, fueling her dread.

Neith looked back to Thrane, to the home she'd never left. To the safety of the Obsidian Mountains, snowcapped, black, and cold. It was a grim sight paralleled by the endless sea of green opposing it. But it was known. It was home.

"*Neith,*" her brother said with a disgruntled urgency, companioning the wrinkle in his brow.

Neith knew she was standing on a boundary of more than one kind, once crossed, crossed forever. She swallowed, stroking the white-and-gray brindled coat of her horse. "Let's on, Storm," she said.

With a gentle nudge, they descended.

✛

They followed their father down the rough path carved out by the soldiers who'd preceded them. Trees had been ripped from the earth and cast aside, roots exposed. She remembered the sounds as they'd watched from above. Like a storm, decimating and destroying all in its path.

The devastation had not diminished the forest's beauty. Little promises of spring were scattered about the earthy floor. Neith marveled at the vivid greens and delicate pastels. Despite the darkness, the abundance of color was an affecting contrast to the barren forests of her homeland.

Neith's understanding of these foreign lands existed only in her mind, drawn from books and stories of others. She envisioned temples with tall marble statues and painted glass. There were no such buildings or monuments in Thrane. There were in fact no such traces of the Faith at all. She wondered if they would still be standing when she walked the streets of Godsreach.

Anticipation pooled metallic on her tongue. Every time she swallowed, it returned, more bitter than before. A feral impulse to flee plagued all her limbs. *Run*, it said. *Before it's too late.* Glancing back at her brother for a sign she wasn't alone, she found his resolve unaltered. His gaze on her tightened with a gentle warning to keep on.

Figures took shape through the trees as the forest thinned. A group of soldiers stood at attention when her father emerged into the clearing.

"Lord King," said the captain, bowing on one knee, fist to his chest, in full Thranean salute. "What little resistance we met has been overruled. The surviving villagers have been gathered by the temple. All is as you commanded."

He looked young to be a captain, Neith thought, but he bore the rank badge on his black leather vest. Perhaps a couple winters her senior, he was tall and slender built, his skin a warm, tawny brown. Loose, dark curls encompassed his face. Neith felt the hum of his ether immediately, considerable and affecting. It would explain his quick rise in the ranks.

"Where is Magnus?" Lorcan queried, stepping down from his horse.

"Waiting for you at the temple, Lord King. I will take you to him now." The captain offered Neith his assistance to dismount. When their hands connected, so too did their eyes, and she felt the full impact of his power, undiluted by the fabric of her gloves. It was unlike any she had felt before, and it sparked curiosity on what his particular strengths might be.

He had a lightness that reminded her of air. Something gentle, but could rage and destroy if summoned—or pressed to.

Neith considered if she had encountered him before, quickly deciding not. She would have remembered him. She would have remembered that power.

His gaze lingered on hers as if perceptive of her examination. When the moment grew long, he looked down, bowing his head in a gesture for her to pass. She met eyes with her father, who looked from her to the captain before he turned, making his way toward the orange glow of Godsreach.

For every step of her father's, Neith took two to keep pace. The air turned warmer as they grew closer, heating her cheeks in a reverse of the chill they'd so recently possessed. It felt more a warning than comfort, and she wiped the sweat from her brow, telling herself it was the air, and not her dread.

There were no marble statues, no tall buildings, and no painted windows. Dwellings assembled from wood with thatched roofs lined the streets. Some still stood, still burning, the upper levels collapsed. Most were little more than fragmentary remains, black ash, and soot. The smoky air was acrid and scratched at her throat. Neith tugged at the clasp around her neck.

It was all a startling contrast from her home in Necrium. The Thranean capital was built from blackstone mined from the mountains surrounding it. She could not picture it burning. She thought it more likely to melt, the stone returning to the earth from which it was carved.

The dirt streets were turned to mud by the fight. There was not a single cobblestone or stepstone in sight. Her cloak and skirts grew heavy as they trudged on, boots sinking into wet imprints made by another. Every footprint followed the same path. She pictured the townsfolk running, and the Thranean soldiers giving chase.

The further they traveled, the more difficult it became to dull her senses. Neith tried averting her gaze and thinning her breath. It was not long before the efforts proved futile.

Bodies were everywhere, scattered about as if they'd been dancing, only to perish midstep. One could barely distinguish the dead from the dying. Their withering cries haunted the night, pleading for a savior who would not come. Spilled bowels and bloodshed poisoned the air, in testimony to their suffering. To their inevitable end.

A man lay face down in the street. He jerked, not with life, but from the efforts of a Thranean soldier endeavoring to wrench free the ax buried in his back. The soldier looked up and released the weapon, then began to drag the corpse from their path. Neith looked at her brother and again found him unaltered.

A child's cry drew her attention. A boy wept, clutching a lifeless form she could only assume had been his mother. Filth, blood, and soot stained his skin, its paleness of color revealed solely by the streams of tears pouring down his cheeks. Three winters he was, at most, she thought.

Neith had seen men die. She had been present at executions from the time she was a small child. But they were thieves, murderers, rapists, traitors. They weren't farmers and miners. They weren't children.

Terror washed through her, cold, and heavy in her chest, halting her step, the sinister scene threatening to undo her. She wanted to look away, to save herself from the image, knowing it was the sort that sticks. Always there, waiting for you to close your eyes. She did not know one so small could show such despair. It felt wrong in ways she could explain, and in ways she could not.

A hand rested on her shoulder. She looked up to find her father peering down, thoughtful, as if sensing her turmoil.

"These people do not deserve your pity, Neith. They made Gods of ghosts. They are ruled by fear," he said, with evident disgust. "They are weak."

She watched as a soldier lifted the boy onto a cart with children of a similar age, also weeping, or paralyzed in fear. "What will become of him?"

"He is liberated. Freed from the restraints created by his forebears." Her father spoke assuredly, as if no challenge to his words existed. "Look at me."

She did. His furrowed brow told her she failed to keep the terror from her face. His grip on her shoulder tightened, and she could not tell if it was meant to be a comfort or warning.

"Your tenderness to this will harden. Forget not these zealots, these *fools*, are the reason your mother was taken from you—from us."

Neith looked back to where the boy had been, at the woman's body, bloody and lifeless. She spoke low, almost under her breath. "And now we take their mothers from them."

"It is the way of war, Neith."

She tried to pull at that anger. It lived in her somewhere. But it's hard to mourn someone you've never known. Neith could only regret the absence of her. How easily she might have been that boy, crying over her mother's burned body. Raised by the very people who took her life, but too young to remember, too young to understand the injustice of it. *It is the way of war,* she repeated in her mind. Neith turned back to her father and nodded. She flexed her hands and continued walking.

The surviving townsfolk huddled together by the temple—largely elders, women, and children clinging to their mothers' skirts. An old man in gray robes stood forefront. A priest, she assumed, by his adornments. Neith had never seen one in the flesh. Only sketches in books of men with elaborately woven robes that looked more like gowns, and bizarre hats that would seemingly do little to warm one's head. This man seemed an impoverished adaptation. She watched him curiously as he stared down the Thranean soldiers, his arms outstretched as if he could shield those who stood behind him. He clutched a tall staff with a six-point star at its peak. Neith recognized it as the symbol of the Faith of the Hexad, representing the Gods, one point for each. It was wooden and heavy, clearly a struggle for him to brandish. His manner suggested he believed it would protect them. *What fools they are, indeed.*

Her father's soldiers stood in bordering rows, appearing a daunting force. The Thranean patch of silver stitches in the design of tall mountain peaks distinguished itself from the black leather of their uniforms.

The temple was the only stone building Neith had seen on their walk through Godsreach. It was two stories, and finely crafted, with a towering painted glass window, telling stories in imagery of their Gods.

Cassia, Goddess of Light, arms outstretched toward the sun.

Adrae, Goddess of Darkness, holding the moon between her hands.

Pyramus, God of Water, channeling a river's path.

Sydel grew from the earth.

Bacchus channeled the air.

The fire of Thelos burned bright.

All six Gods were represented. It was nonsense, Neith thought, but beautiful nonsense.

As if on cue, fire roared, and the window shattered. It sent a ripple of cries through the townsfolk. Their place of worship now an inferno of violence.

This wasn't what Neith had expected. The scale was unbalanced. It was like asking a spider to survive the bottom of her boot. It had little chance, save for her mercy.

Beside the temple, five knelt, hands bound behind their backs. A group of soldiers encircled them, including Magnus, general of the Second Division. A shield poured from the palm of one of the soldiers, taking on the subtle yellow hue of her power, containing the captives beneath. Neith studied their faces through the iridescent sheen. Their eyes darted frantically from soldier to soldier. Some sobbed, heads hanging low. A middle-aged woman with stark red hair stood out. She stared them down, defiance and hate in her eyes. They were injured, burned, bleeding. They'd put up a fight.

Neith sensed their gifts. All five were Etherborn. Dressed like villagers, they wore no insignia or identifying markers, but she knew who they were. Who they could only be. Elah Esērii.

She'd seen Esērii before, most commonly at their executions. On occasion, they were caught attempting to slip through the wards at the borders of Thrane. No matter how many never returned, the Esērii continued to send them. Lorcan told his children it was indicative of their thoughtlessness for their people. A people her father himself once belonged to.

For over four hundred years, the Esērii, shrouded in shadow, turned the wheels of the world, pulling the strings of kings and queens. Living in secret, among the common man, they believe the world is safer, that Etherborn are safer, if kept secret from those born idle. They believe their cause noble, their actions just. Taking babes from their mothers' breasts and raising them in their ranks to do their bidding. They sacrifice whatever and whomever deemed necessary for their cause. It was why her father rebelled against them so many years ago.

They'd known they would find Esērii in Godsreach. Her father planned for it. Their people were stationed in every kingdom throughout the north and south.

Magnus emerged, making his way toward them. "Lord King," he said, deep voice rumbling as he bowed his head.

"Standings?" Lorcan asked, taking in the scene.

"We lost four infantry, no Etherborn. We found seven Esērii, and two fell. We hold the other five." Magnus gestured to the group.

Lorcan pursed. He motioned for Roman. "Scan the immediate area. I expected more."

Her brother nodded and signaled for Katya, his Second. Her long, ice-white hair was pulled tight in a braid trailing down her back, adding to the severity of her look. Beautiful in an ominous way, like a viper. They disappeared around the temple into the tree line on the edge of town, followed by several others from Roman's unit.

"Hello, little one," Magnus said, coming to stand next to Neith. Towering well over a foot in excess of her, his massive stature was imposing to those who did not know him. His rich umber skin formed a striking contrast to her own. He looked her over, dark eyes analyzing. She sensed concern despite his attempts to conceal it. Magnus was her father's most trusted adviser and the only man she would consider his friend.

Neith only nodded, fearful her voice would come out unsteady.

Her father walked to address the townsfolk. They cowered, taking nervous, collective steps back at his approach. Only the priest stood firm. Most cast their gaze down. It stirred and tugged at something in her, something she wanted to rip free. These were the people who had murdered her kind for centuries. Hunted them down under the fallacy that their gifts were a stolen sorcery. An affront to their Gods. Her father, this war, would restore Etherborn to the ruling class, as it had been twelve hundred years ago, before the Great Quell. As it should be. Neith forced herself to stare them down, grasping at a hate she feared didn't exist for her.

"People of Godsreach," her father called out. "I beseech you hear me. I am Lorcan Dracos, son of Godric, and rightful king of Thrane." That was enough to inspire whispers. Ordinary people had no news of Thrane since the death of the previous king twenty years past, when an already obscure kingdom went quiet. They feared little threat due to the dense mountain range surrounding Thrane's eastern, western, and southern borders. It would have been considered impossible to march a meaningful force through, much less an entire army. Until now.

"Know now you live under my rule," he continued. "Know now you look to me. You will throw down your idols and kneel to your king."

"We will not." The priest stepped forward, the staff clutched tight with both hands. He shook it at her father, which drew patronizing smirks and low chuckles from the soldiers looking on.

"Step back, priest," her father warned. Warnings were not often something Neith heard him make.

The priest lifted his chin.

Her father let out a slow, agitated breath. He raised an arm, and tendrils of silver ether raced from his palm, wrapping around the wooden staff in a blink. He retracted the ropes, ripping the staff from the priest's grasp, securing it in his own. The priest shrieked and stumbled forward, then watched in horror as her father used his free hand to set silver fire to it, tossing it aside with less consideration than a branch torn from a tree.

"You've been living in ignorance," he said, and dusted his hand, as if it had been tainted by some immaterial filth. "You've been blinded by your belief in false gods. It is time you know your true Gods live among you, and you will yield to our rule." He turned on his heels, striding back to Neith with a nod. It was her turn to perform.

She took a breath and stepped forward. Long black waves tumbled out as she lowered the hood of her cloak. The eyes that would not meet hers only moments before were now fixed on her, wide and wary.

Neith swallowed, lifting her hands out before her, palms to the sky. They were slick with sweat both hot and cold. She called to her ether, her life, her power. That which animated her. That which commanded the beat of her heart.

Twin cobalt flames kindled above each palm.

"Sorcery!" the priest shrieked. He stared her down with blazing scorn she wanted to turn and run from.

Neith joined the flames, compressing and tending, heating and growing the etherfire until she could no longer see around it. With one quick movement, she flung her arms into the sky, and the flames surged upward in a constant stream of fire and fury. It was a ferocious blast, sending those closest in the crowd stumbling back. It stretched on and on, burning and snapping wildly until its end was no longer discernable to the naked eye. Cries and gasps broke out among the townsfolk. Some of them began to kneel. The theatrical display was unfolding precisely as her father had intended.

Neith released the call on her power, and the etherfire burned out.

"This is *blasphemy*." The priest stepped forward, distinguishing himself from the crowd. "You will burn in the fires of Thelos for daring to engage the power of the Gods!"

Sweat trickled down her face. She stood, panting, doing her best to keep it vacant of her misgivings.

The priest turned to the villagers, looking for support, but found none as more took to knee. "Do not kneel, good people," he urged them.

Neith turned to retake her place and locked eyes with the captain. He studied her curiously, as if his thoughts mirrored hers when they'd met. When she reached her father and Magnus, both wearing looks of approval, she turned back, stealing one last glance his way.

Roman and Katya emerged from the woods. He shook his head as they approached. "We found no one."

Lorcan looked around, unconvinced. "There should be more."

"The cowards must have fled." Roman shrugged. "I sent a party south in pursuit."

The priest continued his spectacle, walking the lines of townsfolk, trying to pull them to their feet.

Her brother pointed toward the forest. "We searched from the northern—"

"Do not damn yourselves!" the priest squawked, trudging through the ankle-deep mud, the hem of his robe clutched tight in both hands.

Roman snarled. "Be quiet, you *imbecile.*" His hand flicked forward, casually, as one might swat at a fly. Silver etherfire roared from his palm, setting the priest ablaze.

Neith regarded her brother in horror as he smirked, watching the priest flail and fumble, shrieking wordless, desperate pleas. The villagers recoiled from his appeal, fearful of succumbing to the same fate.

The blazing man ran in aimless circles before he stumbled and tripped, then started to crawl. Sizzled flesh permeated the air as his body jerked and writhed. All looked on in amusement or terror as he labored, his movements slowing with each thrust forward, as if it were some sort of perverse performance.

An arm's length from her father's feet, the priest stopped, collapsing into the mud. Lorcan gazed down as he continued to burn, and Neith did not think it was with amusement nor terror. Glacial indifference was the only thing she found on him.

Neith turned to Magnus, chest burning as her heart thumped within. His uneasy eyes were already on her. She flinched when her father spoke.

"Make your choice," Lorcan bellowed. "Kneel now in supplication, or meet the same end."

Those who were not already kneeling now complied. Some in fear, some in exaltation. It mattered not.

"Roman, send them on their way." Lorcan turned from the priest as her brother approached the crowd. Her father looked at her the same way Magnus had, and she did her best to conceal her horror as a soldier dragged the scorched corpse away.

"In two days," Roman called out to them, "we will pass through here again. If you value your life, you will not be here when we do. Go and speak of what you have seen here this night. Go and tell the people of Straeth what comes."

The townspeople stayed fixed, looking to each other, no doubt fearing it was a ploy or trick.

"*Now*," Roman said, irritation growing as a silver flame sprang to life in his hand.

A single man sprinted off toward the woods, faltering in his effort to move with haste. When he was not struck down, the crowd followed.

Roman turned and stalked back, muttering, "Pathetic," under his breath.

Magnus stepped closer to her father. "Rhea Carston is among the captured Esērii."

Her father's eyes widened as he turned to look at the apprehended. "Bind her and bring her to me."

Magnus gave orders, and two soldiers returned with the red-haired woman. Her defiant gaze turned to seething rage as they approached, tossing her to the ground at Lorcan's feet. Magnus lifted her by the shoulders back to her knees before reclaiming his place next to Neith.

The woman slowly lifted her head in dramatic fashion, her rage sealed under a contemptuous smirk. "What took you so long? We'd grown bored waiting to see if you would ever crawl out from behind your mountains and wards."

Lorcan peered down at her. "All things in due time, Rhea." He spoke familiarly, like one catching up with an old friend. "Last I saw, you had a knife in your belly, bleeding out on the council chamber floor."

"A knife you stuck there." She spat, then cocked her head, smirk returning. "I remember the sight of your back as you ran from the Citadel after your little rebellion failed, tail tucked tight between your arse cheeks."

Neith listened intently. His rebellion was not something her father often spoke of.

The curiosity in his eyes broadened. "I'm heartened to see you've not lost your spirit over the years."

Rhea stared at him, her shoulders straight and chin high. "Unbind me, and I'll show you just how spirited I remain."

Lorcan chuckled. "Tempting. But you would do well to remember that did not work out well for you last time."

Rhea shrugged. Her eyes moved to Roman, then Neith. "You've been breeding." She looked them over, lip raised in disgust. "Gods help the woman you whelped these devils on." Her eyes were fixed on Neith when what looked like recognition formed on her. Rhea clicked her tongue several times before speaking. "I see. Where is Lia Throndsen then? She was always following you around like a lost little dog."

Roman stepped forward, but Lorcan raised his hand. The amusement on her father faded.

Rhea chuckled. "Obedient, at least. But that's how you like it, yes? All yielding to your will. How little you've changed, too."

Her father's eyes thinned. "Take care. I enjoy your stealthy indignation, futile or not, but there are limitations. You and I know all too well death is not the fate to fear. If you think angering me is the way to meet yours, you are mistaken."

If his threat fractured her defiance, Neith did not see it on her face. They simply stared each other down.

Rhea sighed, and for the first time, the taunt was absent from her manner. "What are you doing here, Lorcan? What does Godsreach have to offer that you'd risk leaving your wards?"

Lorcan folded his arms behind his back. "Righting the wrongs our kind have endured for hundreds of years. The Esērii would have you sacrifice yourself for the common man. No recognition, no acknowledgment. No power. Living a life of servitude in secret. They would have you kneel to idleborn kings and queens. I would have them kneel to you. Etherborn will rule this world again, as it once was. As it should be."

Rhea groaned. "Not this pretentious rhetoric again. It bored me then, and it bores me now. You always were quite vain, even as a child. What are you going to do? Invade the entire northern continent? With what," she said, her eyes darting around, "one hundred men?"

Her father didn't use words. He let the subtle curl of his lips give answer.

"You can't be serious." Her eyes narrowed, weighted with doubt. "You *are* serious." She studied him for a time before her head took on a lean, some of the playfulness returning. "How many men do you have?"

Lorcan knelt, bringing his eyes to meet hers. "A sufficient sum."

Rhea searched his face for sincerity. She nodded as if understanding Lorcan would not bluff. It was not in his nature. "Which direction will you march them?" she asked, her brown eyes curious and appraising. "West?"

He smiled, and it looked wrong for all the vanity in it.

"Come now, Lorcan. We both know I'm not leaving here, and neither are they." Rhea gestured to the Esērii bound by the temple. "Humor my curiosity."

He leaned closer, their faces no more than an arm's length apart. "Perhaps we'll let you watch."

Neith saw the first crack in her mask. Rhea's eyes flicked from face to face, as if looking for understanding she was unable to decipher in his words.

"I'll give you the same opportunity I give every Etherborn who crosses my path," he said. "Though I have already made this offer to you once before."

Rhea scoffed. "Save your breath. I'd rather spoon out my eyeballs than listen to any more from you. After your speech and that ridiculous performance, I'm quite at my end. Kill me and be done with it."

Her father had told her the Esērii would be clever. They were trained to read between words. To rile. To obtain information. Though they clearly shared a past, Neith could not help but think this woman did not know her father at all. He was not one to be provoked.

He sighed and stood, peering down at her again. Neith thought she saw disappointment on him, but it vanished as quickly as it had appeared. "I see it is time to move on." He stretched his neck from side to side. "How many were stationed here in Godsreach?"

Rhea straightened. "All the ones you see before you. And the two you murdered. One of them was a boy, only fourteen years of age."

Neith paled. *Fourteen.*

"It is no fault of mine the Esērii send children to do their work." Her father gestured around them. "You will find no children in our ranks."

Rhea sneered but made no argument.

He walked in slow circles around her. "I'm having trouble making sense of something. Perhaps you might assist me."

"By all means," she said, with a feigned enthusiasm.

"I struggle to understand why the Citadel would send someone like you here. A shieldmaster sent to monitor the borders at Godsreach? Maybe Westwatche, where an attack is plausible, even Caern, but Godsreach? This post is beneath you."

"I like the north." Rhea gave him a toothy grin. "Cold is good for the constitution."

"See, I think you have only just arrived. Bringing a message, perhaps?" He tilted his head. "No, surely there is another expendable child they could send for that." Lorcan crouched to speak closely in her ear. "Visiting someone?"

Her expression gave away nothing Neith could see.

Lorcan motioned as he stood. "Bring the others."

Soldiers retrieved the other Esērii, who were made to kneel. Neith felt the bindings that had been placed on their power, stifling their gifts.

Lorcan stood in front of each, appraising. Their faces were a collection of resignation and fear. He stopped at the young man. Neith shifted on her feet—the pulse of inevitable violence rendering her unsteady.

"Him?" her father asked.

Rhea gave no reaction.

"No, not him." Lorcan continued. He stopped again, this time behind a young woman. A tendril of silver ether curled from his palm, snaking around her neck. "This one?"

The girl thrashed, her blue eyes wild and wide.

Still, Rhea gave no reaction.

Lorcan released the girl. "Not her either, I see. Let us try this a different way."

He stalked to Rhea, fisting her hair with one hand as silver etherfire sparked to life in the other. Neith wanted to close her eyes, cover her ears. It took all her self-control not to cower behind Magnus, desperate to build a barrier between herself and what was soon to transpire. She looked up at him, but he was watching the scene.

Rhea's steel gaze didn't falter. She stared down the other Esērii. "You will yield nothing. Remember your vow." She spoke far louder than required, given their proximity.

Lorcan held the flame to her cheek. The sizzle was quickly succeeded by a howl torn from her lips. The other Esērii recoiled, casting their eyes aside. But none made to speak.

Lorcan released the flame. The right side of her face was scorched and blistered but not disfigured. He turned to the others. "How many were stationed here?"

When no one spoke, he conjured the flame again. This time, Neith saw cracks of fear as Rhea eyed the silver fire. He paused, giving them one last chance to answer.

"You will yield nothing," Rhea commanded again, between exasperated breaths. "You will do nothing!"

Neith closed her eyes, silently pleading for someone to speak. The beating of her heart continued to climb in pace until it was a constant, steady thrum. It was the only sound. The tension, the anticipation grew so thick, so dreadful, Neith thought it might be the only thing holding her upright.

Something surged in the ether. Goose bumps prickled up her arms as a powerful cast split the stillness. She didn't want to see what it was. Or what it would do.

Heat rushed her, and her eyes snapped open, panicked, as a savage, unseen force heaved her backward. She reached for her neck, strangled by the clasp of her cloak. The air ripped from her lungs when her back smacked the ground. Too fast to understand. Too fast to fight back.

It was such a violent act she only realized she was being saved when a plume of bright green etherfire roared above.

The captain stepped into view, and so did his shield, so fast she could not perceive it take shape. He braced against the onslaught as he peered down at her, brows twisted and eyes wild with a look that did nothing to settle her fright. Her stiff body jerked as she lay staring up, spellbound by the explosion of color behind him. The attack and return fire merged into an all-consuming fusion.

Neith gasped, arching in relief when air finally flooded her lungs.

She rolled on her side, toward her father, still heaving in sharp breaths. He was under shield, shouting commands she couldn't hear as her brother returned fire. Her mind had no capacity for thought. It called only for action.

She pushed herself to one knee, her aim to join the fight. But when she set eyes on Magnus, the air left her lungs once again. He was on the ground, shaking and writhing, the left side of his body burned. He, too, was screaming, but his pleas were not commands.

Neith blinked, and something in her changed.

Her fear fell away as if it had been nothing more than a garment she'd worn, discarded at her leisure, releasing the rage beneath. It channeled through her, twisting her face into a snarl as she scrambled to her feet.

The incoming fire blanketed the captain's shield, heating the air within. Relentless, like a scream that never stopped. As if its source needed no air. Neith closed her eyes, calling to the ether, to the fabric, to all that binds. Tapping in, searching for the source of the assault.

Where are you?

The fire receded, and her eyes flicked open. It came from behind the forest's edge, close to the temple. Neith put all her focus there. Nothing. She detected no one, no wielding.

Her snarl deepened.

The fire came blasting in again, and Neith stepped out of the shield, sending fire of her own to meet the incoming attack. A steady stream of her cobalt etherfire crashed with the green. Sparks flew where the two fires met.

With little effort, she pushed back the green flames, tracing their origin. The wielder caught on, and the fire withdrew again.

But it was too late.

Neith now sensed the shield. It was good. One of the best she'd seen. Nearly undetectable.

She studied it, disassembling the woven threads of ether. It started to break down, and she sensed the wielder abandon it, sprinting deeper into the woods.

Tendrils of her ether raced from her palms into the tree line, ensnaring the runner in a single heart's beat.

It coiled around them, snakelike, and she retracted the ropes, tearing them back through the trees, ripping through branches and bramble.

A pale body with bright red hair emerged, limbs flailing in the air.

Neith wrenched her fist back toward the earth, and the body crashed a few yards from her feet. The considerable force sent a burst of air blasting her cloak and skirts around in a rippling effect. It was a savage impact, and Neith heard the snapping of bones when it hit.

Chest heaving and crazed, she tightened the ropes again, suspending the body in the air before them. It was a young woman, perhaps not as old as she, head slumped. Her limbs twisted at unnatural angles. She was wheezing and scarcely lucid.

Someone screamed. Her eyes were fixed on the girl, but she felt those around her move as their shields came down.

Her father approached the broken body and removed one of his gloves. He lifted the girl's chin with a bare knuckle. Blood poured from a gruesome wound above one eye and bubbled and oozed from parted lips. She tried to speak but only made a gargled, primitive sound.

Someone was still screaming. The woman, Rhea. Even with the ruin, Neith saw the resemblance. Understanding took hold. This girl was her daughter.

"It didn't need to be this way, Rhea." Her father released the girl's chin, and her head returned to its slumped position. "All this power wasted. And for what?" Silver ether swirled from his palm, wrapping around the girl's neck. With a quick twist of his hand, it snapped. "*Nothing.*"

Neith released the body, and it hit the ground with a thick, wet thump. She stared at the mangled corpse. Had she done that? She stood, unmoving, save for the heave of her chest, transfixed at the horror born from her own hands. A heaviness crowded her chest, and she felt as if she were sinking. She thought she might not be breathing.

A figure crossed into her line of sight, breaking her focus on the girl.

Soldiers were dragging away the captives. Rhea thrashed and howled. She wished she would stop. *Why is she screaming?* Neith covered her ears, panic commandeering her person when she remembered it was her doing. She did that. She felt cold and wanted to lie down. *Monster.* That's what the woman was screaming. She was calling Neith a monster. A soldier kicked her until she fell still. Then someone else was yelling. If she could only get her eyes to focus.

"Neith!" Her brother shook her shoulders.

She inhaled, sharp and painful. He said something. *Magnus.* Her eyes flared when she looked down to see an aid squad working on him. She staggered forward, pushing them aside.

Burns covered the left side of his upper body, down his arm to the elbow. The skin on his shoulder had been blasted away, revealing the bone beneath.

Her hands hovered above him, plagued with a violent shake. She called to his ether to feel out the depths of damage, looking over the arteries, ligaments, tendons, and bone. She used her power to call to his, accelerating the healing, repairing what was ruined. A dim, cobalt glow surrounded them as she worked. Slowly, the flesh renewed. The black charred edges turned to dust, carried off by the wind. Sweat beaded on her neck, trailing down her back. It was no easy task to heal such a wound. Her fingers molded and directed the ether until the disfigurement reformed. It was raw and pink, but little more than a superficial burn. Neith slumped, falling back on her hands, unsure how much time had transpired. A group of onlookers had formed, including her father and brother.

"Give the woman to Dryden," her father said to Roman. "If there is any information to be obtained, he will retrieve it. Give the others the offer. If they refuse, send them to Nighhelm when Dryden is done with them. Then finish this. You know what to do."

Roman nodded and began distributing orders.

The aid squad returned to Magnus, wrapping his shoulder and arm. Someone knelt beside her, hand extended. She looked up at the face of the captain. She reached for him, and he pulled her to her feet.

Neith heard her name. Someone said it. Her father, she thought. She turned toward the sound.

His glacial eyes studied her as his head took on a lean. His scrutinizing gaze gave way to something else as a tiny curl formed on one side of his mouth. She blinked when she realized it was pride. He was proud of her.

"Captain," he said to the man standing beside her, though his eyes were still set on hers. "You will gather ten soldiers and escort my daughter back to camp. She needs to rest. I am placing her in your charge until otherwise ordered." He turned to look at him. "Can I trust you to see this done?"

Neith thought she saw him fall into half salute.

Her father's attention returned to her. "It is a long ride back to camp. When you arrive, you will eat and rest. Rebuild your strength for tomorrow." His hand came up to rest on her shoulder, and she turned to look at it. His grip tightened.

"Yes, Father," she heard herself say, but he was already walking away.

The captain appeared in her father's place. "Can you walk, my lady?" His voice was clear and calm. Not particularly deep, but steady and strong.

"Yes," she answered, gazing around as if she'd left some task unfinished.

He stepped to the side to catch her eyes. "Is there something you need, my lady?"

Neith shook her head. "No, I—" She caught sight of the mangled body and turned away, clamping her eyes shut. "I am ready."

The further she walked, the faster she moved. She wanted to be away from that place. Far away from what she had done.

Her horse became visible through the trees before they reached the clearing, her reins bound to a tree. Storm bucked and reared until she snapped free. A couple of quick gallops, and she was in front of her, nuzzling.

"I'm all right, girl," she said, stroking the nervous horse.

Neith felt detached, dreamlike. She could see those around her, hear herself speak, but it was oddly observational, as if something within her had snapped and its severed ends flailed within, desperate, but unable to reconnect. She wondered if this was what losing control felt like. *Perhaps I am mad now.* It did not feel as concerning a notion as she thought it should be.

"Let me help you, my lady," the captain offered, extending his arm.

She looked from his eyes to his hand and back, then shook her head. "I do not need help."

He nodded, stepping back as Storm bowed, allowing her to mount.

They traveled through the forest, making their way back up the mountain. The captain rode beside her, the other soldiers behind. No one spoke. He had not looked her way. Either out of respect or disinterest. Or fear, she considered.

Neith did not marvel at the budding trees or pastel petals this time. She felt suspended and tried to focus on breathing or the sway of traveling horseback. Everything that had happened pursued her, like a rabid animal clawing its way up the edge of her thoughts. She had to kick at it, keep it at a distance. It would be too much. Something inside told her so.

The further they traveled, the more difficult it became to subdue. Every stick snapped under hoof was a bone breaking. The wind howled, and she swore she heard screams in it. Cold sweat beaded on her skin. She gripped the pommel to temper the shaking of her hands.

When they reached the mountain's peak, she turned on the cliff to look out over Godsreach again. It was little more than a series of golden embers in the distance.

Neith told herself this was justice. This was retaliation. They were righting wrongs.

Her knuckles turned white from her distressed grip, and she struggled to draw even a shallow breath. She closed her eyes, but that only provided a medium for the images of the dead—the crying boy. The young woman, limbs bent unnaturally. What had she done? It was as if she'd stepped out of her body, and someone else stepped in. Someone sinister, and wrong. Her father might have snapped the girl's neck, but she was never going to survive the damage Neith had inflicted. It was she who ended the girl's life.

These people were the enemy. They killed her mother. The mother she would never know. Hate should be easy to come by, but she was clawing for it, coming back empty-handed. Her thoughts continued to spin until no longer discernible, and she swayed in the saddle.

Storm stopped, sensing her panic. Neith felt bile rising. She jumped from her horse and fell to her knees, retching.

She heard the captain turn back and dismount. Warm tears streamed down her cheeks as the heaving turned to sobs.

Neith looked up to see him raise his hand, telling the other soldiers to give them space. He knelt beside her, holding her hair away from her face.

"My lady, you are not well. We must get you back to camp." He spoke slow and cautiously, like one coaxing a wild horse.

"I killed her!" She stared at him, waiting, expecting him to say, "Yes, you did, you *monster*."

But he only looked at her, considering, and released her hair. "You defended yourself and your people."

"I don't know what happened." She ran a rough hand across her face to swipe at her tears, fighting her mind's command to sink her nails into her skin and tear away at her flesh.

"Your instincts took over. It is why we train." He spoke in the same steady manner he had before, and it eased her. Neith watched him walk to his horse and return with a flask. "Take small sips."

She frowned.

"It is only water."

Neith obliged, content to be directed. When finished, she glanced back at the group of soldiers waiting behind. They weren't staring, and she was grateful, but shame still scalded her cheeks.

The captain looked back as she had, making the slightest of nods. He stood and walked to the soldiers. "Travel on ahead. We've passed through the wards. There is no danger from here. We will follow."

The soldiers saluted and continued as commanded. Neith took a last drink from the flask and passed it back to him. She quickly realized she had never been alone with someone other than her family, tutors, or castle servants.

"Can you stand?" he asked.

Neith nodded. "I believe so."

Steadying her arms, he helped her rise. The hum of his ether on her skin where they touched was vibrant. She found herself wanting to hold on, to be closer to it.

It caused her to study him, intently this time. His brown eyes had a kindness in them, though weighted with worry. There was something easing about his presence. His manner, even. The way he spoke, how he touched her. She felt like she was in the middle of a stormy sea, and he was the steady land in the distance.

Neith blinked and stepped back. "I am ready." Still shaking, she pulled her cloak around her shoulders. "I should like to walk for a while."

"As you wish. Are you cold, my lady?" he asked, reaching for the clasp of his own cloak.

"No." She was unsure why she lied.

He nodded and turned to retrieve his horse.

They continued on the path toward camp, neither speaking. Walking felt a strange task, choppy and awkward, as though her body could no longer anticipate when her foot would next meet the earth. One step rising, the very next sinking.

Neith chastised herself. No one else was acting so bizarrely. The captain appeared wholly undisturbed, save for the occasional distressed glance her way.

Stepping out of the woods, campfires illuminated as far as her eyes perceived. Thousands of tents lined row after row. Neith recalled the ease with which a single unit of men had razed Godsreach. Looking out over camp, she felt only dread. Her father had over thirty-five thousand men. Nearly four hundred of them Etherborn wielders. What carnage they would unleash.

Faint laughter and conversation swelled. Guards bowed as they passed through the edge of camp. They left their horses with a groom before he walked her to her tent.

Neith's eyes wandered aimlessly around the ground between them. She was fearful of being alone with her thoughts.

"Is there anything else I can do for you, my lady?"

Neith shook her head, then looked up. "What is your name?" she asked, steadily, in an attempt to reclaim some of her dignity.

"Sam, my lady."

Neith pulled back the cover to the tent door, turning back once she'd stepped through. "I want to thank you, Sam, for saving me. And for your kindness. I will not forget it."

He bowed his head. She frowned, confused by her disappointment at the formality.

"Sam?"

"Yes, my lady?"

Neith swallowed. "Will it get… easier?"

He looked at her for a moment, eyes searching hers, and sighed. "Yes, regretfully."

Neith couldn't decide if his answer made her feel better or worse. He was still standing there when she let the cover close between them.

The brazier was lit, and a plate of food waited. Her stomach turned at the sight of meat. She left the plate where it lay.

Though her eyes weighed heavy, Neith did not expect to sleep. Pulling off her cloak, boots, and outer dress, she climbed into her cot, tugging the fur covers to her chin. Fearful of closing her eyes, for what waited behind them, she stared at the canvas ceiling, wishing she could see the night sky. A single tear swelled and crested, trailing slowly down her cheek. She lay still, waiting for the panic to resume.

2

Nara

"In the shadows, we find our purpose. In the shadows, we find our light."

THE WAY OF ETHER

ASHERAH GALANIS, FIRST CONSUL, THE CITADEL, 807 AQ

Nara Nyanthi was tired of traveling. It felt like she'd traversed the length and breadth of the southern continent this year, and it was only the third moon. If Etherborn continued emerging at such a rate, she would never have a day's rest.

The desert terrain of Ahara did her no favors. The midday sun was a persistent foe. Pools of sweat formed at the curve of her back and beneath her breasts. Her long black braids clung to her slick skin, and she cursed herself for not taking the time to tie up her hair.

The team of four had departed the Citadel seventeen days past, taking a boat down the River Sana across the borders of Sibreen. The further south they traveled, the more stifling the heat. They'd left Rahab at dawn on camelback for a desert village so small Nara had not bothered to remember the name.

Nara detested camels. It was a languid voyage, the constant sway an unrelenting sort of torture. She found it an exercise in patience. Something she did not possess in abundance.

As if sensing her thoughts, the animal turned its head to glare at her, baring its crooked teeth. Nara narrowed her eyes at the beast, and it grunted before turning back.

"We should reach Amul by midday," her mother said. They rode side by side with Sanne, their Seer, out front. Harker rode behind.

Nara nodded. She had no appetite to converse. She was restless and tried stretching her neck. When she'd requested to join collecting missions ten moons back, the constant travel had been a welcome distraction. It had since grown monotonous, and she found herself counting the days until her year of assignment would end.

Her mother looked at ease, and Nara envied it, perhaps a touch resentfully. Tora had always been considered a beautiful woman, and age had not diminished it. Even then, traveling through the desert, she looked like royalty on her way to a gala or some other high society event. Her red-and-orange patterned robes were vibrant against her umber skin. Thick gold earrings brightened the copper tones of her brown eyes. She seemed to be enjoying the journey, and Nara had to work fervently not to roll her eyes.

She'd been told her entire life she was a mirrored image of her mother, but she couldn't see it. Nara did not possess the constitution for easiness. There was always trouble, something to do. Chaos that needed reigning. Her peace had only ever existed with Cerys. The council stripped her of it a year ago when Cerys was assigned to the north. It was the only reason she'd joined these blasted missions. The aspiration of reuniting with her was the only thing that kept Nara going.

A gust of wind sent fragments of sand swirling in the air about them. The long ends of her braids whipped up, striking her in the face. She cursed.

"I told you to tie up your hair."

Her gaze flicked to her mother, taking in the sly smile fashioned on her lips. Nara huffed and tried tucking her braids behind her headscarf. "I hadn't realized you'd developed Second Sight, *great oracle*."

Her mother chuckled. "It is not clairvoyance, dearest, only experience."

This time, Nara allowed her eyes to roll. Retrieving her flask, she sipped the lukewarm water, denying her desire to gulp it down. Bits of sand stuck to her lips, but she didn't care. It was everywhere. In her sandals, between her toes. She examined her hands. Her dark skin was dusted with the tiny beige flecks. Nara eagerly anticipated a very long, very cool bath when they returned to the field house in the evening.

She was ready to be done with the events of the day. She dreaded the conversations. She dreaded the goodbyes—the lies. Nara didn't want to take any more children away from their mothers. It was all so much easier when the child was in plight or dilemma, perhaps shunned from their community. Something that warranted rescue. Though, she could not bring herself to hope for that. It was a nasty business, but Nara found that after ten moons and nine collecting missions, her heart was hardening to it. At least she told herself so. She was starting to understand how her mother seemed so indifferent. You had to be.

"Have you been considering your next post?" Tora asked, her tone casual, though Nara knew the feelings beneath it were anything but.

Nara shrugged, but she had. She'd thought about it considerably.

"Whatever you decide, I think we can agree another request for collecting will not be submitted." Tora pulled a cloth from a pocket of her skirt, blotting delicately around her face.

"Eager to be rid of me?" Nara cocked her head, brows raised.

"Of course not, dearest," her mother answered, glancing at her sidelong. "Should you choose to request collecting again, and in the unlikely event it is granted, I will be glad to have you with us."

"So you keep saying." Nara rolled her shoulders, stretching against the tension between them. She wanted off the damned beast.

Tora returned the cloth to her pocket and turned to look at her, eyes tender but firm. "They will not send you north, Nara."

"You don't know that." It was a conversation she'd long grown tired of.

"I fear this little sabbatical of yours will not have the effect you desire."

Nara straightened. "We will see."

Her mother took a quick breath, as if she would speak, but hesitated. Nara felt the apprehension in whatever it was she was about to say.

Tora cleared her throat. "If you were to go to the High Council, and show humility, I believe they would restore you as chancellor."

Nara snorted. "I did not resign the post only to turn around and beg for it back."

"You are not happy, Nara," she said, and sighed. "These last years have been difficult for us all, but there is only so long you can run—"

"I find unnecessary chatter less tolerable than silence." Nara winced at her own abrasiveness but made no effort toward restitution. Her mother's gaze burned into her, but Nara held her face forward.

A long moment drew out between them.

"Very well." Tora urged her camel ahead to ride with Sanne.

Nara flexed her jaw. She was well aware of how quick to strike she'd become, but she had not the desire, nor the wherewithal, to rectify it.

Harker rode up to take Tora's place. "You ought not be so hard on your mother," he said, voice gruff from a life of overindulgence.

"I have my reasons."

"Aye… aye. You do." Chin-length, honey-brown hair peeked out from beneath his black turban.

Nara looked him over and her nose scrunched. They were deep in the Aharan Desert, and the man was wearing brown leather fighting trousers and boots. "You look ridiculous, you know? Gods know what you're brewing in those leather trousers in this heat."

He barked out a laugh, deepening the lines around his eyes, no doubt a consequence of his ever-present smirk. Nara guessed him somewhere in age between her mother and herself. "Days, Nara, I'll miss those daggers when you're off assignment."

Despite her best effort, Nara couldn't keep the grin from her face. "I'll miss such an easy target."

Harker smiled, toothy and wide, his skin uncommonly tan for someone from the north. Considered handsome by those who found men so, Nara found him a bit rough-looking, unkempt. Not in the spirited way Cerys was unkempt. He was untidy and often smelled of whiskey and salt water. He reminded her of a sell sword you might see in Azmar, drunken in the dark corner of some seedy pub, waiting for his next hire for pence. But she liked him. She liked him very much. He was honest, kind, and trustworthy. And he made her laugh. She thought about Cerys and how her hair always smelled of pine and honey. Nara closed her eyes.

Two more moons.

They continued for the better part of an hour before the village appeared, tucked away between mountain peaks. The houses were tan-colored clay, square in shape, with flat roofs. Typical of an Aharan village. If not for the presence of greenery from the sparse collection of trees, one might pass right by Amul, unbeknownst.

Sanne stopped on the edge of town, the others following suit. She turned back with a nod. It was easier to create the ruse if they weren't a part of it.

Nara closed her eyes. Her ether hummed, as restless as she. She called to it, coaxing, and it answered with a caress. A dim violet glow poured from her hands as she wove. The translucent sphere molded to form, casing them in. The shield, and all beneath it, were no longer visible to the naked eye.

They followed Sanne through the village streets. It was her vision that directed them to the Etherborn child. Nara was eternally grateful she hadn't been born with the burden of Second Sight. It doomed the Seer to a life of collecting.

Children scurried between the buildings kicking a leather-bound ball, leaving a plume of dust in their wake. Elderly men sat around a table playing a game with dice. Nara inhaled the citrus notes of their tea. Women walked in groups, chatting and laughing, baskets of fabric, food, and other goods balanced atop their heads. It seemed an ordinary day. For most, it would be. For those they were on their way to see, it would be their worst.

The estate was a mile south, situated alongside a narrow river. Wealthy, considering its distance from a major city. An expansive, single-story house stood forefront of two stables and a large pasture populous with goats. Nara found it picturesque. She envied the quiet life. Perhaps not the goats.

Nara dropped the shield, and a man looked up, taking notice of their approach. He called out to an older man tending the animals. Harker pulled back, riding behind. Experience had taught them a group of women was less daunting to those they sought out.

"Good day, friends," Tora called, raising her arm in greeting, gold bangles shining in the sun.

"Good day," the older man replied, caution in every component of his manner. Villages in northern Ahara were under constant threat from Somonian raiders and had long grown skeptical of outsiders. Wary eyes were cast their way anytime they traveled this part of the continent.

The older man walked with a limp that gave dual purpose to the shepherd's crook he carried. The younger gripped a mallet. His eyes lingered on Harker, naive to the actuality he was not the most dangerous among them.

Both wore knee-length white tunics over tan linen pants, dusted and dirty from the day's work.

Tora dismounted, closing the distance on foot. Nara watched the tension in the bodies of the two men ease. Their expressions changed from guarded to curious.

"My name is Tora." She held a hand above her eyes, shielding them from the sun.

"I am Yassin Fazel," the older man said, "and this is my son, Ziad." Yassin looked at each, taking in their finer dress, perhaps thinking them merchants. "How can we help you?"

"We have traveled a long way, Yassin. My friends and I are weary." She gestured behind her. "Might we fill our flasks and take shade from the sun?"

Yassin held Tora's gaze. His eyes grew heavy as his disposition further softened. There was an uneasy pause, but then he smiled. "Yes, of course, my friends."

Ziad frowned, looking to his father for understanding.

Tora turned to Ziad, stepping forward to catch his gaze. "Ziad, would you be so kind as to help my friend Harker with the camels?"

Ziad's concern tempered. "I would be happy to." His grip on the mallet released, and it fell inattentively to the ground.

Nara had never grown accustomed to seeing someone under Ethereal Influence. Even then, at twenty and six, it still set her ill at ease. They might smile, be obliging, but there was always a disconnect in their eyes. A trancelike quality to their demeanor that unnerved her.

"Come, friends." Yassin gestured for them to follow.

When they entered the house, Nara pulled down her headscarf and looked around, sighing in relief at the absence of the sun.

It was a well-kept home with blue-tiled floors shined to perfection. Yassin led them to gather around a tea table in the common room, surrounded by large sitting pillows in an assortment of bright colors. The monotone exterior was a stark contrast to the home within.

An older woman entered the room as they gathered on the floor. Nara watched the woman's eyes change as her mother's Influence struck.

"This is my wife, Yana." Yassin gestured to the woman. "Will you take tea?" he asked.

"No, please do not trouble yourselves." Tora smiled warmly at the pair. "Yana, will you join us?"

Without responding, the older woman sat next to her husband. Both looked at Tora expectantly. She leaned over the table, giving a presentation of intimacy. "Tell me, Yassin, how many of your family live here on this estate?"

"My wife and I, our son, his wife, and our new grandchild." His empty eyes presented the smallest sparkle of pride. "The babe arrived just last moon."

"What joyous news." Tora gave them a brilliant smile. "And is the babe healthy?"

"Oh, yes," enthused Yana, "most healthy."

"How excellent."

It would have been so much easier to simply subdue them. To proceed straight to the lie and take the child. But Influence was a tricky thing. It had to be layered. The less traumatic, the better it would be for the person on the receiving end. You can't destroy a memory, nor alter it. Memories live in one's ether. Ethereal Influence was more like veiling the truth. It would always be there, underneath the facade.

"Yana, might we see the baby?" Tora asked.

Yana stood, glossy-eyed. "I will take you."

Tora gestured for Nara. "Come with us. Sanne, please wait here with Yassin."

Yana led them to a room in the back. A woman, several years younger than Nara, lay cradling a bundle in her arms. Upon first inspection of the unfamiliar faces, her brows furrowed, and she looked at Yana. Tora sat beside her on the edge of the bed.

"Who are you?" the young woman asked. She had large amber eyes and golden-brown skin. Her long black hair was woven into a simple braid that hung loosely over one shoulder. She looked worn and donned only a tan-colored linen dressing gown.

Influence swelled, thickening the air in the room, causing Nara to swallow.

"We have come to see your child." Tora's voice was warm and honeyed, filling the small space with a gentle ease. The woman's nervousness dulled, and she pulled back the blanket to show the tiny infant in her arms.

Nara's mother was a gifted Influencer. One of the most talented of her time. The small group was well within her bounds of power. Nara had once seen her control a room of twenty and five. She wondered if her mother's thoughtful, understanding disposition was part of what made her so powerful. To influence emotion, surely you needed to possess a profound understanding of it.

"What a beautiful daughter you have." Tora lifted her hand, gently stroking the sleeping baby's cheek.

The young woman smiled. "We named her Laela after my grand-mother."

"Laela Fazel. What a lovely name." Her head took on a minor tilt. "May I ask yours?"

"Raja."

"Raja, my name is Tora. This is my daughter, Nara." She gestured to Nara who stood back by the door.

"I am happy to meet you both. Please forgive my appearance," Raja said, looking down at her dressing gown.

Nara struggled to meet the young woman's eyes, feeling every bit the intruder she was.

"It was not an easy birth," Yana explained.

Nara had learned this was a common theme in her ten moons collecting. Giving birth to Etherborn children was rarely without obstacle, especially for the idleborn. The more powerful the child, the more formidable the task. They'd arrived at three collections this year to find the mother had not survived it. On occasion, neither did the child. Her mother had grown increasingly concerned, fearing the mortality rate was on the rise.

Tora leaned forward, resting her hand on Raja's. "You will regain your strength. I suspect your next birth will not be so taxing."

"I pray to the Gods that is true. Though I would do it again for her." Raja smiled down at the tiny infant in her arms.

Tora nodded. "I am quite familiar with the feeling. There is little we would not do for our children."

The weightiness of their current situation was the only thing that kept Nara from scoffing at her mother's words. She wanted her to get on with it so they could depart. She could scarcely bear to look at them.

"Raja, I must tell you something, and I need you to listen to me very closely, yes?" Tora sat up straighter, pulling her hand from Raja's, back to her lap.

She made a sound of assent, still gazing down at her daughter.

"Laela is," Tora said, "*special*. She was born this way. You see, the Gods favor her. She is meant to do great things, to hold much power."

Raja looked up and blinked. "I don't understand."

"There are some in this world who would use her for this power," Tora added, her gentle tone taking on weight. "Even want to hurt her. You want her to be safe, yes?"

Raja nodded, clutching Laela closer to her chest. "I will protect her."

Tora smiled, tender but tight. "Yes, I know you would, dearest. It is only that for her to be safe, she must leave."

Raja looked at Yana, this time with fear.

Tora reached out and touched the young woman's arm, drawing back her attention. "Laela must come with us."

"*No.*" Raja scoffed, pulling free from Tora's grip.

Nara's mouth watered, and she felt uneasy as her mother's power pulsed through the room. Influence, when used at such an intensity, had an ill-inducing effect.

"It is time for Laela to leave this life so she can begin her true one." As Tora spoke, Raja listened with wide, swelling eyes.

"Where must she go?" Yana asked.

"A place with others like her. Like us." Tora looked from woman to woman. "Where we will keep her safe."

"Can I go with her?" Raja asked. Her free hand rested over her heart. "I am not afraid to leave this life."

Nara looked away, taking slow, deep breaths to stave off the heaviness forming in her chest. They did not often resist.

"I know you are not afraid, sweet one." Tora sighed. "But I fear you cannot. Laela has a purpose to fulfill. It would not be safe for you."

Raja's chin trembled.

"It is time for me to take the child."

Raja didn't speak. Her eyes moved desperately around to the other women in the room. Influence swelled again, and Nara feared she might be sick. Raja lifted her arms, leaving them outstretched long after Tora had taken the baby.

Laela stirred, then cried, as if suddenly aware she was in foreign arms. Tora held a palm above her tiny head. Influence swelled once more as she put the child back to sleep.

Raja stared at her empty hands, her eyes hazy and distant, until they slowly fell, crossing over her chest in an empty embrace.

"You are a very brave woman, Raja Fazel." Tora reached out for her hand. "I vow to you, Laela will know you. She will know her mother's name and the great sacrifice she made for her daughter, whom she loved so greatly." She tightened her grip. "You will grieve this loss, but you will take comfort in knowing she is loved and safe in her new life. One day, when you have other children, you will tell them about Laela. The sweetest girl who had to leave too soon." Tora motioned for Yana to sit and then spoke directly to both women. "Laela fell ill last night, a fever. When you woke, you found the Gods called her home to the veil, to eternal sleep. She was a young babe yet." Yana began to weep. "You built a pyre for her, sending her on her way. Raja, Yana, do you understand what I have said to you?" Her mother still spoke with tenderness, but her tone was direct, precise. There could be no misunderstanding.

"Yes," Raja whispered as silent tears fell down her cheeks.

"I pray, dearest, you do not see me again." Tora stood with the child in her arms and walked from the room, her face set in stone.

Nara made to follow, glancing back from the door. The women sat motionless in their grief. They did not look at Nara. For them, the child was already gone. Nara was not there.

Tora passed the baby to Sanne while she explained to Yassin. Nara left the house, desperate for fresh air. She felt ill, and a bit unsteady on her feet. She told herself it was the Influence.

She found Harker and Ziad waiting out front. Tora came out, asking Ziad to join them inside.

"How did it go?" Harker asked, passing Nara the reins to her camel.

"It was fine." But it wasn't. She didn't want to admit it was the hardest one, yet.

Sanne emerged with the baby in a sling strapped to her chest, Tora not far behind. No one spoke as they mounted their camels and rode away, tensions high as they always were after collecting.

Nara waited for the wash of relief it was over, but it didn't come this time. Guilt pooled in her chest, growing denser, heavier, until she felt cast down, chained to the sandy earth. She wasn't built for this. She wasn't even sure she agreed with it.

Part of her knew it served a purpose. She'd heard the stories. Men, women, and children cast from their communities. Or worse.

She would never forget, as much as she might wish to, being eight years old, secretly listening to her mother sobbing to her stepfather as she described the charred remains of a boy of four. Set on fire by the people of his own village, fearing him a witch. The look on her mother's face, the image her mind created of the boy—it was a memory etched into the fabric of who she was.

But Raja Fazel would not burn her child. Nor would she abandon her. She would love her. Protect her. Just as she'd said.

A wail bellowed from the house. A woman's, raw and guttural, unmistakably rooted in grief. Nara clamped her eyes shut as it rattled through her, replaced swiftly by a flare of white-hot rage.

"*Is there nothing else you can do?*" Nara's words came out in an accusing hiss. She knew there wasn't, but could not help it. She let all the resentment she was feeling pour out.

Tora stopped, halting the group. She turned toward Nara, staring her down. "How dare you."

Nara winced but held her ground.

"I have been tolerant of your hostility these past moons," Tora said as her arm came forward, finger pointed at Nara, "but you go too far. Do you think you are the only one this weighs heavy on?" She shook her head and scoffed. "You turn up your nose at this work, but see here how little you can stomach it. For you, this may be demeaning, a snag in your career, but your insolence is an insult to everyone who dedicates their life to this. I will no longer stand for it. You don't have to like it, you don't have to agree with it, but for the remaining two moons you are on this team, *you will respect it.*" Tora urged her camel forward, riding out ahead.

Nara stared at the back of her mother, lips parted, blinking. She had never seen her so angry. She had never scolded her so. Nara felt she likely deserved it, but it only charged her temper.

Sanne was already riding away. Nara looked at Harker. His eyes were tight, and Nara felt the disappointment in them.

"Come on," he said. "We need to get moving."

Nara swallowed and nodded, urging her camel on.

The ride back to Rahab was silent. Nara stayed in the back, putting space between herself and the others. The desert wind was not enough to distract from Raja's scream repeating in her mind.

They were only a couple of miles from Amul when her mother stopped again. She turned her camel, saying something to Sanne and Harker that Nara could not make out, given the distance. Sanne nodded. Harker glanced back at Nara, eyes imploring her best behavior before the two rode on.

Nara exhaled, pressing her lips together as her mother waited for her to catch up. When she did, she found apologetic eyes.

"I should not have reprimanded you in front of the others," Tora said. "Nor with such anger. I allowed my feelings in the moment to take over my better judgment. For that, I am sorry." She straightened her dress as if it had somehow become out of sorts along with her feelings.

Nara looked away, watching Sanne and Harker gain distance. She knew she should return the apology, but she could not bring herself to say the words.

Her mother sighed. "When we return to the Citadel, I am going to request the council remove you from assignment early. This will be your last collection."

Nara's head whipped back, and her camel shifted beneath her. "*What? You will do no such thing.*"

"You are unhappy," her mother said with softness that sparked her irritation.

Nara bristled. "As if that matters."

Tora directed her camel closer, catching Nara's gaze. "It matters to me."

Nara laughed. It was brief and bitter as she stared at her mother. "As of when?"

Pain flushed through Tora's face, short-lived but resonant. "It was a mistake for you to request this. I know, we all know, it was done out of spite."

The anger in Nara burned brighter, stoked by her mother's words. "Spite? The council pulled Cerys from my team and sent her to some inconsequential post in Ire, halfway across the world. They could have sent anyone. *Anyone.* Walking away from my post wasn't something as trivial as spite. Look to the council for that. What I did was a consequence."

The pain was gone from her mother's face, replaced with disappointment, judgment. It was the look she tried to hide, but it was always there, underneath the kind smiles and understanding eyes. "No one so young as twenty and three has ever been made chancellor, and you held the post nearly three years. You threw it away as if it were nothing."

"It *is* nothing. I only took the post to get you and the council off my back." Nara sat back in the saddle and folded her arms.

Tora exhaled, shaking her head. "You are so young. You think one or two years apart is a long time. They mean to have you take a place on the High Council one day. Surely you see this."

Nara laughed and did not attempt to hide the resentment in it. "I would rather rot."

Tora scowled and flipped her hand dismissively between them. "Go ahead then, wait them out. We'll see how far your stubbornness will take you."

"I'll not be the one who bends."

"What did you think would happen when you requested to collect? That they would put you on a team in the north?" Tora laughed. "You're not that naive, Nara."

"I didn't think they would put me with *you*," Nara said from a clenched jaw.

Tora flinched, but then nodded, as her anger cooled. She looked at Nara with curious eyes. "*Why not?* Everyone knows your anger toward me. It is no secret. If they wanted to punish you, that's exactly what they would do."

Nara leaned forward, her eyes fixed on her mother's. "You might be willing to sacrifice the people you love for this, but I am not." She leaned back, her arms swiping through the air. "I never wanted any of this."

"Ever the rebel." Tora shook her head. "But you do not fool me. I know you care." She clapped a hand to her chest. "I know you are good."

"*Good?*" Nara huffed. "I am not good. I am *angry*. You had a *good* child. They sent him away, remember? You *let* them."

"Here it is," her mother said. "The root of your animosity, and oh, how it festers."

"You let them send your son, my baby brother, away to die in the north. For *nothing*." As soon as the words left her lips, Nara knew she had struck too deep. "You didn't even try to fight it!"

Tora stiffened. "All Esērii must sacrifice." She said the words, but they were hollow, thin, and bare of conviction. "He will come back to us."

Nara looked away, shame heating her cheeks. Every blow she dealt her mother was a double-sided attack. She resented her for not speaking up to the council, though she knew it would have made no difference. Her brother had been most resolved to go. Blaming her mother was wrong, and she knew it, but Gods be damned, she could not help it. Her bitterness had become a sickness. Her resentment had hardened to stone.

She knew she should back down. This was the time to stop, to make apologies. But that was not Nara. When the enemy is weakened, strike fast and strike hard. "He is *dead*. It is time to stop pretending he's ever coming home."

Tora shook her head. "He is not dead."

Nara sighed. "No one sent to cross the borders of Thrane has ever returned. You think a boy of only eighteen will be the first? Even if he managed to get through their wards, a swift death would be the best we could hope for him. He is *dead*, and I blame you. I blame the council. I blame his father. I blame everyone who sat idly by and let it happen."

The two women stared each other down. Tora's eyes swelled. The sight of it sent a strike through Nara's chest.

"I know in my heart I will see him again," her mother said, and swallowed. "You should not abandon him so."

Nara wanted more than anything to believe the same. But as the moons continued to pass, then years, and they received no news, not from a single field house in the north, her hope had died. Slow and painfully. She'd had no choice but to mourn him. The memory of it stripped her of her anger, quickly giving way to remorse.

"I'm sorry," Nara said, the words a struggle. "I feel like I'm losing everyone I love, and I'm being punished for trying to stop it."

Tora reached for Nara's hand. "I know. I know, dearest."

Nara was tired of fighting. She was tired of being angry, but she didn't know how to turn it off. Her mother did not deserve her vitriol.

"When we get back to the Citadel—"

A faint boom caused the women to turn. A cloud of black smoke billowed up from behind the mountain range.

"Is that coming from the village?" Nara asked, squinting, trying to make sense of what was presented.

"It has to be." Her mother's wide eyes studied the plume.

"What is it?"

Tora shook her head. "I don't know."

Another explosion followed the first, sending Nara's pulse rising in pace with the smoke.

"What in Thelos's fire is that?" Harker asked, skidding his camel to a halt.

"We have to go back," Nara urged.

"We cannot," Tora answered. "Our mission was the child, and we have her." She looked at Sanne, who approached, then back toward Amul.

"We must! We don't know what it is. It might be raiders." Nara implored her mother, eyes pleading. "We owe them this."

"Nara," she said, shaking her head, "you know we cannot. We will report this in Rahab, and an appropriate team will be sent to investigate."

"They will be too late." Nara looked at Harker and Sanne for support. Sanne was unmoved, but Harker looked between her and her mother, considering.

"It is protocol," Tora said. "We cannot—"

Nara's face twisted into a snarl. "I don't care what you three do. I am going back." She tugged the reins of her camel, turning it in the direction of Amul.

Tora cursed. "Harker, go with her. Sanne and I will ride for Rahab. Nara, listen to me." She reached for Nara's arm, gripping it tight. "No wielding. You will not have Influence. Be conscious of this. Do not interfere if you cannot assist without it."

Nara didn't respond. She urged the camel forward at a full sprint, feeling Harker on her heels. At the accelerated pace, it did not take long to reach the village.

As they grew closer, the sounds of an attack became clear. Small explosions, the roar of fire. Screams and pleas.

They dismounted on the edge of town, pulling weapons from their packs. Nara tugged off her headscarf and slipped on a scabbard, placing twin blades on her back. Her thigh belts held four daggers, and she placed two more at her waist. She cloaked them in a shield as they approached to get a better look.

The ground shook, and a plume of green fire billowed out above the buildings. She stopped and stared.

"*Is that etherfire?*" Harker's voice was low, but frantic. Nara turned to look at him and was met with the same fearful disbelief she knew plagued her face.

"Surely not," she said, lacking any material conviction. She looked back toward the commotion.

"What else could it be?"

"I don't know. We need to get closer." Nara strengthened the shield as they entered the back side of the village. They slipped through a narrow alley that gave them a free view into the center of town. Peering around a building, Nara saw several men and women, uniformed soldiers, all in black, dragging villagers from their homes. Half the buildings were already put to flame.

"How many do you count?" she asked Harker.

"Six. You?"

"Same."

"Who the fuck are they? Nomads?" he asked.

"Possibly, but this is bold, even for the worst of them." She looked at Harker, weighing his reaction as she spoke. "We can take them."

He shook his head. "There are dozens who will get caught in the crossfire."

Nara sighed. He was right. Her mind raced, unsure how to proceed. There were bloodied faces, but no bodies. They were setting the town ablaze, but as far as Nara saw, they had not killed anyone.

"Where is the child?" a middle-aged man called to a girl who waited back from the others. His voice was gravelly, and he spoke with command.

Nara's gaze snapped to meet Harker's.

"I don't know," the girl replied. "This was the village I saw. I know it." Her arms were crossed as she looked over the faces of those kneeling around her.

Nara's heart thumped. She told herself they could not mean Laela.

The man pursed his lips. Nara tried to make out the emblem on his chest.

"We've checked every house," one of the other soldiers called out.

"Perhaps we have arrived after the Esērii again?" the girl asked.

Nara frowned, sure she had misheard.

"There is no evidence of that." He scratched his chin as he surveyed the crowd. "There must be more homes around here. Take Anders and Lika, search the immediate area. Estates outside of the village are likely to be close to the river. Look for traces of Influence."

"Yes, Father." The girl saluted him with a fist to her chest and walked to gather the others.

"They're headed right for them," Nara whispered, turning back to Harker. "We have to follow."

Hesitation tightened his face, but he nodded. "We'll have to cut back and go around the other side of town."

"Then let's be fast."

They made their way through the alley, sprinting once clear of the village. It was a much longer course, and Nara said a silent prayer they would arrive in time.

It was immediately clear they did not.

Ziad Fazel was in front of the house, lying on his back, mallet in hand. Blood pooled on the ground beneath him. Harker checked for his pulse, but Nara knew he was gone. Fury flared through her, turning her hands to fists, and she didn't fight it. She encouraged it. Nara didn't know who they were, but no longer did she care.

"Stay here," she said to Harker, striding off toward the house. She heard him protest but didn't turn back. Her heel struck the door, and it burst from the hinge. A surprised soldier looked her way as he stood over Yassin and Yana. They were cowering, huddled together on the floor.

Nara didn't hesitate.

Palm striking forward, tendrils of her violet ether speared through the room, wrapping around his neck. She recalled the ropes and, in a blink, he was before her, her hand gripped tight around his throat. He gasped, eyes bulging as she slammed him into the ground at her feet.

He hit with a crack, shattering the blue tiles beneath. She heard his skull fracture on impact, blood spurting by the time she exhaled. His body twitched, but there was no life left in his eyes.

Footsteps pounded from the hall. Nara moved out of view, standing in front of Yana and Yassin, motioning for them to move back.

A female soldier ran past, twin burgundy flames at call in both palms.

Nara sent a burst of air, striking the woman in the back. She slammed into the stone wall, falling back onto the floor in a heap, leaving behind bright red splatters and streaks. She was scarcely lucid and wheezing, the right side of her face hideously shattered. Only one of the woman's eyes registered the threat as Nara knelt over her, snarling, and snapped her neck.

"What is going on out there?" someone called out from the back of the house. It was fearful, timid, and one side of Nara's mouth quirked. She recognized the girl's voice.

Nara stalked down the hall, ether at call, and kicked open the bedroom door to find her standing over a sobbing Raja. A thin trail of blood trickled from her lip.

The girl turned, her panicked eyes darting from Nara's hands, to her face, to the door. Nara felt the girl start to call her ether and shook her head in two sharp movements.

"Don't," Nara warned her.

She stopped, seemingly smart enough to know she was well outmatched.

"Step away from her."

When she didn't move, Nara closed the space, fisting the girl's hair. She shrieked as Nara hauled her across the room.

Nara peered down at her, palms out, speaking with all the malice she felt. "Move one inch, and I'll scorch you to ash so fine not even the birds will come to pick at your corpse."

"I—I won't. I swear." The girl looked little more than an overgrown child, trembling on the floor.

Nara turned back to Raja. The terror in her eyes charged Nara's rage. She knelt to meet her gaze.

Raja looked at her, still frightened, but confusion twisted her features. "I know you."

"Yes," Nara said, nodding. "Yes, you do." She lifted Raja to her feet and guided her to the bed. She leaned over, speaking gently. "Stay here and make no sound. No matter what you hear."

When Nara turned away, Raja reached for her hand.

"It is all right," Nara said, with as much tenderness as she could summon. "I swear to you she is safe."

Raja frowned, but her grip slowly released.

Nara turned back, glaring at the girl on the ground. "Walk out to the front. Do not forget my threat. I will sense your cast before it leaves you."

When they reached the front, a horrified shriek escaped the girl when she set eyes on the two mangled bodies.

"Yana, Yassin, please go to Raja's room and wait with her there. Do you understand?"

They looked as afraid of her as they were of the others, but they didn't protest.

Nara backed the girl up against a wall. "*Who are you?*"

"My—my name is Thalie."

Nara scoffed. "I don't care what your name is." She gripped the girl's vest, pressing her harder against the stone. "Where are you from and why are you here?"

The girl's eyes darted around the room. Nara examined the design of the emblem on her chest, and dread nearly consumed her. She ripped the patch of fabric free. It was all black, save for silver stitching in the shape of ridged mountains. Nara told herself it could not be. She stuffed the emblem into a pocket of her skirt.

Long dry of patience, Nara let her power flare, and the house trembled. "*Where are you from?*"

"Thrane," the girl said quickly. "We are from Thrane."

It was the confirmation Nara knew was coming, but it still sent a chill racing across her skin. She swallowed and did her best to conceal the fear within, now growing at a rapid pace. "What are you doing here?"

"Collecting," the girl said. "The same as you." She glanced at the door.

"How?"

She held her chin high. "I have the sight."

Nara's thoughts spun. She tried to pluck one from the chaos. Knowing the others would eventually turn up, she had to use whatever time remained wisely.

"How many Seers does Thrane have?"

Silence.

Nara conjured a bright purple flame in her left palm. She glared at the girl in warning.

"Please."

Nara fed the fire until the air around them turned to steam.

"Four."

"How long?"

"What?"

Nara gripped the girl's chin, pressing her fingertips into the soft flesh. "How long has Thrane been collecting?"

"Years," she cried. "As long as I can remember." She glanced at the window, and then at the door again.

It couldn't be, Nara thought, casting her eyes to the side. She could not reconcile herself to believe they'd been doing anything outside their wards beyond petty raiding. Collecting would have been the farthest of things considered. The Esērii would surely have known of it. The resources Thrane would need to operate such missions were unfeasible. There would be missing children. *Unless…*

Her eyes flicked back to the girl. "Two children we sought this year died before we arrived."

The girl's expression told Nara all she needed.

"You took them?"

The girl nodded.

Nara held her face steady, but inside, she was all frenzy. Her heart, her thoughts. They continued to spin. What did this mean? How could it be? She considered what might be happening elsewhere. In the north. To Cerys. *Fuck.* Nara shook it off. "The man you're with, your father, he is in command?"

The girl nodded again, her wide eyes heedful of the purple flame.

Nara eyed her. "You have concealed your efforts until now. *Why?*"

No answer.

Nara pointed at the man's body on the ground beside them. They were standing in a sea of his blood. "Unless you want your brains splayed out on this blue floor with his, you will answer the question."

The girl glanced down at the body and swallowed. "We—"

Nara felt them outside before she heard him speak.

"We have your man," a familiar gravelly voice called. "Come out."

Nara held a finger to her lips, warning the girl to stay silent. She walked quietly to the window and inspected the scene. The girl's father and the other two soldiers waited in the yard on horseback. Harker was bound, a soldier's ether wrapped around his arms, chest, and neck.

"Thalie!" the man bellowed.

"I'm here, Father!"

Nara crossed the space and backhanded her. A grunt escaped as she hit the floor. "Get up, stupid girl."

Dazed, the girl tried to stand, only to slip in the pool of blood. She reached up with a red-stained hand to touch her cheek.

Nara growled and hauled her to her feet. Grip tight on the back of her neck, she led her out of the house. Fear, then anger, flared across the man's face when he saw the blood, but he quickly replaced it with a cool indifference.

"Don't worry," Nara said. "It is not hers." She tightened her grip on the girl, and she winced. "But it would be little trouble to spill hers where she stands."

The man's eyes flicked between his daughter and Nara. "Not before we snap your man's neck."

Nara looked him over, taking his measure. "Then it appears a conversation is in order."

"So it would seem." He sat back in the saddle. "We were wondering when we might run into one of you. Didn't think it would be so soon."

"It seems you've come too late this time." She kept her free arm out, ether ready at call.

"Yes," he said, nodding. "I see that. Where is the child now?"

"Far from here." Nara studied the soldiers. The commanding officer was the strongest among them. He had sent his best two with his daughter, but all three appeared calm and confident. There was something distantly familiar about him. Or his voice. Though neither could she place.

"I think that unlikely, given your quick return." He had intelligent eyes, and Nara knew he was appraising her as she had him.

"We ride fast." Nara glanced at Harker, attempting to conjure up some sort of plan. His eyes were cautious but controlled. His head made the slightest of shifts. He was telling her not to act rash.

The man in charge narrowed his eyes, studying her face for a few breaths, then huffed. "Well, well. I know you, Esērii."

"I doubt that."

"Are you not the daughter of Tora Nyanthi?" He smiled. The condescending, knowing sort.

Nara kept her face still. "Don't know her."

"You look just like her, girl. Except your eyes." He smirked this time, and it chipped away a little at her panic, replacing the empty space with focused rage. "I remember you as a child in the Citadel. There were high expectations for you. But here you are," he said, as he cocked his head, "on collecting missions." He appraised her further. "It is not for lack of ability. No, I can feel your gift. How interesting the Esērii have sent someone with your power on these menial tasks."

"It would appear it was not done so in vain."

He laughed and scratched his chin. "Perhaps not." His amusement gave way when he looked at his daughter. "The others are dead?"

"Quite." This time, it was Nara who smiled. "And if you can sense my gift, then you know the odds are not stacked in your favor here."

"We are four," he said, with a cool confidence. "You are two."

Harker barked out a laugh. "You better say something else. You don't want those to be your last words."

The man who held Harker tightened the ropes. Nara let her power flare out, sending a light tremor through the earth. The girl's father held up his hand, and the soldier loosened his hold. He looked around, as if considering his options. "I fear we have come too late today. We have already lost two of our kind. Let that be the end of it."

"I'm listening."

"It is simple. Give me my daughter, and I'll release your man. We go our separate ways." He held his hands out to each side. "We live to meet another day."

Nara knew she could take them, but perhaps not before the man holding Harker snapped his neck. And if she attacked, she would be putting the Fazels in danger. She looked down at Ziad's lifeless body. She'd encountered dozens of nomad Etherborn over the years, many of them hostile, but this was something else entirely. If this was truly Thrane, she was in well over her head. She nodded.

Nara released the girl, and she took off. The bindings on Harker fell away. He climbed to his feet, his ether at call, walking cautiously toward Nara.

"You know," the man said as he pulled his daughter onto his horse, "if they don't appreciate your gifts at the Citadel, I'm sure our king would be happy to find a place for you among our ranks."

Nara spat.

He tugged the reins, but stopped halfway, looking back once more with a smirk. "Tell your mother Wystan Barton sends his regards."

They rode off, heading west. Nara watched them intently, not moving or speaking until they were out of range.

"Did that really happen?" Harker asked. "That was Thrane?"

She slowly turned to face him. "I believe it was."

He cursed. "What do we do?" He faced forward, eyes cast out in the distance.

Nara looked back to see them disappearing behind the mountains. "We ride hard for Rahab."

"Does this mean we are at war?" he asked.

"I don't know." All her thoughts went to Cerys in the north. If war from Thrane was upon them, she was at the front. "Let's go."

3

Neith

"Those who seek morality in war set themselves upon a foolish course. For in war, we find only depravity, guised in fables of honor."

THE COST OF VALOR
AUTHOR UNKNOWN, CIRCA 203 BQ
TRANSLATED FROM OLD ASARI BY MERIAH TURAN
HAIS Z'NOSIŠ, 1200 AQ

Neith opened her eyes, squinting at the brightness seeping through the thin canvas walls. She had slept long and hard, something rare for her. Healing Magnus had taken a toll. She stretched to relieve the heaviness of the night, scarcely remembering removing her boots and lying down. Her mind was foggy, and it took a moment to register someone sitting across the tent, staring at her.

She sat up, swiftly pulling the blanket to her chin.

"Good morning, my lady," the girl said, but it sounded more like a chirp. Long, dark blonde hair framed a freckled face with round, hazel eyes, beaming with enthusiasm and cheer. Far too much for such an early hour.

"Who are you?"

"Apologies, my lady. My name is Ayla. My father is General Dryden." Her voice was high-pitched but soft and songlike. She walked high on her toes as if each step were a small hop. Neith surmised she was of a similar age to herself. "I've been assigned to attend to you."

Neith knew Hywel Dryden. He was a man of whom she was not fond. He had long been stationed in Nighhelm, returning only a moon before the army departed Necrium. His reputation for ruthlessness was well known. As were his eyes. They were as dark as brown could be before it went black. She did not even know he had a daughter.

Neith reached out and was unable to sense the gift. The girl was idle-born. "Did my father send you?"

"He did, my lady." Ayla smiled, and the kindness in it put her at ease.

Neith had no attendants since she'd outgrown her nursemaids years before. Only teachers, tutors, and castle servants had seen to her since. She wasn't sure what to do, nor how she felt about it.

"Your father bid me let you sleep." Ayla took an apprehensive step closer. "We all heard what you did in Godsreach. I wish I had been there to see it." The girl had all but stars in her eyes.

The brief reprieve washed away as the events of the night before flooded in. How had she slept so long and serenely when she had done such violence? She thought she must truly be a monster of the worst sort. She wanted to chastise the girl for her regret at not bearing witness. Why would anyone want to see such a thing? Neith only wished she could stop.

"You rest here, and I'll fetch you something to break your fast. When I return, I'll help you dress."

"I don't need help—"

Ayla was out the door before Neith finished her sentence. Sighing, she stood and walked to pour a cup of water from a pitcher across the tent.

The girl returned promptly with a plate of bread, hard cheese, and wild blackberries. Neith adored blackberries. They were difficult to come by north of the mountains. The short growing season and long winters in Thrane made agricultural efforts difficult. It was possible to grow cabbage, potatoes, and various root vegetables in high summer, but fruit was widely unseen. Mostly persimmons and pears.

Neith had little appetite despite the emptiness in her belly. She picked at the berries while Ayla fussed about pulling fabric from a trunk. She decided on a simple dark blue dress with billowed sleeves and a brown leather belt. Neith had never seen it before. Her dresses in Thrane were often simple, black or gray in color.

"I think this will go lovely with your eyes," Ayla said, holding it up beside her.

She then proceeded to brush and then weave Neith's hair in an intricate plait, starting at the top of her head all the way to the nape of her neck. The remaining black waves fell loose around her shoulders. It was a "Parthenean style," or so Ayla had said. She even cleaned her nails and put some kind of oil on her skin that smelled like flowers. Her cheeks and lips were rouged a light pink. Ayla tried to clean her teeth, but that was where Neith drew her line.

The entire act felt ridiculous. But given the alternative of reliving the night before on a continuous loop, it was a welcome distraction. So, Neith played along.

When she was satisfied, Ayla held up a small looking glass. "See, you're beautiful!"

Neith blushed, studying the reflection. She saw herself, for the first time, more a woman than a girl. For a brief moment, she dared to think she looked pretty. Until she remembered. *Monster.* She pushed the mirror away and stood, straightening her dress. "Thank you, Ayla. I will join my father now."

As Neith walked through camp, she felt the stares. Some fearful, some appraising. Ayla had said everyone was talking, but Neith hadn't truly imagined *everyone*. She pulled up the hood of her cloak.

When she reached the tent, the soldiers outside snapped to attention. They bowed, and one pulled back the cover to the door. Neith found her father, brother, Magnus, and several other high-ranking officers seated around the long table covered with maps and scrolls. A few looked up as she entered, but continued in their conversations. Magnus stood, walking around the table to greet her. His left side was bandaged, and his arm hung in a sling across his chest, but he looked well.

He greeted her, grasping her shoulder with his free hand. "I hear I have you to thank."

Neith gave him a taut smile. It felt wrong to be thanked after all she had done. She pictured the mutilated girl. The way her bright red hair cut through the night as she hurtled toward them. The wet sound her body made when she hit the earth.

The shift in her energy must have read clear on her face. Concern crept into his eyes. He opened his mouth to speak, but she cut him off.

"I am happy to see you so recovered." She meant it. At least she had done one good deed. "Be sure to treat the tissue so it does not toughen, else you may lose range of motion."

He nodded, and Neith took the empty seat next to her brother. Magnus followed to his own, but continued making concerned glances her way.

Her brother appraised her, one brow lifting in jest. "Nice dress."

She scowled and leaned closer to him, speaking low. "Do not tease me, Roman. It wasn't my doing."

"After we cross the mountains, we travel southeast along the River Steyr until we reach Northbridge. From there, the First and Second divisions will cut east, toward Croydyn." Magnus stood and moved two markers on the map to rest over Straeth's capital city. "Dryden and the Third will cross the river at Northbridge, heading south for Ealdtown." The third marker trailed down the water line, stopping south of where it connected to the Iren River. "By the time Ealdtown falls to the Third, the First and Second will have completed the march east to Highclere."

"If the Iren fleet is our aim, should we not march south and take Kingsport first?" Cordero asked, eyes scanning the map. Nikander Cordero was a commander in the Second Division under Magnus's authority. He was one of the many faces new to Neith since they'd marched from Necrium a sixday past. They caught eyes, and he smiled at her.

"Dryden and the Third will march on Kingsport once Ealdtown is under our control," her father answered. He was sitting back in his chair, clutching a silver chalice in one hand.

Neith's gaze drifted to Dryden, seated next to Cordero. His dark eyes were already on her, as they often were. When Dryden was in Necrium, Neith took aim to avoid him. She thought his daughter must take after her mother, for she looked nothing like him. He had an affecting appearance that was difficult to make sense of. His thick, dark brown hair was slicked back, smooth, not a single strand out of place. He was clean-shaven, revealing his square jaw and fair skin. She believed he was considered a handsome man by many, but there was something vacant about his manner that made her recoil. He reminded her of an obsidian mountain cat. Always lurking in the shadows.

"If we hold Kingsport and Highclere, the rest of Ire will fall in time. The fleet is our aim, but securing and controlling the supply chain up the Iren River must come first." Her father lifted the chalice, taking a long drink as his eyes surveyed the map. "If all falls to plan, we will hold all of Straeth and the western half of Ire by the end of the Summer Moon. Highclere is impenetrable to idleborn armies. It will become the base of our operations while we work to secure Parthe and Lochland."

Cordero nodded, taking in all that was said. He looked a vibrant contrast to the man next to him. If there were any at the table she did think handsome, it would be him. His olive skin had depth to it, and his short hair was a lively golden brown, matching the color of his eyes. Typical of one from Balta or even Ostalla. Neith did not know from where his people came. His accent lacked the intonations and rhythms of one from the south. He was the youngest of her father's commanders. She guessed him thirty winters.

His eyes found hers, and he smiled again, which she nervously returned, before restoring her attention to the group.

A number of subjects were discussed in the proceeding hours. Food was served, and Neith found she finally had an appetite. It was a stew of venison and carrots, with bread so fresh steam billowed out when she broke it. She ate the entire bowl, followed by a honey oat cake with blackberry sauce. She savored it, knowing the food would be much simpler fare once they were marching again.

Neith rarely spoke in these sorts of assemblies and only ever when spoken to. Her mind would often wander. Her brother, though, spoke often. Too often. He gave his opinion readily, to the irritation of others. His preoccupation with impressing their father was always plain. He came across unprepared and inconsequential. Constant boasting made him appear desperate. Which Neith, with no pleasure, felt was accurate.

"And if she cannot? What is our alternative? Marching to Westwatche and through Argal will add two moons to our timeline. Marching east through Caern is not an option until high summer when the ice melts. Either way, we would not reach Highclere until the Harvest Moon."

Neith's attention snapped back as she realized the woman was talking about her. It was Maelis Nicomedes, a commander in the First.

"She made easy work of that Esērii scum in Godsreach last night," Roman said. Neith felt her cheeks warm, and looked down, no desire to encourage him. Nothing she'd done felt worthy of boasting.

"Yes," her father said flatly. "The one you missed."

Roman sank back in his chair. Neith started to look at him, but quickly thought better of it. He was growing ever ill-tempered as of late, and his moods were always in tune with their father's approval.

"Are you doubting my daughter, Nicomedes?" Lorcan posed, a hint of jest in his words.

"Of course not, Lord King," Nicomedes assured, "only anxious to see it." Her dark blue eyes flicked to Neith, appraising but not intrusive like Dryden's.

"So you will," Lorcan said to the room. "We reconvene at nightfall."

Neith stood to leave, but her father raised his hand. "Stay a moment, Neith."

Roman glanced between her and their father. When he received no acknowledgment, his face morphed from disheartened to angry. He turned and marched from the tent.

Her father stood and walked to the soldier standing by the door, speaking too low for her to discern. The soldier saluted and followed the others out.

He returned to the table with two silver chalices, setting one in his place, the other in hers. She looked inside the cup to see it half full with wine. Neith had never had wine. She looked at him with question until he nodded. He watched her as she picked up the cup and took a sip. Her face puckered. It burned going down her throat and into her belly. She wondered why anyone would drink something that made them feel more thirsty. She returned the cup to the table, waiting for further direction.

Father or not, she had never grown accustomed to the intensity of his gaze. She fidgeted with the stem of the chalice. When he did not speak, she asked, "Have I done something wrong, Father?"

"I fear I may have made a mistake with you," he said. "I've kept you too close, too sheltered. You are gentle."

She wanted to deny it, but after what happened in Godsreach, she knew it was true. No one else had been so affected. If they had, she'd not seen it. She decided she might as well own it. She released the chalice and sat up straight. "Is that so bad?"

"Not if it were a just world." He leaned forward in his chair, resting his elbows on the tabletop, hands clasped in the air in front of him. "When we rebelled from the Esērii, we knew hard years were ahead. Difficult choices awaited us. Sacrifice. Many people, like your mother, made the ultimate sacrifice." He released his hands and reached for the leather cord around his neck, turning her mother's gold ring between his fingers. It was something he often did when in contemplation. "When we found her body, I made a vow her death would not be in vain. We will remember her always as a martyr to our plight."

Neith was unsure what to say. Her father rarely spoke of such things.

"Many challenges lie ahead, Neith. You are crucial to our success and our most powerful weapon against our enemies. In Godsreach, you showed your strengths and your vulnerabilities."

Neith swallowed. *Weapon.* She combed her mind for the words she felt he wanted to hear. "I only wish to honor you, Father. To honor Thrane." She could not apologize or make excuses. That would look weak. That was what Roman would do. "Last night you said to me my tenderness will harden. I believe you are right."

He narrowed his eyes, but she held his gaze, lifting her chin. Though she worried he would be able to see her heartbeat, pulsing at the base of her throat.

"As you know, in Thrane, one earns their place. Even those with birthright endeavor to deserve it or see it taken by one more worthy." He reached for his chalice. She looked away as he drank, eyes finding nothing of focus behind him. She prepared herself to be chastised, to be cast aside. Part of her could not help but be relieved by the prospect of being sent back to Necrium. He set the chalice down, turning it in circles by the stem, his eyes watching the action until flicking back up to meet hers.

"Father, I—"

"You should know it is not your brother I look to as my heir."

Her breath caught, and she stilled.

"It cannot be a surprise to you. You know he is not fit for rule. Roman has value when handled." He pursed his lips, lifting one shoulder in a lazy shrug. "But he is not a leader of men."

She thought first to defend him, but quickly realized she could not. "And you think I am?" she asked, tempering the incredulity in her voice.

"I think you could be." Whatever he read on her face brought a hint of curl to his lips. It faded, and he looked away from her for a moment, considering.

Neith watched him, struck by the reverse of what she'd expected.

His gaze returned to her with a vague trace of vulnerability that would go unnoticed on most. "I will take life when necessary, but I do not relish in it. In Godsreach, you demonstrated you are capable of the same." He paused, consideration returning to his face. "A strong leader has the conviction to take life. A brave leader has the courage to show mercy. A wise leader understands there is cause for both."

Neith swallowed. She felt an ache and looked down at her hands. Her fingers were laced, knuckles white from how tightly they clenched. "I am not sure I am strong or brave, Father, much less wise."

"There is none more dangerous than one with too high a regard for their own morality, Neith. Self-doubt is not the detriment you think it is. You are young, yet." He leaned back and his indifference returned, consciously, Neith thought, as if he'd taken notice of its absence.

The tent door opened, drawing their attention. The captain, Sam, walked through. He knelt in full salute. "You called for me, Lord King?"

Neith felt her cheeks go warm at the memory of all her humiliations he'd borne witness to. He had been kind, at the least pretended to be, but she had not prepared herself to be faced with it so soon. She had made peace, believing she would have little, if any, interaction with him again.

"Rise," her father commanded, beckoning him forward. He looked the young soldier over, taking his measure. "You saved my daughter's life. For that, we thank you."

"It is my privilege to serve, my lord." Sam kept his gaze low, respectful.

Lorcan looked from Sam to Neith and back. "That is well received, as you are being reassigned. You are now made head of her personal guard."

A brief and dim surprise washed over Sam's face. His eyes darted left to right, scanning the ground in front of him. Neith looked at her father, brows contorted. She started to object, but one look from him stilled her.

"Once we cross the border, we are no longer shielded by our wards and mountains. Our enemies will be able to anticipate us in ways they have not for over twenty years. My daughter is the key to taking Highclere, and her safety is of the utmost importance to Thrane." He looked at her. "It is of the utmost importance to me."

"I am honored, my lord," Sam said, but there was little keenness behind it.

"I do not wish to assign such a task to one so… unenthusiastic." He said the last word slowly, accentuating all the hard sounds.

"I beg pardon, Lord King. It is only that I do not see myself worthy, but I am honored, and I will endeavor to do justice to the post, my lord." He bowed his head.

"Good. Choose two soldiers who were under your command to assist you, with Magnus's approval. At least one of them highly skilled in tracking, and the other a shieldmaster. I don't want any more potential threats to go unnoticed. And I want a guard with her at all times, including outside her tent at night." It was quiet for a moment. "You may wait outside until we have finished."

Sam's eyes flicked up to hers. It was brief, but she saw the hesitation in them. He saluted and left the tent.

"Roman does not have a personal guard." Neith could not keep the bitterness from her tone.

"You are not being assigned a guard because of your ineptitude," her father said. "It is your value that warrants it."

"He is an Etherborn *captain*."

Her father peered at her, head tilting. "You would rather I select an idleborn foot soldier?"

Neith knew better than to argue further. She sighed. At least Ayla had seemed happy with her post. Though Sam had tried to hide it, his disappointment was evident.

A soldier stepped into the tent. "General Dryden sends word he is ready, Lord King."

Her father nodded.

"I have something I need to attend to." He reached across the table and covered her hand. "We'll speak more of this later." She nearly tugged her arm back in surprise, unsure of the last time her father had touched her in such a manner.

She watched the cover to the tent door fall in place, now alone, giving her mind a moment to consider all he had said. She would be heir. A strange laugh burst from her lips, and she reached up to stifle it with her hand. She seized the chalice and took a large gulp, grimacing at the bitterness. It did nothing to calm her nerves. Her pulse continued to rise, and she sprang from the table, feeling the urge to move.

"I will walk for a while," she said as she passed Sam. As ordered, she found him waiting outside the tent. He nodded and stepped in line behind her.

She needed space, unsure of how she felt. Neith wanted so much to be joyful, but something didn't fit. Everyone wanted the approval of her father, and she was no exception. The only thing she was sure she felt was conflicted.

She had no destination in mind. A moment away from the unpleasantries of camp was all she desired. She walked through rows of tents, passing groups of soldiers eating, drinking, and sparring. Some paused to stare, looking down when she met their eyes. They weren't afraid of her because of what she had done, but of what she would do. They didn't care she had killed someone. In all likelihood, they were killers, too. Or would be soon.

The snapping of bones played in her mind. The screams. The wet, slumping sound the body made when it hit the ground. The wind. It all united into a strange, muddled melody. Music for her nightmares, she supposed. She wondered if it would always be like this. Forever haunted, destined to relive Godsreach every day until her last. Perhaps it would end when she committed an act even more heinous. Or perhaps her father was right, and she would harden to it. The concept brought her no comfort.

Disoriented by the cacophony of cackling men, squealing pigs, and sharpening blades, she wanted to slap herself or beat her head against a tree to quiet it. And the damned song in her head. The tightness in her chest returned, and her legs grew heavy. She felt as if she were dragging a cart full of obsidian.

Neith picked up her pace and her feet nearly matched the thrum of her heart by the time she darted into the trees. Twenty paces in, she stopped, bracing against the smooth, papery bark of a birch tree, trying to steady her breath.

"Are you unwell, my lady?"

Neith jumped, and a tiny yelp escaped, so lost in her own thoughts she forgot Sam was trailing her. She glanced over her shoulder at him. "Is this how it will be now? You following me everywhere I go?" It came out far more acidic than she intended.

He stepped closer. "Your father commanded someone with you at all times, my lady."

"Yes, my father bids it. First, an attendant, and now a guard. I'll never have another moment alone." Company was all she had craved for years. Now that she had it, she didn't want it.

She knew she wasn't being fair. He hadn't asked for it any more than she had. He had been a captain, likely on the rise, and now he was little more than a glorified nursemaid. She turned to look at him. "I'm sorry. You don't deserve that. I am not... *adjusting* well. My head is—I keep hearing things, *seeing* things I do not wish to."

He stood, eyes alarmed and lips parted, as if as taken aback by her candor as she. "Please don't apologize. I quite understand, my lady."

Heat scalded her cheeks. She knew she'd over-spoken. Neith realized she had no idea how to speak to someone without saying too much or too little. Panicked tears stung her eyes. Any irritation she was still feeling faded. When the first tear fell, she turned around, feeling sheepish, and a little ashamed. "Will it go away?"

It was quiet for a moment until she heard the crunching of leaves as he moved, coming to stand before her. She looked up with reluctant eyes to find his manner thoughtful. He stepped closer, and she watched but didn't move as he slowly raised a hand and began to blot away her tears with the sleeve of his tunic. "I wish I could tell you that it will, but I think we simply learn to live alongside it. You find violence abhorrent because it is. It terrifies you because you are kind-hearted and decent. This is not a bad thing."

"Some say it is."

Sam frowned and lowered his arm. "Many people say many things. That does not make them true, my lady."

She swallowed. "Then how do we know what is?"

Sam took a deep breath, exhaling it slowly. "A person's motivations are a good place to start. But I fear you will need to find someone much smarter than I to give you an elegant answer. I do not find myself often in possession of universal truths."

Neith huffed. It was light and brought a small smile to her lips. "And you? Are you a decent person?"

He shifted, and his face caught the sunlight peeking through the tree-tops. Neith noticed that his eyes were not brown as she had determined the night before, but rather an intriguing shade of amber. She felt an instinct to lean in and peer deeper. "I used to be," he said. "I hope I still am."

"The Esērii woman called me a monster." Neith looked down to where she was twisting the soft fabric of her dress between her fingers. "I think she is right." She was afraid to look back up and see the confirmation in his eyes.

"We are all a villain in someone's story. A person takes from us, so we take from another. On and on it goes. To change this, you'd have to change the entire world."

Her eyes flicked back up to his, and she found no judgment in them. His mouth twitched. Not quite a smile, but something like it.

He had a gentleness about him that was a peculiar contrast to the power rumbling within. It appealed to her. She felt it then, pulsing underneath his composed demeanor. She found it fascinating, the contradiction of it. Of him.

"You speak with an abundance of wisdom for someone so young. How many winters have you?" she asked, wiping away what remained of her tears.

"Twenty, my lady."

She nodded, appraising him further. "I can see you are decent, Sam, even if you are unsure."

His face tightened, and she feared she'd said something wrong, but then he lifted a brow in jest. "Some might say I am not."

"Many people say many things," she mused. "That does not make them true."

He smiled, fully for the first time, and Neith found herself a bit lighter. She wondered if this was how one made a friend. It was an exciting prospect.

"Thank you, yet again," she said. "I promise I will endeavor to keep the task of consoling me reduced from this day forth."

His smile fell away, caution taking claim of his face. His lips parted as if he would speak, but no words spilled out. Shifting out of it, he looked up to the sun. "We have several hours before sundown. Should we walk, my lady?"

Neith nodded. "But I have a request first."

"I will do my best to oblige." He gave her a playful bow.

"If we are going to be spending so much time in one another's company, I would ask you to address me informally. Please call me Neith." She had no desire to indulge in formalities and would rectify the same with Ayla soon.

He looked at first like he might object, but conceded with an acknowledging tilt of his head. Neith turned, and this time, Sam walked beside her, instead of behind. All traces of camp noise faded away as they trekked deeper into the trees.

He extended his hand, helping her step over a fallen trunk. "Why night?"

She wished she had not worn gloves. "Sorry?"

"Why are you waiting until the sun sets?"

"I'm stronger at night."

He gave her a questioning look.

"My father has theories, but we can't be sure. Even more so when the moon is full."

He frowned. "Could you do it under the sun?"

She shrugged. "Perhaps. I've never tried it on such a scale, so Father says it's safer to do at night." Neith stopped to examine the pale green moss growing up one of the trees. She removed her gloves, stuffing them into a pocket of her dress. Her fingertips trailed over the soft lichen. It was velvetlike. Wonderfully delicate.

Sam walked around the tree to face her. "*How* will you do it?"

One side of her mouth tugged up. "I think it will be best understood with your eyes." Many knew what she would do. Very few knew how.

They walked on for an hour, talking the whole way. Sam told her about his life on tradeships and his travels in the southern continent. He told her about the great city of Azmar and the vast libraries in Nyrovi. Neith found it all exciting. There was such a world out there, and she had seen none of it. It made her feel small, but not in a poorly way. It was a comfort to know there was so much more. So much more than the war.

"I should like to see that someday," she said. "These libraries you speak of."

He smiled at her, and it had a sweetness to it, but fell short of his eyes. "I hope you do."

Neith did not ask about his family. Few Etherborn who came to Thrane had happy stories. She did not wish to deflate the mood. From what he had already told her, she assumed he had been nomad. It seemed the most logical of takes. A defector from the Esērii would never be allowed to hold a captain's rank, and Neith had only known of three.

They turned their heads in the direction of a rustle a short distance away. Sam walked to inspect.

"It is a deer, injured. It must have fled from a hunting party."

Neith stepped around him to see. Leaves ruffled from its quick, labored breaths. The poor thing had an arrow lodged in its shoulder. She knelt, using gentle sounds to soothe.

"What are you doing?" Sam asked.

She looked up at him. "Giving it a second chance."

Neith held her hands over the wound, and her bright cobalt-blue ether poured out, enveloping the arrow until it reached the point. Gently retracting, the arrow released, and she tossed it to the side. She refocused the ether, using the same weaving with her fingers she had the night before, until the damage was fully repaired.

As if startled awake, the deer scrambled to its feet. At first, it appeared it would scurry away, but it turned back, cautiously dipping its head toward Neith, taking in her scent. It crept closer, and she reached out to stroke its cheek.

"Run fast and far, my friend," she said. "They are no doubt on your trail." Neith watched as it dashed off, disappearing into the trees. She envied its escape.

"Why save it?" Sam asked.

"A brave leader has the courage to show mercy," she said, low, still gazing in the direction it had run, remembering her father's words. She would like to be brave.

"I could not hear you."

Neith stood and turned to face him, brushing the duff from her skirts. "If I am going to take life, I will do my best to preserve it. When and where I am able."

He frowned, studying her with an intensity that caused her to shift on her feet.

"We should turn back," he said. "The sun will soon set."

The sky was orange when they stepped back into camp, making their way through the sea of tents and campfires. Neith hesitated when she put eyes on her brother. He was sitting with Katya, seemingly sulking while she comforted him, speaking close, intimately, with her arm around his back. It was not a situation in which Neith had the desire to interrupt. Other soldiers from his unit were spread out in the immediate area. They were a wild, temperamental bunch, but fiercely loyal. She lifted the hood of her cloak and attempted to stride by unnoticed. She should have known Roman would sense her.

"*Where have you been?*" he shouted, standing abruptly.

Neith took a quick breath and approached. The volume of his voice caught the attention of several similar gatherings nearby. "Walking, brother."

"I was looking for you," he said, irritated, nearly accusive.

Neith detected the slight sway in his gait as he stalked toward them. He clutched a mug in one hand.

"I am sorry, I am here now," she said. "What is the matter?"

Roman lifted his chin. "I was worried." His eyes moved to Sam, and he sneered. "You're supposed to be looking after her."

"He has been." Neith took a half step in front of Sam to catch her brother's gaze.

Roman walked around her, getting directly into Sam's face, pressing against his chest. They were both tall, nearly the same height, so their eyes met level. Sam didn't move or back down. He looked calm, but his fists were clenched.

"Who are you, truly?" Roman regarded him with unmistakable disdain. "How long have you been here? A year? First, you are made captain and now personal guard to my sister." He shook his head. "That doesn't sit right with me."

Roman leaned closer until their noses were nearly touching. Sam's eyes were burning with indignation. Neith looked between the two, uneasiness growing.

"I'll tell you who you are. No one from fucking nowhere." Roman said the last words with staccato. He would often find some poor soul to take out his rage on anytime he was upset with their father. Neith wondered what had transpired while she was away. Sam said nothing in return. His lack of defense only encouraged her brother. "You're just some common-born, middling nomad pulled off a tradeship. Ether fodder."

Neith frowned. Roman knew his words were untrue. Anyone with a hint of the gift could feel Sam's power. His aim was to be cruel. He wanted a reaction, cause to escalate.

"Roman, stop this now. This is beneath you." Neith attempted to step between them again, but Roman held out his arm, pushing her back. Sam's eyes flicked to hers, and she shook her head, quietly pleading with him not to react.

Katya stepped behind Roman in support.

"My lord," Sam said, from a flexed jaw, "if I have offended you, I offer my sincere regret."

"You *have* offended me. Your mere presence offends me." A silver flame sparked to life in Roman's right palm.

Neith inhaled, fear crowding her chest in a rush. "*What are you doing?*"

Katya grabbed Roman's shoulder. "Roman," she cautioned. "Let's go. He's not worth it."

He shook her off, the remaining ale in his mug spilling out. He tossed it aimlessly to the side. The silver flame grew brighter, hotter, illuminating the translucent sheen of his skin.

"Brother, *please.*"

Roman looked at her, and for a moment his eyes were unsure, but he turned his attention back to Sam. "Only one day, and already you choose his side?" He spoke to Neith, but his eyes were locked on Sam's.

Neith watched Sam's face change. He dropped any pretense of supplication and let his contempt read clear. Neith felt at any moment the conflict would spiral. "There are no lines between us here, Roman. We all stand on the same."

A tremor rippled through the earth.

"Roman!" All turned to see Magnus striding toward them. "*What is this?*"

Roman took a step back, ether retracting, a taunting smirk formed on his face. "Just making sure my sister's new guard is up to the task."

Magnus stepped between them. "*Back up.*"

He said it with such command that Neith instinctively followed the order. Roman flinched but didn't move. Magnus narrowed his eyes, warning radiating from him.

Roman scoffed but complied. When he did, he stumbled, and Neith cast her eyes aside. It was a difficult scene to witness. As trying as his moods were, he was her brother, and she loved him. Watching him humiliate himself was never easy.

"Take him somewhere and sober him up," Magnus said to Katya. She reached for Roman's arm, but he jerked away.

Roman looked around at the gathered crowd. He turned to Neith and, with a mocking bow, quipped, *"My lady."* He staggered away, Katya on his heels.

Neith looked on, stunned, as tears stung her eyes. Her brother had always been jealous and reactive, but this was extreme. And it hurt—the way he had treated her with such contempt.

They'd been close as children. Less than two winters her elder, Roman had been her constant companion. Her only friend. As they grew, and it became apparent her gifts were far more substantial than his, something shifted in his behavior toward her. She feared his reaction when he found out their father intended to name her heir.

Their father had always been harder on Roman. Where Neith was kept close in the capital, he'd been running supply raids all over the northern continent for years.

Neith felt large hands rest on her shoulders. "We're going to have to keep an eye on him," Magnus said.

"I know," she said low, turning to face him.

"I'm sorry, little one." He sighed and brushed a knuckle across her cheek, then looked up at the sky. The sun was nearly set. "I'll see you soon, yes?"

Neith nodded, and Magnus clapped Sam on the shoulder before walking back in the direction he'd come. The crowd had dispersed, and now only Sam stood, watching Roman disappear in the distance. His ether burned hot like steam, still reeling from the interaction.

"Do not let him anger you. This is what he does." She glanced in the direction of her brother. "Though that was... severe."

Sam didn't respond. No doubt he felt he could not. Roman outranked him now that Sam was no longer a captain, and he was the king's son.

"I'm sorry for what he said to you. They were vile words and untrue. He is a"—she paused to choose her words politically—*"temperamental* person. He has always been. You would do well to avoid him."

His gaze was still locked in the direction Roman had taken.

Her instincts told her to allow him some space. "I will return to my tent to rest."

Sam's eyes flicked to hers, expression flat as he gave her a quick nod.

Neither spoke on the short walk. When they reached her tent, he said, "I will send someone to look over you."

"Goodbye for now," she said, crossing the threshold.

She was now familiar enough with the signature of his ether she sensed him walking away.

4

Nara

"The quest for knowledge drives us forward, but also sets us back. Hasty and sudden, too fast for us to see, until we find ourselves set on the same path we've crossed before."

THE WAY OF ETHER

ASHERAH GALANIS, FIRST CONSUL, THE CITADEL, 808 AQ

Nara dismounted, tossing the reins of her struggling camel to the groom before sprinting toward the field house. They'd ridden hard, her thoughts racing alongside the entire journey back. The sun was nearly set by the time she burst through the door. Her mother, Sanne, and several others were sitting in the common room.

"What has happened?" Her mother stood quickly, striding toward her. Her eyes were wide as she looked Nara over, taking in the blood staining her skirts. "*Is it yours?*" she asked, gripping Nara's arm.

Nara shook her head. She wanted to run through the house screaming *Thrane is here*, but she forced sense to overtake her frenzy. "Gather Sanne and anyone else you believe needs to be a part of a delicate conversation. Meet me in the assembly room in the back."

"*Nara*, what is—"

"*Please.*"

Tora inhaled and nodded.

Nara was met with curious regard as she made her way through the house, fighting her body's desire to sprint. When she entered the empty room, she took a seat at the far end of the table, but the moment she made contact with the chair, she stood and began pacing again.

One by one, they all filed in.

"Nara, what is going on? You are scaring everyone," her mother said, eyes darting between her and Harker.

For hours, she had been holding in the words, and now they hung in her throat, too thick and heavy to expel. She swallowed. "When we returned to Amul, we found it under attack."

"Somonian raiders?" Tora asked.

"No," she answered. "They were Etherborn."

It was enough to yield concerned glances around the table.

"Nomads in *Amul?* Why?" Lain, the field house steward, asked.

Nara shook her head. "They were not nomad. There were six, all in uniformed black leather armor. They were pulling people from their homes, searching the village for the child."

Concerned faces turned to frowns.

"The child we collected?" Sanne asked. "For what purpose?"

"They split into two groups, and we followed one to the Fazel estate. By the time we arrived, they had already murdered the father." Nara watched as reluctant understanding tightened her mother's face. "I killed two and questioned the third. A girl, the daughter of the man leading the operation. She claimed to be a Seer and said they were collecting. They wore the emblem of Thrane."

Scoffs and rumbling broke out around the table as Nara held her mother's quiet gaze.

"How do you know?"

"What did she say?"

"Where are they now?"

"You must be mistaken."

There were too many questions, and the noise in the room grew so loud so quickly Nara could not decipher them all.

Harker stood, fist-pounding the table. "Oi! Let her tell the story."

Everyone stilled, and he sat, motioning for her to continue.

Nara reached into her pocket and pulled out the piece of fabric, tossing it on the table. "The girl confirmed it."

A rush of questions did not follow this time. All eyes studied the patch with mountains etched in silver thread. The faces that had held concern or disbelief now grew fearful.

Her mother's eyes lifted to meet hers. "Nara, you are *sure* of this?"

Nara did not want to be. "I am."

Heavy silence hung in the room.

When no one spoke, Nara continued. "The other three caught up to us. I had no choice but to make a trade of the girl for Harker."

Composure returned to her mother's face, the mask of a leader restored. "Do you know which direction they went or where they came from?"

"They were on horseback with light packs, so they had not traveled far. When they left, they went west toward Somos. Once we were certain they were gone, we did what we could to help and left. We had no one with Influence, so everyone in Amul witnessed the soldiers from Thrane wielding."

Lain reached for the fabric emblem on the table. "Is it possible they were falsifying their identity? There are hundreds of unaccounted Etherborn out in the world. Could this be a ploy by a rogue nomad group? Capitalizing on fear, perhaps?"

"If it was an act, it was a convincing one. The girl gave the information freely, but it did not feel deceitful." Nara looked at her mother. "They knew who we were. Their commander asked I give you his regards. He named himself Wystan Barton."

Alarm widened her eyes. The name was enough to convince any skeptics at the table. All attention was directed to Tora. She was currently the highest-ranking Esērii in Rahab.

"Who is he?" Nara asked.

It was Sanne who answered. "A traitor."

"This is grave, indeed," her mother said.

"He is one of the defectors responsible for taking the children during Lorcan's attempted coup," Lain added.

I know you, Esērii, he'd said. Nara closed her eyes, his voice repeating in her mind. Cold crept over her skin. She wanted to shake it off, pretend she couldn't place it. But it was too true, too real. She knew that she knew him, too.

More than twenty years had passed since the massacre, but the day still lived a vivid existence in her mind. The screams, the explosions, the loss of her father. His face, twisted in despair. His cries. Her cries. Being ripped from his arms. Her mother, covered in blood. The rage on her as she fought. And Barton, screaming. Twenty and seven children had been taken that day. Nara had nearly been the twenty and eighth.

Nara's eyes flicked open, and she looked at her mother, knowing they had relived the moment together, silently in their minds. Some ridiculous part of her hoped she'd return to Rahab to find there was a plausible explanation for it all. The memory, and the looks on the faces around her, shattered the delusion. "What do we do?"

Tora looked at the emblem on the table, considering. "Nara and Harker, you will go to the Citadel and tell the council all you have told us. We will keep this quiet for now." Her eyes moved to Lain. "Have a riverboat crewed with Etherborn so they may travel with haste. Load the boat with enough supplies to get them to Nyrovi. We'll need everything extra we have on hand to take to Amul."

"It will take an hour or two to prepare," Lain said, already standing.

"Then go now. Come back for them when it is ready."

He gave a quick nod and rushed from the room.

"I will travel back to Amul to try to gain control of the situation." Tora continued giving orders until only she, Nara, and Harker remained. "It is likely many have already fled. No doubt some are on their way to Rahab, seeking refuge. It seems unlikely we will be able to contain this. We will need to bring aid. Food, clothing, medical supplies."

"Barton's daughter claimed Thrane has four Seers. That they have been collecting for years," Nara said. "Do you believe that possible?"

Tora sighed. "Yesterday, it would have seemed a wild notion. Now, I don't know," she said, shaking her head. "If it is true, it means we have underestimated them to a truly frightening degree."

Nara watched a thousand thoughts race behind her mother's eyes, none of them good. "If they no longer have cause to conceal their activity here, they have no doubt done the same in the north." It was not a question, but Nara looked at her mother for validation.

Tora's eyes flicked to hers, narrowing. She inhaled slowly, as if choosing her words carefully. "I know what you are thinking. I want you to promise me you will not do anything rash."

Nara looked away.

"Nara, this is serious. We need to be careful how we proceed. Look at me." When she didn't, Tora rose from her seat, coming to kneel by Nara's chair. "You know I love Cerys, too. She is like a daughter to me. We will not help her or your brother with impulsive behavior. Promise me you will not go north unsanctioned."

Nara's expression held the weight of knowing she was going to disappoint her mother. "I cannot promise you that."

Tora exhaled. "At least wait for me to return to the Citadel. Give me that."

Reluctantly, Nara nodded.

"Thank you." Her hand clasped Nara's shoulder as she stood. "I will go and oversee the preparations. After you speak with the council, please tell Sayeed what has happened. Tell him I will return to the Citadel as soon as I can. I should not be more than a sixday behind you."

"And if the council commands I do not speak of it?"

"Tell him anyway. Our son is in the north. I will not keep this from him." Tora leaned down and placed a kiss on Nara's cheek. "Travel safe, daughter." She nodded to Harker on her way out.

The two sat in silence in the otherwise empty room. Nara sighed, resting her head in her hands. They had nothing to do for the next two hours but wait. And think.

Harker slapped the table, and she jumped. "Drink?"

"Gods, yes." She pocketed the Thranean patch and followed him from the room.

The pair sat on the roof of the field house, under the full moon, passing back and forth a bottle of whiskey snatched on the walk up. A dog barked, cutting through the muted sounds of laughter and song from the brothels and pubs below. Nara closed her eyes, taking in the light breeze, rich with smoke and spice.

"In the ten years I've known your mother," Harker said, "I've never seen her so undeterred toward breaking a command." He took a swig and then held the bottle out to her with a calloused hand.

"It unnerved me, too." She tossed it up, taking a sizable gulp. It was her third or fourth, and the tautness in her belly was starting to ease.

"She worries for your brother."

"I worry for *her*." Nara took another drink and set the bottle between them. "At some point my mother will have to accept he isn't coming back." With all they'd learned, any sliver of hope that lived in her had been set ablaze. Her brother was gone. Nara had known it for some time. And now Cerys might be in danger. The thought sent a strike of dread through her, and she reached for the bottle again.

Harker turned to face her. "You can't know that for sure."

"Harker," Nara said, with pleading eyes, "you know as well as I do, he is dead."

Harker turned back to the view. Nara sensed he agreed, but perhaps could not bring himself to put words to it. "Will you really go north?" he asked.

Nara considered. "I don't know. If that is where the fight is." She looked up at the moon and wondered what Cerys was doing in the same moment, under the same night sky.

"Days, Nara," Harker said as he combed back his hair with both hands. "Everything is going to change, isn't it?"

"It already has."

They met eyes and shared an understanding, an acceptance of all that the day had altered. As unsettled as she was, Nara felt a strange relief. One cannot exist in fear of the unknown. There is no peace in it. Decades had passed, and many believed Lorcan Dracos would stay forever behind his mountains and wards. Nara among them. But the day was always with them, lurking underneath the delusion. One could see it in the eyes of those who had survived the *Bloody Day*. Even in those who had not yet been born, as if the heartbreak of the betrayal and the horror of the slaughter had been passed down through blood. She wondered how many generations it would have taken to free the Esērii of it. She supposed now they would never know.

Harker sighed and reached for the bottle. "If you go north, I'll go, too."

"You and I both know the council will drag their feet. Even when they move to send a party north to investigate, it will not include me. If I go, it'll be unsanctioned, and I'm going for Cerys. That will have serious consequences." Nara turned to look at him. "I wouldn't ask you to do that."

"You didn't," he said flatly. The moon was bright, and Nara was able to make out his features clearly. He looked uneasy, fearful even, but also resolved.

"Why would you do that?"

He nudged her with his elbow, giving her a sly smile. "Someone has to keep you in line."

Nara laughed. "You're mad if you think anyone is up for that task, let alone the likes of you. You need a handler as much as I."

That pulled a chuckle from him. "Fair."

"But I would not say no," she said, with grateful eyes. "Thank you."

"Ah, I'm just itching for a fight, is all." He winked at her. "Besides, they'll take one look at you and run right back into Thrane. Just like today. They may have Seers, but I'll bet my boots they don't have anyone like you."

5

Neith

"One does not think to wield, one feels it."

THE WAY OF ETHER
ASHERAH GALANIS, FIRST CONSUL, THE CITADEL, 807 AQ

Neith remained in her tent until the moon was high. Ayla fetched her supper and then talked incessantly until Neith pretended to fall asleep so she would leave. She simply lay there, detaching from time and space. When the dread weighed heavy, she tried shifting her thoughts, but they always came back to the girl, the scream, and the awful music in her mind.

A gentle hand rested on her shoulder. "My lady," she heard Ayla say, her voice low. "Your escort waits outside the tent."

Neith sat up and walked to the basin, splashing cool water on her face. Without prompt, Ayla began fixing pieces of hair that had come loose from the plait. Neith was disappointed she did not sense Sam. And perhaps a touch embarrassed by her eagerness.

In his stead were two soldiers she recognized from her escort the night before. They introduced themselves as Max and Petra Nasseri. Two new members of her guard. They shared the same golden skin, dark hair, and heavy southern accent.

It was a short walk to the south side of camp. A large crowd had formed at the base of the mountain, eager to see what she would do. As in Godsreach, it felt performative. This was court, and she was the dancing fool.

She did not see Roman.

Her eyes trailed the length of the peak as she approached, neck craning to see the top. Chosen for its composition, it was rich in softer minerals like biotite, and coal.

When she reached her father, he narrowed his eyes, a question in them. She nodded, and his hand lifted, quieting the crowd.

"Men and women of Thrane," he bellowed, his solitary voice filling the open night. "Over twenty years ago, I returned to my homeland with a vow to see it restored. I vowed to see our people no longer suffer at the hands of zealots, thieves, and those who would make themselves our masters. I vowed no longer will Thrane cower in the mountains. I vowed then, and I vow now, where my father failed, I will succeed. *We* will succeed. For our cause is just."

Nods and sounds of agreement rolled through the crowd as he walked the line. His shoulder-length black hair was tied back, revealing in detail the enthusiasm and conviction on his face.

He pointed toward the mountain. "The idleborn beyond these borders believe their Gods warred and left this world. They do not know they were flesh and blood. They do not know we have always walked among them, like I, like many of you."

Neith felt the energy in the crowd building. Ether hummed as excitement grew.

"We will bring truth back to this world. We will return to the time before the Great Quell. When Etherborn did not hide, and when the idleborn were not made ignorant." He paused, turning to look at Neith. His eyes moved to Magnus and then over the crowd. "I look amongst you with pride. I see warriors. Some of you born here, and some of you traveled here, in common plight with common enemies. The people of Thrane know what it is to be shunned, hunted, and scorned. *Hated* simply for the nature of your birth.

"For hundreds of years, the Etherborn of this world have been relegated to live in the shadows. Made slave by the Esērii. Made to fight for them, die for them, under the falsehood of honor and dignity." He spat. "The High Council sits in silk robes in the Citadel, gaining wealth and power on the backs of Etherborn men, women, and children. Just yesterday, we found a boy of only fourteen winters in Godsreach, sent by the Esērii to guard the borders of Straeth. A meaningless death. A tragedy of Etherborn blood spilled."

The crowd made whispers of disgust.

"Here, now, we come together to build a new kingdom, a new Thrane, a new empire where Etherborn and those born idle live together, thrive together. We will take back the land that was once ours, what is *rightfully* ours." He stopped walking, coming to stand in front of the gathering. *"Will you build this new world with me?"*

The crowd erupted. Neith found enthusiasm growing within. Her eyes scanned the faces, connecting with Sam's.

The ground trembled from the stomping of boots on earth. It continued until her father held up his hand, quieting the group once more. He turned and walked toward her, gazing up at the mountain as a stillness settled. The air was cool and rich with rabid energy. It sparked off her father, off the Etherborn in the crowd. She wanted to do it. She was ready.

He slowly turned his head, peering down at her. "Begin."

Neith removed her boots and unfastened her cloak, letting it fall to the ground. She stepped forward several paces, distinguishing herself from the still-growing assembly. The grass was soft and grounding under her bare feet.

She inhaled, slow and deep, letting her arms rest at her sides, palms forward. Closing her eyes, Neith tilted her face toward the full moon and let its light saturate. This night was chosen with purpose. The moonlight soaked into her skin, intoxicating. For a moment, she let herself bathe in it. It felt like home. Like an embrace from someone who loved her.

Neith reached out into the ether. Through the earth beneath her, through the air, and into the mountain before her. It answered with a gentle hum. Cobalt-blue power poured from her palms, weaving into the soil and clay. Racing through the fabric of the blackstone and obsidian. In all the space between. Discovering its secrets. She saw every crack, every vulnerability. Her power enveloped the mountain, mapping, marking every part she would take.

What poured from her palms grew warm and bright, flowing faster, setting her hands to shake. Neith called and compressed, forcing it together until it started to combust, feeding the surge, on and on until the backs of her eyes could no longer conceal the light.

Slowly, so slowly, she called again. This time, not to the ether, but to that which is below. She called to the nether. That which is empty, that which is void. Where ether gives, nether consumes, and it is always hungry. She wove her power into the plane between her world and the void. Readying to rip, to tear. To snap.

Tremors erupted around her. She heard cries of surprise. She continued to channel, generating heat, building the pressure. She let herself relish in it. It felt good to burn. When she was burning, she wasn't thinking, only feeling. And she wanted to ignite.

The earth shook, and the wind howled. She cried out with the effort to hold on. One. More. Moment.

The air erupted in a silent crack.

The plane snapped, and it cut through the night. Through her bones. Not something you hear, something you feel. Like lightning in the night sky. Its strike too swift to see. Its psalm too quick to heed. Electric on her skin as it consumed.

It called to her, to its familiar. A vortex drawing her forward.

Neith released the nether to the place it belonged, where it longed to be. She fell to her knees, drained, as bright blue light erupted from the mountain, surging in every direction, climbing high into the sky, racing toward them. Blinding. It smacked into her like a windstorm, and she dug her fingers into the damp earth as the chaos around her raged past.

Jarring stillness followed. She stared at the ground, chest heaving. A steady stream of blood flowed from her nose, pooling on the grass.

It was quiet for a time, the only sound the ringing in her ears until slow, cautious footsteps approached.

Someone knelt beside her. She looked up to see Sam, his eyes wide, surveying. He tore a large strip of fabric from his tunic and held it up to her nose. His eyes were struck with awe. Or fear. Or both.

Black ash filled the air, coming down slow and lazy like snow. He was covered in it. She was covered in it. He caught some between his fingers, and it turned into indistinguishable particles, carried away in the night air.

Neith sat back on her heels, hazy and consumed. People shuffled past, eyes fixed on the mountain. A long, dark corridor now split the stone, rising high into the sky and out into the kingdom of Straeth.

"*Nether?*" Sam asked, turning back from the mountain to look at her again.

She nodded, still panting. Wielding nether always comes at a cost. She touched one of her ears, and her fingertips came away red.

"Your eyes—they're black." He peered into them, and Neith could not discern if it was terror or concern that plagued his features.

"It will pass," she said, from a hoarse throat.

Sam held out his arm, and she braced against it, rising to stand. She was up, but unstable, her body in strange conflict as the exhaustion and invigoration battled. Wielding had flared her senses, and all were on fire. The warmth of his skin where she gripped his arm, the cool night air, his heavy gaze, the damp grass. The lingering emptiness. She felt it all, and it felt good.

Her father appeared beside her, his focus on the space the mountain had once occupied. He glanced at her, and Neith flinched, startled by the eagerness in his eyes. It was feral, and his ether was charged, stirring and sparking around him. His chest heaved in deep, affected breaths as he turned back to the mountain.

Without directing his words to any specific person, he said, "We depart at first light."

6

Thea

"When the Gods warred, the world wept. When the Gods quelled, the world went to sleep."

THE WAY OF ETHER
ASHERAH GALANIS, FIRST CONSUL, THE CITADEL, 807 AQ

Thea set her book aside, then stretched her arms high above her head, taking care not to disturb the man nestled between her thighs. His lips were slightly parted, fostering the slow, steady breathing of one caught in the trance of deep sleep. She was unenthusiastic to wake him. They had so few of these moments in their futures. She wanted to live in them as long as she could.

Deep in the forests surrounding Highclere Castle, the magnolia trees in the clearing charmed in full bloom. White and pale pink petals scattered the quilt and earth beneath. Thea closed her eyes, soaking in the warmth of the sun as a cool breeze from the lake billowed into the thin fabric of her shift, carrying traces of citrus and floral, tickling her nose. Spring would soon turn to summer, but the wind and water still possessed a subtle chill.

Her fingertips explored the peaks and valleys of his shoulders, trailing down the muscles spread broad across his back. She studied the shades of gold his chestnut-colored hair reflected when the sunlight hit it just right. His sandy beige skin was smooth and soft, save for some calluses on his hands from sword sport. Thea didn't mind. He was too perfect without them. Everyone needs flaws, and he had few.

She vowed to commit every fiber of him to memory so she might live in these small moments when he was gone. Her heart ached as she thought in scarce over a sixday's time it would be someone else's legs he'd lie between.

Thea brushed a lock of hair from his brow, causing him to stir. "We should get back," she said, gently.

Marten groaned his objection, nuzzling closer, his breath warm against her bare skin. She felt it slow as he drifted back into slumber.

She chuckled and nudged him. "Come on, sleepyhead. I'd rather not get an earful from my stepmother."

He let out a grunt of acceptance and sat up. Rubbing his eyes, he asked, "How long did I sleep?"

Thea looked up at the sun. "An hour, I think." It was approaching midday. "We need to get back. If we are absent all afternoon, it will not go unnoticed."

Marten shifted closer, tucking a loose tendril of golden blonde hair behind her ear. He smiled, pulling small leaves and petals from her wavy strands. "What will they think if you return in this state?" He feigned concern, but the bend in his lips gave away his underlying satisfaction he had displaced her so.

Thea laughed. "What they have long known. That I seduce you and command you here at my leisure." She climbed to her knees, moving to straddle him.

Marten's hands came around, gripping her hips. "Was it not *I* who seduced you?"

Thea pursed her lips, her head taking on a playful tilt. "Let us think on it for a moment."

She leaned forward and kissed him, her tongue making quiet proposals of what could be. Of what had been so many times before. The warmth of his mouth was a pleasure she was well versed in. A song she knew how to sing. Their bodies possessed a familiarity only those who learned how to make love together could. Her thighs tightened, pulling a low groan from him.

"Forget what I said," he breathed between kisses. His arms wrapped around her back, cementing her body to his. Heat built between them, like a long-burning ember threatening to reignite. Except it didn't. It slowed. It became mournful. Marten pulled back to look into her eyes, and she knew what he was thinking. The same as her. They would be separated soon. "How will we bear it?" he asked.

"As we always knew we would." It was the only answer she could come by, and a lie, as she was not sure she could.

Marten sighed, running a thumb along her cheek. "One day, these green eyes will look at another man the way you're looking at me now, and I will envy him until the day I die."

Thea shook her head. "That will never happen."

"It will," he said, with an air of regret that sent a strike through her chest.

"We will still see each other. You'll return to court throughout the year, and there will be other—"

Marten leaned his head against hers, stilling her words. "But not like this." He breathed the words more than said them as a hand trailed up her back.

"No," she said, "not like this."

They'd always known they would never be allowed to marry. Marten was heir to Aremore, the most prominent duchy in Ire. She was the king's bastard daughter. She offered nothing but a stain on his family name. Marriage for women and men of their status was a matter for the state, and time had finally caught up with them.

In eight days, Marten would be wed to a girl he'd never met. He would be sent away from the capital, back to Aremore, to produce heirs and prepare for lordship. He would come to court four or five times a year, at best. He wanted their relationship to continue after he was wed. His marriage was purely political, but Thea had drawn a hard line against it. It had become a point of contention between them so severe they'd stopped discussing it moons ago as they would quarrel endlessly and fervently about it. He shook his head, dismissing the hard truths of their situation, as he always did.

"So, tomorrow then? We meet at dawn?" he jested.

"Where are we going this time?" It was a game they played when the actualities of their situation became a bit too real.

He pursed his lips, a rueful smile forming as he considered. "Ostalla."

"And what will we do in Ostalla?" Thea leaned back, holding on to his shoulders for support.

"Live on the coast," he mused. "We'll build an olive grove and drink wine. You will love it there. Long summers and endless sunshine. Everyone is happy in Ostalla. It is impossible not to be."

Thea smiled. "It sounds wonderful." She could not muster her usual enthusiasm.

His eyes cast a loose gaze, immersed in the fantasy, until flicking up to meet hers. Thea recognized the look at once. She opened her mouth to cut him off, but he moved too fast.

He lifted her back onto the quilt, kneeling, eyes locked on hers. "What if I were serious?"

"Marten…"

"I mean it, Thea," he said. "What if we left?"

She clamped her eyes shut. Every part of her wanted to run with it, but she knew she couldn't indulge the idea, even for a breath. She had put much practice in building her resolve the past moons, but it was fragile and precarious at best. "Please… please don't. It only makes this harder."

His hands came up on either side of him. "What is stopping us?"

Thea threw her arms in the air, reflecting his position. "Duty?"

"Fuck duty. We didn't ask for it." He looked away. "I don't want this. I don't care about titles or lands or lordship or any of that nonsense."

Neither did Thea. Her objections were more logical, practical. She didn't care about doing the right thing or familial obligations. Thea simply knew it was unfeasible. But practicalities were not reasons Marten would consider. "Your father and my stepmother would hunt us to the end of the world." She had meant it as a jest. An attempt to steer the conversation back to play. He didn't laugh.

Marten continued, undeterred by her protests. The fervor in his words heightened with discontent.

"Consider it," he said, reaching for her hand, "for one moment. We could be on a boat tonight—"

"*Marten.*"

His face went from surprise to anger to ache.

Thea pressed her face into her hands. "Please let us stop this. I have only a few days with you, at best, and I do not wish to spend them quarreling."

His eyes met hers, the frenzy in them cooling. "Forgive me. I'm sorry. Of course." He took a breath and combed his hair back with his hands.

Marten was often excitable, impulsive even. Thea knew if she said yes, he would go. She also knew they would be crawling back to Ire in a couple of years when whatever money they scraped together ran out.

"You must know I would go anywhere with you."

"I know." She cradled his face. "I know you would."

He reached for her hands and lifted them slowly, placing a gentle kiss on each. It tugged at her heart, but she knew she had to stand firm.

"We should get going." Thea moved to stand, but he pulled her back.

"Let us stay a bit longer."

"We really shouldn't."

His fingertips grazed the exposed skin of her chest, trailing between her breasts.

"You're unbelievable." She laughed. "I swear by the Gods, the swiftness in the swing of your mood makes me dizzy."

Marten gave her his most convincing pout. "As you said, we only have a few days together. The worst that can happen already is."

"Your father—"

"My father can piss off. I'm not wed yet," he said, his typical, light-hearted demeanor recovered. He leaned down, placing a soft kiss on the inside of her knee. "Besides, there is still work to be done here."

His lips climbed higher, trailing the inside of her thigh, lifting her shift as he moved. He hovered dangerously close to the summit. Her breath quickened as his mouth connected.

Thea lay back on the forest floor. "If you insist."

Brilliant shades of orange stained the sky when Thea returned to Highclere Castle, having said goodbye to Marten under the cover of the forest. She smiled at her home. Its tall, ivy-covered stone walls glowed beneath the warmth of the setting sun. She was later than she'd hoped. Passing castle staff, she inclined her head to them as she strolled through the gardens toward the kitchen entrance. It was her usual route and where she was less likely to encounter a member of court.

She stopped and plucked a single yellow stem of primrose from one of the beds, tucking it behind her ear.

The kitchen was empty. Only Breeda was present, leaning against a table, arms crossed. Scowling. "You grow too bold, girl."

"I got lost." Thea pranced through the room and placed a quick kiss on Breeda's cheek. In such close quarters, she saw the lines drawn around her eyes, and the hints of graying blonde hair coming loose from the white bonnet tied at the nape of her neck. The air was still warm with the faint sweetness of freshly baked bread.

"I mean it, you ought to be more careful," Breeda said, eyeing her as she walked.

"Loosen your bonnet, Breeda. No one here cares what I do." Thea plucked raspberries from an overflowing pail. They were the perfect balance of tart and sweet, prompting a contented sigh of delight. "Besides, you would no doubt make an excuse for me." She smiled playfully, but Breeda was unmoved. Her eyes were riddled with concern, and it gave Thea no pleasure. Breeda had been her nursemaid since she was shy of a moon old, taking a position as the household steward when Thea had come of age. The woman raised her in every regard. Breeda was the only mother Thea had known and one of the few whose love she never questioned.

"I worry about you," Breeda said, her intensity growing. "You are twenty and one years now. You are the king's daughter, and there are expectations—even if your father indulges you."

Thea stretched her neck against the sting. The last thing she wanted was to disappoint her, but she had little desire to converse, yet again, on that particular subject. "The king's *bastard* daughter. You forgot a word. And quite an important one. Born between two wives and five legitimate heirs." Thea knew her circumstances were not common. All at court were aware of her relationship with Marten, but simply didn't acknowledge it. Even her father. It existed only in whispers and judgmental glances. In other courts across the north, Thea would be shunned, perhaps even sent away to some remote temple to live out her days as a Sister of the Faith. In some places, simply being a bastard could earn her that. It didn't make her afraid. It made her angry.

Breeda stood, stepping a few paces closer, speaking low. "If you develop a reputation, how will you marry well? Marten will be gone soon."

Thea snorted. "A *reputation*?" She looked at the woman in genuine shock. "Come now, Breeda, I think we're well past that." She ate another raspberry, shrugging her shoulders. "Besides, if my father has any intentions toward my future state of matrimony, he has not shared them with me."

The conversation halted as they watched a girl enter the kitchen and take a large tray of fruit. Thea snatched an apricot as she passed. When the girl disappeared through the doorway, Breeda continued. "It is not the same for Marten as it is for you. He is a man."

Thea's arms fell to her sides. "Do you think I do not know this? As you so astutely pointed out, I have lived twenty and one years in this body. I'm quite aware it is not the same for me." She strode across the kitchen, snatching a chalice from a shelf. "If only I had a cock, how different my life would be."

"*Language*, Calithea."

Breeda stepped into her path on the walk back. She looked down and plucked a random piece of greenery from the bodice of Thea's dress. When her eyes returned, they were heavy with question, and a little accusation.

Thea walked around her and placed the apricot on a table in favor of a carafe. "Is this Parthenean or Ostallan?" She took a quick sniff and turned up her nose. "Ah, Baltan. Not my first choice, but it'll do in a pinch." She filled the chalice, bringing it immediately to her lips. She gulped half in one turn.

Breeda didn't speak. Only stared at her disappointedly. It was enough.

Thea sighed, setting the carafe and chalice on the table. "I know he will be gone soon. I have known for years, Breeda. I have never entertained the idea this would end any way other than it is, or will in eight days. But he is the only thing I have for myself, and I won't give him up a second earlier than I must."

Breeda's scowl softened, sympathy washing in, only to be swiftly replaced with resolution. "You want me to feel sorry for you? It seems like you're doing enough of that on your own."

Thea stiffened. Breeda was never one to hold her opinion, but it was not often delivered so roughly. Thea felt exposed and a little ashamed.

"No, I do not want that," Thea said, but wasn't sure it was true. She reached for the chalice, tossing back what remained. Perhaps she did indeed want someone to feel sorry for her. The truth in the accusation sparked her temper.

Breeda stalked across the kitchen, snatching the chalice from her hand. "It is only a matter of time before your brother and sister are set in matches of their own. What will become of you when everyone else moves on?"

Thea thought about it. What *would* she do? Spend her life looking after her nieces, nephews, and younger siblings? Despite her affection for them, it did not seem a life's purpose. She looked at Breeda. Would this be her in thirty years?

Thea felt the dark pull low in her belly—the familiar empty feeling. It always happened in the same order. Dark, cold, panic, pain. She tried to swallow the knot forming in her throat. Light tremors radiated down her arms to her fingertips. She fisted and released them, trying to still the shake.

Breeda's free hand rose to settle on Thea's shoulder, eyes concerned. "Another attack?"

"I'm fine." Thea shook her off. For years, she'd had these *fits*, as the physicians called them. Sometimes they would ease quickly. On occasion, they exploded into terror and panic. Her body would shake and writhe uncontrollably. She would often faint. They were getting worse and more frequent.

"You fool no one, girl," said Breeda, shaking her head. Breeda was one of the few whose judgment she could not bear.

Thea chewed at her cheek. "I wish I were the person you wanted," she said, the sour notes of her tone palpable. "What a marvel she would be." Thea snatched the chalice back, grabbed the carafe, and marched toward the stairs. She didn't look back. "And I am not *girl*. I am your *lady*."

7

Neith

"There is always power to be had, if one knows where to look."

THE COST OF VALOR
AUTHOR UNKNOWN, 203 BQ
TRANSLATED FROM OLD ASARI BY MERIAH TURAN
HAIS Z'NOSIŠ, 1200 AQ

Neith woke to find her belongings packed. A single plum-colored dress lay draped over a trunk. Again, she had slept hard, and again, it unnerved her. Neith was not used to being the last to rise. She was always first to wake, first at the table to break fast, and first to finish.

She tossed the fur blanket aside and stood, a touch unsteady on her feet. A plate of berries and bread waited beside the water pitcher, and her belly growled at the sight. Neith was indulging in both when blinded by a flash of light.

"You're awake, my lady!" Ayla wore the same beaming smile and staggering enthusiasm she had the day before.

"What is the hour?" Neith asked, squinting toward the door.

Ayla stepped through. "Quite late. Over half of camp has marched out. All of First and most of Second. Come"—she gestured—"let's get you dressed."

Ayla handed her a clean shift and then turned to provide privacy.

"Why wasn't I woken?" Neith pulled the dirty one from her body, replacing it with the new. The fabric was soft. Much finer than she was accustomed to. "You can turn around."

"We were under strict instructions not to, my lady." Ayla retrieved the plum-colored dress and held it out between them.

"*Ayla,*" she said, "please call me Neith." Ayla agreed the day before, but thrice Neith had to remind her. Neith suspected the error was based in resistance, not forgetfulness.

Ayla curtsied. "If you wish."

Neith stepped into the skirts of the dress and held out her arms. Ayla slipped on one sleeve, and then the other, before securing the ties on the back. She now understood why women needed aid dressing. Neith wasn't sure she would be able to fasten it on her own.

She looked down at herself. "Is this practical for traveling?"

"It is for a lady. I can pull something else if you prefer." Ayla was wearing a plain brown wrap dress that matched the color of her freckles. Neith thought she would prefer something similar.

"No," she answered, shaking her head. "No need for the trouble." Neith cleaned her teeth while Ayla ran a brush through her hair. "Has my father departed camp?"

"He sent word this morning. He waits for you across the border." Ayla put the brush in a trunk alongside other articles for female groom-ing. "Shall I braid your hair?"

"No, thank you, I will wear it loose." Neith doubted she would ever grow used to being preened so by another. It made her feel silly and child-like, something she needed no assistance with. "I am ready now."

Sam stood a short distance from her tent, speaking with Max, Petra, and four soldiers she did not know. He said something to the others, then made his way toward her.

"Good morning—well, no, it is past midday," Neith said, looking up at the sun. It was uncommonly bright. "Good afternoon."

Men retrieved trunks from her tent under Ayla's direction, stowing them on a cart.

"Good afternoon," Sam returned. He looked down at her dress, and she wondered if he was thinking it as impractical as she had. "We are ready to move out. At your leisure, of course."

"I see." Neith felt sheepish they'd been standing around all morning waiting for her to rise.

"Are you well?" Sam held a hand over his eyes, shielding them from the sun. "If I may ask."

She nodded.

"I am glad to hear it."

They smiled at each other until the silence grew awkward, broken only when Ayla emerged from the tent. Sam cleared his throat, and Neith took a step back.

Looking at the gathering behind him, she asked, "Who are the others with Max and Petra?"

Sam folded his arms behind his back. "They've come to join you."

"To join my guard?"

"No." He paused, frowning. "They… wish to be placed in your service."

Neith laughed. It fell away when she realized he was serious. "*Why?*" It seemed such an absurd notion.

Sam's mouth opened and closed several times before he spoke. "Because like I, and all others present, they watched you evaporate a sizable portion of a mountain last night." He said it as if he was still convincing himself it was true.

Neith swallowed. She spoke softly to Sam. "What do I do?"

His frown deepened. "Has no one told you?"

This was just like her father. Throw her right out into the lake. Sink or swim. "No."

She waited for judgment, or a look one gives a naive child, but it didn't come. Instead, he shrugged. "It is fairly simple. They will make their intention known. You accept or decline."

Neith shifted nervously from foot to foot. "Should I accept?"

"That… I cannot say. There is responsibility in leading, but also great honor in being chosen by your peers."

She looked at him, chewing on her bottom lip. "Were you chosen or appointed?"

"Chosen," he said quickly, before his gaze flicked aside.

Before my father stripped you of it, she thought. "Then, I will accept."

Sam inclined his head. "I will send them over."

In succession, each soldier approached and made their request. All appeared to be of a similar age to the rest of their growing troupe. The first, Raiden, Neith knew immediately as the son of Commander Maelis Nicomedes, having seen him around the castle in Necrium at feasts and similar gatherings for years. He was of average height, with long, Thranean black hair he wore tied back. Stray pieces fell over his dark blue eyes, which were serious and stoic, like his mother's.

Next came a tall boy, Kieran Ashwood, with short red hair and a surprisingly deep voice. Intelligent brown eyes studied her, though done covertly.

Iris Aetos, a petite girl with green eyes, pale blonde hair, and Vikan features, followed. She was confident, and her walk had a boastfulness not common on one with such a small stature.

The last was a handsome boy with dimples, whom Neith assumed to be southern. His accent was subtle. Coastal, most likely, perhaps hailing from Tethos or Balta. Bellamy Silva had deep, olive-toned skin, dark hair, and hazel eyes that gleamed. He wore a subtle grin as he offered his service.

All four were Etherborn. Valuable soldiers.

Ayla approached, dusting her hands. "All packed."

"Then let us be on our way." Neith walked to where Storm waited with the other horses. She stroked her neck, and the horse nuzzled against her. Once she mounted, the others followed suit. Neith tugged the reins, turning Storm, and realized all were waiting for her direction.

Three days ago, she was just a girl—a sister, a daughter, a student. Now, she was riding into a war campaign that would span years, if not decades, with a personal guard, an attendant, and four soldiers under her command. *Very well.*

She nudged Storm, and they started south in the direction of the border. Sam fell in beside her, the others following behind.

Ayla had not exaggerated when she said most had departed. They rode past the remains of campfires, their orange embers little more than ash. Some were still packing and organizing, loading carts with crates of food, clothing, and other essentials.

They passed a prisoner cart, close enough to make out its inhabitants' faces. A soldier turned the key, locking a small group within its bars.

Neith paled when she set eyes on Rhea, the woman from Godsreach. She was leaning against the bars, staring out into the distance. The burns on her face had been healed. She no longer looked defiant. She looked broken, paying no mind to anything transpiring around her. The other captured Esērii were with her, having refused the offer, Neith surmised. All were now on their way to Nighhelm, and Neith shuddered at the thought. Having never been herself, she had only rumors and the stories of others to base her trepidation on, but they were enough.

One could barely call it a city. It was northeast of Necrium and nearly encompassed by unending ice. It was cold, dark, and desolate. To stand out in this regard in Thrane was notable. Nothing could be grown. All goods were brought in from the capital, which meant its offerings were even more destitute. It was where criminals were sent, specifically the

Etherborn ones.

Neith could not help her relief in knowing the woman was being sent away. She did not want to look upon her face again. It would always, as it was then, drive her to dark thoughts.

It was a far more impressive sight under the sun. Where once were obsidian and stone, was now a large gap thirty men wide. One could look straight through to the distant green forests on the other side. Her eyes trailed it from ground to mountaintop, where the dark passage turned into blue sky. Neith remembered what it felt like when she'd called the nether. How she'd liked it.

Tiny flecks of black dust still floated in the air, coating the ground and trees. It was ominous, but beautiful. Otherworldly, Neith thought. The air was painfully dry and rich with sulfur, aggravating her throat.

Neith stopped at the edge. Despite the brightness of the day, the depth restricted the sun's reach, and it was darker than she'd expected.

She looked at Sam. He was looking up, studying, an indiscernible expression on his face. Glancing back at the others, she found them in similar action, some with awe and excitement in their eyes.

Sam formed an etherstar. It glowed with a honey-colored hue that reminded her of how his eyes had looked in the forest, bathed in sunlight. He released it, sailing it down the passage before them. Similar stars were visible in the distance as other parties journeyed through. Neith nudged Storm forward. The other horses hesitated, but followed with some coaxing.

The air turned cooler the deeper they traveled. Clusters of raw obsidian in the rough-cut walls reflected in the light. Neith thought it looked a bit like the nighttime sky.

The emptiness from the nether was affecting. She swallowed at the hollow feeling in her belly, sensing the uneasiness from those behind her. Neith was vividly familiar with how unsettling it was the first time one felt it.

"Will it always feel like this here?" Sam asked, gazing around.

"No. It will ease with time. Though I've never used it on this scale before," she answered, "so I cannot say how long. I imagine it will not fade quickly."

"It is a strange feeling. It is… difficult to describe," he added.

"Empty," Ayla said, "frightfully, empty."

Wielding nether was intoxicating, exhilarating even. The feeling persisted for a length of time after, and Neith could not think of anything that compared to it. Until it faded. Then nothing but bitter emptiness remained.

"What is the dust in the air?" Sam held out his hand, collecting it as he had the night before.

"Remnants of the mountain I missed." Neith looked up. It was a disorienting sight. Tall, black walls stretched high above them. "Snapping the plane is like ripping a series of holes," she explained. "It isn't all encompassing." Though practice had made her quite effective. She'd come a long way from snapping small stones.

Sam looked at her with inquisitive eyes, as if trying to make sense of what she'd said. She wanted to tell him there was no point to it. She'd been wielding nether for years and barely understood it herself.

A silent, collective sigh resounded from the group as they crossed out of the mountain path. It was not often Neith relished in the sun, but in that moment, she embraced it with gratitude.

They continued for an hour through the dense forest. As with the path created for Godsreach, trees and other obstacles had been unearthed, carving out a rough trail.

A group on horseback waited on the other side of the tree line, her father among them. As they approached, he looked around her, taking note of the additional soldiers in her company. They met halfway between their parties.

"Well rested?" he asked.

"I am."

His hair was tied back into a slick knot, and his uniform was immaculately polished and pressed. It was not unusual for him to be properly attired, but he was more refined than the average day. "I see you have a squad now," he said, gesturing with a casual nod to the others.

Neith glanced back at the soldiers who waited a short distance behind. "I have."

He stared at her for a moment, glacial eyes taking her in, then looked up at the mountain, and a hint of the fire from the night before returned to his eyes. "I daresay they will not be the last to join you."

Neith took a slow breath, thinking carefully on what to say next. "Should I earn it, I will welcome them."

An ever-so-slight curl formed on one side of his mouth. Were she not so familiar with the stonelike indifference he typically wore, she would have missed it entirely.

"Very well, Lieutenant Dracos. We travel straight through until we reach Northbridge. It is the last sizable town before Croydyn. Your squad will ride with Magnus and Second Division."

Neith blinked. "I am not riding with you?" This was a change. The plan had always been for her to march with her father and brother in the First.

"No. Roman and I will never be more than two or three days' ride ahead. We will raze on the way."

He did not say it, but she knew this change was because of what happened in Godsreach. They were being cautious, having been taken by surprise. She also knew her reaction held some manner of weight.

"The First and Second will travel together after Northbridge," he continued. "If all stays to plan, we will meet again in a halfmoon." He lowered his voice, his next words intended only for her. "Magnus will look after you. You will see no conflict in the Second."

Her first instinct was to protest, but Neith did not take issue with being excluded from the razing. She nodded.

Lorcan looked at Sam and the others behind her. "I expect you all know your roles. I wish to see my daughter arrive safely."

Half salutes broke out among them. He looked at Neith once more. She waited for him to speak, but he simply nodded and turned, riding off with his soldiers on his heels.

Neith found it surprising how inefficiently an army traveled. It was a sort of organized chaos. Her life before had been so orderly. Now she was watching a tent being erected for her on the side of the road. They had simply stopped when it became too dark to travel.

She felt everyone had a task but her. Ayla rummaged through a trunk. Sam, Max, and Petra discussed safety measures. Iris and Raiden cleared debris to set up camp. Neith felt a bit useless. She wondered what her purpose in leading the squad would be. All seemed to know their jobs better than she.

She picked up sticks and brush, eager to contribute.

Sam approached. "We will take care of this. You can rest—"

"I do not wish to rest," she said, continuing her work. "I've been on a horse all day and I wish to use my legs."

"Forgive me, of course." Sam inclined his head, stepping back.

"There is nothing to forgive." Neith smiled and carried an armful of small branches a short distance, clearing space around the makeshift campsite.

Kieran and Bellamy returned shortly with firewood. It was arranged neatly and set ablaze by Raiden, glowing silver from his ether. The sun was nearly set, and Neith watched similar fires igniting in the distance.

After joining with Magnus and the Second earlier in the afternoon, he'd quickly briefed her on their status and orders before departing together. Overall, they were the largest of the three divisions, but the bulk of horsemen and Etherborn were with the First and Third. Her squad was ordered to ride mid-company. It was an abundance of caution, Neith knew. Once they'd crossed the wards of Thrane, something changed. Magnus and her father were cautious in a way she had not seen. She did not wish to be coddled.

The others sat around the campfire, eating, drinking, and laughing. Neith sat a few paces back, picking at her plate, listening in, though pretending not to. Sam sat next to Petra, seemingly telling her a story. On occasion, she would laugh and reach up to touch his arm or push him playfully. Neith tried to picture herself doing the same. Even in her mind it felt an awkward act.

Neith sat up straighter, trying to emulate Petra's self-assured posture. She jumped when a voice came down from above.

"Is there anything I can bring you?" It was Ayla.

"No," she said quickly, feeling like a caught intruder. Neith hoped she did not appear as gawky as she felt. "Thank you."

"Then I will ready the tent." Ayla smiled and turned to leave.

"Actually," Neith said, halting Ayla's retreat. "Do you drink ale?"

Ayla's brows knitted. "Aye."

"Will you sit and have a drink with me?" Neith patted the empty space on the log beside her.

Ayla grinned like she'd been offered a new pony. Neith saw for the first time she had a small gap between her top front teeth, and it did not look like a flaw. "Of course! I'll fetch it."

She watched her walk to a cart, filling two mugs to the brims. Neith's eyes moved to Sam to find he was also watching Ayla. His gaze flicked to Neith as if taking in what was occurring. It made her feel a bit spied upon, but she supposed he was only doing his job. If she took to drink, surely he needed to know as the one responsible for her safety. She scowled at the notion of being constantly observed. It would be little different from back in Necrium under the watchful eyes of her tutors. Sam turned back and resumed his conversation with Petra.

Ayla handed Neith a mug and sat. She held hers between them. "Cheers," she said.

"Cheers." Neith smiled, giving Ayla's mug a gentle clank. She watched Ayla tip hers back, taking a healthy drink. Neith held it under her nose. It was sour and turned her belly. She took a small sip, and her face puckered.

Ayla giggled. "You get used to it."

"Do you?" Neith wasn't sure which was worse, the ale or the wine her father had given her. She took another drink, much larger this time. Then another. And another.

"*Easy.*" Ayla held up her hand. "You'll be pissed in no time tossing it back that fast."

Neith frowned and set the mug down. She didn't want that. She looked aimlessly around camp, trying to think of something to say. "Did you grow up in Necrium?"

"No, in Nighhelm."

"In *Nighhelm?*" It horrified and intrigued Neith in equal measure. "I didn't realize there were children in Nighhelm." As the words left her mouth, she realized how daft the thought. Of course there would be children. Men and women were stationed there.

"There aren't many. Mostly the children of those in command." Ayla wore her hair in a single plait falling midway down her back. Small pieces had come loose, billowing in the gentle breeze.

Neith wanted to ask about her mother, but was nervous to pry.

Ayla glanced at her, her round, hazel eyes inviting. "You can ask me anything you'd like."

Ayla was something of a wonder to Neith. Neith found her endearing, even if she was still adjusting to her bright manner. Every thought, every feeling she had, she wore on her face, and Neith considered there was a sort of bravery in that. She didn't think she had ever met someone so open, so sweet. Her first inclination was to think it all an act, but each time they spoke, she grew further convinced it was simply who she was. Ayla blinked under heavy blonde lashes. Neith smiled at her and said, "We will share that liberty between us."

Ayla held a straight face, but Neith saw she was fighting off another grin. "If you wish."

"What about your mother?" Neith asked and sipped her ale. "Where is she?"

"Dead."

"Oh," Neith said, and held up her hand. "I am sorry."

"It was a long time ago." Ayla twirled a loose strand of hair around her finger.

Neith nodded. "My mother is dead, too."

"I know." Ayla looked down. "I am sorry for that." Of course she knew. Everyone knew.

"I was barely three winters. I never really knew her," Neith said. "I only wish I had one memory of her. Sometimes, I think I can picture her in my mind, but I'm sure it is fantasy. Father told me there is a portrait of her in the Citadel. He said every Etherborn in the Esērii has their likeness taken. The drawings are kept in a vault."

"What is it you see?" Ayla asked, taking a long drink. "When you think of her."

"Long dark hair and bright green eyes. She is beautiful, but the face I picture is a sad one. Father says I have her face." Neith looked down into her mug, now over half empty. She felt uncommonly eased, despite the bleak subject of their conversation.

"Then she was beautiful, indeed."

Neith appreciated the intention but did not enjoy false praise.

Ayla nudged her arm. "Perhaps one day you'll go to the Citadel to find this portrait."

It was the sort of interaction Neith noticed common among the others in her squad. They were always pushing, nudging, or even wrestling one another. It seemed strange behavior to her, but she returned the gesture. "Perhaps."

They shared a moment of quiet, watching the fire. The conversation and laughter around camp were dying down, replaced with yawns and stretching arms.

Ayla slapped her knee before standing. "Well, I'm off to ready the tent."

Neith gave her a nod and thanks. She looked to where Sam had been sitting to find his spot now empty. Neith continued sipping her ale, letting herself get lost in the cracks and snaps of the burning logs.

A hand came into her line of sight. She looked up to see Sam standing over her. "Magnus would like to see you."

Neith frowned. "Now?"

Sam nodded. He did not seem as taken to drink as the others. His eyes were clear.

"Very well." Neith took his offered hand, and warmth traveled up her arm and into her chest as his grip tightened, pulling her to her feet.

He released her and stepped back. "I will walk you."

"How are you, little one?" Magnus asked as he pulled a chair free from the table in his tent. He gestured for her to sit.

"I am well."

His eyes narrowed as she sat.

"I am adjusting."

Magnus nodded as if the revised expression was more acceptable. "Water?" he asked, walking across the room.

"Have you ale?" She finished her first mug back in camp and was heartily enjoying the way it made her feel. She wasn't ready to part with it.

He turned to look at her with raised brows, and for a moment, she thought he might refuse. But he nodded and, with a faint smile, returned with two mugs. He set one in front of her before taking a chair opposing hers.

She sipped the sour drink, surprised to find it more palatable than the first. Perhaps Ayla was right. Magnus watched her, seemingly amused. She found it a bit irritating. It made her feel like an infant taking its first steps. She took a larger drink, then returned the mug to the table. "Was it my father's idea to have me march with the Second or yours?"

He sat back and blinked. "It was mine."

"I see." She took another drink.

"You are cross about it?" he asked, amusement still enlivening his features.

"No," she answered quickly. "Simply curious." It wasn't a lie because she wasn't sure.

He nodded, sipping from his mug. "We haven't had much time to talk of late, and with what happened in Godsreach, I wanted to make sure you are well."

Neith looked down. Of all the things she might want to discuss, Godsreach was lowest on the list.

He leaned forward over the table, speaking softly. "Have the nightmares returned?"

She shook her head. When she was a child, she had recurring dreams where she hurt people with her gift. Neith feared they would return after all that had happened, but she'd slept soundly the last two nights.

He crossed his arms, his large, dark eyes assessing. "I am worried for you. I warned your father it would be too much too soon."

Neith didn't respond. He was right, but she did not wish to endorse her own incompetence.

"You know you can come to me. At any time. For any reason. So much can change in a single setting of the sun. I know this… all too well." He tipped up his mug, emptying its contents. He would sometimes get this look, the very one on him now, lost in a moment long passed. Neith knew little of his life before the rebellion. Only that he had come of age in the Citadel with her father. Magnus did not often speak of his time there, and when he did, it was purely informative.

"I do not wish to receive preferential treatment. I am a soldier in this army, and you are my commanding officer." She looked down at the purple dress she was wearing and felt anything but a soldier.

"You are a soldier, yes," he said, "but you are new to conflict."

Neith chewed on her bottom lip, feeling a sting. "I am no longer a child, Magnus."

He studied her for a moment. "I suppose you are right. It is only that you are gentle, and I do not wish to see you stripped of it."

Gentle. She was growing tired of that word.

"If you would leave me gentle, you would leave me vulnerable. You said yourself much can change in a single day. If I am to take part in this, I cannot be sheltered from the realities of it. I am in it, or I am not." Neith was taken aback by the sternness in her voice. She wondered if it was the ale. "If I have learned anything these past two days, I have learned that."

"We could have prepared you better. I blame myself for that."

She huffed. "Would it be better to ease one into violence? I cannot see how. I would rather see the worst of what I must do. The worst of what others will do. So that I might learn to live with it."

A mournfulness crept into his eyes. "Do not say that. If you knew the depths of what one will do to another, you would not wish to see it. I assure you. Nothing strips one of their humanity like the pursuit of power. Make a man a promise of it, and you'll see him at his worst."

Neith folded her arms over her chest. "The desire for it seems a necessary condition."

"I assure you, we are all afflicted." He said it begrudgingly, as if he wished it weren't true.

Neith did not like the generalization. She did not want to believe people so rapacious. "You speak rather harshly of humankind as a whole."

He chuckled, low and dark. "Believe me when I say I would rather feel as you do."

"We cannot all be so depraved, Magnus. It seems we would have torn each other apart before now." Neith reached for her mug, disappointed to find it empty.

"Who is to say we haven't many times over?"

Neith conceded it a fair point. "I do not want power, I—" She thought of the things she had done the past days and paused.

"Says the person born with an unimaginable amount of it." He did not say it with judgment, rather as if he was trying to make her understand.

Neith could do many things, but she had never thought of herself as powerful. His response made her question her definition of the word. "I did not ask for it," she said, indignantly.

"You did not have to."

Neith looked away. She would not argue hypothetical desires. His words fueled the constant dread that always lived in her, telling her she was bad. It never said how or why, only told her that she was wrong. "Is that what we are after, Magnus?" she asked. "*Power?*"

Magnus stood and crossed the room, returning with a pitcher. He refilled their mugs. "It may not be our only aim or what sets us on our path, but the desire for it always exists, even when necessity does not. We cannot help it."

"Then how preposterous we are." She let the authenticity of her feelings come out in her tone. Magnus was the only person in the world she expressed so freely with.

"That is why we must always be mindful of it," he said, eyes fixed on hers. He let out a noise that sounded something between a laugh and an exasperated breath. "You've grown quite wise in your short nineteen winters."

Neith shook her head. "I am not wise." She took several drinks from her mug in succession, feeling a gentle sway to her movements. "I often feel I have little to say and very little of it wise."

"Spoken like someone with true wisdom," he said, lifting his mug between them.

Neith shifted in her chair, uncomfortable with his praise. She considered for a moment, then leaned back and peered at him. "I do not find you driven by a desire for power. Your motivation is pure. You are driven by justice, by your desire for peace. To see our kind safe. One might daresay you are driven by the opposite of power," she challenged. "One could say it is love that motivates you."

He smiled, but it quickly turned cautious. He reached across the table, hand clasping over hers. "If you take one thing from my words, Neith Dracos, take this. Power comes in many forms. Love is the most perilous among them."

8

Thea

"A lady's voice should be a whisper, a soft and delicate thing."

ETIQUETTE AND TEMPERANCE OF THE DEVOUT
GEROLD THATCHER, 1052 AQ

All were well into their meals by the time Thea arrived for supper. Three additional tables had been brought to the family dining quarters, prompted by the ever-growing presence of visitors to Highclere. A small band of Parthenean musicians played in the corner.

The marriage of a high noble was no small affair, with lords and ladies of Ire and beyond traveling to the capital city. Marten had told her his father expected guests in from as far as Sibreen. On the morrow, they would outgrow the modest room and feast in the Great Hall for the remainder of the celebrations.

Thea was three glasses of wine gone by the time she arrived. Marten looked up, grinning as she tiptoed her way to the high table. He was seated with his father, next to her eldest brother, Conall, and his wife, Leanne.

"Father." Thea smiled, bending down to place a kiss on his cheek. His graying blond beard was trimmed exceptionally neat. He smiled, sharpening the lines around his eyes.

"Calithea," he said, and patted her hand. "You're early." It was a warning for what brewed beside him. Thea tried not to smile when he winked.

Though Thea was well known for her tardiness, it never grew an exhausted subject for Evelynde.

"Stepmother." Thea curtsied. Evelynde was less than ten years her elder, and it had never felt natural addressing her so.

"We are glad you could join us, Calithea." It was polite enough, but even a small child would be able to discern the scrutiny in her sidelong glance. She was finely dressed in a royal-blue gown with an expansive gold and diamond-encrusted necklace covering her ample breasts. The ornaments in her ensemble increased with every day that drew them closer to the wedding. That evening, an ornate comb of sapphires was pinned into her chestnut-colored locks. She looked beautiful, as she always did, even if Thea thought her adornments gaudy.

"Yes, sister, pray tell us what kept you away all afternoon?" Callum asked from the seat next to Evelynde, a falsified look of curiosity twisting his brow. He forked a piece of meat, chewing it as he blinked at her.

Thea glared at him. "Walking, brother."

"Ah, yes, *walking*." He gave her an impish grin.

Evelynde stiffened. Thea flashed a warning to Callum with her eyes, telling him he would pay for that later.

Thea took her seat at the end, walking past her stepmother, Callum, her elder sister, Catrianna, and the twins—Tamsin and Thomas. Her youngest half siblings turned nine two moons past, and Evelynde had since required them to attend the occasional formal dinner, though neither seemed to enjoy it. Thea could not help but feel it was done with the sole intent to move her further down the line. Bastards were welcome at the high table in Ire, but at the end, after all the legitimate children.

She reached her head forward to stick out her tongue at Thomas, winking at Tamsin. It produced the giggles she'd aimed for. Thea sensed Marten's gaze on her, but didn't dare glance his way. Not with Evelynde watching the room like a hawk perched in a tall tree.

A plate of food sat cold in her place. Roasted pheasant with stewed root vegetables and baked apples with cinnamon. She picked at it, trying to pass time to when all would be finished, and they would be permitted to move about the room.

Callum stared blank-faced forward while Evelynde prattled on to him and Catrianna, no doubt speaking of the wedding arrangements and all the proceeding sixday's events. It was all she spoke of anymore. She had worked tirelessly to arrange not only the wedding but the engagement itself. The girl was her niece. The daughter of an Andaran duke.

Ulric and Conall spoke in close confidence, as they often did. Poor Leanne was forced to make conversation with the duke. Marten's father was a stern man, and Thea could not remember a time she'd seen him laugh. Leanne smiled and nodded along with whatever he said, one hand resting gently on her belly, well swollen with her third child. Thea felt only gratitude for her lonely spot with the children at the end.

After what felt like hours of pushing overcooked carrots around on her plate, a nurse finally came to fetch the twins, and Callum claimed the seat next to hers.

"Gods, I thought I'd have to listen to Evelynde go on for another hour," he said, plopping down in the chair.

"See," Thea said, holding her wine up between them, "do not pity my lowly spot at the end, dear brother. I would fight before giving it up."

"Fair on you." Callum picked up the carafe in front of her to refill his cup. He shook it back and forth when nothing emerged. "Hitting it hard this evening?" he asked with a raised brow.

"Nonsense. It was all Tamsin."

He laughed. "I knew it. Little beast." He stood and reached for another. "Marten tells me we are for the alehouse tonight?"

"Have you other pressing engagements?" She gave him a sardonic smile.

He sat up straight, in a dramatic, haughty fashion. "Come now, Thea, you know the life of a second-born son is full of important meetings and obligations. I've many great and pressing decisions to attend to."

Thea nearly snorted. "At least you're spare parts. I'm the log in the road busting the wheel."

Their banter calmed as they both looked over at Marten in conversation across the room.

"How are you… handling things?" Callum asked.

"With grace and dignity, as a lady should." She smiled and blinked her eyes in rapid succession, mimicking his playacting of before.

He choked out a laugh before turning toward her, a rare display of solemnity casting a shadow over his jestful nature. "I'm serious, Thea. Will you be all right?"

She chewed at the inside of her cheek, meeting eyes with Marten across the room. He smiled at her, which she returned, but it was heavy-hearted. She patted her brother's hand. "I've had four years to prepare, brother. Worry not for me."

He covered her hand with his, unconvinced, but seemingly disinclined to press. Only two years her elder, they'd always been close, sharing a predisposition for mischief. When Marten came to court at fourteen, he'd joined their merry band of troublemakers. The three had been inseparable since.

"Is it strange to think we will be attending your wedding celebrations in just one year's time?" Callum was betrothed to a princess of Ostalla, and next year she would come of marrying age.

"Gods, Thea, do not remind me."

He ran a hand through his wavy blond hair. He kept it cropped fairly close, but some loose tendrils bounced around the crown of his head. Betrothed or not, he often found himself the recipient of the attention of the young ladies at court. He scarcely left the dance floor during a feast or celebration. Thea was quite certain he could ascertain any kind of affection he so desired from them, but that was not Callum's way. He preferred the paid company of the ladies of alehouses in the city.

"How is Marten managing?" he asked.

"He is your best friend, is he not?" Thea asked, sipping her wine.

Callum pursed his lips. "He won't speak on it lately."

She nodded, looking out over the room. "He is… still reluctant to accept it."

Callum filled her cup, then his. "And you? Are you reluctant to accept it?"

She chewed further at her cheek until she felt a sharp sting. "In my head or my heart, brother?"

He shrugged. "Both, I suppose."

"One of us has to keep a strong foot in reality, and it isn't going to be him." She laughed, a little bitter. "He suggested we run away today. In earnest." She brought her cup to her lips and sipped again.

"Seems an unfair burden."

Thea raised her brows. "Seems the way of women and men."

Callum huffed. "I'll not argue that."

Her brother was one of the few with whom she spoke openly about her relationship with Marten, as he was one of the few genuinely privy to it. She was grateful to have him. As close as she was with her sister Catrianna, the relationship existed between them as it did with most. Real, but not acknowledged, like doing so would give it validity. It had been a lesson for Thea in the power of denial. A person could overlook much if doing so aligned with their desires or ideas.

"Should we dance, sister?"

Thea inhaled and looked around the room. She knew she shouldn't do anything to draw attention to herself, but she *wanted* to dance. She glanced at Callum, a sly smile forming. "I believe I am amenable to that."

"Excellent." He stood and held out his hand. They walked together to the only open space large enough to move, waiting for the next song to begin. It was the Labyrinthe, a dance in which the women weave in and out between the men.

She was twirled and spun, giving no care to those who watched or those who did not. Thea threw her arms into the air with abandon and moved her body without concern, laughing wildly. They stayed for two more dances before she retired, bidding her father and family good night.

✛

Returning to her room, Thea found Sylvie, her attendant, readying the bed. Her wild, curly red hair threatened to burst from the bonnet that struggled to contain it. She looked up from her work and smiled.

"We're going out tonight." Thea pulled at the ties of her dress.

"Is that wise with all the extra eyes in town?" Sylvie dropped the pillows and made her way toward Thea. "Let me help you."

"It's all right, I've got it." Thea pulled the dress off her shoulders, letting it fall down her body. She was still sweating from the dancing. "We'll only go to Kyna's, and we'll stay in the back. It'll be fine."

Sylvie peered back with a skeptical eye. They'd grown close since she had come to Highclere. A couple years older and unmarried, she was the fourth daughter of a fisherman from Caern. She'd come seeking work when her father was no longer able to afford her keep. The notion she could not find a husband had seemed unlikely, as Thea found Sylvie an attractive, intelligent woman. She was tall and slender, and her eyes were brown, huge, and round. Complexion fair and freckled, she had an earthy, whimsical charm, like that of a woodland creature. It was later that Thea discovered Sylvie simply did not wish to wed.

"Come on," Thea encouraged, "come with us. It's going to be one ridiculous function after the next this sixday. Who knows the next time we'll be able to."

Sylvie sighed, and a reluctant, slow grin formed. "*Very well.*"

Thea rifled through the trunk where they kept their city clothes hidden. "Where are the—"

"I had to move them. Evelynde was in here rummaging around this afternoon. No doubt planning your attire for said functions." Sylvie pulled a box from behind a trunk in the corner. She flipped it open and tossed the simple dresses and cloaks on the bed.

Thea grimaced at the thought of what she might be forced to wear. Her sister Catrianna was typically in charge of her dress. A responsibility

Thea was content to relinquish. But on occasion, their stepmother would take charge, adorning them all in something utterly ridiculous. Usually pastel and ruffled. Evelynde was a woman fixated on appearances, and her choices were… curious.

They eyed each other across the table in the back room of the Iren Stein, the pile of coins in the middle growing high.

"It's to you, Thea," Callum said. He sat back in his chair, Kyna secure on his lap. Callum had been a regular in pubs around the city before he walked into Kyna's nearly a year back, but the Iren Stein had been his place of preference since. He'd jested, saying it was because it smelled the best, but Thea knew it was more than that. She could never tell the extent of their affection for one another, or if it was simply a mutually beneficial arrangement. She decided it didn't really matter. He provided coin, and Kyna provided… a good time.

Thea liked her. Envied her in many ways. She was her own woman, doing as she pleased. Thea knew it was not that simple, but she could not help but feel Kyna held liberties she did not and never would.

Thea sighed. "Fold." She blinked, her eyes growing blurry with drink.

Marten followed. "Back to you, Callum."

Kyna kept the back room available for their visits. The five would sit around a table, drinking and playing cards until the sun came up. On occasion, they would sing along with the patrons up front. They couldn't be seen. At least not by those they could not trust. At first, Thea thought it was coin that kept their secrets, and she felt to some extent it was true. But over time, she had grown to see a certain unspoken agreement among the common folk. There was no honor in exposing another's mysteries. On occasion, they grew careless, and others would join them in the back. It had not, so far, become an issue.

Kyna and Callum would eventually drift off into a room upstairs. She and Marten would do the same. Thea never knew what Sylvie did during that time.

Callum narrowed his eyes on Sylvie. He looked down at his cards, then back up. "I'm all in." He pushed his small pile of coins to the middle.

"Are you sure you want to do that?" Sylvie asked, brow cocked. "You've a few silver pieces in there."

"Quite sure. I sense your bluff, vixen."

Thea choked on a laugh as she sipped her wine, taking some in her nose. Marten chuckled as he tried to wipe the burgundy stains from her chin. They giggled together, leaning dangerously in their chairs. He left a quick kiss on her lips.

"Very well." Sylvie counted coins from her pile to match, tossing them to the center. "What have you then?"

"You first."

Sylvie shrugged and laid her cards on the table. A royal flush.

"Godsdamn!" Callum tossed his cards to the side. "Must you *always* win?"

"It's not my fault you all make it so easy." Sylvie reached for the large pile of silver and copper coins, a gleam in her eyes.

"Will you not play with us, Kyna?" Thea asked.

"I don't play cards with Sylvie. I prefer to keep my hard-earned coin."

Kyna whispered something in Callum's ear, and he looked up at her with a devilish grin. The sounds of a scuffle broke out in the front. Kyna sighed and stood. "Pardon me a moment."

"Shall I come with you?" Callum asked, reaching for her hand.

Kyna shook her head. "I'm sure it's nothing."

It was not uncommon. They would overhear several skirmishes any evening they spent at the Iren Stein. Kyna would go and address it, returning a short time later.

Marten shuffled the deck and began dealing the cards for a new round. The typical time it took Kyna to squash the fight had come and passed. They all looked at the door.

Callum stood. "I'll go and see what is taking so long."

"Let me," Sylvie said, raising her hand. "I won't be recognized." She started toward the door, but it swung open, and Kyna stepped through.

"*Godssake.*" Kyna huffed. "Fucking Andarans. If it's not them, it's the Lochans. No respect, I swear." She flung her long, dark hair behind her shoulders.

"What happened?" Thea asked.

"A couple of boarders. Traders from King's Cross. They checked in this morning." Kyna pulled a cloth from the pocket of her dress, wiping what looked like ale from her face. "I knew they were going to be trouble. They were giving one of my girls a hard time."

"Where are they now?" Callum asked, a grim look on his face.

"On the street with their belongings." She ran the cloth down her neck and over her chest.

Callum walked to her, wrapping his arms around her waist. "I'll have someone sent over for a few days. To keep watch in case they come back."

Kyna smiled, clutching his tunic. "I would be most grateful."

The two snapped from their moment, and Kyna looked around him at the concerned faces in the room. "Oh, stop," she said, pushing Callum aside. "*All is well.*" She grabbed a carafe from a side table and refilled their cups as Callum took his seat.

Thea put her hand over her glass. "No," she said, shaking her head. "I cannot. I've had too much."

"Nonsense," Callum said, swatting her hand away. "This might be our last night together for a long time."

Thea blinked at him from across the table. Her eyes narrowed, but he blurred into two figures. She was far too deep in drink for his words to sink in.

Marten resumed dealing the cards.

"Fine," Thea said, "but no more wine." She eyed the barrel of ale on the other side of the room. She stood, or tried to. Her legs gave out, and she plummeted to the floor. Laughter erupted in the room. Marten stood to help but quickly found himself beside her. She howled and laughed until her belly ached.

Thea lay on her back. The room spun when she sat up. She nestled against Marten, no desire to move.

"Are you two playing or not?" Callum asked, peering under the table.

Marten lifted his head. "Not."

"You amateurs," he teased, and returned to the game.

"So this is where we stay?" Marten asked. His fingertips caressed gently down her hair and cheek.

Thea nodded against his chest. "This is where we live now."

"I am content." He pulled her tighter into his arms.

"Godssake, I'm drunk," she slurred. When he didn't respond, she looked up, trying to focus on his face. She thought he might be sleeping. *What a wonderful idea.*

"Awake, *my lady*, the day is new, and the sky is clear!"

Thea jumped, then groaned. She opened one eye and lifted her head to see Breeda readying the room for rising. Every beat of her heart thumped through her head like a bailiff knocking on collection day. She tried combing through the events of the night before, and it was a hazy recollection of imagery at best.

"If you think you're going to sleep all day because you were up all night, you're sorely mistaken," Breeda said as the drapery rod screeched.

"Let me sleep, woman." Thea pulled the blankets over her head. The darkness was a soothing reprieve. Breeda continued to speak, but the heavy quilt drowned her out to the level of background gibberish. Feeling sleep take hold again, she smiled, letting herself sink into the warmth of it.

Breeda ripped the blankets away. Startled, yet again, Thea looked down to see she had undressed to her shift, but one shoe remained on. Breeda let out a little snort at the sight.

"I can smell the wine on you. At the alehouse again, I see. You, Callum, and Marten are a troublesome bunch if you ask me." Breeda gathered the blankets and sheets into a pile beside the bed.

"Why are you here?" Thea asked, rubbing her aching head.

"Your father requests your presence in the council room."

"*What?* Why?" Thea sat up. "We haven't even broken fast."

"It is midday, Calithea Ironne." Breeda marched around the room, retrieving Thea's stray clothing from the floor, adding it to the pile of laundry.

"Oh," Thea said, trying to sit up, still blinded by the piercing sunlight. She felt sheepish being called by her proper name. "I need a washbasin."

"You need a scrub down in the lake with vinegar and sea salt. But a quick wipe down with some lavender oil will have to do." Breeda walked across the room and returned with a cup, placing it in Thea's hand.

"Fair enough." Thea sat up and gulped the water.

"My Gods, girl, you have leaves in your hair!" Breeda picked out the debris, combing through the tangles.

Thea looked around. "Where is Sylvie?"

"She is otherwise occupied this afternoon, so you get me." Breeda stood above her, shaking her head.

Thea picked nervously at her nails. "Breeda…"

"Yes?"

"I am sorry about—"

"It is all right. I know."

"I need to say it."

Breeda stopped brushing.

"I am sorry for how I acted last evening. There is no excuse for it." The shame Thea felt was worsened by the fact it had been Breeda on the receiving end of her mood.

"I know." Breeda reached up to touch her face. "Please do not think I care not for your feelings. I know this is not easy for you, my girl."

Thea could not help but feel she didn't deserve such an easy pardon. "It is no excuse."

"It seems you'll be paying for it all day," Breeda said, with a sly grin. Thea would not argue that. Her belly rumbled and turned, and she felt as if she'd not slept a wink.

Breeda held out her hands to help her rise. "Come on, let's get you dressed."

Thea was the last to arrive. Ulric, the king, sat at the head of the table. Her brothers Conall and Callum on his left. Her stepmother on his right, next to Catrianna. They all waited in silence, watching her take her seat. Her head was still throbbing, and she could only imagine how she looked.

She looked curiously at Callum, and he shrugged. He was a sad sight himself. At least she would not be the only disappointment at the table that day.

Thea sat next to her sister, breathing slowly to keep the meager contents of her belly from coming back up. She reached for the carafe in the center of the table.

"It is barely midday, dear." The intensity in Evelynde's gaze caused Thea to freeze. She released the carafe and sank back into her chair. Callum bit his lips to suppress a chuckle, and their father glanced between them, a brow cocked in amusement. It fell flat when his eyes met Evelynde's.

"Right." He cleared his throat. He looked around the table, at each of his children, considering. "I've not called you here simply to look upon your faces, however handsome they may be."

"*Father.*" Callum groaned and rubbed his temples. "The intrigue weighs heavy."

Still, their father delayed, as if searching for the words, or simply hesitant to speak them. It sparked concerned glances around the table.

"Before your mother died," he said, looking to Cat, Callum, and Conall, "I made a promise I would keep you together for as long as I could."

The energy in the room shifted at his unexpected solemnity. Like a preface for something severe.

"Were life not so cruel, you would all have known the love of your mothers. You would have known their hopes for you."

Thea looked at her sister. Cat was staring down at the table.

"Ire has had peace for over twenty years," he continued. "It is something I take great pride in. But we all know peace is a fickle mistress. The strongest ways to maintain her are with trade," he said, eyes growing heavy, "and with marriage."

Thea's belly hardened to stone.

"As heir," their father continued, "Conall's betrothal was planned in infancy. Callum's has been settled for many years. I fear the day has come where I can stall no longer." His eyes moved to Cat. "An offer of marriage for Catrianna has been accepted."

Only Thea and Callum reacted.

"With whom?" Thea asked Cat.

"Osric of Andar. The eldest son and heir." It was their father who answered. Cat had still not looked up.

"Why Andar?" Thea asked. "Surely there were offers closer to Ire, or even within." She looked back and forth between her sister and father. Neither would meet her eyes.

"This is *your* doing." Callum directed his words to Evelynde.

"Catrianna will be queen," Evelynde said with finality, as though it required no defense.

Callum scoffed. "In fucking Andar. The other side of the continent. A place you were all too happy to leave, lest you've forgotten." The words spilled out of him with ruthless disdain that manifested in a blink.

Evelynde flinched, but didn't respond.

"How long have you known?" Thea asked Cat, dipping her head to try to catch her gaze.

"Several moons." She didn't look up as she answered.

Their father's face held regret as he gazed at Cat. "We expect to announce it after the wedding. An envoy from Andar will be here this sixday to finalize the contract."

"She's determined to have everyone in Ire wed to one of her nieces or nephews." Callum's tone grew more heated by the word.

Evelynde shifted in her chair but held her chin steady.

"Callum," Ulric said. "Mind your tongue."

Callum cursed under his breath. "Make sure Evelynde is in these negotiations. She'll no doubt make sure Cat fetches a good price."

"That is *enough*." Their father's voice was low in warning. "You are permitted to dislike this, but you will show respect."

"Brother," Conall said, his face drawn, but his words assured. "This cannot be a surprise."

Callum sat back in his chair, arms crossed. Thea swallowed, the tension in the room rising at a worrisome pace. She looked at her sister, waiting for some reaction or response, but she still stared down at the tabletop, gaze unfocused. "*Cat.*"

"I'm fine, Thea," she said, finally looking up. Her blue eyes were serious and pleading not to press her further. "It was my decision."

"I understand this is difficult news—"

"To Thea and myself," Callum said, interrupting their father. The bite in his tone unyielding. "Everyone else appears well aware of Evelynde's schemes."

Ulric exhaled, his jaw flexing. "Callum, I will take into consideration that your feelings in this moment cause you to lose your better sense. You will cease this."

"What about Thea, Father?" Callum gestured across the table toward her. "Will you receive offers for her hand, too?" He laughed, and Thea nearly tasted the bitterness in it. "Evelynde, I know you'd never scheme so low to wed her off to one of your kin, but there will be visitors from both continents in for the wedding. Perhaps you'll arrange to have her shipped off to Ahara." He cocked his head. "Or a wealthy merchant who could offer coin heavy enough to fill your purse."

Ulric stood abruptly, knocking his chair back. It thudded against the stone floor behind him. Everyone jumped. He leaned over the table, eyes locked on Callum's. "*You forget yourself.*" Callum quieted, but didn't back down. "You will make apologies to your sisters and your stepmother, and then you will remove yourself from this room." Ulric slammed his fist on the table. "In fact, you will remove yourself from this castle for the remainder of the day, for I do not wish to look upon your face!"

All eyes were on their father. Callum looked away, contempt still bubbling within him.

He stood slowly. "Cat, Thea," he said, turning to look at each, "please forgive my ill mood." He said no further words and walked from the room.

"Callum!" Ulric called after him.

The door slammed. Thea looked wide-eyed from the door back to their father. Evelynde stood and walked around the table, returning his chair to an upright position. He thanked her and sat down, his head falling into his hands. He rubbed his eyes as they all sat waiting for him to speak again. When he did not, they began to quietly file out.

Thea called after her sister, but Cat didn't turn back.

Her head pounded harder with the escalation of her heart's beat. Its racing sent feverish energy pulsing through her already unsteady gait. She was sick from overindulgence, exacerbated by her worry at what had occurred. Her father had never yelled so. At least she had not seen it.

She picked up her pace down the long hall back to her room. Needles spread out over her chest, trickling down her arms. Her fingertips went numb, unbearably cold. She tried making fists, but her hands curled together on their own. By the time she crossed the threshold into her room, her breath was catching. Sylvie ran to her, hand running over her forehead and cheek. Thea felt the wild look in her eyes.

"You're freezing. Come lie down." Sylvie helped her to the bed and then pulled the covers to her chest. "Breathe, Thea." She put her hands on Thea's shoulders. "Look at me."

Thea did, gasping for shallow breaths as warm tears spilled down her cheeks.

"Breathe. In and out. It will pass."

The ice in her chest eased. She tried for a deeper breath, and relief came as she inhaled to the count of four.

"Good. It's passing. Keep breathing." Sylvie stayed by her side until the attack ceased, using her sleeve to gently blot the dampness from Thea's face, her own set in kindness.

"Thank you."

"You don't have to thank me." Sylvie gave Thea's shoulder a gentle squeeze before she stood and filled a cup of water, passing it to Thea before returning to the edge of the bed. "What brought it on?"

"Cat is engaged—or as good as." Thea took small sips, her stomach threatening to expel them.

Sylvie didn't say anything.

"You do not seem surprised."

Sylvie considered for a moment. "I don't suppose I am." She took the cup from Thea and refilled it. "Here, drink some more."

"Everyone knew but Callum and I. He reacted rather poorly." Thea still could not believe the escalation.

"How so?"

"He blames Evelynde. It is Osric Cumberly, heir to Andar."

Sylvie's eyebrows rose. "I see." She made a sound of discontent. "How is your sister?"

"I don't know." Thea shrugged. "I could not tell. She seemed dispirited but resigned. She said it was her decision."

"Cat is twenty and two. Most women of royal birth are wed years before that."

"I suppose we shouldn't have been surprised. It is only that it felt as if it came abruptly. With each year that passed, we allowed ourselves a little more hope we wouldn't be split apart." Thea set the empty cup on the bedside table. "Naivety on our part, I suppose."

"Hope is not always naivety," Sylvie said. "But I am sorry, Thea," she added, with a cheerless smile. "It does seem a cruelty for her to be sent so far away."

"I need to find Callum. He and Father quarreled quite alarmingly. Father cast him from the castle." Thea moved to rise from the bed, but Sylvie pressed her back.

"You need to rest. There is plenty of day remaining to seek him out." Her hands firmed on Thea's shoulders. "Sleep for an hour. I promise I'll wake you."

Thea did not want to sleep, but the ache in her bones and sour twist in her belly told her Sylvie was right. She could not understand how Sylvie never seemed afflicted by their nights out. Sylvie looked as fresh and well-rested as Thea had ever seen her. "You will wake me in an hour?"

"Promise."

9

Nara

"One can let go without giving up."

AUTHOR UNKNOWN, C. 1500 BQ
TRANSLATED FROM SUMACIAN BY PARRY HAVERFORD
HAIS Z'NOSIŠ, 1204 AQ
RECOVERED 1203 AQ, SOMOS

"You need to take a break."

Nara opened her eyes, glancing back over her shoulder. Harker was standing with his arms folded, expression even more severe than the last time he'd come. Since they'd departed Rahab, Nara had spent most of her time on the bow of the riverboat. She was eager to get to the Citadel. Desperate for news from the north, for news of Cerys. Power poured from her outstretched arms into the wind, propelling them faster up the River Sana. Nara guessed she could get them there three, perhaps four, days ahead of schedule.

"You were out here all night. And don't try to lie." Harker walked around to face her. "It's well past midday. Time to stop." His tone was sterner than she'd heard from him before.

"I can hold out a bit longer." She closed her eyes, returning focus to her work.

He sighed, and Nara felt the frustration in it. "Let someone else take over. You're no good to anyone if you burn out. And I don't like to drink alone."

She didn't answer, but his mention of a drink captured her attention.

Harker nudged her. "Come on, Nyanthi. Take a well-earned rest."

He *was* right. She did need to rest, and a glass of whiskey sounded just the thing to quench her thirst. Nara opened one eye and peered at him. "Fine. But I want the good stuff. None of that rotgut from Straeth we have on board. I know you've a good bottle on you."

Harker shrugged a lazy shoulder, and a faint mischief crept into his eyes. "I may have a splash or two."

Nara lowered her arms, rubbing at her aching shoulders. A girl she did not know stepped up to take her place. Nara nodded at her in passing, then looked back at Harker. "Lead the way."

They sat at a table in the modest midship cabin. A few from the crew were scattered about, taking respite from the sun. Harker pulled a bottle from his pack and set it on the tabletop. Nara's brows shot up.

"Where did you come by this?" She picked it up, turning the smooth amber glass in her hands.

"I acquired a couple cases the last time I was in King's Cross." He set a pony glass in front of Nara, then a second in front of him.

Andaran wine was shite, but the best whiskey came from the southern region of the kingdom. "Acquired?" she asked.

He scratched his beard. "Found its way into my possession. Let's leave it at that." He leaned a little closer and winked.

She eyed him. "You've been holding out."

"Down to the last two bottles," he said with a sigh.

Nara set the bottle back on the table. "Perhaps then you should save it for a pleasant occasion."

"Nah," Harker said, "whiskey is for sharing. Pleasantries or woes." He grabbed the bottle and filled the small glasses to the brims. He held his up in toast, and they clanked. Nara sipped the whiskey, savoring the smooth, gentle burn. This was not some swill one tossed back, but she was keen to take the edge off, so she finished it.

"Very nice," she said. And it was. Full-bodied and complex. She tasted vanilla and oak.

Harker refilled her glass. His eyes flicked up to hers mid-pour. "You cannot continue the remainder of this trip the way you have the last two days."

Nara groaned. "I came for a drink, not a lecture."

"Nara, I'm serious." Serious was something Harker was not often.

"I know." Nara held up her hands in playful concession before tossing back her drink. "I'll shift out the remainder of the trip."

"Good girl." A copper coin rolled over the knuckles of his free hand, a common pastime for him. It was always the same coin, identifiable by a small chip on the edge. "We'll reach Nyrovi in two days," he said, watching it flip. "That will put us in Kurk a sixday after if we maintain this pace. We're making good time."

Nara nodded. "You know," she mused, "if that last bottle is for sale, I'd be willing to pay a handsome price."

"Not for sale."

She held out her glass for another fill. "Fair enough."

The warmth of the whiskey loosened the knots in her belly. There was little she found worse than sitting still while urgency pulsed through her, unattended to. Nowhere nor way to expel it. Nara felt like she should be running full speed, shouting from rooftops. Her boot tapped the wood beneath it.

"What do you think the council's reaction will be?" she asked him, turning the glass between her fingers.

"Eh, it's hard to say. They tend to lead with caution. Often too much for my taste, but maybe that's why I'm not on the council," he said as he poured another drink. He looked up at her, thoughtful, and his brows drew together, his enthusiasm quelling.

"*What now?*" Nara asked.

"The council would be more likely to listen were you still a chancellor." He eyed her, waiting for her reaction.

Nara leaned back in her chair, resting her finger-laced hands on her head. She took a deep breath in with her nose and let it expel haphazardly from her lips. She had already thought the same herself, but it didn't make it more palatable. His face grew further concerned in pace with her silence. It made her feel a bit guilty he feared such a poor reaction from her. "You are right."

His tension eased, and he shrugged. "Something to think about."

Nara made a grunt-like sound of acquiescence that never made it past the back of her throat. She watched as he tossed the coin in the air, then flipped his hand, catching the copper piece midway on its return. It hovered, a subtle, burgundy-colored glow beneath. He grew the ether, lifting the coin higher, and it started to spin.

Nara plucked some grapes from a bowl in the center of the table. "Cute trick."

Harker chuckled, something more of a snort, and recalled his power. The coin returned to his hand, and the mindless walk of it across his knuckles began once more.

"What do you think is happening in the north?" Nara asked, unsure if she was looking for truth.

"Ah, it'll do no good to speculate, love," he said. "Cerys is a tough bird. Don't worry."

He was right, of course, but quieting one's mind of such speculation was not easily done. Though whiskey helps, she thought, as she sipped. Nara fumbled with the gold chain around her neck, clasping its orange stone in her palm.

Harker gestured at the necklace. "You never take that off."

"I'll be cold on the ground before it leaves my neck."

"Gift?"

"I had it made in Azmar. It is one of two. It makes me feel closer to the bearer of its twin." Nara looked down at the stone. She had picked this very one to match the color of Cerys's ether. Something she ached to feel again. She only wanted to be close to her.

"She's at the field house in Highclere. There isn't anywhere in the north safer to be." Harker spoke with a tenderness that would typically set her ill at ease. She did not enjoy being reassured. Perhaps she had finally reached a state of needing it. "Of all the cities likely to fall, or even be targeted, Highclere is at the bottom of that list."

"I know." And she did. But it did nothing to quiet her dread. She wanted Cerys with her. Where she could protect her. Where she had control. Cerys could be careless, too giving. Too willing to put herself in danger for others. She loved her for it, but Nara feared one day it would catch up with her. If she stayed by her side, she could stop that ever happening.

"What is it?" Harker asked, sensing her unease.

"I cannot help but feel it's my fault she is in the north."

Harker shook his head and poured her another whiskey. "Don't do that."

"It is true." Nara tossed back the drink. "I've not been amenable to the council's designs for me. This is punishment."

"You can't know that's the reason."

"No," Nara said, "but there is no justification for having an Influencer of her talent there. As you said, I can't think of another city with less cause and trouble."

Harker sighed. "I don't know, love. What I do know is that the council will not bend when pressed. At some point, you're going to have to decide what to do. I can't see them giving you another year to figure it out."

"You sound like my mother," Nara grumbled.

He chuckled, and it had a wistfulness to it. "If only that were true."

"None of it matters if what we think is happening, in fact, is." Nara made note of the trepidity in her own voice.

"No," he said, his brown eyes taking on weight. He tipped up his glass. "No, it doesn't."

10

Thea

"The truth we seek often lies within, but it cannot be discovered until we believe ourselves worthy of it."

THE WAY OF ETHER
ASHERAH GALANIS, FIRST CONSUL, THE CITADEL, 808 AQ

The enemy came at her with a fierce swing of sword. Thea parried, throwing her own up in defense. Across the gardens, she saw Callum fall, a sword slicing across his back.

Thea screamed her brother's name as his body slumped to the ground. She was on her own now. The one who ended Callum cheered in victory before dashing toward her. There were too many. Thea knew she would fall.

She took off across the Great Lawn, leaping over the garden wall to safety, only to find an enemy in waiting. The girl ran at her, screaming, sword first, and plunged it into Thea's belly. She cried out, falling to her knees.

"You have defeated me." Thea fell, crawling toward her enemy. "Well fought, young Luce." She collapsed in great dramatic fashion.

A few breaths passed before a little voice called out, *"Aunt Thea?"*

Thea felt the dull edge of a wooden sword poke gently at her shoulder. She sprang up in surprise, pulling her little niece into her arms. She tickled the blue-eyed girl until they were both laughing uncontrollably.

Tamsin and Thomas came running over, Callum on their heels.

"I crown you Queen Lucienne of Argos!" Callum placed a crown woven from freesia and lavender on her head. "All hail Queen Lucienne!"

"All hail Queen Lucienne!" the others echoed.

Callum swept Luce up onto his shoulders, dancing around the gardens, the other children joining in. Thea laughed, rolling onto her back in the grass, still trying to catch her breath. She groaned. Her head still produced a dull ache. The nap had tempered her woes from their night out, but the punishment persisted. *Well deserved,* she thought.

The sun was bright and warm, inviting. She closed her eyes, letting it sink in, extending her arms, pretending to float. She tried not to think of her sister. Cat's sorrowful resignation was enough to swell her eyes.

"Children, come, it's time for your supper," Leanne called from across the gardens. Thea sat up, raising her hand to block the sun. Callum walked into view while Thea watched Leanne gathering the children, little Henri on her hip.

Leanne was average in stature, similar to Thea, but her slim body gave the appearance of height. Her neck was long and elegant, with an ivory, heart-shaped face at its pinnacle. Her dark brown hair fell long to her waist, though she often wore it pinned up.

Thea had always admired her beauty, as did all. But it was her character and disposition that most impressed. While all the children had nursemaids, Leanne chose to care for her children herself. She fed them, bathed them, nursed them, and put them to bed every night. She was gentle and tender in every way a mother should be. Thea couldn't help but feel a touch envious watching Henri and Lucienne have Leanne as a mother, having never known her own. She wondered if Cat and Callum felt the same. Thea vowed if she ever had children, she would do her best to be a mother like Leanne.

Leanne waved with her free hand, and Thea returned the gesture before collapsing back into the grass. Callum fell in beside her.

"Gods, my head aches," he said, pinching the space between his eyes.

"Mine as well." She laughed, which only made it worse.

"How did we get back to the castle last night?"

"I am honestly not sure. We were a bit out of control, I think." Thea had a brief and rather blurry memory of the four of them stumbling through the alleyways just before dawn.

"Wouldn't be the first time."

"No." Thea laughed again and immediately regretted it. "No, it would not."

Callum glanced at her. "Have you seen Marten today?"

"I have not. I am sure his father is doing everything he can to keep him occupied." Thea ran her hand over the soft grass. She thought she could sleep there.

Callum combed back his blond waves. "He's a clever boy. I'm sure we'll see him soon."

"I've no doubt." Thea turned to look at him. "You know you have to apologize to Father… *and* Evelynde."

Callum huffed and moved his intertwined fingers behind his head.

"Callum."

He groaned. "*Thea.*"

"I do not disagree with your sentiments, but your reaction was severe. Especially toward Father." Thea thought she sounded a bit motherly, but supposed he needed to hear it.

"I know, I know," he said, turning to face her. "I will make apologies. I swear it."

"Good."

"Just as soon as I'm allowed back in the castle."

They shared a brief laugh before it slowly died, leaving a somber silence in its wake.

"I'm not ready for so much change, Thea."

"Nor I, but it seems to have found us, nonetheless." She rolled on her side to face him. "I do not think we can continue like this, anyway. Look at the state of us."

They considered one another. Pale-faced and eyes dark circled. They both grinned, but underneath it, Thea felt uneasy.

"It doesn't seem like much is changing for me," she said, though Thea knew something needed to.

He turned on his side to mirror her. "I don't think Father could bear to part with you. You are his favorite."

"Stop that," she hissed, reaching over with a lazy slap.

"Please. Everyone knows it." Callum shrugged. "I do not mind."

"I think you confuse favoritism with pity. I am not legitimate. Not of value in the marriage market. If I wed, it will be as a favor or to a lowborn merchant looking to purchase a title." She plucked a small dandelion from the grass, turning it between her fingers. It had always been a mystery to her why the little yellow flower was so despised. Thea had always found them charming, even more so when they turned to seed.

"Thea." Callum frowned. "Don't insult Father. He would never."

"No," she said, tucking the flower behind her ear, "but Conall would."

Callum didn't argue. Instead, he sat up, leaning on the heels of his hands. "It matters not. By the time Father is dead and Conall is king, you'll be old and gray. What price would you fetch then?"

"Ah! You beast!" Thea sat up and reached over to slap him again, this one with more vigor.

The tease in his expression eased. "In my selfishness, I do not wish to see you married off. I would have you here, in Highclere, with me." He reached over for her hand.

The feeling came through her in a rush. She turned her body away from his. She heard him exhale as a gentle hand rested on her shoulder.

"Thea, I'm one of the few you don't have to hide from." He moved to position himself in front of her.

"I know." She tried for a smile. "I feel… *embarrassed* to be so upset."

"Why?" His brows knitted as if it were truly a question and not simply an attempt to console her.

She shrugged, throwing her arms out to the sides. "Because I always knew this would come to pass."

A starling landed on the lawn in front of her. She watched it peck at the earth.

"Do you regret him?" Callum asked.

"Of course not."

The starling made tiny hops across the grass and resumed its search. Gazing behind it, Thea took in the large orange cat stalking around the long line of shrubs.

"What do you want, Thea?"

She blinked at him, considering. "I can't have what I want."

"Is it truly, though? Do you really want to be the *Duchess of Aremore?*" He scoffed. "A life of bearing children and hosting the wives of delegates in the countryside?" His hand waved through the air as if the notion was ridiculous. "You would be surrounded by the sorts of people we can barely stand."

The starling pulled a worm from the earth. The cat crept closer, lifting its paws in prelude to its attack. Thea looked around and snatched a small pebble from the grass. She tossed it toward the bird. With its prey clutched safely within its beak, the starling took to flight, disappearing into the trees. The cat regarded her, accusive, as if it understood what she'd done. It turned, sauntering off into the garden.

"But I would have him," she challenged.

"Wanting him and wanting that life are not the same." Callum shook his head, his eyes as serious as she'd ever seen them.

She chewed at her cheek.

"Some may say Conall and Cat are the fortunate ones. One day, he'll be king and she a queen. But I say it is us. We can spend our lives in shadows, doing as we please. I don't want to be king. I want freedom. What do *you* want? Truly *want?*"

"Are you telling me I should be his mistress?" she asked, not exactly surprised by his line of questions, more startled by the fact that perhaps she had not already asked them of herself.

"No," he said. "Of course not. But you'd receive no judgment from me should you choose to be."

"He will be wed. In seven days."

"Why does it matter so much to you?" Callum's head inclined, searching her eyes as if looking for an answer her words may not give.

"I don't know. Perhaps I believe in the sanctity of a vow?" As the words left her lips, she knew they weren't true.

"And you would hold someone to a vow they were forced to take?"

She shrugged but then shook her head, dismissing the notion. "No, I would not." She squirmed, uncomfortable with the conversation. "I don't know."

He sighed. "What I am asking is if you have really thought about what kind of life you can have. You never have to marry. You could travel. You can be your own woman. I have no doubt Father will bestow a living on you. But if he does not, I will."

Thea looked down. "I suppose I've never thought about it." Had she? She was unsure.

He dipped his head to catch her gaze. "Perhaps it is time."

Thea was not certain if the idea provoked excitement or fear in her. She'd spent so much of her life reading about the outside world. Stories of excitement and adventure from lands like Ahara, Sibreen, and Zargoza. Deserts and rainforests. Incomprehensible places, people, and things of fascination stood outside of Ire. She knew this. Why had she not considered seeing it? It all felt so impossible. So much effort. It made her tired. They were just stories. "Perhaps."

Callum stood, brushing his trousers, then offered her his hand. He looked annoyingly put together despite the grass staining his white shirt and tan vest. "Come, let's get a pint to wash out these headaches."

Thea laughed, eyes incredulous. "Unbelievable. If there are two perched on my shoulders making whispers in my ears, you are no doubt the devil."

He gave her his most mischievous grin. "That's the nicest thing you've ever said to me."

11

Neith

"The measure of a leader is not determined by triumph in war, but by how one shapes the time between."

THE COST OF VALOR
AUTHOR UNKNOWN, 203 BQ
TRANSLATED FROM OLD ASARI BY MERIAH TURAN
HAIS Z'NOSIŠ, 1200 AQ

Daylight evokes a sinister feeling from violence in a way the cover of night cannot. One expects it to occur under the moon and for it to stay there. Neith and Sam rode through the remains of a small village the day after it had been razed by the First. Residual smoke hung in the air. There were no people. Only bodies. Any survivors had surely run long ago.

They'd been on the road most of the day since heading out at dawn. At her request, they made a quick diversion into the village to look around. There was nothing left to take, no aim other than curiosity.

It was far smaller than Godsreach. A place one passes through. Neith wondered what kind of people had lived there, what their professions were, and if any had made it out alive. She couldn't sense any residual wielding, so there was likely little fight. A few stray animals meandered the streets. Neith supposed it was their town now. There would be no cause to rebuild. The little village would disappear into history. In a couple of generations, it would be like it never existed. She found solace, and dread, in how temporary it all was.

"What is—*was*—the name of this town?"

"Alderford," Sam answered.

Neith committed the name to memory. The town may fall into history long forgotten, but she could at least remember the name. His narrowed eyes inquired after her objective in asking.

"Simply curious," she answered. "What do we gain by burning these villages?" Neith looked over the charred remains. "Would it not be prudent to leave them intact and occupy them? The people of Thrane need good land."

"Fear."

Now it was her eyes asking for more.

"News of these attacks will reach other villages days, even a halfmoon, before we do. Many will flee to larger cities. If we can create enough unrest, many will call for surrender. These small villages are of little use to us strategically, but we need to secure the larger cities. We need as little disruption to trade as possible. We are looking at a long campaign. Armies this size are no easy machine to maintain."

Neith sighed at the ever-growing realization she still had much to learn. "We destroy more now in the hope of less in the future. I suppose there are fewer lives lost in the grand scheme of it all."

"That is one way to look at it," he said flatly, leaving her unsure of his opinion.

She looked at him, trying to decipher his motivations. Her conversation with Magnus played back through her mind. She saw the desire for power in most of those around her. Many were anxious to climb ranks, gain influence. But Sam seemed inconvenienced by responsibility. As though he agreed to it only because it was asked of him. He could have humbled her brother the day before they crossed the mountain. He was undeniably smarter, certainly stronger.

Neith decided she agreed with Magnus, but knew it was not all. Some were simply trying to survive, to find security. She then thought about what else he said about power having many forms. Security could easily be thought of as one. *Or is security a privilege? And what is the difference between power and privilege?* She clamped her eyes shut, rubbing at them. A small ache formed between. Magnus may have been right about people's motivations, but he was wrong in calling her wise. The more she thought, the more she discovered, the more unsure she felt. Everything was a mystery to her. Including the boy riding next to her.

"Are you well?" Sam asked, searching her face.

She sighed. "Probably not."

He stopped his horse.

Neith held up her hand. "No, I am sorry. That is not what I mean. I am fine." She rubbed her eyes again. "Only tired." That was a lie. She wasn't tired at all. She'd slept better the last several nights than she could ever remember.

He frowned but nodded. Neith felt it was not a nod of satisfaction, but rather acquiescence.

They reached the end of the tiny town in minutes. A few soldiers walked the streets, searching for anything of value left behind. Neith looked around, considering. She was pursuing something that she couldn't explain if asked, but knew she had not found it.

"Let's head back. There is nothing here." She urged Storm on the path back out of town.

They fell back in line with the Second, returning to what had become their regular formation. Neith rode in front with Sam at her side. Max, Petra, and Ayla followed with the other squad members behind. She would occasionally glance back and find a nod or a smile. She tried not to think about how lost she was. A pang of guilt struck anytime she thought of the four who chose to join her. They did not know they followed a stupid girl who had no idea what she was doing.

Sometimes Bellamy would sing, and Ayla would join in. They were the only two in the group who could carry a tune. They all made regular disparaging remarks at one another's expense, which Neith now understood to be in jest. She spent most of her time listening, trying to understand them. That made Sam the most difficult to discover.

Though he rode beside her, he said little. He answered her questions and was obliging to her requests, but he made no effort to engage with her. The two largely rode in silence, listening to the conversations behind them. Now and then, she felt as if his eyes were on her, but every time she glanced his way, she found them forward.

When the sun had set, they stopped, repeating the tasks of the previous night. Neith helped set up the campsite, this time setting the fire ablaze herself. When all settled around it, she found herself, once again, on the outside of the circle.

"May I bring you anything else?"

She looked up from her plate to Ayla, standing over. Neith felt she needed a thousand things, but none were something that could be brought to her. She smiled and shook her head.

Ayla curtsied. "I'll ready the tent."

Neith studied them as she had the night before. Petra sat next to her brother, and Sam on his own. Kieran and Bellamy played cards while Iris and Raiden talked. Raiden pulled a dagger from his belt, showing Iris an inscription on the blade.

Neith eyed the empty space beside Sam on the log. Her heel tapped against the grassy floor as she chewed on her lip. If she did not do it now, she never would. Before she could convince herself it was a foolish notion, she stood, striding the short distance to the fire. The chatter quieted at her arrival, and all looked up, waiting for direction, or an order, or request.

Sam stood. "Do you need something—"

"Sit, please." It came out a bit curt, and she winced. She tried to smile through the awkwardness.

He nodded, his expression vaguely strange as he returned to his seat. Neith sat next to him, warming her hands over the fire.

Bellamy extended an arm toward her, grinning, dimples on display. "Whiskey?"

Neith accepted the flask. She'd already sampled wine and ale. Whiskey could not be worse. Without thought, she tipped up the cool metal container. It took all her self-control not to stiffen at the shock of the burn as it washed down her throat. She wiped at the small stream running from the corner of her mouth. Something like a cough or choke was forced from her. If the others noticed, they had the thoughtfulness not to show it. She passed the flask to Sam. He did not take a drink and passed it on to Raiden.

"Have we any ale?" Neith asked the group.

"Aye," said Kieran. He stood, but Neith held up a hand to stop him.

"I will get it."

He hesitated but nodded, pointing toward a cart on the side of their camp.

"Would anyone else care for some?" Even she flinched at her stiff demeanor. The others had an easy way of speaking, a banter of sorts, that she didn't possess.

The group eyed each other, then Iris and Raiden raised their hands. Neith stood, walking to the cart, knowing they were all watching her. She filled three mugs, passed them to those who requested, then retook her seat.

Again, they looked around at one another, unsure, but slowly fell back into the conversations they'd been a part of moments before. Neith exhaled.

Sam was quiet beside her, his eyes on the fire.

"Do you not drink whiskey?" she asked him.

He sat up at the question. "Sorry?"

"I noticed you did not drink."

Neith followed his eyes across the campfire at Iris, who now held the flask. "Whiskey burns a bit bright for my tastes."

"I see." She tipped up her mug of ale. The sour flavor twisted her features.

"Do *you* drink whiskey?" he asked.

She started to answer, but quickly realized he was teasing her. Neith pressed her lips together. "I am that obvious."

Sam leaned closer, speaking low. "A small sip next time." He smiled and nudged her with his elbow. She looked down at where he'd touched her, which caused him to retreat, sitting up straight once again.

"In the last three days, I've had my first taste of wine, ale, and whiskey, so tips are most welcome." When she looked at him, the expression on his face surprised her. Skepticism tightened his brow, as if he was trying to decide if she was speaking in jest.

She set the mug down, her smile fading into one of self-deprecation.

"Were you not permitted?" he asked, frowning.

Neith shrugged. She wasn't sure. "I suppose I never asked."

Sam considered for a moment, then nodded slowly, picking up her mug. He pretended to take a drink, secretly tossing it over his shoulder.

Neith laughed. His eyes flicked briefly to hers with a soft smile as he set the empty mug between them.

She was trying to connect, and he wasn't shutting her out.

"I suppose I will adjust," she said. "I am finding quite quickly there are many things I need to adapt to."

Sam turned to look at her. "You don't need to be anyone other than yourself."

Neith looked back at the fire, surprised by the heaviness in his tone. "I don't want to let anyone down."

"Four people joined you, as you were," he said. "Don't forget that."

They joined her because she turned a mountain to dust, she thought. She wanted to say that he didn't choose to be there, but she feared the look of confirmation on his face if she did.

The flask made its way back to her. This time, she took Sam's advice, sipping it slowly. It burned again, but easier than the last. She passed it on to Sam, who again passed it to Raiden without a drink.

"I don't know how to lead people," she said. "I don't know what to do." Neith stiffened, fearful she was being too open. But then she looked at Ayla, now sitting next to Max, and dismissed the notion.

"When there is something to do, you'll know," Sam said. She wanted to believe his words were true, but also feared he could be placating her. He was more often than not stoic and reserved.

"I cannot tell your aim," she said frankly. "I find myself often unsure of your true meaning. I wonder if you say what you think I want to hear. To make me feel better." She was unsure if the whiskey drove her candor, but she didn't shy away.

Sam looked at her, head tilting. "If I were, as you say, trying to make you *feel better*, would that be so terrible?"

"No," she answered quickly. "It would not be so bad. Though I would prefer your truth."

He smiled, and she did not question its authenticity. It was small, but warm, and she felt it. "Very well, Neith Dracos. I swear to always tell you the truth."

She liked the way he said her name. "Even if it is something you do not think I wish to hear?"

"Even then," he said, his amber eyes reflecting the campfire's flames.

"Then I thank you."

The flask came back around. Neith took a sip and then passed it to Sam. This time, he held her gaze, doing the same.

12

Nara

"The aptitudes of wielding are long lost to history. It is only through science and study that we will achieve the greatness once known to our forebears."

THE WAY OF ETHER
ASHERAH GALANIS, FIRST CONSUL, THE CITADEL, 808 AQ

Nara stood restless on the deck of the riverboat, waiting for it to dock in Nyrovi. The vibrant orange shades of the still-rising sun illuminated the sky. A gentle waking call to the sleeping city.

Nyrovi was a bustling metropolis, the second largest in Sibreen. It sat center of the southern continent and was a trading port for all that surrounded it. Nara had traveled to nearly every major city in the south, and she found it to be the most beautiful by far. One could not help but stop and stare on approach. Buildings in shades of azure and jade spanned as far as the eye could see. The rich architecture was rivaled in splendor only by the lush Azmaran Mountains it directly preceded. In addition to thriving commerce, it was a nexus for the arts and sciences and held the largest library seen on either continent. Visitors from all reaches of the north and south pilgrimaged to Nyrovi throughout the year.

"I want to be in and out as quickly as we can," Nara said to all those around her. "You all know your tasks. We meet back here before midday. Not a moment longer."

She was met with nods and words of acknowledgment.

After the boat docked and everyone scattered, she turned to Harker. "I need you to go to the field house and oversee the supply restock."

"All right," he said, with a nod. "Where are you headed?"

"To find a friend."

It was early, and the streets were not yet alive. Vendors were setting up stalls and sweeping their doorsteps. The scent of citrus turned to coffee and bread as she approached the city center. It tempted her to stop, but the library was a much farther walk than the field house, and she was on borrowed time.

Nara's pace quickened to a light jog as she turned the final corner to find herself facing the tall white pillars of Hais z'Nosiš, or *House of Knowledge*. The massive fountain in front of the ancient building depicted Pyramus, hands outstretched, with water cascading from his palms. The gentle sounds of the streams were the only early-morning noise. She dipped her hand in the cool pool, wiping the sweat from her brow.

Taking the white marble stairs by two, the multistory, ornately carved doors opened as she approached. An old man in white robes emerged, giving her a puzzled look as she passed by.

The foyer of the library never failed to impress. Book-lined walls surrounded a long rectangular pool of still water spanning the length of the hall. Natural sunlight flooded the huge room from the glass ceiling dome in its center. The room was empty of people, save for the old man at the door, but she knew it was a different atmosphere below. Esērii scholars were notoriously early risers, and they were no doubt already nose-deep in thousand-year-old books.

The entrance to access the Etherborn floors was warded tight. No one without the gift could find them, never mind pass through, unaccompanied. The wards recognized her gift, parting as she strode through the open frame and down the spiral stairs.

A single desk occupied the space, manned by an older woman in the traditional purple robes of an Esērii scholar. When Nara reached the desk, the woman looked up, squinting through her spectacles. Her gray hair was twisted back into a low bun, not a single strand misplaced.

"May I help you?" Her voice was wiry, and her tone indifferent.

"I need to see Meriah Turan. Is she in the city?" Meriah would often split her time between Nyrovi and the Citadel. She was a lead scholar, overseeing various projects in the sciences of wielding. Nara's fingers tapped impatiently on the desk.

The old woman looked down at the noise. "Who should I say asks after her?"

"Nara."

The old woman waited.

"Nara Nyanthi."

She sighed and stood, reaching for a cane propped against her desk. "Wait here." She slowly disappeared behind one of the doors.

Nara paced the room. Multiple doors opened several times, and she turned at the sound of each, groaning to find unfamiliar faces. When she feared her patience had finally run dry, a bright-faced, beautiful young woman with dark hair walked through.

"Nara!" The two women embraced, and Meriah kissed both her cheeks. Nearly a year had passed since they last saw one another. "I thought you were on assignment for another two moons." When she pulled back and looked at Nara's face, her smile dropped. "What is wrong?"

The old woman was settling back at her desk.

"I need to speak to you." Nara kept her voice low. "In confidence."

Meriah frowned, but nodded. "Come," she said, wrapping her arm through Nara's. "Let us catch up."

Nara followed Meriah through long halls, past room after room of floor-to-ceiling shelves packed tight with books and scrolls. Scholars sat quietly at desks or passed by with their eyes low. It was quiet. Painfully, quiet.

Stories underground, there was no natural light, but the walls were lined with lanterns burning bright with etherstars. They held the faint glow of their makers. Pale purples, blues, and greens. The ceilings, halls, and rooms were spacious and much taller than necessary. Nara felt it must be intentional. One could go mad left underground all day. She knew she would.

They stopped at a door with Meriah's name etched on a plaque. Nara felt her bend the wards so they could pass through. The air in the large room was thick with the musty scent of old books and tea. It held a gathering table and two desks. One empty, and the other with a boy hunched over its book-covered top. He looked up as they entered, a quill clutched in one hand.

"This is my research assistant, Parry," Meriah said to Nara. "Parry, this is my dear friend, Nara."

Recognition washed over him, and he stood quickly, hitting his head on a low-hanging lamp. He was tall and lanky, with dark brown hair that fell just above his ears. His pale, ivory-colored skin told Nara he was from the north. Andar or Straeth, perhaps. He removed his spectacles. "Nara

Nyanthi," he said, walking around his desk, "it is an honor to meet you." His eyes scanned the ground skittishly, but he reached his hand forward.

"And you." Nara inclined her head, shaking hands with him. She looked back at Meriah with urgency in her eyes.

"Parry, would you go down to the archives and pull some records for me?" Meriah asked.

"Yes, of course."

Nara thought him excessively enthusiastic to be of service.

Meriah grabbed a quill from her desk and scribbled a few titles on a piece of parchment. She held it outstretched. He looked over the list and nodded before glancing timidly at Nara, walking from the room.

"That should buy us an hour or so," Meriah said.

"He's a nervous one."

Meriah chuckled. "He's young, barely twenty summers. He's quite brilliant, though. The best I've worked with. He's made great strides in deciphering Sumacian. We have hundreds of scrolls written in the ancient language collecting dust, and only yesterday, I received a letter stating dozens more were found at a dig site in Zargoza." She said it with the ardor she always had when speaking of such things. Meriah sat at her desk, beckoning Nara to take the seat opposite. "Is everything all right? I don't often see this look from you, and when I do, it is never good."

Nara rubbed her temples, considering where to start. She knew everything she was about to say was leagues worse than anything Meriah might be expecting.

She withheld nothing.

Meriah listened intently, her intelligent eyes taking in and analyzing every detail. When Nara revealed it to be Thrane, alarm plagued Meriah's face, but she didn't interrupt. After Nara finished the story with their departure from Rahab, she pulled the patch from her pocket and held it out to her across the desk.

"Gods." Meriah's fingers grazed over the silver stitches. "If anyone but you brought this to me, I might think it some sort of jest in poor taste."

"If it were only."

The brightness her eyes held only half an hour ago was gone. It pained Nara to be the one to strip her of it. "I am sorry. I wish I did not bring you this."

"Please do not be sorry. I am grateful you have. It is only difficult to grasp. It's been twenty years since his rebellion." Meriah sighed. "I think many of us started to forget. Perhaps we simply wanted to."

"Meriah," Nara said, leaning forward, "if this is happening here, what is happening in the north?"

The two women met eyes, understanding and fear between them.

"Who is aware?" Meriah asked. Nara watched her throat bob as she tried to swallow.

"Only those on my team and a few at the field house in Rahab. I'm not supposed to speak on it. I'm on my way to the Citadel to report to the council. We've stopped only to resupply." Nara leaned further over the desk. "I think you should follow as quickly as you can without causing alarm."

"Yes." Meriah nodded and exhaled slowly. "Yes, of course."

"Cerys is in the north." Nara's chest seized as she said the words.

"I know." Meriah reached for Nara's hand. "Alec is, too."

Nara's brows drew together. "Why?" She tried to think of the last time she'd seen him in the Citadel. Her team had been in and out over the past ten moons, often stopping for only a single night.

"I fear I have some things to share with you, too." Meriah pulled her hand back, perching her elbows on the desk. Her lips came to rest against her fingertips as her eyes darted around the space between them. When they returned to Nara's, they were far graver than before. "There have been reports of attacks on trade routes in Argal, Straeth, and Lochland."

Nara shrugged her shoulders. "That is not uncommon. Could be idle-born brigands. Even a stray Thranean, or nomad."

"Yes," Meriah said, "that is usually the case, but it has been escalating. There were also tradeships that went missing under strange circumstances in Port Lethney. The field house there reported whisperings among the idleborn with concerns of sorcery."

"I see," Nara said, letting the information digest.

"It was assumed nomads, so the council sent Alec north to investigate. He's been gone for nearly three moons."

It was confirmation of what she had hoped not to hear.

"It gets worse." Meriah inhaled, letting it slowly release. "Some of the reports outline abductions. Etherborn gone missing."

Nara's thoughts tumbled, tripping over and on one another. Collections, abductions, supply chain attacks. She remembered how confident Barton had been in Amul. They were organized and trained, not some rogue group of nomadic bandits. "Why doesn't everyone know about this?"

"I'm not even supposed to know. Alec told me in confidence before he left. The council wanted to keep it quiet."

Nara cursed. "It has to be Thrane." She looked at Meriah and knew she was thinking the same. "If the council also suspected as much, that would explain their desire for secrecy."

Meriah held her hands up. "After what you've told me, it seems plausible."

Rage rushed through her. It was infuriating to even consider the council would have reason to suspect Thrane behind the attacks and continue to send Esērii into the world so disadvantaged. She could well understand the desire to prevent unnecessary panic, but those taking the risks deserved to understand them. "I'm going to ask to be sent."

"You're no longer a chancellor, Nara." Meriah's dark gray eyes were tender, but stern. "They are unlikely to do so."

Nara shrugged. "I know. I'll go anyway."

Meriah sat back in her chair, resting her hands in her lap. "That will have irreparable consequences."

"I am not sure I care. I'm not leaving Cerys alone on the other side of the world, blind to what may be happening around her." Nara shook her head, confirming her thoughts to herself.

"You could be cast out."

"That will be the council's doing. Not mine." There was a part of Nara that found the concept of being cast out appealing.

Meriah held Nara's gaze for a breath, as if considering how to proceed. "I know you too well to try to urge caution."

"And I thank you for it."

Meriah smiled, but it was taut and swiftly cut loose.

"Will you take this to the king?"

"No. I would not wish for my brother to act with the limited information we have right now." Meriah was looking down, eyes flickering at a rapid pace, as if considering a thousand scenarios. Nara thought she likely was. "I'm going to organize things here. Parry can take over for me. I will travel back to the Citadel and wait for Alec. See if I can find out anything useful in the meantime."

The door opened, and the lanky boy walked through, arms full of scrolls and books.

"I need to go." Nara stood.

Meriah followed, walking around the desk. "If I don't see you in the Citadel, travel safe, my friend."

Nara pulled her into a tight embrace, hesitant to let go. "Nēn anun qah ukh en erēni." *May we meet again in peace.*

Nara released her and walked past the boy, inclining her head. One of the scrolls came loose from his arms, tumbling to the ground. His attempt to recover it sent another.

Nara bent down to pick them up, stacking them back onto his pile. "Look after my friend."

All were present when she arrived back at the boat. Rowers waited on their benches, oars in hand.

"Ready to go?" Nara asked.

"Aye. We've enough food and water to reach Kurk without stopping again." Harker's eyes lingered on her, taking in her demeanor. "All good?" he asked.

"I went to see Meriah Turan."

"And?"

She gave him a look to say they would speak on it later.

Nara turned to face the crew. "As soon as we are out of sight, cloak the ship. We need to move fast."

13

Thea

*"The intimacy of the Arabonde, not only in posture, but gaze, determines it an
unsuitable dance for modest young ladies of noble birth."*

ETIQUETTE AND TEMPERANCE OF THE DEVOUT
GEROLD THATCHER, 1052 AQ

"I feel ridiculous, Cat." Thea pulled at the ribbons of fabric tiered down
the length of her body.

"Stop fidgeting!" Catrianna scolded her, swatting at her hands. "You
look perfect."

Thea did not often mind the garments selected for her. But this day,
however, was a colossal exception. Pale yellow puffed sleeves rounded
the shoulders of the sweetheart-cut gown. Delicately crafted silk flowers
covered the bodice, and Thea thought she could lie down in the garden
and go entirely unnoticed. The skirt, slightly longer than floor-length for
dramatic effect, was crafted from layer after layer of the same dainty tex-
tile. It was ridiculous and a trial to walk in. Her sister donned a similar
garment in pale pink.

Thea sighed. "I don't know why I have to be here. No one cares if
I'm here." She pulled at the sides of the corset, the bone lining digging in.
Her breasts were pressed so high she thought she might be able to rest her
chin on them, were they not so small.

"Nonsense," Cat said. "I care."

Thea had not seen Marten since their outing at the Iren Stein two
days before. She'd played cards, drank ale with her brother, and made for
bed early. They'd been called to the throne room after breaking fast for

the first official reception. The room was packed wall-to-wall with people Thea had never seen.

Her father and stepmother sat in their respective thrones. Conall, Leanne, and Callum stood on their left, Cat and Thea on their right. The twins sat on a step at Evelynde's feet. Now and then, they would begin to push or argue with one another, only to find themselves quickly reprimanded by their mother. Lord after lord and lady after lady presented themselves and were greeted.

"Lady Starling," the king said, "Highclere welcomes you."

The elderly woman bowed to the best of her aging ability.

"Your Majesties honor me with an invitation." Lady Starling was one of the few women in Ire to hold title and significant lands. Married young to a man forty years her senior, she'd petitioned for the rights to both when he'd died. They'd had no children, and Thea's grandfather, Domnall, king at the time, had granted it. It had been a controversial decision, but one he'd stood by. Though he died before Thea was born, she'd always thought well of him for it. Lady Starling's lands were east of Highclere, not far, but they saw little of her at court. She was known as something of an eccentric, not often leaving her estate.

Lady Starling looked over all, smiling when her eyes landed on Thea. She was one of the few at court who treated her in equal regard with her brothers and sisters. "How handsome your children have grown, Your Majesties."

"Thankfully, they all take after their mothers." Ulric smiled, grasping Evelynde's hand. Thea could not see her face, but Evelynde was no doubt beaming. It was exactly the sort of compliment she aspired for. Lady Starling bowed again before moving on, only for her spot to be filled in a breath's time. One after another and on and on.

Thea smiled, curtsied when appropriate, and tried not to be offended when she was ignored. In time, her mind drifted. Her body acted out the routine, but her thoughts were elsewhere. The temperature in the room increased with its occupation. Sweat beaded on her neck, sliding down her back in thin trails.

"Dear cousin, we are most happy to receive you." Evelynde's voice was shrill, cutting through the noise in the room.

"Your Majesties." It was a middle-aged man with brown hair and blue eyes. His royal-blue vest was trimmed with a gold brocade, as was the leather belt fastened around his waist. He bowed in a deep, theatrical fashion, then repeated the action when his eyes fell on Cat, more ostentatious than the first. "Princess Catrianna, the tales of your beauty do not exaggerate. But that is no surprise as the daughter of Alena of Argal. I was fortunate enough to be acquainted with your mother. You are every bit her equal in beauty and grace. My prince is a fortunate one to be in consideration for your hand."

Thea could not help the rolling of her eyes. All knew the deal was done. It simply had to be put to parchment. She had little talent, nor tolerance, for these performative exchanges at court. Cat, however, excelled.

"I thank you, Your Grace," Cat said as she curtsied. "I have heard much of Prince Osric's own appeal, no doubt only second to his splendor and charm." Her dark blonde hair was brushed out in soft plait curls, mimicking the waves of her dress. A silver diadem rested atop, a single sapphire at its crest. Thea thought her sister deserved every word of praise she'd received that day. And there had been much.

"It is true our young prince is considered a fair one." The duke, whose name Thea had already forgotten, seemed satisfied, perhaps even impressed with her sister. Thea wanted to dislike him, but his intentions, however rehearsed, appeared genuine.

"I look forward to learning more about the prince. Will you join my stepmother and me for tea after the reception, Your Grace?"

"Of course, Princess," he said, his smile wider than ever, "it would be my pleasure." He turned to the king and queen and bowed once more. "Your Majesties."

Cat looked straight on, but Thea knew her sister well enough to know she was masking her nerves under pleasantries. She reached for Cat's hand in secret behind their skirts, but Cat stepped to the side. Thea stiffened, fighting the desire to glance her way. Her sister had never retracted from her so.

Both women continued the charade over the next hour until every new arrival had been received. When they were dismissed, Cat hesitated, as if she would speak, but turned and made for the doors.

"I am fine, Thea. Please stop asking."

Thea followed her sister around the kitchen. "I can see that you are not." She watched as Cat pulled three teacups from a shelf. "What are you doing?"

"I'm having tea with the duke," she said flatly. "Do you not remember?"

"Yes, but you need not prepare it yourself. Someone will do this for you." Thea reached for the cups. "Let me do it."

"I would rather keep busy." Cat moved to step around her, but Thea reached out, halting her retreat.

"Cat, stop."

Her sister's eyes were fixed on the floor. When they flicked up to meet Thea's, they were angry. "What do you want me to do? Cry? Scream? Protest? Mope around the castle day in and day out? That's you, Thea. Not me." She pulled free of Thea's grip, striding past. She set the teacups on a tray, then leaned on the table, head hanging.

"No, I—" The sting of her sister's words stilled her tongue.

"I'm sorry, I do not mean that." Cat turned, reaching for her hands. "Please forgive me."

Thea shook her head, the words unimportant. "Of course I do. I only wish you would speak to me. I know you are not being forthcoming. I can see you are struggling. Please tell me what you are thinking."

Cat resumed her work. "To say what? To tell you I am aggrieved? That I am plagued with resentment born from the cruelty of one granted liberty, only for it to be so dreadfully temporary? I know there are worse places to go, Thea, but Andar is not Ire. I will be little more than a parlor decoration. I'll have no rights if my husband is cruel. I can hold no property." Cat stopped, turning to face her. "In Andar, a common man may beat his wife with no fear of the law. What do you think a prince can do? What about a king?" She paused, and the back of one of her hands came up to cover her mouth.

Thea listened as Cat expressed all the same fears she held on her behalf. "He wouldn't dare. Father would—"

"Father would never know. You would never know. Every letter I write will be screened. Every letter you send me will be read. Every action I take will be watched." Cat filled a kettle with water, setting it over one of the stoves.

"I do not often say things of merit on behalf of Evelynde, but I do not think she would send you into such a situation."

"Nor I," Cat admitted, "but I cannot escape the fear of it. I'll have no assurances." She walked to a cabinet on the far side of the room, pulling a glass jar of tea leaves from one of the shelves.

Thea scrambled. This could not be her sister's future. "Then change your mind, Cat. Say no. Father would never force you to go."

Cat shook her head. "It is too late for that. This is too important."

She clutched the jar in one hand, holding it close to her body. She looked around as if she'd forgotten something. Thea watched her eyes find the cups across the room.

"What do you mean?"

"I don't know," Cat said, shaking her head. "I feel an… unease. Something is happening." She took a step closer to Thea. "Can you not feel it?"

Guilt plagued her as she realized she had been so preoccupied with her own situation she had neglected her sister.

"I feel shame to admit it, but no. I haven't." She reached for her sister's free hand. "Here I am weeping over my situation that pales in comparison to yours. I am endlessly sorry."

Cat looked down. "You didn't know."

"I should have." Thea tightened her grip. "If I had been paying attention, I would have."

"I didn't say anything—"

"Cat, stop. This is my fault." Thea pulled her into her arms.

"Strange things are happening, Thea. I know it." Cat's arms wrapped around her in return. She rested her head on Thea's shoulder. "I'm frightened. I don't want to leave Highclere."

Her heart seized at her sister's words. Not once in her life had she seen such fear in her. Thea felt insignificant. Ill-prepared to comfort someone she wanted so much to. She could find no words of encouragement. In truth, she would see little of her sister once she left. If they were lucky, once every several years. Cat's fears were not unwarranted.

"We'll figure this out. We have several moons, at the least." She brushed the loose strands of hair from her sister's face, tucking them behind her ears. Cat's blue eyes were unsettled in a way that made Thea's chest constrict.

The water in the kettle boiled, and Thea thought she knew exactly how it felt. She took the jar from her sister's grasp. "Let me do this."

Thea sat alone in her room before the feast, drinking wine, consumed with worry for her sister. For both of her sisters. For her niece. For all the women in Ire. For all the women in the Godsdamned world. Her contempt grew with every sip.

I will be little more than a parlor decoration.

Cat's words repeated over and over in her mind. Was that all her sister would become? Cat's mother was revered in Ire and her home in Argal.

Her portraits hung proudly in the foyer and galleries, but it was her beauty and charm that were admired so. Never her intelligence or talent or skill.

Thea's own mother was rarely spoken of. Only by her father, on the odd occasion, and always brief. Her mother wasn't even a ghost. She had been a body, a vessel, nothing more.

Even in Ire, where her father had tried to change the course, it wasn't enough. And it was the kingdom's militaristic might that allowed him to press so. Women were valued for their beauty and status, little else.

Thea couldn't help but wonder the same as Cat. Would it not be better to have never experienced autonomy? Can you miss what you've never known? But she thought of her mother and knew one could. One can ache for the absence of something well unknown to them.

The wine had not tempered her mood. She stood, scowling, toes tapping, glass in hand, looking over the gown that had been pulled for her. Pale purple fabric draped in abundance over her bed. It was cheerful, docile. Chosen for those exact purposes.

Thea finished the wine in her cup, setting it empty on the table. She rushed to her trunks and began flipping through dresses, leaving them scattered on the floor. She had one garment in mind, and one garment alone.

The Great Hall was loud with laughter and music when she arrived, the festivities well underway. Thea would usually slip in unnoticed through a side door, quietly taking her seat. This evening, she took the main entrance, allowing herself to be announced. When she walked through the rows of tables, she did not avert her gaze as she typically would. Instead, she inclined her head in greeting. All she passed took in the black gown she donned. It was simply cut, round at the chest and low in the back, with long sleeves and a floor-length skirt. It nearly covered her completely, but was cut close to her body. A ruse of modesty. What it was not, was docile or cheerful.

Her hair was not styled, hanging long behind her, kissing the curve of her back as she walked. Both her cheeks and lips were bare of rouge, for that night she wore only contempt.

She stopped in front of Marten's table and curtsied deep. "Your Grace."

"Lady Calithea." The duke inclined his head but didn't meet her eyes. The Duke of Aremore never treated Thea scornfully. It was far worse. He didn't consider her at all. She was not his equal, only something his son amused himself with. Any acknowledgment he made to her was out of obligation to his king.

"*Marten.*" Thea let his name roll off her lips.

He stood with a broad smile and bowed. "My lady." His eyes trailed down her body, growing in heat, as if taking in the way the thin fabric clung to her curves. She bowed again, taking her time as she walked away, conscious of the way her body swayed.

Thea took her seat at the end of the high table next to Cat. Callum raised his eyebrows, and Evelynde glared. Her father did not seem to notice anything awry.

"What happened to the gown laid out for you?" Cat whispered.

"I wanted something that better matched my mood." Thea reached for the carafe, filling her glass. She met any stray eyes from the crowd that drifted her way.

Cat sighed. "You are intent on angering her."

"No," Thea said in earnest. "I am not, Cat. It is not my dress that angers her. It is my existence."

When the dancing started, Thea moved about the room. She spoke with visitors from all over the continents, introducing herself without reserve. She did not cower at the table as she usually would. Now and then, her gaze would meet Marten's, neither concealing their admiration for the other. Prying eyes could derive their intention.

She spoke at length with Lady Starling about gardening before making a promise to have tea with her before she departed the capital. She stood at a table, refilling her wineglass, when a gentle breath caressed the delicate skin on her neck. "Dance with me."

Thea smiled at the voice that purred against her. "Would that be proper, my lord?"

Another exhale on her bare flesh sent a shiver down her back she couldn't help but arch into.

He moved closer. "If you did not wish me to ask you, you should not have worn this dress."

She smiled devilishly. "I do not get your meaning. There is very little of me on display." She turned around, and Marten was so close their lips nearly grazed.

"And that is what tempts me so." He peered down at the modest neckline. "The idea of what lies beneath."

Thea leaned closer to whisper in his ear. "Good sir, you are thoroughly familiar with what lies beneath this dress."

He let out a low groan. When she pulled back to look in his eyes, she found them on fire. He offered his hand between them. "Dance with me, you siren."

She grinned, slipping her hand into his.

The festivities had quieted, many guests having taken to bed. Marten walked her to the center of the room, leaving her for a brief moment while he requested a song from the musicians. He strode back, taking his place behind her. The alluring sounds of the Arabonde began to play, some in the hall taking notice.

She turned her face toward his. "We are going to pay for this."

Marten's hand found her waist, gliding around, open-palmed on her belly. He tugged her close. Too close. It sent heat rushing through her. "Then let us make it worth it."

They moved, stepping in synchrony to the left and then back to the right. He turned her around, his hands finding her hips as he lifted her from the ground, letting her body slide down his as she slowly returned to the floor. Their arms intertwined, and they stepped in a circle, only to switch and turn the other way. Thea let herself fall into the music.

She spun around him, fingers tracing along the path of his shoulders. He turned his head to watch her move, eyes scarcely leaving hers. When she'd come full circle, his hands again found her waist, lifting her high into the air. She let her head fall back, hair spinning wildly.

They had danced it a thousand times, but never like this. They didn't try to conceal their intimacy. They paid no mind to those who looked on. Lost in the dance, in each other. They danced like young lovers. They danced like two in love.

When it ended, they stood staring at each other, panting in rhythm. Marten bowed to her before bringing her hand to his lips. They shared a tender, but conspiratorial smile. It was only when she turned around that she realized nearly everyone had been watching. Some looked on in shock, some in anger, others in delight.

Thea straightened her back, chin high, and walked to the main entrance of the hall. She turned back to the crowd and took a final curtsy. She did not look at their faces again as she walked from the room.

14

Thea

"It is not the blush in her cheek nor the curve of her figure that makes a lady desirable. It is per piety and purity. There is no woman more lovely than one demure and obedient."

ETIQUETTE AND TEMPERANCE OF THE DEVOUT
GEROLD THATCHER, 1052 AQ

"You know why I've asked you here this morning."

It was not a question. Evelynde had called for Thea not an hour past breaking fast. The tension between them was heavy and tempestuous from the moment Thea had taken the seat opposing hers.

Thea shrugged. She absolutely knew what it was about, but she had gone to bed angry, woke angry, and the disapproving glare of her stepmother did nothing to temper it. She felt well up for a fight.

Evelynde reached for the teapot on the table between them. Her angry blue eyes flicked up to meet Thea's as she poured. "I speak of your behavior last night."

"If the color of my dress is of such controversy, the dress is not truly the problem, is it?" Thea let her head lean in sequence with the raising of her brow. A gesture of intention, but slight enough one could argue its innocence.

Evelynde returned the teapot, resting her hands elegantly on her lap. "I speak of your behavior with Marten Percy."

"Am I not allowed to dance with my oldest friend?" Thea asked. "We are, after all, celebrating his pending matrimony."

Evelynde sighed, laboring to contain her irritation. Thea could see it, pulsing behind her disapproving gaze. "I've not the patience for this, Calithea. You know what you did—what you are *doing*—and I'll not waste time quarreling with you on your intentions."

"Then speak plainly, Evelynde," Thea said, a challenge in her eyes. She reached for the jar of honey. "You're allowed to do that here."

Indignation tightened her gaze, but to her credit, Evelynde didn't back down. Over the years, they'd shared countless moments of contention, but none had spiraled into a true disagreement. Thea already knew this would be the one to erupt.

"You mean to goad me," Evelynde said, almost amused, sipping her tea.

Thea stirred a honey-covered spoon in her own. Notes of vanilla and citrus traveled up with the steam. She took a sip, holding her stepmother's gaze. The cup made a gentle clink when she returned it to the plate. "Let me assure you, I do not spend my time devising ways to vex you. It clearly comes natural."

Evelynde looked down, her lips pressed thin. She returned her cup to the table, and when her eyes met Thea's again, they were angry. "You want me to speak plainly? Very well. The Percy boy will be wed this Godsday. You will not interfere. You will not cause conflict. You will attend this sixday's events as your status dictates. You will dress like a lady, drink like a lady, and you will hinder your erratic and irresponsible behavior. You will not ruin what I have worked tirelessly to build."

Thea flexed her jaw, feeling heat wash over her cheeks. "You say you don't wish to quarrel over intentions, yet you make clear where you believe mine lie. Do you see me such your enemy?"

"Your *enemy*?" Evelynde asked, the grasp on her temper slipping. "That is how you see the world, isn't it? Look beyond yourself, Calithea. This is not about you. This is not a silly rule for you to break for your amusement or etiquette for you to rebel against."

Thea leaned forward over the table, letting some of her own disgruntlement out in her tone. "If you do not wish me to pull at the restraints, then do not try to shackle me so."

The two women stared at each other, neither willing to relent. Evelynde closed her eyes for a breath, her tightly wound composure starting to crack. "What a child you are. I did not make the world the way it is. We're women, Calithea. We cannot do whatever we please."

Thea scoffed and reached for her teacup, but Evelynde snatched it away, spilling some of its contents on the table. Thea stared at her, brows knitted and lips slightly ajar.

"You may be content to live your life on the outskirts of proper society, carousing and wasting away or whatever it is you and Callum do," she said, flipping her hand between them. "But do not be so arrogant and naive that you expect others to do the same. Your father has indulged you. Far too much. Even in consideration of your… special circumstances."

"You can say it, Stepmother. *Bastard.*" Thea spat the words. "I was *born* on the outskirts of proper society. It is not a door one can simply open and walk through."

"And you are determined to see it sealed forever!" Evelynde slammed her hand on the table, and Thea jumped. Her voice was shrill, and her eyes wide. Evelynde blinked and then swallowed, composure promptly returning. The anger in her face cooled, though the rosy hue of her cheeks remained. "Do not think I am not sympathetic to your situation."

Thea hardened her face, determined not to be conciliated.

"I know I could never be a mother to you, but I have tried to be your friend. What you do affects this family. It affects the prospects of all your siblings. Tamsin adores you. What sort of example are you setting for her?"

Thea simply stared at her, unmoved by her words.

The lack of reception caused Evelynde to retreat from her brief, heartfelt appeal, back into reprimand. "Your father may be content to let you run wild, but I will say to you what he will not. This marriage further seals a critical alliance between Ire and Andar. As will Cat's. It is time for these charades of yours to end."

Thea could not see a way toward understanding between them. "Are you quite finished? I'm late for an afternoon of debauchery and drink."

Evelynde shook her head. "You have no idea how special what you have is. You have no idea the *privilege*. If you want to blame me for trying to ensure my niece also has it, I am quite content to take it. Do you think I do not know this sacrifice myself? Was I not wed to a man nearly twice my age? I have grown to love your father. He is a wonderful man, and I am grateful for him. But I did not choose him."

Thea sat up, lifting her chin. "I can hold feeling for your circumstances, Evelynde, but that does not make me indebted to them. Women are not bound to the same oppressions as their foremothers simply because they are born to them. The world never changes if we roll over and say yes."

"Oh, Thea," Evelynde said, regarding her with pity that set Thea's irritation flaring. "Debt can be inherited, I promise you that." She made a noise, too feminine to be considered a huff. "Do I not live in the shadow of your mother? The woman your father would have chosen for himself had he the liberty to do so." Evelynde spoke low, and far more bitterly than Thea had her from her before.

Thea frowned. She'd not borne witness to any such sentiment from her father. She wondered what her stepmother knew that she did not.

"He has a weakness for you," she said, with a stiff, short-lived smile. "For all his children, but for you in particular. Gods help me, I love him for it." Evelynde looked away for a moment, regaining the resolution she'd worn before. "But I will make these heavy decisions if he will not."

Thea felt a wave of sympathy for her, but it crashed against the wall of resentment she'd built, which was far stronger. "Arrange your marriages, Evelynde. Throw your parties, dance the way they want you to. Speak when and of what is appropriate. That is you. That is not me." The temper in their voices had cooled, but the mood was still unsteady.

"You cannot play the game if you do not have a place at the table."

Thea sighed. "Evelynde, I do not wish to play."

Evelynde reached for a napkin, blotting delicately at her eyes. "That is fine, Calithea, but do not judge those of us who do. And for Godssake, do not impede our efforts."

"You would lecture me on the consequences of judgment?" Thea nearly laughed. "I know judgment well. I live it every day." She lifted her face, narrowing her eyes on her stepmother. "In the words spoken to me. In the words *not* spoken. I see it in the eyes of those I walk past. I see it in yours."

Evelynde's eyes swelled, and Thea felt her own tears coming, and they encouraged her anger. She did not wish to cry. Evelynde reached across the table for her hand and flinched when Thea pulled away. "I am not your enemy, Calithea."

"That does not make you my friend."

Evelynde sighed and sat back in her chair, her defenses giving way. She was yielding. Thea thought she would feel victorious, but she felt only unease. "My actions are not designed, and most certainly not intended, to hurt you. This marriage is political. And of love for my niece." She paused for a moment, letting her eyes make her plea. Blue, glistening, and vulnerable. "Not everyone has a father like yours."

Thea stiffened at the sudden sting of truth. It cut through like a hot blade, and she felt a wash of shame at the realization she had not considered that. She had been thinking only of herself. She had thought only of what she was losing, not of what this girl may be gaining.

Thea knew her actions would change nothing. She was lashing out in anger, in rebellion, just as her stepmother said. She had no desire to open the door to proper society. Thea wanted to kick it down, only to turn and walk away. If she did cause trouble, it would not benefit her. Marten would not be wed to her. She would only be creating more hurt. Her circumstances would not change.

"I am sorry." Thea's eyes darted around in the space between them. "I had not thought about it that way."

Evelynde reached across the table for her hand again. This time, Thea didn't recoil. "Women cannot afford to be adversaries in this world, Calithea."

Thea stood. "I will give you no further cause for concern. I swear it." Without waiting for a response, she turned and left, leaving Evelynde at the table alone.

Keeping to her promise, Thea attended the reception in the afternoon. She smiled, curtsied, and spoke when appropriate. She wore the dress selected for her. She did everything requested and required. When Marten arrived with his father, she did not look at him. She kept to the back of the room, only participating in conversation when approached. Which did not happen often.

Callum had come by several times, but she sent him away at each, feigning a headache. It was clear he didn't believe her, but he didn't press. Even her father had suggested she go and lie down, but she assured him she was well enough. Their courtesy only made her feel more fragile. She wished to be left alone.

She was watching her sister charm the duke across the room when a familiar and unwelcome voice disrupted her.

"Calithea."

Thea sighed. Turning around, she met eyes with her uncle. He bowed, a healthy level of condescension in his manner.

Kenelm was her father's younger brother, though one would not know it by sight. They shared the same dusty blond hair and blue eyes, but little else. Married to the fourth daughter of the king of Lochland over a decade before, it had not been an advantageous nor happy marriage, and he had grown bitter over the years. Never a pleasant man, he went out of his way to ensure Thea was always aware of her lower station in the family.

"Uncle Kenelm," she said as she curtsied. "Always a pleasure." She tried and failed to keep the disappointment from her face.

The king of Lochland was now an old man without sons and yet to name an heir. Callum had told her there would likely be a fight among the husbands of his daughters upon his death. Lochland, like Ire, had never seen a woman on the throne. Thea had no doubt Kenelm would be among those squabbling. She started to turn away, hopeful he would move on, but he continued.

"It is always a surprise to me when I return to my homeland to see how young ladies are permitted to present themselves these days." He looked her up and down, eyes fixating on her bare shoulders. It soured her stomach and picked at the thin veil containing her derision.

"It is a surprise to me, my lord, to find you've an interest in women's fashion. Perhaps Cat can advise you." Thea leaned forward with a faint disdainful smirk. "She has quite the eye."

The amusement fell from his face. "It is not only the way they dress that surprises but also the way they speak. Women in Lochland understand their place." Kenelm straightened his back, looking down as if to make her feel small. "A man has many uses for a woman's tongue. Cleverness is not among them."

Thea felt great pity for any woman who was forced to share herself, in any respect, with the likes of him. "It is good, then, Uncle, that you left us so many years ago." Thea knew if she told her father what was said, Kenelm would receive a swift kick back to Lochland. It wouldn't be the first time he would be reprimanded for his treatment of her. He had not been invited to Highclere in years. The wedding was an exception brought on by Evelynde. Appearances in mind, no doubt.

As if answering a silent plea for help, her father appeared. "Brother," he said, wrapping his arm protectively around her shoulders. "I hope your journey was not too taxing."

"Your Majesty." Kenelm bowed. "I daresay it was quite pleasant. You see, the bride and her family passed through Kilney, and we traveled among their party. What a delightful girl." He looked at Thea. "Very beautiful, young, obedient. I suspect she will make quite the happy match for young Marten Percy."

Thea felt she'd been slapped. Heat rushed her cheeks in shame and rage. In part at the intended cruelty, and in part it had worked. Taking in her reaction, he smirked, triumphant. Tears flooded her eyes, and she tried to swallow them back.

"Darling girl," her father said as he grabbed her hand and kissed it. "Your sister is asking after you. Will you go to her now?"

Thea glared at Kenelm until her father's words took hold. Her throat was too tight to speak, so she nodded and turned, retreating with haste until reaching an unassailable distance. She glanced back to find her father leaning forward, speaking directly into Kenelm's ear. Whatever his words, they were enough to wipe the smirk from his brother's face. Kenelm paled, and her father patted him on the shoulder before moving on.

Thea moved as quickly as she could without drawing attention. The room was loud and crowded, and her eyes were heavy with tears she did not wish another to see. She felt the attack coming, the cold panic spreading from her belly. Once she was in the corridor, she ran.

She rushed around a corner, into the long hall leading to the royal quarters, and in her urgency, tripped on the long skirts of her gown. The delicate fabric ripped beneath her feet, and she fell forward, hard, her knees and hands scraping against the floor.

Something between a grunt and a groan escaped between her ragged breaths. She pressed her burning palms into the rough stone, using the pain to focus, to fight the fit.

Breathe, she thought in Breeda's voice.

Black boots stepped into view. Thea trailed the length of a man's body, his trousers and tunic also black, to find a face she didn't know. He peered down at her, hand extended.

She lifted a shaking arm, and he grasped it, holding it tight in his as he pulled her to her feet.

"Pardon me," she said, gaze lowered.

"You're bleeding." His voice was deep and honeyed, with a mild southern accent.

Thea looked down to find her dress stained red at both knees. "Oh— I," she said, wiping at it only to find more blood left behind. Her palms were smeared red, as were his where he had touched her. "Oh, Gods," she whispered, and sheepishly glanced up at his face. "I am dreadfully sorry."

Dark gray eyes swept her from top to bottom, brows creasing, head tilting when he met her eyes again. Black, loose waves did not quite meet his chin, where a close-cropped beard shadowed the lower half of his golden-hued face. Thea was unsure if she should chastise him for his appraisal of her or thank him for his assistance.

"May I help you?" he asked, his manner still undecipherable to her.

"No, thank you," Thea said and stepped back. She clutched her arms around herself, wiping at the numbing sensation taking over. *No, no, no,* she thought, but she felt it coming. Needlelike pricks crept across her chest. She fell back against the stone wall.

He stepped closer. "Are you unwell, my lady?"

Her vision clouded as she tried to produce an answer. She could no longer discern his face. There was only a blur of golden skin and black hair.

"No—I must go. Please forgive my impertinence." Thea turned and scrambled down the hall, bracing against the walls to stay on her feet.

Picking up speed, she yelped when a hand grasped her arm from behind, spinning her around. She had not even heard him approach. Marten took one look at her face and pulled her into his arms.

"You shouldn't—be here." Her words came out in a whisper between labored breaths.

"I don't care. I saw what happened. What did Kenelm say to you?" He grabbed her hands, turning them over. "*Gods,* did you fall?"

She said nothing, only pressed her face into his chest. Her hands trembled, and her lips numbed. Marten pulled back to look at her, and Thea collapsed.

She felt him catch her, lowering her to the ground as her body seized and jerked. He turned her on her side, holding her head in his hands.

"I've got you," he said as he stroked her hair.

Thea gasped as pain erupted over the whole of her body. She felt it in her bones. Like glacial water cascading through her veins, transforming all it touched to ice. There was always pain, but this was unlike any before. She feared it was too much. She feared she couldn't take it. It sent her arching and writhing as her vision tunneled. She heard Marten speaking. No, he was screaming. A blur of red hair came into sight right as she blacked out.

Thea came in and out of consciousness, vaguely aware she was being carried. She heard commotion around her, but could barely open her eyes, and what she was able to see was a muddle of color and light. The pain was gone, and for that she was grateful, but she was cold, terribly cold.

Her body trembled as she was laid on a bed. Her bed, she recognized. She tried to sit up, only to feel a firm hand pressed to her chest.

"Lie back," someone cautioned.

Marten's face came into focus, staring down at her, terror plaguing his features. Breeda pushed him aside, tucking the blankets high up around her neck.

"Rest now, love," Breeda said as she stroked her cheek. A warm wash of relief swelled over her as sleep took hold.

By the time Thea woke, the moon was high. She sat up in her bed, and Sylvie sprang from a chair across the room.

"How long was I asleep?" Thea asked, rubbing her eyes.

"Several hours. It is past nightfall." Sylvie held her hand to Thea's cheek and pursed. "You're still cold."

"Where is everyone?" Thea looked around the empty room.

"At the feast. Your sister left only moments ago." Sylvie continued her examination, peering into Thea's eyes as if they held the answer.

Thea's head pounded. She reached up, palming her forehead with a bandaged hand. "Did I hit my head when I fell?"

"I don't think so. Marten was there."

Thea remembered. The pain. "Gods, that was the worst one."

"How do you feel now?"

"Like I've fallen from the parapet."

Sylvie's eyes grew heavy with concern.

"I jest… I am fine." Thea held up a hand. "I'm sorry."

Sylvie was not convinced. She reached for Thea's hands, pulling back the bandages. "We can take these off." The remnants of a familiar green paste tinted her skin. It was some kind of herbal concoction that Sylvie made anytime Thea injured herself, which was a fairly common occurrence. It smelled like honey and grass. "The scrapes on your knees are a little deeper. We'll take the dressings off in the morning."

Thea flexed her hands. "I suppose I should dress and join supper." She pulled back the cover to rise from the bed, but Sylvie grabbed it, draping it back over her.

"No," she said, shaking her head, "your father forbids it."

A snort-like laugh tumbled out. "My father forbids it?" She stared at Sylvie until understanding she was serious. "What do you mean?"

Sylvie walked across the room and returned with a cup of wine, placing it in Thea's hands. "He bids you rest tonight. He also excuses you the remainder of the sixday, at your discretion."

Thea balked, unsure if she was relieved. She raised a brow. "Evelynde will not be pleased."

Sylvie leaned toward her to speak in confidence, though they were the only two in the room. A sly smile curled on her lips. "They quarreled about it. Your stepmother was not keen on the idea. You know how she is about appearances."

The two women shared a knowing look as Thea drank.

"What happened?" Sylvie asked, taking back the cup. "What brought it on?"

Thea hesitated, remembering the sting of what he'd said. "Kenelm said some… unpleasant things. I think I am more upset with myself than him. And then there was this… strange man."

Sylvie shifted closer. "What man?"

Thea shrugged, shaking off the thought. She had no desire to relive her humiliations. "No one. It doesn't matter."

Sylvie held her cheek and sighed. "In five days, this will be behind you."

Thea nodded. It was what she kept telling herself.

Sylvie tapped the glass. "Drink your wine. I will go down to the kitchens and fetch us something for supper."

She stood, but Thea reached for her hand. "Sylvie, thank you."

"It is no tall task," she said with a smile.

When the door closed behind her, Thea collapsed back into bed, her pillows whooshing in response to the sudden impact. Humiliation weighed heavy, but it was at least a burden she was familiar with. She winced at the thought her family had been standing over her unconscious body just moments before.

She said a silent prayer to Cassia she would never see that man again. The thought of looking into his eyes after that exchange was mortifying. She had left him standing there with her blood on his hands, running down the hall like a madwoman. Anyone who did not already think her a lunatic surely would once this story made rounds through court. Thea flipped onto her stomach, stuffing her face into the pillow, and let out a self-reproaching groan.

Her thoughts drifted to Marten, and she worked to shut them down. It was all too real now. She would think about him later, in five days.

When he was gone.

15

Neith

"Those who would dare invoke the power of the Gods must be quelled. As the Gods themselves pronounced. All men are duty bound to see it so."

HEXADIC PRECEPTS
ZATHRIAN BYGRAVE, 719 AQ

"What does it feel like?" Kieran asked from his seat across the campfire.

Neith considered. "Do you remember how it felt passing through the mountain?"

"I don't think any of us will ever forget," Petra said as she took the seat next to her brother.

"It is like that, but colder, emptier. But also—" Neith paused, trying to find the words. The best she could come by was *intoxicating*, or *seducing*, but both made her feel too exposed. She glanced at Sam, who sat beside her. "It is difficult to describe."

"How is it different from wielding ether?" Bellamy asked, then tipped up the flask.

"Ether lives within us, within everything. Wielding it feels like blinking your eye or waving your hand." Several nodded along as she spoke. "Calling nether is more like opening a door, persuading what's on the other side to step through."

"Does it hurt?" Ayla asked from her spot next to Max.

Neith shook her head. "It is more like it takes something from you. It's a bargain, and you don't know the stakes."

Raiden and Iris looked at each other as if the prospect was terrifying. Neith didn't think she could explain to them why it wasn't. Raiden turned back to Neith. "When did you find you could call it?"

Regret flooded through her at the memory. She was six years old and learning to wield when instead of ether, nether emerged, penetrating the shield of one of her tutors. He'd nearly died. She had been so terrified by the event they'd had to put bindings on her for years until she was old enough to learn to wield it. She had few memories from her early childhood because of it. At that time, they'd had little understanding of nether, relying on myth and old texts her father had stolen from the Citadel. It had been largely trial and error. They were not memories she wished to share.

"*How* do you do it?" Sam asked.

Neith gave him a quick, grateful smile. "There are two methods I have learned. The safest requires more time. More concentration." She thought for a moment the best way to explain. "Think of the void as something layered with our world. It is draped around it, blanketing it. Connected in fluidity. The planes move like water." Brows furrowed across the campfire. She sighed. It was something she felt, not thought about. Putting words to it was a difficult task. "I can use ether to see the fabric that binds our world to the void. I use it to create a mapping of sorts. I visualize everywhere I want to snap the plane. I open it for a fraction of a breath, letting the nether consume."

"Days…" Kieran ran his hand through his short red hair. "Can you do that to anything?"

"In theory. Though stagnant objects are far easier than something moving… or living." She reached for her mug of ale, taking a sip. "The more ether something has, the more taxing and challenging it is. Ether does not wish to be quelled. It fights back."

The group exchanged looks. It was quiet for a moment. The only sounds were the snaps and cracks of the fire between them. Sam's eyes were still fixed on her as if trying to make sense of it.

"And the other method?" Bellamy asked.

"I can pull a fixed amount through a small portal and then manipulate the nether, here, in our world, not dissimilar from the way we can ether. But it is dangerous. Wielding nether in such a manner drains one rather quickly."

"Will you show us?" The eagerness in Iris's green eyes glowed with the reflection of the campfire.

Neith looked at each of the faces staring back. She couldn't help her excitement that they were treating her as one of them, but their enthusiasm toward nether made her uneasy. They had no idea what it was truly like. Of all those who sat around her, only Sam and Raiden appeared cautious.

Neith held out her right hand, and the group collectively leaned in. Closing her eyes, she called, opening a portal to the void so small a human eye could scarcely discern it. She coaxed it, beckoning the nether to come through. It answered with a gentle whisper, a soft embrace. *Hello, my love*, it would say, could it speak. Neith opened her eyes, gazing at the thin, airy black tendril snaking around her hand and the space above it. She caressed it, and it returned the affection.

"Why doesn't it hurt you?" Sam asked. His voice was steady, but Neith sensed uneasiness beneath.

"We don't know." Neith watched it dance around. Several passersby stopped. She pushed it up toward a branch that hung above. It sliced through, sending fragments falling into their fire. All watched with ultimate attention. No one moved or spoke.

She released her call on the nether and it retreated into the void, to its home, swiftly, as if it didn't belong in their world.

The group blinked, the enchantment broken.

"What happens if you don't send it back?" Bellamy's eyes were robbed of the joviality they usually held.

Neith considered the places and things she'd destroyed. "Nothing good."

They sat transfixed, staring into the flames, unsure of what she'd shown them. All looked up when Sam stood. A collective inhale followed, with the others starting into conversations around the fire. Neith surmised they'd seen enough for one night.

She watched Sam walk to one of their carts, returning with a small muslin cloth. He knelt beside her, holding it out. She reached up and touched the space beneath her nose, fingertips coming away red. A thin stream of blood had fallen down her face, neck, and onto her chest.

Heat washed over her cheeks. She tried wiping at the blood, but mostly achieved smearing it around. She thought of the river down the hill and stood. "I will return."

"Should I accompany you?" Ayla asked.

"No," Neith answered, taking in her intimate proximity to Max. "I will be fine."

"I'll go." Sam stepped aside so she could pass.

The gentle sounds of water and chirping crickets replaced the clamor of camp as they descended through the tall grass. Fireflies blinked in rapid succession, like beacons to the water's edge. The riverbed was not as rocky as she'd expected, but she dug through the smooth pebbles with the toe of her boot, searching for any hidden treasures. She'd found her favorite piece of jasper in a creek not far from Necrium.

Summer approached, but the water still held a chill. Neith knelt and dipped the cloth into the stream, then tried wiping at her face and neck.

"Does it always take so much from you?" Sam asked, standing over her.

Neith looked up at him. "I suppose it does. Sometimes more, sometimes less. So far, nothing permanent as far as I can tell." She had meant the last part as a jest, but it garnered no laugh. She sighed, turning back to the water in even bigger mortification than before. Truth was, she did fear it took something, some part of her, every time she wielded it. She wasn't sure what, but she knew it was something she would never get back. Neith continued cleaning herself until she realized she had no idea of her success. Standing, she turned to him, eyes low. "Is it gone?"

Sam stepped closer, examining. Without answer, he took the cloth from her hand and walked around her to plunge it back in the water, giving it a light wring. When he stood, he paused, holding it tight between his hands. Neith frowned, then realized he was trying to warm it.

He stepped closer, directly in front of her, his eyes looking over her face. One hand rose to hold it steady as the other gently blotted at the blood between her nose and lips.

"At least you did not have to tear off a piece of your tunic this time," she said.

One side of his lips twitched. His eyes met hers briefly before returning to his work. When he started on her lips, she had to look away, grateful for the cover of night. She knew her cheeks must be the color of beets at peak harvest.

She lifted her chin while he cleaned her neck. Neith wondered if she'd ever been touched so tenderly, so gently, and she cursed herself for not bleeding more. The cloth reached the bottom of her throat and stopped. He stiffened, his eyes flashing up to hers, as if suddenly aware he was touching her somewhere intimate.

He stepped back, holding the cloth out between them. "I'm sorry."

"No—I—thank you." Neith reached for the cloth, and he looked at her with something she couldn't quite make sense of. An unease of sorts. She hoped it wasn't fear. Neith stepped toward him, and he eyed her cautiously, but didn't retreat. The desire to ease his discomfort outweighed her nerves. She only wanted to know what he was thinking. She realized she could simply ask.

Her lips parted to speak, and his gaze flicked to them. Just as the words started to leave her mouth, a figure sprinted past, stealing their attention. The blur of a human plunged into the water. Followed by another.

"Fuck, that's cold!" Kieran yelled, splashing around.

Iris screamed in protest as Bellamy carried her in. The others ran down the hill, joining the impromptu swim.

"Should I ready the tent?" Ayla asked Neith.

Neith looked over at Max wrestling with Bellamy in the water. "I can do it myself. Stay, have fun."

Ayla grinned in gratitude, taking off to join the others. When they were alone again, Neith turned back to Sam. She wanted to step back into the space that had existed only moments ago, but it was gone. He now looked indifferent, or was trying to. She couldn't tell. "Good night, Sam."

He gave her an abrupt nod. "Good night."

Only Raiden still sat around the fire. Neith took a seat on the log next to his, and he extended the flask to her. She held her hand up to decline.

His raven hair and porcelain skin were not dissimilar to her own, common traits of those with Thranean ancestry, but his eyes were a far darker shade of blue. Like sapphires, or water residing far below the surface. He was quiet, even with the others, but Neith noticed he was always paying attention. He was the youngest among them at eighteen winters, the minimum age to serve.

Neith looked over her shoulder toward the group down the hill. The sound of their laughter fathered a smile. "Do you not wish to join them?"

Raiden turned to face her with a shy, but jesting deportment. "Jumping into a freezing river? I can't say I do." He had a familiarity that she sensed was not all related to his mother. A stoicism that bled through the boyish surface. The sort that, in time, overtakes the playfulness and marvelment of youth. She wondered who his father was.

"I share your sentiment," Neith said as she warmed her hands over the flames. She glanced at him. "May I ask you something?"

He looked at her curiously but nodded.

"Why do you not choose to be under your mother's command?" It was a question she'd wanted to ask the first day he joined her.

Raiden shifted on the log, reaching for a stick to poke the fire. "My mother wishes for me to make my own path. She says we all earn our place in the ranks. She says I will never be taken seriously if I rise under her command."

Neith thought that sounded like Maelis Nicomedes. She did not know the woman well, but she'd gathered enough over the years to know she was hard. "She sounds much like my father."

His eyes flicked to hers, and the two shared a look of understanding. He held the flask out to her again. She laughed, this time taking a drink.

Neith winced at the burn. "And your father?"

Raiden shifted again but shrugged. "No one of note."

"I see." She looked down, knowing that meant his father was likely dead. She wondered if there were any among them who had not lost one or both of their parents.

"Might I ask you something now?"

"Of course."

"Is wielding nether something other Etherborn can learn to do?" He didn't quite meet her eyes.

Neith inhaled. "I don't know. We do not think so. Why do you ask?"

Raiden's gaze returned to the campfire, hesitant or perhaps fearful to answer.

"If it were, would you wish to learn?" Neith asked, her suspicion raised.

"No," he answered quickly, eyes meeting hers again. "No, that's not why." He looked down, and a strand of chin-length black hair fell over his face. "The idea of the wrong person holding that sort of power terrifies me."

It was the sort of judgment she feared. The sort she feared could be true.

As if sensing her thoughts, he looked up. "I did not mean you."

"I understand what you mean." She smiled at him, but it was taut. "You are smart to be afraid of such a thing." Neith handed him back the flask and stood. "I will retire now."

Raiden nodded and returned his attention to the fire.

Neith turned back when she reached the door. "I do not know if I am the right person or if such a person exists, but I will do my best not to be the wrong one." Something behind him caught her attention, and she looked up to see Sam, half-concealed in the shadows. His gaze was intense, scrutinizing, and far removed from how he had looked at her down by the water. She stepped backward into her tent, almost in retreat, and let the cover fall in place.

She tried to strip off her dress, struggling to pull at the ties on the back. It felt suddenly restrictive, and she desperately wanted it removed from her body. Her mind tried to make sense of the look Sam had given her.

When the dress finally fell free, she kicked off her boots. The cool grass on her bare feet helped to ground her. She sat on the edge of her cot, head falling into her hands. Every look she'd received that night replayed in her mind. Fear, most prominently among them.

Neith did not want them to fear her, but nor could she blame them. She had done herself no favors with her party trick. She groaned and fell back onto the cot. Her father would not care about such things. Her brother would likely enjoy knowing he was feared. Magnus would tell her to use it responsibly. None of it fit.

Neith wondered what her mother would think.

16

Thea

"There are four species of mountain cat residing from Argal to Ire. The obsidian mountain cat being the most deadly. It stalks its prey for hours, as if it enjoys the hunt."

THE ILLUSTRATED GUIDE TO NATIVE ANIMALS AND PLANTS OF
THE NORTH
OLIVER BIRCH, 925 AQ

It was a beautiful day for sport. The sun was high and bright, but a gentle, late-spring breeze cooled the skin. Thea sat beside her sister in the stands, watching their brothers compete.

Callum, as expected, was winning all his contests. He looked handsome in his iron armor, blond waves shining under the sun. The tucks of his polished plates overflowed with the dainty and colorful favor of a rather large group of young ladies. They'd followed him from event to event across the grand field, crying out in concern one moment and cheering him on in the next. It was all a bit theatrical for Thea, but he well played the part of charming prince.

"I should like to learn sword skill," Thea said to her sister.

Catrianna choked on her drink. "*Thea,*" she said, blotting delicately at the corners of her mouth, "you only wish that because you are not permitted to."

Thea considered there was likely *some* truth to that, but it wasn't the whole of it. She found the idea of being able to take down a man quite thrilling. "Northern women used to go to battle."

Cat peered at her, sidelong. The gentle breeze fluttered the delicate fabric of her yellow dress. "In stories, Calithea. Myths. From thousands of years ago."

Thea shrugged. "It might not all be myth. Isn't myth supposed to be based on something true? In some kingdoms in the south, women are permitted to train. They fight alongside men, against them."

Cat brushed her hair behind her shoulders. It was silky and smooth and nothing like Thea's own wavy, frizzy mess. "We do not live in the south. We live in the north. The *high north* at that."

Thea sipped her lemonade, considering. It was a touch too sweet. Reason did not deter her. "Women fought in Icena."

"And nearly all of them died twenty years ago." Cat turned to face her. "Thea, what is this about?"

Thea looked out over the tourney. "I don't know. It seems like it would be far more diverting to be out there than sitting here."

It had come down to the final match in sword sport, and the opponent who had been winning on the other side of the field was now making his way across.

Black leather fighting gear and bronze armor set him in stark contrast to her brother. The visor of the opponent's helmet was up, but Thea could not make out his face through the narrow gap. The helmet was not round but peaked, like a castle spire. Southern, in style, she surmised. Aharan, or Sibreenean. In place of a sword, he wielded a long spear, the bronze metallic plating shining like gold. He was slightly shorter than her brother, but Callum was leaner. She thought it looked fairly matched.

Seeing him approach, Callum donned his helmet, meeting the man in the middle of the ring. They bowed to each other before stepping back and taking position. The announcer began to read out the rules and names of the contenders.

"Oh, look, Conall has won his joust." Cat's arm extended across Thea, pointing to the other side of the field.

"Good on him." Thea tried to sound eager, but these types of events rarely held her attention, let alone her enthusiasm.

Cat elbowed her. "Oh, come now. Is it not exciting to see our brothers winning?"

Thea threw her arms up in mock cheer. Cat laughed and shook her head. They watched Conall remove his helmet and walk to Leanne, kneeling before her. It was customary in Ire, and much of the north, for a gentleman to kneel before a lady of his choice after winning a tourney or competition. It signified winning in her honor.

Thea usually found such gestures winceworthy, but her eldest brother's devotion to his wife and children was well known. Though they were the only ones who could extract such sentiment from him.

Distracted by Conall's win, Thea had not noticed Callum's match had begun until the clanking of metal pulled her attention.

Callum swung his sword toward his opponent, backing him up. The man in bronze parried the blows, turning and twisting his spear to fight them off. Callum struck down hard from above, and the man fell to one knee. At first, it appeared a result of the strike, but he quickly swept his spear at Callum's knees, knocking him to the ground before rolling away and back onto his feet. It was an elegant move and drew gasps from the crowd.

Callum recovered as his opponent walked to the other side of the ring before turning back, the spear in his grip.

They moved in a circle, slowly, both watching, waiting. Callum came in with another fury of strikes. Again, the man parried or evaded them. He moved as if dancing, and Thea found herself unexpectedly intrigued.

Thrice more, Callum attacked. Thrice more he was knocked down. After smacking the ground for a fourth time, he was slower to rise. She had never seen her brother struggle in a match. He was long considered one of the best swordsmen in the north, even at the age of twenty and three.

Watching it unfold, Thea suspected his opponent was toying with him, wearing him down. It irritated her, and she screamed for her brother to fight on. The exposition garnered her more than one look of dismay from ladies in the vicinity.

Callum attacked but lacked the swiftness he had before. The southern man twisted and brought the spear down on Callum's arm, knocking his sword from his grasp. He flipped his weapon, flat end forward, striking Callum in the chest. Callum stumbled back several paces before landing on his back. The spear flipped again, thrusting forward, the point stopping mere inches from Callum's throat. The crowd gasped. Then grew as still as the fighting circle.

"*Yield*," Callum called out.

Reluctant applause started in those around her, seemingly as surprised as she at her brother's defeat.

The man in bronze stepped back and bowed before offering Callum his hand to rise. Both men removed their helmets, and Thea saw that her brother was laughing. Callum moved to shake the man's hand, and she saw his opponent's face for the first time. She knew him immediately. An infinitesimal shriek escaped her lips, and she cowered behind the body of the woman in front of her. It was the man from the hall.

Silently cursing, she gathered her courage and slowly peeked around to get a better look. His chin-length black hair was tied half back, revealing his angular face in full. Under the sun, his skin was not dissimilar in color from his armor, warm and sun-kissed. He seemed very different than he had before. His features were drawn into amusement as he conversed with Callum, light-hearted and cheerful. Thea frowned. It was a very different picture than she had painted in her mind.

As if sensing her investigation, his gaze flicked up into the crowd, connecting with hers. One side of his mouth quirked, teasing, and she ducked behind the woman again. Thea felt her face flush. *"Gods,"* she whispered to herself, drowning in mortification.

When she looked his way again, she found he had returned to his conversation with her brother.

"Cat, do you know—" Thea started, reaching for her sister, frowning when she found only air. Cat had moved, now standing with Evelynde and the Andaran duke further down the row. Looking back at the fighting circle, Thea watched the exchange with strange curiosity. She wondered what the man was saying to her brother to garner such merriment. Callum grasped the man's shoulder as he doubled over in a full-body laugh. It pulled a quick snort-like one from her.

The announcer called out the winner right as Thea felt small hands wrap around her waist.

"Aunt Thea!"

Thea turned to see Lucienne and pulled her into her lap. "What are you doing here, little flower?" She tickled her, and Luce laughed, squirming in her arms.

Leanne approached hand-in-hand with Henri, who was still wobbly on his not-yet-two-year-old feet. "I fear Callum is not used to losing, but he seems to have taken it in stride," she said, taking Cat's now-empty seat.

Thea leaned toward her, brows raised. "Well, he needs no assistance in confidence, I assure you."

Leanne laughed. "Indeed."

The swarm of ladies now encircled him, his opponent nowhere in sight. Leanne's hand moved to rest over her swollen belly as she winced.

"Are you unwell?"

Leanne waved her hand. "I'm fine. Or I will be when this baby is born. He gives me no rest. I know he will be the biggest yet."

Thea lifted her hand. "May I?"

Leanne smiled. "Of course." She took Thea's hand, placing it on the other side of her belly. Thea returned the smile when she felt the baby kick.

"How can you be sure it's a boy?"

Leanne shrugged. "A woman knows these things." She turned toward Thea. "As you will see one day."

Thea was not so sure about that. She turned back to the match to see the crowd dispersing. Twice she had the opportunity to learn the man's name, and twice she was distracted.

Callum had removed his chest and shoulder plates and was leaning back against a fence, elbows perched atop. The women surrounding him laughed in over-the-top manners, sometimes reaching out to touch his arm. Thea wondered if they would continue to swoon for him once he was wed to his foreign princess.

"Are you coming to the feast tonight? Conall told me your father granted you permission to excuse yourself this sixday," Leanne said as she attempted to wrestle free her braid from Henri's determined grasp. He relented, walking clumsily onto the field with the other children.

Thea bit the inside of her cheek. "I don't think so."

Leanne nodded. She reached for Thea's hand. The two women watched Henri, Lucienne, and Tamsin run, chased by Thomas wielding a wooden sword. She remembered that feeling. Running through the gardens with Callum and Cat. No worries, no cares. It pained her to know that one day it would be taken from them, too.

"Thank you," Thea said.

Leanne frowned. "For?"

Thea turned to look at her. "For being such a wonderful mother. A wonderful friend."

"Sister," Leanne corrected her.

Thea smiled. "Sister."

Their gazes returned to the children.

"We have a wonderful life here," Leanne said as she leaned closer to nudge her. "It would not be the same if you were gone. The children adore you. *I* adore you. Whether or not he shows it, Conall cares for you, too."

Thea's brows creased.

"I'm serious, Thea."

Thea shook her head. "It is different with him."

"He was older when his mother died," Leanne said, her gaze finding him across the field. "He remembers her. Cat and Callum were far too young."

Conall had always kept Thea at a distance. Seemed nervous when she was with the children, as if he did not trust her. He never spoke it so, but she felt it. Thea well knew the pain of never having a mother, but she did not know the pain of having one so briefly. She had often wondered which was better. Thea never considered herself a particularly clever person, but there were some truths she knew. *We will never understand another's pain.* She kept that truth close to her at all times.

"I'd better get the children inside for supper," Leanne said. "Their bedtimes call soon. If I do not see you tonight at the feast, I bid you sleep well." She kissed Thea's cheeks before standing to leave.

Thea watched as the crowds continued to thin. She huffed when the orange cat from days before scurried through the grass. It stopped and turned its head toward her, presenting the limp starling clutched between its jaws.

Fair on you, she thought.

After sneaking into the kitchens for a bottle of wine, Thea took to the woods. She had one destination in mind. Her favorite place.

The trek to the ruins was not an easy one. One had to traverse the dense woods, cross two creeks, and climb a large tree-covered hill to reach them. She stumbled on them by chance while exploring at the age of ten and three. There was no path, and she always altered her approach to avoid making one. Thea had never brought another, and as far as she knew, not another earthly soul knew of their existence. Or cared about them, at the least.

They were nothing impressive. Three crumbling walls and a couple half-standing pillars. The remnants of a statue stood in the middle. A woman without a head and only one arm. Thea did not know who it depicted. Little was known about the old Gods. She had been told of such ruins across the north, but these were the only ones she'd ever seen.

She would come to read, think, or simply lie on the moss-covered forest floor. When she was still a girl, she dreamt up stories in her mind about who built them and why. What they looked like. What became of them.

Thea undressed down to her shift and spread out a quilt, lying back to gaze up at the orange sky. She tried to keep her thoughts away from Marten. She said a silent thank-you to her father he had granted her leave. She did not trust her own behavior.

Taking the last sip of wine, she chastised herself for not grabbing two. The sun had begun its descent, but Thea didn't fear the woods at night. She could find her way back to the castle blindfolded. She yawned, letting her eyes close. *I'll only rest a moment.*

Thea was not sure when she'd fallen asleep, but when she woke, the moon was high.

"Oh, Gods," she mumbled as she scrambled to sit up, wiping the thin trail of drool from her chin. She prayed the feast was still underway. If not, someone would be looking for her. Many someones.

She tugged on her boots, cursing, until a rustling caught her attention. She froze, fearful she'd been caught, knowing her father would be furious.

When no sound followed, she exhaled, but another, much louder, rustle halted her once more. "*Hello?*"

There was no reply, only the sound of a snapping branch. Thea stood, arms loose at her sides, chin high. "If someone is there, declare yourself."

Again, no answer. She squinted across the clearing, but it was far too dark to see beyond the trees. Thea shook her head, scolding herself for being so silly. *It is a rabbit, or simply the wind, you fool.* She reached for her dress and stepped in before slipping one arm through and then the next.

A slight, nearly indiscernible sound drifted toward her. Low in pitch, like a pulse, repeating its rhythmical pattern, until the last beat echoed past. She paused again, chewing nervously at the inside of her cheek, unsure if it was her mind, or the wine, playing tricks. Thea quickly decided she did not care to know. She secured the ties on her dress and knelt to collect her quilt and satchel.

The sound returned, louder, fuller, stilling everything but the wild darting of her eyes. Dread prickled through her chest when she realized it was a laugh.

It dwindled, and she stood, refusing what her ears proposed. A quick rustling followed, and her head snapped in its direction. She told herself to move. Fighting her desire to run, she turned and made it ten paces before the rustling started again. When she swung around, it stopped.

"I am Calithea *Ironne*, daughter of the king, and I am expected back! There are no doubt guards looking for me at this very moment." She immediately regretted revealing herself.

The laugh renewed, unsettling, attesting sinister intent. Belly tight, heart thumping, she tried to swallow as she turned in circles, squinting into the dense trees as it mocked her.

"*Stop it!*" she screamed. It complied. She stood still, wide-eyed, listening.

A twig snapped, and she turned. She inhaled, and it hurt.

Another snap.

Thea stared into the darkness, chest heaving, fear taking command as a figure took shape in the shadows. The rustling started again, but this time it didn't stop.

It came straight for her.

She bolted, dropping everything in her arms, bounding through the trees as her heart pumped sobering fright. Sticks and branches tore at her dress, but she didn't stop. Even as they cut into her flesh. Her mind had only one command.

Run.

She wanted to turn around, to see what stalked her, but the terror drove her forward. If she could not see it, it might not be real.

Discernible footsteps pounded the ground behind her, each more thunderous than the one before. She pleaded with her legs to move faster.

The laugh echoed again, more maniacal this time, and she couldn't stop her quick glance back. It was only a shadowed blur. Whoever it was gained on her, unimaginably fast. She knew she could not outrun them. A throat-scorching cry burst from her lips, uncontrollable and without intent.

She made it to the edge of the hill, now traveling down. She heard a thump, and a gust of wind sent leaves flying in the air around her, like a villainous breath on the back of her neck.

As her back foot left the ground, she felt resistance, something tugging at her hair. She screamed again and started to turn, to fight, but something crashed into the back of her, sending her flying. A soft green glow swelled around her line of sight.

She didn't have time to understand before the light suddenly flashed, blinding, and she braced for impact.

She smacked the ground with a crack.

Pain was all she could register as the green light dulled, and darkness consumed her.

17

Thea

"If you cannot discover truth in one's words, look for it in their eyes."

AUTHOR UNKNOWN, C. 1500 BQ
TRANSLATED FROM SUMACIAN BY PARRY HAVERFORD
HAIS Z'NOSIŠ, 1204 AQ
RECOVERED 1203 AQ, SOMOS

Thea's eyes snapped open. Her heart beat right into the space between them, aching, and she grimaced at the pain. The woods. She remembered the woods. She looked around. She was in her bedchamber. Had she dreamt it? She inhaled, sharp and jagged, clutching at her aching chest.

A figure leapt from a chair across the room. Her father, running to her side, Sylvie on his heels. Both regarded her, wide-eyed and assessing.

Thea sprang from the pillows and pulled back the quilt. Her legs were covered in small cuts from thigh to heel. She had not dreamt it.

She began to cry, almost as if she had never stopped.

"Lay back," her father said, grasping her shoulders. She started to fight him, but she looked at his face and the familiarity in it grounded her. "It is all right." He looked on the verge of panic himself, and Thea wasn't sure if it was said for her or for him.

Thea heaved, chest burning, but she relented, falling back against the bed. Sylvie moved, nearly casting her father aside. Her hands came on either side of her face, eyes searching Thea's.

"Breathe," Sylvie said. "Just breathe."

Thea tried. It was shallow coming in and shaky coming out. She looked from Sylvie to her father. Warmth radiated from the crown of her head. It eased the seize in her lungs, and she took a deeper breath. She continued like this, each inhale expanding. "What happened?" she asked, little more than a hoarse whisper.

Her father looked at Sylvie before he spoke. "You were attacked by a mountain cat." His eyes searched hers, trying to present ease, but they were wild and distraught.

"A *mountain cat*?" Thea remembered the laugh, and the terror returned. She shook her head. "That cannot be." Her breathing was nearing normal, but her hands still trembled. She clenched the bedsheets.

"Take deep breaths or you're going to have an attack." Sylvie's hands still held Thea's face.

Thea nodded, warm tears streaming down her cheeks.

"I went out with a party, searching for you. We heard you scream and found you just in time. You fell and hit your head." Her father was wearing a white tunic and tan trousers. Both were dirty as if he'd crawled around on the forest floor, wallowing like a dog. Thea frowned, wondering if she'd ever seen him so disheveled.

She reached up and felt a bandage at her hairline and winced.

"You're very lucky," he said. The concern in his eyes melted to anger. "What were you *thinking*?" He kept his voice steady, but Thea could see he wanted to scream. "Out in the woods alone at night? Have you lost your senses?"

Thea stiffened. She didn't want to tell him it wasn't exactly uncommon. "I'm sorry. I fell asleep."

He exhaled, shaking his head.

Sylvie released her face and stepped back. She walked to the other side of the room and returned with a cup. "Small sips," Sylvie said as she handed it to Thea.

Her father helped her to sit up, propping pillows behind her back. She reached for his arm. "But, wait, it was a *mountain cat*? Since when do we have mountain cats in Highclere?"

Sylvie sat on the edge of the bed. She took Thea's free hand between hers. "It is not unheard of, Thea. Mountain cats have been spotted in Highclere before."

Thea regarded her, head leaning. She guessed that could be true. The animal was a far less horrifying prospect than what she had imagined in the woods. The sinister laugh. The strange green glow. It didn't make sense.

"That cannot be," Thea said again, shaking her head. She moved to rise from the bed.

Sylvie's grip tightened on her hand, holding her firm. "Thea," she said slowly, "be still before you hurt yourself."

Thea stopped. Her head throbbed, and her chest felt like someone had hollowed it out with a red-hot spoon.

Sylvie smiled at her, reassuring and tender. "The cat chased you, and you fell down a hill. You hit your head."

She remembered being pushed. No, falling. Something grabbed her hair. It must have been tangled in a branch. But the laugh. "You are *sure* of this?"

Sylvie's hand came to rest on her shoulder. Thea glanced at the contact. "Not many people survive an encounter with a mountain cat." Sylvie pulled Thea's face back to meet hers. "You are very lucky to have done so."

Thea frowned. She did feel lucky. She'd believed she was going to die. "But—"

"We found an empty wine bottle, Thea," Sylvie said, her round brown eyes taking on a narrow gaze.

"Yes," Thea said, nodding, a touch ashamed. She glanced at her father, and he looked away. She had been drinking, and it was dark. And she'd been afraid, so terribly afraid. But all was well now. Her father had never lied to her. She saw no reason he would start with this. Warm relief washed through her, and she sighed. She looked from her father to Sylvie. "I am sorry."

"You are all right," her father said, taking her hand. He gave it a gentle pat. "That is all that matters." He looked worn, even sickly, and she felt guilty she'd worried him so.

"Who knows?" Thea asked, humiliation quickly becoming her primary concern.

"Only the two of us and a few household guards." His face turned steely. "And it will stay that way. We do not want to cause panic with so many visitors in the capital. The beast is dead, after all." He glanced at Sylvie. "We will keep the forests guarded in the meantime to keep any others from drifting out."

Thea yawned. "What is the hour?"

"Nearly dawn. You should get back to sleep. You need rest." He brushed the hair from her face. "You hit your head quite severely."

Thea nodded. "I am sorry again."

"Do not go out into the woods again, Calithea. That is not a request."

"Yes, Father."

He leaned forward and kissed her head. Thea watched him walk to the door. He turned back to look at her before leaving. The look on his face only added to her bafflement.

When the door closed behind him, Sylvie spoke. "When you didn't come back, I panicked. I had to tell your father."

"If you had not, I would be dead." Thea felt the bandage on her head again. "Is it bad?"

"Nothing that won't heal." Sylvie sighed. "You gave me quite the scare, Thea."

Guilt pressed down on her like a steel cloak. "I did not mean to. I really am sorry."

"Stop saying sorry. You're the one all beat up and bruised." One side of Sylvie's mouth twitched up.

Thea chuckled and then flinched at the pain it brought forth. "Was it really a *mountain cat*?"

"Yes." Sylvie inclined her head. "Why do you ask?"

"I don't know," Thea said. "It seemed more… human." She shivered at the memory of the laugh. Though it was starting to feel more like something she'd dreamt.

Sylvie's expression didn't change. She shrugged. "I watched them bury the beast myself."

Thea rubbed her eyes and felt a wave of nausea run through her. "I'm sure I imagined it. It is only that I would swear I saw… This will sound mad, but I swear there was a sort of glowing green light."

Sylvie peered at her, a touch teasingly, and entirely unconvinced. "Your father is right. You need to rest."

"I don't know if I can." Thea wanted to spring from the bed and run clear across Ire.

"Sure you can." Sylvie's hand gripped hers.

Thea yawned again, nestling back into the bed. "I suppose I am rather tired."

The following morning the castle was frantic with preparations. The kitchens were busy, and the castle staff ran wild through the halls, cleaning and ready-making for the reception. Among them running wild was Evelynde. She was hosting a luncheon in honor of the bride-to-be. The girl would remain unseen until the wedding, but it was customary for a small group of women to host an afternoon in her honor. While Thea had been officially invited, it went without saying she would not be in attendance.

No one spoke or asked about the night before. The events seemed to have passed without notice. Thea did not like lying to her siblings but knew they would make a fuss. Especially Callum. Her father had asked her to keep it quiet, and she would oblige. When the wedding was over and the guests were gone, she would tell them the truth. The bandage on her forehead was explained away as a simple fall. The scratches on her legs were easily hidden under her skirts. It had already begun to feel like a distant memory, a dream.

She'd kept close to her quarters since waking. She was tired, and her body still ached. Sylvie had not been more than ten paces from her all day. They didn't speak about the night before, but from time to time, Sylvie would send a concerned glance her way. She had already changed the poultice on her head twice, and it was scarcely past midday.

Her bedchamber had windows overlooking both the lake and public gardens. She gazed out over the sea of men taking tea six stories below. Thea had not seen Marten in two days. She scanned through their faces, searching for him, without success.

Sylvie stood from her chair and again checked her head.

Thea pulled back. "I wish you would stop. I am fine, I swear."

"If you reserved your protests of *I'm fine* for times when you actually were, I wouldn't need to fuss so." Sylvie fixed her stare, and Thea relented.

"We need to get out of this room," Thea groaned.

"I don't think your father would approve." Sylvie walked back to her chair, settling in with her book. "You need to rest."

"A walk in the woods then?"

Sylvie looked up under a heavy brow. "Not. Funny."

Thea sighed. "Let's take tea in the private gardens. We need *fresh air*. All the other women are at the luncheon. We'll have them to ourselves."

Without looking up from her book, Sylvie said, "The window is open. We have fresh air."

"*Sylvie.* Come on, I know you're dying to leave these walls as much as I."

Sylvie's eyes flicked up to meet Thea's. The two women held gazes until Sylvie's lips curled in defeat. She stood. "I'll go down to the kitchens and order tea, then I'll come back up and get you."

"I'm quite capable of walking on my own," Thea said, and stood, taking several slow, playful steps forward. "See?"

Sylvie rolled her eyes, and at first looked as though she wanted to object. She gave Thea a look that felt like a subtle warning. "You will go straight there?"

Thea held her hand to her heart. "On my honor."

✛

Thea kept to the private wing of the castle on the walk down. She had no desire to cross paths with another and be forced to explain her bandaged head. Nearing the door leading to the private gardens, she jumped when she heard her name called from down the hall.

Thea turned on her heels, seeing Marten peer out from a doorway. She giggled, trotting lightly back down the hall. He reached for her arm, tugging her inside.

"What on earth are you—"

Marten pulled her against him. One hand held her face, the other tightened around her back, drawing her closer. "I've been waiting all morning. I'm supposed to be hunting with your brother," he said between kisses.

She sighed against him, only then understanding how much she'd missed him. She craved his lips, his warmth. Desire stirred low in her belly. It felt good to be touched.

He pulled back to speak. "My father has done his best to keep me under lock and key." He frowned as his fingertips traced the bandage on her forehead. "What happened?"

She reached up, covering it with her hand. "I fell. Think nothing of it."

"Think nothing of it?" He scoffed. He tried to lift the edge of the bandage to peer underneath.

"Stop." She swatted at his hand. "I am fine, I swear."

He was undeterred, so she misdirected him with another kiss. After the last few days, she wanted to feel something. Something good. Knowing they did not have long, she reached between them and began unlacing the ties of his trousers.

"*Here?*" he asked.

Her hand moved beneath the fabric, and he firmed in her grasp. She stroked the length of him, smiling against his lips when her effort earned her a soft pant. "It feels you are up to the task."

He leaned back to gaze at her. Apprehension thinned his eyes as he searched hers for sincerity. When her brows rose in challenge, he flipped from curious to wild. He was on her like a windstorm, pulling desperately at the straps of her dress. His mouth covered hers as he slipped it off each shoulder until it hung loose at her waist, hands coming up to cup her breasts. She moaned into his mouth, and it charged the frenzy igniting between them.

Thea tugged on the buttons of his vest but quickly abandoned the task. The need was too urgent. There was no time for buttons. His hand moved beneath her skirt, diving straight to her softest part. Heat built as he touched her, gentle at first, growing in urgency. His lips moved to her neck and then to her breasts, but as he knelt to descend lower, she took his face in her hands.

"No. I want you now."

In one swift movement, he was back on his feet, and she was off the ground. His fingers pressed into the soft flesh of her thighs as he hoisted her up. She gasped when her naked back made contact with the cool stone wall. Where she was soft, he was hard, and she locked her legs around him as he eased into her, the first thrust tender. He moved, and she curled her hips forward so every part of her touched some part of him. They moaned and panted in rhythm. Her body responded in familiarity to his touch, to his sounds. It was savory and satisfying, but she wanted more.

Her lips moved to his ear, teeth grazing as she whispered, "Do not be gentle."

He unleashed himself. Tender thrusts turned hungry, possessive, and she could not contain the sounds escaping her lips. She didn't care to. Every muscle in her body seized before shattering in a blast that sent waves of pleasure from the crown of her head to the tips of her toes.

She bit his lip, hard. He hissed against her, and she savored copper on his tongue as it plunged back into her mouth with desperation so consuming she found herself clenching around him again for more.

Her hands fisted in his hair as he thrashed against her, and she was nearly at peak again when he buried his face in her neck, crying out with the swell of his release.

They stayed clutched around one another as his efforts slowed, then stilled, and they panted together against the wall. He slowly eased them down to the floor, kissing her the entire way.

He moved to sit beside her, lifting her legs onto his lap. She relaxed, satisfied, as they recovered. A hand trailed up her calf, and he stiffened, then lifted her skirt. The scratches and cuts covering her from knee to ankle were now fully on display.

"Thea," he implored, his hands hovering above the wounds. "*What is this?*"

She moved to cover her legs, but he stopped her. "I told you I fell."

"*Where?* Down a fucking mountain?" His eyes were still taking in the cuts.

"Well, yes, sort of."

He gaped at her.

"Don't make a fuss," she said, and tousled his hair. "I was out in the woods. I fell asleep. When I woke, it was dark. I tripped. Think nothing of it."

She leaned forward to kiss him, but he pulled back and huffed. "Stop saying that. I should have been there."

"No," she said, shaking her head, "you should not have."

He looked like he would argue, but a stern gaze from her stilled him, and he settled back against the wall. Reaching up, he touched his lip, coming away with a small spot of blood.

"Gods," he said, grinning. "What is into you today?" He reached over to her with his bloody fingertip, tracing the spot on her lip where she knew his blood already stained. She pulled the finger into her mouth, running her tongue across its length. "Careful," he cautioned. "You'll rouse me again."

She smiled coyly, giving his finger a gentle bite before releasing it.

"How will I explain this?" he asked, though the mischievous look in his eyes told her he did not care to.

Thea shrugged. "Hunting accident."

He laughed, then leaned forward, placing a soft kiss on her lips. One hand rose to hold her face, fingers curling in her hair. She leaned into it, closing her eyes, letting herself slacken against him. Granting herself the moment. He kissed her with an aching gentleness, a near antithesis of their lovemaking only moments before, and she adored him for both. She opened her eyes and smiled.

"Will you be at the feast tonight?" he asked, ripping her from the daze.

Thea sat up, backing out of his grasp. "No. I… can't." She slid her arms back into her dress. "In fact, I should get back before we are discovered."

"Already?"

"Marten, we weren't exactly quiet," she said. "I have no doubt we were heard."

He slumped against the wall. "If we are caught, perhaps they will call off this charade."

She stopped dressing to give him a stern look. "That is not funny."

He laced his trousers. "I do not speak in jest."

Irritation flared through her. She stood, but he reached for her, pulling her against him.

"Please do not go."

She tried shrugging off his grip. "I must. We cannot be found like this."

"It wouldn't matter."

"It wouldn't matter for *you*."

He leaned closer to kiss her again, but she turned her head. Her irritation progressed to anger with how he had so quickly spoiled their moment. He never thought about the consequences their relationship imposed upon her, and what he was always asking. She stood, trying to straighten her appearance. She looked around the room for anything that would give her reflection, a little unnerved at how swiftly her mood had changed.

Marten sighed at her lack of reception to his plea, watching as she wiped the blood from her lips and then combed through her hair.

"You look fine, Thea. You look… beautiful. You are always beautiful." He looked up at her with a sad admiration, and it cooled her hostility.

"Come, get off the ground." She extended her hand, waving him up.

He looked away, folding his arms. She sighed, watching him pout. She had nothing else to give him. There was nothing else she could say. It was time for him to make peace with this on his own.

"Marten… I cannot do this for you," she said, not withholding her vexation. "I cannot manage my own feelings and yours as well."

He stood to face her. "I'm not asking you to—"

"But you are. You are forcing me to be the one to walk away. You are putting the weight of this on *my* shoulders. You want something more from me, but I have nothing else to give. I have given you everything."

"And now you take it away."

She watched his expression melt into regret as hers twisted into fury.

"I'm sorry. I don't mean that." He reached for her, but she stepped back.

"You have some nerve saying that to me." She moved to step around him, but he grabbed her arm.

"Please don't go."

"There is nothing else to say." She tried to pull free, but his grip tightened. She looked up at him with angry eyes. "Let go of my arm."

His eyes were unsure, but he didn't let go. "When you leave, this is over. I don't know when I'll see you again."

"You will see me tomorrow."

"You know what I mean."

"*Why do you persist in this?*" she snapped.

"Because it doesn't have to be this way, and I am desperate!" His chest heaved, eyes pleading. "And I am not ashamed of it."

Her lips trembled, and she felt the sting of tears. She swallowed, calming her voice. "You know where I stand. My mind has not changed. It. Will. Not. Change."

His gaze dropped as his eyes swelled. Thea exhaled. She had never seen him cry. The sight sent an ache through her chest, causing her first tear to spill.

"I do not wish to leave you like this," she said, "but you give me no choice." She quickly wrestled her arm free from his grip, her action taking him by surprise. She passed through the door to find Sylvie waiting in the hall. Urgent footsteps quickened behind her.

"Thea, wait!" He reached for her again, but Sylvie stepped between them.

"My lady would take her leave now."

Marten scoffed and moved to step around her, but Sylvie pressed her hand to his chest. He looked down at the woman, disbelief at her boldness. His attention shifted, transfixed.

"I *said*, my lady would take her leave. And you will not impede her, Marten Percy." Sylvie said his name with authority, almost strangely, like one commanding the attention of an unruly child.

Marten looked from her to Thea. When his eyes landed back on Sylvie, they changed. The anger in them released, and to her surprise, he stepped back. Thea felt a little uneasy on her feet.

Sylvie turned, wrapping her arm through Thea's. "Come, my lady."

They walked at a speedy pace down the long hall. Thea looked back to find him standing there, watching them walk away. When they crossed the threshold back into her room, she looked at Sylvie expectantly. "What was that?"

Sylvie shrugged. "I've had enough of him."

Thea laughed, a touch maniacal. "I—thank you." She looked at the woman, drawing a new picture of her. "Were you outside the entire time? Did you *hear?*" Were she not already flush, she would be now.

"I was. I wasn't eavesdropping, though, I swear. I wanted to keep watch in case someone else came through."

"I am grateful."

Sylvie smiled, but her manner was hesitant. "I know it is not my place to say anything, so I hope you'll forgive me. I think you should be done with this. You are only causing yourself more grief. If you are drawing a line under it, then draw it firm."

Thea smiled, wiping a tear from her cheek. "That is good advice. Were I not so weak, I could put it to practice."

Sylvie pulled a box from under the bed. She popped the cork of a small glass vial, handing it to Thea. "This is the last one."

"I don't think I'll be needing it again for a long time." Thea tossed back its contents, grimacing at the bitter flavor. "Four years, and I still haven't grown accustomed to the taste."

"It tastes better than pushing out a baby would feel."

Thea would not argue that. She'd borne witness to both of Leanne's births. She sat down on the edge of the bed, Sylvie taking the place beside her.

Thea glanced at her. "Have you ever cared for someone that you had to walk away from?"

Sylvie inhaled, shifting on the bed.

"I don't mean to pry."

"No," Sylvie said, "it is all right. And the answer is yes, I have."

"How did you do it?" Thea asked, desperate for words to help harden her resolve.

"I didn't have a choice." Sylvie reached into her blouse, pulling out a gold chain necklace with a bright purple gemstone on the end. She rolled the stone through her fingers.

Thea couldn't remember having seen it before. She sensed there was a story, but perhaps not one Sylvie wanted to share. "I'm sorry."

"Don't be," Sylvie said. "I will see them again."

18

Neith

"I fear the time when we will again see our gift as a weapon. I fear it will come upon us wearing a mask of moral authority. Preying on mankind's most dangerous flaw."

THE WAY OF ETHER
ASHERAH GALANIS, FIRST CONSUL, THE CITADEL, 808 AQ

Neith could smell the smoke from the raze all morning, despite the rain falling since dawn. It had become a relentless drizzle, the sun well hidden in the overcast, gray sky. It was the first day she had been reminded of home.

The rain had made for a troublesome day of journeying. Carts were continually stuck in the thick mud, slowing down the entire train. Neith guessed they were still several hours from nightfall when Magnus ordered them to stop for repairs.

Eynsbury, as she discovered it to be named, was the largest village they'd encountered on the First's reign of terror. Many from the Second wandered into town, seeking refuge from the weather or to scavenge through the remains.

Neith left Storm at camp, walking into town with Sam, Max, Petra, and Ayla. There weren't as many bodies as she anticipated, and the ones that remained were burned beyond recognition. Even the air felt scorched, leaving it acrid with a wet metallic tinge. This was different from the razes preceding it. Her father had unleashed the Etherborn of the First, and they'd burned it to the ground.

She closed her eyes, calling to the ether in the area. She could feel the remnants of a fight. There had been wielding. Significant wielding.

"Can you feel it?" Neith turned to look at Sam and the others.

All three Etherborn nodded.

"Feel what?" Ayla asked.

"The traces of wielding." It was Petra who answered. She was on one knee, one hand hovering above the earth.

The five trudged through the muddy streets in the direction of the trace. It led them to a modest town square where the wrecked remnants of shops and stalls lay about in disorder. Neith pulled back the hood of her cloak. Rain still drizzled, but she was already soaked to the bone.

Large holes and gaps had been blasted through the buildings. In the center, a large craterlike hole cut deep into the earth. Fog hung above, and in the immediate space around it, as if the ground were still warm.

There was something awry, something unsettling about the scene. Neith couldn't place it. She exchanged glances with Sam, Max, and Petra.

"I believe I'll return to camp to help set up," Ayla said, taking small steps back, as if picking up on their uneasy energy.

Still in thought, Neith nodded. "Max, please escort her. There could be Esērii in the area. We must keep in mind what happened in Gods-reach."

Max acknowledged with a half salute and followed Ayla back through town.

The ether signatures of many persisted, her brother and father among them. She stopped counting at twenty and two. Bodies—and parts—were scattered about, and she did her best not to linger on them.

"What do you make of this?" she asked Sam.

"I'm not sure." He surveyed what remained of the town.

"This is odd, no?" Neith walked to the hollowed-out space where the peculiar pull seemed to be sourced.

Neith, Sam, and Petra stood on the edge, peering down. It was little more than a rough-dug hole, ten feet deep and twenty feet wide. Tiny, nearly indiscernible flakes of yellow crystal were mixed in among the dark soil. A chill shivered through her that was not brought on by the rain.

"We should get back," Sam said. No objections were made.

By the time they arrived back at camp, the rain had finally relented. Neith wanted to speak with Magnus about what they'd found in town. She had intended to go alone, but Sam ordered Petra to accompany her.

There hadn't been another moment between them like the one three nights ago by the river. Neith felt he had been avoiding being alone with her. She considered she was perhaps misreading the situation, not often confident in her understanding of interactions with others.

Petra and Neith changed into dry clothes, warming their pruney fingertips by the newly lit fire. She removed the braid from her wet hair, and it hung in thick clumps around her face. She ran her fingers through the tangled waves, trying to shake loose some of the rain.

Glancing across the campsite, she met eyes with Kieran, then Bellamy, both turning away the moment they connected. She frowned and inspected her dress, assuming she must look odd or that something was amiss. When she turned toward Petra, she was met with a look that only added to her discomfort. The sort that someone cannot hold back when they understand something you do not.

Magnus's camp was a good walk from their own. Neith and Petra were quickly ankle-deep in mud, their fresh clothes tainted. Still, she was grateful to be dry, or at least on her way to being.

They'd been trudging for a while before Neith had the courage to ask. She stopped walking and turned toward Petra. "Is there something wrong with—Do I look... odd?" It embarrassed her endlessly, but she thought she would feel far worse if she continued getting strange looks.

Petra was only a couple winters older, but Neith thought she looked womanly in a way that she did not. Confident in her golden skin, her dark hair was woven back into twin braids, as it often was, and her brown eyes were large with heavy lashes. She had full lips and a figure that men admired. Neith felt like a child in her shadow.

"Do you really not know?" Petra asked, head leaning.

Neith looked over her clothes again, patting her hair for some sign of the impairment.

"There is nothing wrong," Petra said, shaking her head. "They, and many others, look at you all the time. Is this the first you've noticed?"

Neith wrapped her arms around herself, suddenly desirous to hide.

"I'm sorry. It was not my intention to make you uncomfortable."

"You didn't," Neith said, but she was agonizingly so. She pulled her bottom lip between her teeth.

Petra's gaze narrowed, her tone turning protective. "I will tell them to keep their eyes to themselves, lest see them carved from their sockets."

"No," Neith said quickly, shaking her head. "Please don't—please say nothing."

Petra huffed as if she'd been eager to make the threat, but shrugged a shoulder. They started walking again, and Neith fought a silent struggle not to ask who the *others* were Petra had mentioned. Not that she had anyone particular in mind.

Magnus, Cordero, and several other officers communed around a table in his tent. He looked up at Neith's entry, waving her over, gesturing toward an empty seat on the end. She met eyes with Cordero, and he smiled.

"The rain should only set us back half a day. We will be able to recover the time if we continue to press," said one of the women.

Magnus nodded. "Good. What else?"

Cordero sat back, hesitating before he spoke. "There is an outbreak of the sweating sickness in one of the idleborn units."

"How many infected?" Magnus asked, sipping from his mug.

"Twenty and seven ill, but two have died." Cordero weighed his words as one does when the current circumstance does not represent the gravity of what might lie ahead. "Given the quickness it came upon us, I suspect it started before we crossed the border. It could turn into nothing," he said, looking from face to face, "but I think we should isolate the unit. We have more than enough men, and keeping them with the division puts too many at risk."

"I agree," Magnus said. "Order the unit to stay behind. Ensure they are properly supplied to see it out."

Cordero nodded. The tension in his eyes eased.

Neith found the news concerning. There hadn't been a major outbreak of the sweating sickness since she was twelve. Thousands of idleborn Thraneans had perished.

Magnus looked around the table. "Spread the word and be diligent about isolation if there are any other signs of it in the ranks. Though Etherborn are unlikely to be affected, they can still spread it. It is better to arrive late and whole than on time and in pieces. I want to know immediately if there are any reports of further illnesses in Necrium." He glanced at Neith. "Let us break. We reconvene tomorrow at march's end."

Magnus stood, and Neith matched the action, nodding at the departing soldiers. Cordero stopped before her, bowing his head. "I hear I am to call you Lieutenant now."

"It seems so, Commander. However surprising it may be."

Cordero shook his head. "I do not find it surprising at all." He smiled, kindly, and it plucked one from her. He had a courteousness about him that was not a common trait among her father's commanders.

Magnus cleared his throat, drawing Cordero's attention. He inclined his head again before turning to leave.

When they were alone, Magnus reached for her, arms extended. She fell into the embrace, grateful to be with someone known, someone she understood.

"Tell me how you are. How is your squad?" He held her shoulders, looking down from his massive stature.

She laughed, a bit nervously. "I am figuring it out a little every day."

He nodded and smiled, then gestured for her to sit, taking the opposite chair. He moved maps and pieces of parchment, then filled two mugs, passing one to her. She could smell the ale from its place on the table. "And your guard?"

She tilted her head, lips pursed, considering. "Overqualified?"

Magnus laughed, his large body bouncing as it tumbled out. She only realized at that moment how much she missed him the past moon. He had been a figure in her life nearly every day she could remember.

As the laughter died, Neith thought back to what prompted her visit. "Magnus…"

"Hmm?"

"We walked through Eynsbury today, and there was something… *strange.*"

"Strange in what regard?" He reached for his mug.

Neith shrugged. "I'm not sure. The others felt it as well. There were remnants of wielding, but something we couldn't quite understand was concentrated in the town center. Where the fight had taken place."

He sat back, taking a breath. "I told your father we should inform you. I knew you would sense it. But you know how he is about information."

Neith knew *exactly* what her father was like. He loved his secrets, and it often seemed like he had an infinite quantity of them, some years, even decades, in the making. He used them like weapons, kept hidden, like one does precious jewels, only to one day unearth them and strike with an indifferent casualness, as if the victim should be abreast of what ascends upon them. It was a disorienting experience to be on the receiving end of. Neith sighed, perhaps regretful she'd asked. "Inform me of what?"

Magnus reached for the pitcher, refilling his mug. He set it back down and hesitated. His eyes flicked up to hers briefly before returning to the table. "Something Dryden has been working on."

She waited for him to continue, but he took a drink as if enough had been said. "And what is that?" she asked.

"Ways to imbue ether."

Neith frowned. Ether was already a part of everything. How could it be imbued? She found herself quickly irritated at the slow reveal. "Will you explain, or shall I be required to ask questions and piece it together myself?"

Magnus let out something between a snort and a chuckle. He watched her for a moment, and Neith worried he would not say. "Dryden has found a way to imbue an ethercannon into certain types of stone. Citrine, moldavite, and others. He calls them 'charges.' He's been working on it for years in Nighhelm." He took another drink. "Once the ethercannon is imbued, it is maintained by the stone's own ether. For a time, at least."

Neith sat up. "Do you jest?"

"I do not."

Her mouth fell open, and she looked away for a breath. "To what purpose?"

"Weapons. Warfare. You saw the damage. Ethercannons require active wielding and have a lifespan once launched. These charges can be created long before a battle takes place. It gives us an advantage over the Esērii. We have that now with surprise and numbers, but in time, they will send many our way, and they have thousands. We are hundreds."

Her heart thumped at the implications of such a weapon. She closed her eyes. It had never occurred to her to use ether in such a way, but now, hearing of it, she wondered why it had not been attempted sooner. "How does the imbuing work?"

"I cannot speak on it in depth, but my understanding is it is a form of Influence."

Neith reached for her mug, taking a large gulp. "How has this been kept secret? Why wasn't I told?"

"Lorcan feared the Esērii gaining knowledge of the work. Very few knew of what was happening—*is* happening—at Nighhelm. I thought we should bring you in, but my protests fell on deaf ears." He tipped up his cup, seemingly saying less than he desired. It was not often Magnus and her father were in conflict.

"Does Roman know?"

"He was involved."

Neith thought of all the times Roman had been away from Necrium the last several years. There were so many secrets. Her father intended to make her his heir, but continually kept her in the dark. She couldn't make sense of it. She sighed, and Magnus reached across the table for her hand. "Neith, you will keep this quiet for now, yes?"

"Of course," she answered with a nod. "Will my father be cross you've told me?"

Magnus looked like he didn't much care. "I suspect it was by design for you to come across the remnants. I knew he intended to test them on the march to Croydyn, but he did not inform me when. If he wanted it to continue to be concealed, they could have cleaned it up. They knowingly left the traces behind."

Neith rubbed her eyes and then reached for her ale. She would have much to think on before they reached Northbridge. "Thank you for telling me."

He gave her a tender smile and patted her hand. It was a fatherly gesture, and she wondered if Magnus was always trying to fill the gaps left open by Lorcan. Her father never seemed concerned, much less threatened by it. She stood. "I will return to my camp now."

They embraced and said their goodbyes.

Petra waited outside the tent, leaning against a tree, arms crossed over her chest. She took in Neith's face and frowned. "Fruitful conversation?"

"Fruitful," Neith said, "but not ripe."

They returned to an empty camp. Following the cracks of wooden swords, they found the others down the hill, sparring by the river. It was nearing evening time, and the sun had finally made itself known as the rain clouds drifted on.

Max was showing Ayla basic defensive moves. Neith thought it simply an excuse for them to touch one another. Sam sparred with Iris and Bellamy, Kieran looking on. Petra walked to retrieve a training sword of her own, gesturing for Kieran to join her.

Neith sat in the grass next to the water bucket to watch. She tried strategically to observe both matches but found her attention continually drawn to one. Sam wasn't wearing a vest or tunic, and she was acutely aware of how his muscles turned and worked, stretching with every swing. Sunlight peeking through the clouds illuminated his golden skin, and she watched beads of sweat trickling from his dark curls, trailing the length of his back. His shoulders were broad and round, his body slender but rippled. He spun twin swords as he turned in a circle between his two opponents. A sly, taunting smile formed as he waited for one to strike. The sight caused an itch at the back of her throat. She eyed the water bucket next to her, deciding against it. Something told her it would not help.

Iris and Bellamy came at him in a fury of strikes. He parried the blows from Bellamy, and a swift kick sent him sprawling back toward the ground. A slash from Iris came down, and Neith was sure it would land, but Sam dipped, leaning forward, and she stumbled as her strike had nothing to bear its weight.

Bellamy was already back on his feet, shield and sword in hand. This time, he stood back, waiting for Sam to strike. Sam came at him, feigning a blow from above but turning, sweeping his second sword up with full force. Bellamy's shield caught the impact, his own sword striking forward. Sam parried it with his free sword, stepping to the side as Iris attacked again. He brought both swords up, catching her strike between them, then thrust his swords apart, ripping hers from her grasp. As she scrambled to hold on, he kicked forward, striking her shield, sending her sprawling on her back into the mud. Her body made a thick, wet sound on impact.

Iris huffed and slammed her fists to either side. "Yield."

Bellamy came at him again with a sweeping attack designed to slash across one's back. Sam turned, parrying the blow at the last breath. He went on the offensive before Bellamy could regain his footing. Sam swung both swords in a fury, and Neith could not make sense of how Bellamy was able to elude them for as long as he did. Each blow sent him stumbling further until he, too, was in the mud.

Bellamy lay on his back, panting. "Fuck. *Yield.*"

Sam pointed a sword at him. "Never forget your shadow tells on you." He tucked the wooden blade under his arm and offered Bellamy a hand to rise.

Iris laughed as she stood, rubbing at her backside. She gave Bellamy a teasing grin and shook her head. "Undone by your own shadow."

Neith bit her lips to conceal her amusement.

Bellamy nodded and chuckled. It had a sense of mischief to it. "I see how it is, Iris, darling." He reached down, taking a fistful of mud.

"Don't you dare," Iris warned, backing up.

He grinned and hurled it. It struck dead center in her face. She yelped on impact, wiping it off in clumps.

"Oh, Bells… you're dead." Iris sprinted after him. Neith laughed, watching as they wrestled in the river, trying to plunge the other beneath its surface.

Sam approached, reaching for the ladle in the water bucket. The first dip he drank, the second he poured over his head, shaking off the excess. He pulled an apple from an adjacent basket and took a spot on the grass next to her.

They watched Iris and Bellamy fight it out. He glanced over at her with a smile. She returned it, mindful to keep her eyes up, so as not to watch the water still trailing down his chest. He bit into the apple, and Neith cleared her throat. Of all the things she thought she'd want to be in this life, a piece of fruit was not among them.

On the other side of the field, Petra was striking down on poor Kieran as he struggled to stay on his feet.

"I believe I would like to be trained in sword skill," Neith said. "Hand combat, too."

Sam turned to look at her. "May I ask why you haven't already? It seems a rare thing in Thrane. I had fourteen moons in Necrium and rarely saw a boy or girl over twelve without a sword in their hand."

He held the apple out between them. She blinked, the act taking her by surprise, but accepted, turning it in her hand. She wanted to put her lips exactly where his had been, but took a modest bite from the opposite side.

"Father did not think it a good use of my time." She passed the apple back to him. "He prioritized anatomy, geology, language. And history. No time for sword skill."

"I see," he said. "How will you defend yourself if you burn out?"

"Perhaps that is why he believes I need a guard." She raised her brows. "But I would like to learn. I do not want to be the only person in this army who cannot throw a punch or swing a sword. As hopeless as the prospect may seem."

His eyes narrowed on hers, considering. Just as the night by the river, she wanted to reach within and pluck out his thoughts. Desperate for a glimpse.

When his lips pursed, she looked away, eyes lowering. "I understand if it is too much. I know I am a novice, and it is a lot to ask—"

He stood and tossed one of his swords in the air, catching it by the dull wooden blade, extending the grip toward her. "Well, come on, then."

19

Thea

*"It is the crown's duty to wed its lords and ladies, and our nobles' duty to
oblige. For peace, for prosperity, to honor the Gods. Those united in Cassia's
light are bound forever in grace."*

HEXADIC PRECEPTS
ZATHRIAN BYGRAVE, 719 AQ

The muffled chatter of women's voices was audible in the hall as Thea approached her stepmother's quarters. She, as covertly as she could manage, opened the door and stepped through.

Evelynde was admiring her cerulean gown in a large mirror. Sylvie and several other attendants scurried about the room, completing various tasks. Cat sat at a dressing table as the finishing touches were put on her hair. It was pulled back into a large bun at the nape of her neck, with pastel-colored flowers pinned around. She looked stunning. She looked like her mother.

Cat's gown was a pale lavender silk, sitting just off her shoulders. Pink and white twists of fabric intertwined across the bodice, cut low, celebrating her ample breasts. Cat made everything she wore elegant. Thea felt she'd look ridiculous in such a gown.

"Thea! You aren't dressed!" Evelynde was standing across the room, hands on her hips. Thea looked down at her pale green gown. One she'd worn more times than she could count. It was plain, no doubt, but Thea did not consider it an inappropriate choice.

She frowned and turned in a showcasing circle. "I am dressed."

"It is a *wedding*, Calithea, you have to wear a corset." Evelynde folded her arms, leaning into her hip.

Thea groaned her protest.

"And your hair. You cannot wear it wild like that." Evelynde gestured furiously with her hands. "Come quickly. There is much to be done."

Thea sighed and set her book on a table crowded with teacups and tiny sandwiches. *The Illustrated Guide to Native Animals and Plants of the North*, by Oliver Birch, had become of great interest to her as of late.

She reluctantly trudged toward them.

"I had a dress made for you," Cat said, her blue eyes gleaming. "It's Parthenean silk, your favorite colors." Cat turned, looking around the room. "Sylvie, will you fetch Thea's gown, please? It is hanging behind the dressing wall, just there." Cat pointed.

Sylvie returned with an abundance of green and gold fabric draped over her arm. She held the dress up for review. The fitted bodice had been painted to look like solid gold. The neckline was cut low, trimmed with metallic gold appliqué that extended onto the shoulders, raised to look like armor, with several layers of the same gold fabric. The skirts were long and loose in green silk. Rich and emerald-like, but distinguishable somehow, Thea thought. Deeper, with more blue. A thin cape in the same silk attached to the back of the dress and billowed out behind it. It was the most beautiful dress Thea had ever seen.

It looked like a gown for a goddess or warrior queen. It warmed her heart her sister had done this for her, its intentions clear.

"What do you think?" Cat asked, expectant and grinning.

"It is beautiful, Cat. Beyond anything I could dream up." Thea tried to smile, but it fell before taking enough shape to be considered so. "It is only that I have no desire to stand out as such. If I were able to go unnoticed altogether, I would."

Cat gave one final look over her completed hair and thanked the attendant before standing. She walked to Thea, taking her hands. "Do not let them make you hide. That is not who you are. Get through this day with your head high for all to see."

Thea inhaled, glancing over at the dress.

"Besides," Cat said, eyes narrowed, looking Thea from top to bottom, "if you wear that old thing, you will most definitely stand out. And not in a good way."

Thea couldn't stop her chuckle. She nodded and sighed. "Very well."

Cat smiled and kissed her cheeks. Thea held out her arms begrudgingly as Sylvie unlaced her dress.

"You'll be the most beautiful woman in Highclere today," Cat said, helping Thea step out of the pale green smock.

"There is little chance of that if you're around." Thea looked at her sister and knew truer words had never been spoken. Cat was the most beautiful woman Thea had ever seen. Even more than the famed beauty in the painting that was displayed proudly in the castle gallery. The portrait of Alena of Argal hung next to one of their father, which was flanked by one of Evelynde. There were no portraits of Thea's mother. A soldier's daughter from Icena did not have a place on the walls of Highclere Castle. Not that such a portrait existed.

Thea was dressed, prodded, powdered, and perfumed for the better part of an hour. When the fuss was complete, she held up her arms.

"Well?" she queried the room.

"Go and see for yourself." Cat pointed to the large mirror in the corner.

Thea scrunched her nose. "I don't want to."

"For Godssake." Cat grabbed her hand, leading her across the room. Resigned not to disappoint her sister, Thea looked up.

The dress fit with immaculate precision. Thin layers of silk hung close to her body, the skirt somehow both airy and full. It created an intriguing contrast with the armored breastplate. The deep cut of the bodice lay naturally between her smaller breasts, enough to be provocative, but not scandalous. One could not help but feel powerful wearing it. Her hair had been woven with golden ribbons in a similar fashion to Cat's, but twisted in a loose braid that trailed long down her back.

"Wait," Cat said and turned to retrieve something from a dressing table. She reached for Thea's hand and slipped a golden band up her arm, then raised her eyebrows expectantly.

"I think you've outdone yourself," Thea said to her sister.

Cat grinned.

Evelynde walked to Thea, resting her hands on her shoulders. "You look lovely, dear."

Thea gave her a reluctant smile.

"Come along, girls, we must make haste." Evelynde clapped her hands in three quick strikes.

Cat started toward the door, but Thea reached out for her hand, gripping it tight. "Thank you."

Cat wrapped her arm around Thea's. "Come, sister, let us be done with this."

❖

It was a short walk to the temple. The streets were crowded with celebration and cheer, parting only for the royal procession. Her father had commissioned a citywide feast, and the air was fragrant with fresh bread and roasting meats.

Callum offered Thea his arm. The sanctuary was wide and long, with row after row of mahogany benches arranged in a half circle around the altar. It was packed full, save for the reserved spaces up front. The chatter quieted as they walked forward, and Thea sensed eyes on her already.

"Everyone is looking at me," she whispered to her brother.

He gave her arm a gentle squeeze. "Because you are beautiful."

They traversed the length of the long aisle, and Thea stopped to take her place in the second row. Callum held tight and did not release her, tugging her forward. She looked at him, brows knitted, but he didn't react. When she sat down next to him, Evelynde stiffened, but said nothing.

The room grew so silent Thea feared breathing. She thought surely everyone could hear the pounding of her heart. She could not sense the lapse of time while the Duke and Duchess of Aremore took their seats, followed by the bride's mother and siblings. She fidgeted nervously with the skirts of her dress. Her gaze darted around the room, growing blurry if she focused on one thing for too long.

She studied the marble statues of the Gods lining the back wall. Sunlight poured in from the domed ceiling into the outstretched arms of Cassia, as if she cast the light herself. It had always been her favorite.

Marten was now at the altar. She kept telling herself not to look, but the urge conquered her resolve, and she glanced his way. She was grateful she could not see his face and clamped her eyes shut.

Regret overcame her at the way they'd parted. She cursed herself for leaving him so. She should have held him, kissed him every moment they could steal. Never letting go until they were ripped apart. This was that moment, and now it was too late.

It was a malicious sort of torture. Being forced to sit quietly when all she wanted to do was scream. When all she wanted to do was grab him by the hand and run.

The bride approached the altar, cloaked in a white, floor-length, lace veil that trailed out long behind her. Her father pulled back the blusher, revealing a pretty, round face with light brown hair and blue eyes, bearing a strong resemblance to Evelynde. Thea knew she was past her eighteenth nameday, but she appeared not a day over fourteen. Her tiny stature and nervous disposition made her appear a child playing dress-up in her mother's gown. Her blue eyes scanned the room, and Thea saw that she was shaking. She remembered Evelynde's words. *Not everyone has a father like yours.*

The priest began to speak, and Thea worked to drown it out. She let herself imagine a different future. One where she and Marten would take that tradeship to Ostalla. Spend their days in a villa on the coast, surrounded by rolling hills and wildflowers. Marten would pick them for her. Maybe she would wear them in her hair. They would make love as often as they pleased, wherever they pleased. She saw their children running in olive groves under a warm, orange sun.

Thea flinched as cheers erupted around her, ripping her from the fantasy. Belly taut and chest heavy, she felt a single tear fall down her cheek. She quickly wiped it away.

She stood to join those around her. Cat and Callum both looked her way, and she gave them her most convincing nod. She could not see Marten through the crowd, and she was grateful for it. Conversations started as the wedding party paraded from the temple.

Thea used the opportunity to flee, making her way to the back of the room, knowing there was a door leading to the alleyway behind. She needed fresh air. She needed to breathe.

She weaved through the crowd discreetly. Not that it was an easy task in her armored dress. Nearly to the door, she moved to step around a small gathering and bumped into someone, stepping back from the impact. It was a man in black, but she kept her gaze low, fearing tears would spill should her eyes meet with another's.

"Pardon me, sir."

He didn't move, so she stepped around him, but he sidestepped, blocking her path. She stepped to the other side, but again, he mirrored her stride. Frowning, she looked up and was met with familiar gray eyes.

He looked curiously over the length of her face, then down her body, and she felt herself flush. When his gaze met hers again, it was altered, now heavy with what she thought might be contempt. It startled her. The moment drew oddly long, but before she could speak, he stepped aside, gesturing for her to pass.

When she reached the door, she turned back. He was watching her. Heat crept up her cheeks, and she bolted from the temple.

Thea tried to swallow back the beating of her heart as it pulsated, inching its way up her throat. *Scream,* it said. She put her hand on her chest, taking deep, slow breaths. She did not want to have an attack. Not there. Not in front of all those people.

Looking around, she found herself alone on the small veranda. Tears were coming, and it made her angry. *I will not cry today.* Grasping the rail, she dug her fingers into the wood until she felt the sting of her hands taking on small cuts.

Thea lifted her chin up to the warm sun, and it took her back to her dream of Ostalla and their villa. She shook her head, banishing it from her mind. She could not continue like this. The door clicked, and she looked back to see Callum walking through.

"I turned around, and you were gone. I only saw you walk out right at the last moment," he said. "How are you?"

Her resolve cracked, and her face crumbled. He wrapped his arms around her, and she shook her head as tears fell unrestrained.

"I feel silly," she said. "I should be able to endure this."

"You *are* enduring it. You are here, are you not?" He held her tight against him.

"I can't abide the eyes on me. They're laughing at me. I dread this feast. There will be nowhere to hide."

He pulled back to look at her, hands firm on her shoulders. "Then don't go. No one will blame you."

"But then they win."

"Thea, you don't need to prove anything to anyone," he said, blotting the tears from her cheeks.

As much as she might wish to agree, she could not.

He sighed, pulling her back into his arms. "One more day, Thea. Then this is done. The charades will end. People will move on. I swear it."

She nodded against him. "One more day."

He pulled back again, giving her a once-over. "Besides, I don't think anyone is going to mess with you in this dress. You look like you take the heads of men to pass time."

Thea laughed, wondering to herself if she'd ever felt more grateful for her brother. "Why did you pull me to the front, Callum?"

He looked at her with a sadness she knew was on her behalf. "Because that is where you belong."

"Evelynde will not be happy about it," she said, with a cocked brow.

Callum scoffed and made a crude gesture toward the temple. "Evelynde can speak to me if she has an issue. She got what she wanted."

Thea chuckled, but worried it would not be that simple. "It brings me great comfort knowing I still have you."

"You always will." He kissed her cheek.

She patted away what remained of her tears. "I can't walk back through like this. Will you take me home through the alleyways?"

"Of course. Let me tell Father, else he will worry for you. Wait for me here."

She nodded. As the door swung open, she peered around to see if the gray-eyed man was still there. He was not.

The walk through the alleyways was faster than the procession. They passed few, as most were celebrating in the streets. Callum left her in her room to straighten up before she joined the feast. There was a little redness in her face, but she was mostly unaltered. She rested a cool, damp cloth over her eyes to reduce the swell while she sipped directly from the bottle of wine snatched from the kitchen on the way up. It could not have been half an hour before there was a gentle knock at her door.

Thea groaned. "Yes?"

The door opened, and Sylvie walked through. "I'm sorry, your step-mother is asking for you."

Thea set the bottle on her dressing table. "You should not be sorry, Sylvie. I'm simply wallowing in disappointments I should have known better than to allow to manifest. You've interrupted nothing of value."

"I am glad to see the events of the day have not stripped you of your positive disposition."

They shared a laugh.

"Should I tell her to expect you shortly?"

"No, I'll go now. Better to be done with this." Thea stood, straightening her dress before walking to the door.

As she passed by, Sylvie reached out for her arm, turning her back. "Do not let them make you feel small." Sylvie tightened her grip, giving her arm a subtle shake. "Your value is greater than the lot of them."

Guests were still filing into the hall when she arrived. She was able to slip in unannounced and take her chair next to Cat. When all had taken to their seats, her father stood, and the room quieted.

"Good people, I thank you for joining us on this most joyous occasion. This union between the noble houses Percy of Ire and Cumberly of

Andar will further strengthen what is already a sacred and strong alliance." He reached for his wine and held it high. "Please join me and raise your glass to the happy couple."

The room cheered. Thea stole a look at Marten and found him staring directly at her. It startled her, causing her to spill her wine. Scrambling to recover, she felt her father purposefully not noticing, and her stepmother noticing most purposefully.

"No one will blame you if you retire early tonight," Cat said, low into her ear.

"I'm fine." Working hard to carve out a smile, Thea reached for a carafe, filling her glass to the brim. "Besides, as Father said, this is a joyous occasion." She made a mocking toast before taking several large gulps.

Her father's speech had brought attention to their table. There wasn't anywhere to hide. Cat reached for her hand, giving it a gentle squeeze. It felt like everyone was looking at her, waiting for her to react. She was determined to give them nothing.

Glancing back at Marten's table, she found him engaged in conversation with his father, his new wife seated on the opposite side. She looked miniature next to him. Her eyes darted around the room. They connected with Thea's and rather than look away, Thea offered her a soft smile. The girl looked down and did not look her way again. Thea couldn't help but feel her indifferent demeanor justified. No doubt Thea was a villain in her story. She determined indifference was likely the best she deserved.

Once all had their fill of the feast and the dancing had begun, it was easier to sink into the background. The members of her family were about the room, engaged in conversation or dancing. Thea was content to sit at the empty table, lost in drink. Just as she considered sneaking out for the night, she heard footsteps. She glanced back to see Kenelm approaching.

"Perfect," she said under her breath. She tipped up her glass, finishing its contents. It was her third.

"Lady Calithea." Kenelm dipped his head before taking the seat next to her. He set a mug on the table.

"Uncle." She kept her gaze forward, pretending to watch the dancing.

"Are you enjoying the festivities?" He didn't try hiding his triumphant grin. It was stretched so far from ear to ear that Thea saw it beaming from the corner of her eye.

"Of course, Uncle." Thea scrunched her nose. He smelled like smoked meat and sweat, as if he had gorged himself sick. She had to stop herself from shifting away. Everything about the man repulsed her.

"It doesn't look like it." He leaned closer as he spoke, his breath stale from ale. "Come now, surely you didn't believe you'd be wed to him."

She straightened. "I do not know your meaning."

"Please, girl, everyone knows you're his whore."

He said it so casually it took a moment for his words to register. Her relationship with Marten was commonly known, but no one spoke about it, least of all in such a brazen manner.

Kenelm reached for his mug. He tipped it up, gaze steady on hers as he drank. He lazily wiped at the ale streaming down his chin. "Your father should have left you in Icena, like he did your whore mother." He moved to return his mug to the table, and she had to fight the instinct to strike it from his grasp. "Your father was always weak for women."

Fury twisted her brow as she stared at him. Struck. Kenelm had never been friendly to her, much less treated her as kin, but this was blatant disrespect. She remembered Sylvie's words. *Do not let them make you feel small.* "Yes, my father, the *king*. Should I call for him now? What do you think his reaction will be when I tell him his own brother called his beloved daughter a *whore?*"

Kenelm recoiled, taken aback by her insolence. It encouraged her.

She deepened her sneer. "Go and find someone else to toy with. I'm no longer a child, and you'll have no more words with me from this day forward." She grabbed the fork in front of her, holding it out between them. His eyes went wide. "Now leave me before I do your wife a kindness and relieve you of your tiny cock. Crawl back to whatever Lochan province my father sent you to."

He gaped at her, unmoving, until he snatched his mug and stood. "Watch yourself, girl. Bastards aren't given keep in other parts of the world like they are here." When his attempt to intimidate her proved impotent, he turned and stormed off.

Thea dropped the fork, her head falling into her hands. She thought she must be losing her mind. Looking up, she searched the room, trying to assess if anyone had been watching the exchange. The last thing she wanted was another lecture from Evelynde. It appeared all were otherwise engaged. She exhaled.

Then she locked eyes with *him*.

The man with the gray eyes. He was looking right at her, brows creased. Thea couldn't be sure if he was angry or confused. His gaze was intense, and she felt scrutinized. She looked away. At least she had not tarnished someone's good image of her. He likely already believed her to be unbalanced.

She needed air. She stood and made for the door.

With relief, Thea found herself alone, walking out to the edge of the balcony. The moon was bright over the lake, its crescent shape reflecting in the water.

The familiar sting of tears struck. It was too much. She tried to swallow them back, but they flowed warm and silent down her cheeks. She had promised herself she wouldn't cry, and she was failing miserably. Thea felt like jumping in the water and swimming all the way to Straeth.

"I do not wish to startle you," said a low voice from behind.

"Oh," Thea said, turning and quickly wiping away her tears. "I did not know anyone was—" Her eyes narrowed, and she scoffed. "It's *you*."

"*Me?*" He walked up beside her, back leaning against the balcony wall, elbows resting atop.

Thea stood with her hands on her hips, making no attempt to conceal her irritation. "What are you doing?"

"Taking in the moonlight," he said coolly, looking up at the night sky. "Just as yourself." His voice was deep and honeyed, just as she remembered. When his eyes landed back on hers, he smiled. It was light, perhaps a touch facetious.

"Who are you?" she demanded, further irked by his playful demeanor.

He shrugged. "No one of consequence. Sorry to disappoint." He studied her again as he had each time before, searching every part of her face.

Confused by his manner more than ever, she folded her arms across her chest. "Why are you watching me?"

His brows rose at the question, eyes taking on more amusement.

"I can feel it. This afternoon at the temple, what was that?" She released her arms and stepped forward. "And at the tourney." Maybe it was the wine or what had happened with Kenelm, but she was feeling bold. "Are you laughing at me, too?"

He frowned. "If I recall correctly, it was you watching *me* at the tourney." The slight twitch of his lips pulled her attention to them.

Thea scoffed, feeling her cheeks heat. "You are quite mistaken," she said, straightening. "I was doing no such thing. And you did not answer me."

Ignoring her question, he turned his body to look out over the lake. "Does he often speak to you that way?"

"What? *Who?*" She studied the designs woven into the back of his vest. They were intricate and detailed, unlike any she'd seen before. The patterns were stitched in black, nearly matching the fabric. One would only be able to discern them in close proximity. It was finery, but subtle.

"Your uncle." He glanced back at her, saying it with a touch of contempt.

"You were all the way across the hall. How could you possibly know what he said to me?" Her hands came to rest on her hips once more.

He tilted his head side to side. "It wasn't hard to read. I was hoping to see you stick him with that knife, though."

"It was a fork."

He laughed. It was spirited and puckish, resonating around her, warm, like a welcome fire in high winter. She nearly joined in.

"Even better." His gaze was intense and confident from beneath a strong brow and dark lashes. She found him charming, and it only further fueled her irritation.

"I'm asking you again. Why are you watching me?"

He shrugged a shoulder. "It was not my intent to spy on you. I considered interfering, but you seemed to have it well in hand."

Thea frowned. "That is not an answer."

His gaze lingered, softening with each breath. "Do not let any of those people make you feel less than."

Thea stepped back. "You speak rather plainly."

"Not often," he said, before tipping up a wineglass she only now realized he was holding. Moonlight caught the single gold ring he wore. Wings of what Thea thought might be an eagle spread out across it.

She hated that she found him attractive. "You don't know me. Why do you care?" Thea turned to face the lake.

"I don't know you. But I do know people like your uncle. You should not let his words affect you so. He is not worthy of it." The contempt in his voice toward Kenelm increased.

"That is easy for you to say. You're not the *whore*. You're not the bastard daughter." Thea blinked, reeling at her own frankness. Now knowing, no longer questioning, she had finally lost her good senses. She glanced at him, expecting judgment or shock, frowning when she found neither.

"Well, see, that's not fair, *you don't know me*. Perhaps, I am much more a whore than you. You don't even know my name." He gave her another smile, this time broader, warmer.

Thea could not decide if she disliked him. She could not even make sense of him. She turned her body to face his, taking a step closer. "Whose doing is that? I have asked, and you have not said. *Who are you?*"

The jest in his manner eased, and for a moment, Thea thought he would answer, but he shrugged and turned back to the lake. "No one of consequence."

Thea sighed. "Do you avoid every question asked?"

"I answer you," he said with an air of feigned innocence. He peered into her eyes as if he were trying to see through them, into her thoughts.

"Yes, you do, but they're not really answers, are they?" It felt like he was toying with her, holding the answers over her head, dangling them above, just out of reach. Tempting her, daring her to jump higher, try harder. "It's quite maddening," she said, her irritation threatening to ignite.

"So I'm told."

Thea wanted to stamp her feet. She made a throaty roar, shaking her fists between them. He turned around, watching her like one does a drunken brawl—with a sense of excitement and guilty delight.

"I don't know why I'm still here." She started to leave but paused, turning back. "You're very vexing, do you know that?"

He smiled as if she'd complimented him, and the sight of it did something to her she was not willing to acknowledge. He stared at her, unbothered by the ever-growing silence between them.

She narrowed her eyes and pointed a stiff finger at him. "There is something not right about you."

Her words only broadened his grin. "More than one thing, I hope."

Thea huffed and stormed off, sensing him walking in behind her. She didn't turn around. Looking over the crowd, she spotted Cat across the room and marched toward her.

"Cat!" She beckoned her sister with her hand. Thea watched impatiently as Cat excused herself from her conversation and made her way around the long table.

"How are you?" Cat kissed her cheek.

Thea didn't answer. "Who is the man from the southern continent? Dark hair and gray eyes, always in black."

Cat frowned. "I'm afraid you'll have to be more specific."

Thea scanned the room. She spotted him across the hall, staring at her. She gave him an indignant smirk, making no attempt to hide her inquiry, and pointed directly at him. "Him, there! Sitting at the table with Lady Starling."

Cat looked, and he shifted his gaze. "Ah, him. Cousin to King Dorian of Sibreen. His name is Alec. Alec Turan."

"Alec Turan," Thea repeated, letting his name linger. It felt familiar, as if she'd known it all along and only needed reminding.

Thea watched him with Dianna. He was smiling and gesturing with animation. Dianna burst into laughter at whatever was said, swatting him playfully on the shoulder. He glanced at Thea from the side of his eye and smirked. Thea scowled. "What else do you know about him?"

Cat exhaled, tilting her head. "Hmm, let me think."

Thea tapped her boot.

"He is a military commander. Quite revered, if I recall correctly. Not married. Obviously quite handsome." She elbowed Thea. "Twenty and eight summers, give or take. He is a favorite of his aunt, the dowager queen."

Thea stared at her sister and blinked. "Gods, Cat, you really do know everyone."

She smiled tightly. "Information is power, Thea, and in this part of the world, women have little opportunity for it. Why do you want to know about him?"

Thea didn't know what she would do with these facts or why she even cared, but it felt like a small victory.

"Thanks," she said, returning her sister's kiss.

"Thea!" Cat called after her, but she was already striding away.

No one of consequence. Thea huffed. Narrowing her eyes, she marched directly toward him. He was staring at her again, a taunting smile having formed on his lips. It only made her more flustered. She was halfway to her destination when someone grabbed her arm, spinning her around. Marten.

"*What are you doing?*" It came out in a whispered hiss. Thea tugged her arm free, eyes darting around the room in concern.

"I can't say hello to you?" He looked worn and sullen.

"Of course you can, but by the time I count to ten, everyone in this room is going to be looking at us."

"Please meet me tomorrow. Midday, our spot?" His eyes were pleading, and it tugged at her heart.

She nodded. "Yes. But now go, *please.*"

Hope washed over his face as he turned and strode away. Thea swallowed, trying to suppress everything she'd felt hours before. The exchange had sent her spinning.

It took her a moment to remember what she had been doing. Turning back to task, she found Alec missing from his chair. She was so cross she wanted to scream.

She waited for an hour, but he didn't return. Having checked the balconies and dining hall top to bottom, she deduced he must have returned to his room. Cousin to a king would surely be staying in the castle.

What kind of way was that to behave? Thea didn't understand how he had managed to get under her skin. It was almost as if she could feel him there, now, still smirking in her shadow. They had spoken mere minutes, but he had been messing with her for days. After the exchange on the balcony, she was sure of it.

Storming through the dark hallways back to her room, she grew angrier by the step, cursing under her breath. She turned a corner in a fury and yelped—part in pain and part in surprise—when she ran smack into a black wall. The impact sent her sprawling on her backside.

Except it wasn't a wall. It was a man. With black hair and gray eyes.

She slapped the ground, palms stinging on the stone. "*What is going on?*"

"You fell," he said, his right hand extended toward her. "Again, I might add."

It was becoming a far too familiar scenario for her taste. She didn't take his hand and scrambled back to her feet. He retracted his offer, clasping his hands behind his back, standing straight, noble-like. Thea brushed and blew loose strands of hair from her face, then shook her shoulders in a sort of reset.

She pointed her finger at him, the same way she'd done on the balcony. He looked down at it with mirthful eyes. "If you don't tell me what you're doing in this part of the castle, I'm going to get the guards." She did her best to speak with authority, to not appear as disarmed as she felt.

He held his hands out to his sides in a gesture of supplication. "I got lost on my way back to my room. Everything looks the same here," he said, as he looked around, "so gray."

"Oh." She huffed. She knew she had such a reason to be angry, but if someone asked her to explain, she would fail to find the words.

They stood for a moment, appraising one another. He was not as tall as Marten, but she still had to look up to meet his eyes. Black wavy hair fell around his face, soft and wistful, as if he were to rustle it about, it would always find its way back in an appealing state. He looked at her with curiosity, no trace of the hubris from the balcony. His beard was clipped, appearing more of a shadow on his angular face than a cover. It was the first time she noticed the fullness of his lips. A small scar cut through one of his thick eyebrows. Otherwise, his golden skin was smooth and unsullied. The prominent bridge of his nose held the slightest of bends, as if recently broken. The makings of his face were somehow hard and soft in parallel. Like finely crafted art, possessing a natural regality.

The front of his vest was as ornate as the back. Solid black with a rounded collar and bronze clasps running down the front, stopping at the waistline, secured by a black belt, also trimmed in bronze. It was cut high at the shoulders, revealing a black linen shirt he had rolled up over his forearms. He looked polished, but somehow casual, undone. She wanted to deny she found him appealing, but he was devastatingly so.

She realized she was looking too long when his mouth took on a bend, the hubris returning. Whatever she was thinking a moment ago vanished. She straightened her dress. "Do you remember anything about the part of the castle you're staying in?"

"Close to the library, I think."

Thea sighed. "The library is on the other side of the castle."

He leaned forward as he spoke. "Hmm, well, I probably need someone to show me the way."

Her eyes narrowed on his as she tried but was unsuccessful in inventing a reason to say no. "*Fine.*" She turned, stalking back down the hall, hearing his footsteps in tow.

They walked for a time in silence. He had an affecting presence, and she couldn't help but steal a few glances his way. His confidence and collected disposition intrigued her. She was so often frantic and unsure. He looked natural, insouciant. Thea wondered what it would feel like to be so at ease. She envied it.

"Are you enjoying your time in Ire?" It was a silly question, and she felt her face flush when she asked.

He bit back a grin. "Indeed. Indeed. It is very *different* from Sibreen."

"I've never been to the south," she said, glancing at him. "Not anywhere but here. I can't compare."

He stopped walking and turned toward her. "You have never left Highclere?"

She shook her head. "Well, Father used to take us to the sea when we were children, but we stopped going at some point. I'm not sure why." Thea thought he might be looking at her with pity. She shifted on her feet, preferring his teasing.

"Tell me, Lady Calithea—"

Thea held up her hand. "Thea."

He smiled. "Tell me, Thea, if you never travel, how do you spend your time?"

"I don't know." She shrugged. "How does anyone? Riding, reading, gardening. I like to walk."

"Do you not wish to see the world?"

"I suppose I haven't given it much thought. As a woman and the daughter of a king, you learn quite early that your life is decided *for* you, not *by* you." She crossed her arms, her tone turning to jest. "But I don't have to explain that to you, do I? Cousin to a king. *No one of consequence*, you said, Alec Turan."

He looked at her lips as if he liked the way his name sounded leaving them. "No, you do not, Thea Ironne." His eyes said much more than his words. Thea could sense the magnitude of thoughts racing behind them. Ideas, notions, musings, considerations. She wanted to know what they were. "I suppose I am asking if it were up to you, would you stay in Highclere?"

"Yes, of course. This is my home." It was an instinctual reply to an odd question. As soon as the words left her mouth, Thea knew they were false. She started to correct herself, but she stuttered, her mind unable to construct the words. The pity returned to his eyes as if he understood her struggle. But then she couldn't remember what she was about to say. *Oh, never mind*, she thought. He was fixated on her face. Thea thought he might look concerned. She blinked, inclining her head. "Why are you looking at me like that?"

As soon as she asked, his expression changed, falling flat. He cleared his throat and started walking again. "What will you do now?"

"What do you mean?" she asked, taking quick steps to catch up.

"Now that Marten Percy is leaving."

She stopped, and he turned to face her. She took a step back. "What kind of question is that?"

"A very straightforward one."

She wrapped her arms around her body. "Why would you ask me that?"

He stepped closer, his expression imparting no clues. She inhaled sandalwood and something smoky. "I would like to know."

Thea frowned, unable to comprehend his intention. She stared up at him, lips parted, brows knitted, shaking her head. She was growing tired of his games. He was hot and cold in a way that infuriated her. One moment, he was kind and amusing. The next, an entitled brute. "So you're leaving tomorrow then?" She didn't try to mask her irritation.

"I am."

She pointed down the hall. "The library is through that corridor. I trust you can find your room from here. I bid you good night and wish you safe travels." She held out her hand for him to shake.

A gentle laugh shook his chest as he reached for it. "I hope our paths cross again, Thea Ironne."

He was warm and gripped her tight. A feather-like touch glided up her arm and over her chest. The intensity of his gaze surged, and she felt a pull to him, an instinct for more contact, to be closer. He studied her again, intently, perplexity returning to his brow. When he looked at her lips, heat flushed her cheeks.

"Your eyes," he said, as his returned to hers, "are a remarkable shade of green."

Thea swallowed and dropped his hand, breaking the spell. She took two steps back before looking up again.

He slowly lowered his hand, tucking it behind him with the other. She had no means to make sense of the look on his face.

"Goodbye, Alec Turan." She had intended to say it with contempt, but it came out soft. She turned, retreating with a hasty pace. When she reached the corner to the next hall, she looked back. He was still standing there, watching.

She raced out of sight.

Thea rubbed her head. It ached. From the wine, from the crying, from the day's events. From that insufferable man. On the walk back to her room, she reconciled herself not to spend another moment thinking about him or trying to decipher his motivations. She was never going to see him again. It mattered not.

Exhausted, she tugged at the laces of her gown. It was a difficult task to remove on her own. She craved a bath, but it was late, and she had no desire to wake the staff. She slipped into a clean shift and started untangling the braids from her hair. Taking notice of the wine bottle she brought up earlier, she reached for it and tipped it up, downing the remains in one attempt. She didn't care how much she would regret it in the morning.

After washing her hands and face in the basin, she crashed into her bed, delicious sleep consuming her within minutes. Right before it took hold, she realized she hadn't thought about Marten for hours.

20

Thea

Marten was already waiting under the magnolia tree when Thea arrived at their clearing. He was sitting on the ground, elbows resting on his knees. Neither spoke as she knelt across from him, sinking into the grass still tender from the soft rain that fell in and out all morning. Hazy fog lingered around them, rich with flora and earth.

His eyes, which had not yet met hers, were red-rimmed and inflamed, and he looked to be wearing the same clothes he had the night before, save for the dress jacket. His white tunic was half tucked, and he looked unusually unruly. Marten was always clean and well-dressed. Always prepared for the day.

"How long have you been here?" she asked, breaking the silence.

"Since dawn." He kept his eyes down as he spoke.

Thea lowered her head to try to catch his gaze, but he didn't oblige. "Have you slept?"

"A little. And you?"

"A little."

Marten looked at her for the first time. She had never seen him so distraught, and it pained her. All her instincts were to rectify it, to ease it however she could.

"This is it?" he asked. "It is truly over?"

She swallowed and nodded. He took on an air of resentment and looked away, jaw flexing. Thea readied herself to take it on, to bear the break on her own. She could do it one last time. She hoped. "When do you leave?"

"As soon as I return." His fingers tugged at the hem of his sleeves. "My father is anxious to return to Aremore."

"Anxious to get you away from me."

He was wholly unreceptive to the jest, and she knew it was the wrong thing to say. When he looked up at her again, it nearly cracked her heart. "Yes, because finally he understands what you are to me." He ripped a handful of grass from the earth, tossing it mindlessly aside. "I couldn't do it, Thea."

She squeezed her eyes shut. It was the information she had anticipated, unsure of what she wanted to hear. "She is your wife. You must."

"I have the rest of my life, no?"

"Yes, I suppose you do." She felt she should warn him of the consequences should the girl tell someone, but Thea knew this was no longer her concern. This was Marten's life now, separate from hers. These were his decisions to make. Light rain returned, but neither moved. "I have much regret for the way I left you last we met." A single tear she had not felt coming trailed down her cheek.

He brushed it away. "Please don't cry. I can't bear it. Everything you said was right. I know I've not been fair to you. I know I ask too much."

She hoped her eyes presented the gratitude she felt.

"But I'm going to ask again."

And it was gone.

He moved, lifting on his knees, gripping her shoulders. "I can go to Aremore, I can do that, all that is being asked of me, but only if I know I have you still. I don't care how often you'll see me, only that you will."

She pulled back. "Marten…"

"Thea, please say you will see me again." He looked at her, begging, pleading, and it caused a second tear to fall down her cheek.

"Of course I will see you again, but—"

"You know what I mean." He moved closer, their lips only inches apart.

Thea turned her face away. "Please do not ask me to be your whore."

"It wouldn't be like that."

"For me, it would." She reached for his hand, holding it between hers.

"One day, you will look back on our time together with fondness. But your heart will belong to someone else. Just as you said to me nine days ago."

"You are wrong." He wrapped his free hand around the back of her neck, leaning in. His lips brushed hers with the softest of kisses, gentle and loving, but heated, as if to show her just how wrong she was.

Every part of her wanted to fall in sync. To kiss him, to hold him, to feel the weight of him as he made love to her as he had so many times before, there on the forest floor. Thea steeled herself. "For once, I need you to be the one who walks away."

"I can't. I love you."

She leaned back, putting space between them so their eyes could meet. "Love was never our obstacle."

His arm moved around her back, drawing her closer. "Is it not? If I did not love you, I would not feel like this. I would not fight like this."

"Please go," she whispered.

He shook his head, pressing his forehead against hers. "Don't do this."

She released his hand, arms falling loose to her sides. He tried to kiss her, but her lips were like stone. She closed her eyes, fearful if she looked at him, she would falter.

He held her for what felt like the length of sunrise to sunset. When he finally yielded, falling back into the grass, she kept her eyes closed. It was longer yet before she heard him stand. "I cannot leave you out here like this. It is not safe for you to be alone."

When she didn't respond, he sighed.

She remained fixed in silence. She heard him walk around, curse, and huff. In time, his footsteps drew further, quieter, until ceasing entirely. She didn't dare move or speak until she was certain he was far gone.

Then it ripped from her. A sob, wretched and consuming. Everything she was holding on to escaped from her body. Every thought was a question. She wanted to run after him. He loved her, truly loved her, and she was letting him go.

Dread crept along her skin. It tingled and slithered, serpent-like, stealing the air from her lungs, her belly, spinning into a vortex that contaminated her thoughts, stripping them of reason. *No, please, not here.* She dug her fingers into the damp earth, but it did nothing to ground her.

With shaking hands, she removed her boots and stood, taking off toward the lake. Her pace grew quicker, more desperate, tearing at the ties of her dress as she ran. When she reached the edge, she was down to her shift. She dove headfirst. The water struck like chill-kissed fire. She swam until she could go not one moment longer without a breath. When her face finally broke the surface, she gasped, heaving for precious air.

She turned to float on her back, gliding through the lily pads as her breathing returned to normal. She watched the clouds pass by. The only sound was her heart. Broken, but still beating. She knew in that moment it had always been. Perhaps since the beginning, since the first time he'd kissed her, always knowing how it would end.

Thea trampled through the dense brush, wet shift in hand. Many were still leaving Highclere, and she needed to be cautious on her way back. She could only imagine how she looked. Dripping wet and carrying her undergarments in her arms. Oh, the stories they would tell. She smiled when she understood, for the first time in her entire life, she didn't care.

Distant voices caused her to halt. She jumped behind the cover of a thick trunk, back bracing against the rough bark, cursing under her breath. She frowned when she realized the voices were familiar.

Timidly, she peered around and squinted through the trees to find two figures in a clearing. Her fear turned to bewilderment as she saw Breeda with… Alec Turan. Wilder still, they appeared to be arguing. He was furious, hands flying as he paced back and forth.

However animated they were, their voices were low. Too low for Thea to discern. Curiosity tugged, and she considered sneaking closer. Something in her gut told her to stay put.

They continued for a short time until Alec stormed off in the direction of the castle. Breeda walked in circles before stopping abruptly, head snapping in Thea's direction.

Thea darted back behind the tree. A long moment passed before she was brave enough to dare another look. When she did, Breeda was gone.

She exhaled, slowly, dumbfounded by what she'd seen. Starting back to the castle, her mind spun with possibilities, but she could come to no plausible explanation. She couldn't even remember seeing the two in the same room the past sixday.

Something told her she needed to keep this to herself.

Dread crept its way back in. Her sister had told her strange things were happening. Perhaps she was now ready to pay attention.

21

Nara

"A field house is a safe haven and its steward the keeper."

ESĒRII BIJRAH Z'OURA
ADE NYANTHI AND PHILOMENA TALIESIN, 805 AQ

"We'll be in and out," Nara said to Harker. They were standing on the riverboat's deck, watching Kurk grow closer. "I'm going to ride hard, straight through each night. Follow behind as quickly as you can."

"Understood."

Nara looked down at herself, then at Harker. Neither had a proper bath since Rahab, and they smelled and looked exactly as one would expect.

"We are fortunate Amena is the steward here," Nara said. It was policy to give an official report when passing through field houses. They did not have the time for that. They needed horses, supplies, and to be on their way. Amena would give them no trouble. If not for Nara's sake, then for Harker's. The two had been warming each other's beds for years.

"Well," Harker said, "I hate to be the one to disappoint."

Nara turned to look at him. "*What?*"

"Amena isn't here," he answered, shaking his head.

Nara frowned. "She was here when we passed through on our way to Amul."

"She was reassigned to Azmar. Was scheduled to leave five days after we came through."

Nara groaned, which turned into a growl that rang down her arms into her fists. "Do you know who replaced her?"

Harker grimaced, and Nara prepared herself. "Rogen Borley."

"*Fuck.*" Borley was an avid rule follower, anxious to climb ranks. He would ask questions, force policy. He would slow them down.

"Yeah," Harker said, sharing her sentiment. "How do you want to handle it?"

"The same. If he makes trouble or delays us in any way, I'll go into town and steal two fucking horses."

Harker chuckled. "Aye."

This was why she liked him. One of the many reasons.

Nara watched anxiously as the crew worked to port the riverboat. The moment Nara and Harker stepped on the dock, they took off sprinting in the direction of the field house, weaving through the late afternoon thinning crowds. When they reached the building, Borley was already waiting in the frame of the door, arms folded across his chest, scowling.

Nara sighed. They were off to a poor start.

"I felt you coming a mile away. What's the rush?" The short man had lost another inch from his hairline since Nara had last seen him at the Citadel.

"May we come inside?" she asked, leaning forward with her hands on her knees, trying to steady her breath.

Borley looked out behind them. "Where are Tora and Sanne? We weren't expecting you to pass through for several days. It is not protocol to show up without the team leader. And where is the child?"

"Must you have answers on the doorstep, or may we pass and have our interrogation inside?" Nara eyed him, already irritated.

He peered at her but stepped back, ushering them in. There were several others on the far end of the room. Conversations stopped, and some turned to look, no doubt confused by their urgent demeanors and disheveled states. Nara could smell something cooking. The tantalizing scents of a stew drifted past her nose. Potatoes, carrots. It caused her mouth to water. She cast the desire aside.

"Borley," she said between breaths. "I need you to listen to me. We haven't the time to explain, nor have we been granted permission to do so. We need two fresh horses packed with enough supplies to ride straight through to the Citadel. We need them *now.*"

"Just hold on a minute," Borley said, his round eyes narrowing. "This field house is my responsibility. There are procedures to follow." He lifted his chin as if to assert himself.

Nara walked up to the man, looking down at him, several inches shorter than she. "Listen to me," she said. "I do not have time to squabble with you, little man. I said we need two fresh horses, and we need them *now*."

He squirmed under the intensity of her gaze but wasn't yet ready to yield. "You are no longer a chancellor. You do not outrank me." He held his head higher. "I'm not going to be the one to explain to the council why I let two collectors prance through my field house without giving proper report." He turned up his nose. "And you should bathe. You stink."

Nara closed her eyes, inhaling slowly, rallying her patience. She felt Harker step up.

"Rogen," Harker said with a much softer tone than she. "We're on Citadel business. Sent by our team leader to travel straight through. You're breaking no rules."

Borley pursed his lips. "Have you a signed parchment detailing this?"

"No."

"Then I cannot supply you until proper report is given." Borley held up his hands and stepped back, as if the gesture put a finality on it.

Harker sighed. He looked at the man with pity, as though trying to impart he was making a grievous mistake.

Nara stepped forward, closing the space he created. "This is of the utmost importance. We don't know how else to explain it to you. If you do not let us pass unabated, *that* is what you'll be answering to the council for."

Their exchange drew a small crowd. There were more people in the room than when they'd first entered.

"You will sit down, you will give report, and then you'll have your horses." He folded his arms.

"This is your last chance." Nara did her best to be sure her words reflected the warning they were. Her power flared, just a touch, and it heated the air around them. She felt Harker step back.

Borley shifted on his feet. "I know you think you can do as you please, Nara *Nyanthi*, but—"

Nara hauled back her fist and punched him right in the nose.

He let out a pained squeal as he collapsed. She stood over him, looking at the gathered crowd. Some wore expressions of shock, others amusement. "I need two fresh horses packed with supplies to get us to the Citadel. This is not a request. Please don't make me ask again."

For a moment, no one moved. Borley moaned on the ground, holding his face. A young woman whom Nara did not know stepped forward and nodded, then strode from the room.

The bloodied man stumbled to his feet. "I think you've broken my nose!"

"I have."

"The council will hear of this!" He pointed at Nara, moving his finger between her and Harker. "Of all of this."

Nara shrugged. "You have a few minutes before we leave. Write it up, and I'll deliver your report to them myself."

Borley sneered at her before turning and marching away. The crowd slowly dispersed, some chuckling, others concerned, whispering among themselves.

Harker clapped her on the back. "Well, that's one way to do it."

The girl returned, ushering them out back. Two horses, good horses, were packed as requested. Nara took the reins from her. She looked of Bacran descent. And young. Perhaps not yet sixteen. Her demeanor was oddly assured for one of such an age.

"What is your name?"

"Hira." A polished knot on the crown of her head held her silky, straight black hair, revealing her features in full. Her dark, monolid eyes exhibited confidence and intelligence, and perhaps disinterest as she walked around Nara's horse, checking the latches on the satchels.

Nara combed through her mind for any flickering of recognition. "Hira Yesen?" she asked as she mounted her horse. "Yul is your—"

"Brother," Hira said, as if vexed to be reminded.

Nara knew Yul as a close friend of Alec Turan. She'd known Yul had a sister, but could not recall meeting her before. She seemed considerably younger than her brother. Nara narrowed her eyes. "How old—"

"Twenty," the girl said, almost involuntarily, like she was accustomed to being asked so at an aggravating recurrence.

"No consequence will come to you for this, I swear. If Borley gives you trouble, send word to me at the Citadel, or to my mother."

"I can handle Borley."

Nara nodded, no doubt she could. She studied her for a breath, taking her measure. She was powerful. Her ether airy and light. Not dissimilar to her brother. And Nara, of course, had a soft spot for those who didn't mind bending a rule here and there. She made note to remember her. "You haven't asked any questions," Nara said to her.

"I assume you'd say if it were my business." Hira turned to the other horse, securing the buckle on Harker's saddle.

Nara could say nothing, but tried to portray the gravity with her eyes. "Are you stationed in Kurk?"

Hira shook her head. "Port Lethney. I leave for Azmar in the morning."

"Ah," Harker said, pausing, foot in the stirrup. "Give my regards to Amena." He gripped the saddle, hauling himself atop his horse.

The girl looked up at him expectantly. "Who should I say passes on their regard?"

Harker frowned, taken aback he wasn't known. Nara laughed, heartily, from the belly. She would not forget the girl now. "Harker," she said, her laughter carrying on as they rode away. "His name is Harker."

22

Neith

"All those of able body and sound mind shall serve, pledging oath and life upon one's nameday of ten and four."

ESĒRII BIJRAH Z'OURA
ADE NYANTHI AND PHILOMENA TALIESIN, 805 AQ

Neith rose before dawn. Sam, Petra, and Bellamy had offered their mornings and evenings to train her in sword skill and hand combat. She collapsed into bed every night exhausted, only to wake the next morning excited to start again.

So far, the efforts had yielded her a black eye from a stray elbow and a broken fifth metacarpal in her left hand. But she could now hold the training sword steady, defend somewhat against an attack, and was no longer a complete embarrassment throwing a punch. She hadn't worn a dress in days and was not sorry for it.

"Keep your guard up," Sam said from the side of the circle.

Bellamy barely moved. He swung the sword down in an almost comically slow fashion, and she lifted her own, bearing the limp impact. Neith felt like a child tinkering with toys.

"Good," said Sam. "Remember, when you step forward to strike, lean into the opposite leg, out of your opponent's line of attack."

Neith stepped toward Bellamy with a blow from the right. He easily knocked it aside.

"I don't understand," Petra said. "Why does someone who can wield nether need to learn sword skill?"

"Don't stop moving," Sam encouraged.

Neith and Bellamy circled each other. He winked at her before attacking on the left. She parried the blow. Then on the right. It struck her lightly on the shoulder. She dropped her arms. "At some point, you're going to have to actually hit me."

Bellamy cocked his head. "Eager for another black eye, are we?"

"Eager to be able to knock you down." Neith gripped her sword with both hands.

"Whoa ho ho." Bellamy grinned and then flashed his brows. "Come on then, Princess."

Her face twisted into a sneer. She hated it when he called her that. It started four days past, and he used it anytime he wanted to work her up. "I'm not a *princess*." She attacked, swinging left, then feigning right but striking straight from the left again. It made contact.

He pursed his lips as he walked around her, flipping his sword in his grasp. "Not bad. What else you got?" She ran at him. He avoided all her strikes, sweeping her feet out from under her with ease. She hit the ground hard on her back.

"Easy, Bellamy," Sam said, weighty with caution.

Bellamy stood over her, hand extended. "What? I'm just giving the lady what she wants."

Neith refused it, climbing to her feet on her own.

"Wasn't your mother a revered swordswoman?" Neith heard Petra taunt from somewhere behind her. She fought the urge to look back, keeping her eyes on Bellamy. "Did that skip you?"

"Petra." The warning in Sam's voice was growing. "That is too much."

"She can take it," Petra challenged.

Bellamy attacked again, making contact before Neith had a chance to ready herself. The strikes pushed her back as she struggled to defend against them. The satisfied smirk on his face sent a flare of irritation through her. She bellowed and, with all her strength, kicked him square in the chest. It wasn't enough to get him off his feet, but he stumbled back a couple of steps. Neith didn't hesitate. In a move that took even her by surprise, she turned full circle, swinging the sword down from above. The wooden blade cracked against the side of his face, and he toppled to the ground.

"That's more like it!" Petra ran into Neith's line of sight.

"I'm sorry!" Neith dropped the sword and moved to kneel beside him. "I thought you would block it."

Bellamy lay on his back, holding his face, blinking. "Well, shit, Princess. Didn't expect that." He laughed, flexing his jaw. "I think you've knocked a couple of teeth loose." He turned on his side and spat. It had a faint crimson tint.

Her hands came up on either side of her face. "I am sorry. I'll heal it."

"Don't be sorry," he said, with a toothy, bloodstained grin. "That was great. I'll let you heal it, though. Don't want to mess up this handsome face."

Neith laughed, and Petra scoffed. Neith held her hand up to his cheek to inspect the wound. She healed a small cut and the ligaments around some of his bottom teeth.

"Handsome face saved," she said, smiling. She thought it most certainly was. His thick, dark brown hair was clipped short on the sides, but left longer on top, neither curly nor straight. The constant shadow of a beard darkened his square jaw, and his hazel eyes were always jovial, but it was his smile that drew one in. It was brilliant and infectious, just like him.

Petra stood over them, hand extended. "Come, let's get something to eat before we ride out."

The sun was nearly up, the orange glow turning to daylight around them.

Sam stood with his arms crossed on the other side of the circle. "That was too rough. She's been training for four days."

"I am not made of glass." Neith smiled, attempting to jest.

Sam's face was stone, wholly unreceptive, as if he had not even heard her. "Petra, you are a member of her guard. I should not need to remind you of your only task."

Petra cocked her head. "You asked me to help train her. That is what I'm doing."

Neith looked from Petra to Sam. "I'm fine. This is what I want."

"Take it easier next time," Sam said, eyes narrowed on Bellamy. "That is not a request." He turned, marching off.

Bellamy walked up to Neith and Petra, and the three watched Sam walk away. "What was that about?" he asked.

Neith shrugged. Petra looked at her, studying, lips pursed.

"What?" Neith asked.

A slow curl formed on one side of Petra's mouth. She turned to Bellamy, and they shared a look.

"Ah, I see," he said.

"*What?*" Neith asked again.

Petra started gathering the swords into a muslin bag. "Ah, he's just moody. It's his way. I wouldn't worry about it."

Neith frowned. "Did I do something wrong?"

"No." Bellamy laughed. "A little too right, perhaps."

"What does that mean?" Neith asked, frown deepening.

Bellamy wrapped his arm around her shoulders. "Let's just say that—"

"*Bellamy.*" Petra's tone was a clear warning. He lifted his hands in submission.

"Come on." Petra gestured to Neith. "You need to eat so you can build muscle. I want to watch you knock Bellamy on his ass again."

"You want me to eat all of this?" Neith took in the large bowl of stewed beans and cabbage. She looked up to Petra, wide-eyed.

"You want to train? You have to eat." Petra left and returned with another plate of cheese, bread, and cherries.

"*This too?*"

"That too." Petra sat next to her with a similar sized portion for herself. Bellamy joined soon after.

"Neith knocked Bellamy on his ass today." Petra popped a couple cherries into her mouth, spitting out the pits.

Neith felt compelled to clarify. "It was a lucky strike," she said before taking a spoonful of the stew. It savored strongly of thyme and spring onion.

"I would like to see that." Iris reached across the table for a portion of bread.

"Iris, darling, you can have me on my back anytime you like. All you need do is ask." Bellamy raised his eyebrows in invitation. Several at the table chuckled.

Iris snatched a cherry from her plate and launched it at him. He caught it, popping the fruit in his mouth with a satisfied smirk.

"The only time I'll ever be on top of you is if I have a blade pressed to your throat." Iris pulled a dagger from her belt, twirling it between her fingers.

Bellamy shrugged. "That isn't usually what does it for me, but for you, I'd make an exception," he said, and winked.

"In your dreams, Bells." She tossed her long, pale blonde hair behind her shoulder.

"Every night."

Neith's cheeks warmed. She was growing accustomed to their banter, but on occasion it still brought about a flush. She might be inexperienced, but was not dumb to the ways of men and women. An understanding of what occurs when two of them sneak off in the night was not lost on her. Or, in Bellamy's case, sometimes three.

Neith finished half of what she was brought before conceding. "I cannot eat another bite."

"It'll get easier," Petra said. Her plate was empty.

They returned to camp to pack and found Sam gathering their horses. Their entire site had been broken down and loaded onto carts. He had made himself busy while they were eating. Once the long train of soldiers began to move, her guard and squad fell into formation.

They spoke little through the morning journey, the sun beating down on them, not a cloud in the sky. Brief respites of shade came sparingly from the odd collection of trees. They were traveling south, away from the mountains, and the terrain was changing from rocky to rolling hills. Neith wiped the sweat from her brow. The sun was now at its peak, midday upon them.

"Traveling is so dreadfully boring." Bellamy huffed. Storm tossed her head as if in agreement. "Let's race across this field and back."

"You'll tire your horse," Petra said. "We have a long day of riding ahead."

"Why must you always be so *practical*, Petra?" Bellamy groaned, and Neith bit back her smile. "A short race," he said. "We'll be back in line within an hour."

Neith looked at Sam, knowing he would not approve. He gave her a wary look. Neith's lips took on a curl, and he made a slight shake of his head. Storm nickered, tossing her head again. Neith glanced back at Bellamy and found his brows set in challenge.

"I'm in!" Neith charged off with Storm into the open field. She looked back to see Bellamy, Max, and Ayla on her heels.

"Let's go, Storm!" Neith urged her on. She closed her eyes and inhaled. It was fresh and light, all grass and sun. Neith was not the strongest rider, but Storm made up for her inadequacies. The only sounds were howls of excitement and thudding hooves.

The field sloped down, and Neith spotted a small pond in the distance. Someone approached on her left, and she looked over to see Bellamy sporting a broad grin. "To the pond?"

"To the pond!"

He edged her out right as they reached it. Max and Ayla weren't far behind. They dismounted, breathless, but thrilled.

Clusters of short trees enclosed the pond on all sides. Lily pads and other greenery covered the water, which carried the slight scent of stagnation, though it wasn't unpleasant. They led their horses to the trees, letting them drink and rest. Max and Ayla walked a short distance, hand in hand, no longer concealing their attachment.

"Well," Bellamy said, looking around, "that was over fast." He removed his boots and tunic, walking knee-deep into the water. He splashed it over his face, shaking out his hair.

"You're a good rider," Neith said to him.

"My family bred horses in Balta."

Neith pulled off her boots, rolling her black trousers to the knees. "How old were you when you left?" She stepped into the cool water and had to fight the desire to dive in.

"Thirteen."

She tried to remember how many winters he had. Twenty and one, if her memory served. "How is your jaw?" she asked, with a sly smile, taking a seat at the water's edge.

He chuckled as he emerged from the pond. "Joining in the banter now, are we?"

Neith shrugged. "Attempting to."

Bellamy smiled, and Neith took in the dimples etched into both cheeks. She well understood why he did not want for admirers. He took a seat next to her, using his tunic to wipe the water from his face.

"What was it like?" she asked.

Bellamy frowned.

"Living nomad in Balta," Neith clarified. Bellamy and Sam were the first nomad Etherborns she'd known. It was a life she was largely unfamiliar, though desperately fascinated, with. It was a wild concept. Living outside of order among the idleborn.

He turned to look at her, brows creased as if surprised by the question. He studied her for a breath before turning back to the pond. "Quiet, peaceful. We lived in the countryside. My grandfather started a horse farm when he left the Citadel."

That piqued her interest. "Why did he leave?" She only realized it might be an inappropriate question after it left her lips. He seemed unbothered by the familiarity of it.

"He hated the Esērii, but I never knew why. He never wished to talk about it."

"He is not alone in that. Many do." Neith lifted her hair from her neck, letting the damp skin breathe. "My father has built an army from it."

"Was," Bellamy corrected. "Was not alone. He died many years ago."

"Oh. I am sorry. I did not mean to pry," she said, now regretting her inquiry.

He gave her half a smile and shrugged. Neith sensed there was much more to his feelings than what showed on the surface. He tossed a pebble at her. "I do not mind. Pry away."

She envied that. The openness. It was becoming clear to her that if she wanted friendships, she would have to find a way to overcome her avoidance of it. "Did you have contact with the Esērii?"

"They would come to see us once a year, but Grandfather said they were always watching. They would try to convince him to come back or, at the least, send me. My parents are not Etherborn, you see. Neither is my brother." Bellamy rolled his head in a circle, stretching his neck.

Neith watched damselflies dance on the water. She recalled the sketched image of the narrow-winged northern damselfly, with its distinguishable green wings, from her favorite book as a child. "How did you come to be in Thrane?"

"Civil war. My mother wanted to leave, but my grandfather refused, and she would not leave him behind. I was twelve, but my brother only four. I think she feared having me on her own, without Grandfather." He paused for a moment, skipping pebbles across the pond's surface. Neith well knew the feeling of being the source of another's fear. It was isolating, and she could only imagine how so if it was one's own kin. She saw the feeling reflected in his eyes. "My father left us to fight in the war. He didn't return. Grandfather died the following year."

"I am sorry, Bellamy," she said. She thought to reach for his hand, but feared he may find her uncouth.

He skipped another rock. It bounced further than its predecessors. "Losing the ones we love is inevitable. All we can do is be grateful for the time we share with them." It was the first time she'd seen him serious, much less melancholy. She wished she could relieve him of it. It was a great deal of loss for someone so young, and she admired how he governed it. Not allowing it to cull his spirit. It made her see him differently. Deeper. "Not long after Grandfather died, a Thranean soldier turned up on our doorstep. Barton, was his name. He offered us a place in Necrium, safety for my mother and brother if I chose to join. The war in Balta was growing worse, and I knew it was what my mother wanted."

"What did you want?"

He skipped another rock. "I wanted them to be safe."

"Thrane seems a far different place from Balta. It could not have been easy." Neith still worried she asked too much, but Bellamy seemed more at ease than she. She kept her stories, her feelings, strapped close to her chest. Only letting them escape in small, strange doses. Usually at the wrong time. More often than not, she felt she could not find words that fit.

"It wasn't," he admitted. "Most of the others my age had grown up in Necrium. It wasn't easy to find friends. Not at first. Grandfather had trained me to wield and Father in sword skill, so I at least had that advantage."

Neith now understood how this charming person came to be, formed from necessity. She saw what was beneath the smiles and jest. Someone good, generous, and kind. She could not help but feel she did not deserve someone like him in her service.

"Why did we never see you in Necrium? We saw much of your brother." He pulled a waterskin from his pack, taking a long drink. "You were always something of a mystery."

"If I wasn't training, I was studying. Tutors were my constant companions." Neith pulled her knees up as a rest for her arms. "And my father feared discovery."

"That sounds a rather lonely childhood."

Neith shrugged. "I haven't thought about it." Except she very much had the past halfmoon. Watching the others bond and laugh had made her acutely aware of a part of life she had missed out on.

The sounds of a galloping horse pulled their attention. Sam appeared on the crest of the hill.

"Fun's over," Bellamy said, nudging her with an elbow.

"Stop that," she said, trying not to laugh. "He is only doing what he was tasked to. A task he did not ask for. I am not making it easy for him."

Bellamy shook his head. "You are far too understanding for your own good."

"And you're far too charming for *your* own good." She pushed him playfully, and he grinned.

"Be sure to tell all the women you meet."

"You're falling behind," Sam called down from the hilltop.

Bellamy sighed, standing. He held out his hands to help Neith rise.

"Back in line, Lieutenant." He turned, but she reached for his arm. He looked down at the contact with creased brows.

"Thank you," she said. "For sharing your story with me."

The frown on him deepened. He made a strange sound, not quite a huff, but something more drawn from surprise. She thought he would speak, but he simply smiled and nodded, then made for his horse.

Neith wasn't sure what it meant, but she did not think it was bad. She brushed the grass from her trousers and stepped into her boots. Max and Ayla were already on their horses, trotting back toward the line.

"I'll meet you back there," she said.

Bellamy looked from her to Sam, where he waited on the hill. He grinned and mounted his horse, giving her a teasing wink before riding off.

When she and Storm peaked the hill, she greeted Sam with a grin of her own, playful but apologetic. He looked away, jaw flexing to fight the bend in his lips. His tawny skin glowed under the blazing sun. As if it were made to live beneath it. Or perhaps forged from it. When he looked back, the hint of the smile faded. "I want to apologize for the way I acted earlier. I know you're not… *fragile*. I only—"

"You're trying to do what you've been assigned to." Neith looked down the long line of soldiers in the distance. "I will try not to make it a difficult task for you."

Sam stiffened, and it looked unnatural. She disliked being the cause of it. "It is not that," he said, though the tautness of his brow said otherwise.

"You are not happy in this post." Neith held up her hand before he could protest. "I do not blame you for that. You should be in command of soldiers. As you were. That is lost on no one. Especially me. Magnus still relies on you. You're doing half the work I should already know how to do as lieutenant. You are stretched thin." When he didn't argue, she continued. "Petra and Bellamy can oversee my training on their own. I can at least do that for you. It was selfish of me to ask."

"I don't want to stop."

"I will make sure it doesn't go too far. You needn't worry—"

"I don't *want* to stop." He looked surprised, as if his voice rose louder than he'd intended.

Neith's lips parted but quickly rejoined. She had no words. She stared at him, trying to make sense of his disposition. The tightness in his features softened, and it did something to her. Something she didn't quite understand.

Sam sighed and ran a hand through his curls. "I like to see you smile," he said, with a startling openness that sent her further spinning. "Training makes you happy, and…" His amber eyes were downcast, perhaps uncertain, but not sad, she thought. When his eyes met hers again, he gave her the same look he had the night by the river. It made her breath, her heart, and other parts of her, quicken. The look, his words. He sighed again, but this one lacked the uneasiness of the one before. He held her gaze and said, "I would very much like to be your friend."

"I would like that." The words left her lips like a whisper, but quickly. "I would like that very much."

Sam smiled, and it inspired her own. They stared at each other for a moment before he held out his hand. "Friends?"

"Friends," she said, taking it. He was warm, his grasp tight. His power poured out, or she pulled it. She couldn't be sure. It came in a rush, traveling up her arm and into her chest. His eyes told her he felt it, too. He let go, looking back toward the line.

"We should get back," he said, turning his horse and trotting off.

They rode back to formation, falling in place at the front of their squad. Her thoughts continually found their way back to what he said. The way he looked at her. She was unsure how to interpret his intention. He had said *friend*, but she was sure his eyes had said something different.

When she could no longer fight the temptation, she glanced at him, assuming she would find his gaze forward, as it had been all times before. But this time, he returned the look. There was apprehension, but also a smile. A small smile, just for her.

23

Thea

"Truth, even when cold and hard to bear, is warmer than a well-dressed lie."

AUTHOR UNKNOWN, C. 1500 BQ
TRANSLATED FROM SUMACIAN BY PARRY HAVERFORD
HAIS Z'NOSIŠ, 1204 AQ
RECOVERED 1203 AQ, SOMOS

Thea received a formal invitation from Lady Starling for afternoon tea at her lodgings in the city. Her father granted permission, but under the condition that Sylvie accompany her. In a carriage. Under guard. It felt excessive, but given recent events, she lacked the courage to press her luck. Thea did not receive many invitations. It had meant so much to her that she tucked the handwritten note in her favorite book so she could pull it out and reread it anytime she pleased.

The two women rocked back and forth to the sound of hooves on cobblestone. Thea adjusted the window cover so she could peek out. Some of the common folk paused their pursuits to bow at the passing of a royal carriage. They did not know it was only the bastard inside.

In the days since the wedding, save for the absence of Marten, High-clere had returned to its ordinary routines. Thea had not divulged what she saw in the woods. If Breeda had taken notice of her, she'd given no indication.

She kept herself busy helping Leanne with the children, gardening, and reading. And drinking with her brother. When she became idle, her mind turned to questions. Had she done the right thing? Would she regret her decision? Her stomach churned at thoughts of the future. She wondered how Marten was faring. She told herself all would resolve. Only time was required.

The carriage stopped at a multistory townhouse in the center of the city. Ivy grew tall on its pale blue stone walls. Potted plants and flowers sat on the stairs, window ledges, and other surfaces, most of which Thea could identify. She thought it was exactly the type of home she would choose for herself. Not that it would ever be something she could do.

She insisted Sylvie join her inside, but she could not be convinced.

Thea was greeted by a member of Lady Starling's household staff and shown to an elaborately decorated sitting room. Floral tapestries in hues of soft blues and pinks hung on the walls. There was only one painting. A portrait of a young woman in an outdated, but extravagant gown. She had long blonde hair, a pretty face, and an even finer figure.

She was still gazing around when the door opened. She stood when Lady Starling emerged, bracing on her cane, a silk lavender shawl draped over her shoulders. Her gray hair was down, brushed out in soft waves. It was uncommonly long and thick for a woman her age.

"How are you, my dear?" she asked, her voice as bright as the large clusters of diamonds adorning both ears.

"I am quite well, thank you, Lady Starling." Thea walked across the room to kiss her cheeks.

"Call me Dianna, please." She smiled, her blue eyes kind. "Come, let's sit."

Attendants followed Dianna into the room, crowding the small table between them with platters of sandwiches, fruits, and small cakes. Thea looked them over, her belly growling at the sight. It was enough to feed ten.

"I'm a bit indulgent these days, I'm afraid," Dianna said. "One finds there isn't much else to do but eat when you're as old as I."

A pretty young girl with brown hair and a freckled face filled their cups from a steaming teapot. "Will there be anything else, my lady?"

Dianna smiled at her. "No, thank you, Nerissa dear. We have all we need."

The girl curtsied, then turned to Thea, repeating the gesture.

Thea reached for the honey, stirring a heaping spoon into her cup. She eyed the spread before her, deciding on a lemon cake first. She sighed at the bright, sugary aroma that wafted under her nose. "This is lovely, Dianna. Thank you for the invitation."

"You are most welcome." Dianna sipped her tea, watching Thea eat. It did not feel like an examination, more like a motherly affection. Thea could not help but like it.

"Why do you not stay in the castle?" Thea asked, using her thumb to brush icing from the corner of her mouth. "I'm sure my father would be happy to provide you with rooms when you visit Highclere. You do not need to lease a home in the city."

"This house is mine," Dianna said before sipping from her cup. A brow was quirked, ever-so-slight, as if there was a story to tell.

"Oh. I did not know." She looked around the room. "It is a *beautiful* home."

"Thank you." Dianna returned her cup to the table and stacked a variety of small sandwiches on her plate. "I've owned it since shortly before I was married."

Thea was unsure how that was possible. Noble women were not permitted to hold property unless it belonged to a title. Even that was rarely granted. She thought to ask, but felt it might be impertinent. Thea sipped her tea. It was exotic and spiced, with notes of orange and cinnamon.

"Tell me how you are, my dear."

Thea frowned. Dianna had already asked. "I am well."

"You needn't hide yourself here, child." Her expression was light, but sincere.

Thea sat up. "I—don't know what you mean."

Dianna sighed as her fingers tapped on the wooden edge of her chair. "This house was a gift."

"That's quite a gift," Thea said, grateful for the change in topic.

"Yes, it was." Dianna looked at her, considering. "It was a gift from your grandfather."

Thea set her teacup on the table. Domnall Ironne died in the war before she was born. Stories were all she had to build a construct of his character. The portrait in the gallery showed a tall man with an imposing physique. He preferred an ax to a sword and always fought on the front line. He was known as a man of few words, a stoic to most. But a good king, well respected by his allies and foes. Her father once told her something Domnall had said to him when he'd come of age. "To lead men, you must have the gift of words or steel. If you cannot speak to inspire, you must fight to. It is no secret which I lack." It had made her believe she would have liked him. When she received no explanation, she asked, "As a… wedding gift?"

"Something like that." The older woman gave the impression she was considering what to say, or perhaps *how* to say it.

Thea frowned, trying to uncover what she was missing.

"Williard," Dianna called toward the door.

The door creaked, and an old man limped into the room. Thea thought he could be twenty years Dianna's elder. He was dressed in a traditional butler's uniform, something one did not often see in the present day. But the material was expensive, and his boots were brand new. Thea had also noticed the dress Nerissa wore was a good deal nicer than an attendant could typically afford. Whatever Dianna was paying her staff, it was well above the going rate.

"Yes, my lady?" the man asked as he rounded the table.

"My young friend and I require something a bit *stiffer* for our conversation. Will you be a dear and bring us a bottle of something nice? You choose." She spoke to Williard, but her eyes were on Thea.

"Of course, my lady." He inclined his head, and Thea watched him exit at the same leisurely pace he entered.

Thea sat quietly, intrigued and a bit nervous to hear whatever was going to be revealed. Her father was often tight-lipped about the past.

Williard returned with an elegant bottle and two glasses. "A '94 rouge de grat, from the southern Ostallan coast," he said as he poured. "Will there be anything else, my lady?"

"No, thank you, Williard," Dianna said, and smiled. "I think this will see us through the afternoon."

When the door hitched behind him, Dianna grabbed her glass and took a healthy drink. Thea did the same.

"This house was a gift from my lover."

Thea choked, wine splashing up her nose.

"Oh, my dear." Dianna reached for a napkin, tossing it across the table. "Forgive me, I was never one for polite conversation, and it has only worsened with age."

"No, please." Thea wiped the wine from her chin. "I assure you it offends me in no way. It was only unexpected." She looked at Dianna, acutely absorbed.

"When I was seventeen, I was brought to court by my father in hopes I would catch the eye of a lord or a wealthy merchant." She pointed at the solitary painting in the room. "You see, I was considered quite fair then, not that you can tell underneath all these wrinkles." She tossed her hand aimlessly through the air, and Thea smiled. "I had no desire to wed, but as you well know, even today, our desires mean little as women. When it was the attention of the young king I caught, well, my father was less than pleased. I had no delusion he and I would ever marry." She chuckled lightly to herself. "We were so young. Like you are now, my dear."

Thea hung on every word. Riveted by the scandal of it, but also the secrecy. She had never heard it spoken of, not even hinted at. But she supposed that made sense. Thea's own situation had been challenging enough. She could not imagine what Dianna would have had to endure in that time.

"We did love one another, I think. It was certainly a passionate affair. But more importantly, we understood one another. We were friends. The best of. You need friends in this life, Thea. It was your grandfather himself who arranged my marriage. Lord Starling was a wealthy man, never married, no children." Dianna leaned forward in her chair. "You see, his preferences toward the goings-on in his bedroom were not especially inclined toward women. He was wed to me as a favor. A request of his king. My father was satisfied. It was the perfect solution."

Thea was leaning so far forward in her chair that she jumped back when she felt it start to tilt.

"In time, Domnall was married, had children, your father among them. He had a full life outside of the one we shared. I did, too, in my own way. But we still had ours. We even had a daughter." She paused, her lips thinning. "Though she only lived a few short days."

"I am so sorry," Thea said. Her mind was in a flurry from the story, caught in its highs and lows. "I had no idea."

"Oh, don't be sorry. I've lived a life of peace and luxury, as my own woman. Neither your father nor his brothers knew of me, nor did your grandmother. The only souls who knew were Lord Starling, and the people who worked in this home. I'm quite good at keeping secrets. As I suspect you are, too."

Thea smiled. "I believe I am."

"So you see, my dear, I understand what you are going through. If there were ever any secrets you needed kept, you could come to me. Aremore is not far from Dunclere."

Thea set her wine on the table. "I see."

"Let me ask you again. How are you?"

Thea swallowed, and the wall she'd built cracked, swelling her eyes. She had pushed it all so far from her mind that the thought of him now brought a rush of emotion crashing through. "Well, I try not to think of it."

Dianna nodded. "That is probably what is best." She reached for her glass, turning it a few times in her hand before looking up. "But it is not your only avenue. I cannot say what is right for you. I can only advise you not to deny yourself something you want. Something that brings you happiness. Life is painfully short, Calithea. Take it from someone nearing the end of theirs."

Thea held her gaze, considering her words. Dianna lived a content, full life. She'd found a way to have the man she loved, or at least the man she'd chosen. But Thea knew she was not her. She did not believe it would be enough. Even then, as she ached for him.

"And I'll leave it at that." Dianna reached forward, patting her hand across the table.

They talked for an hour over two more lemon cakes and another glass of wine.

Dianna yawned. "You'll have to excuse this old woman. I grow weary in my older years, and an afternoon nap calls to me."

"Of course." Thea stood, offering her arm to Dianna. "Thank you. For your company and for your kindness. It is nice to feel understood."

"Oh, my dear," she said, squeezing Thea's arm. "Do not thank me for such small things. Your expectations should be much higher than that." She reached up and touched Thea's cheek. "You will always be welcome in any of my homes. Accompanied or not. For whatever you need. I mean that." She grabbed her cane, leaning into it. "Please come and see me in Dunclere."

"I would like that very much." She would. But her father would never allow it.

The carriage waited where she'd left it. Sylvie sat on the driver's bench reading, feet propped up.

"Pleasant time?" she asked, looking up from her book.

Thea smiled to herself. "Quite."

Thea had made plans with her sister to go riding when she returned from tea. It was something they had done together since childhood, both accomplished horsewomen. They would go to the open fields southeast of the city and ride until they tired their horses. Often staying out until close to sunset.

She was stepping out of the carriage in the castle's courtyard when clamoring hooves stormed through the gates, capturing the attention of all.

"I have a message for the king!" The rider dismounted in a fury, not bothering to pass off the reins of his horse before sprinting into the castle.

Thea and Sylvie exchanged a look. She couldn't remember a time when someone arrived with such haste. Her mind flooded with possibilities, none of them a comfort. She took off into the castle in pursuit.

The man ran at a pace Thea could not keep. She followed the muddy imprints of his boots through the halls until she saw her father enter the council room, doors closing behind him.

Thea sprinted down the corridor, but the two guards standing by barred her entry. She frowned and took a seat on a bench, fingers tapping the cool marble. She looked around, unsure where Sylvie had gone. Not long after, Callum came racing down the hall.

"What is it?" he asked. "I was told of a rider." He looked from her on the bench to the guards. Sweat beaded and trailed down his face as he unbuckled the leather gauntlets on his arms.

"I don't know. I saw him come in. He is with Father now," Thea said, pointing to the door. Callum approached to gain entry, but the soldiers barred the path.

"Step aside," Callum ordered.

"I'm sorry, Your Highness, we are under instruction from the king not to permit entry."

"Step aside," he repeated, with increased command. The guards looked nervously at one another, but neither relented.

"Callum," Thea said, "for Godssake. Sit down."

He grumbled but took a seat beside her. "Did you recognize the man?"

"No, it happened quickly. I didn't have time to make out his face."

"What was he wearing?"

"I don't know." Thea shook her head. "Our colors, perhaps?"

"Was he a soldier or a messenger?"

She widened her eyes and spoke firmly. "*Callum.* I do not know."

He grimaced. "Sorry."

"It is all right," she said, exhaling. "I am nervous, too."

Thea could not measure the time passed before the doors swung open, and the same man, whom they could clearly see now as a soldier, exited the room. Exhaustion plagued his features. He had ridden long to deliver whatever news it was that put such fear in his eyes.

Commander Orin Pryde followed. The older man looked worn and wary. Thea watched him cover it upon seeing them. He stopped, inclining his head. "Your Highness, my lady."

"Commander." Thea curtsied. "Is all well? We saw the rider."

He smiled, but it was half-hearted. "Quite well, my lady. No cause for concern." The lines around his eyes drew tighter. "If you'll excuse me." The commander inclined his head again and turned to follow the path the messenger had taken. Thea and Callum looked at one another before taking off toward the door.

When she entered the council room, Thea could have sworn she had seen a glimpse of Sylvie's red curly hair disappearing through the back. She shook off the notion as ridiculous because it was. Their father was seated alone at the head of the council table, his easy demeanor taking Thea by surprise. He did not seem like one who'd received news of the unfavorable sort.

"Ah," he said as he looked up from the parchment in his hands. "Why am I not surprised to find you two dawdling outside the door?"

"What is it?" Callum asked.

"What is what?"

Callum huffed. "The *news*, Father."

"Oh, some minor disputes on the northern border of Straeth. Nothing of concern." He brushed it off, turning back to the documents spread out on the table.

"The messenger seemed awfully concerned," Thea said.

"Did he? Well, the concerns of a soldier are quite different from yours, are they not?" His tone was teasing, and he glanced up under heavy brows to give them a playful smirk.

Thea groaned. "*Father*, you know what we mean. He stormed in here screaming for you." She threw her arms up on either side. "It put us in a fright."

Ulric stood and rounded the table. He lifted his hand to cup her cheek. "It is nothing," he said, and smiled. "I assure you. Do not trouble yourselves with worry." He kissed her head and patted Callum on the shoulder before taking his leave.

The two stood in perplexity as the door closed behind him.

"Did he just lie to us?" Callum asked.

Thea turned to look at her brother. "I believe he did."

"Why would he do that?" Callum narrowed his eyes in the direction their father had taken, as if searching for an answer that might have fallen off as he fled.

Thea shrugged. "You heard him. The concerns of a soldier are not the same as ours. Does this not also apply to a king?"

The family moved back to the royal dining chamber, now all guests had departed Highclere. Leanne allowed Henri and Lucienne to join even though it was well past their bedtime. The mood was jovial and upbeat. Evelynde boasted about the successes of the wedding. The twins recounted, with spirited enthusiasm, the day's lesson about the Godswar and Akvar the Bold's great victory at Evoire. Thea thought they all must have missed their family dinners as much as she.

The cook announced the meal as roasted goose with a parsnip puree and an assortment of root vegetables. Her belly growled at the sight of the still-steaming food, having worked up quite the appetite. She and Cat had ridden long, bareback as they always did. Her thighs and backside ached, but it had been worth it. The carrots were sweet, and she helped herself to seconds, unable to consume another bite until a raspberry pie appeared. Her favorite. They dined, laughed, danced, and jested. It was a wonderfully ordinary night, and Thea didn't want it to end.

Cat, Leanne, nor Evelynde seemed to know about the rider. She and Callum had agreed to keep it between them until they understood what it was. They'd not burden another with worry if there truly was no threat. And if there was, they had no helpful information to support it. The only person who seemed out of sorts was Conall. Though never boisterous, he was even quieter that night. He ate little and spoke less. When Leanne looked at him, he would smile. If someone addressed him, he replied. But it felt performative. Far more than was routine. *Strange things*, she heard in her sister's voice. Thea wondered what Conall was privy to that the rest of them were not.

She looked to the seat on the end where Marten would often sit. It felt bizarre to simply carry on with her life like nothing had happened. Like she wasn't heartbroken. But she didn't know what else to do. There was nothing but what she did before, only without him. One moment she was laughing, only for the pain in her chest to strike again, reminding her of what she'd lost.

She'd declined her brother's offer to the Iren Stein, choosing instead to retire early. Something she did not often do. She was running a brush through her hair, thinking, while Sylvie prepared the bed.

"Sylvie," she said, setting the brush on the dressing table, turning toward her.

"Hmm?"

"You said you saw them bury the mountain cat, yes?"

Sylvie straightened, releasing the pillow she'd been fluffing. "I did."

"Will you take me there in the morning? I wish to see where it was buried."

Sylvie frowned. "That is an odd request, but if you wish."

Thea had expected hesitation or refusal, but Sylvie had given her neither. It wasn't that Thea suspected Sylvie of lying, but it had been nearly a sixday, and something in the back of her mind needed convincing. Of what she wasn't sure. She pinched the space between her eyes. Wild thoughts were driving her head to ache.

"Are you all right?" Sylvie asked, crossing the room. She held the back of her hand to Thea's forehead, then cheek.

"Yes, I think so." Thea sighed. "Though I feel a little on edge."

"I'll go down to the kitchens and make you a cup of chamomile." Sylvie gave her shoulder a quick squeeze. "It will help you sleep."

Thea nodded and smiled. Whatever notions of deception she had been feeling passed. She laughed at herself for the suspicion.

Thea and Sylvie walked together, stepping over fallen branches and other arboreal debris. Sylvie had said the grave wasn't far, but in an inconspicuous spot where others were unlikely to stumble over it.

Half an hour had passed before Sylvie stopped, looking around. She pointed out a short distance in front of them. "There."

Between the trees in a small clearing was an oval area of disturbed earth. A few leaves and small branches had fallen to cover it, but it showed clear indications of a recently dug grave. Thea knelt over it, running the crumbling dirt between her fingers.

"Is there something you're looking for?" Sylvie asked.

Thea sighed. "I don't know. I can't explain. I wanted to see it."

Sylvie knelt beside her. She had a look Thea had not seen before. Behind the shroud of composure, she sensed concern, and what she thought might be fear. Sylvie had a talent for reading her, so Thea worked hard to strike the suspicion from her mind so it would not show on her face. "And now that you have?"

Thea shrugged and stood, brushing the dirt from her hands. "I suppose I'll move on now." That was the first time she lied to her friend.

24

Nara

"A council of six shall be named. To guide, to govern, to rule."

ESĒRII BIJRAH Z'OURA
ADE NYANTHI AND PHILOMENA TALIESIN, 805 AQ

They'd departed for the Citadel two days past, stopping twice for fresh horses at the outposts between cities. Nara rode straight through both nights, Harker having fallen behind the evening prior. The only thing that trailed Nara now was a long plume of dust kicked up by her galloping horse. Its hooves thumped against the dry, sandy soil.

There were no trees in which to take shade. No rivers from which to drink. Not that Nara would stop for either. Sweat pooled in every bend, every curve of her body, falling down the length of her in quick, thin paths. Her hips ached and her belly growled, but still she pressed.

The sun was high on the third day of travel when the Citadel revealed itself to her in the distance. Its tall, golden walls appeared a mirage, blending in with the honey-colored mountains and rocky plateaus running peak to peak. No matter how many times she'd ridden in, the beauty of it still struck her.

The sun poured over it all, nearly blinding, reflecting the pyrite, citrine, and other aureate hues flecked throughout the sandstone structures. The tall spires of the palace peeked over its walls, gold-tipped and shining, like a beacon for those lost in the sandy sea surrounding it.

There were four gates one could use to enter the Citadel, all varying in their anonymity. Nara made way for the most inconspicuous.

As she approached, a guard waved down from the wall, and the gate swung open. Nara slowed her horse, trotting through its narrow passage where a groom waited.

"He needs rest," Nara said, patting the worn animal. "I asked much of him." She leapt from the saddle and her legs nearly buckled when she hit the ground. The only thing keeping her upright was the urgency that had lived in her the past twelve days. It never tired, even when she did.

"Chancellor—sorry—Citizen Nyanthi, do you require medical attention?" The groom, a boy as Nara could now see him to be, looked up at her with alarm.

"No." She leaned forward, bracing on her thighs. "But have you water?" She'd run out the night before.

The boy nodded and ran to the gate station. Several uniformed guards emerged, eyes in her direction, as if to find the cause for the boy's hasty manner. Nara held up her hand to ward them off. The boy returned with a sprint, passing her a heavy skin. It was the best drink of her life. Nara took in every last delightful drop.

"Thank you," she said as she wiped her face. She passed the skin back to the bewildered boy and started toward the palace.

Vivid tones of gold, green, and blue overwhelmed the senses. Dozens were strolling in their brightly colored robes through the gardens that spread out before the main entrance of the palace. Their distant chatter made for a dull hum against the soft streaming of the winding canals. The crystal water sparkled, giving life to the abundance of trees, shrubbery, and floral vegetation that covered the grounds. The palace gave no indication of the bustling city that existed beyond it. It was peaceful in a way she was not. But it was home.

Nara avoided the gardens, darting down the passage running between the north side of the palace and the mountains, making for a utility entrance near to the council chambers.

She passed few citizens on the trek, but their disconcerted eyes told her all she needed. It was not uncommon to see citizens in various states of disarray in the Citadel, so Nara thought she must truly look a ghastly sight.

The entrance now before her, her hasty walk turned to a light jog. She climbed the stairs to the door by two. As she reached for its handle, it swung open, and a woman emerged. The woman jumped, startled by the swiftness and unexpected proximity as Nara passed by, their shoulders grazing.

Nara walked the long corridor, passing storage rooms and supply stations, grateful for the break from the sun. The sand stuck to her sandals felt gritty against the polished marble floor. The simple, painted walls grew more decorated as she continued until the corridor opened into a large chamber. Sunlight poured in from the painted glass domed roof above. One of dozens in the palace. The open space was full of citizens, orderly and clean in their robes and gowns. Some paused their activity to appraise her disordered appearance.

Nara turned into another corridor, this one lined with offices and council rooms. She emerged into another, more elaborately adorned, lobby and was immediately assaulted by the chatter of those queued to see the council. Each voice bounced around, the racket competing in volume with the droning in her head.

She stalked past the long line of would-be petitioners, toward the guards flanking either side of the bronze double doors. Nara didn't wait for permission. She started to go between, but was met with crossed spears in her path.

"I have urgent news," she said, with warning.

They didn't yield.

"*Make way.*" Every time her heart beat it pulsed between her eyes. She blinked, the commotion around and within her starting to distort her senses.

"*Citizen Nyanthi*, what are you doing?"

Nara turned to see Tyr, the palace chamberlain. "The council is in session," he said, his dark brown eyes full of reprimand. He looked her over from head to toe, the scold in his brow twisting into bemusement as his gaze descended. "What in the Gods—"

Nara gripped his shoulders. "I need to speak to them *now*. I have been on the road nearly a halfmoon. I am tired, thirsty, and in no mood to explain. Unless you wish me to pick a fight in this polished hall, you will go inside and bid them see me. *Immediately.*"

Tyr stepped back, swatting at her hands on him. "One does not dictate when the council will see them, Nara Nyanthi. Not even you." The middle-aged man frowned. His dark hair was slicked back, not a strand disarrayed. He straightened the shoulders of his white robes she had displaced.

Nara took a slow, grounding breath. She was so tired she felt herself swaying on her feet. She leaned forward to whisper in his ear. "Even if one brings news of Thrane?"

He stepped back and peered at her with a look to challenge her sincerity.

Nara shook her head. "Not in jest."

Taking in the gravity, he ordered the guards aside. "Wait here," he demanded, glancing over his shoulder at her.

The doors closed behind him, and Nara turned around only to be met with disparaging looks. Citizens waited for hours to see the council, and there she was, queue-jumping. She folded her arms over her chest, daring someone to test her.

Nara hadn't slept, bathed, or eaten properly in a sixday, and the neglect was finally catching up with her. She leaned against a wall, but was fearful to slacken, worried she would not rise again. She stared at the fountain standing center of the room. It was new. An ornate and detailed statue of a woman, twice her height, stood with her hands reaching to the sky. Water poured from her palms, as if it were ether.

Nara was reminded of the time when she was ten, when she added beads of soap to a fountain in the Commons, turning it into a bubbling mess. She and Cerys were scolded endlessly and not allowed sweets for three moons. But Nara had felt it had been worth it. If only to see the look on her grandmother's face.

The doors opened, and she stood. Tyr gestured her through. She passed an older woman who gave her an irritated look. No doubt angry her time was cut short.

The six members of the High Council of the Esērii sat at their platformed table, watching her approach. The expansive room held hundreds of seats between the floor and balcony, but not a single one was occupied. It was quiet, save for their footsteps. Dust and sand fell from her body as Nara followed Tyr past the myriad of rows of oak benches.

She stopped directly before the dais and bowed her head.

"Have we misheard, Citizen Nyanthi?" Lazlo asked, leaning over the table. His robes were a bright green, and his gray hair was shorter than the last time she had seen him. "For Tyr says you've news of Thrane."

"You have not." Nara looked at each of their faces, watching them grow firm.

"Need we pry it from you? Speak, girl," Delphane urged, leaning back in her chair.

Nara took a breath, collecting her thoughts. She recalled the events from the explosion to her and Harker's arrival back in Amul. Unlike when she had told the story in Rahab, no one asked questions.

"They were looking for the child. They split up, and we followed three to the house we collected from. The father had been murdered by the time we arrived." Rage washed through her at the memory of his body lying lifeless on the bloodied ground, mallet still in hand. "I entered the house, killed two, and held the third for questioning. She was a Seer, or claimed to be, at least. She said they were collecting for Thrane and had been for years."

All six consuls stared at her. Thoughts churned behind their eyes, but none gave a meaningful reaction.

"The other three caught up to us. I exchanged Harker for the girl, and they rode off." It was the shortest version she could construct.

"Have you any tangible evidence they were from Thrane? Could they not have been nomads, playing you for fools?" Delphane asked, her dark brown eyes constricting. "Perhaps they followed you." Her straight brown hair was pulled back into a slick bun. She was the youngest member of the council, and her years were somewhere in the fifties.

"They were uniformed and organized. It did not seem a falsehood to me." Nara reached into a pocket of her skirt and stepped onto the dais, placing the Thranean patch on the table runner in front of Seraphine, then returned to her place.

Seraphine picked it up, turning it in her hands before passing it along. Again, Nara sensed an intentionally controlled reaction. Someone gently tapped their foot.

"Wystan Barton was in command of the operation." That sent all eyes flicking to hers. "They were, with intention, no longer trying to conceal their identity, nor activity."

Lazlo sneered. "I'd hoped never to hear his name again."

Each council member studied the patch. Delphane, at the end, studied it longest.

"What other information have you?" Seraphine asked, her face creased with more lines than the ones time had imposed. Her silver hair was braided loose around the crown of her head. It softened the look of concern now etched on her.

"They headed west on horseback, so likely did not travel far. The girl's name was Thalie. Barton's daughter." Nara took a breath, trying to force out the frenzied energy still crowding her chest.

The council continued asking questions for the better part of an hour before satisfied Nara could tell them nothing else.

"Where are the others in your party?" Seraphine inquired.

"My mother returned to Amul to contain the aftermath and provide aid. She and Sanne will return with the child in a sixday's time. Harker is a half day's ride behind me. I rode straight through from Kurk."

"You must be exhausted, child," Desme said. "You should go and rest. We will discuss all that you have told us and call for you later."

Rest was the last thing Nara was interested in. She frowned. She had been on the road for twelve days, given them such news as she had, and this was it? *Go and rest?* "I am fine. What are we going to do?"

"*We* aren't going to do anything," Delphane said. "The *council* will discuss what you have told us and then decide what to do."

"Consul Durand, with all due respect—"

Delphane held up her hand, peering down at her. "I despise when someone starts their words *with all due respect.* It means they are about to say something that utterly lacks it."

Nara flexed her jaw. She looked at each of their faces, searching for an ally, finding none. "There isn't time," she urged. "If they are brazenly attacking here, they are most certainly doing so in the north." Nara shook her head, the frantic energy reemerging. "This isn't the first time they've done this, only the first time they did not try to conceal it. Do you not understand what that means?"

"You are overworked, child. You need to rest." Seraphine looked at her with understanding, but her voice held a subtle warning.

"Send me," Nara pleaded. "I can be in the north in—"

"Need I remind you, Citizen Nyanthi, you are no longer a chancellor? Concerns of political and militaristic unrest no longer fall under your concern," Phelen added. He was the newest member, having been made consul only two years prior. He was still trying to assert his authority at every turn.

Nara gaped at them. She had expected an uproar. Outrage. She thought back to all Meriah had told her. Their reaction confirmed what they'd suspected. "I do not think Esērii in the field will be comforted to know their council sits idle under such news." She couldn't keep the contempt from her tone.

"Nara," Desme warned. "Mind yourself."

Nara wanted to scream her suspicions at them, but she could not expose Meriah, nor Alec. Instead, she glared.

Desme stood. "Go and wait for me in my chambers."

"But I—"

Desme leaned over the table, her face more serious than Nara had ever seen it. "Go, *now.*"

"This is horseshit!" Nara's hands balled into fists at her side, but she turned and stormed out.

It must have been an hour she waited, pacing the small reception room in Desme's chambers. An attendant brought her food, which she eyed. It wasn't long before the alluring aromas of coconut and ginger wafting up through the steam won her over. Nara was finishing up the stew of chickpeas and squash when Desme arrived.

The older woman eyed her. "In my office," was all she said as she walked past. Nara followed, both taking seats on opposing sides of the large desk.

Nara stared her down, refusing to be the first to speak.

"You cannot act so before the council, Nara."

An attendant walked in with a fresh pot of tea and two cups. Desme filled both, setting one in front of her. Nara held the cup under her nose, breathing in the citrus and honey before sipping it.

"We have been tolerant of your behavior these last years in consideration of your circumstances. But we—*I* can no longer show preference toward you. It has not gone unnoticed." Desme's large, almond-shaped brown eyes were fixed on her. A bright purple scarf secured the base of her low bun, matching the color of her robes. Gray dusted the roots of her black braids, forming a halo from temple to temple.

"I ask for no preference." Nara returned her teacup to the desk. She held Desme's gaze. "What are you going to do about what I have told you?"

Desme inhaled, sighing it out slowly. "We do not know, yet, Nara. I can tell you what we will not do, and that is act rashly. If you wanted to be a part of that conversation, perhaps it would have been prudent for you not to walk away from your post."

"If you hadn't sent Cerys north, perhaps I would not have." Nara sat back in her chair, crossing one leg over the other.

"How arrogant you are." Desme shook her head. "You truly believe it was about you. You think we sit around plotting ways to make you miserable?" She laughed without a shred of humor. "Cerys is Eserii. Just as you. Just as I. But unlike you, she serves without resistance. She embraces her pledge."

Nara bristled. Exhaustion weighed heavy, sending her feelings in disorienting directions. The anger she felt facing the council had not cooled.

Her skin twitched and fluttered as what raced within made its way to the surface. She rubbed her eyes.

"How long has it been since you have slept?" Desme asked, the irritation in her tone turning to concern.

"Two days. But not well in… a while," she admitted.

Desme frowned. "Go and rest."

"I am fine—"

"It is not a request, Nara. You are good to no one if you lose your wits."

Nara sighed. She knew Desme was right. She needed to be clear-headed, but she couldn't imagine sleeping when she had no news of Cerys. "I don't know how to do that when—"

"Nara," Desme said softly, leaning over the desk. "If anything is decided, I will send Tyr with word. He will wake you. Please go and rest. And bathe, for Godssake." She sat back, and her nose crinkled. "I can smell you from here."

Nara snorted. She leaned down, trying to sniff under her arms. She could not deny it.

"I will remind you that you no longer have chancellor's quarters within the palace. You can bunk in one of the community quarters in the Commons, in the Barracks, or go to your mother's house."

"I am aware," Nara said, jaw tight. "Is Sayeed in the Citadel?"

"Your stepfather traveled to Barka last sixday. I believe he is expected to return tomorrow or the next."

"Very well. I relent." Nara stood and made for the door, turning back under its frame. "Though there was something very interesting that I noticed today."

"Oh?" Desme asked as she refilled her teacup.

"Not a single member of the council seemed surprised when I told you it was Thrane. Do you not think that odd?" Nara pursed her lips, shrugging. "Or perhaps it was all in my mind. My wits are a bit lost today." Her feigned perplexity took on an air of suspicion.

Desme stilled.

"Did you not notice?" Nara asked, carefully observing her reaction. When Desme did not speak, Nara nodded, tossing her braids behind her shoulders. "As you say, Grandmother. I will heed your good advice and rest. I do look forward to hearing from you."

✥

Nara made her way back through the palace. The lobby was still full of disgruntled citizens who had waited to see the council, only to be turned away for the day. Tyr was doing his best to assure them they would all be seen on the morrow. Those who had been waiting eyed her, as if they'd come to understand she was the reason. She wanted to scream, *It's not me. It's Thrane, you fools!*, but she simply walked on.

She exited via the central west door, crossing the main bridge into the Commons, the central district of the four comprising the city. It was crowded for late afternoon. The markets were bustling with patrons and passersby. Nara wiped the sweat from her brow, trying not to bump into them, fatigue pressing down.

Crossing through the busy streets, she made for the bridge to the Village. To her mother and Sayeed's house. The Village was directly south of the Commons and housed all nonmilitary Esērii and their families. Those in active service lived in the Barracks, west of the Commons. The fourth and final district, the Athenaeum, sat to the north. Man-made channels separated the districts, supplying fresh water to all the homes, shops, and buildings in Qalanēs.

When she reached the bridge, the noise and bustle quieted. The buildings in the Village were mostly multistory townhomes, but high-ranking officials had their own properties with gardens. Her mother and Sayeed were such.

Like the streets of Nyrovi, the smell of citrus was all around. Trees of lemons, oranges, and mangoes lined the red, clay-bricked streets. But, unlike Nyrovi, the buildings were not all in blues and greens. They were bright in any color one could dream up. Shades of yellow, blue, purple, and beyond. Nara stopped at her mother's home, a brilliant orange color, not dissimilar to the fruit that hung on the trees in the green spaces around it.

Nara retrieved the key hidden beneath a clay-colored pot. The lock clicked, and she swung open the heavy wooden door, calling out for Sayeed. No answer. It appeared her grandmother was correct.

She pulled off her boots and tossed them aside, then stumbled into the sitting room. She craved a bath, but it would have to wait. The edges of her vision were starting to blur. She crashed onto one of the sofas, finding sleep in mere breaths.

✤

The sun had set by the time her eyes opened again. Nara sat up and yawned, stretching her arms high and then her neck. She formed an ether-star as she walked, lighting the lamps along the way.

The house appeared to have been empty for some time. There was no water in the kitchen, and the bathing pool in the garden was bone dry. She grabbed a bucket on her way out to the back of the property. She turned the wheel to open the valve, and water flowed through the pipes from the reservoir that ran behind the houses on the street. While the bathing pool filled, she splashed water over the back of her sun-scorched neck.

Nara went back into the house to retrieve soaps and a towel. After dropping her filthy clothes where she stood, she stepped into the cool water. With ripe enthusiasm, she scrubbed every inch of her body twice over before feeling satisfied she was clear of the muck. The water left behind was a dull, sandy color. She turned the inner valve, flushing it through the pipes below.

Wet footprints followed her to the guest bedroom, where she rifled through a trunk. She stepped into an orange-and-green patterned dress, then finished off the ensemble by tying a brown leather corded belt around her waist. She rooted around in the bottom until she found a spare pair of sandals.

Nara cleaned her teeth and pinned her braids in a high bun, which made her think of her mother. She hoped she would return soon. When she promised she would wait, she had meant to honor it, but she knew herself. The temptation to flee north, to find Cerys, would eat at her every day she had to delay.

A knock on the door downstairs drew her attention.

Nara bolted down the stairs, slowing her pace before she reached the door. She leisurely pulled it open. "Took you long enough." Though she was impressed he'd made it so soon.

"*Hah,*" Harker croaked. "We can't all be as fast as you."

She moved so he could step into the house. He looked around.

"It is only us. Sayeed will not return from Barka until tomorrow or the next."

He nodded. "I need a bath, a meal, and a drink."

"Go and have a bath. You know your way around. There isn't any food in the kitchen, but there should be wine. I'll go to the Commons and bring back something to eat."

"You have my thanks." A cloud of dust spread out when his boots hit the marble floor.

Nara looked up at him. "Perhaps disrobe in the garden."

✣

When Nara returned, Harker was waist-deep in the bathing pool, covered in suds, with a wine bottle tipped up.

"What did you bring me?" he asked, rubbing his hands together in anticipation. His eyes held the enthusiasm of a child about to receive sweets. She could not help but feel it, too. It felt good to be clean and fed. And back with someone who understood all she did.

"Pita with lamb, tomatoes, and cucumber. And goat's cheese, I think."

He pursed his lips and took the wrap, giving it a smell. "Not bad." He finished his food and half the bottle before he prompted. "So give it to me."

"They aren't doing shit." Nara spat the words. She moved her plate aside, resting her feet in its stead. "At least not yet."

Harker nodded as if he'd expected as much.

"It seems as Meriah feared. They did not appear as disturbed by the news as one would expect. They were afraid, but not shocked."

"Days," he said, taking another drink. "Then this is bad."

Nara didn't say yes. He wasn't asking.

"So we go north then?" he asked, stepping out of the water.

She tossed a towel at him. "I promised my mother I would wait. I'm going to try to hold true to that." Nara tipped up her own bottle. She was not overly keen on wine, but her stepfather was and had lavish tastes.

"I think that's best," Harker said. "What do we do until Tora returns?"

Nara sighed, looking out into the distance. *Drink*, she thought. "The Citadel seems ripe with secrets. Let us find some to pluck."

25

Nara

"Humility is a skill, contrived or not."

THE COST OF VALOR
AUTHOR UNKNOWN, 203 BQ
TRANSLATED FROM OLD ASARI BY MERIAH TURAN
HAIS Z'NOSIŠ, 1200 AQ

Nara sliced into a pomegranate, cutting it into sections, then passed one to Harker. They'd walked to a dining hall in the Commons to retrieve something to break fast. The hall itself was loud and crowded, and not somewhere they could speak in confidence, so they'd brought their food back to her mother's house to eat in the garden.

She stirred chopped almonds and dates around in her porridge, honey and cardamom rising up with the steam. It was the small pleasures she missed when traveling.

"Coffee?" Harker asked, holding the pot in the air after filling his cup.

"Please." She watched him pour, then topped it with a spoon of coconut cream.

"Where do we start?" he asked, returning the pot to the table.

She took a bite of her porridge and wiped her mouth. "When secrets are the object of one's desire, there are some obvious places they can be sniffed out. Loose lips are always found wherever there is wine or whiskey."

"So we start in the taverns?" He spread butter over a warm slice of bread.

Nara nodded. "We need to split up. Sayeed should return today, but my mother is likely still four or five days out. It is not a lot of time, and we'll cover more ground that way."

"I'll work the pubs in the Commons, and you'll take the ones in the Barracks?" he asked.

"Seems logical." Nara sipped her coffee, sighing in pleasure. "Someone should study this." She held her cup in the air before taking another drink.

"Is there anyone else we can trust? Others that can help?" he asked, then bit into a boiled egg.

"I don't know," Nara answered. "We aren't even sure there is something to discover. And if there is, I don't know how I feel about putting someone else in danger, especially when we don't know what that danger is."

Harker plucked at the wedge of pomegranate. "Aye."

"I'll also need to get into the palace." Nara took another bite of porridge, trying to discern what type of grain it was made of. Barley and millet, she thought.

"How do you plan to do that?" he asked, tossing a small handful of seeds into his mouth.

"Apologize."

Harker made an abrupt hacking sound, and his eyes went wide. Nara considered rising to pat his back, but he coughed, and a couple of the seeds burst free. "*Pardon?*"

Nara cocked a brow. "You heard me."

"Had to make sure." He dabbed the water from his eyes. "Days. Don't do that to me."

She smiled and tossed an almond at him. "I've been thinking it over, and I don't see another way. I'll have to go before the council, make nice, and ask to be reinstated. It is the only way we'll have access to the resources we need. If we're fighting an unknown enemy, let's at least not do it in the dark."

"I have no doubts they'll say yes, so long as you do the appropriate amount of groveling." He said it like he thought her not capable.

"They'll say no."

Harker looked up from his bowl with a frown.

"At first. They'll say they need to discuss it further, pretend to do so, and then reinstate me a couple days later. I embarrassed them," Nara said, and rolled her eyes. "I must make penance."

"Any other plans you dreamt up last night need sharing?"

She pursed her lips, considering. "That's all I have so far."

"Sounds like a good start."

Nara wiped her mouth, tossing her napkin on the table. "Petitioning starts soon. I'm going to get in line." She stood, making for the house.

"Nara Nyanthi waiting in line isn't something I thought I'd ever see," he called after her.

She turned back in the doorway. "I do not intend to make a habit of it. But sacrifices must be made."

Harker chuckled. "I'll see you back here tonight. Good luck."

Twenty were already waiting when Nara took a place in the queue. Midday came before it was her turn.

As with the day before, all six consuls watched her approach. She'd worn one of her finer dresses, a royal-purple silk gown with yellow geometric designs. For the first time in ten moons, she wore excessive jewelry. Gold hoops adorned her ears, and a thick gold torc circled her neck. Ornamental hair clips held her braids in a neat trail down her back. She looked ever the chancellor they wished her to be. The most taxing part of her ensemble was the expression of submission she wore on her face.

When Nara reached the end of the aisle, she inclined her head. "I thank the council for seeing me this day." Her grandmother eyed her, and Nara knew she'd prepared well.

"If you have come for news of our decision, you should know you will leave without it. No decisions have been made," Delphane warned.

"That is not why I have come." Nara folded her arms behind her back and gazed down. She kept a little bite in her tone to make the charade believable. "I wish to apologize for my behavior upon my return to the Citadel. It was disrespectful and unwarranted." She looked back up demurely, with humility.

Lazlo and Ceneric seemed pleasantly surprised, but the others were skeptical.

"This council thanks you," Seraphine said, her eyes carefully considering.

"Review of my behavior this past day has given me further drive for reflection. I wish to take responsibility for my mistakes… and to take action to rectify them." She waited to be prompted.

"And what are those mistakes?" Lazlo asked.

"Resigning my post as chancellor, first and foremost."

"I see," Seraphine said.

"I know now that I acted in haste." Nara looked at her grandmother, who didn't speak, but looked on approvingly.

"Go on." Delphane appeared the least convinced.

"The council was wise to remind me it was I who abandoned my post. I have given it much thought the past ten moons, and the events in Amul have shown me I can serve best in the position you had so graciously bestowed on me." Nara shifted on her feet. She needed to look nervous. "I humbly ask the council to consider reinstatement."

Seraphine continued to study her. Lazlo, Phelen, and Ceneric looked pleased. Delphane scowled. Her grandmother surely knew the whole act of submission was a farce. Nara did not think she cared, though, as long as she was coming back into the fold.

"You will wait in the hall while we discuss your request," Seraphine said, pointing toward the door.

Nara bowed her head and returned to the lobby. Tyr's wary eyes lingered on her when she emerged, watching as she strolled toward him. She gave him her best diffident smile, and he scowled. He looked the same as he did every day. Short, black hair slicked back, white robes impeccably clean, thick gold earrings, and a fault-finding look in his dark eyes.

"Did you miss me?" she teased.

Tyr cocked a brow. "Miss you? Does one miss the overbearing sun or a fly buzzing in their ear?" He said the words with the straightest of faces.

"Ah, Tyr, I did not come to bring you trouble." Her modest smile melted into a mischievous grin.

"Nara Nyanthi, trouble follows you, dragged in or chasing." Tyr stood straight with his hands clasped behind his back.

She snorted, feeling she could not in good faith dispute the claim. "Where is your husband? I know Milos missed me, at least."

That drew any trace of amusement from his face. Milos had become Harker and Nara's drinking partner when they were in the Citadel between collections. Much to the chagrin of Tyr.

"Out of the city," he answered. It was stern, even a little curt.

Nara clicked her tongue several times. "That's too bad. We're going out tonight." She raised her hand as if a brilliant idea had struck. "You know… you could come with us in his stead." Her eyes traced him from top to bottom and back. "Though, I do not recommend wearing white in the sort of places we frequent."

His expression held, unaffected by her teasing.

The door to the chambers opened, and she was ushered back in. Nara transformed back into her image of humility, giving Tyr a quick wink on her way.

The look on her grandmother's face told her all she needed to know. It would go as she'd expected. Seraphine was the one who spoke.

"We have decided we need more time to consider your request. We thank you for your amends, and we recognize the humility you have presented here today. We will call for you once we have come to a decision." Seraphine peered at her, the warning in her eyes telling Nara to be on her best behavior. Her grandmother cocked the slightest of smiles. Nara knew they'd already decided. They knew it too. This was simply the price to pay for challenging them.

26

Neith

"Be wary of those who thirst for power. It is not of the kind that can be quenched."

THE COST OF VALOR
AUTHOR UNKNOWN, 203 BQ
TRANSLATED FROM OLD ASARI BY MERIAH TURAN
HAIS Z'NOSIŠ, 1200 AQ

The Second had followed the signs of smoke since dawn, lazing like an idle storm cloud over the city in the distance. They'd ridden hard for three days to reclaim time lost to the rains. Night had long fallen by the time they arrived in Northbridge.

Too late to train, they set up camp with the aim of resuming in the morning. Supper was a sad meal of smoked fish and three-day-old bread eaten crudely around the campfire. Neith could not bring herself to eat the fish.

Iris lifted her arm, sniffing underneath. "Gods, we stink."

Neith felt she quite agreed. Lavender oil could only do so much. First thing in the morning, she would scrub down in the river twice over.

"Not as bad as this," Kieran said, holding a limp piece of fish between his fingers. He wiggled it toward Iris, and she pretended to gag.

Petra appeared, pulling off her pack. "Wash well before we leave Northbridge. The River Steyr continues south, and we'll be without it the remainder of the march to Highclere. It'll be ponds and creeks until we reach Lake Crescent."

Iris groaned. "I'm inclined to go right now."

"Where did you run off to, Petra?" Bellamy looked up and over his shoulder after adding a fresh log to the fire. "I hadn't even noticed you'd left, you sneaky woman."

"Getting us this," she answered, pulling an amber-colored glass bottle from her bag.

Bellamy stood, taking it, turning it in his hands. "Andaran whiskey? You goddess." He kissed her cheek and popped the cork, taking a long swig before passing it around.

When the bottle made it to Neith, she waved it off, her mood not in tune with diversion. Her thoughts were stuck in fear of reuniting with the First. Chiefly with her brother. She had not spoken to or seen him since the day she split the mountain, and they had parted badly. The past halfmoon with her squad had been uneventful, pleasant even. She couldn't shake the feeling it was about to change.

Sam sat on the log beside her.

"And what about you?" Neith asked him. "Have you also been off procuring spirits for camp?"

"Not exactly." Sam held out his hand, revealing it full of blackberries, his skin beneath stained a deep purplish red.

Neith grinned. "Where did you get these?" She took one, popping it into her mouth. It was delightfully sweet, and her eyes closed in satisfaction as she chewed.

"That is my business." Sam smiled and urged her to take another. It was not an offer she'd decline. She took two this time. He watched her as she indulged in them again.

"Camp is quiet tonight," Neith said, desiring to make conversation.

"All are worn. I've no doubt the raucousness will return after a good night's rest." His hand was still extended, acting as a makeshift bowl for the berries. Neith sighed and took another.

"I rather like it quiet," she said as she chewed.

"Then we are one and the same in that." He reached for his mug with his free hand, taking a sip as he held her gaze.

Neith looked down, realizing he had not eaten any of the berries. "Will you not take some for yourself?"

He hesitated, then shrugged. "Truth be told I do not care for them."

Neith frowned as she reached for another. "Then why pick them?"

Sam shifted, and his lips parted to speak, but an approaching soldier caught their attention.

"Lieutenant Dracos," the soldier prompted, falling to a knee in full salute.

Neith stood. "Yes?" She was still growing accustomed to being addressed so. She'd commanded all in her squad to call her Neith outside of a formal setting.

"The king summons you to Northbridge."

Neith looked up at the moon. "At this hour?"

"You are to ride in with General Agbani."

Neith rode between Magnus and Sam, following the messenger through the cobblestone streets of Northbridge. By the time they'd made it through camp and into town, the moon was well past high, and she guessed they were closer to sunrise than sunset. One would not know it by the festivities alive around them.

Cheering, singing, and dancing filled the streets. Soldiers ran around in various stages of undress, chasing one another, whiskey bottles in hand. Some fought for sport. Magnus glanced at her, brows raised. She knew he did not approve of such behavior, but the First was made up of a different sort than the Second. And clearly commanded as such.

Neith wondered if Sam would be taking part were he not in her guard. She could not picture it. He turned to look at her and shrugged, as if to say, *pay it no mind.* When they passed a man and a woman coupling in an alley, Neith inhaled and stiffened, heat washing over her cheeks. She kept telling herself to look away, but her gaze stayed fixed. The woman leaned over a barrel, both making their howls of pleasure as the man thrashed against her with such force Neith could hear the smacking of bare skin. When she finally averted her eyes, they did not move from the path forward again.

They stopped at a large stone home on the edge of town, adding their horses to a rack out front. The house was set against a creek running south, and were it not for the sounds of the debauchery behind them, Neith thought it would be a peaceful place. It was wealthy, perhaps home to the mayor or a prosperous merchant.

Her father sat at the head of a long table, on the far side of the room, standing immediately at their entry. His eyes found hers, and she blinked several times to be sure she saw correctly. He had been laughing. A cup of ale sat in front of him. He walked toward her, a muted elation in his manner.

"Daughter."

Neith bowed her head. "Father."

"You look well." His eyes were red-rimmed and a little unfocused. She could see he was heavy on the drink.

"I am," she said.

He smiled, or something like it, then turned toward Magnus. "My friend." They clasped arms. "It is good to have you back with me."

Magnus clapped him on the shoulder. "It seems all is well with the First."

"Indeed. Indeed. We are celebrating our victories, as should you." Lorcan gestured for a servant to bring ale. He took two mugs from the tray she carried, handing one to Magnus.

Neith surveyed the room and did not see her brother. Nicomedes was seated in the chair next to where her father had been, watching.

Magnus and Lorcan clanked mugs, both taking long drinks.

Magnus leaned closer to her father. "They are *celebrating* in the streets."

Lorcan's eyes flicked to Neith, which sent hers to the ground. She knew her face must be the color of beets.

He exhaled, grumbling, then motioned for one of the soldiers standing by the door. "Go and tell them to take it indoors."

When the soldier left, her father turned back to her. "I only wanted to set eyes on you. To know you are well," he said, with the trace of impairment. "The hour is late. Return to camp. I will send for you before we depart."

"As you wish, Father." She bowed her head, trying to conceal her irritation he had dragged her out of camp for this.

"There is much to discuss, Magnus. Come, my friend." The two men turned and walked toward the table, her father's arm wrapped around Magnus's shoulder.

When the door closed behind them, she looked at Sam, her brows knitted in disbelief. "I think my father is drunk."

"I think you are correct."

They shared a quiet laugh. Sam looked as if he found the notion amusing, but also a bit frightful. Neith thought she felt quite the same. She had never seen her father indulge in spirits. He would often have a glass of wine or a mug of ale, but never in excess.

She sighed, looking back toward town and what awaited. She had no desire to see it again. "Let us walk for a while."

"Walk?"

"Into the woods."

"Is that wise?" He asked, one brow cocked.

"Are you afraid?" she teased.

Sam gave her a sly smile. "With you by my side? Never. But the sun will soon rise."

He protested, but Neith sensed he was not truly opposed to the idea. She had grown to understand his expressions and hidden sentiments the past days. In some measure, at least. In many ways, he was still a mystery to her. They talked more than she could remember speaking with anyone. He asked about her life. Her childhood in Necrium. Her training. Something had changed since the day by the pond. The day he'd asked to be her friend.

Though he had many questions for her, he spoke little of himself. When asked, his answers were short, informational. In this regard, he reminded her a bit of Magnus. He often seemed sorrowful when speaking of his past, so Neith did not push.

"We're not leaving for another day. We've been on the road for a halfmoon. Let's walk." She looked up at him, pouting her bottom lip in a subtle, but intentional, act.

Sam narrowed his eyes, considering. "Not far."

They followed a crude path north that ran alongside the creek. She wanted to be far enough that the sounds from town would cease. They walked leisurely for the better part of an hour before she stopped to pick yellow wildflowers.

"I wonder what these are called," she mused. She could not recall them from her studies.

"Agrimonia."

Neith turned, looking up with a skeptical eye. "You know about flowers?"

"This kind grows only in the north, but there is another variant in Zargoza." He knelt beside her, plucking a stem from the earth.

"Is that where you were born?" she asked, gauging his reception to the inquiry.

"No, my father was Aharan, and my mother Zargozan, but I was born in Sibreen."

Excitement sparked through her, and she wanted to ask a thousand questions. When she had decided on one, she started to speak, but he stood.

"I am sorry you had to see that back in town," he said, with apology, as if he had been tasked to, and unable to protect her from it.

Heat crept over her cheeks. Sure of what he spoke. She turned back to the flowers. "See what?"

He was silent for a moment. "Things someone like you should not."

Neith stood to face him. "Someone like me?" Her words were laced with a hint of irritation. "A *child*?"

"No," he said quickly, shaking his head.

"I'm not a child."

"I know." He took a step toward her, holding one hand out in caution. "That is not what I mean."

Neith straightened her back, holding her chin high. "Then what *do* you mean?"

She watched his throat bob as he swallowed, confused when she realized he was nervous.

"You are… gentle." He said it with subtle affection, with a tenderness in his eyes that tugged at something tethered between them.

Gentle. That word again. Though it felt different coming from him. "Is that so bad?"

"No." He shook his head. "It is not something I would see you lose." Sam extended a hand toward her. It held a small cluster of purple flowers Neith had not realized he'd picked. She smiled, reaching across the narrow space that separated them. When her fingers grazed his, she held on much longer than required. His skin was still stained from the berries he'd picked. The berries she now realized he had picked for her, and her alone.

"And what do you know about these?" she asked, looking over the flowers.

"These only grow here, in the north. Straeth, northern Ire, and Argal. Icena and Thrane are too cold, Lochland and Andar too warm."

Neith felt him watching her examine the delicate little blooms. "What are they called?" She twirled a stem between her fingers.

"Sydel's kiss."

When he said the word, her eyes instinctively flicked up to his lips. She studied the fullness of them, curious if they would feel as soft, as *gentle*, as they looked. She cleared her throat. "That is an odd name. Where does it come from?"

Sam reached for the flowers. This time, his fingers lingered on hers. She found it perplexing how one could feel so much from such a small touch.

"When Argos fell during the Great Quell, and the Gods left our world, parts of them remained in their natural forms. Cassia as light, Adrae in darkness, and Pyramus in our streams and sea. Thelos burns in our fires and Bacchus in the air we breathe."

Neith nodded, familiar with the myths of the Faith of the Hexad. "And Sydel was of the earth."

Sam nodded. "This flower gets its name from a poem about Sydel and her lover, an idleborn man."

While Neith had been educated on the beliefs of the Faith, poetry on the subject was not something she had the liberty of. She doubted such books even existed in Necrium. "What does this poem say?"

"I cannot recite it verbatim, nor as elegantly as the prose deserves, but it is about her lover's plea for her to stay. He says he could not live without her and that he would gladly give up his life to go. Sydel told him she would always be with him. She told him to come to the forest when she was gone. That he could find her in the trees, in the earth beneath his feet, waiting. That when he was old and gray and met his end, to have his body put into the ground, and together they would grow, reuniting for eternity. But he protested still. He told her he couldn't live in a world without her. The trees, the earth, they weren't enough. That he couldn't live a lifetime without her touch. Without her kiss."

Neith chewed her bottom lip, thinking it over. "Why wouldn't she take him with her?"

"Out of love, I suppose. She wanted what was best for him. For him to live his mortal life."

Neith frowned, unfamiliar with that sort of sacrifice.

"Sydel reached down and took a pebble in her hand. She held it up to her lips, and her ether poured into it, turning the stone the color of her power." Sam held the purple flower between them. "The stone would always hold her kiss. All he needed to do was touch it to his lips, and he would feel her."

Neith listened intently, hanging on his words. "What happened to him when she left?"

"He tried to live as she wished. He fashioned a cord around the stone to wear around his neck, close to his heart. When he died an old man, he was buried with it. These grew over his grave." He handed her back the flowers. "Or so the poems say."

Neith stood silent for a time. "I should like to read this poem."

"The libraries in Nyrovi are full of books with the old myths, poetry, and philosophy. I imagine you'll find some selection of it in Highclere." Sam smiled at her in a way she had not seen on him before, or perhaps only now understood. There was a wonder in his eyes, a curiosity for the world that she wanted to feel, too. It was like looking at someone who had lived an entire lifetime with the yearning to do it all again.

A distant laugh sent both of their heads snapping toward the sound. Sam's eyes narrowed, and his finger came up in front of his lips as they listened.

The tension eased in his body. "Soldiers. Ours."

"What are they doing out here?" she asked. "It is nearly dawn." She closed her eyes, searching through the ether. "There are three men, and—" She opened her eyes to look at Sam. "I believe an idleborn woman."

His face fell.

"What?" she asked, feeling dread pool heavy in her chest.

"Let me take you back to camp. I will return and take care of this." He reached for her, but she stepped back.

"Take care of what?" Neith looked toward the men. *Oh. Gods.*

She took off in their direction. Sam called after her, but she kept on, quickly feeling him on her heels.

Two soldiers stood outside of what looked to be a small hunting cabin sitting next to the creek. They were laughing and stumbling around. She thought she might recognize one from her brother's unit.

The cabin door creaked, and the third man stumbled out. "She's all used up, boys." He was still tying his trousers.

Neith looked at Sam, feeling her dread ignite to rage. His gaze was fixed on the men. He slowly turned his head toward her, and she thought for a moment he would try to persuade her away again. Neith was not certain what he was feeling, but it did not look like caution. She saw her own fury mirrored back.

"Ah, I've had my fun, and we're out of ale. Let's go back to camp," one of them said.

"We should tie her up. Come back tomorrow," said another.

Neith stepped out of the trees with Sam at her side.

"Who are you?" one of the men questioned, his eyes squinting at them. He started to call his ether, but Neith sent a blast of air, hurling him backward.

The others turned in surprise, straightening at the recognition of who she was.

"Watch them," Neith said to Sam. He hesitated, but nodded. She walked to the cabin, dread compounding with every step, begging under her breath not to find what she feared was waiting. She pulled open the door and gasped.

A young woman was lying across a table, not moving save for the rise and fall of her chest. She was completely nude, beaten, and bruised, blood streaked between her thighs. Her long, light brown hair draped around her. It looked as if they'd kept her there all day. Neith clamped her eyes shut, steadying herself in the doorframe.

When the girl took notice of her, she pulled her knees to her chest, arms wrapped tight, eyes wild.

"Do not be afraid," Neith said. She was trying to be gentle, but knew her voice trembled.

It did nothing to quell the girl's fear.

Neith opened the clasp on her cloak, pulling it from her shoulders. She took slow steps toward her, and the girl watched her every move, inching back on the table. The terror in her blue eyes sent rage boiling up from her chest, tightening in her throat. She tried to swallow it so she could speak. "All three of them?"

The girl hesitated, still unsure, but nodded. Neith draped the cloak around her, and she sat up, clutching at it. The girl continued to watch her, eyes full of mistrust and contempt.

Neith pulled the dagger from her belt, and the girl flinched. She flipped the blade in her hand, holding the hilt out to her. "Take it."

The girl looked at the dagger, then back to Neith. She snatched it from her grip, then slid off the table, backing up in the room.

"Stay here," Neith said, clenching her hands to fists. "They will not hurt you again." Entirely unconvinced, the girl eyed the space between her and the door.

Neith turned and stormed from the cabin. Sam had the men standing next to one another, waiting. His power flared out around him, and when his eyes met hers and confirmed what they'd feared, the air heated, turning to steam.

Neith examined the three men closely. She wanted to scorch them to ash where they stood. They were cautious, but not quite concerned. Nowhere near as much as they should have been. "I will seek justice for this. You will answer for these crimes. What are your names?"

The man she recognized scoffed. "We've committed no crimes. It's just some Straethan bitch we pulled from the village." He was a short, stocky man who looked as if he had not bathed in a moon. His indifferent demeanor toward his actions turned her stomach as much as his smell.

Neith flexed her jaw. "Sam, step aside, please."

He did as asked. She felt the tremble of his ether, ready at call.

Neith let her anger fuel her, and ripped open the plane, calling to the nether, to what lies beneath. She didn't take care. She let it funnel out of the void, curling and twisting wildly above her hands. All three men stepped back. One stumbled, plummeting on his backside.

A steady trickle of blood trailed from her nose. She smiled at them, wicked and threatening, as her eyes snapped black. "Do you know what this is?" Their eyes followed the shadowy snakes twisting and turning in the air, wrapping around her arms. "Do you know what it does?"

The cabin door burst open, and the girl darted through, sprinting into the woods. Neith turned to Sam. "She needs help. I can heal her." He took off after her.

"You—can't kill us," one of them stuttered.

"If I turned you to nothing, who would know?" She tilted her head, studying the fear on them, making them believe she was delighting in it. Perhaps she was. "If I let the void take you, who will tell your tale?" As much as Neith wanted them dead, she wanted them held accountable more. She wanted justice. The punishment for rape in Thrane was castration. She would see all three removed from whatever repulsive excuse for manhood hung between their legs. "Do not make me ask again. What are your names?"

Their reluctance now remedied, they answered her question. She committed the three names to memory. All were from her brother's unit.

Neith recalled the nether, letting it slither back to its home. When the cold rush fell over her, she inhaled, taking her time as the air left her lungs. "Get out of here. My brother and father will hear of this."

The men stumbled and scampered off in the direction of town. She stood with her eyes closed, trying to still her breath, intoxicated from the nether. It was dangerous to call it like that, but she was angry. Like ether, it fueled whatever she was feeling, and in that moment, it was rage. She opened her eyes at the sound of rustling to see Sam limping toward her, his leather vest unbuttoned.

"Where is the girl?" she asked, puzzled. It was not as if she could have outrun him.

"I do not think she wants our help."

Neith frowned. "She refused you?"

"She stabbed me." He lifted his tunic to reveal a small wound on his left side. Neith's eyes went wide. "I'm fine, it's nothing."

She ran to him, holding her hands over the wound, ether assessing.

He was right. It wasn't deep. "I'm sorry, this is my fault. I gave her the blade," she said, looking up at him with apologetic eyes.

Sam laughed and then flinched. "Of course you did." Neith smiled and then worked to close the wound. "Can't blame her," he said, voice heavy.

"No," Neith said, as she worked. "No, we cannot."

The last bit of skin fused, and he was left with only a thin, pink line. He ran his fingers over it.

Neith stood, looking toward the forest where she'd run. "Do you think she will be all right?"

Sam looked around. "I don't know. She knows this land better than we do. There are several villages not far from here."

Neith sighed. "I have to go to my brother. They need to pay for this."

Sam's eyes thinned.

"What is it?"

Hesitation tightened his face, but he did not make her ask again. "I fear your brother will do nothing."

"No." Neith shook her head. "Roman is many things. Impulsive, unpredictable, perhaps even cruel on occasion," she said, and looked down. "But he would not condone this. He would not condone rape."

"He might not condone it, but he would look the other way," he said as he buttoned his vest.

Neith huffed. "Is there a difference?"

"Not to me," Sam answered. "But—"

"You are wrong. I know my brother."

"Wait out here," she said, glancing back at Sam. She'd inquired with the quartermaster about her brother's tent and marched directly there.

Sam's eyes were already apologetic as he nodded. It did not feel condescending, but it flared her irritation. She worried it angered her because perhaps he might be right.

Neith pulled back the cover and stepped inside with no warning. Roman and Katya were asleep beneath furs, identifiable by the contrast of their black and white hair. The room was in chaos. Clothes, empty mugs, and all other sorts of mess were strewn about.

"Roman."

Neither stirred.

"Roman!"

Her brother didn't move, but Katya shifted to her elbows, squinting toward the noise. She scowled when she found Neith.

"Get out," Neith commanded.

"Who are you to make such demands to me?" Katya sat up in the cot, rubbing her eyes. She looked disheveled. Her ice-white hair was not in its usual high braid.

"Someone that could turn you into little more than particles with a passing thought." Neith had no patience for her antics.

Katya appeared hesitant for a breath, but her face quickly twisted into a snarl. She pulled back the fur cover and stepped out. She was completely nude and gave no indication of being sheepish of it. It was only Neith who reddened.

She sauntered in front of Neith as she tied back her hair, clearly perceptive of Neith's unease toward her nakedness.

"Get dressed and get out," Neith said low and in warning.

Katya rolled her eyes and walked around her.

"Roman, *wake up*." Still, he didn't move. Katya chuckled behind her. Neith turned to find her splashing water on her face from the basin at the far end of the tent. Neith marched toward her, snatching the bowl from the table. When she was close enough to hit the target, she dumped the water across Roman's face.

He howled, scrambling to sit up. When his eyes focused, he looked from Neith to Katya and back.

"*What the fuck?*" Roman tugged the blanket to his face, wiping the water away.

"We have a visitor," Katya called from the other side of the tent.

Neith turned to glare at her. "I have told you to leave. If I have to tell you again, it will not be with words." Katya looked to Roman for direction.

He held up his hand. "Give us a moment."

Katya scowled as she pulled on a tunic and trousers. "I'll be outside."

Roman rubbed his eyes. "What do you want?"

After a halfmoon apart, it was the only greeting she would get. "Three of your men were found raping a girl."

His lack of reaction set an ominous tone. She had expected shock, horror. Disgust. Instead, he groaned and rose from the bed. He was also nude, and Neith instinctively turned around.

"Did you hear me, Roman?"

"I heard you, Neith." She heard him rustling through clothes behind her. "What do you want me to do about it?" He walked around her to the table, now wearing trousers, but no tunic. He poured a mug of ale, tossing it back.

She scoffed. "What do I want you to do? I want you to hold them accountable. As is your responsibility as their commanding officer."

He chuckled. "Oh, little sister."

"Rape is *illegal* in Thrane, Roman."

"Was it a Thranean girl?" he asked, one brow cocked.

"What would that matter?"

Roman set down his mug, coming to stand directly in front of her. His eyes ran the length of her, appraising. "Where are your pretty dresses?" She ignored his attempt to divert her.

"I found the girl beaten and bloody in a hunting lodge in the woods. Your men Glendin, Harold, and Thorley were laughing and boasting about it when I happened upon them. There is no doubt of their guilt."

He sighed like one does at a child. "Murder is also illegal in Thrane. Did you not kill someone, also a girl?"

A rush of self-reproach washed over her. "That is different."

Roman inclined his head. "Is it? You didn't have to do what you did. You could have stopped her without *mutilating* her."

Images flashed behind her eyes, uncontrollable and horrifying. She tried to still the tremor in her lips.

Roman leaned closer, speaking directly into her ear. "But you were angry, weren't you? You wanted to make her pay for what she'd done. Right in front of her poor mother, too." He clicked his tongue several times. "I still remember how she wailed." When he moved back to look at her, he smirked, satisfied his words had worked.

He walked back to the table and grabbed a pitcher. "War changes the rules, little sister," he said as he refilled his mug. He brought it to his lips, tipping it up high. Thin streams of ale trailed down his chin as he drank. He wiped lazily at his mouth and gestured at her with the empty mug. "The sooner you learn that, the better."

Neith stared at him, shocked, half panicked. She swallowed, desperate for some of the determination she'd felt only moments before. "If you do not hold your men accountable, you give me no choice but to go to Father." Her voice did not hold the conviction she'd hoped.

He barked out a laugh. "You do that." He set the mug down and climbed back into his cot, pulling the furs high over his body. "Now get out. This whole purity act bores me."

A single tear trailed down her cheek, and she wiped at it roughly before turning and retreating from the tent. Katya was waiting with a knowing smile, no doubt having heard the exchange. She stood with her arms crossed. "Not the reaction you were hoping for?"

Neith glared at her with what would have not long ago been disbelief. Now she felt only contempt. "You are a woman. How can you not care?"

For a moment, Katya's face fell, and Neith saw a hint of regret. "A woman, yes, but not the daughter of a king. Not all of us have the privilege of outrage." She turned and stalked back into the tent.

Neith felt Sam standing behind her. When she had the courage to turn around, she found his face regretful. "Go on, tell me you were right."

He shook his head. "I would rather have been wrong."

She looked around. The sun was rising, and most of camp was still sleeping, but she cloaked them in a shield to speak privately. "Should I go to my father? Speak honestly."

"He may do something to placate you, but it will not be the outcome you're seeking. If he were to truly punish them, it would not bode well with much of the First." He said it gently, but with the same assuredness as he had spoken of Roman. Neith was fearful to find out if he would once again be right.

She ran her hands across her face, then through her hair. "So rape goes unpunished? I'm supposed to look the other way?" Neith could not see a way to resign herself to that.

"No, I'm not saying that." Sam paused, inhaling as his eyes fixed on hers.

Neith frowned. "What should I have done? *Killed* them?" she asked, part in jest, part not.

"I'm not saying that either, but if you had, I would not have objected." He shrugged as if murdering those men held little consequence. "That sort of outcome tends to send a strong message. Whispers of it are often more effective than the whip itself." His eyes were red, and she knew hers were as well. They were approaching a full day without sleep. "If you choose to bring this to your father, I would wait until he has had time to sleep off the ale."

She huffed, frustration eating at her. "Why are people like this?"

"There are over thirty thousand soldiers in your father's army. If you want to build a force that size, many of them will not be good."

She started to say she should keep to herself, to mind her own business, but if she had, the girl would still be tied up in that dirty cabin, where she would likely have died. At least she had a chance.

"What are you going to do?" he asked.

"I don't know," she answered, rubbing her eyes. "Think on it, I suppose."

He nodded as if agreeing it was the right decision. Sunlight broke over the horizon, and a yawn pulled from Neith's lips.

"It is a long walk back to our camp, and you need to rest," he said.

"I won't be able to sleep with this on my mind."

He studied her for a moment, as he often did when considering what to say. "Justice is not always delivered justly. If we are too hasty to see it dispatched, we may lose hold of it on the way."

She let out an incredulous laugh, shaking her head. "How is it you are only twenty winters and speak the way you do?"

The same considering look returned to his face. For a moment, she was returned to the woods before they'd found the girl. When he handed her the purple flowers. She sighed. "Very well, Sam. Back to camp."

27

Neith

"There is no snake more lethal than the obsidian viper. Inhabiting the mountains of Thrane, distinguishable by its glowing crimson eyes, it preys on all, both inferior in size and not."

THE ILLUSTRATED GUIDE TO NATIVE ANIMALS AND PLANTS OF
THE NORTH
OLIVER BIRCH, 925 AQ

Having slept past midday, Neith spent the bulk of the afternoon training with Petra. She had not seen Sam since they returned to their campsite at dawn. It wasn't exactly uncommon. He would often be out for afternoons or evenings, and Max or Petra would be sent to her side in his stead. It hadn't been something she'd thought to question.

Neith slashed at the fabric target, most of her blows falling clumsily to the side. She could barely lift the sword. It was the first time Petra had given her an actual one. Before, she had used only wooden training swords, learning simple strikes and steps. Neith thought the entire thing akin to dancing, and she wasn't known for her lightness of foot.

"Your grip is too close. Separate your hands," Petra said, watching her closely. Neith slid her left hand down the handle. "Yes, good. Now, step back with your left foot. When you strike, use the same foot for leverage and push off. It will put more force into your blow."

Neith nodded, stepping forward as instructed. Her strike came down through the target.

"Good!"

Neith had been thinking about the girl all day. And the men who were probably still sleeping off their drunken stupors, warm in their beds. She struck the target, and a corner of it went flying off.

It felt good to destroy something. She cut at it again and again, letting out all the rage she felt. At the men, at her brother, even at her father, for his reaction she hadn't even seen. Slashing and striking, she grunted with the effort, her arms and shoulders burning. She attacked until it was a pile of straw at her feet. Then she struck at the wooden post beneath, chipping away at it strike by strike until the sword fell from her arms, and she collapsed to her knees. Chest heaving, she looked up to see Petra staring down at her, brows raised.

"You all right?" Petra asked, clearly amused by Neith's display of rage.

"No." Neith fell back onto the ground. "No, I am not."

Petra retrieved the sword, turning it in her hands as she examined it. "I think this might be done for. I'll send it off to see if it can be repaired." She sat on the grass in front of Neith. "You want to talk about it?"

"Yes," Neith admitted, "but I can't. Not yet."

Petra nodded, holding her gaze. "All right." She nudged Neith's shoulder. "Will you at least let me watch when you destroy whoever it is you're angry with?"

Neith laughed, feeling a little lighter. She was starting to understand why the others were always sparring. "Do you know where Sam is today?"

Petra's eyes narrowed, and caution crept into her face.

"It is not him I'm angry with."

The tension eased. "He said he was called away and that he would return this evening. He didn't say more, and I didn't ask." Petra shrugged. "He's probably with Magnus. They spent a lot of time together when he was a captain. He was responsible for much in the Second."

Guilt washed over Neith when she thought how ridiculous they must feel following her around. "I'm sorry you were pulled into this."

"I wasn't. I was asked, and I accepted. Neither Max nor I were forced." Petra leaned back in the grass, bracing on her palms.

"Why?" Neith asked. "Do you not feel yourself wasted here? It seems a silly task for soldiers like you three."

"I joined Sam's first squad for a reason. I followed him when he became captain, and now I'm here. If he asks me to follow him again, I will."

"You were his Second?" Neith asked, and Petra nodded. Neith admired the loyalty. So far, Sam had shown himself worthy of it. "What makes you trust him so?"

Petra considered for a moment. "His actions match his words. He will stand up for what he believes in, regardless of the consequences. But he is not some righteous fool. He understands that *when* demands equal consideration to the how." Petra spoke assuredly as if she knew Sam well, as if they were old friends. Neith could not help but feel a pang of jealousy as she wished she knew him the same.

"Yes," Neith said, her thoughts escaping. "I'm seeing that."

Petra stood, brushing the grass from her trousers. "I'm starving. Let's go and find something to eat."

The dining tents served the best meal Neith had seen since departing Thrane. A stew of venison with vegetables and fresh herbs called to the empty space in her belly. She dined with her squad and guards, save for Sam.

"Enjoy it while it lasts, kids. It'll be salted meat and hard cheese once we're back on the road," Bellamy said with a grin from his spot next to her.

"Do we have orders yet?" Iris asked, looking to Neith.

Neith glanced around and realized all eyes were on her. Sam usually answered such questions. "Not yet."

"Where is Sam?" Kieran asked, forking a piece of meat. What was once an orange shadow on his face was now taking shape into a full beard. Neith thought it suited him.

"He was out early," Raiden said. "Gone by the time I woke, not long after dawn."

Petra shrugged. "With the general, I suppose. What business is it of yours?"

Iris pointed across the tent. "No, General Agbani is there."

Neith and Petra exchanged glances. On cue, Sam sat down at the table, bowl of stew in hand. "Did I hear my name?"

"Is that what you think we do?" Petra jested. "Sit around and wonder where you are all day?"

"Do you not?" Sam asked, straight-faced. It melted away into a grin, and his words garnered a collective chuckle from the table. He looked like he had not slept at all. "We're marching out in the morning." He glanced at Neith with a soft smile. She returned it and tried desperately not to watch him eat.

They finished their meals, most having seconds, before returning to their campsite just past sunset. Kieran and Iris retrieved fresh firewood, and Neith and Ayla brought back pitchers of ale. They settled into their usual spots, some playing cards, others chatting. Sam was showing Neith different grips one could use with a dagger when she felt her brother's ether.

She sat up straight, Sam taking notice as her head snapped to the side, feeling Roman advance from behind. Sam's eyes were still searching hers for understanding when she screamed, "Get down!"

Heat roared above them as she was thrown to the ground on her belly. Silver etherfire roared through their camp, careless and wild.

Shields in an array of colors sprang up around her as the fire recoiled.

Neith looked up in horror to see Roman standing at the edge of their camp, face twisted in outrage. Twin silver flames still at call on both palms.

Neith looked around, taking in her squad. They were sprawled on the ground, dazed, trying to make sense of what had happened.

Sam was already standing in front of her, his power sparking and snapping, electric in the air. He, too, had honey-color flames at the ready. Neith scrambled to her feet and marched around him in a fury.

"*Have you lost control of your senses?*" she hissed. Roman was in a rage, so she met it with her own. "You nearly scorched us all!" Neith glanced back to see they were now standing, brushing dirt from their clothes, with angry looks all around.

Roman sneered. "If that was my aim you would all be ash."

"*Roman.*" Neith stepped closer to him, and she felt Sam follow. "*What is this?*"

He was so angry that Neith thought he should be foaming at the mouth. "What did you do with my men?"

Katya and four others walked up behind him from the shadows. All wore his insignia, the obsidian viper, its red eyes commanding attention, with the words *Soktes en Noxa* stitched below it. *Seeker in the Night.*

"I don't know to what you speak." Neith gave all in his party a flat and cold stare. Sam and Max appeared on her left, Ayla behind them, Bellamy and Petra on her right.

"Three of my men have not reported in." Roman pointed at Neith as he said, "And I know *you* had something to do with it."

Neith laughed, dripping with irony. "The three men I found raping a girl this morning?" A crowd formed from the other camps around them.

Roman stood up straight, rebuffing the accusation. "That is hearsay. And if it were truth, it was not your justice to serve."

"I served no justice. I came to you for that and found none." Neith found herself growing angrier. She was tired of dealing with this. With him.

Roman looked at those around her. "If it wasn't you, it was one of yours."

"Do not look at them," she said, shaking her head. "Look to me." He did, with a shock at her words that she also felt. "If anyone in my squad acted, it was under my command. You will direct your words to me." From the corner of her eye, she saw Bellamy smirking. Iris appeared. Lavender-colored ether twisted and snaked around her arms. Raiden was a step behind her, silver flames at call. Kieran was now next to Max. Neith glanced at Sam. His entire body was shaking, the air around him heating to steam. It seemed all were up for a fight.

Roman stared at her, lips slightly parted. He was not accustomed to her pressing back.

"After I found your men raping the girl," Neith said, speaking louder so the growing crowd could hear her, "I sent them on their way, and I haven't seen them since." She stepped forward, distinguishing herself a safe pace in front of her squad. A shield swelled around her, and she felt Max's ether. Its delicate and intricate weaving poured over her skin like silk. It was so unlike any she'd seen before it nearly distracted her. "But, if they have gone missing, you'll find no sympathetic ear from me. If you have come here with evidence of your accusations, brother, let us hear it. Else be on your way. The ale grows stale in our mugs." A few chuckles emerged from the onlookers.

Katya stepped next to Roman, scowl in full display. Neith met it with her own snarl, letting her power wash over her skin, taking on a subtle cobalt glow. This time a threat.

Roman looked from Neith to the faces around her, sizing them up. Neith let her power flare, and shook her head in warning.

She knew he had come expecting her to fold, as she always did. Neith decided in that moment it would never happen again. He had gone too far. Put her people at risk. If he wanted a fight, she would give him one.

Chest heaving, he stepped back, his silver flames recalled. "If I hear of any wrongdoing on your part toward my men, we will be back," he said, his voice losing its bite.

Neith smiled at him, cold and full of malice, but her words were soft. "You do that."

His face twisted with rage at his own ambivalence thrown back in his face. He turned, storming off, his soldiers on his heels. Only Katya remained. She stepped closer to Neith, but Petra blocked her path.

"You heard her," Petra said, low, nose nearly pressed to Katya's. "Get the fuck out of our camp."

Katya held her ground, one side of her mouth curling up. "See you soon," she whispered, before turning and walking away.

Neith waited until they were far from view and the crowd dispersed before she turned back to her squad. Several of them were grinning. Max released the shield, and Ayla stepped out from behind him.

"Is anyone injured?" she asked, looking each one over.

All shook their heads. She met eyes with Sam and felt his rage.

"This is going to start something," Kieran said. "We'll need to watch our backs."

Iris laughed. "Let them try."

"How many are in his unit?" Raiden asked.

"Two squads, one of twenty, the other fourteen. Give or take three," Sam answered, his gaze fixed on Neith.

It was a high enough number to send some nervous glances around the group.

"I don't want anyone walking around camp on their own. If you leave, you go in pairs, preferably more. Understood?" Neith looked around the group for confirmation, receiving nods from each.

She turned back to Sam. Rage, dread, and thrill surged through her. "I want to speak with you alone." It came out sterner than she'd intended. The others looked away as if she'd scolded him. He seemed unaffected and followed her into her tent. When she heard the door cover close, she turned to face him, throwing up a shield so they could speak in confidence.

"Where were you today?" She observed him carefully, determined to pick up anything his words withheld.

He held her gaze, arms folded behind his back. "Away."

"Where?"

He took a step closer to her. "What do you want to ask me, Neith?"

She inhaled, considering her words. She was afraid to ask the wrong question, or perhaps the right one. "If I asked you if you had something to do with the missing men, what would your answer be?"

"If I told you I did not?"

"I would say that is good, but I still hope they do not return."

He took another step closer. They now stood less than an arm's length apart. "And if I told you that I did?"

She thought about it. Neith imagined him executing them. Turning their bodies to ash. She could hear their screams, pleas for mercy. "I would tell you that I hope they suffered." The words left her without intention. It was simply truth, coming out of its own accord. The only thing she had trouble picturing was his face as he did it. She thought perhaps she did not want to see it.

He didn't move. His eyes stayed locked on hers. "*Are* you asking me?"

Her thoughts raced in pace with her heart. If he had and she knew, she would be obligated to turn him in. The thought sent a strike of fear through her chest.

Neith looked down, shaking her head. "No. I am not." He had been telling her without words since he walked into the tent that those men weren't coming back. That would be good enough for her. She closed her eyes, trying to regain governance of her unruly mood. It frightened her how quickly it had come on.

The intensity in Sam's demeanor eased with her own. "Kieran is right," he said. "This conflict is far from over. I fear it will escalate."

"If they bring conflict to us, we will meet it twofold. It is time for us to start training as a squad. We will learn to fight together."

He inclined his head. She thought he might look pleased.

So much had changed in less than a moon. Neith had believed her time as a student was over, that her education had ended. She now knew it was only beginning. If Sam was right and this was how justice was found in times of war, then she would not shy away from serving it. She needed more people and more power. Her only regret was that she did not have the opportunity to know what her father's reaction would have been. But Sam had been right about many things. She knew, in that moment, that she trusted his judgment, and she would not question it again unless given cause.

The following morning, they rose before dawn. Neith and Sam spent an hour the night before creating a rotating schedule of subjects and drills they would work on as a group. Max would lead shieldwork. Sword skill and hand combat fell to Bellamy and Petra. Sam would teach aspects of warfare, including etherfire, cannons, and defensive measures, leaving Neith to instruct manipulating the elements and other advanced wielding techniques.

As they trained through the morning, seven new soldiers came to join her. Three sisters of Zargozan descent, Sada, Anika, and Zinnia. Another girl, Thora, from Vikandal, and three Thranean boys, Wilkin, Aeron, and Evander. All strong wielders.

Neith warned them joining her squad may put a target on their backs. Not a single one seemed deterred. If anything, it was the standoff with Roman and whispers of what had happened that sent them to her.

A messenger arrived early, summoning her to her father.

"I suspect we'll be moving before I return. We will meet you back in line," Neith said to the group. She and Storm set out east to meet him, accompanied by Max.

They rode through the town in the direction of the house by the creek. The streets were quiet, save for the sounds of soldiers readying to march.

The destruction of Northbridge revealed itself in a way it had not in darkness. Without the distraction of drunken men and women, one had little else to take in but the wreckage. A monument in the town square had been blasted into rubble. It looked to have been an elaborate depiction of the six Gods, with only one still standing. Adrae, The Goddess of Darkness, of night, held the moon in her hands, high above her. The others were now a pile of rocks at her feet.

Neith studied the way the fabric of her robe appeared to ripple in the wind and the detail of the thin lines on her lips. She had known such art, such craftmanship, existed, but seeing it true, before her now, brought forth a diverse assembly of thoughts and sensibilities, all in contrast with one another. Someone made this with their own hands, crafted from an image in their mind. Why? To honor the God it depicts? Perhaps. But everything about it—its beauty, its flaws—was so very human.

Everything lovely the statue provoked was not enough to exile her guilt. She had so long desired to see the world, and here she was, tearing it down.

Roman's horse was already tied to the rack out front when they arrived. She wondered how much her father knew about what had occurred. Likely all, she thought. He usually did.

She found her father and brother dining alone. Her father glanced up at her arrival, gesturing for her to join them. He examined her clothing as she approached. He had been too intoxicated the other night to realize she'd not been wearing a dress. She couldn't get a read on his thoughts. If he had any.

A plate of two boiled eggs, blackberries, and bread was placed in front of her as she sat. Roman didn't acknowledge her arrival. He didn't even look up from his meal.

"Would you care for a drink, my lady?" a young servant in a white bonnet asked, head bowed.

"If you've the capabilities for a cup of tea, I would be most grateful." Neith smiled at her, and the girl curtsied, scurrying back into the kitchen.

"Eat," her father ordered. Neith eyed the plate distastefully. She found the entire spectacle odd. The last time they'd dined together outside of council, was a moon or two before departing Necrium. She thought at first this was her father attempting to solve the conflict between them. When she connected eyes with him, she knew that wasn't it at all. She found them appraising but also encouraging. *Ah*, she thought. *This is a test.* Not for her brother. This was a test for her.

She tilted her head, watching Roman eat. "Good morning, brother."

He finally looked up, his expression flat. She wished she knew the words that had been spoken before her arrival. Picking at the blackberries on her plate, she leaned back in her chair, waiting for him to speak.

"Your sister wished you good morning," their father said.

"I heard."

Lorcan's power flared.

"Good morning," Roman mumbled between bites.

The servant returned with a mug of tea, a small tin of honey, and a flagon of milk. Her hands shook nervously as she set the tray on the table, no doubt heedful of the tension in the room.

Neith thanked her, and the girl wasted no time returning to the kitchen. Neith stirred honey and a small splash of milk around before sipping. "Roman was kind enough to visit my camp last night."

"Oh?" Lorcan looked up from his plate. "And how was that?"

"Enlightening," she said, one side of her mouth twitching. "We are looking forward to his next visit. All in my squad."

Roman snorted. "All four of them?"

"Yes." She sipped her tea again. "And the seven who joined this morning."

Roman looked up, unable to conceal his surprise. Her father's eyes narrowed. She returned both looks with a duplicitous smile. It was clear that while information spread fast to her father's ears, there was still a modicum of delay.

"That reminds me, brother, did your men return?" Neith tossed a blackberry in her mouth. It wasn't as sweet as the ones Sam had picked for her. "I speak of the ones that were missing. You were so very worried."

"No," he snarled, "and I suspect they will not." His tone hid none of his contempt.

Neith sighed. "Perhaps that is for the best." She cracked an egg on the table, picking leisurely at the shell. "There is no room for cowardice in our ranks. Better to weed it out now." She leaned forward. "Do you not think?"

"How many of your men are missing?" their father asked. She could tell he was feigning ignorance, and that confused her. She tried to think what purpose or aim he could have to do so.

Whispers of it are often more effective than the whip itself. Sam's words repeated in her mind. Realization struck so fast she almost laughed out loud. Fear of vigilante justice in the ranks could be useful, but it was temperamental. Too much would undermine the structure of authority. There could be no evidence of what had occurred and, more importantly, who had perpetrated it. She thought back to her father's words the day after Godsreach. He had told her Roman had value when handled. He wanted to see if she could handle him.

"Three." Roman dropped his fork. It clattered on the plate. "Three good fighting men." He looked to their father as if he expected this to garner favor.

Lorcan pursed his lips. "That is a tragedy indeed. But," he said, musing, "as your sister says, if they are truly cowards, then perhaps it is for the best. He speared a piece of meat with his fork, chewing it slowly.

"They weren't cowards." Roman's anger seeped out in his ether around the table.

"You speak of them in the past tense. Do you suspect foul play?" Neith bit into the newly shelled egg.

Roman's fist struck the table. "*What is this farce?*"

Neith held up her hands. "I am simply trying to assist."

He leaned over the table, slow and smooth, moving not unlike the snake stitched on his chest. "You know *exactly* what happened to them."

"I assure you, I do not," she said in earnest. "But, if you do not believe me, brother, then perhaps you should make a formal complaint to your commanding officer. He sits just next to you." Neith gestured at their father, who sat back in his chair, arms crossed.

Roman's gaze darted between the two. He was cracking as she designed. It felt dirty, disgraceful even, but he'd given her no choice.

"I would warn you, though," she said, pausing to sip her tea. "An accusation without motive is a weak one. What possible aim could I have to harm your men? That seems far-fetched. I'm new to leadership, it's true, but that seems an obvious misstep. Unless you can speak to my motive, of course."

Roman looked away. Her brother was volatile, petulant, and, as now she knew, complicit. Neith could poke at these flaws, even use them against him, but he was not stupid. "I cannot."

"That is welcome news," Lorcan said. "Because I heard a rumor your men were found raping a girl from town." He turned his gaze to Neith. "I am glad to hear that's all it was. Only rumor." It was a clear message to her. Talk of it ended there. She nodded.

"Because if it were more than rumor," he continued, "I would tell you to get your men under control." Roman's expression fell into disbelief as Lorcan's tone turned colder with every word. "If it were true, I would tell you that if your men cannot find an obliging partner, tell them to fuck their fists, or each other. I do not care which."

Only days ago, Neith would have paled at the abrasive language, but something in her had since changed. Finding the girl in the woods and the events that followed had given her perspective. While she would not be grateful for it at someone else's expense, she could at least learn from it.

"But you are telling us that it is not true. Is that correct?" Lorcan's eyes were locked on Roman.

Roman flexed his jaw. "Yes." He stared at his sister across the table, eyes like daggers. Neith didn't flinch or look away. She didn't give at all.

"Then we are done with this?" Lorcan looked from one to the other.

"Yes, Father. We are done with this." Her eyes told her brother a different story.

Roman smiled and nodded, as if accepting a challenge proposed.

"Then we are done here. Neith, stay a moment." His eyes landed on Roman, and her brother stood from the table, not bothering to look at either of them before he left. When the door closed, her father turned to her.

"Seven more, you say?" His manner turned light, almost jovial, as if the contentious meeting from moments before had not transpired.

She blinked through the whiplash from the shifting of his mood. "As of this morning."

"I am glad to hear it." He returned to his meal. "I understand you have begun training in sword skill."

Neith leaned back in her chair. "Keeping a close eye on me, Father?"

He raised a brow at her, but his lips exposed his amusement.

"Sword skill and hand combat." Neith prepared herself for an objection. A reason why she should not waste her time. He was still gazing at her, and she had to fight all her instincts to pull back beneath it.

He shrugged. It was casual and looked unnatural on him. "I suppose there is no harm in that now."

Neith sipped her tea, hiding her surprise. It had gone cold during their conversation. She sent a tiny spark of ether through the cup to warm it.

Her father cut through the ham on his plate, sawing at it until a bite-sized piece fell away. "When we arrive in Croydyn, I expect the city will surrender quickly."

"Then your plan is working."

He made no reaction to her praise. "You will accompany me to the parley."

She inclined her head. "As you wish."

"Good," he said, pausing to chew. "Let us enjoy our meal."

There was something predatory in the way her father ate. As if straight from the carcass, having slain the animal himself. Juxtaposed with the straightness of his posture, and the dignified way in which he held his fork, it created a strange inconsistency. Neith felt the contradiction of it quite summed him up in a way she had not quantified before.

Neith finished the egg and all the berries, eating in silence for a time. When it was clear the meal would end soon, she decided to ask. "Father, there is something I wish to discuss with you."

He wiped his mouth with a linen napkin, tossing it over his plate, his full attention now fixed on her. It only added to her apprehension. She swallowed against the knot in her throat.

"In Eynsbury, we came across what appeared to be an explosion of sorts. There was a very *strange* signature in the area. Something I'd not encountered before." Neith paused, waiting for some sort of physical reaction from him that didn't come. "I went to Magnus, and he told me of Dryden's research."

"What is your question?" he asked, his gaze unmoved.

Neith blinked. "I have many. How do these *charges*, as Magnus called them, function?"

"An ethercannon is cast and imbued into the stone's own ether, sustaining it for a period of time. We've found it works best with certain stones. Citrine, quartz, selenite, among others." He spoke about it as if it were common science. "That is what we tested in Eynsbury."

Neith tried to think through the mechanics of creating such a thing. It intrigued and terrified her in equal sums. "Why would the stone itself simply not explode?"

"They did. At first."

"Influence?" Neith asked.

One side of his mouth quirked. "Dryden is calling it Transformation. Though it is not a new science. It is a power our kind once held, lost in the Quell." He seemed eager to speak of it now. "Influence does not change, it creates a facade, an illusion, a spell of sorts. Transformation alters the state of the host, no longer able to distinguish itself. Once altered, altered forever. Charges are only one example, and a rudimentary form at that."

Neith paused, taking in all he said. She could not make sense of the mechanics of it. "Magnus said the charges were one of many weapons and tools being constructed."

"We need every advantage we can create, Neith. We are only beginning to explore the possibilities."

She found that a frightening thought. "How does one do this? Is it a born skill?"

"Several with Influence have learned, but it requires a *notable* level of power that few possess. Dryden was the first." Her father watched her intently, as if measuring her reaction.

She worked to give him none. "Do the Esērii have similar capabilities?"

"Not yet, but they will. They have a team in Nyrovi that appears to be close to making breakthroughs on Transformation. But they are years, if not decades, behind us in this."

Neith's blood ran cold at what a war with such weapons could do. She wanted to ask why she would be kept in the dark about a power she herself may be able to wield. Something told her to wait. "Did you anticipate I would detect it?"

"I aspired for you to."

"*Why?*" she asked, her tone dripping with frustration.

"I think you know why."

Neith sighed, sitting back in her chair. "Why is everything a test, Father? Why must all be a game?"

"Not games, Neith. Lessons."

But they were games. It was all a game, and her father controlled the pieces, moving them around the board at his leisure. "When do the lessons conclude? I'm nineteen winters, no longer a child. If you want me as your heir, as Thrane's Praxa, when am I to stop being on the receiving end of revelation after revelation? Would it not be pertinent to bring me in?"

"The lessons never conclude, Neith. When we decide ourselves master and no longer student, we are at the beginning of our end." He leaned across the table. "Look what it has done for you. You are inquisitive, insightful, and strategic beyond your own comprehension. And you will only grow more so."

You have fashioned me as you saw fit, she thought. "I am not clay to be molded, Father."

"We are all clay," he said. "We require others to shape us before we can shape ourselves."

She snatched her teacup from the table, finishing it in one gulp. "And if we do not like the shapes our makers leave?"

"Add water and start again."

Neith grumbled, folding her arms. She should have known better than to attempt a battle of wits with her father.

"You are proving yourself to be everything I hoped you would be. You earn your place in Thrane. These are our ways." He leaned back, his expression softening. "I can see that you are cross with me. I understand. I need you to trust that I have your best interests—and those of Thrane—in all that I do." He reached across the table for her hand. She looked down at the unusual point of affection. "Do I have your trust, daughter?"

"You do." It came out quickly, but it was true, she thought, or perhaps hoped. She started to apologize for questioning him, but hesitated. That was not what he would want.

"Once we take Highclere and stabilize the city, I will formally announce you as my heir."

She frowned. "So soon?"

He nodded. "Until then, I need you to continue to show all why you deserve it."

"I will do my best."

"Good." He stood abruptly, and she looked up in surprise, standing when she realized it was a signal for her to leave.

28

Nara

"A chancellor is the personification of the High Council in all manners
militaristic and political, acting as its representation to the world."

ESĒRII BIJRAH Z'OURA
ADE NYANTHI AND PHILOMENA TALIESIN, 805 AQ

Nara hit the ground with a thud.

"Fuck." She coughed, inhaling copious amounts of dust.

"You're out of practice, Nyanthi." Fintan spun a wooden sword in his hand. "You couldn't find any time to spar in those ten moons on the road?"

Nara turned on her side, climbing up to one knee. "With whom? My mother?" She struggled to catch her breath.

Fintan laughed. He leaned over her, hand extended, grin wide. "Don't worry, I'll whip you back into shape." He was one of few who could best her with a sword.

Nara took the hand of the huge Vikan man, and he pulled her to her feet. His blond hair was pulled back into a knot, revealing all the small scars marring his face. Years as a ranger were not easy on the body, as well she knew, having done two herself before being offered a position as a chancellor.

They'd come up together in the same class and courses, forming something of a friendship along the way. It was, at the very least, a mutual respect.

"Again?" he asked, brows cocked.

"I need a break." She tossed her two training swords into a crate, and they walked together to the water station, filling fresh cups. They drank and watched the others sparring across the yard.

"Have you heard any news from Barka?" Nara asked.

"Of what sort?" He turned to face her, combing back stray pieces of blond hair falling into his eyes.

"My stepfather was expected to return two days past."

Fintan frowned. "Nothing of trouble. Why? Are you concerned?"

"Not yet," she admitted, "but it is unlike him. He is more often than not painfully prompt." She sipped the cool water again. Her arms were so fatigued it felt a task to simply lift the cup.

"A couple of days isn't out of the ordinary. I wouldn't worry." He gave her a reassuring smile. Nara could only think that if he knew what she knew, he would not think such a thing. The information felt like a rot in her gut.

"I'm sure you are right." Nara sighed. "So, what have I missed around here?"

Fintan shrugged, fanning his tan tunic away from his body. They were both pouring sweat. "Nothing exciting I fear."

"Come on," she said, giving his shoulder a playful nudge. "I'm sure there is something to whisper about. I've been on the road for ten moons. Scarcely back for a day at a time." She refilled her cup, pouring its contents over her head, wiping the dust from her eyes and mouth.

He tilted his head, blue eyes gleaming with a theatrical display of shock. "Has Nara Nyanthi come to gossip? How uncharacteristically common of you."

She huffed. "Says the nephew of the great Consul *Seraphine Nielsen*."

"What are you going to do when your assignment is up?"

Nara noted the abrupt change of subject. "Who says I will not reenlist?"

"For fuck's sake." Fintan glowered, like one begging another to give up an act.

"You are one to talk," she teased. "Infamous ranger turned instructor. You are far too young for that sad story."

A bark-like laugh sprang from his lips. "Between you and me, it was not my idea. My aunt asked me to accept this post."

Nara thought that odd, but perhaps the reason for his recoil at the mention of her. "I suppose you cannot say no to the council."

He turned to look her square in the eyes. "You do."

"And look where that has gotten me."

"Oh, how the mighty have fallen," he mused.

Nara laughed, but his words struck a bit too true for it to reach her belly. She glanced at him. "Why would she ask that of you?"

Fintan shrugged. "She had reasons, but I suspect she wants me close to the Citadel. She's grown… *cautious* in her later years." Gloomful consideration cast a shadow over his features. "I'm all she has left."

Interesting, Nara thought. If the council was truly abreast of Thrane's escalated activities, that would explain Seraphine's desire to keep her nephew close.

A tall, lean woman with a long, red braid approached. She was dirty and dust-covered, like Nara and Fintan. The sway in her walk accentuated the curve of her hip. "Nyanthi," she greeted as she pulled leather gloves from her hands. Even that seemed a lascivious act.

"Carston," Nara returned. "Have you also turned in your ranger badge to instruct?"

Seline Carston laughed. It was songlike. Alluring, like her figure. "Not anytime soon." Her eyes flicked to Fintan before returning to Nara. "How long are you in the Citadel?"

"Not long," Nara answered. "Yourself?"

"Another moon or so. I'm waiting for my mother." Seline grabbed a clean cup from the tray, filling it with water. "We're back on the road as soon as she returns from the north."

Nara took a breath so as not to seem eager. "What is she doing in the north?"

"Visiting Maisie," Seline answered, tipping up her cup. "She's stationed in Straeth through the Frost Moon."

Nara nodded, swallowing the guilt creeping up her throat.

"Why?" Seline asked, frowning, as if picking up on the concealed tension.

Nara shrugged. "Only making conversation. Cerys is in the north as well." Seline already knew that. Nara silently cursed herself to get it together. She never struggled to lie. But this was different. This information was dangerous, and she was lying to people she cared for.

Seline eyed her but seemed to shake it off and turned to Fintan. "See you tonight?" she asked, heavy with suggestion.

He nodded.

"Safe travels, Nyanthi," Seline said as she turned away.

"You as well," Nara called after her. She glanced at Fintan watching Seline saunter across the yard. "That's a new development. Aren't Seline and Alec still warming each other's beds?"

A wide grin spread over his lips. "You've been away a while."

Nara chuckled, shaking her head. "Is there a woman in the Citadel you've not bedded?"

He turned to face her, brows rising.

Nara scoffed. "I'll not argue you're pretty, but you've one too many cocks for me."

He laughed, and she pushed him, trying not to join in.

As it died, so did the lighthearted mood. "Don't think I didn't notice you evaded my question."

"What question is that?" Nara asked, feigning ignorance. When he simply stared at her, she relented. "No." She huffed. "I will not reenlist."

"Good," he said, nodding.

"I have asked to be reinstated."

His brows jumped. "Have you?" Fintan set his cup on the cart beside them and folded his arms. "And what was their answer?"

"I suspect I'm about to find out." Nara pointed across the field to Tyr, who approached. "You'll dirty your robes out here, Tyr," she called to him.

Tyr scowled. "Then make haste, Nyanthi. The council calls for you."

"After careful consideration and much discourse, we have decided to reinstate your post as chancellor." All eyes were fixed on Nara as Seraphine spoke.

Nara stood before the council, dirty and sweat-drenched, not unlike she had only days before. "I thank you." She bowed her head. "Most graciously." The display of thankfulness was not a total fabrication.

"It is not conditional, but we expect a certain caliber of behavior." Seraphine's eyes narrowed. "I hope I do not need to explain further."

"No, Consul." Nara looked down, doing her best to appear meek. "You do not."

"The exceptions that have been made for you are not common, Nara," Seraphine continued. "Please do not force us to make difficult decisions on your behalf again. The outcome will likely be far different if we do."

"I understand." She bowed her head again, as slight as physically possible. She feared saying too much and having her mouth get away from her.

"The region in which you previously resided has been reassigned to another chancellor. Your new region has yet to be determined." More games, Nara thought. They were hanging the possibility of the north over her head. If she was a good girl, she could be rewarded.

"I am grateful to be reinstated and will gladly serve whatever region the council decides." Nara looked each of them in the eye.

"Your previous quarters remain empty and are being prepared for you," Lazlo said and set the gold eagle pin on the council table. "Your badge, Chancellor."

Nara walked up to the dais and clipped it to her chest, then returned to her place. For a moment, no one spoke.

"We have decided to hold a closed session when your mother returns. We will form a plan of action on how we will proceed regarding the Thranean threat, not only in the south but in the north." Delphane was sitting back in her chair, watching Nara's reaction.

Nara looked from face to face, trying to keep her expression still, fearing to show her desperation to attend.

"We would like you to attend."

"Thank you," Nara said quickly, looking up to Lazlo.

"As a guest," Delphane clarified.

"I understand."

"In the meantime, you will continue to keep the information you brought to us about the attack in Amul confidential." Desme's eyes were fixed on her, clearly a warning.

The silence grew again.

"As all of the officers on your previous team have been reassigned, new ones will be selected soon," Seraphine said.

Nara nodded. "If it pleases the council, I have one in mind."

He was seated at the end of the bar. It was the dingiest of pubs in the Commons. Dark, and a bit dreary. It smelled like stagnant water and mistakes. Just her sort of place.

Harker looked up, taking notice of her approach. His eyes moved to the gold eagle pinned on her chest. "Nicely done, Chancellor."

She sat next to him and held up her hand, signaling for a glass. It was the middle of the day, and the pub had few other patrons. The barkeep set a clean pony glass in front of her.

"Have your efforts produced?" she asked, voice low.

"Not a damn thing." He tossed back his whiskey. "If there is anything being buried here, they're digging a very deep hole."

Nara sighed. "As has been my experience."

"I'm not sure if it's a comfort or concern," he said. "No one seems to know anything."

Nara nodded. She'd taken interest in some of the things Fintan had said, but that's all it was… interest. Nothing tangible. "The council will hold a closed session when my mother returns to decide on a course of action."

Harker lifted his glass in mock cheer. "Well, that's something."

"They invited me to attend."

"That's something even better." He turned to look at her. "It must have been some apology you made."

Nara scowled. "It was not my favorite day." She reached into the pocket of her trousers and pulled out a gold pin in the shape of an eagle's wings. Similar to the one she wore, but smaller. She set it on the bar in front of him.

He eyed it. "What is that?"

"That is the pin of a deputy chancellor."

"I know what it is, love. Why are you setting it in front of me?"

She didn't answer.

Harker picked up the pin and turned it between his fingers. "You are serious?"

"Quite."

He cleared his throat, jaw flexing. "That's very generous."

"It is not a favor, Harker," she said, with all the seriousness she felt. "I need you."

His eyes searched hers, as if looking for jest. She gave him none. "Well, in that case…" He clipped the pin to his chest.

Nara grabbed the bottle to fill their glasses. Only drops came out when she turned it up. She held it aloft. "Barkeep, another bottle for my deputy, please."

29

Thea

"It is not the false words spoken in which the greatest deception lies. It is in those left unsaid."

THE RECOVERED JOURNALS OF SONIA THRONDSEN, 1181 AQ

Thea was too afraid to sneak away the same day Sylvie had shown her the grave. It was not only the risk of being caught she feared, but what she would find. Or worse, what she might not. She wanted to forget, to leave it behind, but with each day that passed, the memory of what occurred in the ruins only grew more vivid. When she closed her eyes, she could see the shadowed figure, feel the terror. In her chest, in her belly. The laugh haunted her thoughts. It felt so real she struggled to understand how her mind had pushed it aside for so many days.

She was determined to go back. Something wasn't right. When her mind wandered into considering herself delusional, she would think of the look in Sylvie's eyes at the grave. The way her father had lied about the messenger. Alec Turan and Breeda arguing in the woods. *Strange things*, her sister had said.

The day Thea decided it was time, she waited until the moon was high and the castle quiet. She crept through the halls down to the private gardens, well familiar with how to go unnoticed at night. All the visits to and returns from the Iren Stein had made her quite skilled at sneaking around. She stopped at one of the sheds, retrieving a small handheld shovel on her way.

Thea followed the path Sylvie had shown her, grateful it wasn't far. Since the incident, she had been scared to wander, not that she'd been allowed to do so without guard.

She found the scene as it was six days before. Eyeing the disturbed earth, she gave herself one last chance to change her mind. If she walked away, she could forget everything and return to her life. It was an appealing alternative. Part of her wanted to turn back, unsure if it was fear of what awaited or fear she was a fool. She imagined how she would feel if she dug up the decaying body of a mountain cat. Certifiably mad and utterly ridiculous. But in her heart, in her guts, she knew the question would never leave her. She would have no peace without knowing.

She dropped to her knees and began to dig. She tore into the earth, ferocious, desperate, the garden spade hardly up to the task. Her arms and shoulders ached from the effort. She had to take several breaks, panting and staring up at the moon, her concern of discovery growing with each rake of the small shovel.

Hours passed before she hit hard clay and accepted that the grave was nothing more than a four-foot-deep deception. She climbed out of the hole, spent, trying to make sense of her feelings.

She was relieved she wasn't a lunatic. That her gut had been right. She no longer entertained the idea it had been an animal. They had sold her a lie. *But why?*

What had truly chased after her, and where was it now? The thought sent her looking around frantically in the dark. Whatever it was might not be dead. It could be stalking her now. She forced herself to breathe and gain control of her thoughts. She was a short walk from the castle. If she screamed, a guard would hear her. She hoped.

She could still hear the laugh, feel the blast of air on her neck, the tug on her hair. Like her body remembered as explicitly as her mind. So real she questioned if it was remembrance or evocation, and her fear had called her assailant forth. And it was there, now, just behind her, its sinister breath on her neck. Panic rippled through her like a rock skipping water. She scrambled around on her knees in all directions, finding only darkness and trees.

She stood to run but realized she couldn't leave the grave unearthed. Thea worked quickly to fill it back in, the task taking nowhere near the time it had taken to dig it. She stomped on the ground, scattering leaves and sticks. When it was an acceptable ruse, she sprinted back through the woods toward the castle. She made it to the edge and stopped, hands resting against the rough bark of a tree, trying to steady her breath.

Looking down at her arms, she realized the remaining evidence was her person. She was filthy, covered in soil and duff. Her absence could be explained. Her current appearance could not.

She made her way to the lake, to a place she knew she couldn't be seen from the guard towers. Stepping out of her dress, she thought how wise it would have been to do so before tearing into the earth like a madwoman.

Thea stepped into the cool water, scrubbing at her arms and legs. She hid the wet shift under brush, planning to return for it another time. Her dress was dark enough to hide its sullied state. She looked herself over and cursed, clearly not skilled in the art of deception. If she was going to play the investigator, she would need to be much smarter from there out.

When she made it back to her room, she turned the lock and collapsed against the door. The early glow of dawn seeped in through the window. She pulled off her damp and dirty dress, hiding it behind one of her trunks.

When she was dry and in new undergarments, she fell into bed, pulling the covers high to her chin. She had to tell someone. But who? Callum? She wasn't sure how he would react. She still hadn't told him, or Cat, or anyone else, for that matter, about the attack. He might be cross and tell someone else. A wrong someone. Then her secret inquisition would be foiled.

She couldn't think about it anymore. She needed sleep. She needed to get her thoughts aligned. Thea let her eyes close, feeling herself drift. A strike of panic ripped them back open when she realized she'd forgotten the spade.

Thea feigned illness the following morning. It wasn't exactly a falsehood. Her head did ache, but mostly from the absence of sleep. She had too many things to do. Evidence to hide, evidence to retrieve.

She didn't have a plan, but she was certain she had to keep her suspicions to herself. If she was found out, it would be over. She'd have no answers. Her heart ached a little at the understanding her father had lied to her. Not once, but twice. Sylvie, too.

Sylvie brought lunch, setting the tray across her lap. It was a clear broth soup that smelled of garlic and onion. The sort of thing one eats when one is ill.

"How are you feeling?" Sylvie opened the curtains, filling the room with sunlight.

"Much improved." Thea sipped the broth from the bowl, breathing in its comforts.

Sylvie sat on the edge of the bed, watching her eat. Thea didn't know if it was her own paranoia or if she was being appraised. All her thoughts were to act unsuspecting. She was going to need to get better at it.

Sylvie looked down at Thea's hand resting on the tray. When she did too, her heart thumped. The undersides of her nails were black. Thea swallowed and then smiled. "Gardening."

"Ah."

Thea couldn't get a read on Sylvie, and it added to her trepidation.

"Should I call for a bath?" Sylvie asked, eyes narrowed.

"A bath would be most welcomed." Anything to get her out of the room. Thea considered simply asking her. If Sylvie was lying about that night, she had probably been commanded to. But she was her friend. She might tell her the truth.

"Is there something you want to ask me, Thea?" Sylvie sat facing her, the same strange, unidentifiable look about her face. Thea thought for a moment it was a taunt.

"No," she answered, and shrugged a shoulder.

Sylvie held her gaze for far longer than was natural. "Very well." She stood. "I'll return shortly."

Thea watched her walk from the room, practically counting the steps. When the door closed, she sprang from the bed with the tray in hand, leaving it on the center table. She stepped into a simple dress and boots, and ran from her room. It was lunch hour, so the only people who watched her leave the castle were kitchen staff and a gardener clipping shrubs. But still, it was a risk she'd have to take. Once she hit the tree line, she sprinted. She was back to the spot of the grave in a quarter hour's time.

But the grave was gone.

She turned in circles. She must have made a mistake. *No*, she thought, *this is the place*. But the ground was now grass-covered and indistinguishable. Her hands came up to hold her head, breath hitching. She looked around desperately, eyes swelling with the sting of her panic renewed.

Determined not to have an attack, she leaned forward, palms resting on her knees. "Breathe," she said out loud. "Breathe, Thea." Someone had created this ruse just like the first. She transformed her fear into anger, a snarl twisting on her face. Someone was messing with her. All of this had been done to hide something. And by the Gods, she would know what.

⁘

It took an hour to return to the scene. She closed her eyes, counting steps, trying to find the spot where she'd fallen. *No*, was pushed. She was sure of it now. The more she remembered, the less she doubted. She stumbled over a large rock with a dark reddish-brown stain. She reached up to touch the fading cut on her hairline, shivering at the memory of the crack, black closing in around her, believing she would die.

Determining the path she'd run down was difficult. It had been nearly a halfmoon, and in that time the forest had changed much. She could find no evidence of a chase or anything else out of place.

When she crested the hill, she closed her eyes again, trying to replay what had happened. Where the laugh had come from. It had to be the north side of the clearing. Walking in that direction, she noticed the ground was oddly bare, almost as if it had burned. It was covered over with leaves and fallen branches. Thea cleared the debris, and a crude, ashy path led directly into the woods. The trees on the edges also appeared to have been scorched. She looked around, stumped.

"Calithea."

Thea jumped, falling forward into the trees. When she scrambled around, she found Breeda standing over her. She had been so distracted she hadn't even heard her approach.

"Gods!" Thea exhaled, some of her panic residing. "You scared the life out of me!"

Breeda said nothing at first, simply peered down at her sprawled on the forest floor, a single brow cocked. "What are you doing out here?" Her strangely unruffled demeanor added to Thea's discontent.

"I—um—"

"You know your father doesn't want you traveling this far into the woods." Breeda's hands were clasped together, resting in front of her body.

"How did you know where I was?" Thea tried to steer the conversation.

Breeda reached down, pulling Thea to her feet. "I didn't, but this is where you usually run off to when you're on your own. Sylvie was running the castle searching for you. I found her in the gardens. You've given her a right worry, Calithea."

"Oh. I am sorry. That was not my intention. But—" Thea's head cocked to one side. "How do you know about this place?"

Breeda scoffed. It was dry but not meant to belittle. "I've been looking after you since you were a babe. Did you really believe I didn't know?"

"No," Thea thought out loud. "I suppose not." She brushed the leaves from her skirt. "Did you tell my father?"

Breeda folded her arms. "No, but I should. Why are you out here?"

This was the moment to decide. Should she tell her? Thea felt Breeda would likely think her unstable. But she needed someone she could trust. Perhaps she simply needed someone. "Breeda, I—"

The older woman stepped closer, eyes narrowed. "What is it, my girl?"

Thea thought she detected that same hint of a taunt in her tone that Sylvie had. Like someone asking another to ask. "Nothing. It's nothing. I only wanted to get out of the castle. I know I left oddly. I will make my apologies to Sylvie."

Breeda stared at her, wholly unconvinced, but nodded. "Come on, let's get back. It looks like rain."

30

Nara

"Order is best kept under an inquisitional eye at all times, lest it harden, trapping mankind in place alongside it."

THE COST OF VALOR
AUTHOR UNKNOWN, 203 BQ
TRANSLATED FROM OLD ASARI BY MERIAH TURAN
HAIS Z'NOSIŠ, 1200 AQ

Nara and Harker were having lunch in the Commons when they received a summons to the palace. Her mother had returned.

They were not led to the council chambers, but a smaller room not far from it. It held a table at its front where each member of the council sat, facing several others. Tora and Sanne sat at one. They looked up as Nara and Harker entered. Nara moved with urgency as her mother stood. She was dirty and worn. Nara wrapped her arms around her, holding her tight.

Tora pulled back, taking Nara's face in her hands. "You look well, dearest." Her eyes moved to the eagle pin on her chest, and she smiled. "I see there is much to discuss." Her focus moved to Harker, taking in the smaller pin on him. "Quite a lot."

"I am glad you have returned," Nara said with a tenderness she did not often express. They embraced again before Nara and Harker took their seats.

Tora recounted her return to Amul. By the time they'd arrived, nearly half the town had fled. They tracked down as many as they could, covering memories and providing aid, but some were still out there with a full account of what had happened. She believed many would return in time and that it would be worthwhile sending a team to continue the cleanup.

Everyone in the room sat quietly for a time, taking in the story and its implications.

"We have resolved greater challenges than this," Lazlo encouraged. "And I agree with Tora. We should send not one but two teams back to Amul to scout the area. We can handle whispers, but frantic and fearful crowds will have consequences only leading to a much larger disorder."

The consuls all nodded their agreement. Seraphine gestured for Tyr. She spoke low and directly to him. He nodded and left the room.

Nara tapped her foot quietly, choking back the words that wanted to fire from her lips. The laboriously slow pace at which the council moved was not an easy burden for her to bear.

"We have received no further sightings of anyone wearing the insignia of Thrane. I believe we should continue to keep this quiet until we have a better understanding of what we're dealing with," Delphane said to the room. "We received no such reports from the north."

"Any such report would still be in transit." Nara failed to keep the irritation from her tone. Tora's eyes jumped to hers. A warning to keep her mouth shut.

Delphane glared at her. Her dark hair was pulled away from her face in a low bun much tighter than usual. "We will not weaken our position in the Citadel by sending a force north based on assumptions, Chancellor Nyanthi. If there is unrest, we will hear of it soon and address it as good sense dictates."

Seraphine sighed. "I agree with restraint here. Six Etherborn in black is not something worthy of the panic this would create."

Nara's toe-tapping grew audible in the room. "You don't need to send a force. Send me—"

"Your eagerness to volunteer yourself is noted." Her grandmother's eyes narrowed on her.

Nara exhaled. She couldn't understand if they were frightened, inept, or malicious in their inaction, but she was starting not to care. "The longer we wait, the more we will have to regret when what we suspect is confirmed." She stood, leaning over the table. "For Godssake! I put in your very hands a patch with their insignia that I ripped from one of them myself. Thrane is over two thousand miles north. If we wait for word, we might as well turn our backs! Why must I state what is *obvious*?"

"May I remind you, Chancellor, you are here by invitation. If you cannot contain yourself, you will be escorted out." Delphane met Nara's glare with one of her own. "Return to your chair."

Nara looked around the room for an ally. She met eyes with her mother and received a sympathetic gaze. Nara fell back into her chair, arms crossed.

"I am inclined to agree with my daughter," Tora said. "I myself saw the destruction of what occurred in Amul. The consequences are severe and grow more so the longer we wait. They made it quite clear they did not fear discovery. Let us not be fools to what that means."

The council looked at one another. Nara looked to her mother, eyes teeming with gratitude.

"I do not think it harmful to send Chancellor Nyanthi north," Lazlo said. "To investigate," he clarified. "Not to take action."

"Sending someone north is not what concerns me. It is sending *her* north that does." It was clear to Nara that if any votes had not gone her way on reinstatement, Delphane had been one of them. "She has been reinstated for mere *days*," Delphane continued. "Her behavior the past year has been erratic and disrespectful. I cannot sanction sending a chancellor that I do not, at this moment, have full confidence in. What if the outcome is a fallout worse than what we are currently facing in Amul?"

"You cannot mean to suggest she is responsible." Seraphine peered down the table at Delphane. "It is clear to me had Chancellor Nyanthi not pressed to return, the outcome would have been far worse."

Ceneric and Phelen nodded their agreement. Delphane straightened. Her grandmother remained neutral.

Nara knew they were all afraid. She did not blame them for it. She was as well.

"We need to speak on this more," Lazlo said. He looked at his fellow consuls. "We will give you an answer on the morrow."

Nara exhaled. She could see on their faces they had no intention of sending her. The council did not know that she knew they had already sent Alec Turan. They were buying time. She had waited five days. She could wait one more. When she defied them, they would have only themselves to blame. Nara nodded.

Each member of the council filed out of the room. Sanne followed.

"I'll give you two some time," Harker said, standing. "It's good to have you back, Tora."

Her mother looked up and smiled.

When the door closed, Nara reached for her hand. "Thank you for your backing."

"You are most welcome, dearest, but I simply acted as my conscience dictated." She looked down at the eagle pin. "You are fortunate they agreed to reinstate you."

"I know." And she did.

"But now you will risk it and travel north with or without sanction?" It used to annoy Nara how easily her mother anticipated her, but she was growing to be grateful for it.

"They give me no choice, Mother. I will not leave Cerys ignorant of such a threat." She considered whether she should tell her all Meriah had shared.

"I agree it is wise to send someone north, but I am not sure I agree it should be common knowledge. Not yet. There are too many unknowns."

"It is the right thing to do," Nara pressed. "They need to tell people what is going on."

"Is it? Decisions like these seem easy to those who do not have to make them. The pure panic that it would cause..." Tora shook her head. "You young people do not understand. You can't remember. Many of you were not yet born. You didn't watch brother turn on brother. Sister slaying sister. Your father—"

Nara glared at her in warning. "You know I do not wish to speak about him."

Tora reached for Nara's hand, holding it between hers. "Our world will look very different very soon, dearest. If Thrane brings Etherborn to wage war, I fear the future. The last time our kind warred, we were nearly wiped from the earth. The world fell into ruin for hundreds of years." She sighed. "I don't know anymore. I think we have been foolish to believe we could carry on in secret. This feels an inevitable future, Lorcan Dracos or not."

Nara would not argue that.

"When the idleborn come to know of us, there will be chaos. We cannot Influence the entire world. The kingdoms that are not privy to our existence will act on the defensive. And I, quite frankly, will not be able to blame them. I fear we've been arrogant and naive."

The look on her mother's face as she spoke both pained and terrified Nara to see. She had always been composed, optimistic. Sure of a resolution.

"Very well," Tora said, giving Nara's hand a squeeze. "I will not try to stop you. I know my children well enough to know it is useless to try to dissuade them from something they are determined to do." She stood. "I am road weary. I wish to go home to my husband and rest."

Nara inhaled, hesitating.

"What is it?" Tora asked, returning to her seat.

"Mother, Sayeed has not returned from Barka," she said softly.

Tora cocked her head. "When was he expected?"

Nara's face grew further grim. "Five days past."

Tora looked away, eyes scanning the ground. Her bottom lip disappeared between her teeth.

"I am sure he will return soon. Something must have delayed him." Nara tried to sound confident, reassuring, but knew she was failing.

"I must ride to Barka," Tora said to herself.

Nara shook her head. "You must rest. I will send a page to inquire after his whereabouts. Will that suffice for now?" Nara cursed herself she had not already done so. She readied herself for further opposition, but her mother nodded.

"When will you leave?"

"Not before the council gives their decision."

They stood and embraced. Nara didn't want to let go.

"Thank you, dearest," her mother said, and pulled back. Once again, her eyes were drawn to the eagle pin. "I am proud of you. I know words were said that were not easily drawn from your lips to get that pin back on your chest."

Praise for such a simple task made Nara feel like a child. She supposed, in some ways, she had been acting like one as of late. "Come, Mother, let's get you home."

31

Nara

"The only secrets we truly keep are the ones we do not tell ourselves."

THE RECOVERED JOURNALS OF SONIA THRONDSEN, 1182 AQ

Nara spent the morning sparring with Fintan. It was the first day since returning to the Citadel he had not knocked her on her backside. She was starting to feel like herself again.

She made her way to the Village with the intention of checking on her mother and packing her traveling clothes. The council would call for her soon with their decision, but Nara knew she would be leaving on the morrow, either way. She hoped it would be with their blessing, but she did not require it.

As she approached the house, she squinted, trying to see who stood out front. She thought it might be Tyr. Taking off into a light run, her thoughts were confirmed as she drew closer. "Does the council call for me?"

"No," he answered, then looked toward the door. "You should go inside." His eyes were hesitant, perhaps apologetic.

Nara swung the door open, following voices to the sitting room. Her mother, grandmother, and Seraphine all stood, facing something Nara could not make out.

"Mother?" Nara called. Tora turned, revealing Sayeed on one of the sofas. A healer stood over him. Her pale yellow ether poured out over the right side of his body. Nara strode to join the other women. All eyes were grave. "Sayeed, are you well?"

Sayeed gave her a strained smile. "A few broken bones, nothing to fear." His dark curls were disheveled and wild. Splattered blood stained his golden skin. The beige tunic he wore was dirty and torn. He looked a far cry from the composed man she'd always known, but whatever his ailments, he appeared healed. Unless it wasn't his blood.

"What has happened?" Nara searched every face in the room.

There was a faint clicking sound, and Sayeed flinched. He rolled his shoulder, shaking out his arm.

"Sayeed was attacked on the road," Tora answered, her eyes still fixed on her husband.

"Gods…" Nara's chest grew heavy with dread. "By whom?" She asked but already knew the answer.

Sayeed thanked the healer, and she helped him stand. "A group of soldiers in black leather armor." He looked at Tora. "The Thranean insignia on their chests."

Her mother walked to him. She ran her hand over his cheek.

Nara had to summon courage to ask. "Did we lose anyone?"

"No," Sayeed answered. "I was traveling alone. I injured two of them, but they escaped. They came out of nowhere. It was unprovoked." He leaned against Tora, limping as they walked across the room.

Nara exhaled. It was an odd thing to have one's fears confirmed. She'd known since she ripped that patch from the girl's chest in Amul that the moment she found herself in was inevitable. War was upon them. In part, she felt relieved that finally the council would have no choice but to act. But it was thin and strange and wrong. It was burning up, turning to ash in her body with each breath. Terror took its place. Oily and smooth, slithering through every empty space. She felt it in the tremble of her hands, in the ache in her bones. In the seizing of her chest and the thumping of her heart. *Fury is hot*, she thought. *But terror… terror is ice cold.*

Nara moved with swiftness, stepping in front of Desme and Seraphine. "Has the council come to a decision on my request to travel north?"

"No," her grandmother answered. "But you should go, regardless."

"But the council—"

"We will take care of the council," Seraphine assured. Her eyes moved to Desme, and she nodded.

"You will observe and report. Do not engage in conflict unless given no choice." Desme's hand rose to rest on Nara's shoulder. "Nara, please tell me you understand."

"I understand, Grandmother."

"Once the council agrees, we will send more to follow. Leave instructions for them at the field house in Azmar. Go now. Make haste." Desme pulled her into a tight embrace. "And be safe, child."

Nara nodded, a bit frantically.

A hand grasped her arm, turning her around. It was her mother. "We must speak."

✤

Nara followed her mother to the garden. When Tora cloaked them in a shield, she grew more nervous. She had not thought that possible.

"I do not have the time to tell this to you elegantly. So, I will lay it all out and ask your forgiveness after." Tora's eyes were heavy as she spoke.

"Mother…"

"Cerys is in Highclere, this you know. But she is not stationed in the field house."

Nara swallowed against the dread knotting in her throat. "Please do not make me ask questions."

Tora nodded, taking an audible breath. "She was sent to watch over a girl. Well, she is a young woman now. An Etherborn."

Nara frowned.

"It is a long and rather complicated story."

"Make it a simple one."

"The girl is the daughter of Sonia Throndsen."

Nara blinked. She waited for her mother to correct herself. She did not. "Sonia and her unborn child were murdered by Lorcan Dracos over twenty years ago."

Tora sighed, and her shoulders slumped. It was a far cry from the elegant posture she normally possessed. She looked nervous, and perhaps guilty, like one telling another's secrets. "That is only half of the truth. It is what the council wants everyone to believe. Very few know the whole."

Nara's irritation flared as she prepared herself for more. "And what is the whole truth?"

"Sonia left the Citadel to return to Icena. She did not wish for her daughter to be Esērii. She had her reasons. While I did not agree, I respected her choice. Sonia believed we could do more for the world, for the idleborn, living in the open, in peace. Working together. It was Sonia who inspired Lorcan's beliefs." Tora looked away. Anger formed behind her eyes. "But he twisted them, distorted them."

"Her beliefs are well known, Mother," Nara said, leaning forward in her chair. She was doing her best to be patient, to listen, but she wanted to know what in the hells it had to do with Cerys.

"Sonia returned to Seahenge to give birth and raise her daughter among her own people. We were friends, *good* friends, but she would not name the child's father. Not even to me. It was two moons later that Lorcan staged his coup. Most of it you know. When it failed, he fled north with his followers. They sacked Seahenge and several other Iceni villages. Sonia died defending her home and her people." Tora paused, wiping a stray tear falling down her cheek. "As you know, Lorcan disappeared into the mountains, and the world heard nothing from him since. What you and most others do not know is that Sonia had given birth only hours before and put her daughter on a ship with three Iceni Etherborn warriors, bound for Ire, to the girl's father."

"For *Godssake*," Nara hissed. "The deceptions never end." Nara rubbed her eyes. "Who is the father?"

"She is the daughter of Ulric Ironne. Her name is Calithea."

Nara let the implications of that sink in.

"They kept her hidden for nearly ten years. It wasn't until the girl grew too powerful and they reached out, that we learned of her. One of the Iceni came to the Citadel. She came to me first, and that is the only reason I know of this. Together, we went to the council and, after a very contentious meeting, came to an agreement. The child would be allowed to remain in Highclere as Sonia wished, but bound, with the help and shared guardianship of the Esērii. It was thought that their ability to successfully hide the girl for so many years unnoticed would not look well on leadership. We were just getting back on our feet after the rebellion. At the time, it did not seem so problematic. She lives an idleborn life, bound, wholly unaware of her gift."

Nara recoiled. "I've never heard of such a thing."

"It was deemed necessary—"

"It is *cruelty*." The very notion was appalling to her. Nara had seen Etherborn who had been bound for long periods of time. It was punishment. It was no way to live.

Tora looked away. "Would it have not been crueler to take a ten-year-old child away from the only life she's known? A good life. A peaceful life of privilege with a family that loved her."

Nara sighed. Any question of her distrust of the council vanished. "Why are you telling me all of this?"

"I'm tired of keeping secrets, Nara. The time for that has passed. And—"

"And *what?*"

"Lorcan Dracos is many things, but he is as far from a fool as any man I've ever known. We do not believe he knows the girl lives, but if he does or finds out, he will seek her out. To bring her to his cause. The girl is thought to be quite powerful, and their families are connected. His own wife, Lia Throndsen, is the girl's aunt."

Nara shook her head. "Cerys would have told me this before she left."

"Cerys did not know until she arrived in Highclere."

Nara closed her eyes. She felt unstable, even sitting, as thoughts tumbled through her, pulling her in every direction. She stood. "I have to go. Thank you for telling me. I wish you had told me sooner, but I understand why you did not." Nara knew, and so did her mother, she would have been northbound the very moment she heard.

"This is not an officially sanctioned assignment. We are going to avoid traveling through Kurk," Nara said to Harker as she strapped a satchel on her horse. "Once we step foot in the north, no one will be any the wiser. We will need to procure a ship in Azmar. Preferably with an Etherborn crew so we may travel fast."

"Amena will give us one," Harker answered.

"Confident in your charms, then?"

He chuckled, but it was stripped of its usual zeal. "Some of them."

"It's going to be a long, hard ride to Azmar. Ten or eleven days. Then at least that long at sea to Kingsport." Nara stopped loading her pack and looked at him. "You can still change your mind, Harker. I have no idea what I am asking you to walk into."

He closed the latch on his pack and mounted his horse. "Get on your horse, Chancellor. Like you said, we've a long ride ahead."

32

Neith

"We can find no relevance to the color of one's ether. It seems simply a trait passed down among generations, no more significant than the shade of one's eyes."

THE WAY OF ETHER
ASHERAH GALANIS, FIRST CONSUL, THE CITADEL, 807 AQ

"If your shield is too dense, the cannon will not break apart on impact. If it is not dense enough, it will disassemble before reaching its target." Sam formed a thin shield, taking his time, letting the fibers of his honey-colored ether weave and work. It grew into a sphere around the compressed ball of amber fire. When it was complete, he withdrew his ether, and a translucent veil remained. He held it out before him, hovering above his palms so all could examine. "Creating an effective ethercannon is no easy task. There is good reason why only the most experienced among us will undertake this during battle. If done incorrectly, the wielder is likely to cause more damage to their own forces than the enemy."

The First and Second had been camped outside the gates of Croydyn for a full day, and Neith's squad had spent the morning training in a field not far from camp. In the days since departing Northbridge, five more had joined her squad.

Bellamy, Iris, Raiden, and Petra were all advanced in cannonmaking. Sam gestured to them to demonstrate the same. The others in the group watched intently, all anxious to learn.

"Once the cannon has been formed, it will immediately begin to burn out. How long that takes depends on the compression of it."

A moment later, the four held cannons of their own. Bellamy's looked like a cluster of emeralds, sparking and snapping, ready to ignite.

"There are several ways to launch, depending on your skill level. The most effective is the manipulation of air. Compress the air around it and release." His hands glowed, and his brows furrowed as he worked. With a quick gust, the cannon fired from his hold toward the forest. It split a tree in half, burying into the larger tree behind it. Honey-colored fire roared into the sky as shards of bark and limb scattered the ground around it.

It was an impressive display.

Sam gestured to Petra and Bellamy. Both stepped forward, hurling their cannons into the tree line as Sam had. An explosion of sapphire- and emerald-colored fires poured out, joining the honey, now fading to the orange embers of burning wood.

"The second method is more effective with smaller cannons and close combat. You use your own strength, heightened by your ether."

Sam walked back and forth in front of the group as he spoke. Teaching, *leading*, seemed a natural occupation for him. He stood tall with a straight back, his hands clasped behind him. The respect the others held for him was exhibited in their attention. Neith tried to mimic his posture and confident demeanor.

"It will not travel as far, and for many, not as fast, but creating a smaller cannon and launching it in this manner is a much speedier attack than the first demonstrated."

Sam nodded to Iris and Raiden. Both stepped forward. Raiden held his silver cannon in one hand as he turned his body quickly, building momentum. When he'd come full circle, he released his cannon, and it soared through the air, crashing into a tree. Iris circled her arm in a windmill fashion three times, generating velocity. She grunted with effort as it, too, sailed through the air, crashing into the same tree as Raiden's.

"And that leads me to our next discussion. Accuracy."

Sam instructed all to stand with distance and practice. Neith watched as an array of colored fire sprang to life. Sam walked from soldier to soldier, assisting and giving critique.

Neith formed her own cobalt-colored cannon, a small but fierce one. She aimed for a tree several yards back from the tree line and launched. Warm air gusted around her as it soared, striking its target. The tree exploded. Cobalt fire roared through the sky, twice as high as Sam's had. A satisfied smile curled on her lips. When she turned, she found all eyes were on her. Some in awe, some in, well, she was not sure. Her hands fell to the side, and she stepped back.

"Is it your aim to burn down the entire forest?" Sam asked, mouth quirked as he approached.

Neith shrugged a shoulder.

"That is impressive," he said as he moved behind her. She felt him step closer and lean, whispering in her ear. "But can you hit the same target again? Aim for the tree directly behind the one you decimated." His breath was warm, and she wanted to lean back against him to close the space.

"Let's see." Neith cocked a brow. She turned her face toward his, finding it dangerously close. "You should step back," she said, though the language of her body might have been screaming the reverse. Her second cannon, even more powerful than the first, cut through the air, passing just right of the tree.

She huffed, lips pursing.

Sam stepped around to look at her, a mild taunt tugging one side of his lips. "It appears there may be something I can teach you after all."

Neith felt heat rise in her cheeks. His eyes were heavy on hers in a way she could not mistake his words held double meaning.

"Lieutenant Dracos."

Neith turned to see a soldier falling into salute. "Yes?" She beckoned the soldier to rise.

The soldier's arm extended toward her. Neith wiped the sweat from her brow, taking the scroll presented with her free hand. She broke the seal, reading silently from the parchment.

"Tell my father we will ready and join him promptly," Neith said to the messenger.

"A summons?" Sam asked. Petra approached on his left.

"We are requested at the parley this afternoon," she answered. Her eyes scanned her squad as they returned to practice.

"We?" Petra asked.

"Myself, my guard, and two from my squad."

Neith knew she would take Bellamy but would need to decide on another.

"You'll need to select a Second and a Third soon. With the squad at seventeen, you'll need to create a chain of command," Petra said. "When your numbers grow beyond twenty and five, you'll become a unit. You'll need squad leaders. This is a favorable time to select."

"Should I not let them decide?" Neith believed standard protocol was to allow a squad to choose its own leader. Though exceptions did occur.

"Yes," Sam answered, "but this is how you make your preference known. They may choose against you, but that is not likely."

Neith looked from Sam to Petra, knowing she would choose them if able. "My choices would be Bellamy and possibly Zinnia, but I will take more time to think on it."

Both nodded as if in approval of her choices. The last few days they had begun to step back, encouraging her to make decisions. To take charge of the squad. She wondered if she would ever be able to truly portray to them how grateful she was. Failure would have been the only thing she would have achieved without them, and she was acutely aware of it.

"Bellamy and Zinnia will accompany us to the parley. We will see how things progress from there."

The walls of Croydyn were tall. The spires of the palace within even taller, rivaling the reach of the castle in Necrium. It was the largest city Neith had seen in person. She knew Croydyn was half the size of Highclere, which was half the size of King's Cross, the largest city in the north. The thought sent her spinning, unable to imagine such a place, or how it might feel to stand before it. She wondered if she would get a chance to see what lay behind its walls before her father tore them down.

Neith was directed to a tent where her father, Magnus, and Commanders Nikander Cordero and Maelis Nicomedes were huddled over a table discussing strategy. She took a seat, listening as they planned the siege that would start that very night. Unless, of course, Croydyn surrendered. Less than an hour passed before a messenger came with the news the envoy for Straeth had arrived.

Neith had some idea what to expect at the parley. Since her father had told her she would participate, Sam had been guiding her on what would likely happen, how it would unfold, and likely end. The king of Straeth was an old man of sixty and seven who rarely left his walls. Sam believed there was a good chance he would cower behind them, ignoring the parley altogether. Neith was glad it appeared that was not the case.

A large canopy had been erected before the city gates. Neith tried to calm her nerves on the walk. A surrender would save thousands of lives.

Two groups of chairs were placed opposite the other. Two on the side of Straeth, three on their own. Neith did not look at those sitting for Straeth as she followed her father, taking the seat on his left. Magnus sat on his right. The remainder of their party stood behind them. She felt Sam, Petra, and Max within reach.

When all were seated, she finally looked up to a face far younger than she'd expected. The one in a crown that sat before them could not be a day over thirty. He was dressed in a fine red vest with gold brocade. The crisp white shirt beneath it was bright and without stain. Lean but soft, he did not appear to be a fighting man. Neith could sense his internal struggle to appear confident. Fear radiated from him, so thick it nearly held scent. The stories had no doubt done their deed, but there was still an indignant demeanor about him, despite the uneasiness.

"His Royal Highness, Royce Cawthorne, crown prince of Straeth," a man in the Straethan party spoke. "Accompanied by High Commander Silas Wierland of His Majesty's armed forces." Unlike Royce, the commander did not appear fearful. His jaw was locked, eyes stern. He was of an age he would have fought in the Third Iren War. Neith thought he must be battle-hardened, unlike his prince. Like the other soldiers standing behind them, he bore the sigil of Straeth on his chest. A scale in perfect balance.

A Thranean captain stepped forward. "Lorcan Dracos, king of Thrane. His daughter, Lieutenant Neith Dracos, and General Magnus Agbani."

Both men regarded Neith with quizzical eyes. She knew women in Straeth were not permitted to serve in positions of power, nor the military, as in most of the north, but she was not used to such scrutiny. There wasn't a single woman in their envoy. There were many in Thrane's.

Lorcan raised a hand, and a servant approached with a tray of silver chalices. He took one, as did Magnus. Neith waved him off.

"There are only two reasons a king does not come to speak for his people," her father said. "He is either a coward or unfit. Which is it?"

"My father is no coward," Royce Cawthorne returned, haughty and resentful. Pampered, like his appearance. "I come at his request, under his authority, to discover why you bring war to our country."

Lorcan inclined his head, pretending an affront. "I bring an offer of friendship."

"*Friendship?*" The prince scoffed. He turned up his nose when a chalice was offered to him. "You have burned our villages, our holy city of Godsreach, murdered our people all along the northern border, and you speak to me of friendship?" He folded his arms across his chest. Neith thought it made him look weak.

"Warnings, Prince. Warnings of what marched toward you. That is all of little consequence if you consider what and who will burn inside your walls." Her father's demeanor was relaxed. Neith sat up straight, but not too straight, hoping no one could see the thrumming of her heart. It beat so fiercely it turned her belly.

"Our walls are high. We've provisions to last a year." The way Royce's eyes darted between them told the truth, but they already knew the bluff. Straeth was not a wealthy country and had very little army to speak of. It had never recovered after the last war, over twenty years ago. They had a couple moons of provisions at best. Not that it mattered. The whole of Straeth would stand little chance even if the entire Thranean army were idleborn.

Lorcan sighed. "You have heard what we can do."

"I know only what I see," Royce countered. "We do not listen to gossip and whispers." He leaned forward to glare at Lorcan. "My youngest sister was in Northbridge when you attacked. She scarcely made it back alive and had many things to say about what your men can do." He spat on the ground between them. His commander shifted in his seat.

Neith gripped the arm of her chair, recognition and dread racing through her. She thought of the girl in the cabin, her light brown hair and blue eyes. The same that were sitting across from her now.

Her father either did not understand or did not care. Likely both, Neith thought.

"How many of your sisters will burn when we raze this city?" he asked Royce.

Royce paled but straightened. "Make your demands so we can be done with this farce."

Her father smirked, seemingly unaffected by the prince's hostility. "Straeth will retain its status as a kingdom under the Thranean Empire. Your father will remain its king. You will remain its heir. We will see it returned to its militaristic power and wealth of the past."

Neith studied the faces of the Straethan soldiers as her father spoke. There was little consistency among them. Some were fearful, some as indignant as their prince. Others studied her own party, skeptical, as if trying to decide if they believed the stories.

"As I said, a farce." Royce waved for the servant, seemingly regretting his decision to rebuff the wine. "You mean to slowly dissolve our nation, or tax us into ruin."

"No," her father said. "I seek allies. And you will find the tax and militaristic obligations of our agreement to be more than fair."

Royce scoffed. "An ally does not show up on one's doorstep with a sword in hand."

"Would you rather it were a blade to your back?" He said it with a cold indifference that had the prince shifting in his seat. "Allies are bonded by mutual interest, nothing more. Your father knew that when he joined with mine decades ago. Straeth has no wealth, no military, and little opportunity to change it. What I offer you is a gift."

Royce's chin lifted higher as Lorcan spoke as if to maintain dignity despite the odds. "And if we refuse?"

"If you refuse," he mused, "I will allow you to return to the city. To scurry back behind its walls. Hours will pass and the sun will set. You may even believe you are safe. But when the moon is high, we will return. A small force, only a fraction of our army, will turn Croydyn and all its inhabitants into a distant memory. You will turn into nothing more than another warning for the doorstep we land on next." He leaned forward in his chair, and Royce retreated. "I will send a rider to our force that waits outside Ealdtown with instructions to raze it to the ground. We will rebuild over your ashes, and in ten years, it will be as if you, your entire lineage, and this filthy, stinking kingdom never existed." Her father had not raised his voice, but the certainty with which he spoke gave his words a lethal edge.

"*How dare you.*" The prince stood. His face gave away that his words did not carry the conviction he hoped.

"Your Majesty," said the Straethan commander, but the prince held up a hand to silence him.

Magnus rose slowly from his chair. Royce was not a short man, but Magnus towered over him. "Return your arse to feathered pillow, Prince."

Royce had the good sense to look uneasy, but it wasn't enough to deter him. "How dare you come here with such threats. You heathens from the north." He pointed at them, his eyes landing on each as his finger moved in quick lines. He dropped his arm and pushed his shoulders back. "My father may have been enough of a fool to cower to yours twenty and five years ago, but I am not him." The tension among the group catapulted with the shrillness of his voice. Magnus took a step forward, and the soldiers behind the prince reached for the hilts of their swords. "We are done here," Royce said, and gestured to his party to file out.

Neith cast aside her nervousness for irritation. The fool was going to see thousands of his people dead because of his pride. Without a plan, she stood. "You are not done here." All attention snapped to her.

The prince scoffed, then snarled, aghast a woman had dared speak to him so. "This is the army you believe we should fear?" He directed his words to Lorcan, but pointed at her. "Little girls?"

Lorcan raised his brows, turning to look up at Neith. This was of little consequence to him. He would burn all of Croydyn if need be. He may even have preferred it. Straeth had few resources to offer them. Surrender was simply faster, less trouble.

Neith released the hold on her power. It swelled in the small space. The men on the side of Straeth looked around, aware of the energy but with no understanding of what it was. "If you leave," Neith said, her eyes fixed on Royce, "you are securing the deaths of your people, all because you cannot set your pride aside. Turn around and look into the faces of your men and tell them tomorrow they watch their children burn."

The prince flexed his jaw, uncertainty returning to his eyes. She let even more of her power free, her skin taking on a subtle cobalt glow.

"Sorcery!" a soldier cried out.

Her ether crackled and sizzled around her. When Royce still did not speak, she held out her palm, and his eyes went wide as a blue flame ignited. Several of their soldiers stumbled and darted off, sprinting toward the city.

Neith retracted her ether, trying to calm the irritation it had inflamed. "When your sister arrived at your gate, was she in possession of a cloak and dagger?"

Royce's eyes narrowed. She watched him work through the story. "That was you?" he asked, with a skeptical brow.

"Will you walk with me, Your Highness?" Neith asked, beckoning him to follow her.

He hesitated, but looked back at his men, gesturing for them to remain behind. She did the same.

Royce walked beside her toward the city, stealing quick, nervous glances her way. When they were far enough to speak in confidence, Neith reached down and picked up a small pebble, twirling it between her fingers.

"You must know you cannot win, Your Highness. We are twenty thousand come to your door. Sorcery or not, your city will fall."

"I know nothing of the sort." He was a good deal taller than her and peered down as if exceedingly aware of it.

Neith did not think arguing with him would yield. She had to discover what appealed to him. "Will you condemn the men, women, and children on the other side of this gate to a bloody and violent end? That is their fate if you do not surrender." She dropped her facade of indifference and turned to face him. "My father does not make idle threats. And nor does he lie. If he promises you safety and prosperity, you will have it."

"I have no assurances you won't simply burn it all down once I open my gates to you." He continually glanced down at her hands as if fearful she would call a flame.

"I assure you," she said, "neither your gates nor your walls are deterrents to us. They are mild inconveniences at best. Our offer of treaty is made in good faith."

Royce studied her, wholly unconvinced. And why wouldn't he be, she thought. High walls had been enough to keep them safe for hundreds of years. She would need to make him understand. She tried to think what a man like him would want to hear.

"Are you not tired of watching the kingdoms around you grow wealthier while Straeth declines? Where is the fairness in it? Do your people not also deserve opportunity and wealth? We Thraneans well understand the struggle. But we grew tired of going hungry behind our mountains while those around us feasted. There is good reason our kingdoms have allied many times before." Neith watched some of his distrust ease as she spoke, but nowhere near enough. "Your father is an old man. It will be your reign the world soon sees."

Royce looked toward the city, her last words seeming to strike.

"You said yourself you are not your father. Well, neither is mine." Neith stepped around to catch his gaze. "Where they failed, you could succeed."

His eyes returned to hers, thoughtful. "I need time to consider."

"You do not have it." She saw no reason to mislead him. Her father would not be convinced to delay. The thoughtfulness on Royce washed away, the indignance and contempt returning. It was as if he suddenly remembered he was speaking to a woman, or perhaps a *heathen from the north*, as he had said.

Neith sighed. He was no more convinced than when they started their walk. Reasoning with him was not fruitful, nor was stroking his ego. She had no means to charm him. There was only one tactic remaining.

She turned back to face the city, scanning its walls. "When I want to tear something down, I think first of what it is made. Glass shatters, earth crumbles. Such high walls seem so steadfast from this view. You feel safe, protected, secure." Neith held the pebble out in her palm between them. "What are these walls but a collection of small stones? Stone crumbles, too, Your Highness." She watched his eyes turn wild with terror as she snapped the plane, turning the stone to dust. "How easily it can be as if it never existed."

Royce swayed on his feet, but to his credit, he didn't flee. "You are a sorceress."

"If only," she answered with earnest. "Then you might stand a chance." She felt a single drop of blood fall from her nose.

He swallowed, looking back toward the city. "The men who shamed my sister?"

"No longer draw breath."

Royce exhaled. Neith considered whatever his faults, he appeared to hold love for her. "My people would never forgive me."

"Yes, they will. But that should not be your first concern. If we march on Croydyn, you'll have no people with which to redeem yourself. You will have nothing. Not even your life."

"I'll have my honor." He said it with less than convincing conviction, straightening as he spoke.

Neith shook her head. "Dead men only hold honor if the living decide it so."

When he looked back at her again, she knew she had him. Nothing she was willing to do could strip him of his arrogance, but now he was afraid. Truly afraid. It was a look Neith knew well.

"I will take your offer to my king." He said it begrudgingly, as if the words caused pain.

Neith nodded. "You have until sundown. That is the most I will be able to convince my father of. We will assume the absence of an answer is a refusal and will march on Croydyn this night. *I* will march on Croydyn."

Neith watched him work to keep the sneer from his face. Royce nodded and turned, striding toward the gate.

"Tell your sister she may keep my dagger," she called after him. "She will need it if her king refuses."

Royce faltered, pausing for a breath, but continued without reply. When he was behind the gate, she returned to the canopy.

"Your prince waits for you in the city," she told the Straethan party. Once they were all out of range, she turned to her own. "They will surrender. I gave them until sundown, but I suspect we will hear from them beforehand."

Lorcan nodded. "Very good."

"What did you say to him?" Magnus asked.

"What he needed to hear." Neith turned and walked from the canopy, gesturing for her people to follow.

It was past midday when they arrived back at camp. Bellamy immediately replayed the events of the parley to the squad, in true dramatic fashion. Neith made straight for her tent. She collapsed onto the cot, turning to face away from the door, clenching and releasing her hands, trying to still their shake. She felt she'd become some other person in her conversation with Royce Cawthorne. A version of herself she did not recognize. It frightened her for many reasons, but mostly because she had liked it. It felt good to feel powerful. To command attention. She closed her eyes, trying to drown out the noise around her.

When her eyes opened again, she blinked, feeling time had escaped her in an instant. She was facing the other direction on the cot.

Ayla watched her from across the room. "You're awake," she said softly.

"How long did I sleep?" Neith yawned, her head heavy.

"A few hours. It is not quite evening time." Ayla poured from a pitcher and extended a cup toward her.

Neith sat up, accepting the offer. She gulped the water, finishing every drop. Her brows twisted against the pain radiating behind them. "Have we heard from Straeth?"

"Not yet." Ayla replied, concern etched on her face. She knelt beside the cot. "Are you unwell?"

"My head aches." Neith rubbed her eyes.

"Shall I fetch you a tincture?" Ayla seemed eager to be able to do something. To contribute. Neith knew a tincture would not help.

"That would be very helpful," Neith said, and tried to smile. "Thank you."

Ayla nodded in quick succession. "I'll return as soon as I can." She took the empty cup from Neith and stood, but paused, turning back. "Oh, and Sam is outside. He asked to see you when you woke. Should I tell him you are indisposed?"

Neith swung her legs over the side of the cot. "Send him in."

The tent door had closed scarcely a breath before it opened again. "Ayla said she was to fetch you a tincture," Sam said as he crossed the threshold. "Are you ill?"

"A headache."

He frowned. "Can you not heal it?"

"It is not the kind of ache caused by physical ailment." She looked up at him, towering above her. So far away.

"I see."

Neith gestured toward a chair, and Sam pulled it across the room to face her. He sat down, and they stayed in silence for a short time, barely an arm's length between them. "You were incredible today."

She huffed. "I do not feel incredible."

"You saved thousands of lives." The sincerity in his eyes made her wish she could abandon her feelings about it for his. Adopt them somehow. See it the way he did. But Sam didn't see the way Royce had looked at her. With such loathing, such fear. Like a *monster.*

"We shall see." Neith cocked a brow, trying to mask her discontent. If Sam continued to be kind to her, she feared she might shatter. "He has yet to surrender."

"He will."

Neith looked away, feeling her eyes sting. She sighed in frustration at always being drawn to tears so quickly.

"I know this is not an easy part to play. I know that it weighs on you." He looked at her with a gentle affection. It eased her discomfort, as it always did.

"Is that what I am doing? Playing a part?" Her head tilted slightly as she studied his face.

Sam shrugged. "You tell me."

She didn't answer, unsure what it would be.

"If it helps, you should know Royce Cawthorne is not a good man. In fact, there are few to be found in the entire Cawthorne family."

"How so?" Neith closed her eyes, pinching the space between them.

"They live a life of luxury while their people starve. He has few concerns outside of the palace walls. Whatever he portrayed to you is seated more in fear of losing his own wealth and privilege than concern for his subjects. His father has done nothing but rot away in his castle since the war ended decades ago."

Neith opened one eye to peer at him. "It does help… a little."

"Give me your hand." Sam leaned forward in his chair, elbows resting on his knees.

She shifted closer to the edge of the cot, timidly extending her hand.

He held it in one, then pressed his thumb and index finger with the other into the soft flesh between hers.

She flinched at the pain from it, then looked up at him with a frown. "What are you doing?"

"Wait." Sam moved his fingers, pressing harder. He held for a few breaths and then released, eyes meeting hers in question.

"That's incredible." A light laugh pulled from her lips. "It's nearly gone. How does that work?"

"Misdirection?" He shrugged. "You're the healer, not me."

"It seems there are still many things for me to learn." Her smile slowly faded, and she swallowed, apprehensive to say what was on her mind. "Sam?"

"Yes?" he asked. He was still holding on to her hand as his fingers lightly traced the now-inflamed skin he had pinched.

"I do not wish for you to feel as if it is your duty to comfort me. It is not your responsibility—"

"I don't," he said, releasing her hand, gaze low. "We are friends. Did we not agree?"

"Yes. It is only that I feel this is a very one-sided friendship. You are always helping me. I feel like I have nothing to give in return."

His eyes flicked up to hers. "That is not true."

"No?"

He shook his head. "No."

Neith studied the design of his face. The fullness of his lips, the slight ridge of his nose. "There are moments where I feel I understand you," she said, "but others not at all. So often I wish to know what you are thinking."

His brows drew together. "Why do you not ask?"

Neith thought on it for a moment. "I think I am afraid of being wrong. If I don't ask, I'll never get the answer I fear. I can live on in my mind."

His eyes moved from hers, trailing the length of her face, lingering on her lips. She watched the bob of his throat as he swallowed. She felt she could spend hours studying the subtle movements of his body. Analyzing them, trying to understand their nuanced meanings. She wondered what it would be like to touch him. Not like when they were training. She imagined her hands running up his chest and over his shoulders, over the dips and peaks of the muscle stretched across them. Her heart quickened at the thought.

"What are you thinking right now?" she asked, her voice little more than a whisper.

"Right now, I am thinking I have never met anyone like you."

Her eyes flicked back to his and found the look she loved. The one she could melt under. She had to look away, fearing something dreadful would escape her lips and the moment would pass. "And that is good… or bad?"

The look in his eyes told her it was not bad. It was like a fire she wanted to throw herself into.

She only realized she was touching him when she looked down. Her hand rested on his chest at the base of his neck, fingers curling in a subtle movement across his skin. The beat of his heart against her palm felt like an embrace of its own.

Neith watched the thoughts race behind his eyes so intently that she saw the change. He looked down and moved to sit back, but she grasped a fistful of his tunic. His eyes widened with surprise, but he didn't pull away.

"And I have never met anyone like you," she returned. Her free hand moved to hold his cheek, unsure of what drove her actions. His eyes closed, and he leaned into it. He was so wonderfully warm.

"I only wish for what is best for you," he said, almost mournfully.

"And you do not think this is it?"

His gaze turned grave, giving her the answer she feared. She released him, but he stayed still.

"My resolve wears thin, Neith." He said the words slowly, painfully, as if it cost something to say them. His head fell into his hands.

"Then tell me what I must do to unburden you of it."

He looked up at her with heavy, heated eyes. Like someone pulling against restraint. Her lips parted when she felt his hand grasp the outside of her thigh. He exhaled, and it had a hint of a rumble to it. It stirred something inside her.

"My lady," Ayla called from outside the tent.

"Not now," Neith returned, holding Sam's gaze.

"My lady, your father arrives," Ayla said, a bit frantic.

Neith jumped back, and Sam sprang from the chair, racing to the other side of the room. The door opened, and her father stepped through, eyes taking in the situation. They landed on Sam. "I would speak with my daughter."

Sam glanced at her, eyes apologetic, before saluting her father and leaving.

Lorcan looked at the chair sitting across from her, taking in the intimate proximity. His fingers wrapped around the back, and he pulled it a few paces away from her, his eyes locked on hers. As he sat, she brushed back her hair, trying desperately to breathe and quell the flush from her cheeks. She knew they burned with it.

He leaned back and crossed one leg over the other. His hands rested in his lap, a scroll clenched in one. She bristled under his gaze and eyed the parchment, desperate to move the visit along. "Do you bring news, Father?"

He held it out to her. "The full surrender of Straeth."

She took it, reading through the document before handing it back. "Congratulations."

"This is yours, Neith. It is I who have come to congratulate." There was a jovial air about him, even if it was slight.

Neith shook her head. "That is too generous."

"It is not. It is well deserved." His lips took on the subtlest of smiles. "But I did not expect to find you so"—he cocked his head—"distressed."

Her lips disappeared between her teeth. She thought she might detect a hint of amusement in him. It eased her nerves, but also irritated her to be teased. "I was ill earlier, that is all. I am much recovered."

"That is good," he quipped, his demeanor cooling, "because we dine in Croydyn tonight. Make yourself ready in formal attire and return to the gate. Bring all in your guard. There may be Esērii in the city. We will take no chances."

Neith nodded. "As you wish."

He stood, and she joined him, bowing her head as he turned to leave.

Ayla returned to the tent, excitement radiating from her. "We were just told of the surrender. It's being heralded as yours." She held out a small vial.

Neith felt that was a stretch of the truth, but did not have the appetite to debate it. All she had done was frighten the man. She took the vial and popped the tiny cork, tossing back the bitter tincture. "I am to dine in Croydyn tonight. I need to dress appropriately." She scowled. "Like a lady."

Ayla beamed.

Neith laughed. "Try not to look so excited."

"Well, forgive me if I finally feel useful," Ayla jested.

Neith reached for her hand. "You are useful to me every day. In more ways than one."

"Thank you," Ayla said, pulling her into an embrace. Neith straightened at the unexpected affection. Ayla pulled back, clasping her shoulders. "Now, what would you like to wear?"

For the first time since Godsreach, Neith allowed Ayla to fuss over her appearance. She selected a royal-purple gown trimmed in silver brocade, with long sleeves that billowed and tucked until hooking around her middle finger. It was low cut and fell slightly off the shoulder, exposing the length of her collarbones and pressed edges of her breasts. She felt vulnerable and unsuitable, fearing her father would not approve. Ayla assured her it was appropriate and in line with the style of the ladies of Straeth. Her hair was pulled away from her face in multiple braids, culminating in a single weaving that fell long down her back. After much debate, Ayla convinced her of cheek and lip stain. Neith decided she did not mind it all so much when she saw how the result caused Sam's gaze to linger.

An escort of twelve guards met their party at the gates of Croydyn. Each soldier donned a fine, vibrant red tunic with the seal of Straeth etched on their silver chest plates. Neith recognized none of their faces from the parley, but fear weighed heavy in each. *Whispers of it are often more effective than the whip itself.*

A single street ran from the gate straight through the city. Neith saw the palace in the distance, but little else. Flowering trees and shrubbery lined the cobblestone from end to end, obscuring what existed beyond it. After all Sam had told her, Neith suspected that it was by design.

"Father," she beckoned.

Lorcan turned around, halting the rest of the group.

"I wish to see the city," Neith explained. "I wish to see what lies beyond this decorated promenade."

His brows creased as he searched her eyes. He did not seem opposed. More like he was trying to understand why.

"It is important to me," she said, keeping his gaze.

He studied her for a moment longer, then turned to the Straethan guards. "You will take us through the city."

Their already nervous disposition turned into mild panic. The one who looked to be in command cleared his throat. "Your Grace, I fear the king is expecting—"

Lorcan's power snapped, and the soldiers winced. The same look of fearful uncertainty that had been on the faces of the soldiers at the parley now plagued the ones before them. Neith could not help but feel it an unnecessary threat. She thought a stern look might send them running in erratic directions. "It is not a request."

The guard nodded, and Neith saw the tremble in his chin as he passed her by, leading them north. He was defying an order, and what looked to be an important one.

The real Croydyn was even more destitute than she'd feared. The streets were oddly quiet and empty, the cobblestone quickly giving way to muddy paths. They came upon startled common people in tattered clothing, ducking into doors and alleyways. Dirty faces watched fearfully from windows. The homes and buildings were all in disrepair. Neith wondered if they'd been ordered to remain indoors, and if so, she doubted it was for their safety. She blotted at the water swelling in her eyes from the stench of overflowing sewers and slaughtered pigs. The guard had made the decision to take them this way, which told her it was not the worst.

Her father glanced back at her as if to say he now understood.

The palace itself was surrounded by a large wall and a heavily guarded gate. An antithesis to the city proper. Lush green gardens encompassed ornate and elaborate architecture. Pavilions with pillow-covered seating and fountains were found at every turn. Even the air was a jarring disparity, sweet with the fragrance of late-spring blooms.

Neith looked back at Sam to find his brow tight, eyes thin. It was all as he had said. The disproportion in the quality of life between the royals and the commoners was stark. Rage-inducing. She thought of their sigil, the scale in perfect balance, and it set her sight to red.

The limestone of the palace walls glowed a warm yellow against the lanterns scaling it. Neith looked up as they approached. Conical stone spires peaked with orange-tiled ceramic roofs, a single flag flying from the tallest.

Servants stood in long lines, adorned in matching uniforms, flanking both sides of the palace entrance. They bowed in unison. It was performative and strange, and Neith felt sheepish on their behalf.

The interior of the palace was the equal of its gardens. Paintings in ornamental gilded frames hung next to detailed tapestries in royal blues and reds. The floor was marble, polished so finely it reflected the candlelight in the sparse places a rug did not cover.

Too many people to count stood waiting in the foyer. Men in bright, brocaded vests. Women in gowns trimmed in gold and silver, their faces painted to the point of absurdity. Royce stepped forward. His mouth was pressed so tight he struggled to force it into a smile. Neith thought it insincere and vapid, likely a direct representation of his thoughts.

Royce bowed. "Your Grace, may I present my brothers and sisters, cousins, their husbands and wives." His hand rolled as he spoke. "I'll not take up our evening introducing each one."

Neith did not see the girl from Northbridge among them.

A woman with blonde hair and blinding red lips stepped forward.

"My lady wife, Talissa," Royce said, gesturing at the woman. Her breasts were bound and lifted with such desperation that Neith wondered how the woman managed to breathe.

"You remember my daughter." Her father said it with a trace of threat.

"How could I forget?" The tight line of Royce's lips remained. "My lady, you look lovely." The prince bowed, and the other Straethans followed suit.

Neith tried to hide her chagrin behind a frown. Better for them to find her unpleasant than uneasy.

The heavily painted ladies of Straeth eyed her critically. Neith vowed to thank Ayla for her persistence. These people had expected some kind of heathen. Judging by their reactions, she was not the picture painted to them by the prince. But the night was young, and she would make no promises.

"If it pleases you, we will dine together before we meet with my father to formalize the terms of our agreement," Royce said.

"Surrender," Lorcan corrected him.

Royce's mouth twitched. He flexed his jaw and nodded. "As you say, Your Grace." He gestured with his hands. "If you will follow me."

Her father seemed to hold as much enthusiasm as she. At best, he seemed mildly amused by the charade.

They were shown to a dining hall, warm with the glow of candlelight. Balconies lined two walls, with a small stage front and center. Two men played an upbeat tune, one on a lute, and the other a vielle. The vielle she knew only from study, having never heard its sound before. It was somehow soft and piercing all in one. Like a knife so sharp one does not know it struck until it caresses bone. Neith found it beautiful and mesmeric, and thought she did not mind so much to dine with these people if she was able to sit and listen to its song.

The elegantly fashioned table was set with silver chalices and cutlery. Roasted meats, vegetables, and a variety of breads ran from end to end. Neith thought again of what Sam had told her about the suffering of the people of Straeth. It seemed the Cawthorne royal family lazed around pampered in fineries, stuffing their mouths with cakes and wine while the people outside the palace walls lived in squalor.

Neith was seated next to Royce on her left, who sat at the head of the table, her father and Magnus on her right. Royce's *lady wife* sat directly across from her, followed by an assortment of princes and princesses, lords and ladies.

Neith tried to drown the conversations in a glass of wine. The shrill laughter of Talissa snapped her out of it more than once. On occasion, she caught a hint of disapproval or superiority on the strange woman's face. She spoke of jewels and fine foods. Spices they imported from Sibreen and wine from Parthe. A thick silver chain covered in diamonds and what Neith thought might be some kind of pale sapphire or topaz hung heavy around her neck. It sparkled in the low light. She wondered how many homes in Croydyn could be repaired for the cost of it. She wondered how many such jewels Talissa owned.

Neith told herself none of it mattered. They had secured a surrender. Whatever trouble remained could be solved without violence. She was heir. She would have power. One day she would return to Straeth and see this masquerade dismantled.

Neith made note of the excessive amount of wine Royce consumed. She wondered if it was common. He was oddly nervous for someone under such an influence. His hands shook lightly, only noticeable when he held his fork. When he detected her observing, he returned the utensil to his plate.

"What do you think, my lady?"

Neith glanced at Talissa, realizing the question had been for her. She ignored her and turned back to Royce, but Talissa inclined her head, catching Neith's gaze.

"Or should I address you as Lieutenant? Forgive me, women do not serve in our military, so I do not know what is proper." One side of her red lips curled.

"I leave it to your discretion. Either is appropriate." Neith stretched her neck, feeling tension rise, but unsure of its source.

"Very well, we shall call you Lieutenant. How *exciting*," Talissa said to the other women at the table, with unmistakable condescension.

Neith felt her father's gaze shift toward her. A light laugh shook her chest. She couldn't help but be impressed by the woman's brazenness. Neith reached for her wine, turning it by the fine silver stem. Her eyes flicked up to Talissa's. "Now that we have established what you shall call me, may I do the same?" Neith looked down the long line of painted women. "Quite similarly, I find myself at a loss. Is it princess or *lady wife*, as your husband declared? I am not familiar with a society where women hold no position."

Talissa's smile flattened, and she set her chalice on the table. "Princess or Your Highness." She recovered her smirk. "I leave it to your discretion."

"Then I shall surprise you next we speak. How *exciting*." Neith did all but roll her eyes as she looked back to Royce, irritated the woman had distracted her so. She felt Sam's ether heat behind her.

Royce's eyes wouldn't meet hers. They darted nervously around until fixing on something across the room. Neith followed their journey to a balcony facing her party, and she searched the empty ledge for the object of his attention. The light caught something metallic or glass, but it disappeared, concealed behind a heavy red drape. Unease settled around her.

She turned back to Royce, who was now nearly panting. He looked sick. Ashen and glazed in cold sweat. He wiped at it, surreptitiously, and twice picked up his fork, only to return it to his plate unused.

Neith's heart thumped in a drowsy rhythm as time seemed to slow. The music swelled. Talissa laughed. The sound stretched on, morphing from its shrill pitch to a deep, resonant cackle.

Royce reached for his wine glass. He stopped shy of his mouth, clutching the delicate stem. A brief uncertainty spread over his face, but then he nodded, to himself, Neith thought, and brought the glass to his lips.

Thump, thump, thump, her heart continued.

He tipped it up. Higher still, until surely vacant of its contents. When it returned to the table, he finally met her gaze. The vicious look in his eyes caused her to stiffen. Every hair stood on end. She watched, her understanding still taking shape, as he looked up to the balcony and made a nearly indiscernible tilt of his head.

Movement caught her eye. The red curtain fluttered. Neith saw the crossbow first, then the man who wielded it. The weapon kicked, and cold dread consumed her as an arrow launched before he completed his step. It sailed through the room with remarkable speed, and she studied it, transfixed, her aim to trace its path.

A flurry erupted on her left, of what she wasn't sure. It came at her, fast and forbidding, but she couldn't look. There was only the arrow. The arrow she now knew to be bound for her father.

Ether surged around her. Shields in all colors expanded around the room. A wild gust of wind sent her hair flying forward, striking plates and cups from the table.

She raised her left hand to intercept what besieged her. It fell upon her heavy and heated, but she pressed back, and it stopped, sudden, as if she'd repelled it with ease.

There was no time to think, to scream, to warn. A loud splintering cracked the air as she snapped the plane, nether consuming the arrow as it sailed between the heads of two heedless Straethan royals.

She caught the wide eyes of her father as the dusty remnants bounced harmlessly against his shield, right as it fell into place.

The music stopped, replaced by the echoes of clattering dinnerware. She remained frozen, blinking, staring at her father, as her mind struggled to grasp all that had happened.

A woman screamed, and Neith flinched, the harrowing sound ripping her from the muddle. She turned, paling when she came face to face with the sharp end of a blade. Blood oozed from her hand down her arm in winding patterns, turning the royal-purple fabric of her dress near black. A dagger had been buried in her hand until the hilt met the flesh of her palm. Her eyes flicked up to the one who wielded it.

Royce stared down at her, but there was something… *strange* about him. His eyes held no fury, no fear. The viciousness of before was gone. He looked nothing like what one might expect to see on one plunging a blade into another.

The fireplace burned and cracked behind him, drawing her already impossibly wide eyes to the flames. But they did not move around him. Neith looked through him. A large, gaping hole had been blasted through his chest. Blood and other material poured from the wound as his grip on the blade released. What remained of him slumped to the floor.

Sam stepped up beside her with a look of wild rage. The remnants of his cast snapped and sparked around him. He grabbed her arm at the wrist and elbow, and the rage resided, replaced with horror as he examined her hand. His eyes found hers, apology pouring from them. Neith looked again at the blade, still stunned. As soon as she realized it didn't hurt, it did. Searing agony radiated up her arm, and she doubled forward, her free hand fisting the tablecloth. She bit her lips to stifle the howl that wanted to escape.

The Straethans around the table slowly recovered from their befuddled states. Some screamed, some cried. Others simply gazed around like lost children.

Her father stood slowly, peering down at the petrified faces. He wiped his mouth and tossed the napkin over his plate. "How disappointing."

Talissa whimpered as she beheld the broken remains of her husband. She was covered in wine and bits of food that exploded when Sam had nearly split the prince in two.

Lorcan kicked his chair aside and walked to Neith. He studied her hand. A flurry of unreadable thoughts raced behind his steely countenance. When his eyes found hers, they held a subtle but peculiar sort of affection, and he brushed his knuckles across her trembling cheek.

Her father released her and turned, and as he cornered the table, he lifted his hand, and a quick burst of air sent Royce's body soaring across the room. He leaned over the tabletop, palms flat. His gaze moved down the long line of Straethans. "Is anyone else a comparable fool?" Every single person shook their head. "Who knew about this *plot?*"

It was evident on their faces who did and who did not. Lorcan gestured, and Thranean soldiers put a sword through each. No one spoke on their behalf. The others simply winced and whimpered with each execution of their kinsmen. She only then noticed the deceased Straethan soldiers bleeding out in various locations throughout the room.

"Who is now the eldest heir?" All faces turned to a young man who Neith thought to be in his early twenties.

"What is your name?" Lorcan asked.

"Ri-Ricard, Your Grace."

"Do you share his sentiments, Prince Ricard?"

The young man stood, shaking his head. "I didn't even like him," he said, with an abundance of dramatic disdain. He lifted his chin. "In fact, I'm glad he's dead."

Lorcan looked around the room. "Then I will assume this will serve as a lesson for you all?"

His query was met with enthusiastic nods.

"Very well, Prince Ricard, should we retire to the council room?"

The two men departed with Magnus and the remaining Straethan men, leaving their women behind.

Sam was back by her side, holding her arm again. She looked up at him. His face was all regret, guilt, remorse. He didn't speak. Neith thought if he opened his mouth he might scream.

Her fingers were like ice, telling her that tendons, vessels, ligaments, and more were ruined. It would not be an easy wound to heal. "I need to get to a surgeon," she said, short and winded. "I do not know if I can heal this on my own."

He nodded and gestured for Petra. She was standing over the lifeless body of a Straethan soldier.

Neith met eyes with the trembling woman across the table. She was terrified, but retained her scorn. Behind Talissa, in the distance, the girl from Northbridge appeared in the doorway. She winced at the sight of her brother's body. Her eyes moved across the room, finding Neith, her face twisted with rage.

Neith exhaled and, in a fury of her own, reached for the hilt of the dagger. She ripped it free, eyes locked on Talissa's as blood sprayed across the table, splattering across Talissa's face and chest. Neith heaved and grunted, not drawing her eyes away as the woman recoiled, horrified by the display. The pain of it echoed as if she had ripped it from her hand not once, but thrice.

Blood oozed from the wound in a steady stream, and Neith was made uneasy at the sight. She wanted to cry. More than she ever remembered. But she wouldn't give them a single tear. Not even if it killed her.

Sam regarded her with wide, but quickly narrowing, eyes as he applied pressure, using dinner napkins to tie up the wound.

Neith turned the bloody blade in her free hand, laughing to herself as she realized the dagger was her own. When Sam finished, she stood from the table, making her way to the girl.

The bruises had faded, but the evidence of what she endured still marred her skin. Like Talissa, she was fearful, trembling even, but it wasn't scorn that sharpened her intelligent eyes. It was defiance. Immoveable and unyielding, and Neith knew with certainty it was she who had devised the plot.

Neith flipped the blade in her grasp as she had in Northbridge, holding it out to her. She leaned close, intimate, so only the girl could hear her speak. "If I offer you this blade a third time, take note, it will not come hilt first."

33

Neith

*"The ethercannon is the most effective form of battle weaponry, taking on the
strength and ferocity of its maker."*

ETHEREAL WARFARE
SYMOND TALIESIN, 945 AQ

Neith flexed her fingers. The newly healed muscles and skin were stiff. A
thick line of soft pink scar tissue now ran through the middle of her left
hand.

"Could it not have been healed without the scar?" Kieran asked.

Neith sat with her squad, taking supper in a dining tent.

"It could have," Neith answered, "but I wanted to keep it."

"Why?" Iris asked as she passed a piece of bread to Raiden. He looked
up as if also interested in her answer.

Neith locked eyes with Bellamy. He gave her a curious look. "As a
reminder that I am far too understanding."

A slow grin spread over his lips. Neither Iris nor Raiden had been part
of their conversation by the pond, but seemed to understand the words
held meaning between them.

They had one more night in Croydyn before departing for Highclere.
Neith had not returned to the city nor the camp of the First. Her squad
kept close to their campsite, only venturing out for food or to bathe in a
lake a short walk south.

"That's mine, you bastard!" Two men quarreled at the table adjacent
to their own.

"If it's yours, come and take it," the other taunted. The first man reached across the table, grabbing a fistful of the other's tunic, yanking him across. Plates and cups clattered and spilled. The others at the table grunted and grumbled their displeasure, and it was quickly a fight of five. Fists were flying, and bodies rolled around on the dusty earth. All over a bottle of whiskey.

Soldiers in the Second were growing restless. They'd seen no battle or conflict on the long journey. Skirmishes like this one were breaking out on increasing occasions. It took Neith to thoughts of her brother. Several in her squad stood to watch.

Neith sighed. She had no desire to spectate. "I'm heading back to camp."

"I'll go with you," Sam said, and stood, offering his hand to help her rise.

The noise from the dining tent quieted as they walked.

"All are growing restless. It will be good to get back on the road if for no other reason," Sam said, mirroring her thoughts. "This idleness is opportunity for those with an agenda. I fear the fallout of a second visit from your brother."

Neith nodded. "Fortunately, we've heard nothing from Roman or anyone in his unit since Northbridge."

"That is what worries me." Sam glanced toward her. She met his concerned eyes.

"I do not think he would be so thoughtless as to harm anyone. Not now." Though, she could not be sure.

"You said yourself he is impulsive and unpredictable."

"This is true. I do fear what he will do when he hears—" Neith stopped herself, realizing she was about to say when he heard of her being heir.

Sam stopped walking and reached for her arm. "Hears of what?" he asked, reading the panic in her eyes.

Neith looked around, biting her bottom lip. Her eyes moved with reluctance back to his. "I cannot say right now."

Sam looked displeased, but didn't press. He released her arm. "All right. But all is well?"

She nodded. "All is well."

They continued the walk to their campsite in silence. When they arrived, he turned to her. "May I ask you something?"

"Of course." She frowned. "You know you needn't ask to ask, Sam."

He looked around as if to ensure they were on their own. "Why did you let the girl go? It seemed clear she knew of her brother's designs, if she herself were not the one who orchestrated it."

Neith took a breath, considering. "I'm not sure, if I'm honest."

"And you gave her back the blade," he added. Something like amusement tugged on one side of his mouth.

Neith shrugged. "She still needs it more than I do. Probably to defend from her own kin. It would be comical how ridiculous they are, if it were not so tragic."

Sam's brows drew together. "I don't feel badly for them."

"Why not?" Neith did not either, but she wanted to know his reason.

"There are too many people in this world far more deserving of our thought, and there is only so much to give." He said it with confidence, as if it were something he had considered often. "If you live for everyone, you live for no one."

Neith nodded. With every day that passed since Godsreach, and the dreadful people she'd encountered on the way, she could not help but believe it true. She also knew that, to many, she was among the undeserving. And the sum of those that believed her so would only continue to grow.

"We won't have much time to train on our way to Highclere. We'll be on the road early and stopping late. An army this size moves slowly. We'll need to make the best of what time we can carve out," Neith said to Bellamy and Zinnia as they watched the last remaining trunks from their camp being stowed on carts.

"How long before we reach Highclere?" Bellamy asked.

Neith scratched Storm's neck, receiving a nuzzle in return. "Magnus says fifteen to twenty days."

"I cannot decide if that is a long time or short," Zinnia said, looking from Bellamy to Neith as she twisted her braids into a high bun, securing it with a leather cord. The gold ring in her nose caught a flash of sunlight, heightening its contrast to her dark umber skin. Her round, brown eyes were bright, despite the hesitation in them.

Neith well understood the sentiment. She felt the battle hanging over her. Over them all. Taking Highclere was only one small part of their long campaign, but it was the first of significance. Their journey across Straeth was child's play. They had not yet faced an equivalent foe. She worried for the soldiers under her command. For her friends, she dared to call them.

She watched as dirt was kicked over their dying fires, and her squad mounted their horses.

"I suppose it is time," Bellamy said. Though no one spoke to it, Neith felt the shared unease between them. "I will go and ready the squad. Zinnia?"

Zinnia nodded.

As they departed, Sam approached with carrots in one hand, the reins of his horse in the other. Jaspar trotted behind, his tan-colored coat sleek and smooth, and his black mane brushed to perfection. Neith thought Sam doted on his horse more than she did Storm.

"We are ready to ride out." Sam smiled, but it was weighted with the same dread she had seen on Bellamy and Zinnia. He held out a carrot to Storm, and it quickly disappeared between her teeth.

"I see you are trying to win her over," Neith teased.

"Is it working?" he asked as he fed a carrot to Jaspar, stealing a quick glance her way.

She resisted the smile tugging on her lips and patted her horse's gray brindled coat. "I would say so."

They held gazes for a moment, and Neith waited for him to turn away or break it in some fashion. He didn't. He stayed, his eyes still locked with hers, when he asked, "Are you ready?"

Neith inhaled, sensing the question held more depth than its simple words presented.

She wanted to say no. That was the truth. But she simply nodded and turned back to Storm. "When we reach Highclere, you'll be free of this saddle, I swear."

The long line of soldiers started to move.

After mounting her horse, Neith turned to her squad to find expectant faces. She took each in before calling out, "To Highclere?"

Cheers and whoops broke out among them.

She met eyes with Sam.

"To Highclere," he echoed.

34

Thea

"One hopes the blood spilled on earth and water will serve as a warning to those who come after, and a Fourth Iren War will never come to be."

THE THIRD IREN WAR

LEWIN LEAR, 1185 AQ

It rained for five days. It was weather to match her mood. Thea told no one what she had found in the woods. She apologized to Sylvie for running out, blaming her distress over Marten as the cause. She didn't think Sylvie believed her, but she wasn't sure she cared. Thea stayed in her room, fearful she would not be able to hide her distress. The rains had brought about minor flooding in the city, so most in the castle were distracted, and she was left to herself. Sylvie mentioned the installation of new drainage tunnels and spoiled grain stores. Thea scarcely heard. She was lost in thought, nodding mindlessly as Sylvie spoke.

She'd replayed everything over in her mind so many times she was starting to question if she'd imagined it. The alternative was that two of the people she loved and trusted most in the world were lying to her. Deceiving her. Letting her believe herself mad. That was far more painful than the loss of her sanity. When her siblings pressed, she told them she missed Marten. It wasn't a total fabrication.

After several declined invitations and feigned illnesses, Callum finally showed up at her door, refusing to leave.

"Thea, if you do not *let* me in, I will *break* in. Surely you know that I do not jest!" Three consecutive bangs struck the door.

"I am tired, Callum," she said from her room. "I will come and find you later.”

"Open the door, Calithea." He was serious in a way he was not often.

"Callum—"

Crack.

Thea jumped. "For Godssake!"

She unlocked the door and swung it open. Callum stared her down as he marched through. "What is going on?"

"I have told you I am tired. I am still upset and—"

He shook his head. "Lie to them, Thea, but do not lie to me. I know you're not sitting up here pining over Marten. I know you better than that. If that were the case, you would be lost in a bottle or two."

Lying to her brother through the door had been a much easier task than lying to his face. She swallowed against the guilt constricting in her throat.

"That, there, that look." He pointed at her. "Why do you look afraid?" He stepped closer, resting his hands on her shoulders. "You have been hiding in here for five days. You are scaring me. I am not leaving until you tell me what is going on."

Thea felt her eyes swell and her resolve waver. "I think I have lost my mind," she whispered.

Callum's eyes widened then narrowed, running the length of her face, a slight panic fluttering in them. He considered for a moment, then cleared his throat. "Well, tell me what has happened, and if your mind has truly run off, we'll go and fetch it back."

A bark of laughter escaped her lips, which wrenched one from him.

Thea told him everything. About being chased in the woods and the grave. How she'd found it empty and the strange burn marks on the trees. She told him about seeing Sylvie leaving the room the day the messenger came and finding Breeda and Alec arguing after the wedding.

Callum paced the room, his furrowed brow telling her he was trying to make sense of it all. She wanted to save him grief and tell him there was no point. He paused several times to look at her, and she thought he would speak, but each time he returned to his march. Eventually, he made his way to the carafe on the corner table, pouring a short glass of wine. He tipped it up, taking it all in one go.

"Alec Turan?" he asked with a frown. "You are sure of this?"

"Yes," she said, nodding.

"Could it have been he that attacked you?"

"It crossed my mind like a thousand other wild possibilities, but no.

I feel confident it was not him." She felt he was involved, but she could not imagine how.

He huffed and sat beside her on the sofa. "It doesn't make sense. Why would they lie about it being an *animal?*"

"I don't know," Thea said with all the frustration she felt. "It seems such a ridiculous story now, but I believed it, Callum. For a time, at least. That is why I'm going insane. It is all I can think about. When I say it out loud, it all sounds so absurd."

He looked at her, his expression heavy with concern.

"You believe me… don't you?" she asked, fear quickly crowding her chest.

Callum scoffed. "Of course I believe you. Why would you ask me that?" He spoke like he found the suggestion offensive.

"Thank you." She closed her eyes and nodded, inhaling deep. She watched him work through it in his head. He glanced at her from the side of his eye. A look she knew all too well. "What is it?"

"Nothing." He shrugged, but Thea saw through his attempted veil.

"Callum."

"It is only rumor." He ran his hands through his blond waves, then glanced at her. "It sounds absurd anyway."

Thea gaped at him, her arms flying up on either side of her. "What could sound absurd in comparison to all I've said?"

He laughed nervously, tilting his head from side to side.

She turned her body toward his, irritation flaring. "If you do not tell me this *instant*, I will reach down your throat and extract the words for myself."

He held up his hands in defeat. "All right, all right. But you'll laugh when you hear it."

Thea waited, eyes fixed on his, trying to transmit some sense of urgency.

Callum leaned closer and lowered his voice, though they were the only two present. "Kyna told me of some talk that has been making its way through the city. There have been raids in Straeth along the northern border."

Thea shifted closer to him. "As Father said. The messenger?"

"Yes, but it is more than that. Some are saying entire villages have been razed."

"Gods," Thea whispered. "That is terrible. I am sure Father will send aid and a force to Straeth."

Callum hesitated. "There are whispers of sorcery."

Thea laughed, but it died quickly when he did not join. "Callum… there are always whispers of sorcery. Especially in Straeth."

His eyes took on an uneasiness, her words doing nothing to water down his thoughts. "There are mentions of fire and light in bright colors unknown to nature. Fire that burns green and blue and silver. That the people razing and raiding can control it. That it comes from their own hands."

Thea's belly turned cold. She pictured the bright light from the woods. "*Green?*"

Callum nodded. "And more."

Thea swallowed. "That *is* strange." A nervous chill spiked from the base of her spine to the crown of her head. She shook her shoulders.

He looked at her with wide eyes and said, "Some are whispering the Gods have returned."

A quick barking laugh drew from her lips, snapping her out of it. "The Gods? Callum…" Thea shook her head. "If the raids are as bad as you've said, then yes, that is concerning, but whispers of Gods are nothing more than fear in talking form." She tried to say it with confidence, but something weighed her words.

"I am sure you are right." He did not appear fully convinced in either regard. "It will do us no good to indulge in such tales."

"Indeed," she said. Her belly tumbled with uncertainty, but she didn't have the capacity to consider things like sorcery, let alone talk of Gods she wasn't even sure she believed in.

"We shall speak no more of it," he said, holding up his hands.

"Callum, I need you to swear to me you won't say anything or *do* anything. I mean it." It was the tallest ask of him, and she knew it. Inaction.

"I swear." He rubbed his face with both hands before his arms swung out to his sides. "How am I supposed to walk around with all this and pretend everything is normal?"

Thea shrugged. "Why do you think I've been hiding in here?"

"You're going to have to come out today. I won't be the last visitor you receive if you do not." He peered at her, brows cocked.

"I know." Thea sighed and turned to gaze out the window. The rain had finally stopped, and the sun was shining for the first time in nearly a sixday. It cast a cool yellow glow through the sheer curtains.

Callum reached for her hand, taking it between his own. "What do you want to do, Thea?"

"I want to forget about it all and pretend it never happened. But I don't think I can. For now, I—*we*—have to sit with it. See what happens."

"I'll do whatever you think is best, but please… and I need you to swear." His hands released hers and grasped her shoulders, turning her toward him. "Do not go back out in the woods on your own. If you want to go, find me first and I will take you."

Thea nodded, pulling him into an embrace. "Thank you, Callum."

His arms tightened around her. "Thea, please do not keep things from me. You don't need to do this on your own."

Her brother had always kept her secrets, and she his. She regretted not telling him before. He was often heedless of what escaped his mouth, but he would keep this secret for her if she asked him to. *You don't need to do this on your own.* She exhaled at the thought.

Callum kissed her cheek and stood. "Now get up and get out of this fucking room. It smells like stale wine and self-pity."

Thea spent the afternoon in the gardens clearing the mess wrought by the rains. The task had given her the first reprieve from her racing thoughts in days, but her belly still fluttered. Every noise or movement around her distracted. Waiting for something to happen, she realized, was terribly dreadful. Thea was elbow-deep in mud when a page came to call for her on behalf of her father.

"I'll clean up and meet him shortly."

"I beg pardon, my lady." The boy looked down. "Your father bids you come right away."

"Very well." Thea pulled off her apron and washed her hands in one of the clean buckets. The boy was still standing there. She looked at him quizzically.

"I beg pardon, again, my lady, he commanded I wait and escort you myself. With haste," the boy said, and looked down.

"Of—course," she said, as her heart quickened. She toweled off her hands and asked the staff to continue without her.

She followed the boy through the halls, struggling to keep pace without her walk giving way to a run. Dreadful thoughts plagued her all the way. The boy stopped short of the council room door, and the two soldiers standing guard stepped aside for her to pass.

Her father, Leanne, Conall, Evelynde, and Commander Pryde were already seated around the table. No one spoke as she looked from person to person. Leanne's face was washed with alarm, her hands clutched around her swollen belly. Conall stared at the tabletop. Thea took the empty seat next to Evelynde, who looked on the verge of tears. Her father gave her a soft, reassuring smile. The kind one gives another right before dire news.

Ease settled over her. The fear was still there, but she'd become accustomed to it in the past days, and now she was about to understand why.

The door opened again, and Cat entered the room, followed by Callum. Commander Pryde stood and moved to pull Cat's chair free, assisting her into the seat. She smiled at him, and he bowed first to her, then to Callum.

Thea shrugged when Callum looked at her with question. When Pryde returned to his chair, all faces turned to Ulric at the head of the table.

"I will not attempt to ease you into this news. For it is grave." He cleared his throat. His mouth opened and closed several times before speaking again, eyes moving over each of his children, lingering on Thea. It stretched on, and she couldn't help but feel it was some sort of apology.

"Last moon, a man by the name of Lorcan Dracos marched an army through the Obsidian Mountains. A sizable army, under the banners of Thrane."

Cat, Callum, and Thea exchanged looks. They were clearly the only ones not privy to this information. He paused, letting the weight of what he had said saturate. Of all the things Thea had expected to hear, that was not one of them. The air felt instantly warmer, thicker, more of a task to take in.

"But," Cat said, "Thrane doesn't exist. Not in any meaningful way. And who is Lorcan? I do not recall a Dracos by that name."

"It very much does," Ulric said. "And Lorcan is the second son of the last king, Godric. After Godric and his heir were killed in the war and the scraps of the Thranean army retreated, Lorcan returned to Thrane with a small force, claiming the throne for himself." Their father spoke with sharp disdain, as if saying the names left a distaste in his mouth. No doubt it did. He had fought against Thrane, against Godric, in that very war.

Cat cocked her head, her eyes flickering at a rapid pace. "There is no mention of a *Lorcan* Dracos in any of the books on the Iren Wars or Thrane." Thea watched her sister sifting through her mind for anything of similarity.

"No," their father answered. "There wouldn't be. Most never knew he existed."

"Why?" asked Callum, his gaze shifting from Cat to their father.

"That is… complicated." He didn't look at Callum when he answered. His eyes were on Thea.

For a moment, she had forgotten all she'd been holding. Her own concerns quickly washed away, replaced by a new one. War.

Callum followed their father's gaze to Thea but turned back before he spoke. "And how would they march an army through the Obsidian Mountains? That would take several moons, and they would never be able to carry enough supplies to maintain a sizable force."

Ulric clasped his hands on the table. "We do not know, but we have ideas. That is also complicated."

"You are not making sense, Father," Callum challenged.

"Be patient, brother," Conall said to Callum. Callum took a breath and leaned back in his chair.

Cold sweat beaded on the insides of her hands. She swallowed as the tension compounded. Her father continued to steal glances at her, and she worried what her face was saying.

"The important information in this moment is that he has an army, a rather large one, and he is marching it to our borders as we speak."

Thea inhaled, and it felt collective. She wanted to ask why, but it seemed a foolish question. Thrane had done so thrice before.

"How large is the army?" Callum asked.

Commander Pryde cleared his throat. "At least twenty thousand, likely more."

Callum choked on his drink, and Cat gasped. Thea was sure her heart stopped.

"Surely not," Cat said. Thea was not confident whether it was a statement or question.

"It is one of the few things we are sure of. Only days ago, they marched on Croydyn, and the city surrendered."

"Gods save us." Evelynde's hand came up to cover her mouth.

For a moment, no one spoke.

"How long have you known?" Thea asked.

Her father sat up straight. "Information has been sparse coming in—"

"Father, how long?" Thea repeated.

Ulric looked between Cat, Callum, and Thea. "A halfmoon. We only discovered Ire to be their destination this morning."

"The rider…" Thea looked from Callum to their father. "You lied to us."

"I did." He didn't attempt to conceal it, and it brought forth an appreciation in her for him. Perhaps now she would have answers, though many of her questions no longer felt important.

"What rider?" Cat asked.

"A rider came to Highclere twelve days past. It seemed urgent, but we were assured it wasn't," Thea answered.

"Oh," Cat said, looking from Thea to Callum.

"I'm sorry, Cat. We didn't want to worry you without cause."

Her sister didn't respond, only looked down.

Callum sat up straight in his chair. "If they are in Croydyn now, they will likely march to Kingsport. We have time to meet them at the border if we depart without delay."

"It does not appear they are marching south," Pryde said. Thea thought he had aged years since she saw him only days before. She noticed his gaze continually shifting to Cat.

"That makes no sense," said Callum, looking from Pryde to their father. "Why would they march on Highclere? Surely they are not foolish enough to believe they can take the castle from the west?"

"Not all heed the lessons imparted to us by the past," their father said. "But we do not know their designs," he continued. "As I said before, we are working with limited information, but it appears the bulk of their army marches directly for Highclere from Croydyn."

"A ruse then?" Cat asked. "To draw our attention from the south?"

"Perhaps," answered their father. "In response, we are deploying a sizable force. It is being readied now. On the morrow, Conall will ride north, first to Caern and then Calcheth, to order our reserve forces south. Half to Highclere, half to Kingsport. He will then hold in Eastwatche, taking command of the fleet." Their father turned to Callum. "Callum, you also depart in the morning for Aremore with orders for Percy to join with the forces heading south. Leanne, Cat, and the children will accompany you. You will then travel to Eastwatche, where you will all remain until we know better of Thrane's plans."

Callum nodded, the gravity of the situation starting to weigh in. "Why to Eastwatche?"

"In case Highclere falls," Cat answered quietly, gazing down.

Thea and Callum exchanged a look.

"Fear not, Princess, Highclere has stood strong for a thousand years. It will not fall under my watch," Commander Pryde assured.

Thea swallowed, and it was an arduous task. She looked at Conall and Leanne. Neither had moved, and Conall had barely spoken. His hand rested protectively on her lap, her own arms clutched around his. When Thea finally connected eyes with Leanne, she looked at her with something like pity. It charged her dread. Something told her that not all had been shared.

Reading the faces of his children, Ulric spoke. "Do not worry. We are acting out of an abundance of caution. Our forces are greater in number than theirs, and we have ample time to reinforce our borders."

"Why isn't Thea going to Eastwatche?" Callum asked.

Thea straightened. It hadn't occurred to her she wasn't mentioned.

Her father's eyes flicked to her for what felt like the hundredth time since she'd entered the room.

"Do not say that it's fucking complicated." Callum's tone was laced with warning.

"And what about Evelynde?" Thea turned to look at her stepmother. "Are you not going with the twins?"

Evelynde shook her head. "My place is with your father. It is the duty of a queen to set an example of character for her people at all times, but expressly in those of peril."

Ulric flexed his jaw, telling Thea he did not share his wife's position.

"What about Thea?" Callum asked again.

"There is more to tell, but first, I must speak with Thea alone," Ulric answered.

All eyes shifted in her direction, and she shrank back in her chair.

"Me? Why?" She looked nervously around at her family.

"Please give us some time," he said to the group. "Stay close. I will call for you all again soon."

Thea met with apprehensive eyes as all filed out. She searched each set for understanding, finding none. They either looked at her with pity, or with the same bewilderment she felt. Callum gave her a questioning look.

"I'm all right," she said to him.

He sighed, but nodded. "I'll be right outside."

When they were alone, her father rose from his seat, moving to the now-empty one beside her. His eyes were mournful and nervous, like one about to make apologies. Thea's stomach twisted and rolled in knots, her mind unable to make a single speculation of what he was about to say. She only knew it would be bad.

"There are many things I must tell you, dear girl, that I hoped I would never have cause to."

She shifted in her seat, beginning to question her previous eagerness for answers.

"Please know that everything I have done was what I thought best. What your mother thought best. I wish there was more time. To tell you the whole story."

Thea clutched her belly, fearing she would be sick. "Father, *please*, you are frightening me."

He reached for her hand, holding it tight between his. "Thea, your mother's name was not Eadda. She was not the daughter of an Iceni soldier."

Thea blinked and then shifted back, pulling her hand from his. She frowned, struck again by a subject far outside of anything she could have expected. "I don't understand. Why would you lie about her name?"

"Her true name was Sonia Throndsen," he said, bypassing her question. "Throndsen as in Faela Throndsen, the last queen of Icena. Sonia was her eldest daughter."

An abrupt laugh burst from her lips. When her father simply stared at her, she stilled. Thea sorted through her knowledge of the history of Icena. It did not take long. If only Cat were there. "But… Faela had no children."

Her father nodded. "That is what is believed to be true, but she had two daughters. Sonia and Lia. Do you understand what I am saying?"

"That I am the granddaughter of Faela the Fallen?"

His eyes probed hers as if desperate for, but also fearful of, her reaction. Thea tried to take it in. Her mind tumbled with so many questions she couldn't put a single one to her lips. When she said nothing, he continued.

"Your mother and I fought alongside each other during the war. That is how I came to know her."

"I don't know what I am supposed to say. Why lie?"

"For your safety."

"My safety?" she asked, frowning. "Father, why are you looking at me like there is something more severe to tell?" She felt herself starting to spin and gripped the table's edge. "And what does this have to do with the war?"

He reached across the table for a carafe, filling a chalice, taking two large gulps. She watched his fingers tremble as they clutched the stem.

Her heart beat so quickly it felt like a constant thrum with no reprieve. "For Godssake, please just say it."

"Your mother was… gifted." He set the chalice back down on the table, then turned to look at her again. "She could do things."

"I don't know what that means." The ice-cold prickle of needles spread out through her chest. She swallowed against the feeling as it tried to rise in her throat. She released the table and raised one hand to her chest, as if she could soothe it away.

He watched her movements. "It is difficult for someone like me to explain."

"Someone like you?" The ice radiated down her arms to her fingertips, and her hands fisted. She grunted, struggling to take in a full breath. Seeing the signs on her, he stood abruptly as the door burst open. Thea heard footsteps coming toward her. She looked up to find Breeda standing over her.

"Breathe, Thea." Breeda rested her hands on her shoulders. Warmth radiated from them, causing the icy panic to retreat.

Thea looked up and frowned. It was Breeda, but she looked... different. She wasn't wearing an apron, but was dressed in what looked like fighting leathers. She wore no bonnet, and her gray-speckled blonde hair was braided down the length of her back. As if reading her bewilderment, Breeda said, "All will be explained, my girl."

"You knew all of this? Both of you?" Thea looked from one to the other. "You lied all these years? Why?"

"I did." Breeda took a seat at the table. "It was I who brought you here from Seahenge. I know you have many questions—"

Thea shook her head and then turned back to her father. "What do you mean she was *gifted?*"

Ulric looked at Breeda. She waited for her father to explain, but it was Breeda who spoke.

"This will take some time for you to understand," she said slowly. "There are people who can connect to the energy in our world. To the energy that powers life. They are born with this gift."

Thea didn't intend to laugh, but it burst free of its own accord. She turned to look at her father. His eyes were heavy on her, studying her reaction, as if it would dictate what he would say next. She frowned, then laughed again. "I don't—that doesn't—what *energy?*" she asked. "And do what with it?" Thea asked the questions, but assumed at any moment they would correct her. Tell her she misunderstood.

Breeda took a breath. "Many things. Control the elements, generate fire. Some can manipulate others' thoughts and feelings. People with these abilities are called Etherborn."

Thea choked out another laugh, looking again from face to face.

When neither joined in, hers stilled. "What is this?" She grew irritated they would make such a jest.

Breeda leaned forward to take her hand, but Thea pulled back. "There is no easy way to explain it all, and it will take time to understand."

"You said that already." Thea's reason battled their words. Were these more of their games? "Why are you saying these things? We are about to be at *war*."

"Because many of the people marching with Thrane are Etherborn," her father answered.

Thea's eyes went wide. The implications of what that could mean sent wild thoughts spinning in her mind. Not that she believed them. She most certainly did not.

"Because, dear girl, *you* are like this," Breeda said low but clearly.

A small, nervous laugh escaped her lips, and she shook her head. "No, I'm not." Her eyes shot to her father's, and she found them serious. "Stop this," she hissed.

"She speaks truth, Thea."

"I think I would know if I had some kind of powers, Father." She scoffed. Her fear was quickly burned up by animosity. It boiled within. In her belly, in her blood.

"There are ways it can be suppressed," her father said.

"We believe it is why you have the attacks. What is in you wants out," Breeda added.

"Why are you doing this?" She fisted her hands, fingernails digging into the flesh of her thighs. "I think you've both lost control of your senses!"

Breeda reached forward, grasping her arm. "It is a long and complicated story. It will take time to understand."

"Stop saying that!" Panic burst through the thin barrier she'd been grasping at. "Is this more of your tricks? More *lies*?" She glared at her father and then at Breeda. "I dug up the grave. I know it wasn't a Gods-damned mountain cat. I've known you've been lying to me. Sylvie, too, as I'm sure you forced upon her. You let me think myself delusional." Her chest heaved, breath quickening. "What—*who* chased me?"

"Thea, calm down, or you'll bring on a fit," Breeda said.

"*Who?*" she screamed, and it felt like ice crystallizing through her.

Both flinched at the measure of her voice. Her father's face twisted into one of alarm and guilt.

"We didn't know then, but we now believe it was a Thranean spy,"

Breeda answered.

Thea closed her eyes. *Wake up.* She dug her fingernails further into her flesh until the tiny half-moon impressions stung. *Wake up!* Had everyone around her gone mad? Perhaps it was her. She thought of all that had happened the past moon. Surely, she was dreaming. At any moment, she would wake.

They never allowed her to leave. Her fits. How Breeda was the only one who could calm them. Until Sylvie came. Callum's stories of whispers. The green light in the woods. So many things were left unexplained. But it couldn't be true, she thought. Because if it was, the world was mad, and everything she knew about it, about herself, was wrong.

Thea blinked her eyes open, gaze flicking to Breeda. "You are like this."

She nodded.

Thea stared at her. "Sylvie is like this."

Breeda nodded again. "She is."

"No—no." Thea stood from her chair. It flipped, crashing onto the ground behind her. "I'm not doing this."

"Thea, please sit down," her father beckoned, reaching for her.

She shook her head, backing up, pointing at them. "You are wrong. This is wrong." She turned, striding for the door.

"I'll go with her," she heard Breeda say.

Thea turned back. "No. Do not follow me. Both of you stay away from me. You are liars. You are all liars!" She burst through the door to find Callum waiting in the hall.

"Thea?" Callum stood, expectant. "What happened?"

She held up her hand to warn him off, shaking her head. Storming down the hall, mind spinning, she made for the south side of the castle, toward the forest. She could hear footsteps following, but she kept going. Turning a corner, she crashed into a kitchen girl carrying a large tray. It clamored against the stone floor.

"I'm sorry," Thea cried, her pace now picking up to a run. She had to get outside. She couldn't breathe. She didn't slow when she crossed into the woods. There was no destination in mind, only space between her and what was. What used to be. She ran until her lungs burned and her side ached. Until her legs could move no more.

Falling to her knees, she braced on her hands, fingers digging into the earth. Her chest burned as she battled between breathing and sobbing. She knew Breeda was behind her. Some distance away, watching.

She stayed that way for a time, releasing all that had collected the past moon. Every question, every lie, every suspicion. In time, her breath calmed, and her tears stopped, but her heart ached the same.

"Why are you doing this?"

No one answered, but light rustling started. Breeda came to sit on the forest floor before her. Breeda's manner was calm and steady, and Thea wanted to be angry for it, but it helped to calm her, too. "There are many answers to that question."

"Give me one," she pleaded.

"This is what your mother wanted." Breeda shifted closer, but Thea retreated, scooting backward through the duff.

"You talk about her as if you knew her."

Breeda closed her eyes and sighed. "I did, Thea. I knew her very well. We were not sisters by blood, but were of a sisterhood forged by oath."

Thea's face distorted as her tears returned. "Is there anything I know that is true?"

"My love for you. Your father's love for you. And though you have never known it, your mother's love, too."

"How can I believe such things? You tell me you love me, then tell me you lie to me. You speak of things that are not real."

"It is all very real, my girl." Breeda moved closer again, her voice tender. "Your mind will make sense of this in time."

Thea laughed, rich with lunacy. She was unsure what was more difficult to believe. The stories of her true mother or that she was some sort of sorceress.

"How many are like this?" Thea asked, not even sure what they were, shock in herself she was entertaining it.

"There are thousands of us all across the world."

Thea scoffed. "How is this not known? How could people with abilities you described be unknown to the world?"

"Because we have worked for hundreds of years to keep it so." Breeda paused, as if deciding how much to say, or how to say it. "After the Godswar, and the Great Quell, as many call it, Etherborn were nearly eliminated from the world. Centuries passed, and what remained of our kind lived in secret, in fear, hunted by those who misunderstood our gifts. But as our powers returned, so did our emergences, and over four hundred years ago, a society was formed in Sibreen. Its purpose is to protect our kind, to find a way to use our powers for good. With order and governance, so another war of such magnitude will not come again. It is called

Elah Esērii. I was a part of it, as was your mother."

Thea simply stared at her, lacking the capacity to consider most of what was said. She folded her arms. "You say we have powers? I want you to show me."

Breeda shook her head. "Not yet."

Thea pressed up on her knees. "If you want me to believe you, then show me. Right now. I am done taking people at their word."

Breeda sighed, and Thea thought at first she would say no. "Very well." She held up a hand between them, palm facing the sky. "You are sure?"

"*Show me.*"

A small, pale blue flame sprang to life. Thea fell back as a startled yelp escaped her.

"We call this etherfire," Breeda said. "It is one of the simplest forms of wielding."

Thea moved closer, limbs shaking, circling the flame. She blinked in rapid succession, now certain she was dreaming. It was fire, but not, iridescent and luring, calling her forward. Heat pulsed from it, warming her cheeks. It felt charged, alive, animated by forces beyond its own combustion. She looked at Breeda, knowing her wild thoughts were all over her face. "This is madness."

"It is a certain type of madness, I suppose," Breeda said, with a trace of amusement. The fire retreated, replaced by rays of light that twisted and turned through the air, bending into the open space. "This is ether. *My* ether, better put. Ether lives within you, too, Thea, and it is different from mine." The vines of light grew high, and Thea looked up, following the path. "It lives in everything in our world. The trees, the earth, even the air we breathe. It is all connected." The light retracted, snaking back down, disappearing as quickly as it had emerged. Breeda lowered her arm. "Those of us born with the gift, the Etherborn, can harness it. Manipulate it. Some of us only our own, but many can control the ether around them. Influence it in many ways."

Thea fell back onto her heels. She clutched at the denial now slipping from her grasp. "You said I am like this." Her hand came up to rest on her chest, palm over her heart. "But I do not feel anything."

"We have you bound. We can use one's own ether to bind their abilities. It is difficult to do and even more difficult to maintain, as we have found with you."

"Why would you *bind* me, as you say? Is there something wrong with me?"

"No, Thea. There is nothing wrong with you." Breeda's hands came up to cover her face, and she rubbed her eyes. When it was revealed again, a mournful cast had taken hold of it. "Most Etherborn children are raised among the Esērii, learning to use their gifts from an early age. Sonia did not want that for you. Binding you was the best way we could think to keep you a secret. If we had not, they would have come for you." Her eyes swelled, despite her stonelike expression. Thea tried to think if she had ever seen the woman cry. "Your mother made us swear not to let the Esērii take you. We made a vow to her. You were born, and then I was holding you in my arms on a ship headed to Eastwatche. It all happened so fast."

"What happened to her?" Thea asked. "To my mother."

"We were under attack. She stayed back to give the rest of us time to escape." Breeda shifted closer, taking Thea's hand in her own. "She sacrificed herself for us. For you."

Thea looked down. There were too many questions, but she had to start somewhere. "Do you know *how* she died?"

Any sympathy or tenderness on Breeda's face dissolved. "She was murdered by Lorcan Dracos when she would not join him. As he has done to many others."

Thea's eyes flicked up at the name.

"Yes, Thea. The same man marching here now."

Thea's head fell into her hands. It was too much. Her head ached with the effort to work through it all. For a moment, she considered that it all sounded far too fantastical to be false. Powers. Secret societies. Thea started laughing and couldn't stop.

Breeda watched her with wary eyes. "I am so sorry, my girl."

"You said I am *bound*. Can you not simply take away whatever this is? I do not want it."

"I fear it does not work like that."

Thea closed her eyes, causing warm tears to spill down her cheeks. "I think I have had my fill of truth today," she said as she stood, clumsily. She felt a certain relief that she wasn't mad after all, but dread that it seemed the world was. "We are at war, or so I'm told. That seems far more pressing." Thea turned and started walking in the direction of the castle.

✤

She made her way back to the council room to find her family had also returned. It was clear on all faces at the table that they'd been told what she had. Sylvie was present and, like Breeda, now looked different. Her curly red hair was unbound and wild. She, too, was no longer in an apron, but trousers, tall boots, and a loose tunic. When Thea looked around at her family, they could scarcely meet her eyes.

Thea looked at Sylvie. "You, too?"

"I am sorry," Sylvie said. "Lying to you was never easy."

Thea nodded. "There is much of it going around."

Cat wiped tears from her eyes. She looked truly frightened. Callum looked at Thea as if trying to see whatever it was they had told him about her. Evelynde stared off into the distance. Conall looked uncharacteristically calm, almost relieved.

For a time, no one spoke. What was there to say after finding out things they only thought possible in stories and myths to be true?

"What can I do?" Callum asked her.

Do not look at me like that, she thought. She shrugged her shoulders.

Many questions were asked. Thea drowned them out. For the first time in a moon, her mind was empty. Blank. She reckoned it had received too much. It was now in tantrum, refusing participation. Now and then, hearing her name would draw her attention, but it would soon fade again. She felt dreamlike, wandering in heavy fog.

She looked up to a hand on her shoulder. Breeda stood above her with a sad half smile. Looking around the table, she saw lots of sad smiles. All were standing to leave.

"When you are ready, come and find me. I'll tell you anything you want to know." Breeda gave her a pat and turned to leave with the others. The doors closed, and only her father remained.

"What else can I tell you?" he asked. He looked devastated, and it pained her to see him suffering.

"Everything," she answered. "But not today."

He nodded, and Thea could not tell if it was from relief or disappointment.

"I need some time to think." She wiped a tear from her cheek, surprised she had any left. "Some time to make sense of it."

"We will grant you space, as much as you wish. I only need you to agree to stay close to the castle. It is not safe to go into the woods or even the city."

"I promise. You should go," she urged. "I know you are needed." He started to object, but she held up her hand. "I am all right. I swear it."

He stood and walked to her, placing a kiss on the top of her head. "I am so sorry, dear girl."

All had come to the courtyard at dawn to say farewell. Conall and Callum were both red-eyed and weary, as if they hadn't slept at all. Not that Thea had, either. Her father wore the same clothes as the day before.

Thea watched her eldest brother across the courtyard. He held both of his children before returning them to their nurses. When he reached for his wife, he withheld nothing from his face, whispering words for her alone. His hands tangled in her long hair, and he kissed her, without reserve, no care of who looked on. Thea turned away, part in feeling an intruder on their moment, and in part from the pain of witnessing their separation.

Conall released Leanne, bidding his family, even Thea, with a farewell nod. He mounted his horse and rode off, unceremoniously, with the northbound party.

"I'm sorry, I don't know what to say," Cat said, tears falling in a steady stream down her cheeks.

Thea nodded. "I know. It is all right." She reached for her sister, pulling her into her arms. "We will have time for words when this is over."

Cat sobbed. Thea pulled back to look at her, using the sleeve of her dress to blot her sister's tears. She found it much easier to bear her own pain than to see the like on another.

"Go on," Thea said, and released her. Cat looked back one last time as Commander Pryde helped her into the carriage.

Thea kissed Henri and Lucienne before turning to Leanne, holding both her hands between them. "Is it safe for you to travel?"

"Your father has three midwives accompanying us," Leanne reassured.

Thea nodded, but all knew the baby could come at any time. Leanne had to be well into her eighth moon by now. "Then I look forward to meeting my new nephew."

Leanne nodded and smiled, kissing each of Thea's cheeks before climbing into the carriage with her children.

Thomas and Tamsin ran across the courtyard into Thea's arms. She held on to them as tightly as she could manage. "I will see you soon, littles. Yes?" They nodded, Tamsin not wanting to let go.

Ulric and Evelynde kissed the twins goodbye, and Thea could not watch as Evelynde was forced to pry Tamsin from her body. When the carriage door closed, Evelynde turned away, hand covering her mouth as she cried.

"I can't believe I'm leaving you," Callum said.

Thea straightened the top button on his vest. "You're not. We will be together again soon." She struggled to meet his eyes.

"Do you swear it?" he asked. His voice broke, and it nearly destroyed her.

"I swear it." Thea tried to smile, but every time she looked into his blue eyes, it cracked.

Callum tugged her against him, cradling the back of her head. "If at any time it's not safe here, go to Aremore. Go to Marten. He will see you to Eastwatche."

"I will." Thea wondered what Marten knew.

"You can come with me now," he offered. "You do not have to stay here."

"I can't, Callum." Thea shook her head. "I don't know who I am. Or *what* I am. It might not even be safe for others to be around me."

He scoffed and gripped her shoulders. "Don't you dare say you don't know who you are. You are Calithea Ironne. Daughter of the king and *my sister.*" His eyes grew heavy until overwhelmed, and the tears spilled freely. The sight of it ripped through her. It was a strange thing, she thought, being in a moment like this. Desperate for the agony of it to end, yet dreading when it did.

He leaned closer, speaking into her ear. "I've given Kyna coin and horses. I told her to ride to Eastwatche if the worst happens."

"Good," Thea said, nodding. "That is good."

They wrapped their arms around each other one last time, neither wanting to be the one to break it. She watched each carriage, and then her brother on horseback, cross beyond the castle gate. He glanced back at her and waved. When he finally turned around, she allowed herself to fracture. Her father's arm came around her, and she leaned into him, letting her fears come out in sobs. She thought soon she would be getting used to seeing the people she loved leave.

35

Neith

"The Esērii are only as strong as the sacrifices each citizen endeavors to on its behalf."

ESĒRII BIJRAH Z'OURA
ADE NYANTHI AND PHILOMENA TALIESIN, 805 AQ

The rains returned with a fury. For three days, they had woken and retired to a constant, steady fall. The roads had long turned muddy, and carts were continually stuck. Even the horses seemed to be sick of it.

Etherborn took turns projecting shields, but in time, even that grew tiresome, and they eventually gave in to what nature was determined to give them. By midday, Neith's father made the call to halt travel. By late afternoon, the rain had slowed to a drizzle. All anyone wanted was reprieve and a hot meal.

"At least the rain isn't cold," Kieran said.

"Says you." Iris wrapped her arms around herself. Raiden pulled a dry cloak from his pack and draped it over her shoulders. She looked up at him with a grateful smile.

"I can't sit here until nightfall," Bellamy said, standing. "Who will walk with me?" He turned toward the woods that ran north alongside the road. "There has to be something interesting around here."

"I'll go." Petra stood beside him.

"Neith?" Bellamy asked her.

"For a walk then," Neith agreed. Her hips were tight from the long, slow ride.

Sam, Ayla, and Max also voiced their desire to join.

"Bring back dry firewood!" Iris yelled as they trudged through the mud into the dense tree line.

The wet earth quickly turned solid, their boots no longer sinking. The thick, lush greenery provided coverage from the drizzle. Neith and Sam stopped counting the different species of trees at fourteen. Pine and honeysuckle fragranced the damp air.

"We might be able to find some wild strawberries," Ayla said, looking around. "Maybe even some elderberries. That's if the rabbits and squirrels haven't taken them all."

They trekked deeper into the woods, searching for said berries or even a rabbit to catch. It seemed as if all the creatures of the forest had found some place to bury their heads. It was the better part of an hour before there were signs the storm clouds had moved on.

"Is that the sun?" Bellamy pointed a short distance north. "It looks like a clearing up ahead."

"That's the perfect place to look!" Ayla took off, Max, Petra, and Bellamy on her heels.

"How is your hand?" Sam asked as they followed leisurely behind.

Neith looked over the rough scar, flexing her fingers. "Still stiff. Sometimes it hurts, but I think it is only in my mind." A chill crept up her arm at the memory of the pain, and the horrifying feeling of the cold metal tearing back through her flesh when she ripped the dagger free. She now thought herself a rabid dog in that moment.

Sam stopped and turned to face her with a sorrowful look that confused her. "I am sorry. I should have been faster."

"If memory serves, you nearly cut him in two." Neith laughed. In jest, and in a little madness at the image of it burned in her mind. It was not one she would soon forget.

"I won't let anyone get that close to you again," he said, his somber demeanor persisting despite her jest.

"Has this worried you?" Neith frowned when his eyes answered with a resounding *yes*. He'd scarcely left her side since the night in Croydyn, but she did not realize that it plagued him so. "I am fine." She waved her hand in front of his face. "See?" She grinned, giving him a playful push.

He smiled, but it stopped short of his eyes. He reached for her hand, holding it in his, tracing the pink scars on each side. It sent an ache through her.

"I swear," she whispered. "I am fine, Sam." Her words did nothing to quell his conflict. "You saved me. *Again*, I might add."

A soft, sad chuckle quaked in his chest, and he shook his head. It pained her he had been bearing such guilt. It was the first time they'd been alone since the night in her tent in Croydyn.

"I'm not sure what I would have done had something worse happened." He said the words, but it looked more like his private thoughts had escaped, and he was making sense of them out loud. "Or what I will do if someone tries to hurt you again."

She wanted to ease his burden and tell him nothing would happen, but saying such things in war meant nothing. They had agreed there would be only truth between them.

"Royce Cawthorne should count himself lucky he was granted a quick death." His eyes fixed on her with an intensity that not long ago would have sent her running. Now, she wanted to step into it. Drink it. Drown in it. Even so, she couldn't help but wonder how much his feelings were influenced by his position, being tasked with her safety.

There was danger in this for her, and she knew it. This was more than a dalliance, or could be, at least. At some point, they would have to decide what it was, one way or the other.

"I feel quite the same," she said, holding his gaze.

He cocked his head as if unsure of her meaning.

"I'm not sure what I would do if something were to happen to you."

His hand tightened around hers, and he exhaled. She thought he looked worried.

"What are you thinking?" she asked.

"If I say what I am thinking, there is no turning back."

She nodded. "I think I understand."

He looked away as if not agreeing that she did.

She reached for his face, turning it back to hers. "I trust you will tell me if and when you feel it is right."

He studied her for a drawn moment, as if remedying something in his mind. She ached to understand. But despite her desire to know him, she would not achieve it through means of coercion. She would not tarnish this with impatience.

He covered her hand with his, and a subtle but tender smile tugged on his lips. It drew her attention to them. When it faded, she looked back up to find his honey-colored eyes fixed on hers, removed of their hesitation, transposed with what she both feared and yearned for. What emanated from him drew her in, like gravity, and she took a step closer. She watched with unmitigated attention as he slowly brought her palm to his lips, brushing them against the scarred pink flesh. It sent her pulse thrumming.

"Sam, I—"

She felt his hand on the small of her back. He drew her body against his, causing her lips to part, and she craned her neck to keep his gaze. The look he gave her sent heat resonating through every part of her, and she tried to swallow, finding she could not.

"Neith! You have to see this!" Ayla called out.

They stared at each other until Neith ran a hand over her face and sighed. It felt like she'd dove headfirst into the icy waters of Lake Storna. "Will we never have a moment uninterrupted?"

Sam smiled and brushed hair from her face, tucking the loose strands behind her ears. "We have time."

She wanted to tell him he promised he wouldn't lie, but then she supposed hope and deception weren't the same.

As they approached the clearing, the sky grew brighter. When Neith stepped out of the tree line, her eyes closed in relief as warm sunlight washed over her. When they opened again, she nearly gasped. Dozens of trees brimming with bright white and pink flowers filled the open space, their fallen petals covering the ground. She inhaled a sweet, floral, almost lemonlike scent. She turned back to Sam, who was already looking at her, and she smiled.

A tall stone formation stood center of the trees. The remnants of something once grand. Neith studied it in wonder as they drew closer.

It looked to be the ruins of a large stone room, with twin pillars. Only the remains of two walls still stood. Rays of sunlight pierced through its open spaces, making for a sight of which Neith had never seen. It was more than beautiful. It was storylike and made her think of poetry. At least what she believed poetry to be.

Moss- and ivy-covered, it stood twice the height of Sam, and Neith climbed the six crumbling stairs by two to place her hand on one of the pillars. The stone was warm like the sun that shone down, and surprisingly smooth.

"What is this place?" she marveled, turning in a circle.

"A temple ruin," Sam answered, stepping up beside her.

"Faith of the Hexad?" she asked.

"No," Petra answered. "Much older than that. There are several similar ruins in Straeth and the northern parts of Ire."

That would be something to look forward to, she thought. "What

Gods were these made for?" Neith asked, still in awe.

Petra shrugged. "No one knows. They are thousands of years old."

Neith's fingers traced over the ornate engravings on one of the pillars. Small faces were carved into the stone, connected by knots and other symbols. The etchings were impossibly small. "How is it someone made this so long ago?"

Sam moved to study the designs alongside her. "We believe that time always moves us forward, but I fear more than once in history we may have fallen back."

Something tightened in her chest. It felt such a terrifying prospect. The idea that humanity would be the cause of its own undoing, its own regression. She thought of the charges, of what they'd seen in Eynsbury, and what her father told her of Transformation.

"What does this say?" Ayla stood on the inside of one of the walls, tracing an inscription. She tried to read it.

Sam walked around to stand beside her. He held a finger under each word as he spoke. "*Luxa en Umbraxos.*"

Neith joined them. "It is Argothan."

"What does it mean?" Ayla asked, still studying the words.

"Light in the Shadows," Sam answered.

"That's right." Neith smiled at him. Though parts of the old language were still used across the north, it was not common to find one who understood it fluently.

"That is beautiful," Ayla said, and sighed. "I wish I could read it."

"Why don't you learn?" Sam asked her.

Ayla laughed. "Sure."

Sam shrugged. "I could teach you."

Ayla turned toward him with a questioning look. "You would teach me?"

"When we are gifted something of such value, it is our responsibility to share it." He leaned a little closer and smiled. "And I would be most glad to share it with you."

Her smile slowly faded, and she looked down. "I do not think I am clever enough."

"You are." Neith stepped closer to her, taking her hand. "And I will help to teach you, too, if you wish." It pained her that Ayla would not think herself capable. Neith could only imagine Dryden had something to do with it.

Ayla looked from Neith to Sam and back, a slow grin forming on her mouth. "Very well."

"Ayla," Max called for her from across the clearing. "Strawberries!"

The excitement in Ayla compounded, and she gave them another quick grin before prancing away.

"That was kind of you," Neith said, as they watched her run to Max across the field.

"I fear she has not had enough kindness in her life."

"No," Neith agreed, wincing against the sting the thought brought to her eyes.

Neith looked at the boy standing next to her and could not make sense of how someone could be all the things he was. The captain demoted to guard, enduring it with humility and grace. The soldier offering to teach language to an attendant. The boy warming a wet cloth by the river, who picked blackberries only because she liked them. She considered for a moment that he might not be real. Perhaps she was seeing what she wanted. It sent fear through her, and she worried her feelings were already stronger than she grasped. Losing him, in any circumstance, seemed a terrifying prospect.

Sam frowned. "What is the matter?"

"Nothing." Neith smiled and cleared her throat. She stepped down from the ruins, toward the cluster of trees beside it. "What kind of tree is this?"

"These are magnolia trees." Sam reached up and brushed some of the petals as if he admired them as much as she.

Neith examined the elegant blooms and thick green leaves. "They are beautiful."

"They aren't native this far north."

"Then someone planted these trees here?" she asked.

Sam nodded. "They're temperamental. Even a mild frost affects the bloom. They do best in clearings like this. They get protection from the wind, but also the sunlight they need to thrive. Given the right conditions, they root deep and strong. They symbolize perseverance, living a hundred years or more, if well looked after."

Neith knelt, taking a fallen petal between her fingers. She thought about what that meant. Someone looked after this place. Someone loved it. Perhaps they well understood what Sam had said about history and humans. This place was a symbol, a message, perhaps even a warning that we could always fall back. She vowed to carry that with her. To receive the message someone had worked so hard to create.

"Sam, I—" A prickle crept along the back of her neck, and she reached up to touch it. Her gaze snapped to the tree line. She looked out over the clearing, brows drawn. Something stirred.

She stood and turned to Sam. His eyes widened, taking hers in.

Looking back toward the feeling, she found Ayla picking berries, laughing with Max, who was barely a step behind her.

Neith felt it again on her neck. Cold dread pooled in her belly, crowding her chest. By the time she realized what was coming, it was nearly too late to scream.

"Ayla!"

Ayla stopped, looking up from where she knelt, frowning at the desperation in Neith's voice.

Neith heard the cracks, each louder, more terrifying than the last, and watched in horror as an ethercannon broke from the trees.

Max jumped forward, shoving Ayla to the ground as it pummeled through the open air, violent and brutal. It grazed his shoulder, spinning him around, blood spraying as it passed.

It continued on its path, and Neith met it with a shield. It exploded, and emerald-green fire poured out on impact.

She hadn't time to blink before another hit.

And another.

Neith looked back to see Sam safe under a shield of his own. His frenzied eyes were fixed on her as he tried to press forward as cannon after cannon exploded above him.

Six, seven, eight, nine she counted in an array of colors. She strained against the onslaught, heels digging in the damp earth, trying to push aside her panic to think.

They were being attacked. *Why?*

The sounds of impact were deafening. The heat from the fire turned the air in her shield to steam. Pieces of the ruins exploded, mixing with petals, splintered wood, and mud.

Her friends. She needed to find her friends.

Ayla crawled toward Max's body, limp on the ground. "Stay down!" Neith screamed, though she did not think Ayla could hear her.

She caught a glimpse of Petra and Bellamy by the ruins. Both were struggling to hold their shields. If it continued, they would have to run or fight back. Neith hadn't the time to consider which before the assault suddenly ceased.

Her wild eyes darted around the clearing. Leaves and petals fell lazily through the air. Max was now lying on top of Ayla, covering them in a shield. Sam, Petra, and Bellamy also looked around, panting, eyes wide but focused.

Neith saw no one else, at least not with her eyes. She snapped them shut, tapping into the ether. There was no one close.

Letting her shield go, her range extended, and she sensed them. So many of them. Her chest seized. They were moving in odd patterns, making it difficult to count. They surrounded the clearing, casing them in, slowly edging closer.

Neith held her finger to her lips and then extended her palm forward, signaling to everyone to keep quiet and still.

She felt Sam step beside her, encompassing her in his shield.

"Twenty," she said, low, "probably more."

"Godsdamn," Sam hissed under his breath. "We need to run."

Neith opened her eyes to look at him. "We can't. They're surrounding us."

"*Who are they?*" he asked, stepping closer.

Neith looked at each of her friends scattered across the field, taking in their frightened faces. She wasn't going to wait to find out. "They are about to be no one."

Neith clamped her eyes shut, returning to the ether. She set her sights on one. They were still at a distance close to the edge of her reach, but she snapped the plane anyway, hoping to consume enough to take them down. Whatever else was in the way be damned.

A distant scream, rife with horror, cut from one of their throats. She found another, locked in, and snapped. Another screamed.

She wasn't taking them whole, but she didn't need to. She could afford to be reckless at this distance. She took down four more and stumbled back.

Tremors started in the ground below. Cannons returned in twice the number. They bounced off Sam's shield, the roar so loud Neith could not be sure if her ears were bleeding from it or the nether. She continued to snap as the attackers grew closer. "They're coming straight for us!"

The tremors continued to escalate, now a consistent shake. She was about to snap for what she counted to be the eleventh time when her eyes flicked open. Sam's shield dismantled around them.

No.

Without warning, she was flying through the field, the earth having detonated beneath her.

She hit the ground hard on her back, the sun blinding as she looked up into blue sky. A cannon hurtled through the space right above her, and she twitched, writhing, trying to draw a breath.

A deafening ring reverberated in her head. She inhaled, sharp, painful, clutching the ground and air around her, searching for something to anchor herself to.

Another cannon passed over, this one closer, and she held out an arm, projecting her shield.

Pain like fire radiated through her right side. She reached down to the feeling of wetness and warmth. She decided she did not want to see and climbed to her knees, then to her feet, bracing against the relentless onslaught of incoming cannons. Every move felt like razors ripping through her.

Neith looked around, trying to orient herself, finding she'd been blown to the other side of the clearing, tearing through trees along the way. She could no longer see Sam, Petra, or Bellamy. Max and Ayla were still bracing under his shield.

Neith tried to focus, feeling the attackers drawing near. She snapped three more. They would be on them in a breath, but she had at least cut their numbers in half. She hoped.

A woman with long, blonde hair was the first to break from the trees. Bright orange etherfire poured from her palms, pummeling down on Max and Ayla. Tendrils of cobalt-blue ether ripped through the air from Neith's right palm, wrapping around the woman's neck. She hadn't the time to register what was happening before Neith sent her flying high into the air, then crashing to the ground, punching a crater in the earth, bursting with blood and pulp.

A cannon pummeled into the back of her shield. It sent her stumbling forward, and she snarled. Neith turned to see a man sprinting directly for her from the woods, encased in a shield of his own. Etherfire raged from her palm, halting his progress, quickly pressing him back.

Another cannon hit, but her shield held steady. She watched with satisfaction as his shield broke down. He was close enough she could see the look of terror in his eyes when he realized it would fall. She made it a quick death.

An explosion across the field drew her attention. There was so much debris she could barely see. Petra and Bellamy were fighting someone close to where they'd entered the clearing. She yelled for Sam but received no answer.

Another man emerged from her side of the woods. She snapped him, unconcerned with efficiency. Blood and other bits swirled through the violent air.

A furious assault of cannons smashed into her shield, and alarm whipped through her when it cracked. Someone was working to dismantle it. It was taking more and more effort to maintain, and she was growing weaker. Blood now streamed down her entire right side from rib to foot. From her nose, ears, and black eyes.

She heard Ayla scream. A man had etherfire bearing down on Max's shield. Neith knew she could not use nether so close to her friends. She sent her ether flying toward the man, but it bounced off his shield.

She limped toward them, working madly to dismantle it, feeling blood ooze from her side with every step.

A deafening boom close to the ruins sent pieces of stone flying into the air. Both walls were down, and she thought she saw Sam's honey-colored shield on the other side. She had to get to him.

Another cannon hit from behind. She turned and snapped its wielder into nothing. No idea if it was a man or woman.

Her focus returned to the man attacking Ayla and Max, feeling his shield crack. He turned around, now aware of Neith's effort. He abandoned task and started to run back into the trees, but Neith had already entangled him. He flailed and fought, and he was strong, but Neith had not given him time. He hit the ground with a wet thump.

Etherfire hit her shield from the right. It held, but the impact nearly sent her to her knees. She knew she was wearing down. She was losing too much blood.

When she turned to see her assailant, she stumbled, weak on her feet, but with none of her friends around to risk, she snapped the man. It was a half effort. Only portions of his chest and abdomen vanished, but it was enough to end his life. Blood, organs, and bowels spilled out from the gaps as what remained of his body slumped to the ground.

She was close enough now to see Petra fighting a woman, both under shields. The woman was gaining on her, purple etherfire burning wild. Neith's heart sank as she knew Petra would lose.

The attackers were wearing them down. They could not hold out much longer. *She* could not hold out much longer.

Neith focused her efforts on dismantling the woman's shield, knowing it was making her own vulnerable. Bellamy emerged at Petra's side, adding to the fire. It cracked, and they pressed on. The woman's shield fell away, and their combined etherfire scorched her until she lay lifeless on the blackened earth.

Neith turned in circles. The clearing had gone quiet. Wild, frantic energy raced through her body, and she knew it was all that kept her upright. She wanted to scream, to run, to tear someone apart.

Petra and Bellamy took off toward Max and Ayla. Neith moved to circle around the other side, desperate to put eyes on Sam.

She was panting, feeling herself starting to fade as he emerged from behind the rubble, sprinting directly toward her. A cry tore from her lips at the sight. He skidded to a halt in front of her, his shield washing over them both.

His panicked eyes took her in. He had a nasty cut above his left eye, and blood trailed down one of his arms, but he had no serious impairments she could see. Relief cascaded through her, and she nearly made praises to Gods she didn't believe in. His hands ran over her face, neck, and arms, but stopped when he took in the blood. He lifted the torn remains of her tunic and paled. He recovered his face quickly, but Neith had seen the look on him. It was bad.

Sam searched frantically around the tree line, waiting for another to emerge. When they didn't, he turned back.

"Neith," he said, holding her face. His hands were warm with her blood. "Look at me. Can you sense anyone else out there?"

She closed her eyes, searching through the ether.

"There are two. And one of them is a shieldmaster. They keep trying to take mine down. I can feel it."

He helped her move to sit against a large stone. It was a piece of one of the carved pillars.

"I won't last much longer," she said to him. Her mind was hazy, and she knew it was not only from the nether.

His eyes burned into hers and he snapped, *"Do not say that."*

"There is too much damage, and I cannot heal it. I cannot run." Neith looked at the others across the field. Bellamy was looking around as if searching for her and Sam. Petra and Ayla were helping Max sit up. "Get the others out. Go for help."

Sam moved to kneel in front of her. "That is not happening." He ripped the buttons off his vest and shrugged it off his body. He pulled off his tunic, then worked frantically to tie it around her waist. She winced and cried out as he tightened and tied it off. "I'm sorry," he said, taking her face in his hands again. His desperate eyes fixed on hers, and he exhaled. "I was thinking that I choose you."

She searched his face for understanding as tears fell down her cheeks.

He wiped them away with his thumbs. "The answer to your question. In the woods, you asked me what I was thinking," he said. "I was thinking that I choose you."

She watched tenderness break through his fear. All of the desperation she felt was magnified by his words. Both sure and unsure of what they meant. She clung to them. Grateful. Even if she would only have them for such a devastatingly brief time.

Neith felt a surge as cracks tore through the air like thunder. Both looked up as trees came crashing down all along the forest edge, exploding when they hit the ground.

He gripped her shoulders. "Stay here under your shield, no matter what happens!"

She reached for him, to beg him to stay, but he stood to stand in front of her.

The cracks stopped, quickly replaced by the howl of a windstorm. Violent gusts of air ripped through the clearing, sending shards of wood and fragments of stonelike shrapnel around them, beating up against their shields.

Neith closed her eyes, searching for the source. If she did not find the wielder, her friends were going to die. Sam was going to die.

She raged inside, desperate for anything, thoughts scrambling. But there was nothing. She could feel no one.

Then she remembered Godsreach.

She remembered the girl's shield and how it had been designed to resemble the ether that surrounded it.

Her heart leapt when she discovered it, not at all far from where they took shelter. She could see it, clear as day, nestled between the trees.

She wasted no time. In mere seconds, it started to give. Any moment, it would crumble, and they would be vulnerable. She readied the nether.

But something reinforced it. There were two. She roared, knowing that she could not maintain her shield and take theirs down. She looked up at Sam, barely visible through the debris-riddled air. *I choose you, too.* She thought of her friends. *I choose all of you.*

Neith let her shield fall and threw all her power into taking down the other. It started to crack.

She wondered what her father would do when he found her broken body. If Roman would care.

Crack.

Something sliced across her left arm. It burned, but she couldn't look. She couldn't break her focus. *Crack.* It was only pain, she told herself.

Another *crack.*

Something struck her right leg, and she feared she would not get the shield down in time. That they would tear her apart, piece by piece.

Neith ripped at the shield, tearing through its threads and weaving with so much savagery it felt almost material. As if she could feel it within her own hands.

She was struck again but didn't quit. If they were going to end her, if she was going to die, she would do so fighting.

Then she felt it. Hope. A flicker in the darkness. A thread splintered, and she went wild. Neith screamed, out loud, and gave it all she had left. One last chance, one last try.

And the shield shattered.

It came down, and without hesitation, she snapped. The nether consumed the wielder whole.

She opened her eyes to call for Sam. To tell him of their victory. To tell him it would end.

But everything stopped. Her heart, her breath, her thoughts. For a blink, suspended in the space between measurable time, Neith watched in horror as Sam's shield crumbled, falling away like gentle rain.

A violent gust crashed into him, snapping her out of the trance, and her eyes followed his path as he was sent flying.

The storm stopped, and Neith screamed.

She scrambled to her feet, frantic and clumsy, stumbling around in search of him. She spotted him through the dusty air a short distance across the field. He lay on his side, facing away. Neith limped, wincing with every unstable step.

Behind him in the distance, Max was leaning against a fallen tree, Ayla kneeling over him. His right arm hung loose, only partially attached above its elbow. Blood poured from the gruesome wound. Petra crawled on her hands and knees toward her brother. Bellamy was just getting to his feet, stumbling in her direction.

When Neith reached Sam, she rolled him over onto his back, and the sight nearly sent her to the ground. Countless shards of wood were embedded in his chest and abdomen. One protruded from his right cheek. He convulsed, eyes rounded and projected. His fingers dug at the earth as if desperate for something to cling to.

"Tell me what to do!" Ayla screamed. Petra removed her belt and wrapped it around the top of Max's arm, securing it tight.

Neith knelt next to Sam, hands hovering over his chest, using her ether to peer inside. She was weak and swayed, which fueled her panic.

Bellamy fell to his knees next to her, paling at the sight of her and then of Sam.

"Bellamy, *run*," she said. "Run back to camp. Bring as many surgeons as you can find on horseback." Neith was trying to yell, but her words came out slow and garbled. "As fast as you can. Go now." He regarded her, horrified, but nodded and scrambled to his feet, sprinting back through the trees.

The sounds of the explosions and fighting had surely been heard. It was likely many were already on their way, but she couldn't take the chance.

"I'm sorry," she told Sam. The agony in his eyes tore through her. "This will hurt."

Neith used her hands to pull free any of the shards she could get a hold of, healing the flesh as she worked, focusing her efforts on the larger pieces causing the most damage.

With every shard she pulled free, he gasped, his eyes going wider. She didn't have the luxury of time. She couldn't be gentle. She quickly repaired the tissue, skipping over anything superficial.

The pain in her right side returned, traveling up to her shoulder and across her chest. So intense it sent her spinning. She blinked, trying to refocus her vision.

She heard Max cry out, then Petra was running toward her and Sam. She crashed to the ground on his other side.

Neith knew she had to work fast. She would lose consciousness soon, probably die. And if she did, Sam would die, too.

"What can I do?" Petra asked.

"Hold his hand."

"*What?*" Petra looked at her, blinking.

"Hold his Godsdamned hand!" Neith said with a sob. "He's scared."

Petra nodded frantically, taking his right hand in hers. "He can't breathe," she cried.

"I know," Neith said, lips trembling, her hands hovering over his chest. They were shaking wildly.

She healed the last severe wound she could see, but he wasn't improving. Her hands scrambled over him again, ether searching. He was getting worse.

Sam looked up at her, and blood spurted from his lips. Her heart dropped when she found the large shard embedded in the right side of his neck. It was deep and barely discernible under the blood oozing from it.

His gaze grew distant. The convulsions calmed. He reached up with a bloody hand and touched her cheek.

"Don't you dare," she said, and glared down at him.

She grimaced as she held her hand over the wound. The shard had pierced through his windpipe, flooding his chest. "He's drowning in his own blood." Neith cursed herself for not seeing it first. She coughed, and blood splattered in red specks over her arms. Petra looked up at her, terror twisting her face.

"Petra, I need you to listen to me. I have to pull this out. When I do, he is going to bleed out fast. I have to work quickly to stop the bleeding and repair the damage. I'll start on the inside, so press down on the wound as best you can." Petra nodded in quick, frantic motions. Neith looked down at him. He was fading. "Please hold on," she whispered to him, but he was too far gone to hear her.

Using her ether, she tore the shard free. Blood spurted in every direction, then turned to oozing when Petra's hands covered it. Neith closed her eyes to focus. The wound was not difficult to repair. The problem was the blood pooled in his chest. But she had no tools. She started spinning again, one hand grasping her side while the other worked on his wound.

"It's almost closed," she said, or at least thought she said. Her gaze drifted toward the woods, thinking she heard galloping horses. Maybe it was only in her mind. She blinked continually, but her vision tunneled. She was falling into darkness. When she felt the last bit of tissue reform, she fell back onto her hands.

Neith gasped, realizing Petra was now holding her up. She knew she'd lost time but had no idea how much.

Neith grabbed Petra's tunic, pulling her close. "Tell them they have to drain the blood from his chest." She thought she was being lowered to the ground.

"Petra!" she tried to scream, but it barely registered sound.

"I understand," Petra cried, "I'll tell them, I swear. Hold on." Petra's eyes snapped toward the woods. "I can hear them coming."

Neith turned her face toward Sam. He was still, eyes closed. *Open your eyes*, she willed him. *Open your eyes, Godsdamn you.* She reached toward him, arm outstretched. Her fingertips grazed his cheek.

She felt herself being pulled away. She was so cold. Black closed in as she fixed her gaze on the ever-slowing rise and fall of his chest.

36

Neith

"Healing is an art as much as it is a science."

THE WAY OF ETHER
ASHERAH GALANIS, FIRST CONSUL, THE CITADEL, 807 AQ

Neith blinked through the haze as the blurry outline of a figure came into focus. She inhaled, sharp, and alarm raced through her, savage and unforgiving. The terror sent her reeling, waiting for an explosion, waiting for pain. She saw her father, saw herself in a med tent, but it was obscured with a slowly dissipating veil of blood, fire, screams, and fear.

The heavy scent of vinegar turned her belly. She thought she would be sick. Neith tried to move, but strong hands pushed down on her shoulders. A surgeon stood over her, his ether radiating through her body.

"Careful," the surgeon said, "you suffered a ruptured spleen and—"

She thrashed and felt an ache in her side, but she shook him off, shifting back until she was sitting upright.

"*Neith.* Be still," her father said.

"The others?" she asked, grimacing at the pain of speaking from a dry, coarse throat. A scream readied at the back of her tongue, both dreading and desperate for his answer.

He poured water from a pitcher and extended the cup toward her. His movements were painfully slow, and it felt intentional.

"The *others?*" she repeated.

His eyes moved from hers to the cup and back.

She snatched it, taking a large gulp. The water nearly came back up. "*Father,* what of my people?"

Lorcan gestured for the surgeon to leave them. His demeanor was controlled, but Neith saw the residual effects of worry in his eyes. "Samad Hassan recovers."

She exhaled. "And Maxson Nasseri?"

Lorcan nodded. "Our surgeons were able to reattach the arm, but it is yet to be known what functionality he retains."

Neith pulled back the blanket draped over her. "I can fix it."

Her father's arm came down to halt her, strong and steady. "You nearly died, Neith. You suffered damage to several of your organs. You had multiple broken ribs, and a fractured collarbone. Among other lacerations and breaks. Lay back."

"He needs my help," she pleaded.

"A few hours will change nothing. And it is not a request."

Neith wanted to protest, but his eyes told her it was not a good idea. She settled for a bargain. "*One* hour."

He grumbled but nodded.

"How long have I been asleep?" The sun glowed through the canvas, but she did not know if a day had passed.

"It is just past dawn. You slept through the evening and night." Her father sat back in his chair, crossing one leg over the other.

"Were they Esērii?" she asked, knowing it could have been no one else.

He flexed his jaw. "Yes."

"How many?" She lay back against the bed, trying to calm her senses. Every single one was still on fire.

"It was difficult to determine the sum of bodies. But the signatures of twenty and six were detected."

Neith thought about how she had so wildly and recklessly snapped the plane. Images of it flashed behind her eyes. The blood, the gore, the horror of it. All that she had done. But the memory of Sam dying on the ground in front of her, the lost look in his eyes, the way he reached up to touch her cheek, all of that dissolved the guilt she felt, replacing it with resolution. She would do it all again. She would do more. "One of them ran," she said. "A shieldmaster."

He nodded. "We tracked their path and believe they have been following us since Croydyn, waiting for an opportunity. The shieldmaster you sensed is a woman named Rowena Winstone. She's a warden in the north. Hers was among the signatures identified." Lorcan grabbed the pitcher and refilled her cup.

She took a drink, and then another, until his eyes told her she'd had enough.

"You should not take this lightly. Twenty and six came for you." He spoke sternly, but there was apprehension in him. Neith realized he had been frightened. She feared he was about to tighten the leash. To take her back to how it had been in Thrane.

"Twenty and six came, but only one escaped," Neith said with authority, but it still sent a sting through her.

His brows rose. "So it is. But I will remind you again, you nearly lost your life."

Her hand instinctively went to her side at the memory of the pain. The searing, burning agony. The thought of it put a bitter taste on her tongue.

"You are my daughter—"

"I am a soldier." She would not lose the liberties she'd gained the past moon. She would not lose her friends.

He folded his arms, his piercing pale blue eyes never leaving hers. "Yes, I believe you are."

Neith exhaled and then swallowed, nervous for what she would say next. "Father, I want you to disband my guard."

He made a noise somewhere between a scoff and grunt. "I'm inclined to double it."

Neith took a moment to think. She knew what happened next would likely be determined by her words. She decided truth was her best path. "I'll not have people stand in my stead because they are ordered to."

He eyed her, sitting back. The sternness in his gaze softened. "Neith—"

"You want our people to follow me? To *believe* in me? I must give them cause. You said so yourself." She set the cup on the table beside the bed and sat up straighter, flinching at the tenderness in her side.

He sighed, staring her down as one hand trailed the sides of his jawline. Neith thought she detected the trace of amusement. "Very well."

Neith reared back. She had expected much more of a fight. *"Thank you, Father."*

He gave her a rueful half smile, and she closed her eyes, relaxing back onto the bed. "I suppose a captain does not need a guard."

Her eyes flicked open to find the other half of his smile had formed. "Captain?" she asked, brows knitting.

"News of what you did is well through the camps of the First and

Second. Last I was told, twenty and two wait to pledge their service."

Neith blinked. "To whom?"

"Correct me if I am mistaken, but that puts your numbers at thirty and eight, no longer a squad, but a unit. That makes you a captain." He shrugged a shoulder. "Should you decide to accept them, that is."

Neith could not help her lips parting, replaying his words three times over to be sure she had not misheard. She swallowed. "Twenty and two?"

Her father's smirk turned into a subtle but pleased grin.

"I am honored." She was, but also terrified. She could not think on that now. "Where is Roman?" she asked, unsure if she wanted to know.

"He was here. He left when it was clear you would survive. There was a moment when we were not sure." His eyes held regret, but before she could react, he stood. "I'll leave you to rest. We agreed on one hour." She nodded, and he reached down, clasping her hand. "It brings me great comfort to see you recovered." He released her and walked from the tent.

As promised, she waited the hour, but it had felt like four, every moment spent replaying what had happened and deciding what she would do.

A fresh uniform waited, folded neatly beside the bed. There were new boots, undergarments, and even leather cords to tie her hair. Nothing remained of what she'd worn during the attack. Neith hoped they'd burned it all.

She slipped out of the linen dressing gown and studied the countless soft pink lines and blemishes now marring her skin. They covered her arms, legs, and nearly the entire right side of her body, from breast to hip. She would have few scars. Whoever healed her had worked hard to make it so.

Neith had been told by the surgeon that Sam and Max recovered in the Second's camp. She had been brought to the First, to her father's personal surgeons.

Storm was waiting outside the tent. She stroked the nervous horse, soothing her concern before mounting. She departed with a warning from the surgeon to tread lightly on her newly reformed bones and tissue. It was a warning she'd not needed. She ached from the crown of her head to the tips of her toes.

Stopping first to see Max, she found him sitting up in a cot, Ayla at his side. His right arm was bandaged from elbow to shoulder.

Ayla sprang from her chair, running to Neith. She wrapped her arms around her, and Neith winced.

"I'm sorry," Ayla said, pulling back.

Neith tried to smile, but she could only see the two of them huddled under a shield, covered in blood. Hear Ayla's screams. Feel the heat from the etherfire pouring down on them.

"They wouldn't let any of us in to see you," she said. "Bellamy stayed outside the med tent until ordered away, assured you would recover."

Neith swallowed. She could already feel a sting in her eyes. She cleared her throat. "Where is Bellamy now?"

"With the squad." Ayla smiled and raised a brow. "There are many new people."

"So I hear." Neith touched Ayla's shoulder and walked to Max, taking a seat on the edge of the cot. The golden hue of his skin was cast with a sickly paleness. "How is your arm?"

"Nearly healed," Ayla answered, as she stepped around. "The surgeon does not believe he will lose function."

Max looked down at his injured arm, lifting it slightly.

"May I take a look?" Neith asked.

He nodded. Max was a person of few words, his eyes more often than not speaking on his behalf. They were darker now, plagued with the shadows of anguish. And terror. She knew her eyes looked the same. It was a look she'd seen countless times on those she'd healed over the years. But now she knew what it felt like to wear it. To see it on someone she cared for.

Neith unwrapped the bandage. The arm had been repaired well, but would leave a nasty scar. She studied his bones, ligaments, tendons, and vessels. "I cannot see any issue, but I would like to keep an eye on it. Rest it today, but get it moving tomorrow. We don't want the tissue to harden too quickly."

"What about you?" he asked.

"Tender," Neith answered, "but I'll survive."

"What you did out there... I've never seen anything like it. You saved us." He looked down, shaking his head. "I'm sorry. We were supposed to be the ones protecting you."

"We saved each other." Neith smiled, but knew it was thin. "Besides, you wouldn't have been out there if it wasn't for me." Max started to speak, but she stood. "Where is your sister?" she asked, though she felt both Petra and Sam only feet away.

"With Sam," he answered. "In the tent next to this one."

"Ayla, will you sanitize and rebandage his arm? The skin is still soft, and we need to keep it clean. And use clear alcohol, not vinegar. If it takes to infection, it will not be pleasant."

"Of course." Ayla walked to the supply cart in the corner of the tent.

"And you have my leave until Max is recovered."

"Thank you," Ayla said, turning back, arms full of supplies.

Neith nodded to both before walking out. She knew it was odd and abrupt, but it was the best she could do.

Sam was sleeping when she entered his tent. His brows were twisted, as if pained, but he was breathing, slow and steady. He was covered in bandages from his neck down to the top of the linen blanket tucked around his hips. Her chest constricted at the sight.

Petra was resting her head on the cot. She looked up when Neith entered. Her left arm was in a sling, and she had numerous light pink lines on one side of her face. She stretched her uninjured arm high above her head and yawned. "He was awake earlier. He would only go back to sleep after hearing you were well."

Neith flexed her jaw, trying to contain her tears, but they fell silently down her cheeks.

Petra stood and walked around the cot, pulling Neith into her arms. "He's all right." She stepped back and looked Neith over from top to bottom. "What about you?"

Neith nodded. "You told them about the blood in his chest?"

"I did." They both turned to look at him. "The smaller wounds have already healed. Two on his chest, one on his right thigh, and the one on his neck will scar and are still healing."

"I thought he was going to die." Terror washed over her as if flung right back into the moment. Neith closed her eyes, but it brought no reprieve. "I thought you were all going to die."

"But he didn't. No one died. Thanks to you."

Neith walked to the cot and reached out to touch him but hesitated. "Petra," she said, eyes and voice low, "I need to tell you that you are no longer tasked as a member of my guard."

"What do you mean?" Petra walked around the other side to face her.

"My personal guard is being disbanded." Neith struggled to meet her eyes. "The three of you are now free to join the squad of your choice."

Petra's brow twisted, but it quickly faded, growing heavy, and her eyes cast down. "We failed to protect you."

"No," Neith answered quickly. "No, it was at my request." Neith held up her hand at Petra's protest. "Not for fault of anyone. I'll not have people fighting for me if they haven't chosen to. That is my right."

"I chose—"

"You came for Sam," Neith said. "Not for me." She looked down at a light touch on her arm. Sam's fingers closed around her hand. She looked up at his face to find his amber eyes aware and fixed on hers.

"I'll give you two some time," Petra said, and walked from the tent.

Neith sat in the chair, shifting it closer to the head of the cot. Sam's hand rose toward her face. His fingertips ran along the curve of her cheek. Just as they had when she thought he was dying. She covered his hand with hers, leaning into it as her tears returned.

"Don't cry," he said, his voice weak.

She rested her head gently on his shoulder, still convincing herself he would be all right. He leaned toward her, and she felt his lips brush the space above her brow. They stayed for a moment, like that, breathing.

"Neith," he whispered.

"Yes?"

"Are you sending me away?"

His question sent a strike through her, rivaling the pain she'd felt in the clearing. She clenched her eyes shut, steadying herself before she sat up to speak. His eyes were inquisitive, searching hers for the answer. What would she tell him? That seeing him dying had nearly killed her, and it had nothing to do with her injuries?

"I'm not sending you away," she said. "I'm undoing what should never have been done."

Sam looked at her, through her, and shook his head. "You are sending me away."

Neith ignored the accusation. "May I look at your wounds?" She walked to retrieve a medical blade from the cart in the room. He didn't say anything as she cut away the bandages. "These smaller ones will not scar." She sent her ether through him, examining him internally, finding no issues. She'd worried in her haste to heal him that she may have made mistakes. "All is well." She avoided his gaze and returned the blade, grabbing fresh bandages.

"Look at me."

"I can't."

"Please."

She did, and her face fell into ruin, using all her self-control to contain a sob. She wiped the disobedient tears from her cheeks. "I need to go."

He reached for her, but she stepped back. Surprise, then pain tightened his features, and she felt ever the villain, knowing she was the cause. She used the opportunity to flee.

Petra was waiting outside, stroking Storm's neck. She looked at Neith and then at the tent behind her. "Where are you going?"

"I need to return to my squad. There is much to do."

"All right," Petra said, her manner consistent with one unsure how to proceed, likely in realization it was no longer her concern where Neith went, nor what she did.

"Thank you for everything you have done for me." Storm bowed, and Neith mounted. She looked back at the tent once more. "You will look after him, yes?"

Like her brother, Petra looked like one who wanted to say much, but she only nodded.

Neith urged Storm on, fearing the tears would return should she linger.

37

Thea

"There is much power in a lie. Often more than the truth."

THE COST OF VALOR
AUTHOR UNKNOWN, 203 BQ
TRANSLATED FROM OLD ASARI BY MERIAH TURAN
HAIS Z'NOSIŠ, 1200 AQ

Thea spent the following three days after her family departed in the library, pulling every book she could find on Icena, Thrane, Sibreen, and the Iren Wars. She rarely left, even dined there, returning to her room only to sleep.

As Cat had said, there wasn't a single mention of a Lorcan Dracos, nor could she find anything on Sonia Throndsen. Faela was recorded as having two daughters, both passing in infancy. After Faela died in the war, Icena disbanded back into tribes, many Iceni resettling in northern Vikandal.

Godric Dracos and his only son were also recorded as having perished in the final battle when the Iren and Iceni forces pushed what remained of their army, retreating into the mountains. Thrane, as a kingdom, fell into obscurity.

After skimming through four books on Sibreen, she could find not a single reference to an *Elah Esērii*, as Breeda had called it. The only references to ether were in obscure religious texts. She was deep into a book about the Third Iren War when the door creaked. It caused her to spill her tea. She quickly wiped it from the pages.

"You won't find what you're looking for in those," Sylvie said as she walked around the table, taking the chair opposite her.

Thea sighed. "That is becoming clear."

Sylvie lifted her legs, resting her boots on the table. She picked up *The History of Iceni Tribes*, flipping lazily through the pages. "A bit of light reading?"

Thea kept her eyes on the page. "My sister once told me that information is power. I suppose I'm trying to find some."

"Wise words," Sylvie said, nodding. She slid the heavy book back on the table. "But the information needs to be true."

"Perhaps I want to know the lies before the truth." Thea didn't attempt to hide the irritation in her voice. "Is there something you need from me?" She kept her eyes on her book, pretending to resume reading.

Sylvie dropped her feet and sat up in her chair. She dipped her head, trying to catch Thea's gaze. "I would like to apologize to you."

Thea pointed to the page in front of her. "It says here that over four thousand Straethan soldiers died when they attacked Highclere. Many by arrow. The rest drowned trying to cross the lake. You'd think that would be a warning to Thrane."

"Thea, you have every right to be angry."

"I'm not angry," she snapped, eyes flicking up to Sylvie's. "I'm furious." Thea flipped the page even though she had not finished the one before.

"As I said, you have every right to be." Sylvie's round brown eyes were drawn, and it tugged a little at Thea's resolve, but not enough to set it free.

Thea sat back in her chair, folding her arms. "Breeda said there were others that came with her from Icena, but you cannot be more than four or five years older than I."

"I am not Iceni."

"Elah Esērii?"

Sylvie nodded. "An agreement was struck between your father and the council to allow us to watch over you. For the last year, it has been me."

Thea eyed her. "Who was it before you?"

Sylvie hesitated, as if knowing what she would say next would not help her cause. "You can't remember them."

It didn't. It stung, and Thea recoiled. As a woman, she'd never felt she'd had true sovereignty over her person, but the thought that she was stripped of her own memories was enough to fill her with rage.

She studied the face of the woman she'd only days before considered one of her closest friends. Her curly red hair was unbound, and every time she moved, it billowed, gentle, cloudlike. Thea felt like she was seeing her for the first time without a screen. Without something distorting her image. But her eyes were the same. Tender and kind, perhaps a touch mischievous.

It was an uneasy paradox. One moment, all felt the same as it had before, as if she knew her and they could carry on. The next, she was a stranger. Totally unknown to her. Thea did not like the way it made her question her own judgment. "So you were sent here to mess with my head."

"No," Sylvie answered. "It is not like that."

"Then what is it like?" Thea challenged. "You say you are sorry, then tell me what you did—what you *do* to me."

"Maintain your bindings and control your attacks. And protect you if need be. But we also tried to help you live normally... as best we could." Sylvie shook her head. "I did not agree with it once I was here, but I could not see a way to change things for you, not without disrupting your life."

Thea searched her for authenticity, but quickly remembered Sylvie could control how she felt, at least to some extent. Perhaps it was a futile task to try to understand. "Did you change my feelings, my thoughts?"

"I did."

The abrupt honesty took her aback. She hadn't expected it. "Tell me."

"As little as possible, and mostly around thoughts regarding leaving Highclere, or if you had a desire to do something that wasn't feasible given the circumstances. We needed you to want to stay here. To feel content."

Thea nodded, thinking through what that meant. In the last three days, she'd felt anything but content. "And you have stopped this?"

"Yes," Sylvie answered quickly. "There is no need. I swear no one will use Influence on you again. I won't allow it. We will maintain your bindings because it is too dangerous not to, but no one will manipulate your feelings or thoughts." Sylvie's hands moved forward as if to reach for Thea's, stopping short.

Part of Thea had wanted more of a fight. Cause to rage at someone. "Perhaps if I knew what being Etherborn meant, it would be easier for me to understand."

"You will understand. And soon. You cannot continue as you are."

Fear picked at her fragile resilience. She was not sure she wanted to understand. "Is your name even Sylvie?"

"No."

Thea took a sharp breath.

"My name is—"

"I don't care." Thea looked back down at her book, but couldn't manage to read a line. Sylvie waited as if she had nothing but boundless time and patience. It only stoked Thea's irritation. "Why did you pretend to be my friend? It seems you could have done your job fine without making me believe you cared for me."

"I wasn't pretending." Sylvie's hands extended further. "I do care for you."

Thea scoffed. "As you can see, I'm busy."

Sylvie waited, as if hoping Thea would change her mind. When she did not, Sylvie retracted her hands, sitting back in her chair. "Your father wants you to sit in on the council meetings. I'm here to bring you."

"I thought you were here to apologize." The words came out so bitter Thea could nearly taste them. She closed her eyes and exhaled, knowing her bite was a little too sharp.

"You need to be there," Sylvie said, drawing out her words. "Don't let your anger toward me or anyone else keep you from the things you need. You are a part of this. A big part, and—"

Thea laughed, eyes set on Sylvie in wonder. "Why? Unless they want to plant a garden or select a wine to match their meal, I have nothing to offer."

"You said you wanted information, did you not?"

Thea sighed, drawn and exasperated. She *did* want information, and her eyes were starting to cross from three days in the library. But she didn't want to give in. The lies, from all, still felt like a slap. Like a bruise on her cheek that had not yet healed. With Callum and Cat gone, she felt she was on her own. She had no one to talk to. No one to confide in. "I told you things," she said, feeling her eyes sting. "*Intimate* things."

"I know." Sylvie had looked sorry before, but now she looked truly regretful.

Thea could not help but believe her to be genuine. It still did little to quiet the resentment that seemed her constant companion as of late. "So you are what? My bodyguard or something like that?"

"Something like that," Sylvie said.

Thea tapped her fingers on the tabletop. She looked at the gold chain with the purple stone around Sylvie's neck. She remembered Sylvie holding it when she spoke of someone she loved, someone that she had to leave. "And you were agreeable to that? Coming all the way from Sibreen to be a glorified childminder?"

Sylvie frowned. "You are not a child, Thea."

"Aren't I, though?" Thea fisted her hands, a familiar numbness setting in. Sylvie sat up. "I'm fine," Thea lied, rubbing her eyes. She stood trying to shake the needles from her arms. "Let us to council."

Ulric, Commander Pryde, Breeda, and several others she did not recognize stood around the council table. A large map of the north was spread out, and her father was setting up markers around Straeth. He looked up, motioning for her to stand next to him.

"Reports tell us twenty thousand march directly east toward Highclere. This we've known for days. Today's report tells us another smaller force of ten thousand are marching south, and we are not yet sure of their destination. It is likely Ealdtown or Kingsport. Controlling the supply chains up the Iren River would be the smartest move. There are nearly four thousand men already stationed in Kingsport, but an additional three thousand are marching directly there as we speak. Aremore has a force of four thousand, giving us the slight advantage in numbers."

"But not for Etherborn," Breeda added. "The field house in Kingsport might have anywhere from twenty to thirty wielders at any time, but not all are fighters. We're sending an additional ten, but that's the most we can spare without making Highclere vulnerable." A couple of the men shifted on their feet, clearly uncomfortable at the mention of Etherborn. Thea well knew how they felt. At least she was not the only one adjusting to a new world. "Today's report tells us they have nearly one hundred Etherborn with their force marching south. We have messengers on their way to other field houses in the north, and to the Citadel."

"How many can we expect to come to our aid?" Ulric asked, eyes scanning the map.

"There are thousands of us," Breeda answered. "How many can we expect?" She shrugged. "I cannot say. It will take time. Things in the Citadel tend to move slowly. We need to focus on stalling Thrane. We could be under siege for many moons. Even a year. The longer we draw it out, the better our chances."

"How many men does it take to be effective against a *wielder*, as you call them?" asked one of the men Thea didn't know. He bore a captain's badge on his uniform.

"There is no consistent number to plan with, Captain Roth. Someone with minor powers could fall to a single idleborn man," Breeda answered, and a look of relief washed over him. "But there are some of us so powerful they would not fall to a hundred."

His relief was short-lived. He now looked regretful for asking. "I see."

"How long will it take Percy to reach Kingsport?" another asked.

"A moon, most likely. It will be close." It was Commander Pryde who spoke. Even Thea knew this was optimistic. The duke would likely be marching toward a city already fallen. She wondered if Marten would march.

Her father gave her a reassuring smile. "They are under instruction to hold outside the city if they find it under Thranean control. They are not to attack."

Thea listened intently over the next hour while they planned the defense of Highclere. Archer stations were being erected all along the northern and southern coasts of the lake. If Thrane attempted to cross via boat or ferry, they'd burn them. If they attempted to cross the coastline, their archers would take them out. It was not dissimilar to what she had been reading about during the Iren Wars. That was until Breeda and Sylvie talked about ethercannons and etherfire. Shields and wards. She listened to them describe this thaumaturgy as if it were no different than sword and arrow. As if it weren't madness. Thea drank in every word, doing her best to make sense of it.

"We have done all we can tonight. We reconvene in the morning," her father said. He waited across the table with a question in his eyes as the others gathered papers and departed.

"Breeda," Thea called after her. "May we talk?"

Breeda paused, turning back, glancing between Thea and the king. "Of course."

Thea tried to ignore the sting on her father's face. He stood. "I'll leave you to it," he said, and kissed her head as he left.

When the room emptied, Breeda sat quietly, waiting with the same look of inexhaustible patience Sylvie had before.

"You will only tell me truths now?" Thea asked.

Breeda nodded. "Do you wish to know about your mother?"

"No," Thea answered quickly. "No. I wish to know about the Esērii. There is no mention of it or anything similar in any book I can find."

"There wouldn't be. The only texts on the Esērii exist in the Citadel." Breeda reached for a glass, filling it with wine. "Or in Nyrovi," she added. It was notable, as Thea scarcely saw Breeda drink. She gestured, asking if she wanted a glass. Thea nodded.

"Why in secret?" Thea asked. "If people possess these powers, surely they could be used for good?"

"That is what your mother believed." Breeda smiled, gazing at her like her father sometimes did, as if searching for someone else behind her eyes. She cleared her throat and looked down. "But what can be used for good can also be misused."

Thea thought that true. Power is neither good nor evil. Neither just nor inequitable. Power is what the person who wields it crafts it to be. "What is Sylvie's real name?"

"Cerys," Breeda answered. "Cerys Hawthorne." She inhaled to speak again but stopped, eyes apprehensive.

"What is it?" Thea asked.

Breeda considered for a moment, sipping her wine. "I am not attempting to sway you one way or another. You want truth, so I am simply giving it to you. Cerys falsified reports to the Citadel on your behalf. She withheld information that would have given them cause for concern. Cause to want to come and take you."

Thea shifted in her chair. It was difficult to hear herself being spoken of as if she had no control. That at any moment in her life, someone could have shown up and taken her in the night. "Perhaps that would have been for the best. Maybe then I would be someone that could help and not an invalid that needs constant minding." Thea swallowed, flinching at the acid in her words. She tipped up her wine.

"You might be right." Breeda nodded. "You probably are. I cannot change that now." She looked down, tilting her wineglass back and forth. "We tried to keep your existence a secret, but as you grew, we realized we were not capable of suppressing your gift on our own. It was not an easy decision to get the Esērii involved. To say they were unhappy with our deception would be a significant understatement. But with the help of another in the Citadel I was able to work out an agreement. You would remain here under a joint guardianship. Even in the Citadel, you are known to very few. The Esērii had their own motivations for wanting to keep you a secret."

Thea leaned back, resting her clasped hands on the table. "Which were?"

"The Esērii value secrecy above all else. They seek to control all to keep it, demanding absolute loyalty and confidence from their followers. It would not look favorably upon that presentation if we were so easily able to hide you for nearly ten years." Breeda refilled her glass, and it was growing ever apparent that she was uncomfortable speaking of the past.

"You said before that my mother did not wish for me to go to them." Thea tilted her head, brows knitted. "Why not?"

"That is a long story, but toward the end, she questioned their motives. She believed, as you yourself said, that our gifts could be used for good. Your mother was powerful, as well as popular. She was well-loved in the Citadel. When she spoke, people listened. It caused an uproar when she walked away."

Thea sighed. "I don't feel anything." She held her hands out in front of her. "I can't conceive of something I can't feel."

"We believe the attacks you have are caused by your suppressed gift. That is why they tend to occur when you are angry or upset. Your power creates cracks in the bindings we have on you, trying to break free. I fear it will only get worse, Thea. Very little seems to work anymore." Breeda reached for her wine. She looked up with a weightiness that suggested its origins were far more diverse than a lack of sleep. "Many options have been considered. Last year we nearly told you everything and sent you to the Citadel. It got better when Cerys arrived."

"But you have made me forget?"

"Yes." She did not look proud of it. "We have made many people forget many things."

Thea knew the intention was well-meaning. Breeda had sacrificed her own life to care for her. She did not doubt the affection and concern to be true. But it encouraged the helplessness that seemed to be her new and constant companion. She had no control. She never really had. "What do I do, Breeda? I don't know what to do. I'm scared." She felt *terrified* might be a more suitable word.

"You are not alone." Breeda reached across the table for her hand. "You never have been, and you never will be. We will help you. Right now, we need to keep you safe."

"Will you send me away?" Thea asked. "To this *Citadel?*"

Breeda hesitated. "It might be what is best, but no one will send you anywhere you don't want to go." Breeda's grip tightened on her hand. "You have my word."

38

Neith

"You cannot march men to battle and expect placidity. If you wage war, you will have conflict long before you take to the front."

THE COST OF VALOR
AUTHOR UNKNOWN, 203 BQ
TRANSLATED FROM OLD ASARI BY MERIAH TURAN
HAIS Z'NOSIŠ, 1200 AQ

It was, in all, twenty and seven who had been waiting at camp to join her. They were now a unit of three squads. Bellamy, Zinnia, and Thora were all selected as lieutenants. Iris, Raiden, Kieran, and nine newcomers chose Bellamy's squad, and the rest divided up among the other two.

Four days had passed since Neith woke after the attack. She'd heard nothing from Sam or Petra. Max came by once a day so Neith could examine his arm. She didn't know where the three had chosen to go, or if they even stayed together. Though she thought it likely. Neith didn't ask, and Max didn't offer. Several times she started to inquire with Ayla or Magnus, but couldn't bring herself to follow through. She avoided common areas, keeping to her unit's camp.

The days were long and full. They rode out early and stopped late. Her father was determined to recover time lost to the rains. Bellamy and Zinnia now rode beside her in formation, and they spent the long hours on the road discussing training subjects and theorizing battle tactics. Neith was anxious to keep her mind and body busy. They used any spare time to train, both as a unit and individually. Something changed after the ruins. There was a tangible connection between people who knew they would fight for one another.

Neith spent much time talking to Raiden, finding their childhoods quite similar. As the son of Maelis Nicomedes, there were high expectations of him. Her designs for his ascension extended beyond her own post as commander. She aspired for him to rise to general. Neith found him resigned to his fate. As if his feelings and desires did not matter. Part of her wished she could do the same. She thought it would be better than the conflict that never seemed to leave her.

She sat around a campfire most nights, sipping whiskey with her original four. Zinnia and her sisters would often join them. One night she spent with Thora and her squad, getting to know the new people.

One of the new recruits plucked a somber tune on his lute, humming along at the fire adjacent theirs. It felt appropriate for the mood around camp.

Raiden passed her the flask. She tipped up the cool metal, grimacing at the sour flavor. He shrugged. "We're down to the swill."

Neith held the flask out to Bellamy on her right.

He took it, looking less than excited. "I bet there will be quite the selection in Highclere."

The others mumbled their words of hopeful assurance.

"How many days out are we?" Iris asked. Her right eye was black and swollen from the sport fighting between units in the Second. Neith had gone to watch one night, quickly deciding she wouldn't return. It was brutal, and nothing like sparring. Many walked away with broken bones and dislocated joints. Some did not walk away at all and had to be carried to med tents. She did not find it entertaining.

"Seven or eight," Neith answered. "Less if we can continue to make good time."

"Not soon enough if you ask me," Kieran said, passing the flask to Iris. Like Iris, his face held the evidence of sport. His bottom lip was split, and every time he laughed, he winced, reaching up to touch the wound. Neith had offered to heal them, but was declined by each. They wore the injuries as a sort of token.

"Captain!" someone called from behind.

Neith stood, turning to find two of the new girls from Thora's squad running toward her.

"What is it?" she asked, gaze moving back and forth between them.

"It's Thora," one of the girls said, turning to look behind her. Aeron approached with a limping Thora on his arm.

"*What happened?*" Neith asked, her concern spiking as she took in Thora's face. It was red and already swelling. Her nose was certainly broken. And badly.

Thora spat blood. "An arse from your brother's unit. He challenged me, accusing someone from my squad of stealing. It was horseshit. Just a reason to pick a fight. I declined the challenge, but he attacked anyway. The cunt broke my nose and my wrist." She held it out in front of her. It was visibly displaced. "And I think a couple of ribs."

"*Who?*" Neith asked, low from between her teeth.

"A big guy, bald, with a long beard," one of the girls answered. "His name is Ulf."

Neith flexed her jaw, trying to retain her rage. "And where is *Ulf* now?" Roman had waited long enough for her to get comfortable to strike. Or perhaps he felt bolder knowing she was without Sam, Petra, and Max.

"He is in our dining tent with others from Roman's unit," Aeron answered. "Boasting about it."

"Is that so?" Neith turned back to Bellamy, Kieran, Iris, and Raiden. They were already standing. Bellamy and Iris were grinning.

"Finally," Kieran said, stretching his arms above his head.

"Weapons?" Raiden asked.

Neith shook her head. "No weapons." They'd been itching for a fight, and she knew it. The sight of Thora's broken face had relieved Neith of her aversion to one. "No one moves without my command. Understood?"

All nodded their agreement.

"Aeron, take Thora to see a surgeon." Neith pointed to the girls. "You two, go with them. Pairs don't seem to be enough." She gripped Thora's shoulder. "We will have recompense for this."

Thora grinned, bloody and ruthless.

Neith had not seen nor spoken to her brother since the morning in Northbridge. News that so many had joined her no doubt set him to ill-will. This was a trap to get her to respond. She would give him his wish, but not the way he hoped.

"Let's go."

The dining tent was packed full of soldiers, both idle and Etherborn. It appeared a typical night. Most were fairly lost in ale. There was chatter and laughter, but the mood was unruffled.

Square in the center, at the largest table, sat the soldiers from her brother's unit. She recognized the viper insignia on their chest. Neith made her way toward them, her gait casual, her manner unbothered.

"Which one of you is Ulf?" she asked, but it was immediately evident. Even sitting he looked massive. She thought him somewhere around thirty and five winters. He looked up at her, a jeering grin on his scarred face.

Ulf rose from his place on the bench, walking toward her with the haughty satisfaction of one who believed their scheme had worked. He stopped two paces away, standing with his arms folded across his chest. "I am Ulf."

Neith looked him up and down, then frowned, as if his size was of no consequence. "You attacked one of my lieutenants."

"I made a challenge." Even at two paces, Neith could smell his sour breath. "One of hers stole from us. She accepted as honor dictates."

"Godsdamn they did." Neith glared at the other faces at the table. Some held the same taunting sneer as Ulf, but a few looked nervous.

"Are you calling me a liar?" He cocked his head, feigning insult. The exchange drew attention. The music that had been playing stopped.

Neith spoke loudly so all could hear. "I am calling you something far worse than liar, you pig's arse. I call you coward."

His face flushed, as if he had not expected such a reaction.

She stepped closer to him. "If you want to challenge someone, challenge me." Neith felt those behind her step closer, but she held up her hand.

Ulf scoffed, peering down at her. He was at least a foot taller and nearly twice as broad. "You can't be serious." He looked at her like the notion was absurd. It was. There was no world where Neith could win against the man in hand combat.

"Make a challenge to me and I will answer with one of my own." Neith moved even closer, holding his gaze. "I will make one of grievance and of blood. It will not be a challenge for dominance. It will be one for recompense. A blood challenge. Morx Skoro. We will meet not fist to fist, but power to power."

For a fleeting moment, he looked nervous, but he quickly recovered his arrogant form. He spat on the ground beside them. "Only a fool would accept a blood challenge with you. There is no fairness in it."

"You sought out to challenge one of mine, half your age and half your size. You set this tone, not I." Neith's power poured out around her. The already warm air heated to steam.

His eyes narrowed and mouth twisted, as if he might growl. He was still foolishly trying to intimidate her. She wanted to laugh. People like him were so easy to anticipate. He was trying to find a way to walk away with his pride intact. If Neith let him walk away with anything, it would not be his pride.

"You need cause to make a blood challenge," he said, and took a step closer to her. "What cause do you have?"

"Cause that you dragged me out here, away from my fire, having to endure the stench of you." A few low laughs rumbled through the growing crowd. Neith shrugged. "Cause seems to be a rather fluid concept for you. I'm sure we can find something."

Neith stared him down and took delight as she watched him start to crack. He was furious, nearly shaking. "I do not make a challenge against you," he said, low.

Neith leaned forward, tilting her ear. "I could not hear you."

"I said I do not make a challenge against you!"

She stepped back, anxious to draw a fresh breath. "Then you are smarter than you present yourself. I think you'll find the ale more to your liking back in the First. Our camp is full."

Ulf snarled as more chuckles emerged from the crowd. He made some sort of grunting sound, then turned and stalked away. Neith stared down the others at his table until they followed in tow.

When the last man disappeared into the night, she exhaled, feeling as if her heart might burst from her chest. She was made further unnerved when it was the inclination to laugh she realized she was fighting. She started to turn around, but froze midway when her eyes connected with Sam's across the tent. He was standing in front of a table with Petra. Both had been watching the exchange. He stared at her, blank-faced, and the surprise of it only added to the heave of her chest.

Neith turned away. The only thing she would allow herself to feel was grateful that he had not intervened.

Neith grabbed the flask, tossing back a quick gulp of whiskey before bidding the others good night. She sat on the edge of her cot, letting her head rest in her hands.

She knew she would hear from Magnus, perhaps even her father, over what she had done. Morx Skoro was not something one used lightly. She laughed when she realized she didn't care.

Exhaling, she stood and unbuttoned her vest, tossing it over the chair. The look on Sam's face was fixed in her mind. Like she'd painted it on the back of her eyes. It pained her to think it looked like mild interest, at best.

And it fueled her fears that she'd been wrong about his feelings. About him. She shook her head, grasping the back of the chair. *I choose you*, he'd said. And she'd said nothing in return, then sent him away. What had she thought would happen? That he would join her? She wondered if she'd ever felt more foolish.

Neith had been trying to convince herself she'd done it for him, but the truth had been slowly eating away at her since. Seeing him that night destroyed any remaining shred of her delusion. She hadn't done it to give him a choice. She'd done it because she was scared. Scared to care for someone so wholly. To have something so profound that she could then lose. She was terrified to give in to it. She wasn't only a liar, she was a coward.

"Neith?" Ayla called.

Neith took a breath. "I'm here," she answered.

"I heard what happened," Ayla said, stepping into the tent.

Neith nodded. "News travels fast."

"That kind of news does." Ayla peered at her, brows raised. "Did you really threaten Morx Skoro?"

"I did," she said, and sighed.

Ayla nodded slowly, lips pursed. "If that is not a deterrent to leave us be, nothing is. Surely Roman is not that daft."

"Let us hope." Neith wanted to believe that. "I am fine, though. You needn't have come back. Is Max waiting for you?"

"No," Ayla answered, fidgeting with the skirts of her dress. "He walked me, but I wanted to stay here tonight if that is all right."

"Of course it is."

Ayla smiled, but her eyes were unsure.

Neith frowned. "Is something the matter?"

Ayla shook her head. She pulled her bottom lip between her teeth and reached into her pocket. "I wanted to give you something. Something I made."

"Something you made?" Neith asked, her concern easing.

Ayla nodded. Her hand emerged from the pocket of her skirt with a round piece of black fabric between her fingers. "It's for you. For all in your unit. If you like it, of course."

Neith turned it over. It was a patch with a moon sewn into it in silver stitching. Underneath it bore the words *Luxa en Umbraxos.*

"When Sam told me what the words meant on the wall at the ruins, *Light in the Shadows*, I thought of you," Ayla said, gaze low. "That is how I see you. How we all see you."

Neith's fingers traced the delicate threads.

Ayla stepped closer. "If you don't like it, you don't have to use it. I only wanted you to have an insignia of your own."

"I love it." Neith looked up, choking back tears that had been threatening to fall for four days. She wrapped her arms around Ayla, pulling her friend against her as tightly as she could manage, and whispered, "Thank you."

Ayla pulled back. She beamed, her smile so broad and sincere it caused Neith to form one of her own. "Shall I take it to the tailor and have them made for all?"

"Please," Neith said, nodding. "But I would like to have this one. I would like to wear the original."

39

Thea

"There is no direct translation for king or queen in Sumacian so far discovered. Nor any for title relegated to distinguish male or female."

ANCIENT SUMACIAN, A STUDY IN TRANSLATION
PARRY HAVERFORD, HAIS Z'NOSIŠ, 1203 AQ

"They are, at most, three days' march from the western bank. The force has not split. All twenty thousand march this way." The messenger was still breathing heavily as her father read from the parchment. It was the first report they'd received in days.

Thea divided her time between council meetings and the library. She had not spoken with Breeda, nor her father, about the past again. She had no energy for it and would not take theirs. None of it mattered if Highclere fell.

Her father crumbled the parchment in his fist. "Godsdamn." He looked at Breeda. "What is their play here? How will they attack?"

Breeda looked at Cerys before she answered. "Our best guess is they intend to carve out a path through the woods, but even that seems illogical. There is not enough of a stretch of flat land. Lorcan is too smart to try to boat across. Even if they came with or built hundreds of ferries, it would be a fool's errand." She spoke as if forming her thoughts out loud. "We've been reinforcing our wards for a halfmoon and our shields for a sixday. They won't be taken down easily. But they will have high numbers, and we must assume many powerful wielders will be among them. Lorcan is formidable on his own, as are many who left with him during the rebellion."

Cerys held up a scroll. Her red hair was bound in a tight braid, show-ing off in full the concern that etched deeper into her face with each passing day. Thea had twice called her Sylvie by mishap, and neither time had she corrected her. "We have been working to create a record of those we know, considering their strengths, to help us anticipate how they will attack. But based on the intel we have on their numbers, we know Lorcan has recruited hundreds of wielders over the years, and we have no knowl-edge of who they are or what they can do."

Ulric sighed. "How many Etherborn have we now?"

"As of this morning, we are forty and six," Breeda answered. She glanced at Cerys again. "That will likely be our final number by the time they reach the shore."

"And their count?"

"We have only rough and unreliable estimates from sixdays prior, but over two hundred. Once they draw closer, we will scout to get a better understanding," Cerys explained.

"How do we plan for this?" Pryde asked, scanning the map of High-clere spread out on the table between them.

"There hasn't been a war of wielder against wielder since the God-swar," Breeda said. "That was twelve hundred years ago, Commander. No one knows. We can make assumptions about the tactics they will use, but that is all."

"These *shields*, as you call them, how do they work?" he asked.

"Weavings of concentrated, threaded ether. They can be designed to allow energy to flow one way or not at all. The former is what we are building around the castle. We'll be able to attack from behind them, but their assaults on us will not land." Breeda hesitated, once again glancing at Cerys. "Unless they break."

Thea, nor anyone else at the table, asked what would happen if they did.

Ulric sat down in his chair. He surveyed the parchments strewn about the table as if they might provide some well-desired answer. Thea sensed the weight of it all pressing down upon him. Neither he, nor Breeda, nor Cerys, would speak to it, but she saw fear in them. It not only pained her, it terrified her beyond measure. She wondered what else they were speaking of when she was not around.

"For over twenty years, Ire has had peace. Half of our army has never seen a day of battle," he said, almost to himself.

"But they are well-trained, Your Grace," Pryde added. Of all in the room, he seemed to be the one with the most hope. Thea appreciated it from him, but could not help but wonder if it was simply naivety.

"Do we tell our people the truth of what comes?" Ulric looked around the table at each, searching for direction.

"I do not see how," Breeda said. "It will only create more panic. They know war is coming. They see the shields in the sky. That is enough."

Thea was not sure she agreed, but could not deny there would be no good way. She was right in the middle of it all and still had no idea what it meant.

"Very well," her father said, though he did not seem at peace with it. He turned to Captain Roth. "How are the city preparations coming?"

Roth cleared his throat. "We've moved all of those outside the city walls in. If their plan is to approach us from the east, we will be locked down and ready, Your Grace."

"Good," he said, nodding, then reached for his wineglass. "I want those without shelter brought inside the castle when Thrane reaches the coast. Set up food and cots in the gardens and courtyards. The queen will assist with this. We have three days."

Roth bowed his head. "Your Majesty."

"I would like to assist you, Captain," Thea said to Roth. "Please let me know any way I might be of help."

Roth hesitated, turning to her father, which caused her to follow. He was staring at her, also hesitant, nervous, even.

"What is it?" she asked.

The room grew quiet in unison with his uncertainty. She frowned at her father, but he still didn't speak. Thea glanced around the table to find Breeda and Cerys in a similar state. All three had tentative, but conspiratorial, eyes.

"No," Thea said, shaking her head. "I know what you are thinking. I'm not leaving."

"Thea," Breeda said, with a cautious persuasion. "It is the only way we can guarantee your safety. If we send you to Eastwatche—"

"If you send me away, you'll have to send people with me, yes? To *contain* me. I won't be responsible for anything that will make Highclere weaker." Thea folded her arms and stiffened her brows to show them it was pointless to press.

"One or two will not turn the tide," her father answered.

"You don't know that. I'm not an heir nor betrothed. You can make no political justification to send me away." Thea shrugged. "Besides, Father, as you have all said countless times, Highclere will not fall."

He stared at her, lips thinned, unable to argue her point.

"There is nothing you can do here," Breeda said, her tone gentle but assured.

Thea turned her whole body to face her. "Whose fault is that? If you had trained me instead of *bound* me, as you call it, perhaps I would not be so useless. I would at least not be a burden."

Breeda sighed. "We cannot right mistakes of the past by making more today."

Thea started to protest further, but her father held up his hand. "Give me the room with my daughter, please."

He stood, refilling his wineglass as the others filed out. When he sat back down, he had the same look he had a sixday ago when he told her everything she knew was wrong.

"We need to speak, Thea. I've waited for you to come to me, but I fear we are out of time."

"I do not wish to leave."

He sighed and ran his hands through his graying blond hair. Her father had always worn a beard, but neat, and trimmed. Now, it trailed high on his face and low down his neck, its wiry threads unkempt. He looked frayed somehow, as if someone had run up and disheveled him. "I knew Lorcan Dracos." He took a drink before his eyes moved back to hers. "We fought alongside each other for nearly a year."

Thea frowned. "He fought for Ire in the war?"

"For Icena," he answered. "Sonia had a younger sister, Lia. She… chose to side with Lorcan. Reports tell he has two children by her, a boy and a girl. Well grown. They fight in his forces." He paused, letting her work through all he had said.

"You are telling me I have family, but they come to wage war on my home?" Thea thought she would be more moved by the information. "Do they know who I am?"

He sipped his wine before returning his gaze to her. "Very few knew about your mother and I. That is how we were able to conceal your true identity. But Lorcan Dracos was among them. He was—" He paused, shaking his head. "That doesn't matter. What matters is that he knew, and he is far too clever to be fooled. He will know you on sight, if he does not already."

"I fear you will have to spell out your point." She sat back in her chair, resting her hands in her lap. Determined not to be moved.

"Calithea, you are the heir to Icena."

She scowled. "I—No. There is no Icena, and even if there were, I am not its heir. I'm a bastard." She inclined her head, brow cocked. "I should not need to remind you of this, Father, as you participated in my making."

"It brings me joy to hear you jest again." He smiled, but it was half-hearted. "There is no such thing as a bastard in Icena, Thea. You are, by birthright, its heir. Whether you would pursue it or not."

Thea exhaled, understanding starting to take hold. Lorcan's children by Lia would also be heirs. If they knew she lived, they would likely aim to execute her. She bristled. "Highclere will not fall, so it does not matter."

"We have underestimated them in every regard. We cannot afford to continue to do so."

"I'm not leaving," she said, trying to conceal her uneasiness. "Is there anything else you wish to discuss?"

He sighed, and it turned into a groan, weighted with frustration. "Gods help me, you are just like your mother."

Thea didn't know how to react to the sentiment. "What would she have said if you were asking her to run away and hide?"

He chuckled. "She would tell me to piss off."

"If I tell you to piss off, will you stop asking?"

"Probably not," he said with a lopsided grin. "But I won't ask you again tonight." He stood and held out his hand to help her rise, holding on to it longer than required. "We need to talk about her, Thea. You deserve to know her."

Thea knew what he meant. In case he died, or she died, or they all did. She nodded. "I know."

He smiled and kissed her head. "Your mother deserves it, too."

Thea opened her eyes to the recognition of touch on her shoulder. Cerys stood over her, a torch in hand.

"Thea," Cerys said softly. "*Come quickly.*"

Thea sat up. "*What is it?* Have they come?" She swallowed at the cold rush of alarm racing through her, still trying to blink the haze of sleep from her eyes.

"No," Cerys answered. "But we've had a rider. Your father has called council."

Thea nodded, moving to stand. "I will dress and come down."

"I will wait for you in the hall."

Thea struggled to keep up. Cerys was a good four inches taller and all legs. Thea looked through every window they passed that overlooked the lake. There was nothing visible in the distance. But the urgency in Cerys told her it was not good news they ran toward.

The halls were quiet until they emerged from the royal quarters. They passed one soldier, then another, on tasks unknown. Alarm had been thrumming through her since she woke, now growing with every step, with every soldier they passed. Every moment was a fight against the inclination to ask what in Thelos's fire had occurred.

Her father sat at the head of the council table, wearing a tunic and no vest. Evelynde sat on his left, still in her dressing robe, her hair in a long braid. On his right, in similar states, sat Commander Pryde and Captain Roth.

Thea took the chair next to Evelynde. They were all waiting to hear whatever it was that pulled them from slumber. The door creaked, and Breeda walked through with a dark-haired, middle-aged woman Thea had never seen.

Thea frowned as they drew closer. The woman was disheveled. Her clothes torn and dirty. She wore a braid in her long brown hair, but so much had come loose one could barely call it so. Thea thought she looked like she had been caught in a windstorm. As disconcerting as her appearance was, it was the look of quiet terror in her eyes that most affected.

"This is Rowena Winstone," Breeda said. She wore a muted version of the same fear as the woman she introduced.

"Your Grace." Rowena inclined her head, taking a seat at the far end of the table. Cerys and Breeda took the seats on either side of her.

"Rowena is a warden with the Esērii," Cerys said. "She oversees the southern regions of Ire through Lochland."

Thea didn't understand what that meant, but gathered it was not important at that moment.

"She arrived two hours ago with news of Thrane." Breeda gestured for Rowena to speak.

"I was—" Her hoarse voice cracked. Cerys poured her a cup of water. Rowena took several drinks before returning it to the table. "I was in Lochland when I received news of an attack on Godsreach. I immediately traveled north to Croydyn and was told a story of what occurred." Rowena's fingers clung nervously to the edge of the walnut tabletop. "I was reluctant to believe it."

Breeda looked at Ulric. Some sort of confirmation transpired between them.

"A group of Esērii had been tracking Thrane's movements and numbers since they crossed the border. When the reports came back to the field house in Croydyn, the decision was made to abandon it. Straeth had no army to speak of, and the city itself had little defense." Rowena pointed to the carafe in the middle of the table. Thea reached for it, passing it and a clean glass down the table. Rowena poured, tossing it back before continuing. "After the surrender, we decided to continue tracking, waiting for news from the Citadel. We assumed they would move south, toward Ealdtown or into Lochland, but we quickly realized that was not their intent. We waited, watched, and sent riders out to the field houses in all major cities when there was something to report."

Thea noticed the tremble in her hand as she set the glass back on the table. Every eye and ear in the room was fixed on her. She spoke surprisingly steady despite her appearance.

"Five days ago, six of their Etherborn wandered north into the forests. There were twenty and six of us. We thought—*I* thought—we could capture them. Or, at the least, reduce their numbers. We decided to attack." She shook her head. "We were so cautious, given the story we'd been told about Godsreach."

Thea wanted to know what bloody story.

"We had no idea how outmatched we were."

"Twenty and six against six, and you were outmatched?" Commander Pryde asked. It did not feel like judgment, only genuine bewilderment. Thea felt quite the same.

"Wildly so." Rowena took another drink, larger this time. "They walked away intact. Several were injured, but they were still breathing when I ran."

"How many of you remain?" Ulric asked. He was sitting forward in his chair.

"Only I."

He leaned further over the table. "How is that possible?"

Rowena glanced at Breeda before turning back to the group. "One of them, a girl, she was… frightening. I've never seen anything like it. I'm not even sure what it was, but she was killing us faster than we could perceive." She paled as if transported back to the fight. "I will not burden you with the depravity of the manner of their deaths. I do not have words for it. I will only say that there was no defense against it. Her shield was impenetrable, even after she was injured. I tried everything to take it down. I cannot say how many it would have taken to do so."

Commander Pryde looked around the table. "What does this mean for us? You are saying their abilities are beyond yours?"

"I am saying that I cannot say. I do not understand what she is. She was wielding something I had never seen." Rowena reached for the carafe. "We should have come to Highclere. We never should have attacked."

Thea could see the woman had taken the burden of blame upon herself for the lives lost. Breeda rested her hand over Rowena's as if to discourage the guilt.

Rowena gave her a small, grateful smile. "Only Calidore and I were still standing when we realized it was Lorcan's own daughter we battled."

Rowena glanced her way, and Thea's pulse soared. Lorcan's daughter. Her kin.

"You are certain?" her father asked.

"She has her father's coloring and her mother's face. It would be clear to any who knew them."

"Calidore Galanis has fallen?" Cerys asked with wild disbelief.

Rowena nodded. Breeda and Cerys exchanged a look. Cerys shook her head as if she could not believe it true.

"Did you know him?" Thea asked.

"He was one of the strongest among us," Cerys said. "He is—was a good man."

For the first time, Thea felt she was starting to understand the magnitude of what was to come. A war, decades in the making. Built upon bones and secrets. It was not a war between Thrane and Ire. It was a war between the entire world and everything she knew it to be.

"It happened so fast," Rowena continued. "In mere *minutes*, twenty and five were dead. Then I was running. I didn't go back for a horse. I just ran. And I scarcely stopped until I reached this castle." She cleared her throat, wiping a solitary tear from her cheek. "Your Grace, I need to send a message to my husband and daughter in Kingsport. I do not wish to weaken Highclere by sending an Esērii. I would stay and fight alongside you."

"Deliver any messages you need couriered to Captain Roth." Ulric gestured to him, two seats down. The young man nodded at his king. "He will ensure they are dispensed with urgency."

"I thank you."

Thea reeled, trying to make sense of all that was said. She feared looking at her father. She feared finding his eyes on her, telling her she should leave.

"What does this mean for our defenses?" Commander Pryde asked. It was the first time Thea had seen the older man look concerned.

"I cannot say," Rowena answered.

"It means we can make no assumptions, but it does not change our plans. We need to continue reinforcing our shields. Rowena," Breeda said, turning to look at the woman, "you will help us with this?"

"Of course."

"Your Grace, you should fall back to Eastwatche," Commander Pryde suggested.

"I will not abandon my people to the madness described. As Breeda says, our plans have not changed."

Thea finally looked at him, and as expected, he was staring at her, but she shook her head. The news only solidified that she would not leave.

Ulric turned to his wife. "My dear, you should return to bed. There is much to do in the coming days."

Evelynde blinked and nodded. Her eyes held a sort of stoic acceptance. Thea had watched her stepmother grow from petrified to frighteningly calm as each day passed.

"I will join you in the morning," Thea said to her.

Evelynde touched her shoulder as she passed by. Thea shared a look of concern with her father. "You should send her to Eastwatche," she said to him.

"I have tried," he said, a touch terse. "She refuses to go." He narrowed his eyes on her. "*Like others.*"

Thea didn't respond, feeling she could not justly protest. He took up conversation with Pryde and Roth, and she moved to a seat on the other end of the table, next to Cerys. Breeda was at the door, speaking to a red-haired Iceni woman Thea now knew as Porvi.

Rowena reached into her pocket and pulled free a folded piece of parchment, handing it to Cerys. "This is a list of those we have been able to identify who march with Thrane."

Cerys took the parchment and unfolded it. Her fingers traced the length as she read down the list. She suddenly stopped, her eyes darting up to Rowena's. "You are certain of this?"

Rowena nodded.

"Who else knows?" Cerys asked, with a quiet urgency.

"Only I." Rowena reached for her wine glass. "Everyone else is dead," she said, and tipped up her cup.

Cerys nodded, considering. "Are there any other copies?"

Rowena shook her head. "We feared sharing that information. If it were intercepted, it would have put him at risk."

Thea could not tell if whatever Cerys had read terrified her or excited her. Perhaps both. She started to ask, but thought better of it. The past moon had taught her there were some things she would rather not know.

"Tell no one else," Cerys said, stuffing the parchment in her pocket. She glanced at Thea, but didn't explain.

Rowena nodded.

Breeda called for Cerys, gesturing for her to join. Cerys stood, and Thea watched her traverse the room, stopping by the fireplace to toss in the contents of her pocket. Whatever secrets the parchment contained were now lost to the flame.

Thea shifted into the empty seat next to Rowena, who regarded her with curious eyes.

"Thank you for coming. For bringing us this warning." Thea could not imagine surviving an ordeal as she'd described.

Rowena eyed her in a way all Etherborn seemed to. Intrigued, cautious, perplexed.

"I am—"

"I know who you are, Calithea. Breeda told me when I arrived." Rowena flashed her brows. "What a secret."

Rowena reached for the carafe, but Thea grabbed it, refilling the woman's glass. Thea looked at her as she drank, hesitant, unsure if she should ask. "You saw Lorcan's daughter?"

Rowena nodded as she returned her glass to the table. "I understand why the girl would be of interest to you."

"What does she look like?" Thea knew it was a strange question, but could not help her curiosity. "If you do not mind me asking, of course."

Rowena shrugged. "I only saw her from afar, but like every Dracos. Black of hair, uncommonly pale. Terrifying."

Thea tried to paint a picture in her mind of such a young woman.

Rowena gave her a mournful smile. "You look so much like your mother. Especially your eyes. Though yours are a shade lighter if memory serves."

"That is what my father says." Thea chewed the inside of her cheek. "Did you know her?"

"Not well, but everyone of a certain age knew her in some regard." Rowena continued to stare at her, her disposition growing wary. "You should leave, Calithea."

Thea bristled. She was still growing used to the straightforwardness of the Esērii.

"If I go to Eastwatche—"

Rowena leaned closer, resting her hand atop Thea's. "I'm not talking about Eastwatche. You should leave this continent. If Lorcan does not know who you are, he will suspect it on sight. They can keep you safe in the Citadel."

"I cannot leave my father." Thea glanced across the table at him. "And I will not make Highclere weaker. If I am captured and executed, then I will face that fate with my head held high knowing Highclere did not fall because of me."

Rowena sighed. "The only person who speaks of such things with ease is one who has little understanding of them."

Thea thought at first to be offended, but she didn't feel judgment in the words. The woman was looking at her with care and concern.

"Calithea, death is not what you should fear if Lorcan finds out you live."

Cold quivered down the length of her spine. She leaned closer to Rowena. "*Why?* Because of Icena?"

Rowena frowned. "No, because of your mother…" She opened her mouth to continue, but stopped. She had the look of one realizing they'd said too much.

"Rowena," Breeda called from across the room, beckoning the woman. She leaned back from Thea upon hearing her name.

"Why?" Thea asked again. "I don't understand."

"I'm sorry. I speak of things I should not." She patted her hand before standing, leaving Thea alone at the end of the table.

Thea sighed. Though she now had more questions than answers, one thing was apparent. Not all secrets had been unearthed.

40

Nara

"It is the life of Esērii to live in Adrae's shadow. It is our calling. This is our pledge."

ESĒRII BIJRAH Z'OURA
ADE NYANTHI AND PHILOMENA TALIESIN, 805 AQ

The moon was high when Nara and Harker left their horses at the stables in Azmar. They'd been on the road for twelve days with little rest. Nara worried she pressed him too hard, but he hadn't complained. Though the heaviness in his eyes told the truth. Going from a feather bed in the Citadel to the hard ground was never an easy adjustment. As much as Nara wanted to jump straight onto a ship, she knew they needed to rest.

The capital city of Sibreen was the largest and most populous in the southern continent. While it had its beauty like Nyrovi, it was larger, dirtier, and far more densely inhabited. The serene blues and greens of Nyrovi were replaced with bright red, orange, and tan buildings, twice as tall. Nearly one million people called Azmar their home, and that did not include the hundreds of thousands passing through at any given time. It was a city of excitement, of commerce, and fun. There was nothing one could not buy or procure by some other means.

The field house in Azmar, as in most cities, was in a distinct part of town. It was common for Esērii to come and go at all hours of the night, and that was done far more inconspicuously when nestled between brothels and rowdy pubs.

They turned the final corner through the Scarlet District down a long alley, and Nara felt the ward go off, alerting those inside of their approach.

Amena was standing in the doorway, eyeing them skeptically. "Ain't no way the news made it to the Citadel that fast. The lad left on riverboat two days ago." She was speaking low as if to keep those in the house behind her from hearing.

"A delight to see you, too," Harker said as they reached the door.

Nara pulled her pack from her shoulders. "What news?"

"Were you in Kurk?" Amena looked them up and down. Her dark brown hair was covered with a brightly patterned red scarf secured neatly in a knot at the nape of her neck. Thick gold hoops hung from her ears, matching in color the one in her nose.

"*What news?*" Nara asked again, her pulse already quickening.

Amena frowned. "So you don't know then." She stepped aside and gestured with her hand. "Best come inside."

Twenty or so were seated around the common room, engaged in their own conversations. Four played cards, a bottle of something being passed between them. Some looked up and nodded.

"Let's go upstairs." Amena led them to a room at the end of the hall on the second floor. She grabbed three pony glasses and a bottle while they sat around a small table. She filled all, and they tossed them back. Nara understood it was meant to make whatever Amena was about to say go down a little easier.

"We had a courier in last sixday from Port Lethney. The parchment was sealed for the council, but the lad was so spooked he let it all spill out after a couple whiskeys."

"Thrane," Nara said.

Amena frowned again, looking between the two. "For fuck's sake. Do you know or not?"

Nara shook her head. "What did he say?"

"He was stationed in Godsreach," she said, refilling their glasses. "About a moon ago, one hundred Thraneans crossed the mountains and razed the entire town. Thirty or more were Etherborn."

"*Thirty?*" Harker asked, turning to look at Nara. That was ten times what Thrane would usually send out on a supply raid.

Amena's eyes grew heavy as if to say she was only getting started.

"Rhea Carston was captured along with four others. Three died, her daughter among them."

Nara closed her eyes. If memory served, Maisie Carston had only been ten and seven. She thought of Seline at the Citadel, only days from finding out her sister was dead, and her mother likely, too. Or worse, rotting away in a cell in Thrane. "How did the boy escape?"

"Rhea tried to hide the young ones," Amena explained. "He and another girl stayed behind their shields. Maisie did not."

Harker tossed his drink back and reached for the bottle. "Did he recognize anyone?"

"No," Amena said, shaking her head. "Too young. But he described a man with black hair, light eyes, and uncommonly pale skin. He claimed to be Lorcan Dracos."

Nara cursed under her breath. She had expected this, all of this, but it did not ease the burden of hearing it true. "What else?"

"They let some of the villagers go, then crossed back into the mountains, claiming they would return in two days. The boy said the entire thing was odd. He sent the girl to King's Cross to report, but he waited to see if they would return. What he told me was—" Amena poured another drink and tossed it back. "He said the following night he felt a cast like he'd never felt before. When he followed its source, he found black ash in the air, and..."

"And what?" Nara asked, gripping the small glass in her hand.

"And part of the mountain was... missing."

Nara leaned back and frowned. "Missing?" She worried the boy had let his mind run wild.

"Aye, missing. Like someone had carved out a path right down the middle of it." Amena raised her hand high into the air. "All the way to the top."

Nara scoffed and emptied her glass. "Impossible."

"That was my thought," Amena said, looking between them, "at first. He waited until morning and watched an entire army march through it. If I hadn't heard it from the boy's mouth and saw the look on his face, I wouldn't believe it either."

Nara glanced at Harker. His skepticism was as plain as she assumed her own to be. There had to be an explanation for the mountain. Something logical. A path through a mountain would take years, if not a decade. The Esērii would know of such an undertaking.

"How large of an army?" Harker asked.

"The boy wasn't sure, but thousands. And, at least five times the Etherborn he saw in Godsreach. They were uniformed."

"Days," he said, "that has to be a mistake."

Nara thought back to Amul. Their organization, their confidence. How they had not feared discovery. More like they desired it. Dread washed in, threatening to drown out her disbelief. "Have we so grossly underestimated them?" she thought out loud, not directed at anyone in particular. The implications of that information ran like ice through her veins. She tried to do the math in her mind of how many Esērii were stationed in field houses in the north. Hundreds, across all countries, but it would take a moon, maybe more for information to spread. Even longer for them to organize. She cursed herself for not trusting her gut. She should have left the Citadel the moment she stepped out of the council chambers the very day she arrived. She reached for the bottle and didn't bother with her glass. Her fingers held a slight tremor as she tipped it up.

"Good lad," said Harker. "A brave lad to stay."

"Aye," agreed Amena. "The news should reach the Citadel any day now, if it has not already. I kept it to myself, so this is still quiet. But…" She stopped, studying Nara, then Harker. "Why do you two not seem surprised to hear this?"

"I fear we have a story of our own." Nara reached into her pocket and pulled out her chancellor's pin, clipping it on her tunic.

Amena's brows shot up. "I see." Harker did the same with his deputy's pin, and she barked out a laugh.

Nara recounted everything that had happened in Amul and since.

Amena sat for a moment, eyes moving between them. She reached for the bottle of whiskey on the table.

"Well," Amena said, refilling her glass, "war it is then." She set the bottle back on the table as uneasiness crept into her features. "I guess we always knew it was coming, no matter how hard we tried to forget." She took the whiskey in one gulp. "I'll charter your ship. It will be ready in the morning. You two should bathe. Try to get some rest. You know your way around this place."

Nara nodded. "Thank you, Amena."

Amena gestured for Harker to join her as she walked past.

Harker stood to follow. "Don't sit here and stew all night, you hear me?"

"I hear you," Nara answered, but it made no difference. Worry was all she was going to do until she set eyes on Cerys.

"At least we know what we're walking into," he said, turning back in the doorway.

Nara gave him a stiff smile. "Go and rest. I know I've run you ragged."

He sighed but listened, leaving the door open behind him.

Nara sank into the cool water, inhaling the citrus scents from the oils she'd added to her bath. Her mind raced with calculations, timelines, and possibilities of all sorts. The army could be closing in on Highclere, Ealdtown, or even King's Cross with how much time had passed. They would have no way of knowing their destination until they hit the shores in the north. She considered sailing all the way to Eastwatche. That would be the fastest way to Highclere. But there wasn't a field house. If Cerys had moved or if Gods forbid Highclere somehow fell, she would have no way to find her. She couldn't risk sailing all the way to Port Lethney. Kingsport had one of the largest field houses in the north and would likely have the best information. They would have to start there.

She clutched the orange stone hanging from her neck. "I'm on my way," she said to Cerys, halfway across the world.

Nara had hoped she might find sleep, but she'd tossed and turned all night. When dawn peeked through the curtains, she'd made the decision to concede. She was downstairs in the common room, slicing open a mango when Alec Turan walked in.

"Nyanthi," he greeted her. He dropped his pack by the door and stretched his arms in the air. "This is a fortunate crossing of paths. I have something for you." He was dirty and sea-weary in a loose tan tunic and trousers. His eyes fell on the pin on her chest, and he nodded. "That's a welcome sight."

She wanted to tell him *he* was the welcome sight. If he had returned from the north, as Meriah had said, it couldn't be as bad as she feared. At least not yet. His light disposition told her he knew nothing of Thrane.

"Turan, we need to talk." Nara gestured to the chair across from her.

"Now?" Alec asked, brows knitting. "I've just stepped off a boat." He rubbed his eyes and then brushed his hands through his thick, dark hair.

"Now."

He strode across the room, stopping beside her to lean on the table, picking up a piece of the mango she'd been slicing. "Am I in trouble, Chancellor?" He bit into the fruit, giving her one of his roguish grins.

"You usually are, but that's not why we need to talk." She put the knife and the mango back onto the table.

Alec's face fell as he took in hers. "What is it?" He looked around the room. "And where is everyone?"

"Sit down."

He frowned but obliged. "Should I pour a coffee or something stiffer?" he asked as he pulled a leather cord from a pocket and used it to tie his hair half back.

Nara told him all. Everything from Amul to her arrival in Azmar. About seeing Meriah, her time in the Citadel, and then everything Amena had told her. He went from sitting to pacing several times throughout the story.

"I have to go back." Alec's hands clenched the back of the chair so fiercely Nara thought it might snap. He shook his head and cursed. "If I had stayed north only a sixday more…"

"You saw nothing in Straeth while you were there?" Nara asked, desperate for more pieces to the puzzle.

"Nothing," he said, pacing again. He glanced at her from the side of his eye. It told Nara he lied, or was perhaps unsure. "I started in Argal, traveled through northern Straeth, and ended in Ire."

Nara's eyes flicked to his. "Did you go to Highclere?"

"I did. I was there for a sixday." He walked toward the door. "Cerys is well."

"For fuck's sake, Turan. You could have led with that." Nara stood from her chair, glaring at him over the table.

"*Apologies.* Your news of war was a touch distracting." Alec reached into his pack. "I told you I had something for you." He walked back to the table and held out a folded and sealed parchment.

Nara snatched it from his hands and held it to her chest. He sat down at the table, waiting quietly while she read.

Cerys told her about the girl and how she was bound and far more powerful than the Citadel knew. She asked Nara to find a way to come north. To see for herself. That something had to be done. She wrote that she loved her. That she missed her endlessly. Thought of her day and night. When Nara was done, she read it again.

She ran her fingers over the words *all my love*. They'd been burned with her ether, leaving a trace of Cerys's signature behind. Nara closed her eyes. "Thank you."

Alec nodded.

"I knew about the girl," Nara said, folding the letter and stowing it away safe in her pocket. "My mother told me before I left the Citadel. Did

Cerys tell you?"

"I met her by chance. And only because they did not know I would be there. One can sense she is not idleborn, but the way they have her bound makes it difficult to understand her gift. It took some convincing to get them to tell me who she is. She is scarcely permitted to leave the castle. Bound and Influenced beyond anything I have seen." His jaw flexed. "What they've done to her is cruel."

Nara nodded. "That is what I said."

"Cerys told me she has been falsifying her reports to the council."

"Why would she do that?" Nara asked. "If the girl is a risk, then surely the Citadel needs to know."

"They have formed something of a friendship," he said. "I believe she cares for her. She was quite protective."

Nara laughed without a shred of humor. Her head fell into her hands, and she groaned. "Yes, that sounds like her."

"They cannot keep her as she is. I pressed, but the Iceni won't relent. They agreed to let the Citadel send more Esērii, but that was the best I could do." Alec's gray eyes scanned the tabletop. Nara sensed whatever it was he was thinking was not good. He glanced up at her the way he had before, like one withholding.

"Say it," Nara prompted.

"There was a strange incident," he said with guilty eyes. "She was… attacked."

"*Attacked?* By whom?"

Alec held up his hands. "Cerys asked me not to say anything. She did not wish you to worry." He looked at Nara with nervous eyes, as if expecting a poor reaction. "At the time, we had no reason for such concern. It seemed random, a nomad. She was miles from the castle, far into the forests. We assumed he picked up on her gift." His eyes moved in rapid patterns as if recalling the events again in his mind. They grew in concern until he suddenly stood, pacing once more.

"*Godssake*," Nara hissed. "Did you question him?"

"There was no opportunity. He rots in the earth. He was," Alec said, glancing at her, "unrecognizable." He stopped pacing, leaning his hands against the wall. "I should have pressed harder. I shouldn't have left." Nara thought the words were more for himself than her. "If the man was not nomad," he said slowly, then paused. "If he was sent by Thrane to spy… If Lorcan knows she lives…"

Nara listened with dread as Alec voiced her very thoughts. She swallowed, her heart taking on a savage thump. "Then Highclere is likely where they march."

They stared at each other, letting the implications fall into place.

"Harker and I are sailing to Kingsport this morning," she said calmly, trying to steady herself against all that roared within. If not, she would scream. "The boat is being crewed as we speak."

"Good," he said, pushing off the wall, walking back to lean over the table. "I am coming with you." The sleeves of his tunic were rolled to the elbow, showing the twitch and turn of his muscles as his hands clenched the edge.

Nara sighed, considering. "I'm not sure that is our best play." She would normally welcome him. He was one of the few who could come close to keeping up with her. He was hot-headed but clever, and like all of her favorite people, like his cousin, he wasn't overly concerned with proper protocol. But where Meriah might bend the rules, Alec would happily hack through them with an ax.

Alec cocked his head, expression turning indignant. "I'm not sure I care what you think."

"You need to go to the Citadel," she said, still working through her thoughts.

"I'm going back to Highclere."

"No." Nara stood to meet his gaze. She leaned over the table, palms flat.

"What do you mean 'no'? Should I feel inclined to go north, that is where I'll go. The council might have put that pin back on your chest, but you don't command me. Lest you forget, let me remind you, our ranks sit equally."

Nara huffed. "Lest you forget, let me remind *you*. I am one of the few women in this world who doesn't spend her days considering how I might gain your favor. When you're being an ass, I'll tell you."

Alec scoffed. "Fuck you, Nyanthi."

"*Fuck you*, Turan."

They glared at each other over the table. Anger radiated from him, but Nara saw the exhaustion and fear behind his red-rimmed eyes. The beard he normally wore tidy and clipped was unkempt from his time at sea. He looked unruly and a little crazed.

Nara barked out a laugh, which spread to him. Begrudgingly, they both sat down.

"I missed you," he said.

Nara grunted, but a reluctant smile spread on one side of her mouth. "We need you here, for now at least. You have the ear of the council. And the king. They will listen to you."

Alec folded his arms, unmoved.

"Why are you determined to go back?"

He looked away, his body making strange, quick movements as if it wasn't sure what to do next. Nara stared at him curiously as he continued to fidget, starting to speak several times, but hesitating at each. She cocked her head, considering the severity of his reaction to it all. How protective he seemed of the girl. How quick he was to run to her defense.

Nara laughed. "You cannot be serious."

Alec turned back to her with an air of indignation.

"You *like* her."

"Don't be ridiculous," he said from between scowling lips. "I scarcely know her. It is not like that."

Nara could see that it most definitely was. "You need to go to the Citadel, Alec. *You* can get the council to act. I could not. And you must go to the king. I told you the numbers. Thousands of idleborn soldiers. We will need the Sibreenean army."

Alec sighed, running his hands through the stray pieces of hair that had fallen in his face.

"It's getting long," Nara noted. "I like it."

He ignored her praise, continuing to work through whatever thoughts were dancing around in his mind. There were few whose judgment she trusted, and he was among them. She needed him in the Citadel. For now, at least.

"You know I am right," she said, and his eyes flicked up to hers. They were heavy and drawn like so many she'd looked upon since Amul. She was tired of being the cause. Tired of telling bad news. She felt like the Godsdamned town crier. "And if it as you say, as Cerys says, the girl cannot stay in Highclere. She will need to be brought to the Citadel to train. We need her in the hands of people we trust."

"You have to swear to me that you will get her out. If Lorcan gets his hands on her, he'll try to turn her. If he cannot, he will execute her. She is defenseless as she is."

"How can I promise such a thing? He might already have her. He might have Cerys." Nara's chest seized as the words left her lips.

Alec leaned forward over the table. "If you want me to go to the Citadel, you will make this promise. Else, pack a few extra bottles as we've quite the voyage ahead."

Nara groaned. "Fine. I swear." She shrugged. "I was already going to."

Alec glared at her, then shook his head, a low chuckle tumbling out.

"I will get her out," Nara said, more seriously.

He sighed, collapsing back into his chair. "Then I will go to the Citadel."

41

Neith

"No man fights so fiercely as he who chooses to."

THE COST OF VALOR

AUTHOR UNKNOWN, 203 BQ

TRANSLATED FROM OLD ASARI BY MERIAH TURAN

HAIS Z'NOSIŠ, 1200 AQ

"Breaking your own rules?"

Neith had felt Bellamy approaching long before he spoke. She had walked a short distance from camp on her own before dawn, but hadn't been reckless. Her guard was up, and she was keenly aware of every living, breathing creature around her. She would not be taken by surprise again. "I suppose I am."

The terrain turned rockier as they drew closer to Highclere. She'd hiked a small peak and now sat on the edge, legs dangling over.

"I guess the day in the ruins proved you don't really need protection," he mused.

Neith didn't reply as he sat next to her, and they looked out over the Iren Mountains in the distance. They were impossibly green, save for the snowcapped peaks.

"We're getting close," he said.

"A couple days out if the weather holds."

Bellamy sighed, and she sensed a familiar unease in it. He looked at her. "Are you all right, Neith?"

She met his gaze, considering whether to drop the mask she'd been wearing since the attack. "I don't know."

He nodded slowly, considering.

"Are you?" she asked.

He shrugged. "Some of the time, yes."

"But some of the time, no?"

He didn't say anything. Their eyes moved back to the mountains.

"I killed many people," she said. "I don't know if they were men or women. Or how old they were. If they had brothers and sisters." She glanced at him, fearing judgment.

"Do you truly want to know?" he asked, turning back to look at her again. His hazel eyes were tender, but serious. "Or do you feel as if you should?"

It was her turn not to answer.

"You can't hold on to that," he said, shaking his head. "It will consume you."

Neith knew there was some truth to what he said. But understanding it and acting on it were not the same.

"They were trying to kill us, to kill *you*. And if you need reminding, they almost succeeded." His eyes took on a haunted look as if seeing it all again in his mind. Neith well understood. It was a look shared among all those who'd been in the ruins that day.

"I know," she said. "I know that."

Bellamy tossed small pebbles over the edge. "May I ask something? Not as one of your lieutenants, but as your friend."

"You needn't preface with that."

He turned his body toward hers. "Why not speak with him?"

"Am I so obvious?" she asked, followed by a bitter laugh.

"No. As a matter of fact, you do well hiding it." He nudged her with his elbow. "But I am your friend."

She gave him a half-formed, but sincere, smile. "Yes, you are."

Bellamy grinned, and she knew if her feelings weren't so attached elsewhere, he might win her over with that smile alone.

The amusement fell from his face. "There is something I want to tell you."

Neith frowned. "What is it?"

He hesitated, and Neith could sense that whatever he was about to say was not his original intent. "I want to thank you. For saving my life. For saving all of us."

She wanted to know what he was truly thinking, but Neith did not like being prodded, so she would not do so to her friend. "You do not need to thank me for that."

He still looked worried, but Neith would trust that if it was something she needed to know, he would tell her.

Bellamy cleared his throat. "Back to what I was saying. I think you should talk to him."

Neith had a strong desire to lighten the mood. "Is it wise for me to take this sort of advice from the likes of you?"

He laughed, resonant and from the belly. It echoed out over the canyon. She couldn't help but join in. "Absolutely not."

When their laughter quieted, she looked at him intently, gauging his reaction. "Is it because we need him as a unit? Because I am not an… effective leader?"

His face twisted into a frown as he recoiled. "No, and fuck you for asking."

Neith inhaled, feeling some measure of relief. She still worried others may think so.

"Twenty and seven soldiers didn't come to join Sam. They came to join you." He held his hands up. "Don't mistake me. He's formidable. An asset. But he is not why they came." He turned to look back over the mountains. "He is not why I came," he said with a little sadness that confused her.

She shrugged, shaking off her discomfort. "He doesn't wish to speak with me."

"I wouldn't be so sure of that." Bellamy stood, brushing the dust and gravel from his trousers.

"Why do you say so?" Neith asked, looking up at him.

"Because he's in our camp, with Petra, and Max, asking for you."

Neith grew more nervous with every step on the walk back to camp. She wasn't even sure she wanted to see him. She only now realized how angry she had become the past sixday. She hadn't expected him to join her unit, but he hadn't come to see her once. *Not bloody once*, she thought.

She stopped when her eyes fell on them. Sam, Max, and Petra were standing next to her tent with Ayla and Iris.

Bellamy turned back to her, eyes asking.

"Send Sam out, please."

Bellamy gave her an acknowledging nod and strode off. She kept her eyes on Sam, trying to read anything the language of his body might say.

He was simply standing there, staring out at her, too.

He walked the distance toward her, their gaze never breaking. When he reached her, she turned, and they walked together until Neith was satisfied they could no longer be seen or heard by others.

Neith looked him over, eyes lingering on the scar on his neck. She wasn't prepared for this, and she knew her feelings were all over her face.

"You are angry with me," he said. Neith couldn't get a read on him.

"I'm not angry," she said, lifting her chin, but her chest was heaving.

"I thought that you might be." Sam looked down, his eyes finally showing something. She thought he looked uneasy. He took in the patch on her leather vest. "I like it."

"Ayla made it. Why are you here?" she asked, folding her arms behind her back.

"You know why I'm here."

"I really don't." She couldn't decide if she wanted to run up and smack him or wrap her arms around him. Perhaps both.

"Very well," he said, standing up straight. "I have come to make a formal request to join your unit."

An abrupt laugh tumbled out from her lips, quieting when his face didn't change. "*Why?*"

"I have many reasons." His face took on a gentleness that made her worried she would crumble and say yes immediately.

"I would have you name them."

Sam took a full breath, letting it slowly and intentionally release. His eyes studied the whole of her face. She almost told him to stop looking at her like that.

"Over the past moon, I've watched you become a leader. A good one. You have the empathy and heart for it, but you're also intelligent and objective. It has become clear to me that you desire to do good when and where you are able, even in the face of war. That is the kind of leader that inspires loyalty. That is the kind of leader that inspires me."

Her heart thumped in her chest. She hardened her face, refusing to let the quiver in her lips show. She stepped closer, studying him for sincerity. "You speak truth?"

Sam took his own step closer, folding his arms across his chest. "I do."

"And when did you decide this?" she asked, eyeing him skeptically.

"When you left me in the medical tent." His lips took on the slightest of curls, briefly dragging her attention to them.

Neith worked ardently not to return it. "Then why did you wait a sixday? And I'll remind you," she added, narrowing her eyes, "you said you would only tell me truth, even when it is not something I would wish to hear."

He uncrossed his arms, the jest leaving his face. "I wanted to make sure you knew you could do this on your own."

Neith swallowed and closed her eyes, laughing lightly to herself. "Of course you did." All the indignation that was pulsing through her dissolved.

Sam smiled again, fully, and he looked more like the young man of twenty winters he was than ever before. As if something had lifted from him. A weight she had not realized he carried. She had always considered him handsome, but now she found him beautiful. His amber eyes reflected gold in the growing sunlight, dawn fully upon them. Her eyes drifted to the scar on his neck again, sending images of the attack flashing through her mind. She remembered how it felt reaching for him, believing he would die as she fell into darkness.

"Do you wish to know my other reason?" His eyes were accessible, asking her to ask.

"No," she answered. Though she did want to know. She wanted to know more than anything in the world. But if he was coming back to her, to fight alongside her, she needed it to be for a reason she could live with. What she thought he would say next, or rather hoped for, could not be the reason he risked himself. She needed this moment to be about his belief in her, and that alone.

Sam looked down, not masking his disappointment nor surprise.

Neith stepped closer, intimately so, resting her hand on his chest. Her fingers curled around the collar of his vest. She swallowed, slowly raising her eyes to meet his. "Not yet."

42

Neith

*"The Straethan soldiers found themselves upon burning vessels as they attempt-
ed to lay siege to Highclere. The water became their grave, home to the bones of
three thousand men."*

THE THIRD IREN WAR
LEWIN LEAR, 1185 AQ

The Iren Mountains bore little resemblance to the Obsidian Mountains
of Thrane other than their snowy caps. The ranges surrounding Highclere were green and lush, and reminiscent of life, singing with it. Neith
had not traveled far, but she could not imagine a more beautiful place.

Vast turquoise waters split the peaks, stretching as far as the eye could
perceive. Every direction one looked was a magnificent array of blues
and greens. Cyan, cerulean, sapphire—not a single one seemed to suffice.

The water was clear and pure, reflecting the images of the pine trees
that hedged it. Wildflowers covered every surface of land a tree did not.
Pine, earth, and flora consumed each breath. It was still, and quiet, save
for the gentle current sweeping up onto the pebbled shore.

She now understood why so many wars had been fought for it.

When their forces arrived the night before, Neith had not been able to
appreciate its beauty. After training in the morning, Neith, Sam, Bellamy,
and several others rode through camp to the coast of the lake, viewing
Highclere Castle in the distance. The west side of the coast they now
inhabited had been abandoned. Too small to be considered a hamlet, it
was more a collection of buildings and docks. All ferries and boats had
been pulled to Highclere or sailed south down the Iren River.

"It feels strange to finally put eyes on it," Ayla said. "After all this time traveling."

It was too far away to discern in any real detail, but it was still impressive. Whatever Neith had previously thought of as a castle paled in comparison. She thought it had to be ten times the size of the palace in Croydyn. But unlike Croydyn, it had no modern spires or conical roofs. Highclere was far older. Its walls were lined with parapets and battlements. Built for warfare and defense. It looked like a mountain itself, natural in its place between the peaks.

Even with the distance, the iridescent sheens of the shields surrounding the castle were visible, reflecting an array of colors against the sun. Oily and hazy, ribboning in the air.

Neith could now make sense of the geographical concerns the war council readily discussed. There was no effective way to attack from the west. The mountains were too high, the coastlines too thin, and the forests too dense. The castle had towers built at each corner, and one more, the tallest, in the center. Anyone attempting to approach would be ripe for picking.

"We should search through these buildings for anything missed," Bellamy said, looking around the abandoned area.

"Go on," Neith said. "I will be here a while, and then I am to council. I will meet you all back at camp tonight."

Bellamy nodded, and all but Sam followed.

Neith dismounted Storm, walking to the edge of the water. She looked over the massive lake, scanning its depths through the ether. It was far deeper than she'd expected. Twice that of Lake Storna in Thrane. She sighed.

"Do you see an issue?" Sam asked as he came to stand next to her.

"No. But I do not think it will be easy." She pursed her lips, considering the task.

"More difficult than the mountain?"

Neith nodded, eyes moving to meet his. "The mountains here are too large and too deep. It would take a sixday or more to carve through them. The lake is our best option, but the water is far warmer here than in Thrane, where this has been practiced."

"Is there any risk to you?" he asked, looking her over as if the signs might already be there.

She shrugged. "Burning out? I cannot say."

His concern prompted her to say something to comfort him, but she could not think what. Neith turned back to the lake.

"Have you ever seen such a place?" she asked.

"It reminds me a little of Nyrovi, in Sibreen. The colors, the green mountains." His tone lacked its usual wistfulness when he spoke of such things.

She looked at her insignia on his chest, newly sewn. Cold dread washed in at the thought of battle. She thought of the ruins. There had been so much blood. And it was nothing of what would be spilled in Highclere on the morrow.

As if sensing her unease, he reached for her. But then he looked around, releasing her hand as quickly as he had taken it.

Neith took a step back as soldiers walked past. "I need to go."

Sam nodded, and she turned to leave, but paused, glancing back at Highclere once more. "It is a beautiful place," she said, with a somber cadence. "I hope we do not destroy it."

"We will form like this." Lorcan arranged pieces on the map representing the Etherborn units at the front. "I will lead the charge on the left, Magnus on the right. Followed by Roman's unit and yours here, Cordero." He moved the last in line behind Magnus's. "Nicomedes, you will lead the middle and last Etherborn unit in the center. One legion of infantry units will bring up the rear, with a second on reserve."

"No horsemen?" Cordero asked, sipping his wine.

"We will bring no horsemen. If they fall, it will slow down the idleborn units. We will take fewer casualties the faster we move. We need to bring down their shields before they do ours."

All nodded around the table. They were in a building that looked to have been a fishery. Any signs of sea life or machinery had all been taken when the coast was abandoned, but the smell lingered. It soured Neith's belly.

"What of my unit?" Neith asked.

"They will remain on the western coast with you until the battle is over," her father said while holding her gaze. He was telling her not to challenge him. What he didn't understand was that she had no desire to.

"Once we take down their shields, I suspect they will attempt to flee. Our idleborn units will proceed through the city with a small force of Etherborn to weed out those that run within these bounds." He drew a line on the map a short distance from the castle. "I want the city as untouched as is feasible." He looked up to meet the eyes of all.

A servant set a bowl of what she assumed to be a stew of fish and potatoes in front of her. Its wafts of garlic, onion, and dill overwhelmed, and Neith waved it away.

"Did you get what you needed?" her father asked.

"I did," Neith answered, as the others ate.

"And?"

"It will not be a problem." Neith poured a short glass of whiskey and sipped it lightly. Her aim was not to indulge, only to stave off the stench of fish in the air.

"Good," he said, looking up from his bowl.

The door swung open, and Roman strode through. He looked around the table, hesitating on Neith for a heart's beat. She sat up. It was the first time she had seen him since Northbridge. He leaned over the table between Nicomedes and Cordero.

Roman gestured for a bowl of stew, then began setting markers along the eastern coast of the lake around the castle. "They have people placed all along the northern and southern coasts. Etherborn and idle. Their wards start here." He reached for a piece of charcoal and drew a line across the map. He looked tired and dirty, as if he had been out all night.

Lorcan stood, setting his bowl aside, reviewing the markers Roman continued to place.

"Their shields run tight along the castle walls and persist beyond what we could see," he continued. "They are… significant. They've been building them for a sixday, perhaps two."

"We expected as much. We will set up our own wards here," Lorcan said, gesturing to a spot on the map on the western coast, "and here. We need to protect our camp if any of the Esērii flee west."

When Roman finished, he took the empty seat across from Neith. A bowl of stew was placed in front of him. He didn't look her way again.

"They're spreading themselves thin because they do not know how we will attack. Once it is apparent, they will pull these units back to the castle." Lorcan returned to his chair, resuming his meal.

"Even so, their numbers cannot compare to ours," Cordero said, reaching for a piece of bread.

"No," Lorcan agreed. "And whatever their numbers, they are twenty and five less." Everyone but Roman turned to look at Neith. "Tomorrow, Magnus and I will ride to parley. Roman, you will accompany us."

Her brother sat up straighter in his chair, his manner immediately lighter, more attentive. "Yes, Father."

Hours passed as they continued to plan. Servants lit torches and candles as the sunlight grew dim. When her father called it over for the night, Neith stood with the aim of speaking with Roman, but her father stopped her.

Roman didn't acknowledge her as he left with the others. Neith wasn't sure what hurt more. His contempt or his disregard.

Neith sat back in her chair, turning her glass in circles. She was in no mood for a lecture or lesson.

"Morx Skoro?" her father asked, an eyebrow raised. He reached for a bottle on the table.

Neith shrugged. "He gave me cause."

"That is not something one should throw around so easily, Neith." He eyed her as he refilled his wineglass.

"I assure you, it was not done so."

He made a strange sound, and she was not sure of its meaning. Truth be told, she didn't really care. "I am told after your guard was disbanded that Petra and Maxson Nasseri, as well as Samad Hassan, chose to join your unit.

"They did." Neith sipped the same pour of whiskey she'd been working on all evening.

"Hassan was a captain," he said, peering over his cup at her. "His unit had two squads, and he was well respected for so young a person."

"He did," Neith said, "he is still. What is your question, Father?"

He repeated the cryptic sound. "That will carry weight among the other soldiers. Will you make him your Second?"

"I already have a Second."

"Yes," he said with a curious inflection, "the nomad boy from Balta."

"I have come to rely on him. I trust him. And he is a powerful wielder in his own right."

"Good," he said. "It is important to surround yourself with those you trust." He regarded her with familiar scrutiny, but something was different. Not with him, with her. The intensity of it irritated her. She held his gaze, refusing to collapse under it this time.

"I find you quite changed," he said, withholding any hint of his approval or lack of at the statement.

"I quite agree," she said, without considering her words, something she often did with her father.

"Careful."

He didn't need to clarify. Neith knew what he meant. He wanted her to become a leader. To push the bounds. But there were limits.

"I understand."

"Do you?" he asked, sternly, and it cracked a little at her resistance.

Neith swallowed. "I do, Father."

He sat back in his chair, boots rising to rest on the table. "It seems a rather lazy choice for the most powerful among us to challenge Morx Skoro. No one would accept such a thing."

Neith flexed her jaw, releasing the hold on her irritation. "Roman sent one of his half-witted brutes to challenge my lieutenant, under a fictitious cause. A girl half his age and half his size. How is that any different?"

Her father shrugged a shoulder. "It is not. But is that what you are? A 'half-witted brute,' as you say?"

She didn't answer.

"No," he said, his eyes narrowing. "So do not act like it. Fear is a powerful tool, Neith, but it should not be the sharpest on your belt."

Neith wanted to deny there was any truth in his words. She wanted to open her mouth and roar her rebuttal, but she had none. And as irritated as she felt, she had never raised her voice at her father. Even the thought of how he might react was enough to cool her temper. He was just sitting there across the table, staring at her. Wearing her down. Not smug, but certain. She reached for her glass and tipped it up, finishing what whiskey remained. It returned to the table with a dull thunk. "I understand."

"So you continue to say." He stayed fixed on her until presumably satisfied he had prevailed, then returned his attention to the map. "You may go."

Neith found her way back to the lake, taking a seat on the edge of one of the docks. The sun had completed its descent, and the lights of Highclere were bright in the distance.

She removed her boots, dipping her feet in the cool water, kicking it around with her toes.

Morx Skoro had been a temperamental response. She knew it now, and she'd known it then. Two butting heads, more often than not, resulted in nothing more than two cracked skulls. One could not always meet force with force. Not a leader, anyway. Not a queen. If that was what she was going to be one day.

Roman had wanted her to respond foolishly, and she had done just that. That night, she had thought it was about the fight, but it hadn't been. By challenging Morx Skoro, she made herself look impulsive and supercilious. Nothing like the person who fought, and almost died, for her people. Nothing like the person who earned the surrender in Croydyn. Roman wanted her to look no better than him.

The soldiers in her unit had not joined her because they feared her, and that would never be her aim.

If fear should not be her sharpest tool, as her father had said, then what should it be? Respect? Love? Magnus had said love was the most perilous form of power. Perhaps it was, she thought, but surely it was also the mightiest.

43

Thea

"The Gods of Icena are older than measured time. They are the Gods of our Gods, the embodiment of veil, void, and realm."

THE HISTORY OF ICENA
LEWIN LEAR, 1192 AQ

On the day Thrane arrived at their border, there hadn't been much for Thea to do. The preceding days had been long and hectic. She'd spent them helping her stepmother set up tents, cots, and food stations in the castle courtyard. The last citizens needing shelter were now secure behind its walls. There was an eerie calm about the city. A quiet frenzy of sorts—as when something looms, its threat unsung, but conveyed through darting glances and busy hands.

Thea spent most of the day out on the southwest tower battlement, staring out across the lake. She could make out hazy figures at best. It wasn't until nightfall and she saw the first fire, then another, until the shores were bright with them, that her mind grasped the scale. Twenty thousand, the reports had said, but it had meant little to her at the time.

Thea waited for fear. It didn't come. All she could see were lights. There was nowhere for her to be. Nothing for her to do but watch. And wait.

"You should sleep, Thea. They will not attack tonight." Cerys appeared at the top of the stairs, coming to sit next to her. She had not seen much of her the past days outside of council, but she always seemed to be close somehow. A step behind or around the corner. Thea had still not grown accustomed to seeing her as she was now—head to toe in dark brown fighting leathers. Several daggers were sheathed around her belt, and she carried a longbow.

"Are you going somewhere?" Thea asked, looking over her numerous weapons. She couldn't help but wonder what use they were to someone who could blast fire from their hands.

"To look." Cerys gestured out across the lake.

"We have sent six scouts, and only four have returned," she cautioned.

Cerys grinned. "Are you worried for me, Thea?"

Thea stretched her neck and sat up straight. "I am not inhuman." She glanced at Cerys. "Will you be safe?"

"I want to get a look at their wielders if I can. To try to find any surprises. But I'll keep a safe distance." A firefly flew between them, and Cerys held out her hand. It landed on her thumb, glowing in a gentle rhythm. Not unlike the campfires of Thrane in the distance.

"How does that work? You can see their *powers*?"

"In a way," Cerys said, tilting her head back and forth.

Thea chewed at her cheek, trying to determine if she truly wanted to know what she was about to ask. "Can you see mine?"

"Your bindings make it difficult, but some aspects of it, yes." The firefly took to flight, and they watched it depart, its glow dimming as it gained distance. Cerys turned toward her, lips pursing. "It is potent. Combustive, like it is angry. And it feels… old."

"Old?"

"*Ancient* is perhaps a better word."

Thea slowly turned away, staring out at the lights across the lake, heavy with regret she had asked. "That is—" She swallowed. "That is terrifying."

Cerys shrugged, as if unsure what to say. Thea made note the woman did not disagree.

"Before we were told the truth of it all, Callum told me the common folk were whispering of sorcery. Is wielding—or are Etherborn—what people believe this to be?"

"Many Etherborn have died because of that misunderstanding. I don't know anything of sorcery. I cannot speak on it other than to say it has become a designation for things people do not understand."

A gentle breeze brought the scent of pine under her nose. And something sweet. The air was warm, summer now upon them. "Callum also said some whispered it was the Gods returned to our world."

"Do you believe in Gods, Thea?" Cerys asked, though it felt rhetorical in nature.

"I never gave it much thought. I suppose I assumed it possible, but now," she said, shaking her head, "I don't know. I am told those who live among me can do things I only reasoned possible of a God."

Cerys leaned closer, and it was such a familiar action that Thea nearly forgot she was no longer Sylvie. "The myths say Etherborn are the children of Gods."

Thea dipped her chin. "Is this what you believe?"

"I am no God, demigod, or whatever have you." She gestured across the lake. "And neither are they."

"What do you believe then?"

Cerys paused for a breath. "I don't know," she said, and sighed, "and I am content with that. I know what I am, what I feel, what I see. I know how I wish to live."

Thea wished she could be so content with uncertainty.

"I have to go," Cerys said, standing. "You should sleep if you can. This may be the last chance for it for some time."

"Cerys," Thea called out after her, "be careful."

Cerys turned back with a broad smile, bright even in the darkness. "We will be friends again, Thea Ironne. You will see."

Thea found her father alone on the western balcony, leaning against a wall, eyes on the army across the lake. She joined him, and they stood together in silence. Thea was unsure of the time that had passed when he reached for her hand.

"I have done you such a disservice. I see that now," he said, eyes steadily forward.

Thea didn't respond. She could not know if it was true.

"It is staggering what seems so clear one day can shift so profoundly the next," he added. "But I cannot regret having you with me."

She leaned against him, and he draped his arm around her, holding her close.

"I have tried to give you freedom. As much as I could."

Thea wrapped her arms around his chest, feeling herself a little girl again. "You have, Father. More than I probably deserved."

"You deserve better than this," he said. "I feel so useless to help you. I always have. I should have sent you away the moment you arrived, somewhere safe. But we held out hope your mother would follow. It died when a moon passed and a rider arrived with news of what had befallen her.

And in my selfishness, I could not bear to part with you." He loosened his hold to look down at her. "If you'd had your mother… If she were here, everything would be different."

Her father did not often speak so wistfully. He was always kind and open, gentle even, never withholding affection. But there was a mournful yearning to him anytime he'd spoken of Sonia the past days. "Did you love her?"

"Gods, yes," he said, and sighed. His chest shook, and Thea could not tell if it was a chuckle or a sob he worked to suppress. "But it was more than that. I respected her. Admired her. I would have followed her if she'd let me." Thea sensed guilt in him. "Alena was a good woman, a wonderful mother, and a dear friend. But that's all it was—for her and for me. We did our duty, produced heirs, and allowed each other freedom to find happiness where we could. Don't mistake me, I mourned her. Deeply. For myself and for your brothers and sister. But it was not the same as with your mother. We scarcely had a year together, but I swear I can still picture her face perfectly in my mind. The way her golden hair was always caught in the wind, smelling of lavender and the sea. The precise color of her green eyes and how easy it was to get lost in them"—he paused and smiled—"even when she was cross. I would have happily tossed my crown at her feet."

Thea watched him closely, lost in the memory. For the first time, she saw naivety in him. It was so foreign to her that she found it disconcerting. Her father had always been levelheaded. Pragmatic even. She tried to picture the bold young man he had been. The young man she had never seen.

Her thoughts went to Marten, and at that moment, she wished she had chosen differently. But she supposed it wouldn't have mattered. She could only be grateful that he wasn't with her, in danger. "What was she like?"

"Fierce, stubborn. Outspoken." He chuckled. "She could humble a person with two words. She humbled me once or twice. Above all else, she was good. She wanted to do right by the world. To fight for people."

"She sounds almost…" Thea searched for the right word.

"Fabled?" he offered.

Thea nodded.

"She was. And she had her share of adversaries. People like her always do. But most loved her. Most believed in her. It was what first drew me to her. I had never met someone with so much conviction. I wanted to be like her." He turned to face her, his blue eyes mournful. "You are so much like her, Thea. Sometimes, when you speak, I think for a moment that it is her I'm hearing. I remember the first time I saw her swing a sword. She could cut down five men with little effort. I'd never seen such a thing."

Thea could not think of anything about herself that sounded so. This woman was a warrior and a leader. Thea could not even wield a dinner knife. She felt a pang of regret that her father had lived so much life that she knew so little about.

"She planned to leave the Esērii, to go back to Icena and raise you there. You would be close. It was what she wanted, and I made the decision to respect it." He swallowed, and Thea watched the sadness in his swollen eyes slowly turn to malice. "Then she was murdered." He released her and walked forward to the edge of the balcony. "It is difficult to think the man is there, across the water. So close. If I sleep at all tonight, I'll dream only of his slow and agonizing death. As I have so many nights before."

Her lips parted, and she looked from the back of her father to the camp in the distance. She had never heard him speak with such hate. It sparked a similar feeling in her.

He turned back, walking toward her with haste. "You need to know how much she loved you. From the moment she knew she carried you." His hands came up to rest on her shoulders. "I need you to promise me you'll run. If it looks at all as if Highclere will fall, you will leave. Do you hear me? Cerys will take you to Eastwatche. To your brothers."

She wanted to object, but could not bring herself to.

"Swear to me, Calithea. If I say it is time to go, you will go. He cannot get his hands on you!"

She hesitated, startled by the alarm in him. When she didn't speak, he shook her.

"I—I swear, Father!"

He studied her as if to find she spoke true, then pulled her into his arms. She closed her eyes, leaning into it, and he kissed the top of her head. "I have to go."

She nodded against him, gripping him as tightly as she could manage.

"Do not sit out here all night." He looked back at the lake once more. "What is coming will be here soon enough."

44

Neith

"Ether calls to ether, as like calls to like. It will always seek that which understands it. That which sings the same song. The most fortunate among us find this in another born of ether. A mirrored soul."

THE WAY OF ETHER
ASHERAH GALANIS, FIRST CONSUL, THE CITADEL, 807 AQ

By the time Neith returned to her unit's camp, the moon was high. She'd stayed by the lake, thinking long into the night. Petra, Max, Ayla, and her original four sat around the fire next to her tent. Neith took the empty seat next to Petra.

"Do we have orders?" Petra asked.

"We do."

Looking out over her unit, Neith thought back to their first night on the road when it had been the nine of them huddled around one fire. It felt like a lifetime ago. For her, in many ways, it was. Now, there were four campfires, sometimes five, with many new faces she was still getting to know. She wondered how many would be disappointed to find they would not fight tomorrow. And if any would be as relieved as she. Neith had not lost a soldier, and the prospect terrified her.

Seeing her friends happy and smiling, she did not wish to dispirit the mood with talk of the battle.

"First thing in the morning," Neith said to Petra.

Petra nodded. Her eyes searched Neith's for more, but she didn't prompt.

"Wine?" Kieran held out a tall, thin glass bottle.

"Where did you get this?" Neith held it in front of her, turning it in circles. It was elegantly shaped and delicate.

"Bellamy and Iris found an entire case in one of the buildings on the coast," Kieran answered.

Neith sipped the dark red wine. It was the best she'd ever tasted.

"Ayla said it's Parthenean. She said all the finest wines come from Parthe." Iris took a drink.

Hearing her name, Ayla lifted her own bottle in toast before returning to her private world with Max. He tucked a strand of her dark blonde hair behind her ear. Ayla was laughing at whatever he'd said. Neith smiled, but then Max leaned forward and kissed her, and Neith looked away, feeling an intruder.

She surveyed their camp for Sam.

"He went for a walk," Petra said, leaning close. "Said he would be outside of camp on the south side. Something about constellations."

"On his own?" Neith frowned. "He knows he isn't supposed to go out alone."

"So go reprimand him."

That sort of teasing would ordinarily make her sheepish, but her heart was too heavy for it.

"I'm serious. At some point, the two of you will have to stop dancing around whatever it is that's going on." Petra took a drink and passed the bottle to Neith. "When will be a better time than tonight?"

Neith thought that a fair point but also thought herself a coward. "If anyone comes by—"

Petra nudged her. "I'll come get you."

Neith sighed, taking one last gulp of wine before returning the bottle to Petra. "South side of camp, you said?"

She found him lying in tall grass on a hill. He was on his back, hands tucked behind his head. "You're not supposed to be out here alone."

He didn't move, having no doubt felt her approach. They were well familiar with the signature of each other's ether.

"I'm not alone, now."

"Leave it to you to find a loophole." She lay down next to him, looking up at the same sky. "I've never seen so many stars," she mused. "It is rare to have such a clear sky in Thrane."

"You forget I spent fourteen moons there," he said, glancing at her with a smile.

"Yes, I suppose I do." Neith wondered if it was because she didn't feel like he belonged. He was so warm, and Necrium so cold.

"Look there." He pointed up. "It is Rain of Thelos."

Neith searched the sky, trying to discern what he was referencing. He took her hand, pointing her finger directly at a set of stars that formed what looked like a giant flame with sparks and trails of fire falling from it.

"Do you see it?"

She smiled. "I do."

"It is only visible this time of year, most prominently during the Burning Moon." He continued to move her finger, tracing along the lines of the flame. She was no longer surprised at the things he knew. They seemed endless.

"What is it about the stars that intrigues you so?" Neith surveyed the endless sea above them, ready to seek out his reasons.

"The stories they tell. No one truly knows what they are, but they speak to us. In their own way."

Neith turned to look at him. "Show me your favorite one."

"When I was a boy, it was Aros, Akvar the Bold's warhorse. But it cannot be seen this time of year."

"Then tell me of it."

He considered for a moment. Turning back to the sky, he raised his hands. Honey-color ether poured from them as he formed a cluster of tiny etherstars. She watched as he positioned them, drawing the constellation in the air. It took on the shape of a horse in squares and hard lines. "The myths say Cassia formed it in the sky to honor their victory at Evoire in the Godswar."

Neith loved this part of him. The curiosity and marvel that lived inside. She relished in the small glances he gave her, unsure how she ever found him stoic. She imagined him as a young boy looking up into the night sky at this constellation, full of excitement and wonder.

She turned on her side to face him, and he did the same. "Tomorrow is going to be different, isn't it?"

"Highclere is a formidable castle. The Iren armies are superbly trained and well-commanded, but the bulk of their forces aren't battle-tested. They'll have Etherborn. Nowhere near our numbers, but we will lose people tomorrow. We will take the city, there is no doubt, but it will not be as easy as what we have done so far. They won't expect our attack or what you will do."

Neith couldn't help but feel, yet again, it was ultimately she who would be responsible for the violence. She nodded, breathing in the warm air, rich with honeysuckle and grass. "And if I did not participate, how would the battle go?"

Sam pushed up onto his elbows, brows creased. "Why would you ask that?"

"Call it curiosity." Neith sat up, wrapping her arms around her knees.

"I think it would be difficult. We would have to cross through the dense forest on what little land exists between the lake and mountains. They could pin us back with arrows, and their Etherborn would be able to take us out in high numbers. We would still take the city, but it would take time, perhaps moons, and losses would be high."

When Neith didn't respond, he sat up. "Are you frightened?"

"I'm always frightened, Sam."

He shifted closer to her, his hand resting over hers. "I'll be with you. The entire time."

Neith glanced down at his hand, and he pulled away, but she held on, intertwining her fingers with his. She wanted to touch him, to be closer in some way, any way. *Every* way. Wherever he was, she wanted to be.

"Sam," she said, swallowing the nerves fluttering up from her belly. "Do you... like me?"

He frowned. "You know that I do."

"No—" She shook her head. "That is not what I mean." Her belly rolled and tumbled. "When you came back to me—to us, I mean—you asked me if I wanted to know your other reason."

He stilled, stiff, as if she'd caught him off guard. His eyes left hers, traveling slowly down her face to find her lips. When they returned, they were more serious than she'd ever seen them. "I did."

Heat flushed her cheeks, neck, and chest. She wondered how she was supposed to ask now. "What I mean is—what I want to know is... do you... *want* me?" She felt as if someone had put her face to flame, the vulnerability nearly unbearable. She watched a flurry of thoughts race behind his eyes. The longer the silence, the heavier her belly. She grew terrified he was going to say no, that she had made a grievous mistake.

When she could bear it no longer and started to turn away, he reached toward her, taking her face in his hand. His thumb grazed her cheek, and he tucked a loose lock of hair behind her ear. It was a tender gesture, his fingers lingering on the strands as they slowly trailed the length of it, like he didn't want the journey to end. When his eyes met hers again, they were rich with the look she loved. The one that somehow gave her life and stole the very air from her lungs in tandem.

Neith shifted closer, and he stilled, watching her every move. Her heart thumped, and it was all she could hear. She had never kissed someone. She wasn't sure she knew how. She had never wanted to. Until him.

With all the bravery she could summon, she closed her eyes, leaning forward until her lips brushed his. It was soft and subtle, but still sent a shudder through her. Her body, her power, burned and ached. She pulled back enough to let it linger, breathing, lips grazing.

He hadn't moved at all, save for the heaving rise and fall of his chest.

"*Sam*," Neith whispered. A fragile plea.

He closed the space between them, bringing his lips back to hers, gentle but intentional, giving answer to her request. One hand cradled her face, and she melted into it, into him, as the other wrapped firmly around the small of her back. He pulled her closer as his tongue parted her lips, sending a swell through her, radiating over and within every part. She let herself get lost in the feeling of his hands on her. Touching her, gripping her, *wanting* her.

Her hands found his chest, moving up around his neck until her fingertips grazed his soft curls. He was warm. So warm. She wanted some of it. All of it. Everything he was willing to give her.

His grip on her tightened, and he deepened the kiss, pulling a soft sound from her. The kiss was just like him, tender and yearning, but underneath, power snapped and sparked.

Sam pulled back, resting his head against hers as they panted together in sync. "Is this all right?"

Neith nodded, swallowing, feeling every nerve in her body dance with life. She felt his hesitation, the delicacy with which he touched her. With revelry, with fragility. Every place his body brushed hers burned. Ached. Asked for more.

His thumb traced the curve of her cheek again, eyes racing across her face like thoughts. Like there were so many things to say, but no right way to say them. Neith felt it, too. She could do no justice for her feelings with words.

"I wanted—" Sam started but stopped, swallowing.

"What?" she asked, searching his eyes. "You wanted what?"

"To do that," he answered, brushing the hair from her face, "for a very long time."

Neith exhaled, melting further into his touch.

He pulled her against him, lying back into the grass. She nestled against his chest, and he held her tight. Her eyes closed, hard, as she tried to calm her senses, all of them blazing. Her heart thumped at a frantic pace, and she could feel his in similar rhythm. Neith held on to him, afraid to let go. Fearing if she did, he would slip away into the night. That their moment would leave. There, with him, there was no war. Tomorrow would not rob her of this moment.

They stayed for hours. He told her more about the stars, and she hung on every word. It wasn't until the warm glow of dawn rose behind the mountains that they relented, walking back, hand in hand.

When they neared the edge of camp, Sam hesitated, turning toward her. "If anyone sees us like this, your father will know about it within the hour."

Neith hadn't thought that far ahead. What *would* her father say? Her mind raced with the possibilities. None of them good.

"I think we should keep this quiet," he said. "At least for now."

"Yes, of course." Petra knew, Bellamy knew. Many others close in their group likely suspected. But she trusted them, didn't she? Her thoughts must have read clear on her face because Sam reached up and touched her cheek.

"Don't worry. We will figure this out."

She tried to smile. He leaned in and kissed her, and she wrapped her arms around his neck as she felt her feet leaving the ground. Kissing him felt like living, like breathing. She could not imagine growing tired of it.

"You walk first," he said as he slowly lowered her back to the earth.

She nodded but didn't let go. When she did, the night would be over. Neith looked up at the sun growing brighter by the breath and realized that it already was. But when her gaze returned to Sam, she knew that they were not. They had only begun.

45

Thea

*"There can be no treaty with a tyrant, for a true tyrant does now know himself
so."*

THE COST OF VALOR
AUTHOR UNKNOWN, 203 BQ
TRANSLATED FROM OLD ASARI BY MERIAH TURAN
HAIS Z'NOSIŠ, 1200 AQ

Thea hadn't truly slept. She lingered in and out for hours before deciding
it a hopeless venture. When the sun finally rose, she walked to the window
that overlooked the lake. She had approached it expecting a fearsome
sight. But the distance diluted it. All she could differentiate in the daylight
were the buildings that had always been and an oyster-colored blur of
what she determined must be tents. Their campfires had been a more
menacing scene.

It felt unfitting to go about everyday actions like cleaning her teeth
and brushing her hair while an army waited beyond the lake. Thea broke
fast with her stepmother and then spent the morning distributing food,
water, and medical supplies to the thousands who had retreated behind
the castle walls seeking refuge.

Soldiers marched through the corridors and halls on constant rotation.
There wasn't a stretch of Highclere that went unmanned or unmonitored.
When she looked out over the city from the eastern walls of the castle, it
was quiet, its citizens tucked away in their homes and shops. Street dogs
sniffed the empty alleyways. She hoped they would find somewhere to
hide.

No one knew when they would come, nor how. So, they waited. When it was approaching midday, and she could find no further tasks to occupy her body and mind, she set out to find her father.

He was on the west balcony, looking out over the lake with Breeda, Cerys, and Commander Pryde.

"They will come soon. Lorcan will want to look at you, face to face," Breeda said. "He will try to provoke you."

Ulric nodded. "I am no stranger to his games."

Thea came to stand next to her father. He wrapped an arm around her. "You believe they will come to parley?" she asked.

"They will come to pretend," Breeda answered. "Lorcan did not march twenty thousand men across Straeth to bargain for a surrender he knows Ulric will never give him." Her father held her gaze as Breeda spoke. "He will come to tear at old wounds."

Thea's eyes turned questioning, but her father looked away. It was becoming clearer that the history between them all was long passed but long remembered.

"Will you speak with him?" Thea asked.

"I will. If for no other reason than to show him we do not cower behind our walls."

"Riders!" a soldier on the southwest battlement called out.

Another came running down the balcony toward them. "Your Grace, four riders approach along the northern coastline, bearing a white flag."

Thea stretched her neck over the wall but saw no riders yet.

Ulric turned to her. "You will go inside. You will stay out of sight. This is not a request. Go now."

Thea heeded the command. She watched from the narrow gap between the slightly ajar door and its frame as her father, Cerys, Breeda, and Commander Pryde descended the staircase leading to the castle grounds. As fast as her legs would move, she ran to the southwest wing of the castle to try to get a look. Four Thraneans traveled on horseback, all in black, traveling leisurely along the rocky coast.

Half an hour passed before she could see that it was three men and a woman. Two men were raven-haired with fair skin. Both tall and slender built. The other man had umber skin and no hair she could discern. Even from a distance, he appeared extraordinarily tall and broad. The woman rode first, brandishing the flag. All rode massive black war horses. It was a fearsome sight.

Thea turned away from the window, back bracing against the wall.

She said she would stay out of sight, and she would, but she had to get closer. She had to see the face of the man who had murdered her mother. Her father and party waited by the lake on the northeast coast, not far from the stables. If she could make her way there in time, she could find a window to watch from, perhaps even be close enough to hear.

She dashed through the halls down to the first floor, through the kitchens, and into the workers' courtyard. Many of the staff were peering through windows, trying to watch the parley. When she was sure no eyes were upon her, she slipped through, stopping behind corners and walls to remain unseen. When she reached the stables, she slowed her pace, fearful to startle the horses and make herself known. She opened doors to rooms on the east side until she found a supply closet that had a small square window covered in wooden shutters. She stepped inside, closing the door behind her. She made it to the window right as they approached. As slowly as she could manage, she lifted one row, scarcely enough to peek through. Thea could only see the back of her father, but had a clear view of the soldiers from Thrane.

They dismounted, tying their horses to a tree by the path. The woman with the flag stayed back as the three men approached. A man and a woman Thea did not know, waited inside the pearly wall of the shield surrounding the castle. The man held his hands forward, and a gap opened, parting like water, allowing the Thraneans to pass.

The man who walked first could only be Lorcan. Thea wanted to feel hate and outrage, knowing she had eyes on him, but all she felt was fear. He walked with a serpentlike, confident gait. Hair so black it was nearly blue was tied back, revealing his face in full. She assumed him to be of her father's age, perhaps a few years younger. It was hard to tell with his stern expression. Thea now understood why someone would know his kin by their face. It was unlike any she'd seen before. Severe but somehow delicate, like rough-sculpted marble, difficult to look upon, but even more difficult to turn away from. Even with the distance, his glacial-blue eyes cut through.

All three men donned the same uniform. Different badges and markers were sewn onto their leather vests, but each wore an insignia with silver stitching that she could not quite make out. She thought it might be mountains.

As soon as her eyes took in the other black-haired man, she knew he must be Lorcan's son. They were remarkably similar in appearance, even in their walk. Their only differences were a few inches in height for the younger and a more somber expression. The younger man had a threatening presence, but he was not as frightening as the other two. They stopped ten paces from her father's party.

Collective silence hung between them. She wished she could see her father's face. Thea tried to breathe against the heaviness flooding her chest, cold like winter rain just before it turned to ice.

"It is brave of you to come here." Breeda stood with her arms crossed, a longsword sheathed across her back.

"Breeda Olsen." Lorcan's voice was thick and gravelly. One side of his mouth quirked. It was not a smile, but his face was rich with amusement. "I must admit I find myself surprised to see you returned to the Esērii. It has been a long time, old friend."

"Not long enough." Breeda spat.

"We come under the banner of peace." Lorcan held his arms out in a mocking gesture of supplication. He looked around. "No place for us to sit?"

"We did not think you'd be staying long," Breeda answered.

Lorcan chuckled, and it sent hair rising on the back of Thea's neck. "I hate to disappoint, but we intend to stay for quite some time."

"You may stay as long as you like," Thea heard her father say. "We'll add your bones to the bottom of the lake with all the other fools who dared cross it with a mind to take it."

"Ulric," Lorcan said, inclining his head. "I see your sharp tongue has not yet cut itself free."

"You will address the king with respect." Commander Pryde stepped forward, but her father held up his hand.

"Be on with it, Lorcan." Her father spoke calmly, but it was serrated, edged with threat.

"I rather thought we'd catch up, but if you are anxious to end your reign, we can begin. Though I believe it is rather obvious." He glanced over his shoulder. "You have eyes. If you do not surrender Highclere to me, this very day, we will march when night falls."

"We do not fear the dark." Her father stood tall and confident. Seemingly unafraid of Lorcan's threat. Thea felt quite the opposite.

"If you knew what prowled within it, you might feel differently." Lorcan's hands rested on the hilt of his sword sheathed at his hip. He stood with one leg slightly bent and ever so faintly in front of the other. "I have over twenty thousand men."

"And I an arrow for each," her father said. "Send them over and you will see them fall."

Lorcan looked at Breeda, his demeanor casual. "Do you share his enthusiasm for defeat?"

"I share his enthusiasm to see you bleeding at the end of my sword." Breeda's eyes moved to the large man and then to Lorcan's son. "It is tall enough for all three."

Lorcan laughed, and Thea was taken aback by the lightness in it. "You know what we can do."

"We are not alone here," Breeda said quietly, as if the words themselves were already loud.

Lorcan gazed up at the castle walls. "Yes, I can feel them. But you've brought out your strongest." He gestured with a nod toward Cerys. "A smart tactic. Though I think you'll find we outnumber you many times over."

"How many are you willing to lose?" Ulric asked.

"As many as it takes." Lorcan said it with such ease and without consequence, it sent chills snaking up Thea's spine. A sneer curled on his son's lips. "But there needn't be bloodshed. Surrender Highclere to me. I'll spare you and your family who remain here. Your people need not suffer."

Breeda had been right. He did not want them to surrender. He wanted a fight.

Ulric stiffened. "You know we will not yield. *I* will not yield. Not to you. Not ever."

Commander Pryde stepped forward again, now at her father's side. "Highclere has stood strong for over a thousand years. It did not fall to your father. It will not fall to you."

"It will fall, old man. And it will fall to me." The sinister pitch of Lorcan's voice caused Thea to step back.

All in the group stared each other down. It grew so quiet Thea feared they would be able to hear her heart thumping.

Her father's demeanor changed. His shoulders relaxed. "Why are you here, Lorcan?"

Lorcan frowned. "Did I not make that clear?"

"Are you really here for Highclere? For Ire?" Her father's head took on a lean, his tone turning icy. "Or are you chasing the ghost of someone who did not want you in life, and would spit upon you in death?"

The amusement fell from Lorcan's face, and his jaw clenched. But then he scoffed, recovering his nonchalance. "After all this time, I still cannot make sense of what she saw in you. You're ever the fool you were twenty and two years ago."

If her father reacted, Thea could not see it. She could only assume they meant her mother, and the thought sent her reeling.

"And you are like your father and his father before him. Quick to forget the failures of their betters." Ulric stepped forward. "Go ahead, march your army. It will fail like all those before it that dared to try."

Lorcan took a step to match her father's. "Have you forgotten which side of that battle I stood upon? There are many among my ranks that bled for Ire in the war." Another step. "And what did they see for that blood? *Nothing.* If not for us, my father would stand where you do now."

"I have not forgotten. I also remember those you slaughtered in Icena when they would not bend to your will." Ulric spat between them. Lorcan's son stepped forward only to be met with a halting hand. The third man had not moved, but his eyes were carefully watching all in her father's party, his palms open out to his sides.

Thea felt a strange pulse in the air. Like the moment before lightning strikes or thunder rumbles. Fear constricted in her throat, and she wanted to cry out. Goose bumps crawled up her arms, causing her shoulders to contort. Decades of hate lay thick between them, dry and stale, needing only a single spark to ignite. All those who were able had their power at the ready. She could not explain how, but she felt it in her bones. In her guts.

Cerys walked up beside Breeda, speaking for the first time. "And what of those you slaughtered in the Citadel?"

Lorcan slowly turned his head toward her. "Do not speak of things you know nothing about, girl. You were still pissing your pants when good men and women fell in noble pursuit."

Cerys laughed. "Noble pursuit? Is that what Sonia would have called it?"

Lorcan's face turned to stone. Any trace of amusement vanished. "I will not warn you again," he said, and Thea felt the quiet rage in it. "Do not speak of things you know nothing of."

"Are we done here?" Breeda asked, arms still folded across her chest. The others were still staring at each other, none of them willing to relent.

Lorcan looked from person to person. "You have until nightfall." He stopped and fixed on her father. "I will feast in these halls tomorrow, Ulric. Either as your guest or your vanquisher. That is up to you."

Her father shook his head. "You will not step foot behind my walls, let alone feast within them." He stepped closer again, and they were only an arm's length apart. Thea whispered prayers under her breath.

Lorcan smiled at him, then looked up at the castle. "You have done much with Highclere these past twenty years. I must admit to its beauty." He paused, gazing around in an almost theatrical fashion. "It does hold a certain intrigue. I'm looking forward to seeing what else lies behind its walls."

Lorcan's gaze snapped to Thea's. Her mind screamed *move*, but she simply stood there, transfixed. Eyes like ice bore through her. Sorrow, rage, tenderness, she felt them all. His feelings. Her feelings? Her heart thumped, and it was the only thing she could hear, unable to breathe or move or think.

His mouth twitched before he turned, striding away.

"He seemed eerily confident," Commander Pryde suggested. "A ploy, perhaps?"

"I do not think it so," her father answered. His head was low, eyes scanning the tabletop as if the maps and parchment would provide some answer.

"I had little question before, but he is not looking for surrender," Breeda said. "I have no doubt the attack will start tonight as threatened. We need to remain alert and malleable. Once we see their plan, we will adjust our tactics. Remember, our aim is to draw this out as long as we can."

Thea's focus fell in and out of the conversation. Her thoughts continually shifted back to Lorcan and the way he had looked at her. She thought to tell them several times, but changed her mind at each. She might be wrong. And it would do nothing but cause further concern. Thea could not bring herself to do anything that would add fear to her father's eyes. She was starting to understand why one might withhold information from another they love.

What she'd witnessed had shown her how ill-prepared she was. She knew nothing of conflict, nothing of war. The battle hadn't even begun and there she'd been, shaking behind wooden shutters. Perhaps she should have gone to Eastwatche like her father said.

"A siege like this will likely span several moons. They have no easy means to cross. Our entire eastern border is open. We are not cut off from supply. We can last indefinitely." Her father sat back in his chair, still gazing over the large map on the table. "News of this is soon to reach our allies."

"And the Citadel. We can expect reinforcements within the next moon." Breeda looked around the table. "We need to settle in. This is going to be a long, challenging time."

46

Neith

*"If ether draws from the veil into the realm, so surely does nether from the
void."*

THE WAY OF ETHER

ASHERAH GALANIS, FIRST CONSUL, THE CITADEL, 809 AQ

Neith sat quietly in her tent, waiting to be summoned. Camp had grown
silent hours before, save for the low voices of her unit and crackles of
campfire. There were no clangs of wine bottles or songs on the lute. They
waited patiently, quietly, for her.

Every time a twig snapped or leaf bristled, her eyes flicked to the
door. No word had come from Highclere, nor had they expected it. Units
from the First and Second would march on the castle that very night.

For every disappointed face, two were relieved at the news they would
not fight. Their orders were simple. Neith would be the bridge. The cata-
lyst. Then stand down.

She closed her eyes, feeling for the moon. It was almost high. They
would come for her soon. She had asked for this, her only request. Neith
did not want to hear the battle speech. The claims of blood to be spilled
and brutality unleashed could go on without her. The incitement of violence, the anticipation of it, would be too material, too affecting. She
would play her part. She would do what was asked. As would all.

"Neith," Ayla called.

It was time.

Neith stepped from her tent to a crowd of expectant faces.

A soldier fell into half salute. "Captain Dracos, the king calls for you."

She nodded, dismissing him, and turned to her unit. "Bring your cloaks," she said, and walked on, Sam falling in beside her.

The farther they traveled, the larger their party, as soldiers and camp followers fell in line. By the time they arrived, they were a small mob. Neith paused, gazing out over a sea of black. The stretch of land before the coast was shrouded with row after perfectly formed row of battle-ready soldiers. The First on the left, the Second on the right, with a pathway between them reaching the lake.

"Sam, Bellamy, Petra, with me."

Low chants and dull thuds from spears cast to earth reverberated, imparting an aural accompaniment to the harrowing scene. Her heart beat in rhythm. As they walked the path, some called out to her, "Dotir Um-braxos," in the old Argothan tongue. *Daughter of Shadows.* She met their eyes, determined to fulfill her role.

A long line of trebuchets partitioned the army midway, illuminated by the glow of imbued stones, piled high in carts, in all colors one could imagine. Neith thought of the crater in Eynsbury. Of what the charges could do. What they would soon do to Highclere and those within its walls, who had no notion of what awaited them.

Her father and Magnus stood by the water, twenty paces beyond the last soldier. Magnus's eyes were soft, her father's hard. She kept her gaze forward as she approached, walking past them to the coast. She needed no prelude. The tip of her boot caused a gentle ripple, and she watched it grow until it died out in the vast, dark pool.

The thuds and chants quieted. Even the air grew still, as if not a single set of lungs disturbed it. Beyond the glistening waters, the lights of High-clere burned bright in the distance. No doubt they burned brighter that night. She envisioned chaos and soldiers running the wall walks, archers lining the battlements. She hoped they would yield. She hoped they would run.

Neith closed her eyes and inhaled, lifting her arms, feeling the warm summer air expand her lungs, then belly, continuing until reaching the crown of her head and tips of her toes. Tapping into the fabric of the lake, she retraced the map she'd already drawn in her mind. She knew its depths, apprised of all its secrets. She knew every creature that would die.

On her exhale, she began to call.

Cobalt ether poured from her palms, diving into the depths of the water. It spread from coast to coast as it descended, infiltrating all that was aqueous and lacustrine. Accelerating with each breath, each beat of her heart, it grew stronger, faster, warmer, until blanketing the bedrock with a veil of raw power.

In its center, she compressed, whispering to the ether, bending it to her will. Her star took shape deep beneath the surface, growing as it thieved the heat around it. The vibrations of the water slowed, growing colder, glacial.

Neith called to the star, like a silent siren's song, letting it feed as it ascended, gently at first, crystallizing all it passed through. It continued to climb, combustive as it surged, the velocity amplifying in pace with her efforts. Sweat beaded at her hairline and neck, falling in quick, thin trails down her back. It was working. She could feel it. She could see it in the ether.

Low groans and creaks eclipsed the quiet. She felt water splash up onto the coast. Neith opened her eyes to a swirling cloud of fume and frost circling the candescent surface, bright white light radiating from its depths. The cobalt glow of her ether spread up her arms, covering her heaving chest, blindingly bright. She had never called so much, not even for the mountain.

The ground shook with a rhythmic quake. Trees closest to the water's edge splintered and fell. The cracks and crashes joined her dawning composition, animating the night with the music of transformation.

Wind so cold it burned swept past as the giant etherstar broke the surface. The last wash of water crystallized beneath her boots. She sent the star higher, hypnotized by the harrowing beauty of what she'd forged as it continued to rise in glory, illuminating the scene like a midnight sun.

Relief overcame her, rapid but brief. She had done it. But there was too much heat. In the star, in her. It burned, and she cried out, fearful it would consume her. She stepped back, bracing, struggling to contain it as she sent it higher into the sky.

Neith tugged at the plane between her world and the void. This would not be like the mountain. The star was alive. It would defend. She called to the nether, offering it this gift. Pleading with it to answer.

It did. Eager and ready, as if it knew what she tendered. Blood streamed from her nose—from her black eyes—as if her mind itself were an open wound. A bellow roared from her chest, scorching her throat. She could wait no longer.

Neith closed her eyes and snapped.

A silent crack tore through her, splitting her apart, ripping her from her body, through a tunnel, an empty vacuum, so fast she could not perceive it. So violent she could not survive it. She knew she must be dying. Every particle stretched and malformed, transforming into its reflection. Only horror and agony existed for her now.

Neith wanted to scream, but she had no voice. No eyes to see, no ears to hear. No heart to beat. She was in pieces, tearing through one world and into the next.

Startling, terrifying stillness replaced the rip. She was left in a vacancy, a place of nothing. Whatever she was now was not human. It was basal, primal, elemental. She was essence, a part of the stars, or what lies beyond them. Neith felt no pain. No fear. But no comfort. No ease.

This must be death, she thought.

The moment she accepted—the very moment she agreed—she was ripped back through the vacuum, back into pain and anguish, transforming once more, particles reflecting into human form. She was screaming, or in her mind at least, giving direction to a voice it now recognized. Hands tearing at flesh she could now perceive. Eyes blinded by cobalt and white. It was not relief, only a return to something she understood.

Neith came to with the hazy realization she was being held. She blinked her eyes open, only to close them again, light-scorched and blinded, even the moon too bright.

"*Neith... Neith... Neith...*" someone said. Something shook her.

She tried again. There were so many faces, but so many of them the same. They slowly converged into three. Her father, Magnus, and Sam looked down at her. Sam was on his knees, holding her limp body against his.

Her chest ached, like a heavy knot swelled within. She inhaled, and it was both reprieve and ache. The icy air burned her throat, and she gasped and choked to get it down.

Neith remembered the snap, the rip, the torment. The memory of it sent bile rising from her belly. She turned, twisting out of his arms onto her hands and knees, retching with such savagery she feared she would turn herself inside out once again.

Hands braced her shoulders, securing her upright. She looked at Sam on one side, then at her father on her other. Both were watching, appraising, fearful as her senses returned. She wanted to scream, but felt as if she already were.

She clutched Sam's arm, bracing on him to rise.

"Careful," he cautioned.

Neith could hear him, discern his words, but they repeated, like an echo within her head. She touched her ear, and her fingertips came away crimson-stained and wet. She leaned into him, still unsteady, as his grip tightened around her waist.

A cold breeze blew past, and she shivered, hugging her arms around her as she looked out over the lake. What once was water was now solid ice.

Sam gestured, and she felt a cloak drape around her shoulders. He reached between them, securing the clasp at her chest. Every time he looked into her eyes, he winced.

Sparks fell from the sky, lazy like plump snow. Remnants of the star she'd missed. She hoped it would serve as warning to those across the ice. *Run. Run now.*

Neith felt the weight of a hand on her shoulder. She looked up at her father. He had a feral, eager look about him that was wrong. She wanted to recoil from it, to step out of his touch.

"Rest now, daughter. Tomorrow, we feast in the halls of Highclere." He turned back to the waiting soldiers and shouted, *"Forward!"* with savage inflection, drawing out the word as it thundered through the night.

Neith flinched when the first drum was struck. The vibration of boots in march shook the earth. Commands and orders were shouted down the ranks as those in the front projected shields, the iridescent sheens reflecting in the moonlight. She heard her brother's voice on the left and Magnus's on the right.

Sam brushed hair from her face, blood-soaked and clinging to her skin. "Let me take you back to camp."

"No," she whispered, her voice dry and cracked. "I will watch."

Neith feared what she had done. Where she had gone. The nothing, the void. It couldn't have been. It was far too frightening to believe. But she could still feel it. The terrifying feeling of being torn apart. As if space still existed between the fragments of what she was made. Her body still reuniting with itself. The only word she could come to was madness. But it wasn't. There was no word because it was not of her world.

She let the weight of what she'd done press down upon her as the army marched past. Such violence loomed, and it was hers to bear. She would not run from it. She clung to the guilt to save her from the aberration. She clung to the ache still resonating through her.

Bellamy, Petra, Ayla, and Max appeared. Her friends stayed by her side until the last soldier was no longer discernible to the eye. When the sounds of incitement turned to screams of terror, and etherfire filled the night sky, she finally looked away. They hadn't run. *Damn them.* They hadn't run, and now they would die.

She feared for her father and for her brother. For Magnus, and for every Iren man, woman, and child.

"Let us go," she said, turning away. "We will see it all when the sun rises."

47

Thea

"Humanity has learned nothing from war, yet still does not understand it has nothing to teach us."

THE COST OF VALOR
AUTHOR UNKNOWN, 203 BQ
TRANSLATED FROM OLD ASARI BY MERIAH TURAN
HAIS Z'NOSIŠ, 1200 AQ

The early summer night was warm. There was no wind, no breeze. Like the air waited alongside them in anticipation. Fixed in disquiet of what was to come.

Thea and Cerys stood on the western balcony, looking out toward the Thranean camps. Iren soldiers filled the space between the castle and the lake. Archers lined the battlements and keeps. Scouts surveyed, reporting back at timed intervals. They were prepared. There was nothing more they could do but wait.

"Why haven't they moved?" Thea asked. "They said they would attack tonight." The sun had set long ago, but still their fires burned steadily in the distance.

"I don't know," Cerys answered. "I can't make sense of it. Every approach we have conceived should have started by now. It must be games."

Thea felt Cerys's uneasiness, which only encouraged hers. She had made a promise to her father that as soon as there was any sign of battle, she would fall back into the safety of the castle and join her stepmother in the lower levels.

Thea had not grown accustomed to seeing Breeda and the other two

Iceni warriors in their battle attire. Their hair was braided and woven in intricate detail, revealing the pale blue paint that had been used to draw complex shapes on their faces. Each donned a bow, a longsword, and a seax. She now understood why entire armies turned and ran from Iceni and Vikan warriors. It was a fearsome sight. She knew she would run too.

Hours passed with no action. Thea sank, turning to sit with her back against the short wall. "I will go mad waiting."

"Perhaps that is their tactic." Cerys joined her on the stone. She reached into her tunic, pulling free the gold chain that never seemed to leave her neck. Thea watched her turn the purple stone between her fingers.

"The day before Marten's wedding, you told me you had to leave someone you loved. Did they give you that necklace?"

"She did. She wears its twin."

"Who is she to you?"

"My woman." Cerys clutched it in her palm. "The person I love most in the world."

Thea wanted to know more, desperate for a respite from all that loomed. "What is her name?"

"Nara," Cerys answered. "Nara Nyanthi."

"Nara Nyanthi," Thea repeated. "That is a good name," she said and nodded. "Does she know where you are? What you face?"

"She will have figured it out by now. She's clever. And the most determined person you'll ever meet." Cerys smiled. "Stubborn to a fault, but I would not change it."

Thea thought she must be quite a woman for Cerys to think so highly of her. "Is she like you—like us, I mean?"

"Nara is Etherborn, yes. But she isn't like anyone else. She is one of the most powerful wielders in the Esērii. In the world, for that matter." Cerys yawned, and Thea wondered the last time she'd slept.

"And you had to leave her to come here with me?"

"It was asked of me," Cerys answered, "and I agreed. All Esērii sacrifice."

Thea had her share of being ripped from those she loved and well knew the pain of it. She thought of her brothers and sisters, and of Marten, grateful they were far away. "I am sorry for that."

Cerys reached for her hand. "It is no fault of yours."

"I am sorry for it still." Thea looked the woman over, head to toe in fighting leathers, weapons sheathed at every place. She felt silly in her embroidered dress and heeled boots. Tomorrow, she would ask the dressmaker for trousers and a tunic. *If tomorrow comes.* She shook her head, dispelling the notion. Highclere would not fall. At least not this night. "Where is she now?"

"She is on her way here."

Thea sat up. "You have had news from her?"

Cerys shook her head.

"Then how can you be sure?"

"Because I know her," she said with a sly grin. "And Gods help anyone who gets in her way." Her grin advanced into a light laugh. "She'll have a cross word or two for me when she gets here."

Thea tried to imagine that sort of love. The sort that yields the sureness Cerys spoke with. The deep understanding of knowing another's true nature and loving them for it, flaws and all. She was afraid to ask herself if she felt that for Marten. Would she traverse the continents in search of him? She believed she would, but perhaps not for the same reasons. In that moment, on the precipice of battle, Thea could only feel regret she had wasted so much time feeling sorry for herself. If she died, she would die ignorant of so much. So many of the things she'd worried about a moon ago now seemed silly and insignificant.

"Were you born—" Thea paused, brows knitting as she felt a shudder. She thought she must have imagined it, as no one else stirred. "Were you born in the Citadel?"

"No, I—"

It returned. They met eyes, and Thea knew Cerys had felt it too. Cerys stood, and Thea followed. Both waited, listening, as conversations continued around them.

It came again, stronger, with more command. They turned toward the Thranean camps. Thea saw nothing that signaled approach.

The next was enough to still the others around them.

"What is that?" Thea asked.

Cerys held a finger to her lips.

When it came again, it felt more like a rumble, lingering longer. Squinting across the lake, she took in what appeared to be a strange blue glow. She blinked, watching it grow, now unmistakable as the rumbling returned.

Breeda appeared next to Cerys. "Do you see?"

"Aye," Cerys answered, her focus fixed across the lake.

"What is it?" Thea asked, looking nervously from woman to woman.

Cerys shook her head. Another tremor came, this one the strongest, pulling gasps from those around her.

"What are they doing?" Ulric asked, appearing on Thea's left.

"I don't know," Breeda answered, barely above a whisper.

The tremors started again, but this time they did not stop.

Breeda and her father took off down the balcony, shouting orders to those below. The blue glow grew brighter as the quaking stone began to groan.

The ground shook with a violent fury, sending many to their hands and knees. Thea clutched the edge of the balcony wall, transfixed on the glowing blue light.

"It's coming from the lake!" someone yelled. The tremors and groans escalated into a symphony of warning. *Something is coming*, it threatened. *Run, you stupid girl.*

Trees came crashing down, the splintering sounds harmonizing with the cracking stone and cries of terror. Thea watched in awe as white light radiated from the water. It grew brighter, more luminescent, until a glowing mass of fire broke the surface. The light within it swirled, thrashing against itself, angry, as if it battled.

She shook her head, telling herself what she saw was false. That she had fallen and hit her head, and now she dreamt this.

For a fleeting moment, she was caught in the beauty of it. Like a wandering star traveling back to its home in the night sky. It paused its journey, but it was not still. It ignited, sparked, raced with energy that raged to be free.

Stone crumbled around them. Her father ran along the balcony, yelling at her to get back into the castle. An order she did not disobey. With Cerys on her heels, they bolted through the doors, bracing against the inner walls of the Great Hall.

Pressure swelled like a mighty storm brewing. Her ears felt like they would burst. She covered them with her hands, but it did nothing to ease the strain. Bright light poured through the windows. Unnatural and blue.

Cerys's arm stretched in front of her, and the same pearl-like wall that surrounded the castle poured out around them. Thea sank to the ground, arms sheltering her head. She thought at any moment the castle would surely fall around them, burying them beneath its bones.

A crack like silent thunder ripped through all her senses. Deafening but mute. Somehow both violent and still.

A gust of frosty air sent everything sitting idle swirling around the room. Plates, cups, chairs, forks—all bounced off the translucent screen around them.

Thea wanted to cry, to beg, but there was no answer to be had. The only answer was madness. She closed her eyes and screamed. It ripped from her throat, raw and terrifying, even to her. It continued until it was the loudest sound, drowning out her panicked thoughts.

With a final roar, the storm retreated. As quickly as it had come, it was gone, sucked back through all it had ravaged, like a snap. She was too afraid to look.

The only sounds now were the thrum of her heart and the echoes of all that had crashed around them.

Thea blinked her eyes open. Cerys signaled for her to wait. Only Cerys's eyes moved as she listened. The shield fell away, and she reached down for Thea's arm, pulling her to her feet.

Thea exhaled and could see it in the frosty air. Her arms came up to cross over her chest, hands rubbing at the exposed skin.

Timidly, they peeked through the busted door. Many on the balcony were still climbing to their feet. All those who stood faced the lake.

They walked to the balcony edge, her fear compounding with every step. Icy panic, colder than the air, raced through her body when she looked down.

"It's ice!" someone screamed from below. A couple of soldiers walked out onto it. "It's solid ice!"

All looked on, mystified, as tiny golden flames fell through the sky like gentle rain, dying off as it descended.

Thea stood still, utterly transfixed by the impossibility of what she was seeing. She jumped when the distant pounding of a drum shattered the silence. The stillness erupted into chaos.

Her father appeared. "How is this possible?" he asked Cerys.

"I don't know," Cerys answered, shaking her head. She turned to look back at Thea, eyes so wide Thea saw the white all around them. All the confidence they had built crumbled away, carried off in the bitter wind.

"Can they march across this?" Commander Pryde asked as he came running up.

"The lake is hundreds of feet deep. If it is frozen solid, we could build a keep on it," her father answered.

"Our advantage is gone." Pryde removed his helmet, running his hand through his thinning gray hair.

The horror of what that meant reverberated through them.

"Is there anything you can do?" Ulric asked Cerys, but his tone said he already knew the answer.

Cerys shook her head. She had taken no time to think on it.

Pryde stepped in front of her father. "Your Grace, you must fall back to Eastwatche. Go now, and you may escape under the cover of night."

Her father looked at the aging commander and shook his head. "I will not run, Orin."

Pryde nodded, solemn but resolute. "And nor will your men." He replaced his helmet and bounded down the balcony.

Breeda ran past, shouting orders. She paused to touch Thea's face. She nodded at Cerys and made for the stairs. Thea feared it would be the last time she would see her.

"Cassia protect you!" Thea called out to her.

Breeda turned. "And you, my girl!" She disappeared into the darkness, her warriors on her heels.

Her father turned to her and grasped her shoulders. The alarm on him nearly caused her to cry out. "You promised you would run."

"I—I can't."

"You must!"

A sob escaped her as he pulled her into an embrace.

"Please, dear girl," he said against her ear. "Go to your brothers in Eastwatche. Tell them their orders are to hold. No matter what happens here. Tell them to wait for help from the Citadel and from our allies. It will come." He stepped back to look at her. "Do you understand me?" Thea nodded, dread consuming her. He held her face, his eyes saying more than his words. Regret, terror, grief. "I have failed you."

A loud crack caused them all to jump. He reached for Cerys. "Get my daughter to Eastwatche. Go, now!"

Her father pushed her from his arms, and Cerys grabbed her hand, hauling her across the balcony and into the castle. Thea glanced back from the doorway. Her father watched as they ran. In the distance behind him, fire, *wild* fire, in every color she could imagine, roared through the night sky. She would have stopped, frozen in awe, were it not for Cerys dragging her away.

They ran. As fast as their legs would carry them. It was the only thing she could do. Left leg, right leg, repeat. If she stopped, she would scream.

The halls that had been so calm only moments before were now a storm of chaos. Soldiers, attendants, and anyone of sense raced for destinations unknown.

Earth-shaking thuds continued one after another, nearly in rhythm. Thea looked through a window as they passed, seeing an array of colors bouncing off the glossy shields in the sky. She heard another crack.

They ran through the gallery, into the foyer, and out the main door, spilling into the courtyard. Cool night air filled her laboring lungs as she crashed into the back of Cerys, a sea of people blocking their path.

All who had sought refuge now sought escape. The gate was open, but there were too many people. It became a stampede.

Precious time passed as they tried to find a path through the crowd. Thea looked on in horror as men, women, and children were trampled and shoved aside. Shouts and orders from soldiers to remain calm fell on deaf ears. The thumps of drums grew louder.

"We're going to have to find another way out!" Cerys was screaming, but Thea could barely hear her over the crashing, cries, and thunderous cracks. In every direction, there were too many sights, too many sounds, too much to fear. "It will be slower, but we can get out through the lower levels." Thea felt hands on her face. "Look at me!"

Thea tried to, but the horror around her consumed her awareness. She looked every way but hers.

"Look at me, Thea!" Pain where Cerys's fingertips dug into the flesh of her face brought her back. A loud snap caused Cerys to look at the sky. Bright purple fire roared in the air above them.

"Thea, if I fall, you fall. If I jump, you jump." Cerys looked from eye to eye. "Do you understand?"

Thea nodded, frantic, face twisted in fright.

Something in the sky ruptured. All in the courtyard cowered and threw up their arms. Cerys looked up at the sky again, so Thea did too. She thought she could discern tears in the shields over the city. Another bang shook the ground.

Before she understood, she was being dragged away again.

They raced back into the castle, through the halls toward the western wing. Toward the fight. The signals of battle grew louder with shouts and commands, the roar of fire, and whistles of arrows loosed into the night.

Alarm radiated through her. Primitive and innate. It told her she was going the wrong way. To turn and run.

A gust of wind swept in from the windows along the western wall, tunneling down the corridor, knocking them to the ground.

Thea hit the stone, hard, and it felt like someone had struck a bell inside her head. It rang so loud she tried to find reprieve by covering her ears, but the sound came from within.

She crawled around through the ashen cloud, dust padding her mouth and nose. A gust of wind sent the debris from the hall, and she looked up to see Cerys, hand extended. Thea reached for her, and she pulled her to her feet.

They reached the corridor that led below only to see several soldiers, all in black, descending the very staircase they sought. Terror ripped through her, rough and jagged like a serrated blade. Thea hesitated.

Cerys hissed under her breath. "We have to go. Stay behind me, stay quiet."

Thea wanted to turn and run, but she nodded, too paralyzed with fear to speak.

They descended slowly, Cerys spying around every corner before they took the path. The deafening sounds from above turned muted the lower they fled. Thea heard footsteps and men and women shouting commands.

"There is a door down a corridor off the next that leads into an alley in the northern part of the city," Cerys whispered. "We're almost there. We need horses, but we cannot go to the stables. The shields are down."

The shields are down. Thea felt the words in every part of her body.

"Kyna's," Thea whispered. "We can try the Iren Stein. Callum gave her horses before he left. In case—" *In case of this*, she thought.

She had thought much of this moment and what she might feel. She felt foolish for trying. Anything she imagined was a poor imitation of the realities of what lived in her now.

"Good," Cerys said. "Kyna's is not far from the northeastern gate." Cerys glanced around the next corner. "No matter what happens, stay behind me."

The hall stretched on, unforgivably long as they tiptoed through. Thea heard voices, unsure if they were in front or behind.

They were nearly to the end when a group in black uniforms turned the corner, blocking their path forward. Cerys twisted on her heels, fisting the front of Thea's dress.

"Close your eyes," she said as she thrust her to the ground.

Thea watched Cerys reach for the sword on her back, then heeded her command. She clamped her eyes shut as the sound of clanging steel bounced around the narrow corridor. Something warm and wet splashed across her face. Someone screamed, and she tried to cover her ears with her hands, but the sounds were too loud. Grunts, groans. The horrifying audible indications of slicing flesh. Hot air washed through the space above her, and she bit her lips to stifle a scream.

She was still trembling on the ground when a hand found hers.

"Thea," Cerys said, voice low. "Keep your eyes closed."

Cerys pulled her to her feet, and she felt herself stepping over what she knew were bodies, though her mind tried to contest it. When she slipped, Cerys picked her up, and she dug her face into Cerys's shoulder, far too terrified to feel like a coward.

Cerys set her back on her feet. "Don't look back," she said.

Thea opened her eyes, and they were running again.

They turned a corner and met with a large stone door. Cerys's hand came forward, and orange light poured from her palm, shattering the lock. She kicked the door open, and the muted sounds of battle turned deafening once more.

Cerys led them along the northern city wall in the direction of Kyna's. So many nights they had slipped through the same alleyway, cloaks drawn, inconspicuous. Now they sprinted. Her legs ached, but she pressed on. Terror charged her. Desperation fueled her.

Something crashed into the building beside them. Stone and debris blasted through the air. Cerys covered them with a shield, pausing while it settled. Fragments of what looked like emerald flickered and shimmered, bouncing off the pearly wall. When Cerys dropped the shield, she caught some of the dust between her fingers, studying it with disquieted fascination. It was the first time she'd looked afraid.

Screams, cracks, and thunderous roars resounded from every direction, but they passed few people as they ran. Those who risked fleeing were making for the gate.

They approached the Iren Stein through the alleyway at the back. Cerys held a finger to her lips before she peeked through a window. It was dark. She tried the door. Locked. Cerys looked around quickly before striking it with her heel, sending the door bursting from its hinges.

"Kyna!" Thea called out as she ran through the inn. No answer. It was empty. Cerys cursed. Both knew there was no cause to check the stables.

"Without horses, then," Cerys said, and sighed.

Thea leaned against a table, trying to catch her breath. She burned from collar to navel. The pause in their escape gave her mind time to work.

"Maybe we should go back," she said. She knew they couldn't. It was only what she wanted.

Cerys strode across the room and grasped her shoulders. "We can't go back, Thea."

Thea nodded, feeling her face fall into ruin.

"I know you're tired. I know you're scared." Cerys stepped back, extending her arm between them. "But we need to move."

Thea stumbled forward, locking her hand in Cerys's once again.

They sprinted through the streets, heading for the gate. The screams grew louder. The explosions grew closer. Warnings to move faster.

As in the courtyard, they found themselves against a wall of fleeing people. Those at the front shouted for the gate to be opened, only to be ignored by the soldiers guarding it. Cerys pressed them through the crowd until they were close enough to see.

"Open the gate!" someone cried.

"Move away!" a soldier commanded, swinging his sword at those daring to step forward.

Cerys turned to look at her. "Stay in the crowd. When the gate opens, stay on your feet and move forward. I will find you."

Thea wanted to object, but before her lips parted, Cerys let loose her hand and pressed forward. She approached the gate, yelling something at the guard, pointing back toward the castle.

He swung his sword, but Cerys hit him in the face with her elbow, taking his sword for herself. She kicked him, and he fell back as three other guards charged at her. Thea could not see what happened next.

The gate creaked.

An explosion sent debris flying, cleaving through the crowd and everything in its path. Something sharp sliced her cheek. Panic ensued as every person still on their feet pressed forward in a ferocious tide.

Some fell, those behind climbing over. The pressure of the crowd had her arms pinned to her chest. The desperation of her mind telling her body to do something it couldn't created a fracture between the two. She tried to scream, fight, kick, and thrash, but nothing moved. She could scarcely breathe.

She met eyes with another woman and watched helplessly as she fell beneath the crowd. In her mind, she was reaching for her, but the terrified woman disappeared.

The clamor and dissonance of screams and explosions melted into a dull thread of indiscernible noise. Like standing too close to a waterfall. It consumed her senses.

Thea looked up at the night sky as warm tears spilled down her cheeks. *Just look at the stars*, she thought.

The bodies around her fell away, so suddenly she stumbled, nearly collapsing to her knees. She looked up to a mass of red hair and felt an arm wrap around her waist. She inhaled. Relief swelled as the precious air filled her lungs. Thea was back on her feet, and they were pushing through the crowd before she took her next breath.

The moment they crossed the gate, space opened, and they were running through the dirt streets of the outer city. They headed north, toward the forest, away from the crowds.

Thea looked back at the castle when they reached the trees. The shield was gone. The explosions had stopped. The chaos was now a dimming orange glow. Her heart sank. She knew what it meant.

Highclere had fallen.

48

Neith

"… and when she fell to Godric's sword, Faela Throndsen, the first and only queen of Icena, became forever known as Faela the Fallen."

THE HISTORY OF ICENA
LEWIN LEAR, 1192 AQ

"How long will it stay frozen?" Bellamy asked, tapping his boot against the ice.

"I don't know. We are well through the first moon of summer, but the temperatures are still rising. At least a moon, I think," she answered.

Neith stood on the western coast with her unit, ready to cross. Hours before, she'd received a message from her father. The battle was theirs.

A windless morning left hazy smoke suspended over the city, diluting the aureate glow of the sun as it broke the horizon behind Highclere Castle. With no breeze to thin it, the early-morning air had grown viscous and warm, unassimilable with the cold rising from the frozen lake. The conflicting circumstances for the separate hemispheres of the body made for a disorienting scene.

The ice was gritty and riddled with small cracks. Soldiers, servants, and civilians traversed the makeshift bridge, pushing carts of food and other supplies in both directions.

Neith thought of the girl she had been not long ago. The girl on the mountain, trembling, terrified of what she would see in Godsreach. She felt like someone different now. There was still fear. There was *always* fear. But now she knew violence. She knew what was waiting. She'd spent the last six hours alone in her tent, thinking of little else.

Sam had been there, beyond the canvas wall, granting her the space she'd needed without having to ask. He had not tried to unburden her, and she was grateful for it.

Neith glanced at Bellamy on her left, then Sam on her right. She exhaled and stepped out onto the ice.

The signs of battle began midway. Neith traced where plumes of etherfire had bounced off the Thranean shields and into the tree line, scorching the coast black. The blue, white, and gray hues of ice quickly turned to murky browns and reds. Soldiers were still collecting remains, piling the fallen on carts. Very few of them whole. Horror surged through her, and she winced when, for a terrifying moment, she thought she was back in the ruins. She looked at Sam. *It is all right*, he said, without words. She wanted so badly to reach for his hand.

As they grew closer, they had to bypass larger splits and pits in the ice. The Iren forces had used something to attempt to break it, but they hadn't known how deep it was. That it was useless.

Highclere Castle had been an impressive sight from a distance, but up close, it was breathtaking, even under smoke and fading ember. The main structure stood eight stories high with ivy-covered towers of varying heights. The tower battlement on the northwest side was completely gone. Its twin on the south half-standing. The castle had gaps and holes in its walls, but at first glance, it appeared otherwise foundationally intact. What remained of lush gardens lined the entire western coast, wrapping around to the south. One could discern the original structure of centuries past from its modern improvements. It was somehow both ancient and new. Both daunting and alluring. Neith wished she could have seen it as it was before.

"Captain Dracos," a man called out. He stepped forward in half salute, distinguishing himself from a group of soldiers. Neith thought she recognized him as a lieutenant from her father's unit. "The king requests you and your Second join open council. A page will see you to the room." He pointed to a boy waiting by the door.

"Very well." Neith turned and waved for Zinnia. "I do not know how long we will be. Have the unit meet back in camp at midday."

Zinnia nodded. "We will scout in the time between. Orient ourselves with the city."

Neith glanced at Sam before gesturing for Bellamy to follow.

The interior of Highclere was a far cry from Croydyn. There were rugs and tapestries, but not in excess. Countless windows and courtyards admitted a surprising amount of natural light. The open spaces were lush, filled with small trees and flowering bushes. The castle felt like a forest of its own.

There were no bodies Neith could see, but the evidence of a massacre was all around. Servants mopped blood from the floors and scrubbed at red splatters on the walls. Neith considered the porous nature of limestone, knowing despite their effort, some trace of the slaughter would always remain.

The corridor they traversed opened into a large gallery, its ceiling rising three stories high. Paintings of varying sizes covered the walls, some scorched and hanging loose from their fasteners. Neith stopped to view a long line of portraits.

In the middle was a man dressed in a red vest and fur-lined cape, adorned with a golden crown. He had kind eyes and a long beard. *Ulric Ironne III, King of Ire*, the marker read. Beside him was a much younger woman, Alena Talis, queen of Ire, princess of Argal. Neith thought she was perfection in every way a northern woman could be considered so. Long, dark blonde hair fell around her shoulders. Her blue gown trimmed in silver matched the color of her eyes, which were set in a perfect heart-shaped face. Her nose was small, faultlessly sloped, and her lips were not thin, nor plump, but proportionate. Her figure was comely, her breasts full. Neith wondered if this image spoke true or was a gross exaggeration. She had never seen someone who looked so ideal.

The line continued with one portrait after another of beautiful men, women, and children. She read the names Conall, Callum, Catrianna, and on. They looked like their home. Like spring—airy, and light.

The portrait on the end was of a young woman with golden hair and striking green eyes. The marker read *Calithea Ironne*. She, too, was beautiful, but not in the ideal way of her siblings. Her eyes were slightly too far apart, and her straight nose lacked the desired slope of her sisters'. Her mouth was bigger, lips fuller, the bottom more so than the top, and her eyes were large. She was fair-skinned, like Neith, but her ivory tone had warmth to it. Her eyes told a story of someone who perhaps didn't fit in, as if the portrait itself was aware it sat on the end. If the rest of her family was spring, then Calithea Ironne was summer.

Bellamy appeared on her left. "You're staring at this one."

"There is something about her." Neith could not say exactly what.

He turned in a circle. "I've never seen so many yellow-haired people in my life."

Neith looked around. He was right. The other walls held the Ironne families of the past. The consistency of their ancestral look was as strong as her own.

Neith and Bellamy followed the page down another corridor, stopping at a grand set of doors. Two guards standing on either side turned, ushering them through as the entryway opened, granting her an immediate view into the fair-sized room.

Her father, brother, Magnus, and several officers convened around a table placed center of the room. Their Seconds sat in a row of chairs stationed along the wall, where a sprawling map of the north had been expertly painted, covering its full width and height. All kingdoms were named, save one. Her home was only mountains and ice. As if Thrane didn't exist and never had.

She nodded to Bellamy and walked to join the council, taking a place on the end next to Cordero.

"Captain," he said, inclining his head. A jagged pink line of newly healed flesh ran the length of the left side of his face. It had been skillfully healed, but Neith could see the daunting wound it once was.

Neith returned the gesture. "Commander Cordero."

Several others around the table nodded to acknowledge her. They wore the leavings of blood and ash, but appeared, for the better part, unharmed. A servant approached Neith with a glass of wine, but she held up her hand in dismissal.

"We have several units in the area chasing down soldiers who fled," Magnus said. "Many will make it to Eastwatche, but that's of little concern. The castle and the inner city are fully secured."

"Good," her father said as he looked up from a map, taking notice of her arrival.

A frenzied exhilaration radiated around the table. No one had slept, but the thrill of battle, of victory, fueled them on.

"I want work on the permanent barracks to begin tomorrow. We'll erect temporary tents here in the gardens," he said as he gestured to a spot on the map south of the castle, "until they are complete. Commander Cordero, you will oversee all structural undertakings. Pull four idleborn units from the Second that did not fight to assist."

Her father's eyes scanned the lake and coastlines. "I want a travel route on the north side of the coast. We'll build a small bridge here." He pointed to a skinny stretch of the lake on the northern side. "We need to set up a supply chain. The ice will not hold indefinitely. We will make use of the timber you clear for the new barracks."

Cordero nodded.

The door creaked, and a soldier entered, striding across the room. He waited in full salute until her father gestured for him to rise.

"The girl is not in the castle, Lord King. It has been searched four times over. Nor have we recovered a body matching your description," the soldier explained.

Lorcan exhaled. "They must have fled during the siege."

"What girl?" Neith asked, rubbing her temples. She was so tired she worried she might fall asleep sitting up in her chair.

When he didn't answer, she dropped her hands and looked up at him. He was sitting back in his chair. Neith frowned when she realized he looked apprehensive. Perhaps nervous.

"What girl?" she asked again, this time looking at Magnus.

"Calithea Ironne," Magnus answered. He, too, appeared hesitant.

"Ulric's bastard?" Cordero asked, looking around the table. "What makes her of particular interest?"

"She is Etherborn," her father said. Neith's gaze snapped to his. His eyes were fixed on her as he sipped from his mug. "And she is the daughter of Sonia Throndsen."

Neith blinked, sure she had misheard. Roman and Neith connected over the table for the first time in nearly a moon. His furrowed brow told her he was as perplexed as she.

"She was kept here under the supervision of several Iceni wielders and the Esērii," Lorcan continued. "They kept her bound, wholly unaware of her gift."

Neith scoffed, looking from her brother to their father. She waited for him to correct himself. It didn't come. Irritation washed through her, hot and hasty. "*What?*"

"Why was this kept secret?" Roman asked, his tone as provoked as her own.

"They believed I did not know she lived," their father answered. "I wished to keep it so."

Neith was long accustomed to her father's secrets, his *games*, and she did her best to endure them. But this was different. This was something she had a right to know. She felt her face flush, her irritation rising to anger. Her jaw ached from how ruthlessly she clenched it.

She thought of the portrait she'd been looking at only moments before, unsure of her feelings to find the young woman was her own kin.

Daughter of her mother's sister. It sent her spinning.

She folded her arms across her chest in full disbelief her father had revealed the information in such a manner. She considered perhaps that was by design to quell her reaction. There was a story, and Neith would inquire after it when they were alone.

Lorcan cleared his throat and turned to her brother. "You will take a handpicked squad and hunt her down. They could not have gotten far. She'll likely be with an Esērii, Cerys Hawthorne, the red-haired woman who stood with Ulric during the parley. She is formidable. Do not underestimate her. Use caution and take your best."

Roman nodded. He glanced at Neith before he stood.

Lorcan rose and walked around the table, hands resting on Roman's shoulders. "This task is of the utmost importance to Thrane. Do you understand? I need her back here, alive and unharmed."

"I understand. I will not disappoint you," Roman said with a bowed head, his eagerness to please their father seeming to overrule his discontent.

"I would prefer Hawthorne also alive, but kill her if you must." Their father's eyes moved to Magnus briefly, a slight uneasiness to them, before returning to Roman. "You fought well. I am proud."

"Thank you, Father." Roman fell into half salute.

Neith watched the exchange, still furious but relieved at their reconciliation. It gave her hope she might find the same with her brother. Roman turned, making for the door, Katya on his heels. Her hope faded as quickly as it had come as he passed by with no acknowledgment. Magnus looked at her with apologetic eyes. She stretched her neck, shaking off the sting.

"What of Ulric's other children?" Neith asked as her father returned to his seat.

"He sent them to Eastwatche a halfmoon ago. The princes hold the fortress along with a sizable force of the Iren army and fleet. I imagine all those who fled Highclere are on their way to join them."

"Will we march on Eastwatche?" Cordero asked. He glanced at Neith, something akin to commiseration in his eyes.

"In time," her father answered. "They need to believe they can still win this. I don't want to scare them into sailing the fleet south." He reached for his mug, tipping it up, then gestured for a servant. A fresh pitcher of ale was placed on the table. "Securing the fleet is one of our objectives in marching on Ire, but we need to solidify our position here before we go chasing after it. Ire will call on its allies, so we must begin to form ours. We will aim to spread our reach from Straeth. Envoys will leave for Vikandal, Lochland, and Parthe within the moon. Ostalla, Andar, and Argal soon after. We will close them in, force surrender."

"It will not be easy to sway Parthe," Neith said. "The two have stood together for hundreds of years."

Lorcan looked at her from across the table. "Some allies you sway, some you force."

"Even if not, what threat is an idleborn army to ours? The Iren and Parthenean forces could double in number and pose no threat," Nicomedes said. She was unusually unkempt without her leather vest. Her black tunic was torn at the chest, exposing a bandage running the length of both collarbones. She turned to look at Neith, revealing her right eye, all the white of it drowned red. It looked like a sapphire in a sea of blood.

"It would not be wise to underestimate them." All attention turned to Magnus. "The Iren army is well-trained and loyal. Our high casualties, much higher than anticipated, are testament to that. We do not know the sum of Esērii in Eastwatche, and it will continue to grow. We captured only seven and recovered the bodies of twelve. Dozens escaped. Once news of this reaches the Citadel, they will send reinforcements, even if our plans in the south succeed."

Neith made note of the many plans she was not yet privy to.

The energy in the room waned. Tired faces met all around.

"We will break here," her father said. "Take a well-deserved rest, my friends." He stood, and a satisfied smile tugged one side of his mouth. "Tonight, we celebrate."

Fists struck the tabletop before the others rose, shaking hands and congratulating one another.

Lorcan looked at Neith, eyes beckoning her to stay a moment. She gestured for Bellamy to go on without her.

Magnus clapped her shoulder as he passed.

"Sit," her father said, gesturing to the empty chair next to his. He studied her as she moved. "You are recovered?"

"Once I sleep." Neith reached for a mug, filling it half full. She could not help but feel she would need a drink for their conversation. "It was a more laborious task than I had anticipated."

"It was magnificent." Hints of the wild eagerness from the night before returned to his eyes.

Neith searched the map spread out over the table. She had grown able to endure his scrutiny, but not his commendation. "Thank you, Father."

She tipped up her mug, emptying it of its contents.

"Quarters are being prepared for you in the castle," he said, reaching for the pitcher.

Neith sat up in her chair. "I would prefer to stay with my unit."

He pursed his lips as he refilled her mug first, then his own. "I respect the dedication, but you are heir, our Praxa, our future queen. You will not sleep in a tent if we are not marching."

"If I insist?" she asked, a mild sternness to her tone.

"It is not a request, Neith."

She sighed, intentionally, to show her irritation. "I understand."

"Good," he said, "but do not worry. They will not be far. Your unit is being assigned to castle watch, residing in the new barracks once complete." He took a drink and yawned, rubbing his eyes, showing his first sign of fatigue. "I want Maxson Nasseri on the team assigned to building and maintaining the new wards. We need to put our best on this. Two or three more of your choosing will join him, working with others of Magnus's choosing. You will meet with him tomorrow to create a rotating schedule between your unit and another from the Second."

Neith nodded. "Very well. All will be happy to have task. Many were disappointed they did not see battle."

"Tell your soldiers there will be more than enough in the coming days." He sat back in his chair, resting his feet on the table. "Our losses were higher than we'd expected."

"How many did we lose?" she asked, unsure if she wanted to know. She pictured the carts on the ice, piled with arms, legs, torsos.

"Thirty and two Etherborn. Most of them from the center line," he explained. "After we broke through their shields, it was not long before they were able to do the same. Cordero's and Nicomedes's units took heavy losses."

Neith thought of the newly healed wound running down Cordero's face. Nicomedes's terrifying eye. "And the idleborn?"

"Estimated around a thousand." He ran his hands through his hair, and Neith saw the blood caked around his scalp as he pushed it back, no idea if it was his. He didn't have a scratch on him. "We do not have an exact figure yet."

She thought to ask more about the battle, but decided she knew enough. Her father lived, her brother lived, Magnus lived. Her unit was intact. There were other concerns weighing heavier on her mind.

Neith tilted her mug in circles while she considered how best to broach the subject. "Why did you not tell me about Calithea Ironne?" she asked, looking up at him. His expression was flat as if he'd been expecting her to ask. The lack of concern reignited her irritation. "The existence of one's own cousin seems information one should be entitled to." She tried to conceal her disdain, but her words were edged with it.

"I have already said."

Neith huffed. "Then you do not trust me?"

He exhaled, as if put out he had to explain. His head took on a tilt as he leaned forward, hands resting on the table. "What would you have gained by having this information before now?"

Neith looked down, unsure how to answer.

"It would have given you nothing but trepidation," he said. "I spared you that."

"Because I am *gentle*?" she asked, the words coming out more like a hiss.

He ignored her question, seemingly unbothered by her aggrieved disposition. "You have only nineteen winters, Neith."

Old enough to kill, not old enough to keep a secret, she thought. Neith was sure of only one thing. Her feelings had nothing to do with his motivations regarding the girl. Whatever they were, it was clear he did not wish to share them. "I understand, but—"

"Go and rest," he said, gesturing with a flick of his head. "You are depleted, as are we all. I expect your presence at the feast this evening."

Neith sighed. She didn't have the heart to press. His tone told her it wasn't the time. "Very well."

She stood and bowed. A gesture he returned. As she was making for the door, he called to her, and she turned back.

He regarded her for a moment. "Your mother would be proud of you."

Neith worked to restrain her reaction. Heat flushed her cheeks, and a rush of tears stung her eyes. She inclined her head before she turned, making for the door with haste. Not long ago, such words would have thrilled her, but all she felt was disdain. Blinding, contemptuous rage that came on like etherfire. It washed over her face as she met eyes with Bellamy.

He looked at her, brows furrowed, but she shook her head.

"Let us find the others."

⊹

She returned to camp and informed her unit of their orders. All were excited to hear they would reside in Highclere, anxious to be out of marching camp. Neith packed her weapons and a few personal items on Storm. Ayla would stay back, ensuring her trunks and other effects were couriered to her new rooms.

Having a much smaller task than the others, she decided to ride back on her own, still reeling from all her father had said. Sam had looked at her, questioning, but she wouldn't know what to say if prompted. She needed to be on her own for a time. Like everyone else, she needed to sleep.

The stables in Highclere were spacious. She removed Storm's saddle, as promised, whispering to her that the long ride was over. Handing the reins to one of the grooms, she asked for her to be washed, fed, and brushed.

Neith followed a steward through several long corridors and up multiple flights of stairs. The royal wing of the castle had seemingly taken little damage in the siege. She passed what looked like children's rooms, a school room, and a study. Finally, on the fourth floor, the room assigned to her.

It was expansive and airy. Four tall windows lined the long exterior-facing wall, curtains lightly billowing in the breeze. The bed was three times the size of hers in Necrium. Sheer, pale blue fabric fell from the upper panel, held high by four posts crafted from what she believed to be mahogany. Two velvet-covered sofas were separated by a tea table, arranged to create a sitting area in front of the fireplace, both overflowing with pastel-colored pillows.

A large writing desk was stationed in front of one of the windows, so its occupant could gaze out while they worked. It was well-stocked with parchment, quill, and ink. A sizable shelf stood beside it, packed full, but tidily, of books of all sorts.

Curiosity called her to rummage through the trunks and armoires. She found them half empty. What remained were elaborate gowns, corsets, and other forms of complicated undergarments. She, whoever she was, had only packed her practical clothing.

Like so much of the castle, it felt like the outside flowed in. The point, Neith realized. The windows faced south, overlooking the public gardens. She looked out over the sea of tents being erected and yawned, the high noon sun reminding her how long since she last slept.

The door creaked, and a servant walked through. A young girl in an apron, startled when she put eyes on Neith. "Oh! My lady, I am sorry. I did not know you had arrived." She curtsied. Neith recognized her from the palace in Necrium. Maeve, she thought, was her name. "I am sorry, I am still tidying the room."

"It is no worry," Neith said, stepping back from the window.

"Thank you, my lady—or should I call you Captain now?" she asked, gaze still low.

"You decide." Neith flicked open the buttons on her vest.

"May I bring you anything, my lady? The kitchens are not yet open, but I could fetch you bread, cheese, and wine, or call for a bath."

"Water will be sufficient." Neith let go of her vest, and it fell to the floor.

The girl gestured to a table in the corner. "I brought it up fresh not an hour ago."

"Thank you, Maeve." The girl's eyes lit up, seemingly excited Neith remembered her name. "I have everything that I need. I will try to rest for a while," she answered, kicking off her boots. "Please wake me in late afternoon. I wish to have a bath before the feast this evening."

"Of course, my lady. I will ensure it's ready when you wake." She curtsied again before she left.

Neith stripped off her tunic and trousers, pulling a clean shift from her pack and over her head. She pulled back the blankets and climbed into the bed, sinking into the luxury of it. For two moons she'd slept on a straw cot. This was unbelievably soft.

For a short time, she believed she might sleep. But then she started combing through the faces of the women in the gallery, trying to decide to whom the room belonged. Whose bed she now lay in. She wondered if it was Calithea's. Something told her not.

Neith flipped on her back, studying the floral designs of the embroidered canopy. That was how she stayed for hours.

Neith's eyes were open when Maeve returned. She'd lain in the bed, lingering in the dreadful state between slumber and wake. Anytime she started to drift, her mind would attack, like a jolt spiking through her, snapping her eyes agape. She thought about the battle, the bodies, her father's lies. The poor woman her brother hunted.

Every time she remembered the void, the endless nothing, her chest seized. She wanted to believe she'd dreamt it, a fantasy of her own mind's doing. But the feeling of being ripped into pieces was too real. She could feel it then. Like her skin, tongue, toes, even her eyes, remembered. It sent a sickly chill about her. She wanted to tell someone. But she did not even think she could formulate suitable words.

"Ayla has returned from camp, my lady, and your trunks are in the hall. I sent her to sleep, but I can fetch her if you'd like."

"No, let her rest." Neith sat up.

"Your bath is ready in the washing room," Maeve said as she gathered the soiled clothes from the floor. "I will have these laundered." Neith felt embarrassed she had left them strewn about so.

She threw her legs over the bed and stood, stumbling a step. She blinked, gripping the back of the desk chair until her mind grasped that she was right side up. Maeve made to assist her, but Neith held up a hand, waving her off. A silk dressing robe had been laid over the chair. Neith ran her fingers over the delicate fabric, far finer than she was accustomed. "Will you show me the way?"

Maeve pointed toward the far side of the room. "It's there, my lady. Your chambers have a private washing room."

Neith hadn't noticed the door before. It blended in with the ornate paneling and floral designs of the wall. "I see."

A long window ran the length of one wall, but was set too high to peer from. The glass was decorative and painted so rays of fuchsia and periwinkle reflected around the small room. A second door sat center on the adjacent side. A servant's entrance, she assumed. Rugs ran parallel to the large tub, and a neighboring shelf was stacked with jars of soaps, oils, and salts. The air was heavy with a sweet, honey-like scent, a touch floral.

Neith stripped off her shift, handing it to Maeve, far too tired for modesty. She slid into the lukewarm water, deep enough to go under. It felt like a lifetime since she'd had a proper bath. For the first time since she was a child, she let someone wash her hair and clean her body. De-evolving felt like a small comfort.

She rummaged through her trunks, searching for a dress light enough for the summer weather in Ire. Everything she owned was designed for the brisk climate of Thrane, where a hot day meant no cloak.

Neith eyed the armoire across the room. She remembered a dark blue dress she'd seen hanging. It felt uncouth, but she tried it on.

Its fabric was thin and light. The sleeves were gathered at the shoulder, high on the arm. She'd never worn a dress that didn't reach her wrists. It was made for someone with much larger breasts than she, but it laced in the back, and Maeve was able to pull it tight enough that it didn't gape. The soft fabric of the skirt moved wistfully when she walked.

Neith sat at the dressing table, looking over all the various bottles of perfumes and cosmetics. She dabbed a soft pink color on her lips while Maeve combed through her damp hair. She was unsure what she was doing, or why. Perhaps she was simply keeping busy. *This is your room now,* she continued to tell herself. *These are your things if you wish it.*

A large jewelry box overflowed with silver and gold, sparkling diamonds and jewels, as if the owner had taken nothing with her. Neith ran her fingers over the finery but could not bring herself to pull anything free. She had little jewelry of her own. Only a pair of silver-and-obsidian earrings she'd inherited from her mother, but her ears were not pierced. It only then occurred to her that it was easily remedied.

"Maeve, have you a sewing needle?"

49

Thea

"There are many ways to run that do not require moving."

AUTHOR UNKNOWN, C. 1500 BQ
TRANSLATED FROM SUMACIAN BY PARRY HAVERFORD
HAIS Z'NOSIŠ, 1204 AQ
RECOVERED 1203 AQ, SOMOS

Thea and Cerys ran for hours. They didn't stop until Thea's legs gave way to walking. Until the sun started to rise. Until the fear turned to sorrow, and the distance between them and Highclere grew long.

Thea had said nothing since they crossed the gate. She was too afraid to open her mouth. Terrified at the prospect of what would come out.

Avoiding roads, they traveled directly northward through the forests. Cerys said it would take longer, but they couldn't risk heading east. Not yet.

Thea reached up and touched her cheek as she stumbled through the brush. It was hot to the touch. Her eyes were heavy, and she tried to blink away the hazy lens developing. Cerys glanced at her. It was the fifth time in the last hour.

"We will need to stop soon. You can't continue like this," Cerys said. She looked up to the sky through the treetops. "It will be nightfall soon. Then we will stop to sleep."

Thea didn't respond, only focused on placing one foot in front of the other. She watched the tattered ends of her green dress kick out as she moved. They had no spare clothing and little food. Only basic supplies Cerys kept in the small pack she had with her while out scouting. No one had foreseen Highclere would fall. Not in a single night.

The shock of it still radiated through her. She thought it might be the only thing keeping her upright. It felt like screaming from severed vocal cords or trying to see with sun-scorched eyes. Or worse, a dream where you're trying to move, to run, to do anything, but your body won't participate, *can't* participate, as if moving through mud, agonizingly and terrifyingly impeded.

There were small moments when she would forget. But a breath or a blink and it was back, the truth ripping through her like a blade in her belly, twisting and turning, tearing her to shreds.

Running water slowly discerned itself from the crunch of the forest floor under their boots. When they reached the creek, Thea fell to her knees, scooping the cool water into her mouth. She splashed it on her face, neck, and chest.

She tried to stand and fell back into the brush. Her feet ached. Her legs and hips ached. Her heart ached. Everything ached.

Cerys knelt in front of her, assessing her condition. She looked tired, but nothing like Thea felt.

"Another hour?" Cerys asked. "If someone is looking for us, which I suspect they are, water is something one follows. We need separation from it."

Thea nodded. "I can do it." Her voice came out smaller than she'd expected. Cerys pulled her to her feet, and they stumbled on.

Dusk was upon them when they finally stopped.

"We can't risk a fire or wielding beyond wards, so there will be no hunting," Cerys said as she cleared brush from under a large oak tree. Thea sat in a groove of its roots, leaning back against the massive trunk.

Cerys sat across from her, pulling a small leather pouch from her pack. She reached inside and then held out a piece of salted meat.

Thea shook her head. Warm tears spilled down her cheeks. They came at random times, falling silently without an accompanying lament.

"I know," Cerys said with apology. "But you must. If we can't steal horses, it will be a fifteen-day walk to Eastwatche." She held it out again. "You won't make it if you don't eat."

Thea reached for the rough piece of meat, biting a tiny piece from the end. She was determined to be acquiescent, despite her desire to simply lie beneath the tree and sink into the earth. Cerys had saved her life, risking hers to do so. She would not be a burden.

They sat in silence for a time, eating, taking small sips from the waterskin to get it down.

"Is my father dead?" Thea asked, her eyes fixed on Cerys for truth in her face if she couldn't find it in her words.

Cerys sighed. "I can't say with certainty, but I will not lie to you. It is a prospect more likely than not. I am sorry, Thea."

She held Cerys's gaze for a breath, then nodded and looked away. She tried to banish the image of her father on the balcony from her mind, haunted by the fear in his eyes as the sky behind him filled with fire.

"What will they do with my stepmother? If she lives, will they execute her?"

"If she survived the siege, I think they would move to use her. She is sister to the king of Andar and could be used as a bargaining tool. Andar doesn't value their women, but they value their perceived strength." Cerys searched through her pack.

"I have to tell you something," Thea said, wiping the tears from her cheeks. "I am sorry. I should have told you sooner, but I thought there was time."

Cerys stopped, eyes flicking up to Thea's, sorrowful and understanding. "We all thought there was time." She returned to her search, pulling free a small metal flask.

"I believe Lorcan knows who I am. That I live."

"Why do you think so?"

"I watched the parley from a window in the stables. He looked right at me. I was hidden, but it was as if he could sense me. Or see me, I don't know." Thea shook her head, now questioning herself. "Perhaps it was all in my mind."

Cerys sighed, considering.

"Are you angry with me?"

"Of course not." Cerys extended the flask toward Thea. "Whiskey."

Thea frowned.

"We're not aiming for a night at the Iren Stein. Only to take the edge off. It will quell your gift, and to be frank, I need the help to keep your bindings up on my own." Cerys shook the flask. "A couple sips to calm the nerves."

Thea turned the cap and brought the cool metal to her lips. The whiskey burned going down.

Cerys reached for her pack, setting it down in the space she'd cleared. She patted the top. "Come, lie down here. You need to sleep."

Thea complied. Her body and mind still raced with feverish unease, but the heaviness in her eyes was a warning that sleep was coming whether she lay down or not.

"If you wish, I can help you."

Thea shook her head. "I will try on my own."

Cerys nodded and stood. "I'm going to set up a ward. I won't be far." Thea watched her walk away into the woods.

It had been easier to cast her thoughts aside when they were moving. The pain gave her focus. Lying still, her mind was free to torment her.

She knew she didn't have the wherewithal for hope. If she was going to survive, she needed something harder. Something darker. Something she could hold on to. She pictured Lorcan's face, so arrogant and knowing. She had lost so much, and it was he who had taken it. Blinding rage swept over her at the thought of him, in that very moment, in her father's castle, sitting on her father's throne. It made her sick. If she could not have hope, then she supposed hate would suffice.

50

Neith

*"We are not the children of these new world Gods. Our makers are older, our
power has never been quelled."*

THE RECOVERED JOURNALS OF SONIA THRONDSEN, 1182 AQ

On her walk to the feast, Neith discovered Highclere had several dining
halls. In addition to the numerous private ones, there were also four large
halls for hosting. The Great Hall, as it was referenced, was the largest
among them. Music and cheer rang through the corridors as she approached. Drunken men and women stumbled by. Some inclined their
heads. Some made salutes. Some mumbled, "Dotir Umbraxos."

The mood in the room was palpable. Feverish and frenzied. Wine, ale,
and sweat hung heavy in the sticky summer air. It reeked of debauchery
and the spoils of triumph. Nothing Neith wanted to take part in. She only
wanted to retreat. She would make herself seen and then find a quiet place
to hide.

A long table at the far end of the room sat elevated on a two-step
platform. Lorcan and Magnus sat next to each other, mugs clashing,
laughing, enthralled. Twenty and one years they had spent planning, training, waiting. All for this. At that moment, they did not look like a general
and a king. But two old friends, sharing an evening and drink.

"Daughter!" Lorcan called out as he took notice of her approach.
He stood from his chair, grasping her shoulders, eyes scarlet and shiny.
His jovial smile from Northbridge had returned. Neith wondered if this
character lived inside him always and the alcohol simply freed it, or if it
was the alcohol alone that manufactured it.

His exuberance wavered when he looked at her ears, taking in the silver-and-obsidian jewels that now adorned them. But he quickly regained his spirits. "Your accommodations are adequate, I presume?"

"Quite."

"*Little one.*" Magnus stood, pulling her into an embrace.

Neith recoiled at the sobriquet. It had begun to make her feel like a child. As if he might tussle her hair as he said it. "General," she said, and bowed her head. She turned toward the sounds of a scuffle. A fight had started out on the far side of the room. "The festivities are at peak, I see."

"Join us," her father said, motioning to the chair next to his.

Neith sat, listening to them banter. The table overflowed with roasted meats, bread, and cheese, but it all turned her stomach. Looking out over the crowd, she did not see many she recognized from the Second. The only present from her unit were Bellamy, who was flirting with not one, but two women, and Raiden, who sat with his mother. Catching her eye, Bellamy raised his glass, and she did the same, giving him a knowing look. He grinned, shrugging his shoulders.

She finished a whiskey, then two more, before coyly slipping from her chair. Her father and Magnus were too lost in drink to notice. She looked around for an escape, the racket reaching unbearable heights. She dodged and weaved through the drunken crowds, making for the doors across the hall. Fresh night air hit her cheeks, and she inhaled the sweet relief.

Walking to the balcony's edge, she looked out over the lake, avoiding gaps and piled debris. The faint lights of camp glowed in the distance. She wondered if anyone had stood in that very spot the night before, watching her on the other side.

The gardens below hosted a celebration of their own, but it seemed a far less raucous affair. From the balcony view she could only make out the outliers, but knew that was where she would find her people. That was where she would find Sam. Solitude had not eased her discontent. Perhaps her friends could.

Neith yawned, fatigue settling further in. Whiskey had taken the edge, but her vision was hazy, and her bones ached.

As in the hall, there was drinking, music, and dancing, but the open air and vastly calmer crowd made for a far more bearable scene. Pleasant even. Perhaps it was just the whiskey, but she felt light. She wandered around the Great Lawn until familiar sounds of the lute captured her attention. She found most of her unit gathered at several adjoining campsites stationed at the far side of the gardens. They were playing cards, laughing. Some sat quietly around the fires listening to the music.

Sam looked up from his seat next to Petra, taking notice of her across the yard. Neith thought he must be able to feel her as she could him. He drank from a flask, handed it to Petra, and then stood without breaking his gaze on her. The closer he got, the more she could see that he, too, was feeling *light*.

He stopped closer than he should have, but far enough that he could study the length of her.

"*Sam?*" Neith questioned, tilting her head, one side of her mouth quirked. "Have you taken to whiskey this night? I thought it burned a bit bright for your tastes?"

He didn't answer, but when his amber eyes finally made their way back to hers, he said, "You look beautiful."

Neith laughed, glancing around nervously. "You must be soused." No one was paying them any mind. He wasn't drunk, as best she could tell, but perhaps not far off. It was the first time she'd seen him at all affected by drink.

"I was worried for you," he said, his voice thick and heavy, gaze intense, as if all his thoughts and attentions were fixed on her, and her alone.

"And that drove you to drink?" she jested.

"It drives me to a lot of things."

Heat crept up her cheeks, and she had to look away, her lips disappearing between her teeth. When she looked back, he had not altered from his state of rapt regard. It caused her pulse to spike. "Will you come with me?" she asked. "Just the two of us."

"Are you sure that's what you want?"

Neith frowned. "Why would it not be?"

Sam took a step closer, and she had to crane her neck to keep his eyes. "Because if I get you alone, I'm going to kiss you again."

His warm, whiskey-laced breath sent heat returning to her face and other places. She liked this side of him. Direct. Accessible. She walked by him, slowly, her fingertips grazing his as she passed. She felt him turn, following her back toward the castle.

He kept a leisurely distance as they walked past the Great Hall, through the noise and calamity, making their way to her room. Every time she glanced back, she found his eyes, and the look in them caused her breath to hitch. She remembered how it felt when he held her body against his, the softness of his lips, and the warmth of his tongue as it caressed hers. By the time she reached the door to her room, she felt like she was on fire.

He followed her in, and the moment the lock clicked, he grabbed her arm, swinging her around. He tugged her against him, one hand wrapping around her waist to find the small of her back, the other clutched tight on the back of her neck, holding her steady. Neith exhaled, needing a breath to keep pace.

His lips hovered above hers. "Tell me this is what you want."

"This is *all* I want."

His mouth was on hers the moment the words left her lips, fingers curling in her hair, clutching her tighter. She met his fervor with her own, lips parting, eager. He kissed her, hard. Not with the softness or the tenderness of before. Like a claim. One she was ready and willing to accept.

The hand on her neck moved around her throat, slipping down her chest to find one of her breasts, and a breathy moan escaped her as her head fell back, his lips tracing the path his hand had taken.

It dove further still, then around her waist to join the other, and he dipped, gripping the backs of her thighs as he lifted her from the ground.

Sam walked them back until she was fixed between his body and the door. Her legs wrapped instinctively around him, one foot resting in the bend of his knee.

His lips returned to hers with even more ache. When he pressed against her, between her thighs, she moaned again and clutched around him, arms, legs, mouth. He pulled back, eyes locked on hers, chest heaving. "Tell me this is what you want," he said again, desperate and demanding.

"I want *you.*"

Something changed. Like a switch. He swallowed, eyes shifting rapidly, blinking, and slowly released her back to her feet.

Neith searched him for understanding, finding nothing but concern.

He dropped to his knees, his face pressed against her belly, hands gripping her waist. He didn't say anything. His breath was heavy and warm against the thin fabric of her dress.

Neith slowly lowered to meet him. "Did I do something wrong?"

"No." He shook his head. "Gods, no." His hands rose to hold her face, and he looked as if he would say a thousand things.

"Tell me." She reached forward, clutching the collar of his vest. He grew solemn, and she feared his next words.

"I care for you."

Her lips parted, and she inhaled. That had not been what she'd expected. "You say it as if it is a problem."

"It is a complication," he said, thumbs brushing her cheeks.

Neith sighed. "I don't understand, Sam."

He leaned his forehead against hers. "I don't want to be with you when I am like this. You are more than that to me."

Her perplexity peaked. She felt there must be something she was missing. Something someone else would easily understand.

"I'm sorry," he said, shaking his head.

She reached up and wrapped her hands around his, pulling them down between them.

"Please do not pull yourself away from me." She tried to swallow against the knot forming in her throat. "The thought of being close to you is all that has gotten me through this day."

He tensed.

"I've said too much." She released his hands.

"No," he said quickly, his hands tightening around hers. "Say more," he implored, suddenly vulnerable and open. It spurred a similar feeling in her.

"All day, I wear a mask. I say what I believe people want me to. I do what is asked of me. When I'm near you, with you, it is the only time I am my own person. It is the only time I feel like I can find out who I am. You make me believe there is more to the world than this war. More than my father's ambitions." She moved closer to him, wrapping her arms around his neck. "I don't know why you retreat, and I'm not going to ask. I only want you to know that if it is for some benefit of mine… don't."

Sam's hands returned to her waist, pulling her against him again. "This is not fair to you," he whispered.

"I don't need fair." She brought her lips back to his. He returned the kiss, but when she tried to deepen it, he pulled back.

"I will not make you my distraction."

Neith sighed, studying his face. "Then let me look after you. It is clear to me you are burdened. You have looked after me for two moons."

"I will always look after you." The look in his eyes was so tender Neith was not sure she could bear it.

"I know," she said, nodding. "Please allow me the same."

He gave her a soft, mournful smile. "Have you slept?" he asked, brushing hair from her face.

She shook her head.

"Nor I."

"Stay with me?"

He glanced at the door. "Is that wise?"

"Everyone is swimming in whiskey and wine. No one is coming here. But I don't think I care. Not this day."

Sam nodded and started to stand, lifting her up as he rose. He walked them to the bed and laid her down, climbing in behind. When his arms tightened around her, she wondered if she would ever desire to be anywhere more than there with him.

They lay together for a time in silence. His lips left small kisses on the back of her neck as he drew lazy circles on the inside of her hand, tracing the pink scar.

"Sam?"

"Hmm?"

"I believe I know what burdens you," she said, unsure what drove her instinct.

His fingers stilled, and he was silent for so long she thought he would not speak. But she felt him inhale, and he said, more timidly than she had heard him before, "Many people died here last night."

She turned around to face him. "And this wears on you?"

The look in his eyes was all the answer she needed.

"You are not alone in this."

"No?" he asked, and Neith could sense the fear in it.

"You can say this to me." She held his hand over her heart. "We are one and the same in this."

He smiled, as if remembering his words to her from a moon before, when they were still little more than strangers.

Neith now saw them for what they were. Two people who were made for war, shaped for it, but wanted no part. Neith didn't understand his reluctance to share this with her, and perhaps the motivations didn't matter. From then on, she would remember if she wanted to know something, all she had to do was ask.

She closed her eyes, nestling into his chest. His fingers ran through her hair as she relented, letting sleep take her.

51

Thea

"The common starling is prey to a variety of avian predators. The typical response is flight, as their skill is not commonly matched."

THE ILLUSTRATED GUIDE TO NATIVE ANIMALS AND PLANTS OF
THE NORTH
OLIVER BIRCH, 925 AQ

Thea wiped sweat from her brow. It did not seem hot enough to warrant such exertion, but it pooled, running down her neck and back. She tried to catch her breath as she sat on a log, watching Cerys fill their waterskin from a small stream.

They had been walking a northernly course for three days, but tomorrow they would turn east.

Cerys rested a hand against Thea's cheek, inspecting, as she often did. A cool feeling washed over her face.

"Your bindings are breaking down," Cerys said, not concealing her concern.

It was something Thea herself had feared for some time. She appreciated the transparency, however unsettling it was.

"What will happen?" Better to know, Thea thought, than to let her mind run wild.

"I can't be sure." Cerys was still looking at her, but it felt more like through her. As if she were studying a part of Thea she could not see herself.

"Will I die?" Thea expected to feel more when asking such a question,

but it felt like little more than information. She knew something was happening to her, even if she could not explain it. It was more than fatigue,
more than hunger. Her body was breaking down in a way sleep and food
would not repair.

Cerys grasped Thea's shoulders. "I won't let that happen."

Every day, she grew weaker, slower, walking fewer miles with each
sun that set. Once, they heard horses in the distance, so Cerys made them
travel deeper into the woods. If they were being chased, the gap was
closing. Cerys would not say, but Thea knew it was true.

"You should go," Thea said. "Nothing is gained by us both being
caught."

"Hush, Thea." Cerys pulled the flask from the pack and shook it.
There was scarce a drink left.

It was a difficult thing, being completely dependent on another.
Though Cerys had neither said nor done a single thing to give her the
impression she was a burden, Thea very much felt like one. "I'm serious."

"I won't leave you, and I'll hear nothing else about it." Cerys glared at
her with warning before pulling a small handful of salted meat from the
leather pouch, splitting it up between them. "This is the last of it."

Thea sighed as she bit into the tough strip of beef. "How far north
are we?"

"We are south of Penderly. North of Dunclere," Cerys said as she
chewed.

Thea sat up. "*Dunclere?*"

Cerys nodded, looking around. "I believe so. It is difficult to track
from so deep in the forest."

"You could leave me there," Thea said. "You could go and get help
in Eastwatche."

Cerys opened her mouth to argue, but hesitated. Thea watched her
work the possibility through her mind. "I can't leave you. It would take
at least a sixday to ride to Eastwatche and back. That is too long. We will
steal horses when we are out of the forest tomorrow."

"We can get horses in Dunclere." Thea hadn't given up on Cerys
going on without her, but getting to Dunclere would be the first step.
"Stealing them seems like something that would draw attention. Dianna
will give us food, water, whatever we need."

Cerys took a drink from the skin and passed it back to Thea. "You are
smarter than you credit yourself for."

No. I am desperate, Thea thought. "To Dunclere, then?"

"We will have to turn back south a couple miles. But yes, to Dunclere. *For horses.*"

"For horses," Thea agreed.

Cerys looked up through the treetops. "The sun will soon set. We'll camp here for the night."

They rose with dawn, using the morning hours to track back south.

"Dunclere is a half a mile or so east through these woods. If we continue, we should come out right by the eastern road." Cerys passed her the waterskin. "Here, finish this."

Thea took the skin, tipping it up for the last drink as she wiped the sweat from her brow. "How is it you never seem to tire?" Cerys looked as if she could run for miles.

"We can go longer without food and sleep than those born idle. And we need less of both. We are also far less susceptible to illness and disease. If you were not bound, it would be the same for you."

It was the first time Thea felt intrigued at the prospect of being Etherborn. The only things it had given her so far were pain and dependency.

The density of the forest lessened the further they traveled east, encouraging her to go on. Her feet ached in ways she never knew possible, and her ankles and legs were covered in small scratches and cuts. The skirt of her dress was in shambles, and it felt like an accurate representation of her person. Thea knew she was nearing the end of what her body could endure.

Nearby the tree line, Cerys had her wait as she went to investigate. When she finally called her forward, Thea moved faster than she had in days, eager to feel the sun on her face. When it washed over her, she closed her eyes, giving herself a moment in its comfort.

"Dunclere is not far." Cerys pointed out into the distance. Thea saw the peaks of a small castle over the hilltop. "There is a hamlet on the north side of the estate, so we will approach from the south. I will shield us, but if there are Etherborn in the area, they may be able to detect it." Cerys's hand came forward, and a pearl-like wall encased them. She had not used her power for anything other than wards since they left Highclere. She said wielding would be like leaving a trail they didn't have time to cover.

They were still standing on the edge of the forest when the sound of trotting horses traveled up from the northern road.

"If anything happens," Cerys said, "remember to stay close. Move where I move."

Thea nodded.

A horse-drawn cart appeared on the hill, and Thea reached for Cerys's arm. They watched the man pass by so close she inhaled the fresh, sweet scent of hay stacked high in the back. His attention never pulled their way.

Thea followed Cerys through the open, rolling fields of Dunclere, feeling suddenly exposed. The forest had provided a sanctuary she was not yet ready to part with. When they reached the crest of the hill, the whole of the estate became visible in the valley.

Lush green gardens surrounded the modestly sized, but ornately adorned, two-story castle. It was old, likely built around the time of High-clere. One could see it in the shape of its two towers, and in the manner the limestone was laid. The reminder of her home caused an ache in her chest.

The only bridge over the moat was north-facing, leading into the hamlet. Composed of twenty or thirty brown and white buildings with red clay roofs, one could make no mistake of its wealth.

They traveled down the hill to the southern edge of the property. Thea was relieved to find the moat more ornamental than practical. The water scarcely came to her thighs as they trudged through.

They stepped around a wall of hedges to find Dianna sitting at a small garden table nestled among foliage and flora. An attendant set a teapot in front of her. Thea recognized the girl from their lunch in Highclere.

"Thank you, Nerissa," Dianna said. The girl curtsied and turned, walking back in the direction of the castle.

Dianna sipped her tea, gazing into the distance. A single, long gray braid draped over one shoulder of her lavender-colored dressing robe. Thea had never seen her so informal.

"There is no one else out here," Cerys said as she dropped the shield. "You can go."

Thea made her way through the gauntlet of flower beds, peeking around a tall shrub. "Dianna," she beckoned, scarcely above a whisper, fearful of startling her.

She didn't stir.

"*Dianna*," Thea said, again, louder this time.

Dianna jumped, her tea splashing over the edge of the cup. Turning toward the sound, her eyes went wide when she took Thea in. "Oh, my dear girl." She set the teacup dismissively on the table with a clank.

"I'm sorry," Thea said as she walked closer, shaking her head. "I did not wish to frighten you."

Dianna climbed from her seat, bracing on the backs of the chairs as she rounded the table. She reached out for Thea, pulling her into her arms. Every tear, every sob Thea had held in for four days came pouring out.

"Oh, no." Dianna held her tighter. "You poor thing." She pulled back, looking her over, alarm taking hold of her face at the sight. "Come, we have to get inside."

Cerys appeared, and Dianna's concern deepened. "Come, girls, *quickly.*" She grasped Thea's hand and led them toward the castle.

Dianna sent all the attendants from the house except the girl, Nerissa, and her butler, Williard. She assumed these were the only ones Dianna trusted wholly.

Thea watched with desperate attention as the girl filled her teacup. The moment it was full, she brought it to her lips, breathing in the warmth before taking a sip. She wanted to cry all over again.

They were given a stew of rabbit and root vegetables, bread, cheese, and lemon cakes. Dianna watched them with trepidatious eyes. She hadn't asked any questions, Thea realized.

"You heard of what happened in Highclere?" Thea asked, refilling her teacup.

"We had a rider in two days ago," Dianna answered, her expression grave. "It is true then? Highclere has fallen to Thrane?"

"It is." Thea flexed her jaw so her voice didn't waver. "I only made it out because of Cerys."

"The king?" Dianna asked, her attention moving between the two women.

Thea could not bring herself to answer. She chewed at the inside of her cheek until she felt a sharp sting.

"We do not know," Cerys said.

"What about your brothers and sisters?" Dianna asked Thea.

"They hold Eastwatche," Thea answered between reluctant bites of stew. "Father sent them some time ago."

Dianna leaned forward, elbows resting on the table. "But not you?"

Thea looked at Cerys. "No, I refused to go."

"You refused?" Dianna narrowed her eyes, and Thea nodded. It was not a lie. Not exactly. "I see."

It was clear she sensed there was more to the story, but she didn't press. Thea felt the less Dianna knew, the safer she would be.

"Well," Dianna said, sighing, "it is good the princes hold Eastwatche." The suspicion on her face gave way to worry. "The rider was not the only visitor we have received, I fear."

Cerys's spoon returned to her bowl.

Dianna looked at Nerissa, sitting on the far end of the room. "Nerissa, dear, will you prepare baths for our guests?" The girl stood and curtsied. When the door swung shut, Dianna leaned further over the table, speaking low. "There are Thranean soldiers looking for you."

Thea looked up from her stew, alarm whipping through her at an unobservable pace.

"Two separate groups have been through the past days," Dianna continued. "One this very morning. They are making threats against anyone who offers you aid."

Thea turned to Cerys. "We have to go. *Now.*"

Cerys scanned the tabletop as she considered. "He must know who you are."

Dianna frowned, but she didn't ask. "You cannot leave in the daylight," she said. "You are fortunate you made it here undiscovered."

"We shouldn't have come," Thea said, standing. "I—"

Dianna held up her hand. "I'm old, Thea, not an invalid. No one decides what risks I'm allowed to take but me."

"Dianna is right," Cerys said. "It will be better to leave after nightfall."

"They were here this morning. I doubt they will return until tomorrow," Dianna said with an easy confidence, but Thea knew they were only words. She could not predict such a thing.

Thea looked from woman to woman. Neither showed a sign of yielding. She huffed. "You do not understand the risk you are taking," she said to Dianna. She looked back to Cerys for help.

"I know more than you think." Dianna leaned back in her chair and gestured to Cerys. "It is not lost on me you no longer call her Sylvie."

"It is more than that." Thea sighed, palms flat on the tabletop. "If you knew, you would not—"

"*Sit down, Calithea,*" Dianna said with command that caused Thea to stiffen.

Thea blinked, struck by not only her tone but the stonelike resolution etched on her face. Thea slowly returned to her seat, feeling like a scolded child.

"You will stay until nightfall. You will eat, bathe, and rest. I will have horses packed with supplies to get you wherever you are going." Dianna paused and exhaled, her easy demeanor returning. "It is probably best if I do not know where that is."

"Thank you," Cerys said. "Truly. We are grateful."

Thea quelled her desire to protest further.

⊹

The bath had to be emptied and filled again. The first turned so filthy it had been impossible to get clean. Thea sank into the cool, fresh water, breathing in its floral scent.

Nerissa helped her comb through the tangles and knots in her hair, referring to her as "Princess" several times, to which Thea corrected her at each. Her sisters were the princesses. She closed her eyes, feeling grateful her siblings were safe in Eastwatche, and hopeful she would be reunited with them soon.

A green traveling dress and fresh undergarments hung on the back of the washing room door. Thea had never felt more thankful for such simple things, kindness the most profound among them.

She had wanted to linger in the water for hours, but knew her time was best served sleeping. They planned to leave on horseback after sunset, not knowing when they would find rest again.

Nerissa closed the curtains, and Thea sank into the feather bed. It was still early in the afternoon, and sunlight streamed in around the edges of the heavy drape.

She hadn't the chance for a single thought after her eyes closed. Sleep consumed her.

⊹

"Thea," someone whispered. She felt the warmth of a hand on her shoulder, followed by a gentle shake.

Thea blinked her eyes open, feeling like she'd closed them only moments before. The yellow glow from the window had turned orange, telling her it was late in the evening.

"Is it time—" Thea started to ask, stopping when Cerys's hand clamped over her mouth.

Cerys's eyes were wide with a warning to stay quiet. She leaned in closer to whisper in her ear. "They are in the hamlet, searching homes. They'll be here soon. We need to go. *Right now.*" Cerys held out her hand.

Thea sprang from the bed, immediate terror washing away the haze of sleep. She stepped into her freshly polished boots, her shaking hands fumbling with the laces.

"I believe there are only four, but we need to avoid a fight. It will draw the attention of any others in the area." Cerys handed her a pack, and Thea strapped it to her back. "And it will be difficult to protect the people in this castle. Do you understand?"

Thea nodded. There was no overture for the fear she felt. No warning, or ease in. It came on rapid and all-consuming.

Cerys walked to the window that overlooked the front of the estate. When she peeked behind the curtain, she cursed. "They're coming."

Cerys took her hand, and they crept down the stairs to find Dianna in the foyer with Williard and Nerissa. Dianna was standing by the door, cane in hand as if she would strike anyone who dared come through.

"Go," Dianna whispered, gesturing toward the back of the castle. "We will keep them occupied."

Thea reached out for her arm as they passed and mouthed, *thank you.* It was not enough, but she knew leaving was the best thing she could do to keep them safe.

Dianna gave her an encouraging smile and nodded, but she was afraid. Thea could feel it.

They moved with haste through the long hall toward the kitchen until Cerys jumped back, pulling Thea against a wall. Thea looked on through a window with horror as a woman in a black leather uniform appeared in the gardens. She walked casually, a crossbow clutched in one arm.

Thea thought she could make out a man's voice.

The woman in the garden narrowed her eyes in their direction and stalked toward the kitchen doors. "Ulf," she called to someone.

The largest man Thea had ever seen came into view. He was bald with a long brown beard and a terrifyingly broad build. The woman said something to him, and he smirked and turned, walking back in the direction he'd come.

"If we run, they will kill them," Thea said, turning to look at Cerys. Thea could see she was considering their options.

"Thea," she said, reaching for her hand. "I am not without a heart, but you are my priority."

"I cannot live with that." Thea shook her head. "I can't."

Cerys didn't yield.

"Do you really think I will make it to Eastwatche like this?" Thea asked. "I cannot outrun them."

Thea watched the confidence fall from Cerys's eyes. "We can try."

Their heads turned toward a crash and a girl's scream. Thea started to move, but Cerys's arm struck out in front of her. "Stay behind me."

Thea followed her quietly back down the hall.

"Come out!" a woman's voice called. "We know you're there."

Through a window in the front, Thea saw a woman in a Thranean uniform in the distance. Her ice-white hair was pulled high into a slick knot on the crown of her head. She stood with her hand around the back of Dianna's neck.

When they reached the foyer, Cerys positioned Thea behind the wall. "Stay here until I move you." Cerys took a deep breath, and Thea watched in strangeness as her entire demeanor changed. Cerys stepped into the doorway and crossed her arms, leaning casually against the frame.

"The girl, too," the same voice commanded.

"What girl?" Cerys mused. She pointed at something Thea could not see. "There's a girl." She thought it had to be Nerissa.

"No games, Esērii. I'll scorch this old bitch to ash." The voice was feminine, but she spoke with an eerie indifference that cooled Thea's belly. Thea did not doubt she would do exactly as she threatened.

Cerys shrugged. "Go ahead. She's of no consequence to me."

"Ride out to Roman. Tell him we found the girl," Thea heard the woman direct to someone. More were coming. There would be no way to escape. "Give us the girl, Hawthorne."

Cerys watched with indifference as if they were no more than a neighbor come to call. She picked at her nails. "She is my prisoner. Why would I give her up to you?"

Thea heard Nerissa scream. If Cerys reacted, she could not see it.

"Last chance," the woman said.

"You have a lot to learn, girl."

"And what is that?"

A cunning sort of frenzy spread out over Cerys's face. "If you hurt them, what is stopping me from tearing the three of you to shreds?" Thea had never heard Cerys speak so coldly.

"You are outnumbered, Esērii."

"Stop your bluff. It only hinders our new friendship. You know my name. You know who I am." Cerys stood straight now, her palms resting at her sides, facing forward.

Thea looked around, feeling a tremor in the wood floor beneath her.

It creaked. The chandelier took on a shake, its crystal prisms making a melodic ring as they gently rattled. It softly died out.

"You won't be able to protect them," the woman said.

"Perhaps you are right," Cerys said, nodding. "But perhaps you are wrong in assuming I care."

"Even if you killed us all and fled, my lord would be on you by nightfall. Give us the girl, and you can go. No one will pursue you. She's the only one we want."

Thea could not perceive what happened until she was on her knees in the doorframe, looking out into the courtyard. Cerys tightened her fist in her hair, snapping her head back. "I will kill her myself before I see her in your hands."

A swift jerk caused Thea to cry out, reaching for the hand that gripped her hair. Wild thoughts tangled and twisted in her mind as she struggled to understand. The woman holding Dianna eyed Cerys skeptically and, for a moment, she looked nervous. Like Thea, she seemed to be trying to determine Cerys's intention.

"She lies," said the large man from the garden.

"These are their games, Ulf."

"Katya," the woman with the crossbow said. "Kill her and be done with this." She leveled the bow at Cerys. She was the only one carrying a weapon that Thea could see. Until Thea remembered that they themselves were weapons.

Katya failed to keep the concern from her face. "We find ourselves in something of a standoff, Esērii."

"It appears we do."

Now that Thea could see Katya clearly, she was surprised to find her much younger than she had originally assumed. She did not think she could be older than her at twenty and one.

The grip on her hair eased.

Katya walked to the others, throwing Dianna down to her knees between Williard and Nerissa. They spoke low.

Dianna's eyes were fixed on Thea's. *Run*, she mouthed. Williard looked at the ground. Nerissa sobbed uncontrollably. Thea clamped her eyes shut.

"Barter me," Thea spoke low to Cerys. "Me for them."

Cerys pulled Thea to her feet, her arm wrapped tight around her neck. "No," she whispered.

"They want me alive. Otherwise, they would have attacked."

Cerys was quiet.

"If we run, they'll catch us. This is the only way we can help them." The sound of Nerissa's sobs caught Thea's next words in her throat. "They are about to call your bluff. You know it. I know it. But they clearly fear you. Barter me. You can run to Eastwatche."

The group of three were still talking while Katya eyed them from across the lawn. Thea felt Cerys exhale against her.

Katya turned to face them, palms forward. "Start with an eye."

Ulf moved behind Nerissa, pulling her to her feet. He reached toward his belt, and the shiny metal hunting knife caught the sunlight as he raised it to her face, the blade edging dangerously close to her eye. He smiled and pressed the point into the delicate skin, and a thin line of blood trailed down her cheek as she screamed.

"Stop," Cerys called out, releasing her hold on Thea.

Katya's lips took on a faint curl.

"Let us make a trade," Cerys called out.

Katya folded her arms, a single brow cocked. "State your terms."

"You will give them a carriage and horses and allow them to leave unharmed."

Dianna began to protest, but the woman with the crossbow kicked her, and she fell forward.

"Stop that!" Thea screamed, her eyes fixed on the woman.

Katya held up her hand, and the woman backed up. "And what do we get?"

"The two of us. No fight."

Thea turned to Cerys. "No," she said, shaking her head. She turned back to Katya, hand pressed to her chest. "No, only me."

Katya pursed her lips. "You will allow yourself to be bound?"

"I will."

"No, Cerys," Thea said, her voice growing in urgency. "*No.*"

"I accept." Katya said something to the woman with the crossbow. "She moves away first." She pointed at Thea. "Walk across the yard. And both of you take off your packs."

"Do it," Cerys said.

Thea closed her eyes, shaking her head. A scream ripped them back open. Ulf had the blade back to Nerissa's eye. "Stop!" Thea screamed.

A thicker trail of blood flowed down the girl's face.

"All right!" Thea cried. She glanced back, and Cerys nodded, gesturing for her to go. "I want your word," Thea said to Katya. "They leave unharmed."

Katya looked at the three and shrugged. "You have it. They are nothing to us, dead or alive."

Thea walked ten paces from Cerys and stopped, tossing her pack on the ground.

"*Farther,*" Katya demanded.

She took ten more, glaring at Ulf all the way. The other woman leveled the crossbow at her.

"You will not shoot her," Cerys warned as she dropped her pack, kicking it to the side.

"Not in the head," the woman said, mouth quirked. "But she would find it quite difficult to run with an arrow through her knee." She closed one eye as if setting her aim. "That is entirely up to you."

"You. Old man." Katya nudged Williard with her foot. "Go and prepare a carriage. Do it fast."

He looked at Dianna, and she nodded. He stumbled and stood, limping toward the stables. Ulf dropped Nerissa, and she crawled to Dianna.

They waited in a silence so tense Thea swore the air thickened. The weight of what she'd agreed to settled in. Fear cracked at her resolve.

Williard returned, and Nerissa helped Dianna into the carriage. Dianna hesitated, turning back. Thea inclined her head. *Go,* she pleaded silently. *Go before I am turned coward.*

Thea watched as they crossed the bridge into the hamlet, then headed east and out of sight.

"You will step forward on your knees," Katya directed Cerys, pointing at a spot halfway between them on the lawn.

Cerys did as commanded, moving slowly. She looked back at Thea, for the first time afraid.

"Arnes, bind her," Katya said to the woman with the crossbow.

Katya and Ulf both stood with their hands out to their sides. Pale yellow and deep green flames erupted from their palms, just as Breeda had shown her in the woods in Highclere.

Arnes held her hand above Cerys's head. Cerys flinched and shook lightly as a dim blue glow cascaded over her. It continued for several breaths until the light retracted, and Arnes stepped back. "It's done."

Katya and Ulf released their flames.

"Go to the stables and get rope. Tie them up." Katya motioned to Ulf, a satisfied smirk on her face.

Cerys's head hung heavy. Her eyes were on the ground, unfixed.

"*Cerys,*" Thea called to her. But she didn't look up.

Katya stalked toward Thea, eyeing her up and down on the way. She was tall and slender, with an intimidating carriage. Her eyes were big and dark brown, and filled with a sinister delight, like a spider circling a fly in its web.

She clutched Thea's face with one hand, turning it from side to side. "Such a fuss over you," she said, and frowned. "I cannot see why."

Ulf returned, binding their hands together, then securing them across their chests to a rope around their necks, as if in prayer.

Katya turned to the others. "Should we find something to celebrate with?"

They took them to the dining hall, seating them at one end of the table. Arnes and Katya sat at the other, eating and drinking what they could find in the kitchen. Ulf had disappeared.

They weren't permitted to speak. Every time she looked at Cerys, she wanted to cry. Hours passed, and night fell, giving her a tormentful length of time to think of what awaited them. She knew who was coming, but not what they would do. The woman sitting beside her would likely die, and it was all her fault. *At least Dianna is safe*, she kept telling herself, but it did little to quell her guilt.

Katya and Arnes were laughing when the sounds of galloping horses caused them to pause and sit up. They grinned. Thea glanced at Cerys and instinctively tugged at the ropes binding her hands. Cerys gave her an encouraging nod, and Thea closed her eyes, trying to summon some of the courage she'd felt hours before.

They snapped open, startled by a crack as the door swung, crashing against the wall. A tall, slender young man with black hair burst into the room. She knew him immediately from the parley. Lorcan's son. *Roman*, as she now understood. When his eyes landed on her, he stopped, and a triumphant grin twisted on his lips.

He strode to Katya, where she waited like a child expecting praise. He gripped the back of her neck, tugging her to him. They shared a strange, quiet moment, seemingly unaffected by the soldiers continuing to file into the room. He leaned forward and kissed her, brazenly intimate, in a sort of sordid gesture of appreciation.

Roman released Katya and turned toward Thea, smirking at whatever look of dismay was on her face. He ran a hand through his hair as he stalked across the room.

He made no attempt to conceal his elation as he sat in the chair next to hers, his head tilting as he studied her. His eyes were so striking it was difficult to keep his gaze. They were a pale color she'd only seen once before on his father, almost undecipherable between blue and gray. His hair was slicked back into a low knot, with several pieces falling down around his face. Thea wondered if she had ever seen skin so fair. Everything about him was unsettling, most of all his look of victory. She labored to still the tremor radiating through all her limbs.

"It is all right to be afraid, Calithea." His voice was deep, like his father's, but lacked the gravel.

"I am not afraid of you." It came out with more conviction than she expected it would.

Roman let out a short, quiet chuckle. "Of course you are, cousin."

Thea sneered. "You are no kin of mine."

Her insult did not appear to strike. He continued to appraise her, nodding lazily. "I can see my sister in you," he said. "Same curve of cheek. Same naive indignation. I look forward to watching my father strip you of it."

Thea spat, and it landed across his eye.

He sat still for a breath, and Thea expected rage, but he simply wiped it away, coolly, with a black-gloved hand. "What is it with highborn women and spitting?" He chuckled again, and the other soldiers mirrored the sound.

"Thea," Cerys said, scarcely a whisper. It was a warning.

Roman leaned closer to her, resting his elbow on the table, speaking low. "If you do that again, I'll give you to my men for the night."

Thea looked around him at the soldiers standing at the other end of the room.

"I'm supposed to return you unharmed, so I'll tell them to be gentle. But I do not think you will enjoy it, either way." He watched with satisfaction as a solitary tear fell slowly down her cheek. "Do we have an understanding?"

She nodded, fear crowding out her contempt.

"Good," he said, and slapped the table, causing her to jump. His threatening demeanor turned jubilant in a blink.

The door opened, and Ulf appeared. He nodded to Katya and then to Roman, who stood.

"Excellent timing. Come, cousin, there is something I wish to show you." He grabbed the rope between her bound hands and neck, tugging her to her feet. She flinched as the rough material burned her skin. Cerys started to stand, but he shook his head, finger wagging at her. "Not you, Esērii." He pushed Thea forward toward the door. "Keep an eye on the other one," he said to Katya as they passed.

It was a dark night. Quiet, once the castle doors closed behind them, save for the ambient vocalizations of creatures that rise with the moon. Gravel crunched beneath their boots as he led them through the courtyard and onto the road leading off the estate. She squinted into the distance. Torchlight illuminated a small crowd gathered by the bridge.

"It is important, Calithea, for a kingdom's citizens to not only respect the word of their sovereign, but to fear the consequences should they choose to disregard it." Roman wrapped his arm around her shoulder, as if they were friends on a nighttime stroll. She wanted to recoil but feared his threat. "Do you not agree?"

Thea didn't respond.

"We're at war," he said, his free hand gesturing out before them. "Order must be maintained. Justice must be served. And sometimes the hand that serves it must strike hard." He glanced at her with a condescending brow. "After all, they were warned not to help you."

She stumbled, shaking off his arm, and stopped. The look on his face caused her pulse to spike. She glanced at the bridge. "What are you talking about?"

Roman regarded her the way one does a child, as they are forced to bear witness to them learning a hard lesson. He sighed. "I am sorry for this," he said, shaking his head. "There is nothing exciting about killing an old woman."

Understanding rushed her. Exploding through her at a sickening pace. She swayed, feeling unsteady on her feet.

"Now come along," he said, and reached for her.

She stepped back, shaking her head.

His expression flattened, and he reached for her again, too fast this time, gripping her arm, dragging her forward so briskly she struggled to keep up, tripping over each step. She feared her arm would snap.

Thea could now make out Dianna's carriage by the bridge. "No! Your woman made a trade," she cried. "She gave us her word!"

He laughed, ignoring her protests, shoving her forward until they reached the bridge.

Dianna, Williard, and Nerissa were standing center of the roadway.

Ropes hung loose around their necks, the ends draped over the top of the arch. Thea locked eyes with Dianna. She wore a look of quiet dignity. Williard gazed down, and Nerissa was sobbing, whispering prayers under her breath.

Thea turned to Roman. "*Please.* I'll do anything you want." She looked back and forth between him and Dianna. "I didn't fight. I gave myself up. I won't be trouble. I swear." Thea did her best to show her desperation, that she meant her words.

She fell to her knees, ignoring the gravel digging into her skin. She reached for Roman's hands, restricted by the ropes. "Please, I beg you. Let them go. They are no threat to you." This couldn't be. They got away. She made the trade.

He peered down at her, and Thea could not make sense of his expression. It was neither hard nor soft, neither angry nor understanding. She tried to think what to do, what to say.

"My lord," Dianna said to Roman, drawing his attention. "Please grant mercy on my people. They acted on my order. They are innocent in this. The girl is only fifteen," Dianna continued. "Little more than a child."

Roman grabbed the rope around Thea's neck, tugging her to her feet. He walked them closer to address the crowd. "You were all warned of your fate should you assist any members of the Ironne family or armed forces as they fled. Age does not invalidate crimes against your new lord and king."

Dianna closed her eyes. Thea felt her legs start to give.

"But," Roman continued, "you will not find us without mercy." He gestured toward one of his soldiers. "Release the girl."

Thea exhaled as a soldier walked to Nerissa, cutting the bindings from her hands and the one from her neck. The girl turned to Dianna, tears cascading down her cheeks.

"Go, now, dear girl," Dianna urged her, gesturing with her head. She didn't move. "Nerissa, it is all right. Go now, run to your father."

Nerissa sobbed, stumbling away into the crowd.

Dianna turned back to Roman. "Thank you, my lord, for your mercy." She took a breath. "I beg now for my man. He, too, was not complicit in my crime. He acted upon my order alone."

"No, my lady," Williard said, his voice as frail as his frame, which barely stood upright. "My place is with you."

Before Dianna could further plead, Roman raised an arm. "You heard him. Proceed."

Thea fell to her knees again. "I beg you, cousin." She looked over to Dianna as soldiers grabbed the long ends of the ropes, pulling them taut. It caused Dianna's chin to lift. "*Please!*"

Roman held up his hand again, and the soldiers stopped. He looked down at her and frowned. "I thought I was no kin of yours?" His frown slowly transformed into something sinister. "Continue."

They pulled, and Dianna's and Williard's feet left the ground.

Thea screamed, scrambling to her feet, trying to run for them. Roman grabbed the collar of her dress, heaving her back. His arms wrapped around her shoulders, holding her in place as she struggled against him. The more she fought, the tighter he held her.

"This is the fate of any who help you," he said against her ear. "Remember this before you doom another."

She watched in horror as their fragile bodies thrashed and kicked. Thea met Dianna's panicked eyes. She raged and fought, but couldn't break free. "I'm sorry!" she sobbed. "*I'm so sorry.*"

It was not long before it was over.

When Dianna stilled, so did Thea. Roman released her, and she collapsed. She swayed, suspended, gasping, as if time itself was caught in her throat.

"Tie off the ropes," she heard Roman say. It echoed around her. She looked at him. "Leave them hanging," he ordered, then pointed at the weeping townspeople. "Let this be a lesson to you all."

He continued to speak, but his words faded. Her chest heaved and ached, desperate for anything more than the thin air it was receiving. She sobbed as she looked up into Dianna's vacant eyes. A ringing reverberated through her head, reaching a pitch she'd never heard. It sent a searing pain from the back of her eyes down through her body. She fell forward on her hands and knees and retched, spilling everything in her belly out onto the ground. Roman stepped back and cursed.

"Take her to Arnes. Her bindings are breaking down," Thea heard him say.

Someone picked her up, throwing her over their shoulder. Someone big. Ulf.

Thea bucked and thrashed, clawing at him, but it made little difference. By the time they were back in the castle, she could barely hold her head upright. Silent tears fell as Ulf put her back in the chair next to Cerys.

"They killed them," she said, breathless. "Hung them from the arch on the bridge." Her entire body twitched.

Cerys didn't respond. Thea turned to look at her. "You knew it would happen."

"They were never going to let them live," Cerys said, watching Arnes and another soldier approach.

"Then why agree? Why play along?" Thea asked, feeling ever the fool. Ever the cause. She would die. *Cerys* would die. For nothing.

"I had hoped to spare you their deaths. But I have failed at that, too."

52

Nara

"From the ashes of the Great Quell, so emerged Ire, in militaristic and economic might."

THE RISE OF IRE
LEWIN LEAR, 1198 AQ

The last two days at sea had not been pleasant for Nara. The north was well known for its summer storms, but as they approached the southern coast, the journey had turned into a relentless barrage of crashing waves and sour bellies. She was below deck, trying to keep down her supper, when she was called for.

Her cabin door swung open, and one of the deckhands appeared. "Chancellor," he said between shallow breaths, "you need to see this."

The storm had calmed to steady rain. It fell in thick drops, bouncing off the wooden deck. They were hours from sundown, but the sky was cloud-covered, casting the illusion of near night.

Nara blinked, trying to assure herself her eyes did not betray her. She turned, climbing the stairs by twos up to the quarterdeck for a better view, the deckhand on her heels. She watched a ship approach and sail past. Then another, and another that trailed the second. On and on, stretching in a long line until her eyes took in the distant sight of Kingsport.

"Godsdamn," she hissed under her breath.

Harker appeared on her right. "Well, this ain't good."

Nara reached for the deckhand while her attention stayed fixed on the city. She fisted his tunic, pulling him toward her. "Go and get the captain."

The boy nodded frantically, sprinting down the deck.

Nara turned to Harker. "We can't sail into harbor. Kingsport is either captured or soon to be. It looks as if the entire city is fleeing."

"Will we turn and sail for Eastwatche?" Harker asked.

"No," she said, shaking her head. "We need to find out what has happened. We need information." Nara watched the ship's captain approach.

"What are your orders?" he asked, concern creasing his brow.

"Sail east of the city. Anchor a half mile off the coast. Harker and I will take the tender boat in, under shield."

The captain nodded. "Should we expect you back?"

"No," Nara answered. "Leave at first light for Azmar unless the city goes under siege. If there is danger, do not wait. If the city still stands, I will send a messenger out before you depart."

"Understood," he said, bowing his head. "Adrae protect you, Chancellor." He turned to Harker. "And you, Deputy." The captain turned and distributed orders to the crew.

"I'm still getting used to that," Harker said.

"Getting used to what?" Nara asked, continuing to watch the ships pass, searching for a sail or identifying marker of any kind.

"The title," he answered. "I don't always realize they're talking to me."

She peered at him from the side of her eyes. "Pin weighing a little too heavy on your chest?"

Harker straightened. "I didn't say that."

The moment of jest fell away as another ship sailed by. Nara tried to think through the possibilities of what awaited. If the Thranean army marched to Kingsport, then Highclere was safe. Cerys was safe. She wanted to draw some comfort from it, tried to, but feared she would have none until Cerys was standing before her. Until she could reach out and touch her.

"What in the hells are we walking into?" Harker asked, voice low.

Nara turned to look at him and sighed. "War," she said. "We are walking into war."

It took over an hour to row to shore, and at least another to walk to Kingsport. Night was upon them by the time they reached the city. Nara was relieved to find it had not fallen, but it was apparent whatever waited outside the western gates was daunting.

The city was locked down. Every citizen requesting entry, though there were few, was questioned and searched. Most were leaving, heading up the northern road.

Nara had passed through Kingsport's cobblestone streets on more than one occasion but had never stayed long. Ire had typically been a place of peace, so it was not a kingdom she was often sent to.

Heavy rain and winds had knocked out the streetlamps. Markets and shops were closed. Even the pubs. Windows were boarded up. Those who remained were hidden away in their homes, preparing for a siege.

They approached the field house, expecting to be greeted at the door, as they were accustomed. Nothing and no one stirred.

"That's odd, no?" she asked, turning to look at Harker.

"Aye," he said, scratching his chin. "Can you sense anyone?"

Nara held her palm toward the red-painted door. "No. It's warded tight."

"I suppose that makes sense, given the circumstances." Rain trailed down his face, taking diverse courses over the bends and angles, beading in his shadow of a beard. "Can you break it?"

Nara scoffed. "Of course."

She closed her eyes, sending her ether around the field house. "Someone put a lot of effort into this. It's set to go off like a Godsdamned war bell."

"Well…" Harker said. "Seems fitting."

She weaved and enveloped the ward, bending rather than breaking, just enough for them to open the door and pass the threshold.

Nara pulled back the hood of her cloak, shaking off the rain, and frowned. The common room was empty. There were no candles or lamps lit. Furniture remained, but there were few traces of life. A single teacup and saucer sat solitary on a table.

Nara walked to the table and held her fingertips to the porcelain. "Still warm."

Harker formed an etherstar. Its soft, burgundy-hued light filled the dark space.

"Hello?" Nara called out. "Is there anyone here?"

"State your name!" a girl's voice called from down the hall, followed by the glow of orange etherfire.

"Chancellor Nara Nyanthi and Deputy Chancellor Harker—" Nara stopped, turning to look at him, brows furrowed. She realized she did not know his surname. Or if that *was* his surname. "Just Harker."

The orange glow dimmed but didn't go out. A young woman stepped around the corner, concealed beneath a shield. She had dark brown hair and eyes that were terrified. She kept a small flame at call.

"We've just arrived from the Citadel," Nara said, attempting to reassure the nervous girl.

The shield was recalled, and the orange flame went out. "I'm sorry," the girl said, from the darkness down the hall. "I was told no one could get through the wards. I didn't recognize your signatures, so I grew frightened." Nara heard slow, cautious footsteps.

"It's quite all right," Nara said, taking a step of her own. "We heard what happened in Godsreach. We were sent by the High Council to investigate." Not exactly a lie.

"Oh, thank the Gods," the girl said as she stepped into the light. She was younger than Nara assumed. Not a day over thirteen. She looked at Nara's eagle pin and then behind her, as if expecting others. "How many have come?"

"It is only us."

"*Only two?*" The girl blinked and dropped into a chair, head falling into her hands.

Nara glanced at Harker, and he shrugged.

"But more will be on their way soon," Nara said as she took the seat opposite her while Harker lit the lamps in the room. "What is your name?"

"Aida," she said, muffled by her hands.

"Aida, why are you here alone? You do not look old enough to be on assignment."

"I'm not." The girl shook her head and looked up. "My mother is warden here. My father is the field house steward."

"Ah. You are Ray and Rowena Winstone's daughter." Nara had not seen them in years. She remembered Aida as a babe on her mother's hip. She wanted to rapid-fire fifty questions, but the fear in the girl's eyes cooled her impatience. "But why are you here alone? The last time I came through Kingsport there were at least twenty Esērii permanently stationed here."

"There were more than twenty," Aida said, looking from Nara to Harker as he joined them at the table. "Highclere sent reinforcements, but everyone is now returning north. My father and the others will return soon, and then we are leaving."

"The Esērii are abandoning Kingsport?" Nara asked, omitting the accusation she wanted to weight her words with.

"It cannot be defended. That is what my mother said in her letter." The girl stood and walked to a desk in the corner of the room, returning with a parchment in hand, folded, with a broken seal. "Thrane sits half a day's march from the western gate." Her hand shook as she handed the letter to Nara.

"Do you know their numbers?" Nara asked as she unfolded it.

"Ten thousand."

Nara's eyes flicked back up to hers. "You are certain?"

Aida nodded. "And they have Etherborn. Nearly a hundred. And powerful ones."

Nara glanced at Harker, trying to keep her composure, not wishing to frighten the girl further. "Why would we choose to abandon? Surely we should group here and make a stand?"

"Oh, you don't know." Her voice was low, like one about to give dreadful news. It was something Nara never understood. If there was something amiss, one should say it loudly and clearly, so there could be no mistake, no delay, no error.

Nara leaned over the table. "What do we not know?"

The girl swallowed. "They have two forces. The other larger one marches for Highclere. Or is likely already there."

Panic flooded Nara's chest. It traveled up her throat and down to her belly. Her heart pumped the caustic substance, drowning her in it. It was all-consuming, like falling into a frozen lake. No thoughts, no actions, only fright. She wanted to scream, but instead, she nodded. "I see."

"You should read the letter," Aida said, planting her heels in the chair. She wrapped her arms around her knees, pulling them to her chest.

Nara inhaled, flipped it open, and read. Rowena described two separate forces totaling over thirty thousand. One marching south, the other directly east for the western coast of Lake Crescent in Highclere. She glanced up at the girl who watched her with trepidation, as if she expected a wild reaction.

The letter went on to recall a fight in a Straethan forest. Twenty and six against six. Lorcan's daughter. Disappearing bodies. Nara's hands started to shake. She didn't look up again, but had to pause so as not to react. She was a chancellor. It was her responsibility to present order.

It sounded like fiction, but Nara knew Rowena to be a practical, level-headed woman. Not the type prone to theatrics.

Her letter finished by stating that if Highclere fell, she would travel to Bacebridge to meet them, and they would continue to Eastwatche together.

When she finished reading, Nara sat quietly, trying to control the pace of her heart. She closed her eyes to think, suppressing the dread that filled her belly. Highclere would not fall. It was nearly impenetrable, she told herself. But she recalled what Amena had told her about Godsreach and the mountain, and what Rowena described in the forest.

Nara handed the letter to Harker. "Thank you, Aida. Everything you have told us is most helpful. Rest assured, the Citadel will respond appropriately."

The worry in the girl's eyes eased some, and she nodded.

"Aida, you said you were waiting for your father and others to return, correct?" The girl nodded. "I am going to write a message for the council. When the others return, someone needs to deliver it to a ship that is anchored off the coast. I will write directions to a tender boat hidden on land, not far from the eastern gate. This is very important." Nara reached across the table for the girl's hand. "Do you understand?"

"I understand, Chancellor," she said, sitting up straight.

Nara smiled, and it was one of the best lies she'd ever told. "Have you extra supplies beyond what you and the others need to ride north?"

"We do."

"Excellent," she said. "Will you help us with two packs? As much as you can spare?"

Aida nodded.

"I will also need parchment and quill."

The girl stood and bowed her head before dashing off through the house.

Harker folded the letter and set it on the table between them. He stood, and Nara watched as he made for the bar cart across the room. Not bothering with glasses, he returned to his seat with a bottle in hand, tipping it up against his lips. "What kind of power is that?" he asked as he passed the bottle to Nara.

"I don't know." She suspected, but lacked the courage to admit it. "It might be fantasy," she added, but her words had little weight to them.

He sighed, running his hands through his hair. It was still wet from the rain. "We can't risk the river. Not with what was described in that letter. We'll have to travel north on horseback."

She nodded her agreement as she took a drink. If it burned, she didn't notice.

"To Highclere or Eastwatche?" he asked.

Nara shook her head and shrugged. "I don't know," she answered, passing the bottle back to Harker. "That depends on what we find."

53

Thea

"By hiding our light, we deprive those who live in the dark the opportunity to see."

THE RECOVERED JOURNALS OF SONIA THRONDSEN, 1181 AQ

Dianna's and Williard's bodies were still hanging from the arch when they departed the morning after. Thea tried to avert her eyes, the guilt still sharp and unyielding, but the sight of Dianna's boots swaying in tune with the creak of the ropes was enough to nearly send her from the saddle. She clamped her eyes shut until the sound of hooves on wood turned to dirt once more. Ulf was staring at her, a broad smile on his face. She wanted to sneer, to curse him, to make a stand of any kind, but all she could do was look away.

She had been made to ride with one of the soldiers. He smelled of sour ale and sweat. Thea did her best to sit upright, as far removed from him as she could manage. It caused her back and hips to ache. They rode long into the evening hours, rising each day before dawn. It was apparent Roman was in haste to return.

They were given ample food and water, and privacy when needed. It had been far better treatment than Thea had expected, and she feared angering them. She feared what they might do to Cerys. At night, when they stopped, she listened to their conversations. Eager for any information about the war or Highclere. They didn't speak of anything of use. Only bantered and joked. On occasion, Thea would catch one of them inspecting her as if trying to make sense of what she was.

She wanted to be angry with Cerys for not running. It hurt to see her shackled so. The binding had changed her, as if they'd robbed her of her spirit. Even so, Thea couldn't help but feel grateful she wasn't alone.

It was the afternoon of the third day of traveling when they arrived back in Highclere.

The outer city was relatively unaltered, save for the presence of Thranean soldiers at every turn. They dismounted their horses before crossing the northeastern city gate. The very gate Thea and Cerys escaped through only a sixday before.

The signs of siege began the moment they passed through. Gaping holes marred the walls of homes and shops. Roofs were covered with canvas tarps. More than once, they passed an empty lot. Whatever had been was no more.

Roman paraded them through the streets while the townsfolk looked on. Every time Katya tugged the rope forward, it burned, but she bit her lips to keep from crying out. Thea was not well-versed in war tactics, but their intention was clear. They were showing the people of Highclere that no one could run. No one could defy them. Not even the daughter of the king.

Many carried on with their daily tasks, heads down, as if trying to go unnoticed. But it wasn't long before they gathered on the walkways, watching as the spectacle passed. A brave few called out to her. She tried to hold her head high, meeting any who would look her way. Thea could see the suffering in their eyes. There was loss and fear, but also fury. Quiet fury. And it encouraged hers.

When they reached the castle walls, Thea stopped, turning toward the crowds.

"Fear not, good people," she called out. "Hold strong knowing your princes live. One day, they will return and take back your capital!"

The back of Roman's hand was so swift that she did not have the opportunity to anticipate it. White-hot pain flared across her cheek, and the impact sent her sprawling to the ground. It radiated through her head, vision blurring as she thought she heard light commotion and cries of protest. Roman crouched over her, and she gaped at him, stunned, having never been struck.

"I already warned you," he said, low. "You are lucky my father wants you unmarred."

He reached down, but she recoiled, scrambling back. She stumbled to her feet despite her bound wrists. A thin trickle of blood traveled down her cheek.

Roman shook his head and sighed. "You do these people no service inspiring false hope."

She stood up straight, shoulders back. "We shall see."

Cerys gave her a look of warning. The same one she'd been giving her the past three days. Katya tugged on the rope, smirking, as they continued toward the castle.

Thea knew had she anything in her belly, it would come right up. She did not know what she was walking toward. Her death, most likely. She thought perhaps they had captured her to make a show of it, as they had in Dunclere. She recalled Dianna's face as they raised her up. The fear in her eyes was an image forever burned in her mind. Thea was not sure she had the courage to face her own death as nobly as Dianna, but she would try. For her people. For her father. For herself. They could have her fear. She would give them that. But they would not take her fight.

When the castle gates opened, her heart dropped.

How quickly her home had changed. Soldiers lined the courtyard. Weapons and supply carts filled the space once occupied by fountains and flower beds. The remnants of both lay broken around them. The blue hammer flag of Ire had been replaced by a black one with silver stitching of a mountain range. The gray of the castle walls that had once acted as a canvas for the colors of Ire now felt like those of a prison. Lifeless and empty.

Thea's lips pressed thin, and she pulled them between her teeth. Her eyes swelled, and despite her best efforts, she couldn't stop herself from crying.

The interior of the castle was no different. The paintings in the main gallery were gone, walls scorched where they once hung. All the draperies with the standard of Ire were no more than ash. Statues depicting the Gods were reduced to crumbled marble. A thousand years of history gone.

Commotion poured out as the tall doors to the throne room creaked open. The chatter and laughter quieted as they crossed the threshold, all in the room turning to watch them approach the dais.

In the space between her captors, Thea saw Lorcan Dracos sitting on her father's throne. Her stomach twisted at the sight, and she made no effort to keep the contempt from her face.

A young woman of strong resemblance stood next to him. She wore the black uniform of a Thranean soldier, but the way she stood with her arms folded behind her back and the softness of her raven-colored hair made it clear she was high-ranking or also royal. Thea knew she could only be his daughter.

She was severe, like her father and brother, but only in her coloring. Her features were round and soft, and her skin had a translucency that made Thea think of pearl. She felt an unspoken familiarity with her that she did not share with Roman, as if believing for the first time the possibility these people were her kin. The girl's frost-blue eyes appraised her in the same manner, but whatever her thoughts, Thea could not read them. Her face was set in stone, giving away nothing.

The rope around her neck came down hard, and Thea fell forward on her knees, Cerys beside her. She looked around the throne room, meeting narrow eyes, jeers, and smirks. She forced herself to hold her chin high, despite being on her knees.

"Father," Roman said, gesturing toward her. "I give you Calithea Ironne. As requested."

Lorcan stood slowly, unnaturally so. The quiet threat she'd felt the day on the bank still emanated from him as he made his way toward her. He motioned with his arms, and rough hands pulled her back to her feet. She sneered up at Ulf, tearing herself free from his grip.

Lorcan stopped two paces from her, examining, as if trying to understand from what she was made. To see what existed beneath her skin. Everything about his manner was disquieting. Every alarm, every bell in her body rang with warning. Though she trembled, she stood tall. She thought of Dianna, of her father, and of her home—and leaned into the rage.

He took a step closer and reached out to grasp her face, turning it from one side to the other. His glacial eyes held a wild marvel as he stared into her, through her, like he was looking for someone else. She drew further disordered when she thought she saw a hint of tenderness in them. "Remarkable," he said, under his breath. He released her face. "Do you know who I am?"

Thea snarled. "You are the Usurper King, the Great Betrayer. A coward and a *monster*," she hissed and spat in his face. She braced herself to be struck. But if her words or actions angered him, he did not show it. One side of his lips twitched as he wiped it away.

"Have I so many names already? I see it is not only your mother's face you've inherited." A few in the crowd chuckled. "My next question for you, Calithea, is do you know who *you* are?"

His presumption fueled her indignation. She drew her shoulders back.

Her cheek still burned from Roman's strike. "I know *exactly* who I am."

"Ulric finally confessed to you?" he asked. "He only held you prisoner for what?" Lorcan's head took on a slight lean. "Twenty and one years is it now?"

Thea scoffed. "This is my home. I was no prisoner."

"Were you not?" He walked around her in slow circles, continuing to appraise. "They've bound you so tightly. How do you bear it?"

Thea swallowed. She would give him nothing.

"Does it not pain you?" he asked, leaning close to her ear, speaking softly.

She looked away as he returned to face her.

"I know about the attacks, Calithea. I know how your gift tries to tear itself free. I can feel it." The peculiar tenderness returned to his eyes. He stepped disturbingly close. At the intimate proximity, his skin appeared almost translucent. She could trace the blue veins beneath. "It thrashes against its restraint," he said. "Your power was meant to sing." He reached up and caught a tear falling down her cheek. "This is a crime."

Thea recoiled, shrinking back from his touch. He stared at her for a moment that drew on far longer than it should. Cerys had told her they would be clever. That they would try to manipulate her. To turn her. Whatever he was doing would not work. "Where is my father?" she asked, from between gritted teeth.

Her words seemed to break his trance, and he exhaled, stepping back. "With your stepmother in her quarters."

Thea straightened, shifting between her feet. She had not expected him to answer, much less for those words to be it. "*They live?*"

"They do."

A sob burst from her. Her head fell forward into her bound hands.

Lorcan leaned close to her again, speaking in confidence. "Perhaps I am not the monster you think."

Thea didn't answer, unsure how to respond. Now that she knew her father lived, she was fearful of angering him. She dropped the indignation from her face. "May I see him?" She asked in earnest. A genuine plea.

His eyes narrowed, considering for a breath. Reaching down for her bound wrists, he severed the bonds with a silver glow from his palm. The skin beneath was red and raw. He did the same to the rope around her neck. Without directing the command to anyone specific, he said, "Take her to see her father. Then heal her and clean her up. Put her in her room under guard."

Thea exhaled, letting the tears that sought to fall make their journey down her cheeks unabated. Her father was alive, and now she would see him. However relieved, however grateful, she could not bring herself to thank him.

Roman stepped up beside her. "What about the other one?"

Lorcan looked down at Cerys as if seeing her for the first time. "Put her in a cell with the others."

Thea wondered what others he spoke of. A guard tugged on her arm, and she turned toward Cerys, dreading their separation. Cerys gave her a reassuring nod as they were led in opposite directions.

Thea turned back to look at Lorcan, and then at his daughter. Both were watching as she was taken away.

Evelynde lay on her bed, knees curled to her chest. Her father sat in a chair by the window, facing away from the door.

Evelynde sat up and blinked. "*Calithea?*"

Ulric sprang from his chair, and Thea took off toward him. Disappointment and relief both twisted his face. She leapt into his arms, and he lifted her from the ground. "I'm sorry," she cried, "we tried to run."

"You're alive. That is all that matters." He pulled back to examine her, his thumb tracing underneath the cut on her cheek and then the burns on her neck. He looked back toward the guards waiting by the door, rage burning behind his eyes. "Are you hurt?"

"No." Thea shook her head. *Not in ways one can see.* "No, Father." She reached for his face, turning it back to her.

Outside of a cut above his left eye and bruises running the length of his right cheek, he appeared intact. Evelynde's eyes were swollen and red from crying, but Thea could find no injury.

Evelynde pulled Thea into an embrace. "Have you any news of Eastwatche?" she asked in a whisper.

Thea glanced back at the soldiers. "No," she said, with regret. "Breeda?"

Her father nodded. "Last we saw, she lives. When the shields collapsed, I gave the order to retreat. Many fell, Thea, and many are prisoner."

"Father," she said, reaching for his hands. "How did it happen so fast? We were scarcely out of the city and the battle was over."

"I don't know," he said, shaking his head. "They had weapons and abilities Breeda and the others had never seen."

"That's time," one of the soldiers commanded.

"Please, a little longer," she pleaded.

The female soldier stepped forward. "*Time.*"

"We must stay strong, Father. We must be patient. Our allies will come to our aid."

Ulric smiled despite his swelling eyes. He took her hands, pulling them to his lips. "And so we shall." Thea turned, but he reached for her, pulling her back. "Do not give in to them. No matter what they say to you."

Thea nodded and squeezed his hand.

"If I come to fetch you," a male soldier warned, "it'll be by your hair."

Thea glared at the man as she walked past. He grabbed her arm, tugging her hard. Her father called out in protest, but she gave him a pleading look, and he stilled.

"I love you," she called over her shoulder as the door closed between them.

54

Neith

"The salt and sea call to me, and I fear I cannot resist."

THE RECOVERED JOURNALS OF SONIA THRONDSEN, 1183 AQ

When they pulled Calithea from the room, it quickly fell into noise again. Her father walked to Roman, thanking and congratulating him. Neith stood next to the throne, trying to make sense of the exchange. She locked eyes with Sam across the room. His expression told her he also perceived the oddity of it. Her father had an eagerness Neith had only seen in him twice before. On the mountain and by the lake.

Calithea looked much like her portrait, only thinner. The only thing the artist did not capture was the color of her eyes. They were green in a way Neith had not seen before. Like the way water can be. She knew her mother's eyes were also green, and she couldn't help but wonder if they were the same.

Neith felt her power, just as her father had described it. Tempestuous, like putting a lid on a boiling pot. Her presence was affecting, not one easily forgotten. It was no easy task to stand with your head held high in such a condition. Not before her father. Neith admired her for it but feared it would only bring her trouble.

Lorcan returned to the throne, calling for wine.

"What will you do with her?" Neith asked him.

"That depends on her." He took a cup from a servant, tipping it up. Neith had noticed his habit of drink escalating of late.

"You will make her the offer?" she asked, walking around to face him.

"I make everyone the offer." He cleared his throat, seemingly still flustered by the meeting. He had not looked at her. His eyes were off in the distance of the room.

"And if she refuses?"

He either did not hear her or did not care to respond.

"Father."

He sat up and looked at her, brows furrowed.

"If she refuses, what will you do with her?"

"We will work to persuade her."

It was the answer she had hoped to hear. Neith turned back to the crowd, finding Sam again.

"If you've no further need of me, I will take my leave."

He nodded, tossing back his wine. "Stay close."

"What will he do with her?" Sam asked as they walked through the construction of the new barracks.

"He claims he will try to turn her."

"That seems a high ask," Sam said, glancing her way. "A simple question is usually all that is offered, no?"

Neith shrugged. "I no longer try to understand the motivations of my father." She glanced back, sidelong.

He smiled, but it was a slight thing. "Fair."

She stopped walking and turned her body toward his. "Is everything all right?"

"Of course," he said. He smiled again, and this one climbed higher, but Neith knew it was a veil.

Neith studied his face for the truth. They'd spent the last six days with little time apart. Most nights he stayed with her. On the ones he didn't, he left late. Only Maeve and Ayla had seen him come and go. Maeve gave no indication for Neith to be concerned. She'd blushed and smiled nervously the first time she'd seen him leaving in the morning. A box of small vials had appeared in Neith's room that evening, which caused Neith herself to blush. She had started to tell Maeve she had the wrong idea and did not need them, but thought better of it. Perhaps one day she would.

Neith had taken notice of little moments when Sam seemed to get lost or slip into himself. Something weighed on him. It was the kind of look one recognizes on another only once they have worn it themselves.

She reached for him, withdrawing her hand when she remembered where they were. "Will you come to my room tonight?"

He looked down. "It would be smart for us to spend a few nights apart. I think we have been taking too many risks."

Neith nodded, trying to conceal her disappointment. He was likely right, but it still felt like a rejection.

They approached their unit's camp, and Petra walked to meet them. "What was so important to drag you away from training?"

"Roman returned with Calithea Ironne and the Esērii woman," Neith answered.

"I see," Petra said, looking from Neith to Sam. "And we are… unhappy about this?" Her brow furrowed as she studied both faces, trying to make sense of their shared mood.

"Of course not," Neith said quickly. She felt Sam's heavy gaze on her.

"All right," Petra said, lips pursed. She held out a wooden sword to Neith. "Then let's get back to it."

She'd sparred with Petra until she could no longer raise the sword above her shoulder. Max took the entire unit through shield practice, and they ended the day's training wielding water. They trained longer and harder than any other unit, and it was starting to show.

The Burning Moon would soon be upon them, and the weather screamed of its approach. Sam, Petra, Max, and others from the southern continent appeared unscathed by the heat. It made her curious how hot it was in the south, and if she'd survive it. Every window in the castle remained open throughout the day and night. The only fires that burned were those in the kitchens.

Her arms and back ached, but it was becoming a sensation she had grown to appreciate. She called for a bath and, despite the heat, raised the temperature of the water so high she had to sink slowly into it. Maeve had added salt and oils at Ayla's instruction to ease her stiff muscles.

She'd asked Maeve to bring her supper to her room. As the days moved on, she spent less and less time in the common areas, dining halls, and throne room. Her patience for the antics of many of the other soldiers grew thin. She craved peace. She craved quiet.

After lazing in the bath for an hour, Neith slipped into one of the silk shifts left by the room's previous occupant, retiring to a chair by one of the windows. The soft orange glow of sundown poured into the room. She sat, picking at her supper while flipping through a book on the Ironne royal family she had taken from the library on her walk up.

There was little information on Calithea outside of her date of birth. She was born on the twelfth day of the Blossom Moon, in the year 1183 AQ, making her twenty and one winters. The name of her mother was listed as Eadda Torsney. Neith couldn't help but feel sorrow for her, knowing she'd spent her entire life not knowing half of herself. Neith had not known her mother either, but she'd known the truth of who she was, and there was something substantive to that.

Neith looked up to a gentle knock at the door.

"Enter," she called out, assuming it was Maeve come to fetch her plate.

It was Sam who came through. She'd been so engrossed in the book she had not felt him approach. Neith cocked her head, watching him walk closer. "I thought you said it would be smart to spend some time apart?"

"It appears I cannot stay away," he said, one side of his lips tugging up. He knelt in front of her, his hands coming to rest on the tops of her thighs. "But I have come with an agenda."

"And that is?" she asked, heart quickening at his touch.

"To ask your forgiveness for my behavior earlier."

Neith closed her book, setting it on the desk beside them. "There is nothing to forgive. You do not have to share your every thought with me." She reached up to cup his face. "Even if I wish to know them."

"It is not that I do not want to."

Her brows knitted. "What stops you?"

Sam took a breath, considering his words. "It is simply that I find there are times I cannot speak."

Neith sighed, familiar with the feeling. "I believe I understand. As I said before, there is nothing to forgive."

He gave her a soft smile, one she felt. "I have a gift for you."

"A gift?" Neith sat up. She had been given many things in life, but few felt like gifts. He reached into his pocket and pulled out a silver chain, holding it up between them. A pendant of obsidian carved in the shape of a crescent moon hung from its end.

Her heart skipped as she studied the smooth ripples in the black stone. "Where did you come by this?"

"I made it. Well, the pendant. I bartered for the chain." Sam tucked loose hair behind one of her ears. "It is silver and obsidian, like your earrings."

Neith reached up and touched the black stone hanging from one of her ears. Her eyes swelled, and she cleared her throat. "What did you barter?"

His lips curled into a sly smile, and Neith watched their entire journey. "That is my business."

"It is beautiful." She wanted to spring forward and wrap her arms around him. Instead, she calmly asked, "Will you fasten it on me?"

He gently lifted her hair, pulling it to one shoulder. His hands came around either side of her neck, connecting the necklace around her. She reached up, clasping it in her hand.

"Thank you," she whispered, and swallowed, determined not to cry. "I will wear it always." She leaned forward, bringing her lips to his. His arms wrapped around her, and her legs parted to bring him closer.

Neith had spent much time kissing him the past days. A familiarity was growing between their bodies. A comfort that she craved. Neith often found herself recoiling from touch. With Sam, she found she could not be close enough.

He pulled back to look at the necklace. "I fear it is not worthy of you."

She wanted to say it was she who wasn't worthy.

His eyes trailed down her body as if just made aware only a thin layer of silk covered her. She watched the bob of his throat as he swallowed, fully conscious of how little it concealed the peaks of her breasts.

He started to pull away, but she wrapped her legs around him, leaning forward so that as he sat on his heels, she went with him, settling in on his lap.

"Neith," he said, low. His eyes were heavy with warning.

It did nothing to dissuade her. She tightened her grip on him.

"I fear I cannot stay," he said, leaning his forehead against hers.

"You have a more pressing matter?" she teased.

"Not of my choosing. Magnus has called for me." He did not look happy about it. "I only stopped here on my way."

Neith huffed and pursed her lips. "Very well." She leaned back, grasping the back of his neck for support. "You will return later?"

"If I can." He sat up, lifting her back into the chair, leaving a gentle kiss on her temple before making for the door.

She tapped her fingers on the desk, showing her displeasure at his choice of departure.

He stopped and glanced over his shoulder. Neith slowly lifted the silk to expose one of her thighs, letting the loose fabric drape between her parted legs.

Sam turned on his heels and marched back, leaning over the chair. He stopped just before her lips. "You are intent on making this difficult for me?"

"I simply tap my fingers." Neith stretched her neck, trying to reach him.

"Yet, it is enough."

His hands closed around her face as his lips crashed onto hers. He moved so fast it took her a moment to return the kiss. His tongue explored every part of her mouth, hungry, needy. She reached for him, tugging him closer. *Yes.* This was what she wanted.

His lips left hers, moving to her neck as one hand gripped the outside of her bare thigh. She wanted him to press harder, to hold her tighter, and she tried arching up to find more contact. She tore at his vest, angry she couldn't feel more of him through the leather of it.

The buttons gave way, but he released her, standing and stepping back. His chest heaved as he stared down at her, heavy and heated. Heady amusement teased his features as he laughed lightly, shaking his head. "Know that there is nowhere I would rather be than alone in this room with you." Sam exhaled, making some sort of exasperated groan as he ran his hands through his hair.

Neith smiled up at him, feeling something like satisfied she had stirred him so. He gave her the same look of warning he had earlier before turning to leave.

She watched him walk from the room. All of her thoughts then fixed on how she would extract such a moment from him again.

55

Thea

"There are many ways to break a person. Some are more delicate in body than in mind."

ETHEREAL WARFARE
SYMOND TALIESIN, 945 AQ

Three soldiers led her through the halls of Highclere as if they knew the castle as well as she. Every face she passed was unknown to her. Every tapestry, rug, or décor of any kind bearing the colors of Ire was gone. It was her home, but not, stripped and bare. Thraneans in black uniforms loomed around every corner like a piceous cloud. An infectious disease.

Despite the state of the castle, her room appeared untouched. The last book she'd read was still sitting on her desk, her dressing gown draped over the chair.

"Sit," the female soldier said, pushing her forward.

Thea turned around. "Sit?"

"*Sit down,*" the soldier said.

Thea folded her arms. "Anywhere? Or have you a preference?"

The woman flashed her a look that warned not to try her patience. Thea glared at her, then made for the chair by the window.

A short time later, the door creaked, and an old man in black robes came through, followed by four female attendants. What little hair remained on his head was gray and coarse. He wore thick spectacles and a look of disinterest.

He hobbled toward her, gesturing for her to stand. Without meeting her eyes, he examined the cut on her cheek and the burns on her neck and wrists. He didn't speak to her unless to direct her to move.

When he seemed satisfied by his review, he held his hand out over her cheek. A dark red glow emanated from his palm, washing over her skin. Thea stiffened, waiting for pain. Instead, the sting eased, and her cheek itched. He moved to her neck and wrists.

When finished, he turned and left without words. Her fingertips grazed her wounds, finding them wounds no more. She looked at the guards and attendants around her for an explanation. None was given.

The attendants immediately went to work combing through her hair and unlacing her dress. If she resisted, she was chastised. Any request to do something herself was denied. All questions went unanswered.

The three soldiers never left her side. Even when she bathed. She had been placed in a bathing gown, but it did little to protect her modesty. One of the guards leered at her as the attendant scrubbed her body. He had a long scar that ran from his hairline over his right eye, down to his jaw. Thea held his gaze, telling him she was unaffected by his degradation. She hoped her falsehood appeared true.

The second soldier was a tall, slender man with red hair and a permanent scowl. The third, the woman, whom the others referred to as Calix, had sleek black hair cut blunt at her chin.

After she was bathed, she was dressed in a pale blue gown that fell off her shoulders, crossing over her chest. An elaborate gold necklace and pearl earrings were chosen for her. The attendants had left her hair long and simple, brushed out in soft waves.

When they'd finished, like the old man, they left without speaking. Thea looked expectantly at the guards, but still, they said nothing.

"I cannot imagine you've dressed me up so to sit in my room."

The female guard peered at her. "Sit down."

Exhaling, she turned and took the chair by the window again, gazing out at the now-rising moon. Its reflection in the lake no longer existed. The lake that Thea loved so dearly was still a slab of solid ice.

Sitting idle, her mind began to work. Cerys had told her to be smart and bide time. That help would come. Thea tried to place her faith in that. The door swung open, and another soldier entered, gesturing for her to follow.

He led her down the corridors of the royal wing to the ground level, her guards close behind. He opened the door to her family's private dining room. The room where they ate, laughed, and danced together, nearly every day of her life.

The family table had been moved to the side, and a smaller two-person table put in its place.

Lorcan sat at one end. He looked her over and smiled, if one could call it so. Thea could not think of a word for his manner. It was neither warm nor cold. Neither inviting nor forbidding. He gestured for her to sit.

She obliged and, with wary eyes, watched him fill her chalice with wine. The door hitched, and she flinched, turning back to look in its direction. They were alone.

Lorcan set the carafe on the table, leaning back in his chair, eyes locked on hers. "Tell me what it is you are thinking."

Thea decided there was no purpose in trying to hide it. Her face, her trembling hands, no doubt gave it away. "I am thinking that you terrify me."

"That is not my desire, nor my design."

"I am a prisoner of your war, am I not?" She had spoken too quickly, and it came out with accusation. Thea took a calming breath, reminding herself he held her father, stepmother, and many others she loved. And her home.

His eyes took in her earrings, necklace, then gown, lingering on her bare shoulders. It made her want to squirm. "You do not look like a prisoner."

"A gown and a little gold change nothing."

Lorcan chuckled. "I assure you, a prisoner you are not. But if you wish to experience the disparity, it can be managed." His look was softer than his words. Every instinct told her he was not the sort of man to make idle threats.

Thea bristled, determined not to be intimidated by him. "Why am I here?"

"I would like to know you." He reached for his cup, sipping from the silver chalice, and made a sound of gratification. "It has been a while since I've had Parthenean wine. It is not easy to come by in the mountains." When she didn't respond, he gestured at the plate in front of her. "Eat."

It was piled high with some kind of braised meat, with carrots and turnips. Her mouth watered, and her stomach growled. Thea lifted her fork, taking a small bite. He watched her attentively, seemingly pleased she had heeded his command. Her eyes closed when the food hit her tongue. She was starving. She wanted to tear into the food like a madwoman, but she chewed slowly, returning the fork to the table.

His eyes were so extraordinarily blue they were hard to look into.

His long black hair was pulled back, slick and neat, his face clean-shaven. Deep lines etched his forehead and the space around his eyes. He donned a gray tunic in lieu of the uniform he'd worn earlier. Bathed and changed. For her?

Thea did not understand. His appearance, the meal, her gown. She could not ascertain the purpose of it all. "What do you wish to know?"

"Many things," he said. "First and foremost, I would like to know what it is that you want."

Thea let out an exasperated laugh. "What *I* want?" She shook her head. "I do not think you want to hear what I want."

He gestured his arms out to the sides in invitation. "Try me."

She reached for her fork, twirling it between her fingers. It was not the first time she'd considered stabbing a man with one.

As if reading her thoughts, he smiled, devilish and knowing.

Thea sneered and dropped the fork. "I want you to march your army out of Highclere. Out of Ire."

"Done." He said it so quickly and straight-faced that Thea laughed again. He remained austere.

"I do not understand. Is this some sort of game I am too dense to make sense of?"

He chuckled again and reached for his wine. "I assure you, it is not."

Thea stared at him in perplexity, searching his eyes for sincerity, and found it. It only fueled her bewilderment. She grabbed her cup, pretending to drink, trying to buy time. That was what Cerys would do.

His gaze never left her as she stalled. Her chest tightened when she realized what he was waiting for. She set her cup down, clutching her fingers around the stem so he could not see them tremble. "And what do you want?"

One side of his mouth quirked. "I want you to join us."

"*Pardon?*"

He didn't repeat himself.

Her lips parted in genuine disbelief. "What use am I to you? I would think you'd more likely desire to kill me, but then what would be the purpose of this charade?" She gestured at the table overflowing with food and the gown she wore.

"I want to help you."

Thea laughed with an icy edge. She reached for her wine, taking two large gulps before placing it back on the table, sliding it toward him for a refill. She could not believe he was serious. Her eyes moved to the fork on her plate, a familiar thought returning. She looked up at him, angry, no patience for tricks.

"I can help you with your gift, Calithea," he said, sipping his wine.

She dipped her head in artificial sincerity. "Can you help me be rid of it?"

"No," he said, refilling her cup. "That would be a tragedy. I will teach you to use it. No longer a burden to you, but an asset."

Thea searched his eyes for deception, finding none. "And why would you do that?"

"I offer every Etherborn the same. If I were your enemy, why would I seek to strengthen you?"

He murdered her people and now expected she would join him? She thought he must truly be mad. It was a prospect that frightened her. One could reason with a bad man, but not a mad one. "Did you make that offer to my mother before you murdered her?"

A quick flash of something dark washed over his face, but he flexed his jaw, and it retreated. "Is that what Ulric told you?" he asked, and scoffed. "I suppose he believes that to be true. The fool." He reached for his wine, finishing whatever was in the cup. "Would you like to know the truth?"

Thea didn't speak, so he continued.

"Sonia Throndsen ended her own life."

"*Lies.*"

"No." Lorcan shook his head. "Many people have and will continue to tell you lies, Calithea, but I am not among them." He sat back in his chair and paused, as if settling in for the story. "When we landed in Seahenge, we took the city with little resistance. Faela was gone. Her army decimated. We didn't know it at the time, but your mother had put thousands on ships to Vikandal before fleeing down the coast on horseback. We tracked her and cornered her on a cliff. It had been a ploy to pull our attention while they sailed away. She was just standing there, waiting for us, staring out at the sea." He looked away for the first time. "She was the most courageous person I've ever known. I learned much from her."

Thea shifted. Her inability to detect deception in him sent her spinning. He appeared genuine, and she worried she was not smart enough to withstand his manipulations of her.

"I'll never forget the look on her face when she turned around. There wasn't a trace of fear. Only peace, acceptance... satisfaction. She wore a pale blue dress that billowed out behind her in the wind, her belly swollen with you. Or so we thought. Her hair was wild, golden, like yours. The same defiant green eyes that are looking at me now." He looked over every inch of her face. "It really is remarkable how much you look like her."

Thea felt her eyes swell. She tightened her face to fight it off.

"She could have fought on. She could have killed several of us before we ended her. Her sister pleaded with her to reconsider, to join with us, to think of her child. But Sonia left the pleas unanswered."

Thea looked at him in bemusement as she was sure she saw true sorrow on his face. During the parley, her father had made a comment about her mother to Lorcan that she hadn't understood at the time. "You cared for her."

The look in his eyes gave his answer. "She gave us no warning before she struck the cliff, sending herself plummeting into the sea. To a cold and lonely death."

Thea watched him intently as he told the story.

"I grieved her," he said mournfully. "I am the one who pulled her body from the water. I am the one who put her in the ground. In a place of honor, where she belonged. I can take you there one day. To her grave."

"Why?" Thea swallowed, her voice shaky. "Why would she end her own life?"

"At the time, I did not know. It wasn't until later that we discovered she had given birth to you mere hours before she died. When we were on that cliff, you were on a ship headed for Eastwatche. Sonia's motivations were known only to her."

Thea studied his face. He spoke about her mother as if she was someone he loved. Respected. Not his enemy. Her gut told her he spoke true, but she had no means of assurance. Her father had withheld so much from her it was inevitable there was more. There would be a time for discovering such truths, but this was not it.

"Her sister, my aunt, is she here?" Thea asked.

"No," Lorcan said quickly. He reached for a chain around his neck, turning whatever lay at its end between his fingers.

"Let us say that I believe all you have said. Have you forgotten already that you sit in my father's seat, at my father's table? You murdered our people and waged war unprovoked. In what world do you think I would agree to join you?"

"This one, Calithea. I am not my father. Ire is not my enemy. I do not intend to sit on its throne. My fight is with the tyrants in silk robes at the Citadel. I came to Highclere because I need its resources. Its ships. Its soldiers. *You.*"

She laughed without intention.

He scowled. "Whatever you've been told, make no mistake, if you knew the truth, it is they you would brand your villain. You can dress it up in oaths of honor, but underneath, it rots the same. Corruption, greed… deception. The council doesn't care about justice, or service, or protecting the idleborn. They only care about one thing. *Power*, Calithea. Maintaining what they have and obtaining more. And they achieve it at the expense of indoctrinated children."

"Is that not what you have done?"

"I am going to build a world where people like us do not have to live in the shadows of it. A world where a father does not have to bind and blind his daughter to her true nature. A world where someone like you is revered, not treated like a pet." He spoke with a conviction that was difficult to disregard. "The only wise decision your father made on your behalf was refusing to hand you over to them. What allegiance have you to the Esērii?" He shook his head. "You didn't even know they existed. They, along with your father, lied to you, manipulated you, bound you. It was they who imprisoned you. Not I." He leaned forward in his chair, palms flat on the table. "I would set you free."

Thea could not deny there was some truth in his words. She felt naïve and outmatched sitting across from a man who had built an army unrivaled by another, in secret, for over twenty years. That sort of task required patience, intelligence, and fierce determination. It was not something many could accomplish. "If you do not intend to take my father's throne, what are your plans for it?"

Lorcan relaxed back. "If we can come to an agreement, I will restore your father as king. Your eldest brother will remain its heir. Once we've taken what we need, we will leave. Ire will pledge its allegiance to Thrane. Its army and navy will join our cause. But, in all other aspects, things will return as they were."

"A vassal state."

"I do not care for such labels, but you may distribute them at your leisure." He picked up his fork, a piece of meat speared on the end.

Thea watched him chew. "Why are you bringing this to me? Should it not be my father with whom you make this proposition?"

He wiped his mouth with a linen napkin. "There is no agreement to be had if you do not join us."

Thea tried to think what her father would tell her to do. Knowing she was at Lorcan's mercy, she still couldn't withhold her contempt. She thought of Dianna's lifeless eyes, and her rage returned. Her face twisted into a snarl. "I will never join you. My father will never agree." Her voice grew in scorn as she continued. "Our allies will come to our aid, and my brothers will march on Highclere and take back our home."

"Do not be so hasty, Calithea," he said between bites. "I do not ask twice."

"You need not start with me."

"Unyielding stubbornness." His jaw flexed and exhaled. He looked more aggravated than angry. Impatient. Like one dealing with a petulant child. "I can see that you need time to think it over. That is disappointing, but not unexpected. I would expect nothing less from the daughter of Sonia." He took a final forkful from his plate before tossing his napkin over it. "I've enjoyed our time together, but I can see that it has come to an end. You should finish your meal. It may be some time before another presents itself."

Thea held his gaze as she slowly lifted her hand. His eyes narrowed as he watched. With a quick swipe, she knocked her setting from the table, the metal plate and cup clattering against the stone floor. A guard appeared in the doorway, but Lorcan held up a hand. She was furious, but fearful she had gone too far.

A laugh burst from him, taking her by surprise. It continued, and she watched him in perplexity as he bellowed in genuine delight.

When it quieted, he sat staring, fingers tapping the tabletop.

Without warning, he sprang to his feet. Any trace of amusement vanished, replaced by wild rage. He flipped the table on its side, and Thea fell out of her chair, startled, scrambling back as he stormed toward her.

His boot came down on the skirts of her dress, ripping from the resistance. Reaching down with one arm, he wrapped his hand around her neck and raised her up with ease. She clawed and pried in vain as his fingers sank into her throat, barricading her lungs. He watched her eyes, taking in the desperation in them.

She thrashed and kicked, but he tightened his grip. Thea thought surely her neck would snap.

Her vision tunneled, and just as she feared she would black out, he released her, and she fell to her knees, heaving, palms flat against the cool stone floor. Her lungs and throat burned as she struggled. When she finally inhaled, she gasped, her panic as severe as the pain of it. Her heaves quickly turned to sobs.

He knelt, leaning close, his lips hovering above her ear. "I want you to know what comes next gives me no pleasure. I truly hope you find your way." He lifted her chin, giving her one last look. His free hand rose, and his fingertips stroked her cheek. She didn't have the fight to pull away from him.

"Our lady here needs some time to consider her options. Take her below." Lorcan released her and stood.

She was still trying to steady her breath when a firm grip on both arms pulled her to her feet. She scrambled to keep up with the pace of the soldier forcing her forward. She looked back at Lorcan right before they crossed through the door. He was just standing there, arms crossed, watching.

The soldier handed her over to her guards. The two men held her arms, one at each side.

"I thought you might be smarter than that," Calix said, moving to face her.

Thea tried to straighten herself, eyes defiant, though small cries still escaped her.

Calix laughed. "We'll see how long this act lasts. What do you say, boys? How long before she breaks? Two days? Three?"

The scarred man leaned closer, his breath hot and sour. Thea tried to turn away from him, but he grabbed her face, fingertips digging into the flesh of her cheeks. "Give her to me. I'll have her done in a day."

The red-haired man chuckled.

"Let's find out then," Calix said with a cruel smile. "Shall we?"

They dragged her through the castle to the staircase leading to the lower levels. Thea tried to prepare herself to be locked in a cell. Possibilities of all sorts raced through her mind on the descent. Lorcan had already told her she wouldn't be fed. Would they withhold water? Would they hurt her? Her entire body trembled, and her throat ached from his assault.

As the air grew colder, it also grew darker. Part of her wanted to cry that she was sorry, that she agreed. That she would do anything if they would only take her back up.

She stumbled all the way down to the last level. They continued past every cell, and Thea grew more frightened. When they reached the end of the block, the stone floor gave way to dirt. Calix moved in front and pulled back a thick black fabric cover, revealing a large hole in the ground.

Understanding took hold, and Thea thrashed. The two male guards held her still as the woman took a blade from her belt and cut down the length of her dress and undergarments. The other guards ripped the ruined fabric off her shoulders, leaving her bare.

She screamed and struggled as they forced her forward. She tried to throw herself to the ground, but it was useless. They were impossibly strong. "*Please!* I'm sorry—"

The guards released her arms, and a thump to the back so violent it stole her breath sent her sprawling into the abyss. Thea hit the far wall of dirt and rock, feeling something in her arm snap. White-hot pain radiated through her right side, and she landed on her back, smacking the ground, eyes wide, breath caught. She cradled her mangled arm and looked up as the guard with the scar peered over the edge.

"Sleep tight, Princess." He pulled the fabric over the opening.

She inhaled right as it went dark.

Thea screamed. So severe it burned as it burst free. The terror, the desperation in it, was frightening, even to her.

Scrambling to her feet, she tried climbing the walls with her one good arm, but the earth crumbled in her hands, falling into her eyes and open mouth. It was too dark to see her own hands in front of her face. She could hear nothing but her own pleas.

"Please don't leave me here!" she cried—guttural, and pleading. The horror at her own sounds fueled her fright. "*Please,*" she cried, stumbling through the dark. It was the innate sense of dread, the primal instinct to live, that drove her. Her senses were wild with the understanding that this was a place of pain, a place of danger, and she had to get out. She persisted in trying to climb and dig her way up until every shred of strength in her body was consumed.

Collapsing against the wall, she slowly sank to the ground. The memory of Marten in the room by the garden played in her mind. Of how he leisurely, and so tenderly, lowered them, still in embrace. It ripped another plea from her.

She pulled her knees in, cradling her broken arm like a babe across her chest. Her screams had turned to sobs, which in time turned to whimpers.

"Please," she whispered to no one. "I'll be good, I swear."

Thea had never experienced darkness like this. Silence like this. When the terror overcame her, she would cry out. She tried counting, reciting poetry, anything to distract her mind as the hours passed. Her thoughts would always wander back to the unknown. How long would they keep her there? Could she withstand it? Her arm throbbed, and she was glad she could not see it. When there were no more tears, no more screams, she lay down on the cold earth, praying to fall asleep. Desperate for any kind of reprieve, no matter how fleeting.

One moment, she was terrified they would return. The next, that they wouldn't. She had tried to play their game, to show them who she was, but her indignation had awarded her nothing. They didn't fear her. To them, she was just a girl, and a foolish one at that. Thea knew they would win.

They already were.

56

Thea

"To be bound is to be a prisoner in one's own skin. A captive of one's own mind."

THE WAY OF ETHER

ASHERAH GALANIS, FIRST CONSUL, THE CITADEL, 808 AQ

Thea had never minded the dark. Not even as a child. But she hadn't known true darkness before the pit.

When she first woke, she gasped, paralyzed in terror, fearing she'd gone blind. The terror did not leave when she remembered where she was.

She had no way of knowing if it was day or night or how many days, if any, had passed. When she was awake, all her efforts were engaged in keeping herself calm. She continued reciting verses or hummed the melody of the Arabonde.

When the sound of her own voice no longer soothed, she took to pacing. She counted steps from one side of the pit to the other, trying to determine its size.

They had not taken her jewelry when they'd stripped her. She tried to find some method to turn the adornments into a tool, or weapon, but could not come up with a means. There was little she could do with one arm in the dark. She ended up burying the earrings and necklace with no real understanding of why.

When terror overtook her, she rocked back and forth, soothing herself with mumbled words. Her throat was too hoarse to scream. She had nothing left in her body with which to cry.

Thea tried to think of the ones she loved who needed her. Her thoughts wavered back and forth from lament that she hadn't agreed to Lorcan's offer, to blind rage at what they'd done to her. One moment, she felt resolved to accept. The next, she imagined ways she might kill him if set free. How she might drive a blade into his heart and laugh as he bled out.

She lost count of how many times she'd fallen asleep. Her dreams bled into her waking thoughts, and it became difficult to discern them. Sometimes a comfort, sometimes a horror. If their aim was to drive her to madness, Thea knew it would work, and she did not think it would take long.

She was lying in the dirt, knees pulled to her chest, whispering a prayer to Cassia, when she heard the fabric cover move.

Dim light from a torch was nearly enough to blind. She squinted, trying to determine if it was another dream.

A ladder descended into the pit. Thea looked up expectantly, waiting for instruction. When it didn't come, she eyed the ladder, hesitant. Anxious to get out, but afraid of what awaited her. She also feared it wasn't real. That if she touched it, it would disappear.

"Climb," a man's voice commanded from above.

She was weak, and climbing with one arm was no easy task. When she reached the top, she found the old man in black robes waiting with her guards. She tried to cover her naked breasts with her uninjured arm, unable to meet their eyes.

The old man wrapped a cloak around her shoulders and gestured for her to follow.

He walked down a long corridor, Thea limping behind. She thought she recognized it as the one she fled through with Cerys during the siege, but she couldn't be sure. It all looked the same. And her mind wasn't working properly. She wasn't even sure she was awake.

He stopped at a door a short walk from the pit. A large key turned the lock, and she followed him into the room.

It was small and dark, lit only by the torch in his hand. It held a square table with a single chair, a straw cot, and a chamber pot. He set the torch in a sconce on the back of the door as he gestured for her to sit.

He pulled back the cloak, examining her arm. She whimpered when he moved it. She didn't look. She knew it was malformed.

After reviewing it to his satisfaction, he held his hands above her shoulder. The same deep red glow he used before covered her arm. His fingers moved, and her arm ached. The pain accelerated until she felt a light snap, which caused her to cry out, followed by immediate relief. Thea moved her arm, finding it healed.

"Thank you," she said, her voice barely audible.

The old man's eyes met hers with a crabbed expression. He walked from the room, returning with a pitcher and wooden cup, setting them on the table in front of her. She eyed the stream of water desperately as he poured.

"Drink."

She needed no further invitation. Thea gulped the water until every drop was gone.

"More?"

She nodded, and he refilled it.

"Slow down," he cautioned.

Thea tried to, but she was thirsty in a way she had not known was possible. He watched her as she drank.

"Do yourself a favor," he said, "and don't resist."

Her eyes flicked up to his. She found them in warning, and it reignited the panic she'd somehow put to rest.

He left the pitcher, and Thea drank directly from it until it was bone dry. She sat dirty and alone, too afraid to move. There was no comfort to be had. Her mind lived in a persistent state of fear for what came next.

The room had a heavy, wet smell. Thin streams of water trailed down its stone walls, flowing beneath the sparse layer of straw strewn about. She had known such rooms existed in the lower levels of the castle, but she'd never had cause to see them. It was a sad place, and she would have been happy to go her whole life never having done so.

Thea did not think much time had passed before the door creaked. A woman she did not recognize walked in, dragging a chair behind her. She placed it at the opposite end of the table. Like all from Thrane, she was dressed in black. Her blonde hair was tied back in a slick knot at the nape of her neck. She looked polished, important. She sat down in the newly placed chair, resting her interlaced hands on the table.

"Calithea, my name is Nykka Halvorsen," she said with a heavy Vikan accent. She had dark blue eyes with fine lines at the crease. They weren't exactly kind, but nor were they threatening. Thea thought her somewhere around the age of thirty and five. Her eyes moved, studying Thea in the same manner all Etherborn did. She extended her arm, palm up across the table. "Give me your hand," she beckoned.

Thea retreated in her chair.

Nykka smiled softly. Thea felt the hair on her arms rise as a strange vibration blanketed her skin.

"Give me your hand, Calithea Ironne," Nykka repeated. This time, her words were soothing, almost songlike.

Not wanting to disappoint her, Thea did as instructed. The vibration intensified as it trailed up her arm and into her chest. It set off something inside her, a warning telling her something was wrong. She hadn't wanted to give her hand. Realization smacked into her, and she jerked her hand away.

Nykka cocked an eyebrow. "Interesting."

Thea didn't speak, but watched the woman apprehensively, pulling the cloak protectively around her body. Nykka looked down, pursing her lips as she discovered Thea wore nothing but the cloak. She walked from the room, returning a few moments later with no explanation.

"What did you feel when you pulled your arm away?" she asked. When Thea didn't respond, she leaned over the table. "It is only a question."

Thea bit her lips. She was terrified to disobey, but averse to help them. She knew they could do things. *Influence* her, as Cerys had called it.

Nykka stood, walking around the table to kneel in front of Thea. Her eyes were tender, and Thea did not feel it was deception.

"If we are not successful in our work together, the next person they send will not have such a gentle touch. I am not the person you should fear." Nykka's stormy eyes implored her. "If you are amenable, this is where you stay. If not, those soldiers will throw you back into the pit."

Thea's eyes went wide. She did not want to go back.

"Do we have an understanding, Calithea?"

Thea nodded with sharp, quick movements.

"Good." Nykka smiled and returned to her seat. "What did you feel when you pulled your arm away?"

"Alarm." Thea cleared her throat. Speaking was not yet a comfortable action. "Like something telling me I had not acted willingly."

Nykka appraised her. "But you felt compelled to comply at first?"

"Yes."

The process continued for hours. Nykka used her powers in varying degrees. Sometimes it worked, sometimes not. After, she asked questions and Thea answered them. Repeat.

"We will stop here today." Nykka stood. She walked toward the door, turning back as she opened it. "If your behavior remains agreeable, this torch will remain lit. If you attempt to use this fire in any way, it will be removed. Do you understand?"

Thea nodded, and the door closed. She sat still. She hadn't heard a lock.

Swallowing, she stood, taking slow, timid steps toward the door. She tried to listen and could hear nothing but the water. It was cool beneath her bare feet.

The door creaked, and she retreated until her back met the wall. A young woman walked in, arms full of folded material, followed by another holding a washbasin and pitcher. The guard with the scar watched from the doorway.

Neither attendant looked her way before leaving what they carried and exiting the room. The guard lingered, looking from her to the washbasin. Thea tightened the cloak around her. She would rather remain in filth than let him set an eye on her once more. She sat down on the straw floor in protest.

He huffed, then smirked, as if he found her resistance amusing. When he finally relented, she heard a key enter the lock and turn, sealing her in.

Thea looked through what she'd been brought. It was a simple white shift and a gray linen blanket. She ran the fabric through her fingers, grateful for the dignity it would provide, but vowed it would do nothing to quell the hate she felt.

Thea drank most of the water, leaving scarce enough to wash in. There was little she could do about the dirt beneath her nails and clumped in her hair, but she could at least wash her face. She pulled the shift over her head, noticing a slight ache in the arm that had been broken.

She let herself get lost in time, huddled beneath the blanket, thankful for such a simple comfort. The gentle sounds of running water soothed her to sleep.

She awoke sometime later to the creaking of the door. Thea sat up at the scent of porridge, belly rumbling at the prospect of food. An attendant entered the room and placed a tray on the table. She left without words.

Thea sprang from the cot to find a small bowl of plain oats. There was no spoon, so she tipped it up to her lips. It was bitter and unsweetened. Only oats and water. It mattered not. She ate the entire thing in seconds, using her dirty fingers to scrape the bowl.

It was not enough. Her belly growled and ached.

She returned to her cot, pulling her knees to her chest. The pains intensified, and she feared the porridge would come back up.

Nykka returned, and they resumed their "work," as she called it. Thea did all that was asked of her, not understanding its intent or purpose. She could never be sure how much time had lapsed between visits. Nor how long she slept in between. It felt like it was never more than a couple of hours, as if the intention was to keep her in a constant state of deprivation. However daunting, she was still grateful she was not in the pit.

Thea had no other visitors save for the occasional attendant bringing her food. It was never enough to satiate, and always something plain, like the oat porridge or stale bread. Sometimes Nykka would bring her an apple, only letting her have it once they were done. The first time Thea cried, eating it slowly, savoring every sweet bite.

Compliance was not the only thing Thea feigned. She had discovered nuances in the tests. She could differentiate when Nykka was manipulating her bindings, and when she was attempting to Influence her. The more she understood, the less effect Nykka had.

They were strange sensations she did not think she could describe to another, too complex for her own mind to grasp. They were not thoughts, nor feelings, but something uncharted, as if she were acquiring a new sense. It terrified and intrigued her.

Thea grew worried Nykka was taking notice of her ability to resist, so she played a part, pretending the Influence successful. Her confidence in her ability to playact wavered as Nykka became further frustrated with each visit. She eyed Thea constantly, her skepticism apparent. Thea simply didn't know what to do. Any outcome seemed to anger her. The kindness Nykka had originally shown her disappeared.

During their last visit, she'd grown so displeased she snatched the apple from the table when she left. Thea was not brought food between that visit and the next.

The lock clicked, and the door swung open, recklessly, as if it had been kicked. Thea jumped when it smacked against the wall, watching with wide eyes as Nykka stalked through. The look on her face caused Thea to swallow. She was already angry.

Nykka sat in her chair and gestured for Thea to do the same. She didn't speak. Thea stood, startled by the abrupt entry, but did as commanded.

Nykka stared at her for a moment before she reached for something on her belt. She grasped the hilt of a small blade, placing it on the table between them. Thea's eyes flicked up to hers.

"Take the blade," Nykka said.

Thea shook her head, though she wanted the blade more than she wanted air. She simply knew it would do her no good. The warm vibrations of Influence washed over her.

"Take the blade, Calithea," Nykka repeated.

Of her own accord, Thea reached for it with trembling fingers. The Influence fell away.

"Now cut your arm."

"*What?* No." Thea dropped the blade, and it clanged on the table. The Influence returned.

Nykka's eyes narrowed as she leaned closer. "Pick up the blade and cut your arm."

Hand shaking, Thea grasped the hilt, hovering the blade above her left forearm. She looked up with pleading eyes.

The vibrations intensified.

"Cut yourself," Nykka commanded.

Fearing more what would happen if they found her out, Thea exhaled, sliding the sharp steel across her flesh. She tried to keep the pain of it from her face, but it burned as blood oozed from the thin cut. The Influence fell away.

Nykka leaned back, appraising as she often did. "Again," she said. "Deeper."

Thea looked down at her arm and shook her head. "No."

"No?" Nykka asked, brow cocked. She stood, hands grasping the edge of the table. Her eyes grew dark as she leaned closer. Influence swarmed the room, but it had no effect other than turning her belly. "Calithea, you will cut yourself again."

Thea wished the Influence would work. She did not think she had the will. Lips quivering, she lifted the knife and swallowed, once again drifting the blade above her skin.

Nykka's power amplified, now a buzzing in her head. "*Now.*"

Thea clenched her teeth and sank the blade, quick and deep, before her mind could protest the act. For a breath, there was no pain, only the horrified feeling of being split open. She watched as her skin parted for the sharp metal, blood pooling in the channel of flesh. It trailed down her arm, falling onto the tabletop in a thick, viscous stream. When the pain did come, it came on in a rush, causing her to heave.

Nykka's eyes were wild as she stared her down.

Thea swayed in her seat. Blood dripped from the tabletop onto her thigh. She'd gone deeper than she'd intended. She didn't think she could do it again, no matter the consequences. *"Please,"* she said, and cried. "I have done all you asked of me."

For a moment, Nykka looked hesitant. Thea watched her working through something in her mind. She looked down, eyes flicking back and forth. Her chest heaved, and her grip on the edge of the table tightened.

Thea let herself hope.

But Nykka laughed—so bitterly Thea could taste it—and her hope fell away. Nykka shook her head, and Thea slumped back into her chair, cursing herself for being foolish enough to think, even for a heart's beat, that any of these people would do anything to help her. That they cared at all. Any hint of uncertainty Nykka possessed had been exiled. She looked angrier than she ever had before.

Influence smacked into Thea, and she sat up straight.

"Press the blade to your neck," Nykka said, low and menacing.

Thea's eyes went wide as a dim yellow glow covered Nykka's skin.

Nykka slapped the table. "Now!" Sweat trickled down her face, and her body trembled, like one pushed to its limit.

Thea lifted the blade, holding it far enough from her neck she could see the reflection of the torchlight on it, despite her blood still dripping from its tip.

She could not believe the intention was to have her end her life. If they wanted her dead, they could make it so at any time. But, Thea thought, perhaps they could heal it.

The yellow glow now radiated from Nykka's eyes, horrifying and awe-inducing, concealing their natural shade of blue. "Cut your throat," she said from between gritted teeth, slowly, spreading out the words.

Thea pressed the cool metal to her neck, swallowing against its edge. Tears spilled freely down her cheeks as she pushed. The sting caused her to stop, and she felt a thin trail of blood trickle down her chest. She closed her eyes.

"Cut your throat!"

Thea knew she could not. There was no reason to continue the charade. She sobbed, knowing she'd lost.

"I knew it."

Thea opened her eyes and slowly lowered the blade.

Nykka stepped back from the table, yellow glow subsiding. She stood with her hands on her hips, panting. "I warned you, Calithea. I told you the first time we met that I was not the one to fear. You should not have deceived me."

Thea sprang from her chair, backing up in the room. She held the blade out in front of her.

Nykka scoffed and shook her head. She looked back at Thea with something akin to pity as she walked from the room, closing the door behind her.

Thea stood, like a cornered animal, waiting with the dagger in a trembling hand, determined to sink it into someone else this time. She flinched when the door opened, and her three guards entered the room.

The man with the scar laughed when he saw her standing there, clutching the blade.

He rushed her.

She tried to slash it at him, ignorant of how to wield it. He knocked her arm aside, and the knife clattered to the floor along with her courage. The back of his hand struck her cheek so savagely she fell back onto the cot. A sharp ring filled her head before the pain of it registered. She reeled, arching against the sting.

Strong hands grasped her ankles, tugging her hard onto the floor. She jerked as something made contact with her stomach, sending the air from her lungs. A kick to the back sent her coiling in the opposing direction. She didn't have time to cry, to plead, or even breathe before another blow came.

She looked up to see Calix's face, then her black boot. It grew with a quickness, consuming her line of sight.

57

Nara

"For nearly one thousand years, one family has ruled. Never lost to war or ruin."

THE RISE OF IRE
LEWIN LEAR, 1198 AQ

They rode hard for days. Their horses struggled, and though he wouldn't admit to it, Harker was struggling too.

Nara let him sleep past dawn, but he still looked uneasy in his saddle since departing their makeshift camp.

When their journey started, they rode around carts of families and merchants escaping the city. Most took an eastern road, heading for the coast. The further north they traveled, the less they encountered, often having the road to themselves.

"We will reach Bacebridge before midday," Nara said. "We will stop to rest for the night."

He only nodded, but Nara saw the relief wash over his face.

She had never traveled so far north in Ire. Her familiarity with the geography of it was strictly learned. Bacebridge was a large village but had no walls and no offer of security for its citizens. Nara told herself that was the cause for the quiet roads. Truth tugged at her gut, but she kicked at it.

They reached the town and continued through its dirt streets in search of the field house. They were usually easy to find. All one had to do was follow the ether. But the pull was dull at best. So much so that Nara thought those with lesser power might struggle to feel it altogether.

They passed few people, and the ones they did encounter appeared to be in a frenzy to pack their belongings and leave.

No one came out to greet them as they hitched their horses to the rack. There were no wards, and she couldn't sense a single soul inside. It was almost as if it never was.

Nara looked at Harker. She knew he was holding back his own dreadful thoughts.

"You ought not leave your horses out like that," a gravelly voice called from across the road.

Nara turned to see an old man sitting in a chair on a porch. She gestured for Harker, and they walked together toward the home.

"Good morrow," Nara called out.

"Good morrow," he returned. "Not many arriving. Most are leaving. There's a shortage of horses in town. If you leave yours out like that, someone is gonna take off with 'em."

Nara smiled and nodded. "I thank you for the warning, sir." Deep lines covered the thin skin of his face, neck, and hands. "We are only passing through. We are headed to Highclere."

He shook his head, eyes grave. "You cannot go to Highclere, lass."

"Why not?" she asked, but she already knew the answer.

"Highclere has fallen."

Nara closed her eyes. She heard Harker curse.

"The rider came yesterday morning with news Thrane had taken the capital. We didn't believe it, not at first. Not until more arrived in the night." He leaned in his chair as if to speak in confidence. "There were whispers, tales of sorcery." He folded his arms. "Not that we believe it. But, you see, you cannot go to Highclere."

Nara turned to Harker. "Will you check the field house? See what you can find useful to us. I'll join you shortly."

"Aye."

Nara walked to the porch, kneeling in front of the old man. "If Highclere has truly fallen, then the people who took it will eventually come here. You should flee."

"I'm too old to be leaving, and my wife is poorly." He glanced back toward the house.

"Have you no other family?" Nara asked.

He shook his head.

Nara sighed. "I fear the whispers you heard are true."

He chuckled. "If you say so, lass."

"Either way," she said, "this town stands no chance, I fear."

The old man shrugged. "Then we are all doomed," he said, though he did not appear convinced. His voice was shaky, but not with fear. At his age, he'd likely lived through the first and second Iren Wars.

"Those that came from Highclere, did they carry with them any news of the king?" she asked. "Does Ulric live?"

He shrugged again. "No one knows."

Nara looked out over the town, trying to build a timeline in her mind. If news reached Bacebridge the day prior, then Highclere must have fallen ten, perhaps twelve days before. Those who fled to Eastwatche were already there or arriving any day. *Godsdamn*, she thought, unsure where to go next.

She found Harker in the field house, rummaging through trunks and cabinets.

"They cleared it out good before they left." Harker pointed to a table. "I found a small bag of oats and a half-empty pouch of dried apples." He stood and paused, taking in the look in her eyes. "*What?*"

Nara clasped her hands in front of her and swallowed. "You will take this and whatever else you can find and travel to Eastwatche."

He stared at her expectantly.

"And I will continue on to Highclere."

"The hells you will, Nara." He marched through the room, stopping half a pace in front of her.

"I have no way of knowing if Cerys fled to Eastwatche or if she is still in Highclere. She could have been captured, or—" Nara did not say the alternative. She would not give it words or breathe life into it. "If she is in Eastwatche, I need you to tell her to wait for me there."

Harker started to speak several times, as if taking care to choose his words wisely. "Nara," he said slowly, cautiously. "You read what I did in that letter. There is only one thing that can—"

"Nether is myth, Harker. If it ever existed, it died with the Gods twelve hundred years ago." Her words came out with a threadbare confidence that would convince no one. Not even she believed them.

"I didn't ask for a history lesson. We all know the stories." He glared at her and huffed. "You made me your deputy for a reason. You know I'll go along with most of your wild ideas. But you also know that I'll tell you when you're going too far. When you're about to cross that line between being bold and being bloody stupid. This is bloody stupid."

Nara simply looked at him, brows drawn, wanting to argue but failing to find words. "I know," she said, and sighed. "But I do not have a choice. You know I don't."

"*Godsdammit,*" he grumbled and started pacing the room.

"I won't do anything reckless. I will go and observe." They both knew it was a lie.

Harker turned back to her, eyes angrier than she'd seen on him. "Let me come with you."

Nara shook her head. He continued to pace, and she watched silently, letting him make peace with it. Harker knew her well enough to know arguing with her was a fool's endeavor. He grabbed the back of a chair, and she believed for a moment he might hurl it across the room, but he cursed and let go.

He marched forward, putting his finger right in her face. "If you're not in Eastwatche by the end of the moon, I'm coming after you. Then you'll carry both our deaths on your back." He met her eye to eye. "Do you hear me?"

She nodded, feeling small but steadfast. "I hear you."

"You're bloody mad, woman." He pulled her into a tight, quick embrace, then stepped back, holding her at arm's length.

"Come now," she said, cocking her head, trying desperately for a smile. "It is why you like me so much."

He looked less than inclined to laugh. Though he tried to fight it, one side of his mouth quirked as he shook his head. "Your mother is going to have my head. Or my balls. Or both."

Nara chuckled, but it quickly fell away. She did not want to part with him. "Take both horses. Let them rest the day and night." He started to protest, but she held up her hand. "I'm going to travel through the woods. A horse will do me little good with speed."

He sighed and walked to the table. "At least take this." He tossed the bag of dried apples at her.

"Leave in the morning. If you can manage means, and they are amenable to it, take the old man and his wife with you."

"Aye." He nodded. "When will you leave?"

"Now."

58

Neith

"When Godric fell, so too did Thrane. Into obscurity, lost to the known world."

THE THIRD IREN WAR
LEWIN LEAR, 1185 AQ

Neith arrived at morning council to find an unwelcome, familiar face. Hywel Dryden sat with his feet propped on the table, interlaced hands resting on his lap. His dark hair was slicked back, his uniform clean and orderly. He did not appear as one who'd spent days on a riverboat, and Neith could not think of a time she'd ever seen him disheveled.

Cordero and Nicomedes were the only others present.

Dryden watched her as she traversed the room. Neith sat down in the chair opposite his, determined to no longer be unnerved by him. She was a far cry from the girl he'd last seen in Thrane.

"General Dryden," Neith said, inclining her head. "We welcome you back." She reached for the teapot. Steam billowed out as she filled her cup. "I must congratulate you on your successes in Ealdtown and Kingsport. It was welcome news."

He peered at her in the same manner he always had. Appraising, taunting. But today, with an added air of amusement. His eyes traveled down to the badges on her uniform. "I see I am to address you as Captain now." His dark eyes narrowed. "And what an interesting insignia. *Luxa en Umbraxos*," he read. "Light in the Shadows."

"Made by your daughter."

His eyes flicked up to hers. They shared a contemptuous smirk.

"They also call her 'Dotir Umbraxos,'" Cordero said. Neith smiled at him, too, but this one was warm. The scar from the wound he'd acquired in the battle was little more than a soft line running the length of his face. It took nothing away from his favorable looks.

"Do they?" Dryden's lips quirked, perhaps impressed. "Making names for yourself already," he said. "I am glad to see you living up to your father's expectations. If only all daughters did."

Neith wanted to snarl. It disgusted her he would express resentment toward Ayla to provoke her. She was determined not to let it show on her face. She stirred a spoon of honey in her tea. "Yes, if only all daughters had a father like mine. A leader. A king. A true example to live by." Cordero's brows shifted, and Neith was fairly sure Nicomedes stifled a grin.

Dryden didn't crack, only smiled back as if to say *challenge accepted.*

The door opened, and Lorcan, Magnus, and Roman walked through. They settled in their chairs as servants brought plates of food to the table.

Her father reached for a mug, holding it out in front of him. "We welcome General Dryden to Highclere and congratulate him on his taking of Ealdtown and Kingsport." The dull thud of fists on the table filled the room. "We now have full control of the supply chain running the length of the Iren River."

"A success indeed," Magnus said. He looked down the table at Neith with an acknowledging nod.

"How many ships have we gained possession of in Kingsport?" Nicomedes asked.

"Twenty and two now fly our flag," Dryden said. Neith noted he had not touched his food, which made her think. She couldn't recall having ever seen him eat.

The door opened again, and a woman entered. Neith recognized her as an Influencer from the First. Her blonde hair was pulled back in a low, tight bun, and she looked nervous.

"Halvorsen," her father called out, gesturing to the woman. She stopped a few paces from him, falling into half salute. "Report," he commanded, tearing a piece of bread from a large loaf.

The woman took a quick breath, as if hesitant to speak. "I fear my efforts continue to be unsuccessful, Lord King."

Lorcan dropped the bread, turning toward her in his chair.

"If anything, she gains resistance to Influence." Halvorsen kept her eyes low as she spoke.

"She is bound," her father said. His tone already lacked patience, and

Neith feared for the woman.

Halvorsen shifted. "She gains resistance despite her bindings."

Neith now understood she spoke of Calithea Ironne. "How is that possible?" she asked.

Halvorsen turned to address Neith. "I do not know, Captain Dracos," she answered, bowing her head with respect.

"You have followed my instructions?" Lorcan reached for his mug.

"We have, Lord King. She was kept in the pit for two full days. Since then, she has been deprived of food and consistent sleep. She grows weaker, but her resolve remains. She attempted to conceal her understanding of Influence. I had her beaten for it."

"*Beaten?*" Neith asked, looking from the woman to her father.

Roman chuckled but quickly quieted when their father's eyes bore down on him with warning.

"So what you have come to tell me is that this is beyond your capabilities," Lorcan said to Halvorsen.

She stiffened but inclined her head. "It would appear so, Lord King."

He turned back to the table. "Then you are dismissed to return to your regular duties."

Halvorsen blinked, then opened her mouth to speak, but appeared to have thought better of it. She saluted, and Neith thought she shared a look with Cordero before walking from the room.

"What outcome can you hope to achieve by Influencing her? Even if it were successful, it would start to break down as soon as you remove her bindings," Neith said to her father. She knew he was far angrier than he let on.

"You can shape one's feelings and desires. It requires only time, Neith. Patience. Everyone breaks. Influencing her is simply a start." He reached for his bread, resuming his meal. "General Dryden, you will take over for Halvorsen."

"I will start today, Lord King." Dryden inclined his head, his eyes flicking to Neith.

Her belly turned cold. Whatever Halvorsen had been doing would pale in comparison.

"Surely we move forward with our goal at the forefront of mind? The efforts are meant to turn her," Neith said. "Are there not better ways to bring her to our side than torture?"

"If torture was our aim," her father answered, glancing up at her from his plate, "I assure you we would have her on our side by now."

Neith swallowed, uneasy at the idea of his definition of it.

Lorcan turned to Dryden as he chewed. After he swallowed, he pointed his fork at him. "You will do nothing to cause injury we cannot repair."

"Of course," Dryden said as his eyes met Neith's again. She knew she had made a grievous mistake showing any concern for the girl. She, more than anyone, was acutely aware of the horrors they could heal.

Neith directed her attention to Magnus. He had remained quiet during the exchange. While his discomfort with the situation may not have been as deep as hers, she could sense his uneasiness. She pleaded with her eyes for an ally.

Magnus looked at Dryden, then at her father. "And we must clarify that also pertains to her mind. If you destroy it, she will be of no use to us."

"Indeed," Lorcan agreed. He fixed his gaze on Dryden. "But I will repeat, in case this needs clarification." He looked then at Magnus, then Neith, taking time between his words. "I want her on our side."

"Where are we going?" Neith asked Sam as she followed him through the forests of Highclere.

"I found a place I think you will like." He smiled as he lifted her over a large fallen trunk. "It is not far now."

They'd been walking down the southern coastline for near an hour. She hadn't shared with him the information about Calithea. She did not want to burden him with it, knowing it would disturb him as it did her.

They continued through the dense brush until Neith could start to discern a clearing in the distance. Distinguishable rays of sunlight struck through the treetops. She thought she could hear birds.

Sam gestured for her to go first. She stepped out into the open space and nearly gasped. Bright white and pink magnolia trees filled the clearing. Turquoise water lined the far edge, running between the tall, green mountain peaks. It looked like art. Like something far too imaginative to be real.

"How did you find this?"

"While on patrol. Max and I were out testing the wards when we came upon it."

She stepped further into the clearing, closing her eyes when the warm sun flooded her face. Neith had never considered herself overly fond of the sun but thought she might be starting to have a change of heart. Perhaps she had simply seen too little of it most of her life.

"You loved these trees, and…" He paused, and she turned to look at him. "I want you to have a better memory of them."

Neith closed the half step between them, bringing her lips to his. She wrapped her arms around his neck as she kissed him, drawing him against her. The warmth of his mouth made her think of many fine memories they could make in such a place.

Their kiss stilled, but they stayed wrapped around one another.

"You are happy, then?" he asked.

She smiled against him and nodded, fearful of what amorous confessions might spill from her lips should she open them.

Sam released her and stepped back. "Come," he said, and held out his hand.

He had packed a quilt, food, books, and even two sparring swords. His intention, as he said it, was to "bring whatever they may wish to occupy their time."

Neith lay on her belly, bare feet kicking lazily in the air as she flipped through the pages of a book on the Third Iren War. Her fingers traced stains of spilled tea on the pages. The stains looked recent, and she wondered who had made them.

Sam lay in front of her, head propped on one hand, turning through a book of his own. They passed an apple back and forth between them. From time to time, she would look up and meet his gaze, finding soft eyes.

"It is strange," she said, flipping another page, "to read about a war fought by one's own grandparents. Against each other, no less. The same war my father fought against his own."

"War is ugly enough between strangers," Sam said. "It seems a tragedy if fought between kin."

Neith considered his words, chewing on her lip. "That depends on one's kin, I suppose."

"True," he said. He took a bite from the apple and passed it to her, returning to his book.

Neith regarded the half-consumed piece of fruit in her hand. Its pale yellow flesh was already starting to brown. *How fleeting*, she thought. Such a brief time without its fragile skin, and it starts to wither. "My own cousin sits in a cell only stories below where I sleep."

Sam looked up from his page, turning toward her with curious eyes. "She is your enemy, is she not?"

Neith was unsure how to answer. Her enemies were her father's enemies. He did not appear to see Calithea as such.

"I don't know." She returned to her book, thoughts shifting to fears of what Dryden was going to do to her.

"What's the matter?" Sam's eyes narrowed on her, abreast of the shift in her energy.

Neith closed the book and set it aside. "They've put her to torture."

He did not look surprised. "I see."

"Withholding food, sleep. Beatings." Neith took a breath. "They put her in a pit." She had seen these types of pits in Necrium, and the result of those who spent any significant measure of time in them. They were warded to be sound and light proof. Most succumbed to madness, or something like it.

Sam nodded. "As I said, war is ugly."

"My father is sending Dryden to see her today."

The look in his eyes told her he shared her feelings about the man. He sat up to face her. "This is what weighs on you today."

She thought she must be wildly obvious, or he truly knew her well. She pushed back onto her knees. "I had thought not to say anything."

He shifted closer, tucking loose hair behind her ear. "Isn't that what you asked me not to do?"

"So we burden each other with our attempts not to." She smiled, but it was half-hearted.

"Is there anything you can do?" he asked.

"I tried to dissuade him, but I feared pressing. Dryden seemed to notice my interest in her."

Something like loathing passed through Sam's face so quickly she nearly missed it.

I could help her escape, she thought.

"What are you thinking?"

"Nothing," she laughed bitterly, shaking it off. "Only wild thoughts."

59

Thea

"Of all our power, it is Influence we should fear the most."

THE WAY OF ETHER
ASHERAH GALANIS, FIRST CONSUL, THE CITADEL, 808 AQ

Thea awoke in so much pain she could scarcely move. Every breath produced a wince, which drew another sharp breath. One eye did not open, not that it mattered. They'd taken the torch. She simply lay there on her cot in the dark, as still as she could manage, trying to be grateful she was not in the pit.

She let herself feel every ache, every misery that radiated through her. She was no stranger to pain. Overcoming the fear of it would be one small power she could reclaim. But she knew it could be worse. She thought of how she had tried to sink the blade into her arm, mutilating herself, and how her body screamed and railed against it, forcing her to stop.

In time, the old man came and healed her wounds. There must have been many, as he worked on her far longer than he had before. He gave her water but no food.

"Stop resisting," he warned her again.

"I don't know how," she said in earnest. Not that she would. Would she?

Time passed. It felt like the longest stretch they'd left her alone. She considered perhaps it was simply the dark.

When the door finally opened again, she sat up in her cot, squinting at the torchlight. The two male guards entered. One secured a torch in the sconce. They lifted the table and carried it from the room, returning with another of similar size, placing it in the same position. Thea frowned. The scarred guard smirked at her on his way out. He didn't close the door.

Thea looked at the table. Dread slithered in when she noticed what looked like shackles bolted to the top.

A man walked into the room. He smiled at her, and it was anything but warm. He sat in the far chair, gesturing for her to take the other.

She hesitated, but something inherent warned her not to anger him. He watched her walk to the chair in a way that felt predatory. He was the cat, and she the starling. But there was no one to throw a rock for her. Nor had she anywhere to fly.

When she sat, she kept her eyes low. He dipped his head, trying to catch her gaze. When he did not desist, she looked up.

He had terrifyingly dark eyes. Not only in color, but something in his regard. An eerie indifference. Thea knew this was someone come to hurt her. Her lip trembled. He looked satisfied by her reaction, as if well aware of the effect of his appearance, and he used it so.

"My name is Dryden."

"*Please.*" It was all she could get out.

He sat so very still that every time he blinked, she nearly flinched. It made him appear unearthly, the product of fiction.

Dryden gestured at the table. "Put your wrists in the restraints."

Thea pulled her arms back, shaking her head.

"They are for your benefit, Calithea." His voice was honeyed in a way she'd not expected. Not pleasant, more sickly sweet. Every word came out with steely confidence, as if chosen with intention.

Still, she didn't move. The way he said her name set her belly to ice.

He repeated the command.

When she didn't comply, he stood from the table, rounded it, and backhanded her. Her face lit up in an explosion of pain. The blow was hard, but not enough to disrupt her wits. She had been hit so many times of late she'd learned the harder ones hurt less. It's the ones that don't disrupt you that hurt the most. Something told her he was aware of that.

There was no anger in his action, nor satisfaction. He returned to his chair, all traces of violence gone. He acted like one going through the motions of something performed so often it had become mundane. It required no thought, only repetition. "Put your wrists in the restraints," he repeated.

Thea's arms shook as she extended them onto the table.

"Palms down."

She swallowed, doing as commanded. As soon as the lock clicked, she instinctively pulled against them. Her forearms were nearly cemented to the wooden table, and she had little range to move her body in any direction.

He gave her no warning.

She snapped, frozen, moon-eyed. It felt like she'd been running full speed before slamming into stone.

Memories flashed, playing out behind her eyes. Running with her siblings as a child in the gardens. She and Marten in the forest making love. The attack on Highclere. They were random and convoluted, but they were pieces of her life. Dryden's head twitched, eyes racing as if he was reading at an unfathomable speed. She felt like she was falling, and her fingernails pressed into the wood in a desperate attempt to still the sensation. To find an anchor. Drops of blood fell from her nose, pooling on the table. Unable to inhale, she wheezed and choked, starting to convulse until the acceleration became too much, and she felt herself losing awareness.

Thea woke on the cot. She reached up to a stabbing ache between her eyes. Someone had bathed her and dressed her in a clean shift. Even her blanket was new. She couldn't make sense of the comfort. She reckoned it must be some sort of game.

They had not healed her cheek. It was tender and swollen, and her wrists were red and scratched from pulling against the restraints.

She had no concept of what he'd done to her. It was nothing like what Nykka had. It felt like he had infiltrated a part of her that another person never should. A private place, sacred to her. She felt invaded, intruded upon. A persistent dull ache buzzed behind her eyes that she couldn't blink or shake away.

Nykka had warned her they would send someone worse.

Every time she heard footsteps pass, she eyed the door warily, terrified Dryden would return and do it again. Or that they would take her back to the pit. She had angered them with her deceit. She wanted to be compliant, to do as they commanded, but all she could picture in her mind was jumping across the table and gouging out his dark eyes.

Thea imagined many things while she waited. All of them violent.

She didn't have to wait long. When the door swung open, she moved back as far as she could on the cot until her back hit the cold, damp stone.

"Good evening, Calithea."

Evening. She tried to make sense of the days. She couldn't be sure.

"Ready to try again?" He eyed her with raised brows, seemingly possessing little of the indifference he had before. His newly found enthusiasm was far more unsettling.

The insubordination had been easier to produce when she'd been on her own. Seeing him now, dark eyes peering down on her, sent her heart racing. Thea swallowed against the fear creeping up her throat. She wanted to plead, but she knew that would do nothing but amuse him. Instead, she glared.

"You're an interesting one," he said, walking around the table. "I can feel your fear, but still you resist. It's so thick I can almost taste it. Sweet and ripe." He looked as if he would lick his lips. "Few resist after time in the pit."

She watched as he crossed the cell, crouching down in front of her.

"I want to see what's behind these walls," he said, one of his fingers tapping on her forehead. "To see what you are. And I will, Calithea. Time is the only barrier."

She recoiled, but he grasped her face, forcing her to meet his eyes. He smelled clean. *No,* not clean. Sanitized. Sterile. And of some sort of earthy spice.

"I will tell you something about me that might help encourage your… cooperation. What interests me today rarely does tomorrow. Lorcan and I are very different in this regard."

Thea made note he did not refer to his king by title.

"It is true what they say," he said, and sighed. "You do look so much like your mother." He released her face but didn't back up. "She was a fascinating woman, but a disappointment in the end. She started something, but did not have the gall to see it through." He pursed his lips. "And her sister turned out to be no better."

Thea frowned, unable to conceal her curiosity at the mention of her mother's sister.

He ran his fingertips along the bruised cheek where he had struck her. "It does not give me pleasure to hurt you, though you may believe otherwise. To what degree and how often you suffer is entirely up to you. I will get what I want, Calithea. You decide the path."

She wanted to scream at him, throw her fists, claw out his eyes. Do something, *anything* that would cause him pain. The best she could do was a quiet rebellion.

He stood. "I'll ask one more time. Are you ready to try again?"

Though she knew it was a profitless protest, she simply could not bring herself to comply. Her silence was all the answer he would get.

"Llun!"

Thea flinched.

Dryden didn't take his eyes from hers as the guard with the scarred face walked into the room. "Help our lady here into her restraints." He walked back to the table, taking his seat.

The big man stalked toward her.

Thea leapt from the cot, but he caught her foot, sending her top half to the floor. She kicked and thrashed, one of her heels striking his nose.

Blood spurted, and he released her, hands covering his face. "You bitch!"

She thought she heard Dryden laughing.

Thea used the opportunity to crawl across the floor, but there was nowhere to flee. He was on her in an instant. Fisting her hair, he hauled her up, then pulled back to strike, but Dryden spoke. "I need her coherent."

Llun snarled, carrying her to the chair. He was too strong, and she was too weak. She'd not eaten, barely slept. She could hardly walk, let alone fight. It was an easy task to subdue her.

"I could leave him alone with you for a time," Dryden said as she was placed in the chair. "Perhaps that would cull your spirit."

Llun grinned down at her as he locked the restraints.

"I have no doubt force is the only way you'd get a woman beneath you." Thea spat, and it splattered across his face.

Llun growled, wiping it away. His hand came away crimson-stained from the blood still streaming from his nose. Thea smiled at him, jeeringly, and he grasped her face in his hand, eyes wild and angry.

"Go on," she said, between gritted teeth, "strike me. If we're going to spend time together, something has to get a rise out of that miserable excuse for a cock hanging limp between your legs."

Llun's eyes went wilder still as he pulled back his free fist.

Dryden held up his hand. "*Leave us*," he said impatiently.

"You heard him," Thea said, smiling. Llun's fingers dug painfully into her cheeks, but she didn't let it show. "Your master has given you an order, dog."

Llun growled again, but did as commanded.

When the door closed, Dryden sighed. "As amusing as I find your protests, they will, in time, grow stale. It is not an idle threat, Calithea."

Thea stilled. It was not a subject in which she would test his sincerity.

As before, without warning, he slammed into her mind.

And again.

And again.

And again.

The time between the *invasions*, as Thea began to think of them, was immeasurable and unpredictable. Sometimes it felt like only an hour passed. Other times, an entire day. Every visit, he would do the same. Get inside her head and crawl around, and then she would black out, waking sometime later, alone on her cot.

In the time between, a buzzing reverberated through her like an insect flying around, smacking against glass, again and again. She thought she would go mad from it. At its worst, she clawed and slapped at her face, desperate to subdue it. But the guards would come in and restrain her and threaten to put her back in the pit.

If she asked questions, she was struck. If she didn't comply, she was struck. If they injured her too severely, the old man would come back in and fix it. Llun would threaten to rape her, only to be called off by the woman. He told her sometime soon she wouldn't be around to stop him. He whispered the vile things he would do to her.

With each visit, Dryden grew further disgruntled. Whatever he was doing didn't appear to be working, and his invasions became more severe.

When he came back for the seventh time, something changed. Thea didn't pass out. When he pulled from her mind, he looked something other than angry or eager. He looked perplexed.

On the eighth visit, her nose did not bleed. On the ninth, she stopped fighting the restraint. It was a game now, and she wanted to play. On the tenth, she laughed at him. He sent the female guard in to beat her, but it had been worth it. She was getting used to the pain. Pain was easier to bear than fear, and even that was waning.

Thea had no idea what he was trying to do, but she knew he was failing. She smiled, listening as they argued in the hall. She was starting to believe she could survive him. But hope was a terrifying prospect. Even more than their torture. Better to make peace with it. Better to believe she would die there. Thea vowed if she could do nothing else, she would not make it easy for them.

60

Neith

"Some bonds, once broken, remain so forever."

THE RECOVERED JOURNALS OF SONIA THRONDSEN, 1183 AQ

"It has proved more difficult than I had anticipated," Dryden said. "She resists, but I remain confident."

Lorcan studied Dryden as he spoke. "You have had three days with her," he said dryly.

"The line between breaking someone and bending them is delicate, Lord King. If you want her whole, in mind and body, then patience is required."

Neith sipped her wine, listening to Dryden give report. The topic had grown to take up the body of their meetings the past days. Neith had noticed shared looks across the table from some of the commanders. Her father's strange fascination with the girl was becoming more obvious by the day.

"Perhaps it is time to execute her," Nicomedes said. "Surely, there are other matters more deserving of our time."

Lorcan's eyes darted to her. "I will decide when that time has come to pass."

Nicomedes looked away, but her concern didn't fade.

Cordero shifted in his seat, clearing his throat. "I'm inclined to agree with Maelis. Turning her seems a tall task. If we execute her now, we eliminate the risk of the Esērii taking hold of her."

"She is locked in a cell in a castle we hold," Magnus challenged. "She poses no threat."

"I concur," Roman said. He was sitting back in his chair with his arms crossed. "We should have hung the bitch with the others who offered her aid."

"Need I remind you we remain outnumbered?" Lorcan spoke calmly, but the irritation in his voice rumbled underneath. "Until our efforts in the south conclude, we cannot assume we know what we are truly up against. It would be foolish to think our enemy weak because time and distance separate us."

"She is no more useful than the other idleborn idiots we slaughtered when we took this castle. We do not need her." Roman tried to speak with indifference, but his resentment was clear. Neith could now see it was not only she who sparked jealousy in him. It was anyone to whom their father took an interest.

Nicomedes ignored him. "I'm simply saying that—"

"I would like a chance," Neith said, louder than the other voices around the table. All attention turned to her.

"With all due respect, Captain Dracos," Dryden said, his tone brimming with condescension, "I do not—"

"With all due respect, *General*, as my father said, you have had three days and made no progress."

Lorcan eyed her, waiting to see if she was an ally or foe.

"I would like an opportunity to speak with her," Neith said, holding up her hands. "Nothing more."

Roman snorted.

Neith turned to glare at him. "If you have something to add, brother, speak up. Holding your tongue is not something you often do."

His eyes flicked to hers, unused to her brazen rebuttal. "What makes you think you can speak to me so?"

Neith laughed, rich and bitter. "Because the depth of your desperation to appear relevant is blurring your ability to see how utterly ridiculous you sound."

Roman looked like she'd rounded the table and slapped him. She considered it.

Cordero flexed his jaw to avoid whatever look he wished to conceal. Magnus glanced nervously from her to Roman and then to Lorcan.

Roman stood, his chair screeching against the stone floor. "Be careful, little sister."

Neith joined him on her feet, but slowly, calmly. She leaned over the table, eyes fixed on his. "Or what, *big brother*?"

Roman flinched when a fist hit the table.

"*Sit down*. Both of you." Lorcan's voice was icy and edged with warning.

They obeyed.

Their father took a narked breath, looking from Roman to Neith. "What is it you believe you can do?"

"The morning after you took Highclere, Father, you said, 'Some allies you sway, some you force.' It is becoming apparent that Calithea Ironne cannot be forced."

"And you believe you can persuade her?" he asked, brow cocked.

"I am asking for a chance to." Neith turned to Dryden with subtle contempt. "While there is still something of her remaining."

Lorcan stared at her, fingers tapping slowly on the tabletop. "No," he said.

Neith opened her mouth to protest, but he held up a hand.

"Not yet," he added. "General Dryden will continue his tactic for now."

Neith looked away, exhaling her discontent. She couldn't bear the look she knew Dryden must be wearing.

"And as I said before, in regard to her execution," her father said, glowering around the table, "*I* will decide when that time has come to pass. I take no liking in repeating myself."

His words were met with apprehension, but nods of submission.

"We reconvene in the morning." He waved his hand, dismissing them all. "Roman, Neith, you will remain."

Neith brought her cup to her lips, taking a large drink of the bitter wine as the others started to leave.

When the door closed, their father spoke. "You will not turn my council into a charade between squabbling siblings."

Roman pointed his finger across the table. "She tried to humiliate me."

"She succeeded," their father said flatly. "Not that you make it a difficult task. What your sister speaks is true."

Roman shrank back in his chair. He looked small, like a little boy who'd been scolded for spilling his milk. It cooled her anger toward him.

"Humiliating you is not my design, Roman. But you seem to forget you have done nothing but try to demean me since we crossed the mountain."

"And what have you done?" he asked, scowling. "The same."

"No." Neith shook her head. "I came to you for justice and found none. You attacked my people, and I retaliated. You laugh and jest and attempt to belittle me in council, so I defend myself."

"You speak as if we are adversaries." He said the words as if they were a challenge for her to make them true.

"If I am your adversary, it is because you have made me so."

"*Enough.*" Their father looked from one to the other. "You will find a way to make peace between you. Real or fictitious." He stood, leaning over the table. "Do you understand me?"

"Yes, Father," Roman answered.

Lorcan's eyes moved to Neith.

"I understand."

"Good." He turned, striding from the room.

Roman sat in his chair, arms crossed. Neith recalled the times when they were children, and she would run to his room in the middle of the night, frightened by thunder and lightning. Not once had he turned her away.

She tried to uncover when his feelings toward her had turned. It had happened so slowly, over such a long time, that she could only now, looking back, see just how much their relationship had changed. "Is there truly no way for us to be friends again?"

The anger in his eyes had dissolved into a sadness of sorts. It encouraged her to try.

"You are my brother. Surely, we can—"

"How can there be an amends with so many lies between us?"

Neith sat up. "What lies?"

A bitter chuckle shook his chest. He peered at her with disbelief. "Do you think I do not know?"

"I don't know to what you speak."

He scoffed, running a hand through his hair. It nearly grazed his shoulders now, which made him look more like their father.

"*Roman,*" Neith said, her patience threadbare, "I have no interest in games."

"I know Father plans to name you Praxa," he said from a clenched jaw.

Her expression slipped, giving away the truth. She shifted in her seat and swallowed. "Did Father tell you?"

"He did not need to."

Neith looked nervously around the tabletop, unsure if she should deny it. "Nothing has been decided."

He laughed under his breath, shaking his head. "More lies."

"I didn't ask for it, Roman. I don't even know if I want it."

He turned his body so it fully faced hers, head cocked. "You will say no then?"

"I—" She swallowed.

"I didn't think so, sister."

"Roman, I—"

"You have stolen what was *mine*!"

Neith winced, but held his irate gaze. When he reached for his wine, she closed her eyes and sighed, subduing her desire to chide him. Roman acted like one whom life simply happened to, as if he played no part in it. She had misunderstood his sadness. It was not sadness. It was only pity for himself. "I cannot steal from you what was never yours."

He didn't respond, only stared off into the distance of the room, his face full of contempt.

Neith stood from her chair, leaning over the table. "I will do as Father asks and end my side of our hostility. I would advise you to do the same."

His jaw flexed before his eyes flicked up to hers. "Fictitious it is."

Bellamy lunged forward, the tip of his wooden sword aimed for Neith's heart. She crossed her shield over her chest, blocking the strike.

"Good," Petra said, observing their movements.

Bellamy grinned at her, turning the blade tauntingly in his grip. Without forewarning, he swung it low. She jumped back as the edge grazed her shins.

"You aim to distract with your smile, Bells," Neith accused.

He grinned again, circling her. "Is it working?"

She feigned a strike from above, instead slashing from the left. His sword came up, parrying the blow. "More than I care to admit."

Neith had hoped a sparring match would ease her anger over her fight with Roman. She had done nothing but mull over it all afternoon.

Bellamy struck a series of quick chops that she defended with her shield, causing her to step back from the impact.

"You're distracted," Petra said.

"We've already established that," Bellamy jested.

Petra sighed. "Keep your opponent's eyes. The eyes will tell you where they're going next. Even when their body lies."

Neith lunged, stabbing her sword forward. Bellamy knocked it away, twisting, slashing across her back. She stumbled forward and nearly fell face-first into the grass.

"Come on, *Princess*. You have to do better than that."

Neith huffed and turned around, running at him in a fury.

She slashed, chopped, and stabbed at him. Her last blow grazed his upper right arm.

"Better," Petra said.

"Oh, I see. You came to work some things out." Bellamy nodded slowly, looking her up and down. "You know, Princess, there are other ways I could help you relieve tension." He flashed his brows and winked at her.

Neith let out an exasperated growl. She threw her shield to the side and charged. Again, she delivered strike after strike until Bellamy grew bored of parrying them. He brought his sword down on hers, twisting and knocking it from her hands. She watched it falling, oblivious to his shield coming forward, smacking into her chest. It wasn't a violent blow, but it was enough to send her falling back.

Petra stood over her as she lay on the ground panting. "If you let your opponent work you up, the fight is over before it has begun." She reached down, pulling Neith back to her feet. "But good work. You're getting better."

"Enter," Neith answered to a knock at her door. She looked up from her book to see Ayla coming through. When the door closed, Ayla leaned against it, gaze low.

Neith frowned, setting her book aside. "Ayla, what is wrong?"

When she didn't move or speak, Neith crossed the room. She dipped down, trying to meet her eyes.

Slowly, Ayla lifted her face, and Neith gasped.

"*What happened?*" she asked, her fingers coming up to graze Ayla's cheek. Her right eye was nearly swollen shut, just starting to turn black and blue.

"I can't go back to camp like this," Ayla said. "If Max sees, he'll get himself killed."

"Ayla," Neith asked again, "who did this to you?"

She looked down again, her lips pressed thin. A tear fell from her uninjured eye. "My father."

Neith exhaled. Rage washed over her in a wild rush, guilt on its heels. "This is my fault."

"No," Ayla said, "it is mine."

Neith swallowed, trying to contain her power spilling out around her. "There is nothing you could have done deserving of this."

"He asked me questions about you. I didn't want to answer them."

Neith frowned, concern deposing some of her rage. "What kind of questions?"

"About your habits," Ayla said, "your relationships." She sniffed, another tear spilling.

"I see."

Ayla shook her head. "I didn't tell him anything, I swear. Not willingly." She leaned closer. "But he can see inside my mind."

Neith knew what Dryden could do. Ayla, born idle, had no defense against it.

"Will you heal me? And please don't tell anyone. If Max tries to do anything, my father will kill him."

"Of course," Neith said, and pulled Ayla into her arms. "Of course I will."

Neith led her to one of the sofas and worked on her face, trying to maintain composure at what that beast had done to her friend. Ayla then revealed a trail of bruises starting on her right shoulder, running down her arm. Bruises were easy to heal, but difficult to clear. One had to understand the body's process.

"He knows that I hate him. He saw it in my mind." Her eyes were so fearful they were difficult to look into. Tears fell down her freckled cheeks in continuous streams.

Neith turned Ayla's face toward hers. "He won't get away with this, I swear it."

"There is nothing you can do. You have to dismiss me. Anything I see, he will see."

"No," Neith said, "not a chance."

"You don't want my father as an enemy, Neith," Ayla said, shaking her head. "Whatever it is he is after, whatever his aim, it is nothing good. Why does he want to know about you?"

"Because I angered him. I stood up to him." Neith ran her hands over her face, rubbing her eyes. "I told you, this is my fault. He didn't need to beat you. Or even ask you. He did this to you because I told him you made the patch." She wiped tears from Ayla's face, feeling her own eyes sting.

"You deserve so much better. I am endlessly sorry."

"This is not the first time he has put his fist to me."

"Then he is more a monster than I already believed him to be." Neith stood and started pacing. Dryden was powerful, connected. He even had the ear of her father. Neith could not take him head on. They would have to be clever. "If we make a legal complaint against him, he may do something rash. Pull you away." She stopped, turning to Ayla. "But…"

"But?"

A conspiratorial grin curled on Neith's lips. "If you were under my command, we would not need to. I could protect you myself."

A tiny snort escaped her. "Were that only possible."

"Why is it not?" Neith asked, her excitement growing as she continued to think through her idea.

Ayla shrugged. "I'm not a soldier, Neith."

"You train with my unit, do you not? Nearly every day now." Neith watched the idea bounce around in her mind.

"I do, but—"

"But what?"

"I'm weak. I can't fight. Not truly. I can barely wield a sword." Ayla looked as if apprehensive to even consider it.

"Not yet. But neither can I." Neith shrugged. "We will get better together."

"You are serious?" Ayla asked. She laughed, but the irony was fading.

"Most certainly."

Ayla looked around the room. She glanced back at Neith several times as if confirming her authenticity. "What do I do?"

"It is simple," Neith answered. "You stand and make your intentions known."

61

Thea

"I should like to choose the manner of my death. To know its purpose. To ensure it has one."

THE RECOVERED JOURNALS OF SONIA THRONDSEN, 1183 AQ

Thea was sitting on her cot, knees pulled to her chest when the door creaked open. Dryden entered with another man she had not seen before. He had short blond hair, and while he wore the uniform of a Thranean soldier, he looked more a learned man than a fighter. He was of average height, his body soft. Thick spectacles framed stern brown eyes.

Unprompted, she stood, strolling to take her seat.

Dryden's eased, indifferent disposition had returned. Thea put her wrists in the restraints, and he locked them, finding her eyes with the trace of a smile. "We're going to try something different this time."

"Good," she mused, shrugging a shoulder. "I was growing bored."

"This is my associate, Alister," Dryden said as the second man rounded the table. He crouched down to her level, but didn't really look at her. She felt like a prop or tool, not like a human. Not like a person. He put his palms on her temples, and a gentle hum flowed over her skin. It wasn't painful. It was soft, soothing even. She watched him the entire time, trying to discern what he was doing, but it was a new sensation. Where Nykka's and Dryden's touch felt like ice, this felt warm, like sunlight.

The man retracted his power and nodded at Dryden.

"Remember, put it back if it doesn't work," Dryden told him.

Thea looked nervously between the two, fearful at the prospect of something new.

The man walked behind her, and his hands returned to her head, gripping it in place. The hum returned. But this time more immersive, saturating. Weaving into the minuscular spaces in her tissue and muscle. Her heart beat against it. It caused her to shake.

Every alarm inside rang with warning.

Dryden leaned over the table with a wicked smile. The white around his black eyes took on a sinister red glow. Fear returned, infectious and consuming. She didn't understand what they were doing.

The hum surged in vibration. It grew until it went from warm to hot. From hot to scalding.

Thea struggled against the restraints. She did her best to hold it back, but a cry tore from her heaving chest. Once she started screaming, she couldn't stop.

Just as she felt like she would combust, something cracked.

She was open, uncontrollable, falling through an endless void. Nothing to grasp, no anchor. Dryden's invasion came on, but this time evolved. Before, it had felt probing, like he could see but not touch. Now he could reach in and stir her mind. Walk around and shift things.

Dryden was shaking with rage, furious in his attempt. She could scarcely see him through the crimson glow expanding around him. She knew she had to fight, but she didn't know how.

The memory of Lorcan in the dining room played in her mind, vivid, as if she'd stepped back in time. Except… she didn't throw her plate. He didn't attack her.

Thea grasped at the truth, trying to preserve it. But he was too strong. She couldn't fight him and the fall.

So she gave in.

She embraced it. The less she fought, the less she fell. The less she fell, the more she could push. What was dark grew bright. Golden light illuminated the black space in her mind. She wasn't thinking. Something innate was taking over, and she let it run free. What surrounded her became tangible. She let it cover her, fill her, strengthen her. Thea let it consume her.

She ignited.

The man behind her screamed. Her body whipped back as if whatever had held her snapped. Thea inhaled and opened her eyes. She blinked. Dryden was gone.

She swayed, nearly faint, breathing while her senses returned. There was so much light. She tried to move, stunned when she discovered her wrists were free. The shackles had burst.

Thea leaned on the table, pulling herself to her feet. Dryden slumped against the far wall. Alister stirred on the ground behind her.

Run, was all her muddled brain could compose. She made for the door.

It swung open as she reached it, and Llun burst into the room, taking in the scene.

He snarled and reached for her. Slivers of dark gray light snaked from his palm, twisting around her body and neck. She swung a desperate arm at him, and it burned as golden fire erupted from her palm.

His eyes went wide, exposing white all around the brown. The surprise in them matched her own. Wails of agony drowned the small room as the gray ropes retracted, and he fell backward through the door.

Thea looked down at her hand in disbelief. A faint golden glow still surrounded it. Shaking and terror-struck, she stepped cautiously into the hall.

Llun was on his back—his face and chest gruesomely burned. The horror of it halted her. The sight and smell of his melted skin like wax brought bile rising from her belly. He was stilling, breath stalling.

Die, she thought. *Fucking die.*

Thea stumbled over him, looking around, still disoriented from the invasion. As if Dryden were still there in her mind, like a dark shadow obscuring her thoughts.

The door.

Thea remembered the door. The one she and Cerys had escaped from during the siege. She took off down the passageway, bracing against the walls to keep balance. She tried to run, but she was hot. So terribly hot. Sweat trailed down her face, her vision hazy, head aching, heart racing at an inconceivable pace. She knew she had little time before the others would be on her, but her legs felt like they were trudging through mud.

When she turned the corner, her heart sank.

"*No,*" she cried, closing the distance to where the door had been. She beat her fists, kicking and thrashing at the newly sealed brick wall. Her desperation burned brighter than the flames in her chest. It felt like she was on fire.

Something was happening to her. Something she didn't think she would survive. There was too much heat. The inferno spread. It moved down her arms and up her throat until she screamed, clawing at her skin.

Angry voices and footsteps echoed through the hall. She looked at her hands, trying to recall whatever had burned the guard, but she had no idea what to do. She panicked, her breath hitching. They would catch her. She was going back to the room. Back to the pit. Back to the invasions. To her death. Her little spark of hope had been foolish. A small sob tore from her when she thought that death might be a relief.

Soldiers cleared the corner, and she thrust her hands forward, praying to Cassia for help. She stumbled back when a fury of gold flames surged from her palms. Those who faced her were set ablaze, their wails deafening in the narrow hall.

Thea didn't dare stop it, too afraid she wouldn't be able to call it back. Not that she knew how. She pressed forward, resigned to kill as many as she could. Every step was an effort. Sweat poured down her face and back.

The flames dwindled, and she fell against the wall, panting, as the fire dulled to a glow. Three scorched bodies lay down the hall. The air was hot and heavy with charred flesh. Someone was shouting commands.

Thea looked down at her hands. It felt like her flesh was melting, but it appeared clear and unmarred. Whatever she had started was now spinning out of control, and she knew she couldn't stop it. She clawed at her skin, trying to extinguish flames that didn't exist.

This is what it feels like to burn.

It was agony. Thea knew she would die. At least the torment would be over. At least she could rest.

She closed her eyes and welcomed her end. She only wished she had taken more of them with her.

I'm sorry, she thought. Unsure who it was for.

Ripped from the flames faster than her mind could grasp, every fiber of her body stiffened, frozen, as she was cast into a cold abyss. Her eyes snapped open in shock at the contrast. She gasped.

She was lying on the floor, writhing, pain radiating from the back of her head. She blinked, trying to bring her sight to focus. Dryden knelt on one side, Alister on the other. His scorched hands hovered above her.

Both stared down at her with fear. The red-haired guard and Calix stood behind them, flames at call. Something pooled in Thea's mouth. She coughed and watched as little red droplets fell back onto her face.

"Are they in place?" Dryden's dark eyes were desperate as he looked from her to Alister and back.

Alister nodded, falling back against the wall.

Dryden's fear morphed to relief, then rage. "Put her to sleep."

"I need a moment."

Thea looked up at the guards with a bloody grin. "Where is your friend?"

Calix sneered down at her. Thea laughed, more blood spilling from her lips.

Dryden grabbed Alister by the collar. "I said, put her to sleep!"

Alister pulled free from Dryden, one of his blistered hands hovering over her face. Her vision tunneled. She wanted to fight it, but she had nothing left.

Thea turned to Dryden, giving him one final triumphant smirk. She felt herself fading. Whatever door they'd opened was sealed shut. Their faces blurred and voices grew distant. She swore she saw Dryden smiling back.

62

Thea

"There is only light and dark. It is for every man to decide beneath which he stands."

HEXADIC PRECEPTS
ZATHRIAN BYGRAVE, 719 AQ

Thea opened her eyes to darkness and dirt. She groaned, reaching for the back of her head. It ached so fiercely she almost felt grateful for the absence of light. It pulsed with every beat of her heart. But she was alive. She was breathing.

Running her hands over her body, she could find no serious injury. Dried blood caked in her hair and on the top of her shift. It flaked off her face as she tried to scratch it away.

Thea lifted herself up and leaned back against the dirt wall. If she was in the pit, no one was hurting her, she told herself. No one was invading her. It was quiet, even peaceful.

It had at least started that way.

Time passed at great, immeasurable lengths. She had not been retrieved in what felt like days. Every so often, the cover would open, and someone would dump cold water on her. At first, she avoided it, already frozen to the bone. In time, her thirst grew so desperate she had resorted to catching it in her dirty hands, trying to drink from them. She dug an assortment of small holes in the floor of the pit, hoping to pool some of it.

They brought her no food, and her body was breaking down in ways that terrified her. She now worried they'd left her to die.

Thea tried all she had before. Reciting poetry, humming the Arabonde.

Thinking of her family. Of Marten. Of being kissed. Of making love.

It worked, for a time.

She started talking to her brother Callum, out loud, until her voice grew too hoarse. Then continued in her mind.

He encouraged her. Told her jests.

She became so weak she spent more time asleep than awake. Her thoughts became her dreams, her dreams her thoughts. She no longer had the energy to scramble for the water. If they weren't trying to kill her, they were still trying to break her, and Thea feared it had worked. She thought she'd be better off if she didn't wake. That had scared her more than anything because she knew it was real. She was giving up.

Thea lay in the muddy earth, legs curled to her chest. She imagined her brothers retaking Highclere and coming to find her body. Would they know it was her? Would they bury her bones?

She dug lazily at the place where she'd hidden the earrings and necklace, adorning herself with both. If she was dying, she could do it with some semblance of dignity. She closed her eyes and let herself dream.

When the bag was ripped from her head, she clamped her eyes shut, unable to withstand the light. Thea had no idea when she'd been pulled from the pit. She could hear voices, but in her delirium, she could not discern their words.

Water so cold it burned splashed across her face. She squinted through the haze to see Roman standing in front of her, empty bucket in hand. She was still dressed in her filthy, bloodstained shift, strapped to a chair holding her in an upright position.

He, almost playfully, slapped her face a few times. "Wake up, Princess."

"If it is your disgusting face I must look upon, I'd rather be back in the hole." Her throat was so dry it came out more of a primitive grunt than language.

"That's the spirit." He gestured for someone. "Clean her up, feed her, and heal the bruises. Make her look presentable."

Thea fell in and out of consciousness until a cup appeared at her lips. It tipped forward, and precious water spilled into her mouth. She drank desperately at the thin stream.

"Easy," a familiar voice warned. He pulled the cup away.

She met eyes with the old man.

"I warned you not to fight them."

"More," she begged, "please."

The cup returned, and she drank.

"Thank you."

"Do not thank me," he said. "I am not your friend."

He gave her small amounts of water over the next several hours while she fell in and out of sleep. He used his power on her. She could not say for what. In time, she grew strong enough to sit unassisted.

They brought her a small meal. A single roasted chicken leg and four strawberries. She tore at the food, picking every morsel of meat from the bones. She considered eating them.

When she finished, they put her in a bath. She stole a glance in one of the mirrors, wincing when she took in her reflection. Her face was gaunt and pale, her body bruised and thinner than it had ever been. What disturbed her the most was the empty look in her eyes.

An attendant washed her body, hair, and teeth. Thea wanted to fight, but for the first time in a long time, she felt human. They put her in a pale green silk dress. One of her favorites for the summer.

She could not contain her gratitude for those who helped her. She thanked them in earnest, even though she knew their design. Thea had built a wall against their beatings, the pit, and the invasions. What she could not endure was generosity. When she was down there, she had resolve. She had fight. But they'd brought her back up, given her comfort with reason. She now had the fear of returning. She would do nearly anything not to go back. Thea knew they were smarter than her, stronger than her, and they were going to win.

They left her in the comfort of her room for several hours. She sat motionless in her chair overlooking the lake. She was terrified, starving, and every part of her ached. Thea looked down at her hands, remembering what it had felt like when the golden fire had burst free. She wondered if she'd dreamt it. She could feel nothing now.

The sun was starting to set when Roman came to retrieve her. He took her to the council room where Lorcan was seated at the end of the long table, hands clasped, waiting. He was in his uniform, his sleek, black hair loose around his face.

He gestured for her to sit. This time, the other chair was placed next to his, not opposed. She didn't protest. A large plate of fruit sat on the table between them, piled high with apples, strawberries, apricots, and plums. The sight of it set her belly to growling, but she didn't reach for it.

"It gives me no pleasure to see you in such a state."

"I doubt that."

"You shouldn't."

Again, she didn't protest. Either apathy or exhaustion won. At that moment, she didn't care which.

"Do you know how long you've been below?" He filled two glasses of wine, setting one in front of her. She ignored it.

"I suppose you're about to tell me," she said, staring lazily at the tabletop.

"Eleven days."

Her eyes flicked up to his. He bore the satisfaction of one who'd extracted just the response they'd desired.

"That's correct," he said. "Eleven days, Calithea."

That wasn't possible. She had guessed a moon, if not more.

"When last we dined, you found my offer appalling because you did not know the alternative. Now you do." He paused, taking in her reaction. "How long did you think you were below? A moon? Two? Now imagine how long a year would feel. What about five years? Would you survive it? Would your *mind* survive it?"

She trembled beneath his words. She wanted to believe it falsehood.

Lorcan leaned closer, intimate. "We can take you so close to death, only to rip you right back. Even when you plead for it. What you had was only a small taste." He reached for the plate of fruit, sliding it closer to her. "That is the trouble with hope. It is in our makeup to claw for it, no matter how futile. No matter how fleeting." His eyes met hers again before he sat back in his chair. "You know what I want."

Thea tried to swallow. She could give in, and it would all be over. No more pain, no more hunger. "If I cannot agree?"

"If you do not feel this is something you can amend yourself to, the kingdom of Ire will cease to exist. It will be absorbed by Thrane, and Highclere will become its new capital. Your father will be executed. In time, we will march on Eastwatche, which we will take. Your brothers, sisters, niece, nephew, and every last heir will be executed, ending the Ironne line forever."

Her drowning eyes were overcome, and a tear spilled down her cheek. "You would do all of that over *me*?"

Lorcan slammed his fist on the table, and she sprang back. "You cannot conceive of what I would do!"

Thea trembled, the memory of him flipping the table vivid in her mind. The same violence was present in his eyes again, but this time, there was also desperation. He leaned on the table, staring at her, chest heaving.

Indignation and fear dueled within her. Between shaking lips, she muttered, "Things not going to plan?"

He fell into a low, exasperated laugh. She prepared herself for brutality, already regretting her words. Instead, he stood and combed a hand through his hair. "Let us see what motivates you."

The throne room was swarming with soldiers. They lined the walls, crowded around tables, their low chatter like a dull hum. Her father and stepmother were standing center of the room, soldiers on either side. When her father's eyes found hers, horror took claim of them. Evelynde's hands covered her mouth as she cried.

Thea was led to face them twenty paces out. Lorcan continued, coming to stand between the two parties.

Her father glared at Lorcan. "*What have you done to her?*"

She was grateful they had healed her, sparing him the image of how she'd appeared before. "Father," she said, as softly as she could perform, "I am all right."

His eyes were wild with rage when they returned to her.

She shook her head.

"It has become clear to me you think my threats empty," Lorcan said, walking idly between them. "It has also become clear your own demise does little to sway you. You are your mother's daughter in that." It was subtle, but something like apology weighed his brow.

Let us see what motivates you, he'd said. Her breath hitched.

"Put him on his knees," Lorcan commanded.

"No!" Thea tried to move, but the guard tightened his grip on her arm.

Two soldiers dragged her father toward Lorcan as Evelynde screamed her protest. One of the soldiers kicked at his legs until he fell to his knees, the other ripping his tunic until the top half of his body was bare. Her father looked up at her. This time it was he who shook his head.

Lorcan moved behind him, eyes fixed on Thea's. A silver flame erupted from his palm. She thought of Llun's melted face.

His hand came forward, flames exploding.

"Wait!"

Silver fire erupted over her father's back, only to be withdrawn in a blink. He arched and cried out, the heat of it surging through the space between them.

Thea screamed, thrashing at the man who held her. "No, *please*!" She looked at Lorcan. "I beg you!"

"This is your choice, Calithea," Lorcan said, his steely indifference returned. "He can burn or sit the throne."

"Do not give in to him!" Her father was on his hands and knees, panting, but he looked up at her with purpose. With resolve. He shook his head again.

Thea didn't know what to do. Panicked tears fell as her gaze darted between them. "Father—"

The flames returned.

Again, she kicked and thrashed but made no advancement. The guard was too strong. They were always so *Godsdamned* strong. Evelynde was on her knees, sobbing.

Her father collapsed, and Lorcan recalled the fire. His back was bright red and blistered, but he looked nothing like Llun. Not yet.

"Please," Thea cried. "*Please* stop!"

"You can end this," Lorcan said. His eyes narrowed, sharpening his gaze on her. As if she were far away, and the act would draw her closer. "You know what I want," he said with an insidious tenderness.

Thea had endured their beatings, their torture on her mind and body, and they had not broken her. But she knew she could not endure this. There was no reason to try. She looked at her father, who was back on his knees, face twisted in agony of more than one kind. "I'm sorry, Father," she cried, shaking her head.

"No!" He tried to climb to his feet, but a soldier kicked his back, drawing an agonizing wail as he fell forward. The soldier moved to deliver another below.

"Stop it!" she screamed. Lorcan held up his hand, and the soldier stepped back. She watched her father twisting on the ground and knew it was over. All she'd endured had been for nothing. Perhaps she had always known they would win in the end.

Fully resigned, she looked to Lorcan. "I—"

"*I challenge you to single combat.*"

The room went silent, her father's words cutting through.

Thea inhaled. "*No*," she whispered, shaking her head.

Lorcan scoffed. "Ulric, come now. As much as I would enjoy ending your life, it would give me no pleasure to do so under such... *inequitable* circumstances." Low chuckles rolled through the room.

"Father, no!"

He ignored her, climbing to his feet. "Man against man. Sword against sword. To the death. If you have the courage," he said, then spat on the ground between them.

Lorcan shook his head, dismissing the notion.

"You cannot refuse with your honor intact. Your men will bear witness to your cowardice." Stonelike resolution hardened on her father's face.

Lorcan flexed his jaw. His eyes moved to Thea with an indecipherable look. He walked slowly through the open space, looking at the faces of the soldiers surrounding them. "Is that what you want? *A fight?*"

Cheers erupted in the crowd.

"Then make a circle."

Thea and Evelynde screamed, but their cries were drowned out. Thea pulled and struggled against the man who held her arms until a knife appeared at her throat. Thea stilled, eyeing the blade. Katya smirked at her, resheathing it.

Roman placed a sword in his father's hands. He dropped another at her father's feet. Her father picked it up, swinging it with the nostalgia of one reliving the past.

Lorcan stood with his hands resting on the hilt of his sword, balancing the point on the stone floor. "I will give you one more chance to change your mind. Think of your daughter," he said and gestured at Thea. "And your wife."

Thea looked at her father, pleading. Begging. She knew he had been a renowned swordsman in his day, but she hadn't seen him train in years. He was not unfit, but it was clear his fighting days had passed. It was also clear that Lorcan had not stopped training. He had not stopped fighting.

Her father looked at her with sorrowful, but determined, eyes. She watched them turn to rage as he answered Lorcan with an attack.

He moved with grace and elegance she had not expected. He attacked in a fury, not dissimilar to Callum.

Lorcan parried the blows, but the force of it sent him back several paces. He continued the assault until Lorcan had no choice but to sidestep and flee. Her father's sword grazed Lorcan's shoulder as he passed. It gave her a spark of hope.

Lorcan appraised the wound. He looked irritated but not afraid. He moved into position, waiting for her father's next attack. It came immediately and with more fury than the first.

Again and again he attacked, never relenting until Lorcan fled.

Terror struck as she remembered the tourney and Callum's final match. His opponent had taken his time, worn him down. Thea saw it happening all over again.

She tried to scream in warning, but only added to the cacophony in the room.

Her father attacked, but this time, Lorcan did not move back. He didn't flee. He parried a blow from above, bringing his sword up and back down on top of her father's.

It clamored to the floor.

Lorcan then tilted and swung his blade, and her father cried out as it sliced into the flesh on the right side of his chest.

He stepped back as her father fell to one knee. Lorcan was playing with him. Dread and sorrow consumed her as she understood that her father would lose.

Ulric climbed back to his feet, grasping for his sword. His apologetic eyes met hers for a breath. His free hand held his side, and he charged forward. Heroic, but hopeless.

Lorcan easily parried and knocked his sword from his hand once again. He swung, this time slicing across the left side of his chest. Lorcan then kicked, and her father fell back onto the hard stone, a rough gasp tearing from his lips.

The room spun. Thea's legs gave way, and she stumbled. The hands that held her released. She braced her palms on the cool stone, watching as Lorcan slowly walked to her father, sword at his side, blood dripping from its end.

Some in the crowd were laughing. It echoed around her, the sounds converging. She wanted to look away. Her mind commanded it. But still she looked on.

Lorcan raised his sword. Her father looked at her. *I'm sorry*, his eyes said. She watched the blade rise, then fall, astounded when it stopped just shy of his throat.

"*Yield*," Lorcan commanded.

Thea blinked.

"*Never*," her father choked out between pained breaths, seemingly as surprised as she. He turned on his side, reaching for the sword that lay several feet from him.

"Yield!" Lorcan commanded again.

"No!" Her father tried edging his body closer to the blade.

"Father, please!" Thea's plea rang through the room, quieting the crowd.

He looked at her again, this time frantic and desperate, and understanding took hold of her. He had known she would give in on his behalf. He had also known he had no chance of winning. If he was dead, Lorcan would have little leverage on her. He was sacrificing himself. For her.

"*Please*," she cried.

Evelynde was on her hands and knees. "Ulric, yield! Do not leave us here on our own."

His arm fumbled about for the blade.

Lorcan stroked his brow and sighed. He walked around and kicked the sword far from her father's reach.

He closed his eyes and collapsed on his back. A roar ripped from him, giving voice to his rage, his heartbreak. The sound of it broke the parts of Thea that were somehow still whole. He lay still for several breaths before turning his face toward her.

Please, she mouthed. *Please, Father.*

His body slumped, and he sighed, turning back to the rafters. "I yield."

Thea exhaled, and Evelynde cried out.

Lorcan tossed his sword aside. The satisfied look on his face as he watched her father struggle to get up made Thea want to charge at him. When her father tried to stand, he fell forward, clutching his right side.

Several in the crowd chuckled, Roman among them. Thea glared at them. She started to crawl across the floor, but someone grabbed a fistful of her hair, hauling her back.

"Help him up," Lorcan commanded, amused, gesturing with his hands to either side.

Her father cried out as Roman and another soldier hauled him to his feet. Unable to stand, he collapsed against Roman, and what happened next transpired so quickly Thea was struck for several breaths before her mind could make sense of it.

With an unexpected swiftness, her father pulled a dagger from Roman's belt, launching it in one continuous move. It sailed in a fury across the room, nearly too fast to follow. Thea's eyes went wide, believing it would strike true, but Lorcan shifted, and it sailed by. It hit with a cracking, wet thud, burying itself to the hilt in the head of a man behind him.

All watched, mouths agape.

The man stood lifeless far longer than one would expect. Until, without prelude, his limp frame collapsed.

The room was silent.

For the first time, Thea saw surprise on Lorcan's face. A thin line of blood trailed down his cheek where the blade had grazed him.

A bloodcurdling scream erupted, causing all to flinch. Evelynde. She rocked, her arms covering her head as she wailed. Thea's eyes snapped in the direction of what plagued her.

Everything stopped. Her breath, her thoughts, her heart. Thea watched as Roman twisted his sword before he tore it free from her father's chest.

Her lips stretched around a roar that ruptured from her. As if someone had reached inside and ripped it from within. Stolen it against her will.

Her father fell back onto the floor, writhing and convulsing, clutching at his chest.

Thea reared back, tearing free from her captor, leaving some of her hair in their fist. She scrambled across the floor to his side.

She tried to cover his wound, but warm blood poured out over her hands. "Help me!" She looked around the room. "You can heal him!"

Lorcan knelt beside her, moving slowly, hesitantly, and, with sickening softness, said, "We cannot heal such a wound."

Thea screamed.

Her father reached for her with slow, jerking movements, blood spurting from his lips.

Helpless, she pressed harder against the wound, but his breaths drew further apart, his eyes quickly losing their focus.

"No, *please*, Father," she pleaded, cried, begged. To him, to the Gods, to anyone who would listen. She took his hand in hers, holding it to her face. "Father, I don't know what to do. *Please*," she cried. "Please do not leave me. *Tell me what to do.*"

His body jerked. "Do not—give in," he said, barely above a whisper. The desperation in his eyes faded to tenderness, to love. His love for her.

His other hand reached for her, but he gasped, eyes going wide. With a final shudder, the arm fell limp at his side. Thea felt his hand in hers go loose. She watched as life left his body behind.

Her father, the king, was dead.

Her heart cracked, snapping against its cage in her chest. Again, and again, rising up her throat with each beat until it pounded on the back of her tongue, ringing between her ears. Searing and staggering. It ruptured from her lips in a howl that set her own blood to thickening, guts twisting.

She could not anticipate the attack. It came on her in a rush. Ice traveled through her veins, exploding in her chest. She seized and collapsed, writhing, falling back onto the floor.

Lorcan knelt over her, eyes wide with concern. She met his concern with malice, back arching from the floor.

His hand hovered above her head, glowing silver. "Alister!"

She watched with disgust as it lowered to touch her, and the repulsion that reverberated through her overruled the pain. It turned her grief to rage.

With all the fight she could muster, she reached up with an unsteady hand, grasping his wrist. A golden glow erupted, and he screamed, wrenching his arm free as he fell back.

Alister stood over her, keeping a distance. The ice receded, and the weight lifted from her chest. She inhaled the stench of scorched flesh, delighting in it, vowing to make more.

Thea looked at her trembling hands. *Cassia, help me.* She felt herself start to drift and railed against it.

"She's resisting!"

Lorcan stood above her, holding his injured arm. The sleeve of his shirt was burned away, revealing sizzled, blackened flesh.

What is in you wants out. She remembered Breeda's words. *Give in,* something told her. *Surrender.* To what? All she had was rage. She felt a spark, and small golden flames flickered to life at her palms.

Gasps erupted around her. One may have come from her. With no hesitation, she flung her hands toward Lorcan, her rage fueling the fire. It roared through the open air, those in its path jumping back.

Blinded by the golden light, she heard Lorcan scream, "Bind her!"

Whatever door she had opened slammed shut, and she jerked as the flames withered out.

Lorcan stood over her again, and she laughed with an ice-cold edge, charged by the fear in him. Thea looked him square in the eyes, her smile violent and vowing. *"I'm going to kill you."*

"Take her back to her room. I want two maintaining her bindings at all times," Lorcan commanded, recovering his composure.

Someone pulled her to her feet and started to drag her away.

She took one last look at her father, lifeless in a sea of his own blood. His blue eyes were still open but saw nothing. "I'm going to kill you all!"

63

Neith

"I regret the manner of our parting, dear sister, and I pray it is not too late. I would have you come to Seahenge to be with me when my child greets this world."

UNOFFICIAL CORRESPONDENCE FROM SONIA THRONDSEN TO LIA THRONDSEN, 1183 AQ
RECOVERED AFTER THE BLOODY DAY

Calithea Ironne screamed. It was the only sound in the room. Neith felt it rattle her bones. "I'm going to kill you all!"

She fought, roaring in a rage as she was dragged from the room, leaving behind a crimson path from her saturated skirts. The girl cast daggers into every set of eyes she met. Her own wild, feral-like.

Blood continued to pool under the lifeless body of Ulric Ironne, falling into and traveling the crevices of the stone floor.

Neith blinked, struck, unable to move or breathe as the edges of her vision began to cloud. The beat of her heart thumped loudly in her head as if her eardrums themselves had been struck.

She felt a hand on her shoulder. She turned to look. Sam. His eyes searched hers.

It had all happened so quickly.

Her father scrambled to his feet, storming toward her brother. Without warning, he struck Roman with the back of his hand so severe he flew back, crashing onto the floor.

Roman gaped up at their father, holding his cheek in disbelief.

"Clear the room!" Lorcan commanded. He motioned for Neith, Magnus, and a few others to stay. "Take the queen back to her room. And get these bodies out of here." He kicked the sword Ulric had fought with, and it clattered across the floor.

Sam stood firm by her side, and he was not told to leave.

Evelynde Ironne stared motionless at the body of her husband. When the guard grasped her arm, she looked up at him curiously. He coaxed her gently, and she didn't fight. She simply stood, turned, and walked away.

"You fool!" Lorcan paced in a rage.

Roman climbed to his feet, blood gushing from his nose. "He tried to *kill you.*"

"He was no threat to me." He strode back to Roman, grasping the collar of his vest. *"Do you not see what you have done?"*

Neith looked at Magnus for direction, but he shook his head with the slightest of movements. A warning not to intervene. Dryden sat with his feet propped on a table, unaffected by the violence that had occurred.

Roman's eyes were wide as he took in their father's. "I'm—I'm sorry."

"Any chance we had of her joining us was just destroyed by you." He looked at her brother with such disdain it sent a chill through her. He jerked Roman forward, then released him, and he stumbled back. "Remove yourself from my sight."

Katya appeared at his side, holding a cloth to his nose. He ripped it from her grasp, and she shrank back. "Father, *please.*"

Lorcan turned on his heels and roared. "I said, remove yourself!"

Neith felt it in her chest.

Roman recoiled. He looked at Neith and the fear on him turned to a snarl. He turned and marched from the room, Katya on his heels.

Neith looked down. Her breath was still coming in quick shallow bursts. She could still hear Calithea screaming. Still smell the singed flesh of both their fathers.

"What do we do with the girl now?" Dryden asked, drawing her attention.

Lorcan's eyes scanned the floor. "I don't know. I need to think."

Neith had never seen him so unnerved. So unhinged. It encouraged her distress.

"I could take her to Nighhelm," Dryden proposed.

Neith turned to look at him, making no attempt to hide her disgust.

"I said I need to think!" Lorcan swiped at the table in front of him, knocking its contents to the floor.

Dryden's hands came up in supplication. "Of course, Lord King."

Her father panted, gripping the edge of the table, and looked around the room. When his eyes met hers, he stopped. "Everyone out. I need to speak with my daughter."

Most appeared content to oblige. Dryden was slow to rise but heeded the command. Magnus walked by her with an encouraging nod. When Sam didn't move, Lorcan peered at him as if only just noticing he was present. "Did I not speak, soldier?"

Sam was hesitant, but after a nod from Neith, he followed the others out.

Lorcan collapsed into a chair. "I am satisfied to see you inspire such loyalty," he said, fingers combing back his long black hair, "but I'll ask you to remind your soldiers to whom their ultimate fidelity lies."

"Of course, Father. I assure you, he is loyal. And first to his king." She took the seat next to him, doing her best to appear collected. Neith held out her hands. "Give me your arm."

It took him a moment to understand. She turned his burned arm around, examining the damage. It was deep. A nasty burn.

He stared at her while she worked to heal it. It was distracting, his gaze penetrating, as if he were aware of the wall she held up between them, and he desperately wanted to see what was on the other side. "You wanted a chance with her. Now you will have it."

Neith looked up at him and frowned. "I don't understand."

"I want you to speak with Calithea."

She blinked, ensuring she had heard correctly. "What do you imagine I could say that would overcome this night's events? It is over, Father. If I try to talk to her, it will be *my* face she spits in this time, and rightfully so."

"She is cousin to you, Neith. You are the granddaughters of Faela Throndsen. The first and only queen of Icena. Both born to royal blood. You are connected. Bound to each other as all women of Icena are. As your mothers were."

Neith paused, her ether retracting. "This is why you try so hard to turn her?"

He watched her as she continued to think it through.

"As the eldest living descendant of Faela, Calithea is heir to Icena."

"And?" he asked. He was using this moment to teach her.

Her brow furrowed as she released his nearly healed arm. "And you wish to reunite the tribes under the banner of Icena. United under Thrane."

Her father nodded, his temperament easing further. "Where do we go from here?"

"She'll never join us now. Not after this." Neith looked to the pool of blood where Ulric Ironne died. Calithea's scream echoed in her mind. It reminded her of the woman Rhea, in Godsreach, and how she'd raged at the sight of her mutilated daughter. It sent a chill through her.

"What do we do?"

Neith considered. "We can execute her. That would make Roman heir." It tasted bitter in her mouth.

"The tribes would never unite under him. The Iceni people would not accept a Thranean-born ruler."

Neith could sense there was more to his objection to executing Calithea. He had a clear impartiality toward the girl. She had never seen him work so hard to turn someone. It had always been a simple question with only one chance to choose right. She was special beyond her birthright, but Neith did not yet know why. "If we want the tribes, she must be convinced. Or bargained with. But what we held to bargain with is now lost."

He reached for a mug, peering in to see its contents. He tipped it up to his lips, seemingly satisfied by what he found. "I'm giving you the chance you asked for."

Neith scoffed. "Yes, but now it is an impossible task," she said. "Surely, you see that."

"Spend some time with her. If she can't be persuaded before the next moon, she'll hang from the castle gate. As your brother suggested." He stood abruptly. "Or I'll give her to Dryden to do with as he pleases."

She nodded, and he walked from the room, leaving her on her own.

Neith sat at the table, head in her hands, trying to make sense of what her father had laid at her feet. She had never seen him so impulsive, careless even. It unnerved her. Irritated her.

The door opened, and Sam walked through, taking the seat beside her. He reached for her hand, thumb running softly over the pink scar.

"Are you all right?" he asked. "That was…"

"Horrifying," she said, looking up at him.

He nodded.

"He wants me to talk to her."

"To Calithea?"

"He has given me until the next moon to change her mind. Else she will be executed." She excluded the atrocious alternative proposed by Dryden. Neith turned toward Sam, running her fingers over the moon patch on his vest.

"She watched her father murdered by your own brother, and he wants you to speak with her?" He was evidently as perplexed as she by the command.

Neith shrugged. "I do not understand it either. I do not believe he wants to execute her, but he may feel he has no choice. He would have her sit on the throne of Icena."

Sam's brows rose. His eyes flicked around for a breath before returning to hers with an idea in them. "Many lives could be saved by this. If Icena reunited and pledged to Thrane, Vikandal would be more likely to come to our side without a fight."

Neith did not believe that to be her father's driving motivation, but it was a welcome consequence.

"Will you try?" he asked.

"I cannot see what I could say or do that would mean anything to her. But, yes," she said, and sighed. "I will try."

For two days, Neith considered exactly that. She was terrified to speak to her, to look into her eyes and see the merited hate in them. She hoped she could find a way to get through.

Calithea had not been pulled from her room. She was brought food she did not eat, and wine she did not drink. She didn't speak or ask questions. No protests were made. The guards reported she barely moved from a chair, spending all day staring out a window overlooking the lake.

Resigned that she would never be ready, she made the walk to Calithea's room with Sam and Bellamy.

Neith found her exactly as reported. Dressed in a simple white shift, she was curled up in a large chair, her legs draped over one of its arms. Sunlight bathed her bare feet. She didn't stir or look over when the door opened and closed.

Sam and Bellamy waited by the door as Neith took the chair opposing hers, a tea table between them. A plate of meat, cheese, and bread sat untouched.

"Do you know who I am?"

Calithea didn't answer.

"I am—"

"I know who you are, cousin." Her voice was low, barely above a whisper, and simmered with animosity. Neith only then realized how deep the tone, now robbed of its zest. "Why have you come?"

Neith decided in the moment that honesty was her only option, knowing she did not possess the gift of persuasion. "Because I want to save your life. And hopefully the lives of many others."

Calithea laughed with a dark amusement, gaze still directed at the window. "Why do you care?"

"Our mothers were sisters, were they not?"

"They were also enemies."

"In the end, yes. That does not mean we have to be." Neith took a slow, disguised breath, attempting to conceal her shaking hands under her skirts. She'd changed from her uniform into one of the new dresses Maeve had commissioned for her. It was deep amethyst in color, its fabric soft and delicate, styled like other dresses they'd discovered in Highclere.

"That story was inked to parchment when your brother drove his sword through my father's heart." No part of Calithea moved, save for her lips. She did not even blink.

Neith nodded. There was no rebuttal to be made. "Calithea," she said, shifting in her chair, "my father will have you executed before the next moon."

Calithea turned to face her. The haunted look in her eyes caused Neith to stiffen. "Do you think that frightens me?"

"I do not know," Neith said in earnest.

Her green eyes were swollen and full of contempt, but her voice was steady. "You have beaten me, tortured me, imprisoned me. Taken my home. Murdered my father. You're all monsters."

Neith stiffened at the word.

A trace of grief cracked through Calithea's steely exterior. "He was a good man. A good king."

Neith swallowed. She knew she was not doing well. "I am sorry for it all. Truly."

Calithea scoffed. "Get out." She returned her gaze to the window. "If you've any decency in you."

Neith saw no purpose in attempting to detract from all Calithea had endured. "What is done cannot be undone."

"No," Calithea said, so low Neith could scarcely hear her. "It cannot."

She looked like a ghost of the woman in the painting Neith had seen when she first came to Highclere. The fight she'd witnessed the day her brother dragged her into the throne room was gone, replaced with resignation. A deceitfully quiet, paradoxical acceptance of her fate. It looked unnatural, and there was something devastating about it. "I lost my own mother," Neith said, "like you, before I had the chance to know her."

"Good."

Neith tried to conceal the sting. She took a breath, unable to recall having ever told the story. "I was only three winters. She was on a supply run in Straeth when her party crossed paths with Esērii on their way to Godsreach. There was a fight, and only my mother survived, but she was gravely wounded. A group of townspeople happened upon the aftermath. Rather than help a dying woman, they condemned her. Declared her a sorceress." Neith looked down for a breath. "Do you know what extremists of The Faith of the Hexad do to those they label so?"

Calithea didn't answer. Her posture gave the impression that she was not even listening.

"They cut off her ears. Gouged out her eyes."

Calithea's eyes flicked but didn't find their way to Neith.

"Her eyes were green. Like yours, I imagine." Neith dreamt the story so often as a girl that it had come to feel more like a memory. The images her young mind created were with her always. "Then they cut out her tongue. Though we cannot be sure of the order of all she endured. They believe the cursed soul will wander the void for eternity, deaf, blind, and mute."

Calithea shifted in her chair. "Why are you telling me this? I don't want to hear this."

"After all that, they bound her to a stake to be cleansed in Thelos's fire. Their faith tells them they must." Neith watched Calithea carefully as she spoke. "Her body was still burning when my father found it."

Calithea's head snapped in Neith's direction. Her eyes were angry, but Neith noticed a subtle uncertainty in them. "If you are looking for a sympathetic ear, you are far dafter than you present."

Neith shook her head. "I look for nothing on my behalf. I only ask you to see that one death always leads to another. It never ends unless we decide it so."

"Save your words," Calithea said, unmoved. "Tell your father he has sent you on a fool's errand."

"If you let him execute you—"

"*Let* him?" Calithea laughed, and this time it had a sentiment of madness to it.

Neith paused to choose her words more carefully. "If you accept his terms, many lives will be spared. No one else need die. Your brothers cannot hold Eastwatche indefinitely. I am trying to save your life."

Calithea frowned. "Did you expect to find me grateful?"

"No," Neith admitted.

Calithea's eyes narrowed on her before she turned back to the window, nestling against the chair. "Whose room have you taken?" she asked, with ice. "One of my sisters'?"

A wave of shame washed over Neith, but she straightened her shoulders. "Your sister Catrianna's, I believe."

Calithea had a quiet confidence, a boldness, even in that moment, even broken, that Neith could not help but envy. She could not find a single similarity between them. If Calithea was the sun, she was the moon.

Neith did not question her bravery. That had been evident to all the past moon. What she did question was the presentation of apathy. She questioned Calithea's indifference to her own execution. Something stirred beneath her eyes. They moved too quickly. Neith could discern it in the tapping of her foot, the fisting of her hands. She did not want death. Neith believed she would meet it before betraying her family or her country, but she feigned a detachment that wasn't whole. There was something else to it. Some other motivation. And then she understood.

Neith hesitated, knowing she had only one chance to get it right. "I know what your father was doing. I know why he challenged mine. He was trying to sacrifice himself. So you wouldn't have to choose. Because he loved you, and he knew the love you held for him would break you."

Malice slowly took hold of Calithea's face. "What do you and yours know of love? You have brought only horror and hate to our home." Eyes fixed on Neith's, one of her heels came forward, and she kicked the plate of food from the table. It clamored on the floor.

Sam and Bellamy were at her side in a breath, but Neith held up a hand, ushering them back. She felt Calithea's power raging against the bindings. A hint of her fight returning.

"I also know that is what you are trying to do now," Neith said, her confidence growing as she watched her cousin react. "Do you fear someone will try to come for you? Your brothers? A lover, perhaps?"

Calithea's breath caught, and Neith knew she spoke truth.

She took the edge from her tone. "You can save them by finding a way to align yourself with us. You are the heir to Icena. My father would make you its queen."

Calithea looked at Neith as if she'd lost government of her wits.

"My father is a determined man, Calithea. He always gets what he wants, one way or another. He is also terrifyingly patient. Forget not, he spent twenty years planning this invasion. You are an intelligent woman. Do you think he hasn't thought through every possibility? That he doesn't have a plan and three more if one fails? Do not sacrifice your life in vain. Let your father's death be the last."

Calithea was shaking, her eyes drowning. She looked back at the window. "You are wasting your time."

Neith knew at that moment that she was not. "I have seventeen more days to find out." She stood, brushing crumbs of bread from her skirt. "I will have a new plate of food brought to you."

"It will find its way to the floor with the others."

Neith sighed. "Then we will simply bring another." She started to leave but turned back, resting her hands on the back of the chair. "You are right to question what we know of love. I operate under no falsehood that anyone would sacrifice themselves so for me." Neith nodded, and with full sincerity, said, "I envy you that."

When the door closed behind her, she exhaled, falling back against it. Her pulse raced from the exchange, and relief flooded through her that it was over. As taxing as it had been, she couldn't help but feel she'd done well. The look in Sam's eyes told her so.

"Do you think there is any chance she will change her mind?" Max asked. "It seems unlikely, given all she's endured."

"Very little, but I will try. It is the right thing to do," Neith answered, staring at the fire that cracked between them. She'd taken supper with her friends in the gardens. It was becoming routine. Neith had grown tired of the antics in the dining halls. The drinking and fighting were not how she cared to spend her time.

Ayla appraised her, head tilting. "Do you care for her?"

Neith wanted to answer *yes, of course,* but chose wiser words. "I cannot deny a certain affection for her. It seems natural when one finds another is one's own kin. I have not had much of that and never anything like a sister. But that will never happen. She despises me, as she should. This is the only thing I can do for her."

You can help her escape, she thought.

"Will your father really execute her?" Ayla asked.

"I have no doubt." She did, though, but wouldn't admit it to the group.

"It's unfortunate. You can feel how powerful she is, even with the bindings," Bellamy said.

"A powerful ally but a formidable enemy," Sam added, and Neith met his eyes.

"Can you see her power? What is it like?" Petra asked.

Neith shook her head. "She is bound too tightly. I cannot see what it is, only that it is… significant."

"But, surely not such as yours?" Ayla asked, tipping up her mug.

Neith shrugged. "I cannot say, but I do not feel nether on her."

"I admit I feel for her," Petra said. "That was an awful way to watch your own father die."

The group looked from one to another, their faces telling they shared the sentiment. They also knew they were likely alone in this, and such words stayed between them.

"That depends on the father, I think," Ayla said softly. All eyes shifted to her. She looked up as if surprised the words had left her lips.

Neith couldn't help but feel that a part of her, however small, might agree.

Ayla's cheeks reddened, and she stood, directing her words to Neith. "Forgive me." She turned and walked off toward the woods.

Max was already on his feet, chasing behind. The remaining four looked at each other. They were all familiar with Hywel Dryden.

Neith sighed and rubbed her eyes, the toll of the day weighing heavy. "I will retire," she said to the group.

Sam stood, holding out his hand to help her rise.

They bid good night to Petra and Bellamy and made their way to her room. When they reached her door, she turned to face him. "Will you come in?"

Sam looked down the hallway. Neith had told him about her conflict with Dryden, and how he'd probed Ayla for information. She left out the beating. "I'm not sure that is wise. If we were found on our own, it might—"

"Might what?" she challenged. "You are a soldier under my command. It is no one's business what we discuss in private, nor how often." Truth be told, she was apprehensive to be on her own. She needed reprieve. From the day, from her own thoughts. Sam was the only one who could provide it.

He smiled, then nodded. "As you say, Captain."

"Easily persuaded," she said, and returned the smile. "Are you not?"

He reached up and touched her face. "When it comes to you, yes."

Neith's cheeks grew warm as she turned away. The room was dark, lit only by the moonlight pouring in from the open windows. It was far too hot for a fire.

When the door closed behind them, she turned, pressing herself and Sam against it. Stretched all the way on the top of her toes, she still could not reach his mouth. When her hands came up around his neck to pull him down, he made no hesitation to find her lips with his own. He tasted of wine and warmth, and she wanted more.

Neith deepened the kiss, and his arms wrapped around her, hand trailing up her back. She wanted to know what it would feel like without the barrier of her dress. To be touched, and touch in return. To put her mouth places she had not seen. The thought sent her pulse rising. His hold on her tightened, as if she had shared the image in her mind.

More than once, Neith had hoped their affections might advance, but Sam always seemed to catch himself and retreat. She hadn't yet summoned the courage to be the one to try for more.

She pulled back from the kiss, her aim to take her lips somewhere else. The moment they brushed his throat, he stiffened and let her go.

Neith blinked at the abrupt shift. He leaned in and kissed her again, but it was brief, chaste.

"I'll light some candles," he said as he walked around her.

Neith stood in place, stunned, perhaps a touch rejected. But it was subtle, and she didn't want to derive false meaning.

"It is sort of remarkable how much you look alike," he said, putting a honey-colored flame to a candle.

"Who?" She kicked off her boots and eyed the water pitcher across the room, feeling suddenly parched.

"You and Calithea."

Neith frowned, glancing back at him as she walked. "We could not be more different."

"Your coloring, yes. Which is perhaps why I did not see it at first."

Neith laughed. "That is a bit cruel, actually." She filled two glasses with water and walked to hand one to him.

"I'm sorry," he said, his eyes apologetic as he frowned. "I don't understand."

Neith inclined her head. "She is… *beautiful*, and bold, and confident. And people love her. They're drawn to her, like the sun. Look at the way my own father behaves around her."

Sam searched her eyes for understanding. He peered at her with the perplexity of one being tasked with justifying the sky blue. He laughed, but it was not the sort born of humor. "You do not believe you are beautiful."

Neith turned away, abashment flaring hot on her cheeks. She stood with her back to him, eyes clamped shut.

He stepped closer, the sound of his boot softer than the thrum of her heart. His hand came around her neck, fingers gently pulling her hair behind her shoulder, tracing along its length. Part of her wanted to run from the room. Something underneath said stay. Stay and see what happens.

She swallowed and turned back to him, gaze low, teeth tugging at her bottom lip.

"Look at me," he beckoned.

Her eyes slowly rose to meet his. She found them serious, intentional. He had something to say, and he wanted her to listen.

"It is not the sun I marvel at each night." He touched her hair again. "It is the midnight sky." Both hands came up to hold her face. "It is the moon that calls to me." He spoke assuredly and with an affection that seized her heart. Her eyes stung and swelled, unable to understand why kindness hurt so much more than callousness. "To say that you are beautiful is not enough. In a sea of faces, yours is the one I would look upon."

She struggled to keep his gaze.

His fingertips grazed her jaw, lifting her chin. "Sometimes I wonder what lives within these eyes that causes you to see yourself so falsely."

For the first time, Neith wondered this herself.

His fingertips moved across her cheek, his eyes following the path. They moved down her neck, over the dip of her shoulder, slowly making their way down the length of her arm. His fingers wrapped around her wrist, lifting her hand to his lips. They pressed into the flesh of her palm, leaving a soft kiss on the pink scar. His ether echoed up her arm, setting a slight heave to her chest. He returned her hand to her side, eyes fixed on hers. "Do you understand?"

She nodded, feeling a single tear spill.

Sam stepped forward, and his lips brushed hers. He kissed her without hesitation, telling her how much he meant his words. The warmth of his mouth sent a ripple down her body that dispatched her arms around him, fingertips pressing into his back. His hands tightened in her hair, and her lips parted as a small sound escaped.

He pulled back to look at her. His longing sent a swell of the same through her, and she pressed up onto her toes to close the space he created. She tightened her grip, pulling him back to her lips, and he didn't fight.

Her body ached, as if she could only get close enough it would cease or catch fire—either would suffice.

His lips left hers, trailing soft kisses down her neck and across her throat, as her head fell back. The thought that she had no idea what she was doing wavered in her mind. What if she did something wrong? She waited for the vulnerability to overtake her, to make her run, but it didn't come. Instead, she moved her hands between them, fingers tugging at the buttons on his vest. She pulled at his tunic, slipping her hand underneath. When she touched his bare chest, he jumped back, putting space between them.

He pressed his eyes shut, exhaling.

She wanted to say something, but she knew she would fumble her words. When his eyes opened again, she tried to tell him, with hers, what she was feeling. What she wanted. She knew her affection for him was growing and that she was not alone in it. Whatever it was between them, Neith knew it was not common.

She could not understand it. She could not make sense of how some-one like him, so striking, so powerful, so beautiful, wanted *her*. He could have anyone. *In a sea of faces, yours is the one I would look upon.* She wanted to say something as beautiful to him, but she didn't possess that gift. Nothing she could say would ever compare to his words, nor would they convey the admiration and desire she felt for him.

Neith stepped back and turned, making for the door. Her fingers wrapped around the metal lock and clicked it into place. Heart pounding, belly twisting in knots, she walked back to him. She met his eyes and began to undo the laces of her dress.

His lips parted as he inhaled, and his hands came up to cover hers, stilling her action. "That is not what I am after."

"I know." And she did. She swallowed. "Do you not *desire*, me?" Neith felt her cheeks heat at the use of such a word. She struggled to meet his eyes again.

His brows creased. "Surely you cannot think that my objection."

"Then what is your objection?"

"It is only that I do not want you to wake tomorrow in regret." One of his hands came up to cradle her face, and she leaned into it. "You do not owe me anything."

"I know that, too." She tried to continue her work on the laces, but his hand held firm. His eyes made clear his struggle. He studied her face, her lips, the curve of her neck, down to where her chest heaved and their hands met.

"I want this with you." Her words were a whisper, and as they left her lips, she knew they were true.

She watched the struggle in him slowly retreat. He fought against it, and for a moment, she thought it would win. But slowly, reluctantly, his hands set hers free.

He watched with ultimate attention as she unlaced the dress, pulling it down one shoulder, then the other. Summoning all the bravery that existed within her, she let it, and her shift, fall to the floor.

The quickening of his breath sent her own heart thrumming. His eyes moved down her body, leisurely, with the care and pace of someone in a moment long considered.

Neith fought the urge to cover herself. She held her shoulders back, leaning into the fear.

Sam stepped forward, but her hand on his chest halted him. He frowned, searching her eyes for understanding. She looked down at his body, still clothed.

Eyes on hers, he let his unbuttoned vest fall from his shoulders, then lifted his tunic off his body. She watched him pull off one boot and then the other before his hands moved to the ties on his trousers. Neith swallowed back the knot of nerves tangling in her throat. When she saw him, all of him, something stirred within. Something that had been asleep, dormant, that he alone brought life to.

She traced the lines of the rippled scar on his neck. He leaned into her touch as if they were reliving the moment together, silently in their minds.

They edged closer until their bodies grazed. She ran her hands over his chest, as his hands found her face, raising it until their eyes met. He brushed her hair back. "You are certain?"

Neith nodded. She was terrified, but she was certain. "You will tell me if I do something wrong?"

Sam leaned forward, brushing his lips against hers. So slowly, so soft it felt more like a whisper. "That is not possible."

Neith wrapped her arms around his body, fingers pressing into the muscles tightening across his back as she pulled him against her. The feeling of her bare breasts against his chest had her aching, and she opened her mouth against his. He kissed her deep, unhurried, their tongues exploring as his hands curled in her hair.

They made small, synchronized steps toward the bed until Neith felt her calves meet the wooden frame. His hands trailed down her back, over the curve to her thighs, and he dipped, lifting her from the ground. He laid her down and climbed on, shifting them back in one swift movement.

When he pressed against the softness between her thighs, she moaned, and he captured it with his mouth. Heat rushed her, rolling through her body, heavy and consuming, and she rocked her hips against his to bring it about again.

Urgency sparked between them, and his lips found her neck, his hands her breasts, and she bowed into the touch.

Her fingers tangled in his dark curls as his mouth descended, tongue swirling, her body moving in tune. His hands gripped her hips, and she bowed again when his teeth grazed the underside of her belly.

When his shoulders dipped between her thighs, she swallowed, fighting the instinct to snap them shut and escape the vulnerability.

But then lips grazed her, the softest part of her, and she inhaled, and need like she had never felt consumed her. She whispered his name, and he reached up for her hand, interlacing his fingers with hers.

Neith arched, thighs pressing against him as he kissed her. She wanted to cry, to laugh, to scream. To run. To never leave. Feelings and thoughts raced through her at such a pace she could not perceive them. It was the gentlest of touches, yet she could feel it over every inch of her skin. In the arch of her back, the curl of her toes, the tingle on her lips.

Pressure built and rumbled. Heavy, thick, and full of heat. Her mind raced to make sense of how something so strange was not strange at all. How one person could make another feel such a way. A cry slipped from her lips as her body moved against his mouth.

As she feared it would become too much, that she could not withstand it, every muscle, every fiber in her body seized. She clamped her eyes shut and saw the nighttime sky.

Then again.

And again.

And again.

Neith grasped at the bedsheets, searching for something, anything to anchor herself to as it echoed, quieting with each pulse.

She lay still, tangled in the sheets, save for the heaving of her chest. Sam was still trailing gentle kisses on the inside of her thigh when she called for him.

He moved back up her body, and she reached for him, bringing his mouth to hers. Her taste on his lips, on his tongue, reignited her, and she clutched her legs around him, desperate to return to touch.

Her hips curled in response to the resistance of the firmness converging at her center. He reached between them and watched her, brows drawn, eyes tender, as he slowly pressed himself inside. She stiffened, her fingers digging into his back against the sting.

He paused, eyes asking, his thumb trailing her cheek.

Neith nodded.

His hips rolled forward, and he groaned as his face buried into the curve of her neck, thrusting in until she felt his body flush with hers. She cried out, not at the pain, though there was pain. She cried out at the discovery. At the sensation of him inside of her. At the intimacy of being touched by another in a place she had not touched herself.

He moved slowly, unrushed, as if they had nothing but time. Their hands, their hips, their mouths, never stopped moving. The attentiveness with which he touched and admired her with his body continued until she saw the stars once again.

When Sam cried out, he collapsed against her, shaking, and she held him close to her. Close to her heart. They stayed wrapped around each other, lazily tracing lines on the other's skin. They didn't speak. They didn't need to.

He stayed with her until the fear of exposure drove her to make him leave. When he kissed her goodbye, it hadn't felt like goodbye.

Neith smiled under the morning sun. She'd woken some time ago, but had not risen. She lay lost, reliving the night before, every sensation taking her back. The soreness between her thighs, the salty smell of sweat on her skin. When she stretched her arms, she remembered how his touch had arched her from the sheets.

Her body had been starved for a tenderness it hadn't known existed. And perhaps her heart. Her life had been so small, her world so small, but now she was seeing what existed in the rest of it. And she knew she wanted more. For the first time in her life, Neith considered that her father's path might not be her own.

64

Thea

"We are not fated to the same end because we undertake a task those before us failed to complete. There is more than one path to the same destination."

THE RECOVERED JOURNALS OF SONIA THRONDSEN, 1182 AQ

Thea was angry she'd been so easily read.

Neith Dracos had seen through her in a way she could not clearly see herself. As if she had simply sat in the chair, exposed, naked, helpless to be picked apart. Her cousin had not needed powers to know her thoughts.

All she felt was rage. A rage so consuming that it was silent.

She lay on the bed after waking, not bothering to rise after the sun made its ascent.

Midday passed. A plate of something grew cold on the table across the room. Calix told her that if she did not eat that day, she would be forced to.

Thea watched bits of dust dance around in the fractal hues of greens and blues pouring in through the window. She thought of the ruins, wishing she were there, laid out in the grass, letting the earth slowly consume her. Sinking beneath the moss and stone to sleep forever with the Gods of ancient times.

Her cousin had looked different from how she remembered. The first time Thea had seen her in the throne room, she had been wearing a soldier's uniform. Black leather with patches and badges, her hair secured in a sleek knot. Face like stone. Yesterday, she'd come in a silk dress, with her long black hair brushed out in soft waves. Neith Dracos had regarded her with benevolence. A calculated decision, Thea imagined.

Neith had been the one Breeda and Cerys feared, but she seemed the least frightening of them all. Perhaps that was only because she could not feel their powers. She could not even feel her own. Despite it all, she believed the girl had been genuine in her desire to help, however misguided and naive. Thea would never join them. She would rather burn.

Seventeen days, her cousin had said, until she would be executed. It seemed dreadfully long, yet frightfully short. She could only be grateful she wasn't in the pit.

Thea was afraid to die. She would not deny it. But she feared far more they would not execute her and would use her against her brothers. The way they had tried to use her love for her father against her. She feared Callum and Marten marching on Highclere, naive to the evil that lurked. Ignorant of the foolishness in the attempt. Thea could not have their deaths in her name. There were too many already. If she were dead, they might not march. They could mourn her and move on. Run away from this place. Live.

Do not give in, she heard her father say.

"Never," she whispered.

She saw no other path. Her death was inevitable. The manner of it might be her last chance to choose something for herself. Her mother had sacrificed her own life. So had her father. She could do the same for those she loved. She could strike the cliff. She could fall on the sword.

There were no weapons in her room. The sharpest thing she could recall was a wooden comb. That would give her no death. They were going to force her to eat, so starving herself was not an option. She had no doubt they could. She could attack someone important. Give them no choice but to kill her. But with what means? She was not a fighter, and the power she had somehow called before was gone. She felt nothing but a newfound dormancy.

Thea realized she was lying six feet from her answer.

She studied the latch on the wooden shutters. It would be so easy to simply flip it open, step onto the sill, and jump.

If she jumped, they wouldn't march.

Nervous energy punched through her like small strikes of lightning, causing her to twitch. She glanced at the guards by the door. Their eyes were always on her. Would they reach her before she was free?

Thea wondered if she would die. She worried it wasn't high enough.

The door opened, drawing the guards' attention.

Thea threw back her blanket and sprang from the bed. Her bare feet thumped on the wooden floor as she sprinted. She was swinging open the shutters before she heard one of them yell.

Thea stepped onto the ledge, grasping the frame, eyes wide, taking in the gardens below. She knew if she thought about it, she wouldn't jump.

So she didn't think.

The moment her feet left the windowsill, she felt only one thing. And it was not what she expected. She felt only regret.

The delicate resolve she had built shattered, crumbling away like the walls of the pit. Her arms and legs flailed wildly, desperate for something, *anything* to cling to. But there was nothing. Only the air in the space between her and the ground she plummeted toward.

She'd thought it would happen fast. That there would be no time to think. She had grossly misjudged.

She thought of her brothers and sisters. Cassia protect them. Tell them to abandon this place. Tell them it cannot be won.

She tried to tell herself there were worse ways to die. That this had purpose, honor, dignity. It was a sacrifice for those she loved.

But none of it really mattered. It was too late. She'd jumped.

She stilled the scramble in her arms, releasing them free around her. Her eyes remained open, watching the ground coming up to meet her. The only thing she hoped was that it was high enough to end her. To stop the pain.

Something constricted around her waist.

Her body whipped back against the sudden halt. She cried out as it dug into her flesh. Her upper body smacked the stone wall.

She was in and out, vision blurred, vaguely aware she was being pulled back up. She'd nearly made it. The ground had been so close.

"No!" she cried, twisting her body, trying to free herself from her captor's grip. A steady stream of blood trickled from her cheek. The entire right side of her face throbbed.

Hands wrapped around her ankles, pulling her back through the window. Her exposed skin scraped against the rough stone frame. She thrashed and swung at the hands, at faces, at any part of them she could perceive. One of her elbows made contact right before she fell back onto the wooden floor of her room.

"You crazy bitch!" Calix spat as she kicked her. Thea curled up, fetal, trying to protect herself from the blows, unsure if she was crying or laughing.

The guards peered down at her, open-mouthed, as if fearful she'd finally lost her wits. Thea thought she probably had. Dread overwhelmed her. Dread that she had actually done it, and dread that she had failed.

65

Nara

*"Once one truly knows another's ether, it stays forever, as if remnants of it
reside within."*

THE WAY OF ETHER
ASHERAH GALANIS, FIRST CONSUL, THE CITADEL, 807 AQ

Nara stayed deep within the forests on her trek to Highclere. It slowed her down, but it was the only way to avoid crossing paths with another. She couldn't risk it. Not when she was on her own. Not when what she read in Rowena's letter could be true.

She kept herself tightly shielded at all times despite its drain on her. It was midnight by the time she reached the castle and nearing dawn by the time she'd traversed its perimeter.

It was locked down. Impossibly so. An entire mile around Highclere was warded so tight that Nara had difficulty bending through it undetected. Every entrance to the castle was guarded heavily by both Etherborn and idleborn soldiers. Dread commandeered her thoughts with the realization of their numbers. If they had so many Etherborn they could afford to have them guarding doors, she was in trouble.

The estimates the field houses were working with *vastly* underestimated their depth. Nara could easily handle ten, but a fight would draw attention and alert others. And if the rumors were true of what they could do, she may even be outmatched. It was difficult to assess the threat level of individual wielders when there were so many sharing the same space. It was like trying to listen in a crowded room.

She watched doors for what felt like hours, looking for someone, *anyone*, she recognized. Any sign of prisoners. Her efforts yielded nothing.

Nara retreated to the south side of the forest, a sizable walk from the castle. She considered drawing them out, starting a distraction. She even considered simply going in like a madwoman. But there was only so much she could do on her own. She cursed herself for sending Harker to Eastwatche. Defeat picked at her as she considered she may have to leave and return with help. She did not know if Cerys was even there. Cerys could have escaped, or they may have taken her somewhere else. She could be—no—she would not even think it.

Nara's ether perked at the recognition of others headed her way. She closed her eyes to focus. They were moving slowly, twelve people, eleven signatures.

Her breath caught, and her eyes snapped open. She shook her head. It couldn't be. She tried to dismiss the notion, but as they drew closer, she grew more confident.

Her heart stopped when her eyes fell upon the face of her little brother. It struck her like lightning, stilling her breath, her limbs, her thoughts.

When she finally blinked and he was still there, she had to fight every instinct to call out to him. His soft dark curls were longer, and his tall, slender frame held more muscle, but it was him. She covered her mouth with both hands.

He walked with a group of soldiers, all of similar age. All wore the black uniform she now recognized common for a Thranean soldier. They were listening as one of them, a boy of southern descent, spoke about the wards. He explained how they worked and how to verify their soundness. Nara listened intently for anything that might help her, still trying to accept that her eyes did not lie.

The group moved on, and she followed at a safe pace. Her brother strolled at the back with one of the girls. He offered her his hand as she stepped over a fallen tree, the intimacy between them plain. He glanced back at the others now gaining distance, and then turned around and kissed her.

Nara stepped back, confounded, unable to make sense of what she saw. Power radiated from the girl, and Nara swallowed at the possibility of who she may be. Hair as dark as her uniform framed an impossibly pale face. Even with the distance, Nara could see her icy eyes. The girl didn't look so fearsome, smiling up at her brother, but Nara felt it. So much ether. So much power it felt material.

She could not understand what her brother was playing at. Unless, she thought, he planned to kill her himself.

They walked for an hour as the same soldier continued to instruct, having the others test the wards. It wasn't until they were readying to return that she opened her shield, only a fraction, for less time than it takes to blink. But it had been enough.

Recognition flashed through his eyes. She silently cursed him for the reaction, but he recovered quickly, resuming his conversation with the girl. If any of the others had taken notice, it didn't show.

She considered whether she should attack. Take them out right then and get her brother. Her inability to understand the girl's power discouraged her. If it came to a big fight, her chance of getting Cerys would be gone.

Instead, she watched them walk away with a prayer her brother could—and would—return.

Nara waited through the night. She did not know the lengths he would have to go through to leave. Or if it was even possible. As the hours passed, her hope dwindled. If he did not come before dawn, she would have to leave and seek help in Eastwatche.

She was idly carving a stick when she felt his ether in the distance. It grew stronger, and her heart thrummed as she stood. She could sense only him.

When he stepped from the trees into the moonlight, she nearly doubled over. "*Sam?*"

They sprinted across the clearing, crashing midway. Their arms clung around the other, desperate, as if their minds needed convincing the other was real. Nara only pulled back when the desire to see his face won her over.

"I can't believe it," he said. "I felt you earlier, and I feared I imagined it."

"Let me look at you." Nara held his face. Her lanky little brother was replaced with a sturdy young man.

"*How are you here?*" His warm amber eyes were wide with incredulity.

"It is a long story."

"Who is with you?" He looked around her.

"It is only me."

Sam frowned. "On your own?"

"I did not travel alone, but they wait for me in Eastwatche. I came—"

She clutched his shoulders. *"Cerys?"*

"She's here," he said. "She's alive."

Nara exhaled. She stepped back, leaning against a tree. Every feeling, every fear she'd suppressed came crashing to the surface. But Cerys lived. Her *brother* lived. Against her better judgment, she let herself feel a tiny fleck of relief.

"They keep her and others captured in the battle in cells below the castle. When I first saw her, I feared you were here, too. I searched every cell as soon as I had the opportunity."

Nara swallowed and turned back to him. She still couldn't believe he was standing before her. "I came to get her out."

His face fell. "It will be difficult."

"You will help me?"

Sam grabbed her hands. "Of course I will."

Nara studied his face, nearly laughing. She knew she'd not sleep at all that night, too afraid she'd wake and find she'd dreamt him. "How have you remained undetected for so long?"

"It has not been easy," he admitted.

"Are there any others?" Nara asked, hopeful they'd been wrong about losing so many Esērii over the years.

"No," he said, looking down. "As best I know. Most are discovered as they attempt to cross the wards. I tracked the Thranean raids in Stra-eth and Andar for several moons, pretending myself nomad, working on tradeships and caravans. There were whispers of recruitment, so I put myself in their path, letting them find me."

"Smart." Nara studied her little brother, a deeper and more material intelligence shown through his eyes than he'd possessed when they said goodbye two years ago. She dreaded knowing the causes of it. "You've been posing as one of them since?"

"I had no idea what waited behind the borders. No concept of the army they'd built. The organization, the depth of it all. Nara, they've been collecting Etherborn for years. Recruiting nomads, planning, stockpiling supplies."

"I know. We crossed paths with a team in Ahara." She considered whether to tell him about the attack on his father and decided against it. Not yet, not like this.

She studied the patches on his leather vest. One had a crescent moon stitched into it with the words *Light in the Shadows*, in Argothan.

"Cerys told me you were collecting," he said, appraising her for an explanation.

"I thought you were dead, Sam. The council sent Cerys north." She held up her hands. "It is a long story. And not important now."

"I haven't been able to get any information out. I've been on my own, and the risk too high. There's been no one I can trust." His hands clasped around her arms. "Nara, listen to me. You took a big risk exposing yourself. You cannot do that again. There are too many powerful people here. We are fortunate no one else felt it."

"I have heard stories of what they can do." Nara exhaled. "What of Ulric's daughter, Calithea? Does she live?"

"She does," he said, hesitant, "but they have not been easy on her."

"What do you mean?" she asked, though she knew the likely answer. She thought back to her conversation with Alec in Azmar, and their fear Lorcan knew her, now realized.

"Do you know who she truly is?"

Nara nodded. "Mother explained before I departed the Citadel."

"They put her to torture trying to get her to turn. They make these… pits in the ground that are warded to be light and sound proof. She's been beaten, Influenced, starved."

Nara recoiled. "Then they are truly the monsters we have always believed them to be."

A strange expression washed over Sam's face, almost as if he did not agree. "The king is dead. It did not seem Lorcan's intention, but Calithea was witness to it, and it was… brutal." He looked down. "There wasn't anything I could do. But she's the reason Cerys is still here."

Nara stepped back. "*How is that?*"

Sam held up his hands. "I offered to help her escape, but she refused."

"If you had the means, why would she refuse you?" Nara asked, irritated already.

"She won't leave Ulric's daughter, and there was no way I could get to her. Not on my own. Lorcan keeps her under constant guard. Cerys said she was tasked to protect her and that she won't abandon her."

Nara cursed. "That sounds just like her."

"I told her you'd be cross," he said, one side of his mouth tugging up.

She returned the gesture, and it felt like two years had not passed between them.

"How are Mother, and my father?"

"Well. Worried for you, but well." Nara thought of how their mother had never given up on him and felt regret knowing she had. "We need to get Cerys and the girl. We will go to Eastwatche and—" His expression caused her to pause. "What is it?"

"I will help you get Cerys and the girl. We may be able to free the other Etherborn they hold captive, but I'm not leaving, not yet." He stood up straighter as if he expected a poor reaction.

Nara crossed her arms. "I don't understand."

"I'm not leaving."

"I heard your words, Samar Amad, I ask your reason," she said, her temper flaring.

Sam looked down, shifting between his feet. He opened his mouth several times, but nothing came out.

She scrutinized his manner, trying to formulate what possible motivation would drive him to stay. She considered for a moment he had joined them but dismissed it immediately. Nara would not insult him with even the thought. If they freed the captives, what else was there for him? He said himself it was too risky passing information.

She started to ask again, but then remembered watching him in the woods. The girl. Lorcan's daughter. How intimate they'd been. How familiar. Laughing together, the kiss.

Nara closed her eyes and sighed. "Oh, you stupid boy." When she opened them again, she found him bristling. "Tell me I am wrong."

He lifted his chin. "I am not a child, Nara."

"Yes, I see you believe that to be true." Looking at him now, she knew that it was. He was a man grown, and it tugged at her heart, but his naivety was clearly still intact.

"She doesn't belong with them."

"Only a moment ago, you yourself spoke of their depravity. She's a murderer and the daughter of a tyrant. From what I've been told, she's the entire reason they were able to cross the border into Straeth. Rowena Winstone wrote a letter that I read in Kingsport about the things she can do. Twenty and five she massacred."

"Twenty and four."

"Tell me you did not…"

"It was not me," he said. "Though I nearly died. She saved my life. I live because of her."

"No, Samar, you nearly died because of her. I read the names of the fallen. *Calidore* was on that list!"

Sam flinched. "I know," he said, low. "I felt him, Nara."

She fixed her eyes on his, chest heaving in escalating bursts in line with the delivery of her words. "You were there, and you did nothing as she slaughtered our people? Our *friend*. Calidore was like a father to you."

He looked like she'd taken a blade and plunged it into his heart. Then twisted it for good measure. Nara swallowed. He looked away for a breath, and when his eyes returned to hers, the anger in them caused her to wince. "You have not been where I have. You've not faced what I've faced. I have done all I could. There was nothing I could do to save him. There's been nothing I could do to save *any* of them." He said it with so much sorrow Nara felt it in her bones. His breath hitched, and he stumbled back. He looked lost and a bit frantic. "Do you think I have endured that with ease? Do you not think it weighs heavy on me? *That I struggle to breathe beneath the guilt?* I—" He swallowed. "I have done all I could!"

"I'm sorry," she choked out. "You are right." She reached for him, pulling him against her. "Of course you are right."

He stayed stiff, not returning the embrace. "Think me a fool, Nara, think me a traitor, but know I understand what I do."

She pulled back to look into his eyes and found them wet. "I'm sorry," she said, again, covering her mouth. "I did not mean—"

"I know what you meant. I know what you're thinking, but you're wrong." He shook his head. "She's not like the others. She's not like her father. She's pulling away from him. And it's not only about her. There are others here, too, who given the chance may leave. I need more time—"

Nara sighed, unable to keep it contained, and he recoiled, his eyes growing angry again.

He glared at her. "Who are you to judge me? Should I ask if your presence here is sanctioned? Did you not just run across both fucking continents for Cerys?"

Nara straightened. "That is different."

He looked her square in the eye and spoke slowly. "No," he said, shaking his head. "It is not."

His stubbornness infuriated her. She was well familiar with it. It was the same that lived in her.

"They'll find out who you are, and when they do, they will execute you. From everything you have told me, you'll be fortunate if that is all they do."

"It is a risk I am willing to take."

"Oh, *Gods*, Sam." Nara threw her arms out to either side. "What of the girl? Do you think she will still want you when she finds out how you have deceived her?"

For the first time, he looked unsure, shifting between his feet. "If she decides she does not, I will live with that. At least I will have gotten her out."

Nara could not help but admire his selflessness, no matter how reckless. It reminded her of Cerys.

"My feelings aside, if I get her to leave, they will have lost their most powerful resource. She is the reason they have been able to come this far. If they lose her, they lose their advantage over us."

Nara could not argue his logic in that.

He reached for her hand. "Let us not waste this time, sister. We have little of it, and we need a strategy."

Nara relented, for the moment.

They made a plan for the following night. Once they'd agreed to the details, she told him all that had happened at the Citadel since he left. She told him how their mother had never given up hope, not once, even when she had.

Nara knew their time together could be better spent discussing Thrane's forces and intentions, but she only wanted time with her little brother. However brief. When he talked about the girl, she knew any further attempts to sway him to leave would fall on deaf ears.

They talked and laughed together for the better part of an hour before Sam looked up at the moon and stood. "I have to get back."

Nara could not help from trying one more time.

"Will you not change your mind and come with us?" she asked, eyes pleading.

He shook his head. "I will not."

"We could simply take her," she jested.

"I would never force her," he said. Then his lips curled. "It would be useless, anyway. She would make dust of us with little effort."

"So what they say is true, then?" Nara asked, fearing the answer.

His face tightened. "Unbelievably so."

Nara nodded and exhaled at the unwelcome news. "I could make you go with me right now, you know."

"You could try. Maybe you would succeed." He shrugged. "But you'd never get Cerys out."

"I'm only jesting." Nara tried to force a smile. She swallowed. "It is only that I do not wish to say goodbye to you." She reached up and touched his face. His hand covered hers.

"We will see each other soon," he said. "I swear it."

Nara nodded, knowing he could make no such assurance. Knowing she would likely never see him again.

"Will you send a messenger to the Citadel? Tell Mother and my father that I live?"

"Of course." She pulled him into an embrace so tight her arms shook from the effort. She had to leave, or she would lose her resolve. "We will wait for you at Eastwatche, little brother." She walked away, each step an unbearable effort.

66

Neith

"And there have been no escalations since?" Neith asked.

"Nothing reported," Thora answered, pouring the last of their third bottle of wine into her cup.

"Good," Neith said, "but I fear it will not stay that way. Tell your squads to stay alert. Roman grows restless, and after what happened with the king, he is eager to flex his reach again."

Her three lieutenants nodded. A knock at the door drew their attention.

"Come," Neith called.

Two kitchen servants entered carrying large trays. A bowl was placed on the table in front of each.

One of the servants curtsied. "Venison with potatoes, carrots, and peas, Captain."

"Very good, thank you," Neith said, with an appreciative nod. The empty bottle of wine was retrieved from the table, and a new one set in its place.

The four spoke of changes to the patrol rotation and cabin assignments in the new barracks while they dined.

When the meal was complete and their council ended, Zinnia and Thora excused themselves to return to their squads, leaving Bellamy and

Neith on their own in her room.

Neith took the last sip from what she believed to be her fourth glass. She had not intended to drink so heavily, but the night had gotten away from her. Her head fell into her hands, and she rubbed her eyes, letting her mask fall away.

Bellamy nudged her. "I can see that you are trying to blame yourself."

"Is it not my fault?" she asked, looking up. "She tried to jump from her window after speaking with me. Not after she was tortured. Not even after her father was killed."

Bellamy sighed, his hazel eyes considering. "This is not something I expect to say often, Neith, but you are overestimating your hand here. She did not jump from her window because you tried to help her. I was there."

"Is that what I was doing? Helping her?" Neith reached for the bottle. Bellamy watched as she poured, and for a moment she thought he might tell her to stop. She took several sips in succession, feeling a small stream of the wine trail down her chin. She lazily wiped at it. "They put her back in a cell."

"Will you try to speak with her again?"

Neith shrugged. "I don't know."

Bellamy looked at her with kindness she could not amend herself to feel she deserved.

She tried to smile at him coyly, eager to shift the mood. "Do you not have a young lady waiting for you? I imagine that a far more entertaining evening than listening to me drown my sorrows." Neith lifted her cup in mock toast.

Bellamy laughed, and it was such a welcome, warm sound that she found the force in her smile faded. He shrugged and reached for the bottle, filling his own cup. "I would rather drink with my friend."

Hours passed, and so did the bottle of wine, and much of a bottle of whiskey. Bellamy told her stories from Balta. They played cards, and he won each game. Once they were well soused, he tried to teach her to dance the Basa. When he kicked and fell flat on his back, Neith laughed until her belly hurt. Until she thought she would never breathe again. They ended up on their backs on the floor, studying the painted flowers on the ceiling. The same pink and white flowers from the clearing. And the ruins. Some blossomed, some still blooming.

"I wonder," Neith said, "what kind of life provides the capacity to concern one with painting such a scene on a ceiling." She was taken aback by the slight slur in her speech.

"A peaceful one," Bellamy answered, tossing a pillow repeatedly in the air.

"That does not seem real."

"I hope one day it does, Neith. If anyone deserves peace, it is someone like you."

She frowned. "Someone like me?"

The pillow stilled. He pitched it aside and turned his body toward her. "Someone who cares so much. Who *feels* so much. It is like you are tethered to everyone around you. You feel their sorrows, their joys, their pain. Even when you do not want to."

The drink had washed gaps in her walls. She tightened at the unease of feeling seen.

"I don't know if you've ever known a day of peace," he said, mournfully. She had never heard him speak in such a way. It made her wonder if she knew him half as well as he clearly knew her. It felt like he'd strummed an exposed nerve. She returned her gaze to the ceiling.

"Have you," she asked, clearing her throat, "known peace?"

He was silent for a moment, then shifted onto his back. The pillow returned to the air. "We had good years in Balta when I was young. Before the civil war."

Neith sat up and reached for the whiskey, desirous to exile the feelings his words had called forth. They were sentiments she was not yet ready to face. "Will you go back when the war is over?"

He shrugged. "My thoughts are currently more attuned with surviving. What about you? What will you do?"

Neith took a healthy sip and set the bottle between them. She looked at him, considering. She had told no one. Not even Sam. "My father intends to name me heir." Neith blinked, unsure if she'd made a conscious decision to confide in him or if the words simply escaped her, having grown tired of being held captive.

Bellamy's brows nearly reached his hairline. He let out a short bark of a laugh. "I see."

She watched him carefully, surveying his reaction.

"That is… welcome news."

Neith turned her body to face his. "Is it?"

He frowned at her, rising to his elbows. "Of course it is. I cannot imagine there are many who wish to see Roman rule. Your brother is a cruel idiot. There is scarcely a worse combination."

Even though she agreed, it hurt to hear him called so.

"So," he said, grinning. "You really are a princess."

Neith reached for one of the pillows behind her, hurling it at his face. He laughed, catching it midair with surprising swiftness. "There is no such thing as a princess in Thrane, Bells. The heir is called Praxa. Or Praxo, were I male."

"You Thraneans and your old words," he mused. He studied her face and sat up. "You do not seem pleased about it."

Neith inhaled, letting it slowly spill from her lips. "I do not know what I feel."

"I think you would be a good queen," he said with a grin.

"Do you?"

He nodded. "Truly."

Neith chewed at her bottom lip. "I will need people that I trust when—*if* I become queen."

"Are you saying that you trust me?" he asked, one brow rising to form a pitch between the two.

"I do," she answered honestly. "You are my Second, and if you are amenable to it, so I would have you stay indefinitely."

His playful expression fell away. She thought she saw a hint of regret in him. "Say that to me tomorrow when it's not the whiskey guiding your words."

Neith reached up and touched her head. It was already pulsing with a dull ache. "I will regret this drink in the morning. But not my words."

He looked her over as if searching for jest. When it seemed he found none, he swallowed. "Very well, then. Ask me your question again."

Neith frowned. "My question?"

"What I plan to do after the war."

She smiled, which made him smile. Neith cleared her throat, speaking clearly. "What will you do when the war is over, Bellamy Silva?"

He sighed, slowly, with drama. "I will be at the behest of my queen." The tease in his manner fell away. "Indefinitely."

Neith nodded in rapid succession, feeling a sting behind her eyes. She had come to understand the value of loyalty. She had come to respect the sacrifice it demanded, and the responsibility it merited. There was power in loyalty. She vowed to return it, twice over.

They held gazes for a long, drawn moment. She knew she had made many friends these past moons, and she also knew he was one of the best among them. His eyes fixed on hers, growing in intensity, and she wondered what he was thinking. They both jumped at a light knock at the door.

"Enter," Neith answered quickly.

Sam walked through, taking in the scene. His eyes moved from them on the floor, to the nearly empty bottle of whiskey, to the empty wine bottle on the table. He nodded slowly. One side of his mouth tugged up, teasing. "I see I come late to the gathering."

Bellamy slapped the floor and stood. "I'll be off then."

"You do not need to leave," Neith said, rising to her knees.

"I've a young lady to attend to." He winked at her, reaching for his vest thrown over the back of a chair.

"Do your best work," she jested.

Bellamy turned back, brow cocked. "I always do."

Neith had no doubts. He clasped hands with Sam and made his farewells.

When the door closed behind him, Sam flipped the lock. He walked to the table and filled a cup with water, then moved to stand in front of her, peering down. "Drink," he said and extended the cup.

Neith gulped it all in one take. She looked up at him with an innocent grin. "I fear I am rather drunk."

"I see that." His eyes were serious, but his lips were still set in amusement. His hand came up to hold her cheek, and she closed her eyes, leaning into it. "Are you all right? I did not wish to leave you on your own today."

"No," she said, and opened her eyes. "But I have washed it away with whiskey and wine to think on another day."

Sam lowered to his knees. "Very well."

"Tell me what has occupied your night?" Neith lay back on the floor, eyes focused lazily on the flowers again. She remembered the first day Sam had taken her to the clearing. The way he'd looked at her. How he had cared for her. She'd had some measure of peace that day, however fleeting. Her mind moved to the wild things she'd thought. *I could help her escape.* Recalling it brought forth an uneasiness, and she wondered why. If it was nothing but a passing thought, why did it worry her so? Neith shook her head. "What?" she asked. Sam had said something.

"Reinforcing the wards on the northern border took most of the evening. I've been with Magnus and Max these past hours discussing how we might strengthen them further."

Her brows creased, and she turned to look at him.

"You asked me what occupied my night," he clarified, with a light laugh.

"Oh, yes."

The distraction of the drink had waned. She could drink more, but that would only add to her lament tomorrow. She sat up, looking from the whiskey bottle to Sam.

"What are you thinking?" he asked.

"I am thinking that I do not wish to think."

Something like pity washed across his face, and she frowned. That was not what she wanted. Her eyes were heavy on him, considering. She sprang up and fisted the front of his tunic, pulling him down on top of her. He didn't have the opportunity to object before she wrapped her legs around him, securing him close.

Neith kissed him, attempting to let her body ask, so she did not have to. He returned her kiss but kept a distance between them. She arched up to eliminate it. When she was unsuccessful, she flipped them over, landing to straddle him.

"*Neith*," he said, under his breath. His tone was light, but it had a hint of caution to it.

"What?" She circled her hips over his, enjoying the way it made his face tighten. "I do not like it when you say my name like that," she said from pouted lips. She ground against him again, feeling her core quicken. He groaned, and she delighted in the sound.

"I do not think this is wise. Given your… state."

She felt him growing firm between them. "Your body suggests otherwise."

"Believe me," he said, as his hands gripped her hips. "It is only a thin thread of decency that objects."

"I'm not interested in decency tonight." She leaned forward, bringing her lips to his, determined to sway him. She felt a tremor and thought at first it came from within.

Neith sat up, continuing to move as she tugged at the buttons on her vest. She stopped when she felt the tremor again.

Sam's hand trailing beneath the fabric of her tunic to find her breast drew her back, and she fumbled with the laces on his trousers.

But again it returned, and she paused, looking toward the window. Sam reached for her, but she stood, unsure of what she pursued. She scurried across the room and flung open the shutters, climbing onto the frame. She stretched her neck out as far as she could without falling. A multicolored fire raged across the lake.

Sam's hands gripped her hips, holding her steady. "What is it?"

"*Fire*," she answered, climbing back out of the window. Neith turned around, trying to think through the haze in her mind. "In the marching camp."

Sam frowned. "That's odd."

Neith quickly fastened the buttons on her vest and started for the door. Sam reached for her arm, spinning her around. "You should stay here until we know what it is."

She looked down at the contact and frowned. "It is a fire," she said, confused by his urgency. "And it is all the way across the lake."

His grip stayed, and she thought to protest, but then he sighed and let her loose.

The castle was quiet until they were out of the royal quarters. She ran down the stairs with Sam on her heels toward the kitchens and dining halls. She found Cordero shouting orders.

"What has happened?" she asked him, trying to keep the evidence of drink from her speech.

"Explosion," he answered, "in the camp. It looks like a crate of charges detonated. We do not know the cause. Your father is already on his way over."

Neith looked around the room, considering.

"I think it would be best if you stay here," Cordero suggested. "Until we produce the cause."

"Very well," she answered, trying to conceal her deceit.

Cordero nodded and turned, disappearing into the sea of soldiers.

"I agree with him," Sam said. He looked nervous. Almost desperately so. "I think you should return to your room until this has passed."

Neith understood his desire to protect her. She felt quite the same for him. But his concern seemed excessive. Or perhaps it was simply the drink fogging her mind. She blinked and rubbed her eyes. "All right."

They started the walk back, but Neith halted when they reached the staircase leading to the royal quarters. "I want to put eyes on my unit."

Sam sighed. "I will go and then meet you back in your room. Will that suffice?"

"It seems an abundance of caution," she answered, "but if you insist."

"I do." He looked around before leaning down to kiss her. His hands wrapped around her face and then the back of her neck. "Go," he whispered against her lips. "I will return as quickly as I can."

Neith started up the stairs, glancing back to find him watching her ascend. She stopped past the first corner, leaning against the wall. After a few breaths, she peered around. He was gone.

She shook off the wild instinct and started back up the stairs. After four steps, she turned back. She didn't want to wait in her room.

Soldiers and servants rushed through the halls in all directions. It was not a panic, but all were awake in a haste of curiosity. Neith tried to blend into the hastened crowd, unsure where she was going. Perhaps she did know. *No*, she thought, shaking her head. She simply wanted to get outside. To look out across the lake. She tried to pretend she did not notice a particular door growing closer on her left. The door leading to the levels below. To the cells. To Calithea.

As she approached, she slowed her pace. Two soldiers emerged, and she stepped to the side, turning away so as not to be seen. She stood there, chewing on her lip, considering. She thought she must be mad. A wild laugh escaped her, and she clamped her hand over her mouth.

Go back to your room, Neith, she heard Sam's voice say in her head.

Her hand rested on the knob. The moment it turned, she jerked, stepping back. She laughed again at her short-lived delirium and turned to walk away. She had not made it two steps before her head snapped back, sure she felt a cast.

Palms on the door, she closed her eyes and listened. It came again. It was distant, below ground, but she'd felt it. No one passing through the hall seemed any the wiser.

Her hand returned to the knob. This time, it turned full circle. Her breath hitched as the door swung open, and she stepped through. Still unsure of her objective.

67

Nara

"Bending wards is no quick study. It is more complex than their creation. Not many will find they have the endurance nor skill for it."

THE WAY OF ETHER

ASHERAH GALANIS, FIRST CONSUL, THE CITADEL, 807 AQ

Sneaking into Highclere had been easier than Nara anticipated. Two Influenced idleborn soldiers came to fetch her on a supply cart an hour's ride south of the city. She had not felt badly when she slit their throats, hiding their bodies in an alley.

The city had returned to some semblance of order. Shops and markets were open for business, and damage from the siege was in active repair. But there was heavy uneasiness. Looks of contempt, more often than fear, plagued the faces of the common folk. Nara could see the people of Ire would not be easily swayed to Thrane, even under the heel of their boot.

She'd hidden in the back of a pub called the Iren Stein until nightfall, listening to whispers of Eastwatche, and of the princes and if they would return. The citizens of Highclere made prayers for their king and queen. Others spoke of sorcery and cursed the devils that took their city. Some told dramatic accounts of their failed attempts to flee the city. One woman, whom Nara had deduced to be the innkeeper, wept as she recalled Thranean soldiers dragging Calithea Ironne through the streets.

When the sun completed its descent, Nara made her way to the south side of the castle, searching for a door marked on a hand-drawn map. Sam had told her all but two leading into the lower levels had been sealed.

When she found it, she sank into the shadows to wait.

Nara looked over the list of names of the seven captured during the siege. Two had a thin line running through them, having perished in captivity. Of the five remaining, Nara recognized only one. Rowena Winstone. She thought of the girl in the Kingsport field house, eager to ride out to meet her mother.

As the moon peaked in the sky, Nara grew nervous the next stage would not come to pass. Everything until then had been easy. What came next was the part unlikely to succeed.

A gentle tremor caught her attention. She could not see around the tall castle walls, but a faint polychromatic glow illuminated the sky behind. The door she watched most carefully slowly opened.

Nara peered down each side of the alley. There was no one around. She crept across the dark street, slipping in through the door. Another Influenced soldier stood expectantly, holding two swords and a large linen bag.

"I am the chancellor," she said. He blinked, extending the bag between them. Nara retrieved a harness with dual scabbards, slipping each arm through. He handed her both swords, which she sheathed, before tightening the straps. After securing a waist belt around her midsection, the soldier pulled two daggers from his own, holding them out, hilt first.

"Bad luck on your account," Nara said as she sheathed one, then ran the second over his throat. His hazy eyes went wide, but he didn't fight. He simply slid down the wall, hands on his neck, blood spurting and oozing from the gash.

Nara retrieved the map, flipping it over to review the layout of the lower levels. She'd spent all afternoon committing it to memory, but it was not a time for taking chances. She would have to resist wielding unless given no choice. Discovery would likely end it all before it had truly begun.

Four corridors were all she had to traverse to get to the cellblock that held Cerys and the other five. The one marked as Calithea's was deeper inside the castle.

She heard footsteps and paused. Two, she counted. Both Etherborn. They were talking about the explosion, having been sent to guard the door she entered. She'd hoped to make it farther before crossing paths with another. Nara covered herself with a cloaking shield and stepped back into the shadows.

The soldiers cleared the corner, strolling past in conversation. They moved with haste, but not with the urgency of one who expects danger.

Swords in hand, she crept behind, trailing in pace for several steps before plunging one through the heart of each. They made garbled gasps as she wrenched the swords free, and their bodies slumped to the floor.

Blood immediately pooled, reaching her boots in a breath. There was no hiding this. She returned to task.

As she crept down the first long stretch of hall, she ran into a group of three idleborn soldiers, dispensing all with her blades. The longer her trail of bodies, the faster she needed to be.

She had expected this, but had no real understanding of what it would be like to navigate the halls, nor who they would send. If she ran into someone stronger, she would have to wield, and then it would be chaos. The halls were high, but not wide. A real fight could bring the castle down on top of them.

The closer she drew to Cerys, the bloodier her blade.

Nara reached the last corner. She felt the wards and bindings on the rooms, but not the occupants beneath. She stole a quick glance around.

Four soldiers stood in the corridor between the cells. A woman with slicked-back blonde hair relayed orders to the other three men. She halted, her head snapping in Nara's direction.

Nara didn't give her the opportunity to understand. She hurled a dagger through the air, and it buried itself in one of her eyes.

The three men watched, dumbstruck, as her body collapsed, stepping back when their collective gaze landed on Nara.

Her second dagger found the heart of one. The third soldier had flames at call, but Nara sent a burst of air, blasting him and the fourth backward, crashing into the stone wall. She heard at least one skull crack.

Someone would feel her cast if they did not hear it. The race was on.

Nara retrieved her blades and sprinted to the cell marked as Cerys's on the map. Urgency overtook her as she ripped away the wards. She kicked the door, and it crashed against the wall, light pouring into the dark room.

When she met Cerys's expectant eyes, she wanted to scream. To cry. To get on her knees and kiss her feet. To pray in gratitude to Adrae. Nara wanted to run to her, wrap her arms around her. Curse at her for leaving.

But Nara did none of those things. She simply touched Cerys's cheek and severed the bindings on her gift.

She was dirty. Her red hair matted, clothing tattered. Bruises, both old and new, dulled and discolored her face. Nara watched life come back as the bindings fell away. Cerys covered Nara's hand with her own. Her chestnut eyes were tender, and more beautiful than Nara had ever seen them.

Nara gripped the front of her tunic. "You are never leaving me again. Do you understand?"

Cerys nodded and tried to smile, but it broke.

Nara cleared her throat to stave off a sob. She didn't have time to feel. She unclasped the buckle of her waist belt, wrapping it around Cerys. "Free as many as you can and clear their bindings," she said as she tugged the belt tight. "We have to be fast."

"Calithea?"

"We will get her." They turned and ran.

The first cell Nara opened held an older man with graying blond hair. He was slow to rise, limping as he walked free.

Nara opened a second to find Rowena Winstone staring back. She had not seen the woman in years, but she looked little altered. Nara severed her bindings.

"Welcome sight, Chancellor," Rowena said. She touched Nara's arm as she passed.

Cerys cut the bindings on an older Iceni woman with fire-red hair. Fragments of pale blue war paint still clung to her skin. She pulled a blade from the belt of one of the dead soldiers before she spat and cursed.

Rowena helped a limping woman with umber skin from the cell Cerys cleared. Nara glanced between her and the older man, both of whom had considerable injuries. They would slow them down.

A young man with curly brown hair was the last to be freed. Nara surveyed the group. "Can anyone heal?"

All shook their heads.

Nara sighed and pulled a copy of her map from one of her pockets, holding it out to the injured woman. She gestured for the man. "Head to the south wall in line with the steeple of the temple. There is a gate giving access to a drainage tunnel that channels below the city wall. Four Influenced idleborn soldiers stand guard. Tell them you're with the chancellor, and they will let you pass. Head directly south into the forest. Horses wait for us here." Nara pointed to a place on the map. "Ride hard for Eastwatche."

The two nodded, moving as fast as their distressed bodies allowed.

The remaining four waited expectantly.

"Calithea Ironne is held not far from here." Nara pointed, and their eyes followed. "Down this corridor. We will need to backtrack and make our way to this door. The Thraneans bricked up most of the exits." She showed them the path out on her map.

"Go and get her," the Iceni woman said. "We will wait and hold off any who come. Else we'll be cornered with nowhere to run."

"Aye," Rowena agreed.

Nara tucked the original map into Rowena's hand. "Your daughter and husband were safe last I saw in Kingsport. They planned to ride to Bacebridge. If we do not return, take horses and go."

Rowena's lips parted, and she inhaled. She squeezed Nara's hand and nodded.

Nara took off, Cerys on her heels. Exhilaration thundered through her. Their plan was working. But it was only half achieved. More Thraneans would come, and soon.

Nara projected a cloaking shield as they approached Calithea's cellblock. Sam had said there would be three guards. There were four, and they were waiting, having surely felt her cast from before. Any element of surprise had departed. They would have to beat them, power against power, fair and square.

She glanced back at Cerys and looked down at the daggers on her belt. They did not have the weapons to take them without wielding. It would be like sounding an alarm, but they had no choice.

Nara signaled, and Cerys nodded.

Nara cleared the corner under shield, sending violet etherfire blasting from her palms. A violent wail cut through the roar of the flames as the purple fire engulfed the space.

Two shields burst in an instant. Two remained to fight. Dark green fire pushed back against her own, and she felt a gust of air smash into her shield. Yellow fire joined the green.

She screamed for Cerys to take down their shields as she stepped forward, bearing down on them. The weaker one crumbled. There was a quick, shrill shriek, and the yellow fire retracted.

The other was stronger. She felt Cerys tearing at it wildly. It began to thin. The threads of ether snapped, and a woman screamed. Nara recalled her power when the green fire fell away.

The steam cleared, and Nara stood panting, staring at the scorched bodies on the ground. Sizzled flesh pervaded the sticky air, sending bile climbing up her throat.

Cerys darted past her and ripped down the wards. She swung open the door, disappearing into darkness.

Nara followed, clearing the threshold as Cerys formed an etherstar, its light filling the cell with a dull orange glow.

It was larger than the ones before. A square table sat center with two chairs on opposing sides, its pale wood stained with splattered and pooled blood. What looked like the busted remnants of steel restraints were bolted to the top. It was a sinister sight.

"Thea," Cerys said, her voice gentle.

Nara squinted to see a mess of golden hair. Calithea was lying on a straw cot, facing away from the door, knees bundled up to her chest. She had no blanket, no shoes. She was oddly still. If Nara had not felt her ether, she might have thought her dead.

Nara frowned. Did she not hear her name?

Cerys knelt, one hand resting on the girl's shoulder.

"*Thea*," Cerys said again.

The girl jumped and sat up, eyes wild as she scrambled to the far side of the cot. She took in Cerys and then Nara. Her chest heaved, and she blinked, as if trying to decide if she trusted the story her eyes were telling.

A jagged cut ran along her swollen, bruised cheekbone, protruding from her gaunt face. She was scared, but Nara felt the tempest. Something brewed and raged, barely contained, ready to attack.

The girl sprang from the cot, wrapping her arms around Cerys, who returned the embrace.

"We need to move," Nara urged.

Cerys pulled back to look into her eyes. "Thea, we're leaving. Do you remember everything I told you to do last time?"

Cerys stood and held out her hand, helping Calithea rise. She reached for one of the daggers on her belt, holding it out hilt first. With no hesitation, the girl took it and nodded.

"*Let's go*," Nara pressed, motioning for them to follow as she turned and ran from the cell.

A low moan drifted from the pile of bodies. A woman lay on her back, half propped by the wall. Her body made slow, suspended jerks as she drew husky breaths. She was horribly burned, and Nara was surprised her heart still beat. She reached for one of her swords to end it, then stepped forward to strike.

"Wait."

Calithea appeared, her dagger in hand. She glowered down at the woman, her pale green eyes taking on a shadow. The kind one acquires when they've seen too much. Felt too much. The sort of darkness that can come only from hate.

"We *need* to *move*," Nara urged again.

Calithea knelt and plunged the dagger into the woman's chest, right where her heart should be. The burned woman gasped, eyes bulging, as Calithea tried to twist the blade before wrenching it free, falling back from the effort. She climbed to her feet and watched as blood oozed from the brutal gash. The body stilled, and Calithea spat. "You cannot heal such a wound."

Nara looked at Cerys, brows raised. Cerys shrugged.

Calithea turned and looked at Nara expectantly. "Are we not leaving?"

68

Thea

"Violence begets violence. It has no end."

THE COST OF VALOR
AUTHOR UNKNOWN, 203 BQ
TRANSLATED FROM OLD ASARI BY MERIAH TURAN
HAIS Z'NOSIŠ, 1200 AQ

Thea grasped the dagger, now dripping with Calix's blood. The woman, whom she did not know, peered at her with a short-lived perplexity. She had large, almond-shaped dark eyes, and an intense gaze. She turned to Cerys as if seeking an answer, and when Cerys shrugged, she made a noise that sounded something like a grunt.

"Let's go," the woman said, then turned, sprinting down the hall.

Cerys held out her hand. "We're not coming back this time."

Thea stepped up and gripped her tight. "We're not coming back."

She braced against Cerys, her eyes still adjusting to the dim light. Cool water splashed over her bare feet as they ran. She was struggling to keep the reduced pace of the woman they followed. Intermittent glances back from her told Thea just how reduced it was. She urged her legs on, praying to Cassia for one more chance to escape. That she wouldn't blunder it this time. She would run as far and as fast as she could, not stopping until she reached Eastwatche. Perhaps not even then.

Shouts and commands echoed down the hall, quickly followed by a roar in the air. It turned hot, steam rising, and Cerys tightened the grip on her hand, tugging her back against the wall.

The woman in front stopped. An iridescence sheen poured from her right hand, filling the narrow hall from ceiling to floor as blue fire bounced up against it.

She held up her hand, telling them to stay back as she pressed forward, driving back the incoming fire with her own. She disappeared around a corner, and Thea heard a man scream, and the roar in the air retreated.

Cerys grabbed her hand, and they were running again.

"We're almost to the others!" the woman yelled back at them.

Thea didn't know who the others were but was glad to hear there were more on their side. She did not close her eyes nor look away as she stepped over the charred bodies.

A deafening boom halted them again. The halls shook. Small bits of powdery stone fell from the ceilings and walls, clouding the air.

"*Cannons?*" Cerys asked the woman as they shared a look. "They'll bring the Godsdamned castle down on top of us all!"

The woman's already large eyes widened with alarm. "We have to get out of here, *now*. It doesn't matter how."

The blasts grew louder and more violent the farther they ran. Thea tried to steel herself, knowing they were running right toward the fight. A fight where she would be useless.

The heat in the air rose at a frightening pace. It became difficult to breathe. Sweat poured down her face and neck. It felt like she was running into a windstorm where the thunder cracked without pause. Her ears were ringing, and her eyes stung from the debris and dust.

Cerys's palm came forward, and the dust thinned before another shield spilled out around them. Thea inhaled the cleaner air, coughing out bits of powdered stone. Her mouth was chalky and dry, and her eyes spilled water to wash away what blinded her.

A deafening boom shook the ground, sending them bracing against the wall. Thea watched the stone before them crack.

The woman in front turned, once more signaling for them to stay back.

"Nara!" Cerys yelled after her, but she disappeared around the corner into the chaos.

Nara.

There was an explosion, followed by a gust of air and a wave of tremors that sent Cerys stepping back as she braced to hold the shield in place.

Fragments of stone swirled through the air. Thea heard screams in the roaring wind. Cracks erupted like the snapping of giant bones. Thea's fear transformed from burning to being crushed.

A body smashed into the wall where they waited, leaving a splatter of crimson behind as it collapsed. The horrified scream of a woman cut through, and the howl of the windstorm halted.

Cerys didn't move. Her eyes flicked in rapid motions as she listened with ultimate attention.

Wet footsteps approached, and Nara appeared, sword in hand. She plunged it into the limp body at their feet. It jerked as she tore it free. Face and tunic splattered with blood, she was calm and focused. She gestured with her head for them to follow and disappeared around the corner.

It was carnage.

Bodies were everywhere. Some whole, some in pieces. Burned, sliced, crushed, hacked. Blood dripped from the ceiling. It trailed down the walls, pooling on the floor.

Thea's chest burned when she inhaled the metallic, sickly stench of things she could not identify. Things she did not wish to. When her bare feet stepped into the wet, warm pool, she heaved, but didn't stop.

She waited for the horror to come. To take over, to consume her. But it didn't. All she felt was repulsion. Disgust. And though she did not like it, she hoped they had suffered.

They crossed the cellblock, turning a corner into another hall to find Rowena Winstone, Porvi, and a young man Thea did not know.

No one spoke as they passed, only made nods of acknowledgment. They took off running, and the three additions fell in line behind them.

They sprinted down several halls, short and long, jumping over lifeless bodies in black uniforms. Nara led them like she'd traversed the lower levels all her life. Thea thought of the last time she'd run through the same halls, terrified and disordered, only to find the door she searched for sealed up. She remembered the devastation. The grief. The feeling of true hopelessness, and how she knew it had altered her forever. It was a wound that would never heal.

Thea wanted to cry out when she turned the corner to find a wooden door waiting. Nara reached for the handle and turned.

When the door swung open, moonlight poured into the hall, and Thea gripped the dagger, ready to plunge it into the heart of anyone who blocked her path. She was getting out. No one would stop her. No one would bring her back this time. She would rather die.

The alleyway was empty and quiet.

"We need to split up," Nara said to Rowena. "You three go together. Head east, then cut south. You have the map. We will meet you in Eastwatche."

Rowena nodded, but Porvi looked from Nara to Thea, as if hesitant to leave her.

"I'll get her there this time," Cerys said. "I swear it."

Porvi looked unsure but gave a small nod.

Shouts from inside the door sent the two parties sprinting in opposite directions. Cerys and Thea followed Nara down the alley toward the south city wall.

Nara cautioned anyone they encountered to get inside and stay there until the sun was high. They avoided all major walkways and roads, sticking to the shadows and backstreets.

What started as distant shouts turned to the sound of boots on stone, and Thea knew they were being chased. She pressed on, running as fast as she could, but knew she was slowing them down.

They were nearly to the south wall when the alley ended, and they had to cut east to get through. The soldiers who followed were gaining on them, and dread built in her belly. But she remembered the slaughter Nara left behind and wondered who was truly in danger.

When they turned the corner, Nara stopped, sending Thea crashing into Cerys.

"They're going to catch up," Nara said. She turned to Thea. "Stay behind this wall." She pointed further down the alley. "Go twenty paces and wait. If one of us looks back, that is your signal to run."

"Where do I run?" Thea asked. The blade of the dagger tapped erratically against her thigh. An effect of the shaking hand that held it.

"Anywhere you can." Nara sheathed her swords as the approaching shouts grew louder. "Go," she urged, pushing her forward.

Thea ran down the alley, counting twenty paces exact. She watched as Nara and Cerys readied in the place where the two alleys met. An orange-hued shield expanded around them.

Bright purple flames sparked to life in Nara's palms. She held them out, facing each other, and her fingers moved, turning and twisting as the flames combined into a ball of fire that sparked and flickered.

They waited.

Someone shouted.

Nara grimaced, and the violet fireball launched from her hands, disappearing down the alley. She had another formed and ready by the time the first met its target.

A thunderous boom shook the alley. Thea could not see, but smoke and debris soared over the buildings. There was a brief moment of screams and shouts before the second struck.

Nara launched a third as incoming fire poured down over them, bouncing off Cerys's shield and spilling into the alley. Bright green, blue, and yellow, stopping several feet in front of her. The heat caused her to step back.

Thea could only see flashes of the fight. The inbound fire fell away long enough for her to see Nara ready another fireball and launch it. The trio of incoming fire fell to two.

An earsplitting crack cut through, and a large piece of stone sailed high above the buildings, then came crashing back at an accelerated speed. Only the yellow fire remained.

The assault ceased, scarcely a blink, and Thea saw Cerys bracing behind the shield, but Nara was gone.

Thea felt the hair on her body rise. The ground shook, and violet light splintered into the sky, snapping and fracturing like lightning. She stared, transfixed by the ferocious display.

The yellow fire vanished, and a woman screamed. Only the violet light remained.

Thea exhaled.

The light dissipated as the smoke and dust cleared with a gust of wind. Nara returned to her spot behind the shield. Thea frowned, expecting them to turn and run toward her, but they stayed still, focused, on their guards.

Thea's relief fell away when fear twisted Cerys's face.

A woman's voice called out. Familiar, but its inflection was a marked contrast from the last time she'd heard it. This time, it was hostile and determined.

"Where is she?"

69

Neith

"Is it our conviction that guides our actions or our actions that define our convictions? I am no longer sure."

THE RECOVERED JOURNALS OF SONIA THRONDSEN, 1183 AQ

The door clicked, and the commotion departed. Muffled thuds from her bare feet were the only sounds as she descended into the dark unknown.

The stairs opened into a corridor that split into multiple halls extending in every direction, only torchlight visible in the distance of each. Neith thought there would be soldiers, but she was alone, turning in circles, unsure where to go.

She closed her eyes, listening for signs of wielding. It was no easy task in her altered state. Thoughts tangled and half-formed, she shook her head to clear them. There was nothing but the echo of streaming water. She considered for a moment it was all in her mind.

Her gaze snapped toward a distant blast. A tremor followed, and the shallow pools of water under her feet rippled with the aftereffect. She felt the ether stretch and bend from the cast. Neith took off in pursuit.

Heavy legs and a maladroit gait had her bracing against the narrow walls to stay upright. But she tumbled on, determination giving direction to a body ill-prepared to oblige.

Another boom rumbled down the hall, shaking the ground with a thunderous crack. A distant scream followed, bloodcurdling and brutal, as if it had been viciously ripped from the caller's throat.

Neith stumbled to a halt. She glanced behind her, considering if she should go back. For the first time that night, she was afraid. She wished she were not on her own. But the scream could have been Calithea's. It could have come from one of her soldiers. One of her friends.

She steeled herself and ran. Faster than before, as the traces of the wielding became easier to track.

Rounding a corner in a frenzy, she slipped, grasping wildly for something to keep herself upright, finding only air.

Neith smacked the stone floor hard on her back. Water splashed up around her on impact as she cried out. The force sent a ringing through her head, and she clamped her eyes shut against the sting.

A wave of pain followed, and she groaned, reaching to touch the ache. She frowned when she discovered her fingers sticky and slick. Neith opened her eyes, studying the crimson stain.

She flailed, frantic, trying to stand, but only managed to slide backward, slipping until she hit the wall. She turned her face away. Her mind tried to convince her that her eyes spun a fallacious tale. But the warmth of what pooled beneath her conquered the delusion. She turned back to face the truth.

Bodies lay in heaps. She could not count them. Some lay whole, scorched, unidentifiable. Others in pieces, parts that should be inside, now out. Blood covered the floor and walls. It dripped from the ceiling. Carnage was the only word she could come by.

When she finally inhaled, she gagged on the rancid air, heavy with spilled bowels and the sickening scent of meat. She turned on her hands and knees and retched until there was nothing more to expel. Then the retching turned to sobs.

Using the frame of the entryway to brace, she climbed to her feet and fell back against the wall. When she summoned the nerve, she looked around, avoiding the butchery.

The cell doors were all open.

Neith told herself she should go back. Get help. Or simply return to her room and pretend she was never there. Perhaps she would forget and wake with the nightmare long lost to whiskey. She cursed herself for having come down. She should have listened to Sam.

But it was too late.

She stumbled through the bodies. None wore her insignia she could find, and Halvorsen's face was the only one she knew. Only a bloody black hole remained where her left eye had been.

There was no one alive. Someone had slaughtered them all.

Her hands turned to fists as she took in the bloody footprints trailing down the opposing hall. An enemy, a traitor? She knew not who they were, but nor did she care.

Neith ran, jumping over bodies as she followed the bloody path. Her bare feet burned, taking on cuts from the rough stone with every stride. With every fallen Thranean she passed, her determination surged.

Moonlight poured in from a door as she rounded a corner, bright at the end of the hall. Neith commanded her legs to continue despite their fatigue. Despite their continued unsteadiness. She spilled onto the empty street, falling briefly to her knees. The path split, with one group heading east and the other south. Her gaze flicked back and forth as she considered which to follow. A crash along the south wall provided the answer.

She followed the smoke and dust rising in the air, vowing she would make it this time.

Neith turned into an alleyway to see an explosion of colors down the stretch. Roars of green and yellow etherfire pummeled into the sky. A bright purple cannon struck, and a body in black came hurling through the air, crashing into a building behind them. Violet lightning cracked upward, shaking the ground and buildings around her. Its force rattled her teeth, her bones, and nearly caused her legs to buckle. Neith tumbled into the next alley to find a third body at her feet.

Two women stood at the far end, waiting. She recognized the one with red hair.

"*Where is she?*" Neith snarled. She could sense Calithea was close.

Neither answered.

A violet cannon came plummeting toward her. Neith met it with a burst of power, and it deflected, crashing into the building on her left. The next she diverted into the air and space behind her. A third she flung against the wall on her right. Neith shook her head and screamed, irritated by the immediate bombardment. She had wanted to talk.

She threw up a shield and closed her eyes, searching for a weakness in theirs as the assault continued. It was strong. She picked at the threads and growled, impatient at its reluctance to simply shatter.

But it did.

She found a thread and tugged. It unraveled around them, and she sent a blast of air. Not enough to kill. Its aim to subdue.

The cannons ceased on impact. The two wielders had been sent backward by her blast, slamming against the wall behind them.

In less than a blink, the second woman was already back on her feet, readying a cannon. She moved so fast that for a moment Neith thought time itself had malfunctioned. Long black braids spilled out around her shoulders as she launched, its violet flames surging toward Neith in a fury. She deflected it with ease.

"*Stop*," Neith warned with her eyes as much as with her words as she took three quick steps forward.

The woman stood in front of the other as she climbed to her feet, glancing behind her with concern. She was fearful but determined and seething with rage. She held her hands out, as if to ready another cannon.

Neith shook her head.

The two women stood together, facing her once more. Neith watched with curiosity as Hawthorne glanced at the other woman, communicating without words. Both looked down the opposing alley toward someone or something out of Neith's line of sight.

"Do not run." Neith dropped her shield and held out her palms. Nether escaped in wild ribbons, twisting and turning around her arms. Both stepped back. "Don't," she warned again, shaking her head. Neith studied the face of the woman she didn't know. The defiant look in her eyes wavered as she watched the nether. Neith was not sure how, but knew she had seen those eyes before. "*Who are you?*"

When the woman didn't answer, Neith retracted the nether from one hand in favor of her ether. Cobalt-blue ropes raced from her palm through the alley, wrapping around Hawthorne's neck. Desperate fingers clutched and tore at the noose.

"My name is—"

"*No!*" Hawthorne gasped. Neith tightened her grip.

"*Nyanthi*," the woman answered quickly. "My name is Nara Nyanthi." She looked from Neith to Hawthorne, holding her hands up in caution. "I'm a chancellor with the Esērii. A far more valuable captive than she. Please let her go, and I will go with you willingly."

Neith scoffed. She knew she could end them both at her will. She knew they knew it too. The woman was desperate.

"*Please.*" Nyanthi took a cautious step closer to Hawthorne.

Neith felt her readying her power to strike. She examined her ether, and just like her eyes, it held a familiarity. "Where is Calithea Ironne?"

Nyanthi didn't answer, so Neith tightened the ropes, lifting Hawthorne's feet from the ground.

"Please!"

Neith felt her release her call on her power.

"Please," she said again, more calmly. "I came for her, not for Calithea."

Neith let her disbelief and absence of patience show on her face. She lifted Hawthorne higher. "If you do not answer me, there will be nothing left to take." Nyanthi's eyes grew wild as she called her power again. But a familiar voice halted them both.

"Stop!" Calithea called as she walked into view, dust-covered and bloody like the others. Like her. Wet trails fell from her eyes down her cheeks. Neith's belly twisted as she remembered the boy in Godsreach who had looked the same. Soot-covered and tear-stained.

Neith returned Hawthorne to the ground, releasing and retracting her ether. The woman fell to her knees, choking, as Nyanthi ran to her. Neith watched her cousin move cautiously in front of the other women, their eyes fixed on one another.

"I cannot go back," Calithea said, a dagger clutched in one hand.

"And I cannot let you go." Neith felt a steady stream of blood dripping from her nose and down her face. The shadowy haze of nether filled her eyes, casting them black. It poured from both of her hands, coiling in the space between them.

Calithea watched it dance with wild eyes.

Neith studied the fear on her. The terror she inflicted.

Calithea swallowed. "*Please.*"

Neith flinched but shook her head. She looked down at the body of the Thranean soldier at her feet. No way to tell if it was a man or a woman.

Calithea exhaled and nodded, whispering something to herself. She looked more mournful than afraid. "Then kill me. I beg you."

Neith recoiled.

"I would rather die than go back."

"That is not your decision to make." Neith had tried to say the words with conviction, but they broke.

Calithea's chest heaved, her face twisting into a desperate frenzy. She turned to look at the women behind her. When her eyes met Neith's again, they were fixed in resignation. The dagger rose in her grip until it met the bare flesh of her neck. "I cannot go back," she said, her voice breaking. "I *will* not go back."

"Stop," Neith cautioned, stepping forward.

Calithea sank the blade into her skin, and a thin line of blood trailed down her neck.

"Stop!" Neith let go of her hold on the nether. It twisted through the air, back through her palms, and into the void. Her arms fell to her sides as she took another hesitant step forward.

Neith wanted to believe she wouldn't do it. That she could talk her down. But this was the girl who had thrown herself from her bedroom window only two days before. Neith knew she would drive the blade in.

They stared at each other. Neith was afraid to speak. To say the wrong thing, unsure of what to do. She couldn't let her go. But she couldn't kill her. And she feared nor could she watch her kill herself.

Scenarios raced through her mind. If she slit her throat, could she make it in time to heal her? If the other two ran, perhaps. If they did not, she might bleed out before she could get to her.

As if reading her thoughts, Calithea moved the dagger to her chest, hovering the point above her heart. She gripped it in both hands, and wild determination settled on her face.

Neith looked at the mangled bodies around her. Soldiers in her father's army. Her soldiers. Her people.

Two moons ago, she crossed the Obsidian Mountains believing she was a seeker of justice, a liberator of her people, fighting an enemy with righteousness on her side. Everything that had happened since had cracked at that fragile idea until it lay before her now, in pieces at her feet. She was standing face to face with a woman, her kin, who would rather plunge a blade into her own heart than stand beside her.

There was a villain here, and Neith knew she was it. If she killed Calithea, she would be stepping into that role. Owning it. It would be a choice she could never take back.

The sounds of thumping boots echoed down the alley she'd run from. More soldiers would be there soon.

Neith wanted to scream. Her hands came up over her face, fisting in her hair. She could feel the wild look she knew possessed her face. If she let her go, she would be betraying her people. Betraying her father. But killing her would be a betrayal of herself.

They all feared what Calithea could become, the power she might yield. If she let her go, she would be strengthening her enemy. Her father's enemy. If she let her go, she would be balancing the scale.

Her lips parted, and her arms fell.

Calithea watched her curiously, still clutching the dagger. Neith thought of the sigil of Straeth. The hypocrisy of it. She thought of Gods-reach and how she'd felt in that moment and every day since, watching her people step over or on everything in their path.

If she could not grant Calithea mercy, she could do this. It was something to grasp hold of, a justification she could cling to. Neith inhaled. *Yes,* she thought, *balancing the scale.*

"Go," she said, low and steady.

Calithea didn't move. She only stared at Neith, brows drawn, body shaking.

"Go, *now,*" Neith repeated as the sounds of approaching soldiers grew closer.

The blade slowly fell away from her chest, but her feet stayed in place.

"I will change my mind in three breaths' time." Neith said the words slowly and with a warning that was not idle.

The two women behind her didn't hesitate. Hawthorne grabbed Calithea's hand, dragging her away. Their eyes stayed locked on one another as she disappeared into the alley.

Until we meet again, cousin.

She knew that they would. Only time would dictate the line drawn between them.

Neith stared at the empty space where they'd stood. Relief, shame. Shock at her own actions. She felt it all. And perhaps, already regret. Her muddled brain could not distinguish everything that tumbled through it.

She wiped roughly at her tears as the approaching soldiers poured into the alley. The wild eyes of Bellamy, Iris, Kieran, and Raiden took her in.

"There is no one here," she said, as her mask fell into place. "Gone by the time I arrived."

"Are you injured?" Bellamy asked, grasping her shoulders.

Neith shook her head. "It is not my blood."

They looked at the bodies. Neith felt their rage swell as they recognized their fallen peers.

"They are from the Second," Iris said. She flipped over the remains of a girl. Light brown hair covered her face, and Iris brushed it aside. She was missing her left arm and part of her abdomen. "From the unit on city watch with ours."

These could have been Neith's soldiers.

"We saw the smoke from the barracks." Kieran helped Iris lift another body from the rubble. "We split into smaller groups, and Sam went back to the castle, looking for you."

"Who did this?" Bellamy asked, looking up with angry eyes from the body of a young man, nearly split in half.

Neith couldn't stop the hand that covered her mouth as she turned away and choked. "Esērii," she answered. "It could only be. They released the Etherborn prisoners."

Raiden walked partway down the alley. His eyes studied, as if recreating what had unfolded. When his eyes met Neith's, they held a subtle look of what she thought might be distrust.

"How is that possible? How could they have gotten in?" Kieran asked, looking from face to face.

"I do not know," Neith said. "But we will find out."

70

Nara

"One of wisdom knows when to fight, but also when to run."

AUTHOR UNKNOWN, C. 1500 BQ
TRANSLATED FROM SUMACIAN BY PARRY HAVERFORD
HAIS Z'NOSIŠ, 1204 AQ
RECOVERED 1203 AQ, SOMOS

They ran, unchallenged, the short distance to the drainage tunnel hatch. Four soldiers stood guard as expected, and Nara dispatched all, running a blade across their throats. She could not risk their being questioned and giving up her brother.

Cerys and Calithea were below ground by the time she turned around. Nara made for the hatch, her legs dreadfully heavy knowing she was leaving her brother behind. She said a silent prayer to Sydel to look over him. When she'd left him the night before, she thought it would be the last time she would see him. Her run-in with the girl had given her hope she might have been wrong.

Nara could make no sense of why she had let them go. Perhaps Sam was right. Perhaps she wasn't like her father. Hope sparked within as she lowered herself onto the first rung, ready to flee that wretched place.

She paused. Half above, half below, sure she felt a cast. A shield, she thought, as she listened. Nara looked around. There was nothing, no one, except the tiny pulses of woven ether.

The hair on her neck stood on end when she felt its familiarity. *Their* familiarity. Though she could not say who, she knew she had met this wielder before. She decided she was not going to wait to find out.

Her boots splashed in the ankle-deep water. Calithea and Cerys were nearing the end of the tunnel. She quickened her step to catch up.

"When we come out, we will still be behind the wards," she said. "The ones that left before us likely could not pass through undetected like we will." Nara did not include that it would give them an unfair advantage. The others would draw the attention of anyone giving chase.

"Then I hope their lead will be enough to get them to Eastwatche." Cerys's hand braced against Calithea's back, leading her on. Nara knew the girl had to be tiring. She was barely a whisper of a person when they'd pulled her from her cell. Nara knew well how desperation could carry one for a time, but even that waned.

The tunnel opened south of the castle, and they trudged through the waist-deep water to the lake's edge. Calithea's skirts slowed her down, but she didn't stop. Nara watched the gentle way that Cerys guided her through.

They cleared the lake and followed Nara through the dense brush of the woods. Calithea had no shoes but made no complaints. No one spoke. Their only concern was to get as far away as fast as they could.

When they made it to the horses, Nara sighed, finding six still tied to the surrounding trees. The first two she sent out had made it, but Rowena and the others had not. She glanced back at Cerys.

"Perhaps they ran into trouble as we did and will follow soon," Cerys said, but her eyes betrayed her words. She likely said them for Calithea's benefit.

"Perhaps."

Calithea mounted a horse with ease. She had said nothing since Neith Dracos had let them go. Since she had threatened to plunge a dagger into her chest. The same one she still gripped. Nara considered whether she believed the girl would have followed through.

She walked to the spot where she had left her pack and slipped it on her back before climbing onto a horse of her own.

"We're heading south. Once we're outside of the wards, we will have to ride hard. We'll cut east tomorrow when I'm confident we are not being followed."

Cerys nodded, and Nara turned to Calithea. "If you need to stop—"

"I'll be fine," she answered, turning her horse and trotting off south.

71

Neith

"Loyalty is not something one can demand. It is not born of fear nor force."

THE COST OF VALOR
AUTHOR UNKNOWN, 203 BQ
TRANSLATED FROM OLD ASARI BY MERIAH TURAN
HAIS Z'NOSIŠ, 1200 AQ

As the chaos in the city quieted, the chaos within her burned brighter in pace. She trudged back to her room, as sick from the whiskey and wine as she was from what she'd done. She had betrayed her father. He did not know, but she did. She would always know, and would have to live with it every day for the rest of her life. *Secrets are dreadful things*, she thought. Her trepidation compounded with every unsteady step, knowing he would call for her soon.

She also feared Sam's reaction. She had misled him, and he likely knew. Another assault of guilt rained down. *What is done cannot be undone.*

She was relieved to arrive to an empty room.

Neith ripped at the buttons on her vest until it fell free. Her black undershirt was sticky and stiff. She pulled it over her head, leaving behind the thin fabric of her undergarment. The crimson-stained linen clung to her breasts and belly.

She walked to the washbasin, dunking her entire face into the water, desperate to have some part of her clean. When her eyes met the mirror above, she winced. *Traitor.* She'd earned a new epithet for herself that night. *Monster. Traitor.* She wondered what would come third.

Her gaze snapped toward the door, feeling Sam approach. He was moving fast.

He burst through, taking her in as she stood there, water dripping down her face and neck. He quickly crossed the room, his hands coming up to grasp her arms as if he would shake her. But he simply stared, eyes demanding explanation.

"I'm sorry." It was all she could get out.

Sam scoffed, looking her over from head to foot. He swallowed as he examined the blood covering her body. "Are you hurt?"

Neith shook her head, and it felt like a lie.

Sam exhaled and released her arms. He paced in the space in front of her, occasionally glancing back. She braced herself to be scolded.

He stopped, facing her a few strides away. "*Why?*"

"I don't know—I—"

"I would have gone with you." He moved a step closer, retaining her gaze.

Neith swallowed. "I wasn't thinking. I was… *impaired.*"

"*Evidently.*" His expression was accusing, but it quickly turned to regret once the word left his lips.

She took a step back and straightened her shoulders.

"I'm sorry," Sam said, stepping closer. "I don't—" He paused, taking a breath. "When I came back to this room and found it empty, I panicked. I have been running the city looking for you, going out of my mind." He stepped once more, closing the space between them. His hands rose, passing by her arms to hold her face. "But you are here now, and you are whole."

She covered his hands with her own. "No," she said, "It is I who should be sorry. It was not my intention to frighten you, and I feel only regret for it. I should have returned to my room." It was neither truth nor lie. A part of her, which grew rapidly with each beat of her heart, wished she had.

He pulled her against him, clutching her tight. "Neith, what happened?"

She cleared her throat to stop herself shedding the tears that swelled. His heart thumped against her cheek. Everything she'd felt and witnessed and done, pushed forward, daring to bust through her thin resolve. "I was walking back to the courtyard, and felt a cast in the lower levels. I should have gone for help, I know, but I followed it. I don't know what I was thinking." She shrugged and lost control of her face, and it broke into a thousand pieces. Once the first tear fell, they came like rain. "It was awful," she cried.

"I saw the cell block," he said as she sobbed against him. One of his hands cradled her head.

She wanted to scream and confess and tell him what she had done. "I gave chase, but they were gone before I could reach them. The Etherborn prisoners escaped. Calithea, too."

Neith felt him exhale against her as she wiped at her tears.

A knock at the door drew their attention. She pulled back to look up at him. "That is likely a summons from my father."

Sam's hold on her didn't relax. He gazed down, his anger and panic retreating. He brushed the hair from her face. "You are safe," he said, and Neith thought the words were more for himself than her. "That is all that matters."

She wished that were true.

Another knock. This one harder. "Captain Dracos."

Against all her desires, she let him go and went to retrieve a clean tunic from the armoire.

"Come," she commanded after she tucked the ends into her trousers.

The door swung open, and a soldier walked through. "Captain Dracos, the king calls closed council. All are being summoned and expected to arrive with haste."

She nodded, and the soldier saluted and left.

Neith looked at Sam across the room. He was sorrowful and weary, and it pained her. "I cannot say when I will return. Go back to the barracks. Try to rest."

He looked as if he wanted to protest.

Neith made for the door. Hand on the knob, she turned back to look at him. "I will find you after."

Sam didn't speak, only nodded. When his weariness reformed to tenderness, she turned away. She couldn't bear tenderness, not then. She had created a secret between them. A secret she would have to keep.

Dryden, Cordero, and Nicomedes were already in the council room when Neith arrived. No one spoke as she took her seat.

Cordero stared at the tabletop. He was also covered in blood, his eyes desolate, but angry. Many had died, and the look on his face said at least one of them meant something to him. Guilt poured onto the mountain of it already strapped to her back. She may not have been able to save whomever he mourned, but she could have brought him justice, and she'd chosen not to. Of the three in the room, he would be the last to whom she would choose to bring harm.

Nicomedes looked afraid. Neith thought she was right to. She also dreaded the fury her father would bring to the room when he arrived.

Dryden stared at her. In no mood for his games, she glared back, but he made no taunting gesture as she expected. She couldn't read him, and it only made her angrier. Part of her wanted him to say something so she could act. Take out her rage, blame someone. Pass off some of the guilt.

Neith flinched when the door creaked. She turned to see her father walk through, Magnus on his heels.

He was alarmingly calm as he took his seat. Neith thought he would come in screaming, furious, ready to tear someone apart. He looked at the faces around the table, landing on her last.

When her father looked away, she looked at Magnus. He peered at her like he was searching for something. She gave him a questioning look, but he turned away.

Lorcan inhaled, expelling it slowly before he spoke. "We have recovered three."

Neith went stiff.

"Calithea Ironne was not among them."

She still didn't move, not even to release the breath she was holding.

"Roman and his unit are tracking those who escaped." Her father spoke stoically, but Neith knew what bubbled beneath, waiting for the smallest provocation to spring free.

"Then I have no doubt they will be found, Lord King," Nicomedes said.

Lorcan's gaze moved to her slowly, with the slight turn of his head. It was a warning to hold her tongue. His temperament was so controlled Neith found it far more terrifying than his rage.

Neith tried desperately to tame the tempo of her heart. There was a part to play here. She told herself it was no different from any other council she'd attended. She swallowed and let the mask fall over her face.

"Horses from our stables were found inside our wards, packed with a halfmoon of supplies. Food, spare clothing."

"They had help from within," Neith suggested, holding his gaze.

Her father nodded, then turned to Dryden on his right. "You will question every soldier and servant who had means for this treason. I want to know who. And how."

Dryden inclined his head.

"It is unlike the Esērii to take such a risk," Magnus said.

"Their designs were clearly on the girl. If we had executed her, this would not have happened." Nicomedes folded her arms, sitting back in her chair. She looked unusually disheveled, as if pulled directly from her bed.

"I simply mean that we should remain open-minded to the motives behind this," Magnus challenged. "You read the same reports I do. The Iren people are not conforming as we'd planned. Two idleborn soldiers were killed by a mob of townspeople during the chaos of the escape."

"They loved their king," Neith said flatly. "Perhaps if Roman had not dragged his daughter through the streets or put a sword through his chest, we would not be dealing with such unrest."

Nicomedes gestured at his empty chair. "You criticize someone not here to defend their actions. That is cowardly."

"I say nothing now I would not say were his chair warm with his body." Neith felt Cordero glance at her.

"I'm not concerned with townspeople, Captain Dracos. My concerns lie with our enemy now in possession of Calithea Ironne. We should have executed her a halfmoon ago. Instead, we kept her alive in another futile attempt to turn her."

"It was not futile," Neith said, her irritation flaring. "Were we successful, the Esērii would stand little chance against us. As our king has stated prior, they outnumber us by quite the margin. If Calithea proved herself to be what we believed, she would have given us a well-needed advantage."

Nicomedes scoffed. "She tried to throw herself from a window. If that is not an answer, I do not know what is. Instead of listening to her, our enemy is now made stronger, and many of us lie dead. In *fucking pieces.*"

Neith stood from her chair. "You do not need to tell me, Commander. I wear their blood as I stand here before you." Neith glared at her down the table as she gripped the edge to still the tremble in her hands. Her power poured out despite her effort to keep it contained.

Nicomedes's eyes widened, but she didn't look away. An uneasiness settled in the room as the others watched the exchange.

"Maelis, your grievances are heard," Lorcan said to Nicomedes. "Hold your tongue or see yourself removed." He looked from her to Neith and back. "What is done cannot be undone."

Neith's breath caught as she recalled saying those exact words to herself only hours before. A trickle of fear found its way in.

"Neith, return to your chair."

Nicomedes scowled as if deciding whatever else she wanted to say was worth Lorcan's reaction. When the silence continued, Neith surmised she decided not.

Neith fell back in her chair and rubbed her eyes. She was sick and exhausted and frightened, but also angry. She imagined herself jumping on the table, dancing like a madwoman, screaming down at them in jest that she had let Calithea go. Something like a snort escaped her.

"Is there something you find amusing, Captain Dracos?"

She looked up to meet her father's eyes and chuckled bitterly. "Not in the slightest."

"Then let us continue," he said with heavy irritation.

Dryden leaned forward in his chair. "I would like to speak to the recovered first, Lord King. We need to know who helped them. On the inside and out. It is clear they were aided in both regards. The manner of death of our soldiers suggests Influence was used on the idleborn. And I request permission to"—Dryden paused, eyes flicking to Neith's before he continued—"push the boundaries of the tactics I use. I think the urgency and importance of the matter justifies an evolution in our inquisitional methods."

"You may do as you wish with the Esērii," Lorcan answered. "But you will respect our law when questioning our own."

"As many of the soldiers to be questioned are in my unit, I request permission to be present at their interviews." Neith spoke to her father, but her eyes were fixed on Dryden.

"That is your right," he answered. "But let me be clear, you may observe, not interfere."

"I understand."

Dryden seemed unaffected by her request. If anything, he seemed pleased by it.

"I request the same." It was the first time Cordero had spoken. His face was blank, his eyes loosely focused on the tabletop.

"Granted."

"What happened tonight cannot go unanswered," Dryden said.

"It won't." Her father looked down the table. "Cordero."

Cordero lifted his head.

"If you cannot find the townspeople responsible for the murder of our soldiers, you will select four of your choosing. Hang them from the castle gate. Let it be a warning that future trespasses will be met twofold."

Neith looked from Cordero to her father several times, hoping she'd misheard. "You suggest to hang innocent people?"

All attention turned to her. Dryden and Nicomedes looked amused. Cordero looked nervous, and Magnus's face held warning.

"*Innocent?*" Lorcan asked.

She fought the urge to shift under his gaze. "What I mean is—my concern is that will not help. Surely, that will only build further unrest."

"Then perhaps it should be six."

Neith's mouth fell open. She didn't speak, too afraid to. His eyes were set in warning not to test him.

"Tempers run high this morning," Magnus interjected. "We are all tired. The captain," he said as he glared at her, "does not mean to question your judgment, Lord King."

"The *captain* may speak for herself."

Neith swallowed, fearing she'd gone too far. "It is not my intention to question your judgment, Father."

She said the words with as much authenticity as she could falsify. They stared at each other, and the look on his face, the intimidation, chipped away at the guilt she felt. When she could take it no longer, she looked down, allowing him the win. If she pressed, she had no doubt he would follow through on his threat. Neith did not think she could carry the burden of any deaths by her hand that day, directly or not.

The group squabbled over several subjects in the following hours. There was anger and confusion that the drainage tunnels had not existed in the versions of the city plans they'd had before arriving. Dryden and Nicomedes wanted to set up outposts in the woods outside the wards. Magnus pushed for caution. Anytime Neith thought to give her opinion, she chose instead to hold her tongue.

The meeting faded to background noise as she grew lost in her thoughts. In that moment, she didn't care about outposts and drainage tunnels. She hoped whatever direction Calithea was running, she was running fast.

Neith looked up, her thoughts broken by those around her standing. She had not heard her father call the meeting concluded. He was the first from the room.

⊹

Sunlight blinded as she stepped from the castle, her wet hair soaking the back of her tunic. It had taken twelve buckets of water to wash the filth before she was clean enough to bathe in a tub. Her skin and scalp were pink from where she'd scrubbed herself raw, despite protests from Maeve. The girl had patiently combed through the tangles and knots, weaving her hair in a single long braid now hanging damp and heavy down her back.

Neith trudged past the new barracks and the sounds of hammer and saw, toward the sea of tents. It was sometime between dawn and midday, and she passed few apart from those who wielded the tools whose rackets polluted the amity the sun had brought with it.

She felt Sam as she drew closer. Sensing no one else in the space he shared, she pulled back the cover on the door of his tent to find him sitting up in his cot, wearing only trousers, rubbing his face as she stepped through.

Sam's eyes, heavy with sleep, took her in as she came to stand before him. His arms wrapped around her waist as he nestled against her belly, an act so achingly tender she thought at that moment to tell him everything. Her mind had become a pool of languid hysteria. A listless delirium from the drink and no sleep. Stripped of reason by the violence and gore. It was oddly numbing, in a way. She felt muted. Hazy, as if dreaming.

She'd told him she would come, so there she was.

"Have you slept?" he asked.

Neith shook her head. He moved down the bed, gesturing for her to lie down. She looked at the empty space on the cot, then back to him.

He frowned. "What is wrong?"

So many things, she thought, unable to will her lips to move.

"*Neith?*" Sam moved to stand, but she pressed his shoulders down.

His concern eased as she took his face in her hands, running her fingers along the faultless design of it. He was beautiful in a way she had not known a man could be. She remembered how he had looked when he pressed himself inside of her. How his body shuddered and the cries he made when he spent himself, and how she'd thought it was the sweetest song.

She ran her hands through his hair as he gazed up at her with soft, dozy eyes. She wanted to dive into them. That was what he was for her. Escape. One of the many things. Neith wondered if he would look at her the same if he knew what she'd done. Something in her gut, in her heart, told her he would understand. But she wasn't brave enough to test them. She wanted to put it all from her mind, however fleeting.

Neith lifted one knee and then the other, straddling him on the cot. Surprise flashed through his face as he searched hers for intent. She watched him with definitive regard as she curled her hips. His hands tightened around her waist as he exhaled, brows creasing. He tried to kiss her, but she pulled back, rolling against him again, slow and savoring. She moaned, feeling heat, need, spark to life.

The sound brought a shift in him. Hungry hands moved around the front of her body, trailing underneath her tunic to find her breasts. Neith moaned again at the contact, audible but restrained, and further still when his mouth found her neck. His lips and tongue swirled and kissed, setting fire to every place they touched.

Sam tugged at her tunic, freeing it from her body. He leaned her back, his kisses trailing down her neck, chest, and breasts. She clamped her lips together to stop the cry that wanted to escape.

He held her steady as he loosened the laces of her trousers. When his palm curled over the axis between her thighs, she pressed down against him, desperate for a firmer touch. This time she cried out as her head fell back, abandoning her concern.

Neith braced her hands on his shoulders as she moved, tightening herself around his finger as it slipped inside. Her breath came out in feverish, soft puffs, and she quickened her pace, feeling as if she were running from something. It was on her heels, trying to rip her back.

When he tried again for her lips, she didn't retreat. His free hand wrapped around her neck, holding her tight and steady against his mouth. Their tongues collided in a frenzy of need. She opened every part of herself, inviting him in.

Before she realized she was moving, she was on her back. Sam lifted her from the cot, pulling away what remained of her clothes until she was wholly bare before him. She dismissed the inclination to cover herself. She let him look at her, all of her, without reserve. His eyes ran the length of her body, landing back on her face. His chest was heaving, but he hesitated.

She discerned his manner, desperate to share in his thoughts.

His gaze held longing, but something else was there, something bigger. Sadness, she thought. The same sadness he was often fighting. But that wasn't all. Her heart stopped when she realized it was love.

He was looking at her with love.

Neith reached for him, drawing his body down onto hers, finding his mouth. She tugged at the laces of his trousers until they fell loose down his hips, trying to silence the voice in her mind telling her she didn't deserve this. She didn't deserve him. Every part of her throbbed and ached, even her heart, and when she felt him firm, pressing against her, the sensation, the anticipation, was nearly enough to send her. Every nerve, every particle, every fiber that existed within her, all of what she was made, was exposed, too sensitive, raw, and defenseless. She gripped his hips, urging him on.

When he pressed inside, her face drew tight, stifling her cry. He withdrew, and when he returned, she let it out. *It doesn't matter*, she thought, *let them hear.*

Sam's eyes found hers as he thrust again, and a sob escaped her. He stopped, but she shook her head, wrapping her legs around him, pleading for him to persist.

It was a curious but liberating feeling. Like anguish and elation colliding only to find it is in embrace. Neith felt herself coming undone, and she didn't care. She welcomed it. She wanted it.

His thrusts turned deeper, swifter, her sobs turning to cries of pleasure as she let herself get lost in the warmth of his body pressed to hers, clutching and clawing to keep it close. Every moment was a battle in the desperation to ignite, but not, to live in it as long as she could.

His hand moved between them, trailing between her breasts, over the small swell of her belly. He found purpose turning circles at the crest where their bodies connected. She arched and rounded into his touch.

Unable to resist, she surrendered.

Release rolled through her in waves from her core to the tips of her toes, over her chest, and through her heart. Sam gripped her face, gentle but weighted. He brought his lips to hers and cried out against them.

When he stilled, she tightened her legs around him, imploring him to stay. She was not yet ready to part. The weight of him calmed the tremor in her limbs. She felt safe and hidden. As if no one could find her beneath the mountain that was he.

He kissed her, tender and indulgent. As if time did not matter. As if discovery did not loom. When he pulled back to look at her, she could barely withstand it. His thumb collected a tear she had not realized had fallen. He swallowed, and his lips parted, but voices outside the tent drew their attention.

Neith released her legs, expecting him to withdraw, but he stayed. He brushed away the loose strands of wet hair clinging to her face as she looked from his eyes to the door.

"No one is coming here," he said.

She pulled her lips between her teeth, not made calmer by his words.

"It is fine, I swear. Everyone is sleeping or on post."

The voices drew louder, but quickly quieted again as they walked past, occupied in conversation.

"But—I was… not quiet." Flush stained her cheeks.

A slight but telling smile formed on his lips. "I did not mind."

Her blush deepened, and she turned her face away, but he grasped it, setting it straight. "You are safe with me."

Neith exhaled, nodding, seeking to accept the sanctuary he was offering. All of what she suppressed was finding its way to the surface. This time, she felt the tears before they fell. She had traveled past the point of exhaustion, completing the succession into frenzy, her body making involuntary spasms and shakes.

"You need to rest." He kissed her again before lifting himself up. She winced at the loss of him.

He walked to the washbasin, returning with a dampened cloth. The water was warm like the air, and it felt like an embrace of its own as he ran it over her sweaty skin. She wanted to retreat from the affection. All she could think about were her lies.

Sam dressed her, leaving a kiss on her belly after lacing her trousers. She nearly sat up and screamed her confession. When he finished clothing them, he walked across the room, pulling a box from beneath the other cot. He returned with a small vial, popping the cork before handing it to her. She shivered at the bitter flavor, then returned the empty vial to his hand. He smiled at her, brushing her cheek. She turned, curling up on the cot, and he climbed in behind her.

"I do not think I can sleep."

"You will. Close your eyes." His arm came around her, and she sank into him. Their connection calmed her, as it always did.

She had to decide. Her uncertainty was not something she wished to wake to. She vowed to choose, there and now, if to tell him. If she did not, she never would. She would tell no one. She would forget about it herself. Push it far from her mind as if it had never happened. But Sam would understand. He would *want* to know.

"Sam," she said, scarcely above a whisper. When she didn't continue, he lifted his head. He looked at her the same way he had before, with love. With a tenderness that cracked something within her. With affection she knew in that moment she could not live without. This wasn't something she would risk. *He* wasn't something she would risk. She swallowed as concern crept into his eyes. "I only wanted to say that there is nowhere else I would rather be than here with you."

His concern softened, and the look that remained nearly brought the words *I love you* from her lips. "Then never leave," he said.

She turned her body, nuzzling into him, limbs tangled together. He kissed the crown of her head, and she solidified her decision. She would think of it no more.

His arms tightened around her, and she felt herself drift.

72

Nara

"We cannot always carry all in which we aim to."

AUTHOR UNKNOWN, C. 1500 BQ
TRANSLATED FROM SUMACIAN BY PARRY HAVERFORD
HAIS Z'NOSIŠ, 1204 AQ
RECOVERED 1203 AQ, SOMOS

It was the horses that protested before Calithea. The sun was bright in the morning sky, and Nara knew they had to rest, else risk one to injury or exhaustion. She'd kept them cloaked from the moment they crossed the wards and could use a rest herself.

They'd said little throughout the night, their only aim to travel as fast and as far as they could. When they reached a small clearing, she slowed her horse, letting the shield fall away.

Nara dismounted and tied the reins to a tree. She looked back to find Cerys doing the same. Over a year had passed between them, but time had changed nothing about her. She was the same woman Nara had said goodbye to. The same woman she'd watched sail away.

There weren't many times in her life Nara could remember crying. When she'd fallen from a tree at age seven, breaking an arm. At age ten, when her little dog, Sarri, had died. The day she lost her father.

Cerys turned toward her, their eyes connecting across the clearing. Cerys smiled, and Nara choked back a sob threatening to tear itself from her chest. She started toward her, her walk quickly turning to a run, gaining speed as she moved. She clutched Cerys against her, grasping and clawing at her, all in effort to draw her closer. To forge her lover's body against hers so they could never be parted again.

Nara closed her eyes, inhaling pine and honey, distinct even through the blood and sweat. She let herself, for the first time in a year, feel a sense of peace, however fated to be fleeting it might be.

Cerys pulled back to look at her, her chestnut eyes wet. "I knew you would come."

She always would. No matter the distance or danger. There was no greater threat to Nara than losing the woman in her arms. Her heart. Her purpose. She was not whole without her.

Nara ran a thumb over the freckles sprinkled on her cheeks. She kissed them. Every single one, until her lips found their way to Cerys's mouth. When their tongues grazed, the consuming nature of their connection nearly relieved her of her self-control. She'd gone without it too long, and now she was a woman starved. Every night, she'd dreamt of this. Every day, she thought of little else. All she wanted was to get lost in it. In her. To take her time studying the lines and curves of her. To put her mouth on every part of her body. Use her lips, her tongue, her teeth. To be reminded of her taste. To reclaim her.

Their kiss slowed, and Nara exhaled, forehead pressed against hers. "Have they hurt you?"

Cerys shook her head. "I am all right." Her arms tightened around Nara's waist. "I am now."

Their lips met again before Nara forced herself to let go, wiping the tears from her cheeks. She glanced back toward Calithea to find her dismounted and turned away across the clearing, granting them privacy.

"You found Sam?" Cerys asked, as she sipped water from a skin.

Nara had done her best not to think of him. "I did."

"Will he meet us in Eastwatche?" The hopefulness in Cerys's eyes sent a sting through her.

Nara could not bring herself to answer. She looked down.

Cerys stepped back. "Nara, where is Sam?"

Nara looked up and watched as the easiness she'd just possessed slowly melted into concern. "He would not leave. I could not convince him."

Cerys frowned. "I don't understand. Why would he stay?" When Nara didn't explain, she continued. "Nara, they will find him out. You don't understand." She shook her head frantically, her red, exhausted eyes turning desperate. "They can do things. Things I have not seen before. Influence in ways we cannot."

"I know." Nara reached forward, gripping her shoulders. "I know."

She swallowed against the guilt knotting at the back of her throat as panic took claim of Cerys's face.

"Why didn't you *make* him?"

"If I did," Nara said, feeling her tears returning, "I would not have been able to get to you."

Cerys's hands came up, running over her face as she cursed. "When I saw him there, I couldn't believe it. All I wanted to do was find a way to tell you."

"He made a choice," Nara said, trying to steel herself.

"Why would he stay?" Cerys asked, her tone suggesting it was a most absurd notion. "It is a miracle he has not already been found out."

"That is what I told him." Nara's head fell into her hands, and she laughed, a touch frenzied.

"I fail to see what is funny." Cerys folded her arms and stepped out, widening her stance.

Nara sighed. "He stays for the girl," she said, throwing her arms out to either side. "He believes he can turn her."

Cerys stared at her, blank-faced.

"You know who I mean."

Cerys's eyes flickered as if replaying the past, trying to make sense of what Nara had said.

"He's in love with her," Nara said, helping her along. "At least he believes himself to be. And he believes she feels the same. He claims she is not like her father."

Cerys's lips parted, and she inhaled. She returned to her look of consideration, her head taking on a lean, brows raising. "She did let us go."

Nara glowered and pointed at Calithea, who was still facing away. "She let *her* go."

"Do not be like that." Cerys glanced across the clearing. Her voice lowered. "She's powerful. Don't deny you can feel it."

Nara could not. She'd felt the girl's strange power from the moment Cerys had torn away the wards on her cell. "Perhaps she is, but whatever they've done to break her seems to have worked. Will she even be able to make this journey, let alone learn to use her gift?"

"Thea is stronger than she looks. They have not broken her." Cerys looked as if she was reading the uncertainty on Nara's face. "She is a good person, Nara. A worthy person. You would like her, given the chance to."

Nara scowled.

"If she is what she is believed to be, we will need her. You saw what the other girl did. What she can do."

Nara paled at the memory. Her breath grew heavy as she pictured the black tendrils snaking up from her palms. Twisting and biting through the air.

Neither of them said the word.

"We can't be sure," Nara said, desperate to cling to an alternative.

"I have never known you to hide from the truth."

Nara wanted to argue there had never been a truth so frightening. She didn't have the capacity to worry about anything more than she could control at that moment. She reached up, taking Cerys's face in her hands. "Let us put this aside for the time. We need to focus on staying alive. We can deal with that… later."

Cerys sighed but relented. Nara ran a thumb across her cheek before leaning forward to kiss her once more. It eased some of the tension that plagued every part of Nara's body.

"How did you get here so fast?" Cerys asked. "Your last letter said you were setting out for Ahara."

Nara released her face, taking her hands. "Come, there is much to tell."

They walked a short distance south until coming upon a creek. They set the horses to water and took seats on fallen logs to eat and rest. And talk. Nara told them of Amul and all that had happened in the Citadel. Cerys listened intently, taking in every word. Calithea gazed out, unfocused in the distance, pulling tiny pieces of bread from a larger portion, occasionally putting one in her mouth. At first, Nara thought her attention aimless, but from time to time, Calithea would look up at her, eyes wary or considering.

Calithea had said nothing since they'd ridden away from the city. Answering with a simple nod or shake of her head. Some part of Nara felt pity for her, but another resentment. So much fuss over this yellow-haired girl from Ire. But it was not her fault, Nara had to admit. Cerys seemed to truly care for her, so she must have some merit. She couldn't help but roll her eyes when she thought of the way Alec had acted.

Looking at Cerys, Nara knew she was no one to judge. Nara would climb every mountain, turn over every stone, set fire to the entire Gods-damned world for her. Gods help the next person who tried to take her away. She would tear out their heart with her bare hands. There would be no second thought because there would not be a first.

She watched Cerys sip water from a skin and wipe away at the tiny stream trailing down her chin. They met eyes, and Nara smiled. Cerys's gaze shifted to Calithea, her brow knitting in concern. She reached into one of the packs and pulled out a pouch of salted meat. She took a small piece, holding it out to Calithea.

"You need to eat more than bread," Cerys told her.

"I'm not hungry."

"That will change with time. But you will not regain your strength unless you eat."

She'd likely been starved. Cerys was thin, but Calithea looked unnaturally so.

"She is right," Nara said. "We will be riding hard for Eastwatche, and we need you to stay atop your horse."

Calithea glanced at her, neither disdainful nor in search of approval. She took the meat from Cerys's hand, biting off a small piece. "I will stay atop my horse."

Cerys's lips drew into a grin that she pulled between her teeth when meeting Nara's narrowed eyes. Cerys raised her brows as if to say *see*.

73

Thea

"I do not see how one can be bold without a little madness."

THE RECOVERED JOURNALS OF SONIA THRONDSEN, 1182 AQ

Thea peeled the tattered remains of the dress from her body and stepped into the cool water. At its deepest, the creek rose to her waist. She sank down to her knees until it reached her chin, dipping her head back. Nara had suggested they bathe while the horses rested. That they may have little other opportunity on their journey to Eastwatche once they left the woods on the morrow. Ten days, Nara said it would take.

She used her nails to scrub at her scalp and skin, saturating herself in the soap Cerys had given her. Then she did it all again for good measure. She wanted no remnants of the last moon remaining on her person when she stepped from the water. It was cold coming down from the ice-capped mountains, but she didn't care. She cared far more about being clean.

Thea tried, without success, to push down thoughts of her brothers and sisters. The thoughts made ten days feel like a lifetime.

She wondered if Leanne had given birth. She prayed to Cassia both child and mother were well. She thought of Marten, and if he was in Aremore, and of his wife. They would all know by then that Highclere had fallen.

She could not think of Evelynde locked away in her room in the castle. Thea wanted to vow to find a way to get her out, to save her. Something she would have done only a moon ago. She laughed at herself. At the thoughts of a stupid girl. A naive girl. *You couldn't even save yourself,* she chastised.

Nara and Cerys bathed a short distance up the creek. They spoke low, their eyes regularly landing on her. Not obviously, but Thea could feel it. No doubt they thought her a madwoman cackling naked in a creek. She knew she would be dead without them.

Thea was fairly certain Nara would leave her behind, given the choice, and Thea did not blame her one bit. Not with what happened to those who helped her. Her faulty composure threatened to snap as she remembered the terror in Dianna's eyes when they raised her up by the neck. The desperation in her father as he bled out.

Thea swallowed, letting her sorrow harden to rage. It washed over her in a flash of heat, prickling down her arms, up her neck, and over her cheeks. It wanted violence. *She* wanted violence. She remembered what it felt like to plunge the dagger into Calix's chest. How it had surprised her how much effort it had taken. She remembered the sound it made. Blade slicing through flesh, the grating of steel against bone.

She pictured their faces in her mind. Roman and Lorcan Dracos. The man who called himself Dryden. She feared his dark eyes would forever haunt her dreams. If her dreams ever returned. She thought of each time they'd touched her, hurt her, and the memories of it turned her belly.

Thea rushed from the water, bracing against a tree, breathing deep to stop the meager amount of food in her belly from coming back up.

Cerys called after her, but Thea held up her hand. Her thoughts went to Neith, and the wild look she had as she told them to run. *Why?* Thea could make no sense of it. Nor could she bend herself to feel grateful. She had thought of a thousand reasons as they rode through the night, but could not find one that fit. The look on her face was burned into Thea's mind. Fury, desperation, and something else. Something Thea was not yet ready to call concern. She shook her head, tossing it from her mind. What remained, and what was truly frightening, was how terrified Cerys and Nara had been. Thea knew next to nothing about their powers, but the instincts of self-preservation were enough to tell her cousin's were daunting.

She dressed in the clean tunic, trousers, and boots Nara had given her. They walked south for several hours until the sun set. Nara said they were still too close to Highclere for a fire, but created something Cerys called an etherstar. Thea watched as violet light poured from Nara's palms. She moved her hands as if pressing the energy together. A thin, translucent sheen surrounded it, containing the dim glow.

Even with all she'd seen, Thea could not help but feel in awe.

Stars, fire, shields. Reading another's thoughts. *Altering* another's thoughts. Freezing an entire Godsdamned lake. It seemed so unbelievable, even as she sat cross-legged on the ground, watching it happen before her very eyes.

Nara and Cerys had refused her offer to take a watch, and Cerys didn't argue when Nara said she would take the first. Cerys looked worn. More so than Thea had seen her. She wondered if they'd also done torture to her. If she'd spent time in the pits. She hoped not.

Thea lay down, using her pack as a pillow, turning away from the others. The first time they ran from Highclere, it had not been easy to sleep on the ground. Now, Thea would gladly sleep on the forest floor every night of her life if it meant never returning to the cell. She closed her eyes, saying a silent prayer to Cassia she would awake to the trees, and not a stone wall.

It was still dark when she blinked her eyes open. The gentle noises of what roamed the forest at night were the only sounds.

Thea turned, locking eyes with Nara, who sat against a tree.

"You've only been asleep a couple of hours," she said, slicing through an apple with a small blade. She spoke low so as not to wake Cerys, who slept beside her.

"I do not often sleep well," Thea said. "Without help, at least." She sat up, reaching for her waterskin. She took three large gulps while Nara watched. Nara's gaze was intense and appraising, as if taking her measure. Thea shifted uncomfortably beneath it.

Nara reached into a pack and pulled out another apple. She tossed it at Thea, who scrambled to catch it as it flew through the air, landing in her lap. "We should eat the fresh food before it spoils."

Thea looked at her, mystified by her manner. Nara was abrasive and unnecessarily direct, but also seemed to be concerned with everyone around her. Even when it irritated her. Except for Cerys. She was soft with her. Gentle. It was a stark inconsistency.

The light from the etherstar had dimmed, but Thea could still make out her face. It was the first time she'd truly looked at her in depth. Her umber skin was cool-toned, and she had large, almond-shaped dark eyes that were always watching, always exhibiting intelligence and thoughtfulness. Thea imagined very little escaped her.

Her face was the kind you often found in art. The sort one aspires to reproduce. Heart-shaped with soft, round cheeks. Thea found her beautiful. Wildly so. Despite the scowl now directed toward her.

"I know that you are not happy that I am here," Thea said, looking over the apple in her hand. "That you resent it."

Nara didn't answer.

"I do not blame you. Too many have suffered because of me, and I would not see it happen to another." Thea looked at Cerys again. Her lips were slightly parted, fluttering as each breath moved in and out. "Especially not her."

Nara's gaze followed Thea's. "Cerys cares for you," she said, as if that was the reason she was there.

Thea nodded. "And I her. If it helps my case at all, I did try to convince her to leave me behind. She wouldn't hear of it."

"No." Nara sighed. "She would not. That is her way." Nara looked back to Thea, her expression considering. "I don't resent you." She lifted a slice of apple to her mouth, chewing it slowly as she stared. One of her brows raised. "Perhaps I simply do not like you."

A small, scoff-like laugh tumbled from Thea's lips. She thought at first to be offended, but registered the hint of amusement on Nara's face. Thea cocked her head. "Perhaps I will grow on you."

Nara stared her down, eyes narrowing. "Perhaps you will, Calithea." Her voice was feminine and rich.

"Thea."

"Pardon?"

"Everyone calls me Thea."

Nara nodded. "Thea, then."

Thea bit into the apple she'd been gifted, closing her eyes, relishing in the sweet, tart taste.

"We don't often have apples in the Citadel," Nara said. "It's too hot to grow them so far south." She ate another slice. "I've never had one like this."

"These are honey apples. Notoriously difficult to grow."

Nara smiled, turning the apple in circles as if admiring it. "Then I like them more."

"They do best in the high north. In the cooler climates," Thea added.

Nara grumbled. "Well, nothing is perfect."

Thea laughed but paused when Cerys shifted.

"You should try to sleep," Nara said. Her scowl had softened to a mild uncertainty. "This is the only night we will not travel."

Thea nodded and moved to lie back down. "I know it was not your aim, but I want to thank you for getting me out. It is not a debt I could ever repay, but I am grateful and would endeavor to, given the chance."

Nara looked at her with far less disdain than she had before. She didn't speak, only inclined her head.

Thea turned around, lying back on the ground. A low, slow yawn pulled from her lips. She let the frogs, crickets, and other creatures of the forest sing her back to sleep.

74

Neith

"Whispers of it are often more effective than the whip itself."

THE COST OF VALOR
AUTHOR UNKNOWN, 203 BQ
TRANSLATED FROM OLD ASARI BY MERIAH TURAN
HAIS Z'NOSIŠ, 1200 AQ

"Two of the noble houses of Ire have surrendered," Magnus said, "and one of them its most prominent."

"The rest will come," Lorcan grumbled. He had been in a dreadful mood since the escape. It took very little to send his temper spiraling. On two occasions, he'd taken to ranting and raving about loyalty. The first time, Neith had been frightened. The second had dragged on so long that by the end, she couldn't care less if he found out what she'd done. She had simply wanted him to cease talking.

"In time," Magnus agreed. "Though it seems most will come by force. Four dispelled our envoys on arrival, and six refused an audience altogether. The Duke of Calcheth sent back a box of his own shit after hearing what occurred in Dunclere."

Unexpectedly, Lorcan laughed. "The Iren are a stubborn lot."

Neith wanted to correct him. To tell him loyalty was not stubbornness, and one who ranted about it so often should know the difference. She bit her tongue to still it.

Much had happened in the eight days since the escape. Cordero was unsuccessful in finding the townspeople responsible for the murders of the Thranean soldiers. Four citizens were seized, charged, and executed, as instructed. Two men, a woman, and a sixteen-year-old boy. Three days later, their decaying bodies still hung from the castle gates, spoiling and festering under the summer sun.

As Neith foretold, it had done nothing to quiet the resistance. Two similar attacks had since taken place, and nine more bodies were added to the ones swaying from the gates. As was a captured Iren captain they pulled from a cell. Cordero told her the young man called out for the resistance to continue as the noose was placed around his neck.

Neith had been surprised by his admission. Though he did not say it, it was evident to her he did not agree with the commands he carried out.

Sam asked her not to, but she forced herself to go and see the bodies, then regretted it later when she dreamt of their bloated faces, forever stuck in terror. She'd woken in a cold sweat that night, having dreamt of Calithea hanging alongside them. It had nearly erased any guilt that lingered.

Neith kept her head down. She attended council, spoke little, and spent her time training. Or with Sam. She kept to what she'd decided and told no one what she'd done. Not because there weren't people she trusted. She trusted Sam. She trusted Bellamy, even Ayla. But telling them, asking them to keep her secret, would put them in danger.

As the days passed, her resolve grew. Not that she had made the right decision, but that she had made one, and she would stand by it. She had thought it strong until a soldier marched into the council room.

They were long in morning session when he entered, delivering a message to her father that Roman had returned with some of the escaped in hand. Lorcan's eyes lit up. "Have them brought here," he directed to the soldier.

Neith was sure her heart stopped, but it was only because it fluttered with such tempo it felt more a persistent action than steady beat. If it was Calithea, it was over for her. She would have to run. Where would she go? Would her father execute her? If she ran, would anyone go with her? Would Sam?

The pandemonium in her head stilled when two dirty, bruised, and bloody bodies were dragged in, barely able to stay on their feet. Neith recognized neither. Relief swelled through her, and she inhaled, trying to slow her heart. Roman and Katya followed, falling into half salute before the king.

Lorcan stood, looking over the prisoners before he turned back to address Roman. "What is this?"

"What you asked for, Father."

Neith was surprised at her brother's tone. It lacked the ever-present desperation for approval. He was dirty and travel-weary. Even Katya, who stood behind him, was uncharacteristically disheveled. Her ice-white hair was tangled and murky with grime.

Lorcan scowled. "You brought me two half-dead Esērii. What use have I for this?"

Roman flexed his jaw, then stretched his neck. "I've been up and down the countryside for eight days. We could find no traces of the Ironne bitch."

"You mean the only one we care about." He glared at Roman, saying his next words slowly. "How dreadfully disappointing." He turned and walked back to his chair, gesturing carelessly with his hand. "Take these *corpses* below."

Roman didn't retreat. He straightened his back, eyes defiant. "You mean the only one *you* care about."

Lorcan turned on his heels, rushing forward to meet Roman nose-to-nose. "Would you care to clarify your meaning?"

Roman flinched but held his ground. "I—"

"You *what?* Do not hold your tongue now." His voice echoed, bouncing off the stone walls. "Speak!"

Tension blanketed the room. Neith's pulse rose again, fearful this would be the time a quarrel between them would erupt.

"Lord King," Magnus said as he stood. "Perhaps we should break for now, return to council later?"

Lorcan held up his hand, warning him off.

Dryden seemed amused by the exchange. Nicomedes simply watched. Cordero appeared irritated, as if it were a show he had seen one too many times before.

"I will go back out," Roman said, his eyes losing their resistance.

Lorcan scoffed, stepping back. "There is no use. They could be at the coast by now." He walked to his chair, gripping the back. "You failed." His face contorted, and his power rumbled around him. Neith jumped when the chair back snapped. He picked it up, hurling it across the room. It smashed into the far wall, splintering into a thousand pieces. He stood there, panting, then brushed his hand through his hair. "Get these prisoners in cells. Do not make me say it again."

Roman, Katya, and the others fled the room. Neith wanted to go with them. Instead, she stood and dragged a spare chair around the table. Her father looked at her strangely as she set it in place. He was seated by the time she returned to hers.

"I want to know who," he said to Dryden. "Do what you must."

Neith sat around a campfire in the barracks, sharing bread, cheese, and rabbit Max had caught, and Ayla had roasted on skewers. She was happy to have her friends together, but the mood was somber, heavy with all that had happened since the escape.

"When will they take the bodies down?" Ayla asked. She was in her new uniform. It was all she wore now that she was officially a member of their unit. She trained hard every day, and Max was rarely more than ten paces from her. She seemed happy. But more importantly, she was safe.

Dryden had not been pleased, to say the least. But to her surprise, he had not addressed it directly. His rant to his daughter had been the only words she'd heard on it. And she'd seen no bruises on her since.

"I don't know. Avoid the area until they do." Neith looked down at the skewer of rabbit in her hand and recoiled. She held it out before her. "Anyone?"

Kieran, two seats down, reached forward to take it. Their campfire was dwindling, and Neith thought it a fair representation of their collective mood.

She wished the supper was like the ones they'd had on the road, laughing and jesting. She hoped those days were not all in the past.

"I fear it will only make things worse," Bellamy said, snapping Neith from her thoughts.

"They murdered our soldiers," Petra countered, stoking the fire with a long stick. "Execution is what they deserved."

"Of course," Bellamy added. "It is the manner, I think, that leaves something to be desired."

Neith did not have the heart to tell them that those who hung were not the perpetrators. She was drained from the ever-growing sum of secrets she was now prevailed upon to keep. She did not like secrets. At least not those she had to keep from people she cared for.

Neith glanced at Sam to find concerned, questioning eyes. She smiled at him, as full as she could manage, but knew it was not convincing. Her eyes moved to each of the faces around the campfire. The faces of her friends. She vowed when she became queen, there would be no such secrets to keep.

With every day that passed, Neith knew she grew further from the family she was born to, and closer to the one she'd found.

75

Thea

"Once you are driven to madness, the risk to return always remains. Your mind has charted the course, and it is one not easily forgotten."

UNOFFICIAL CORRESPONDENCE FROM SONIA THRONDSEN TO LIA
THRONDSEN, 1183 AQ
RECOVERED AFTER THE BLOODY DAY

"Make yourself known," a voice commanded.

Thea looked up at the high gates. She could see no faces behind the tall walls of Eastwatche. "I am Calithea Ironne, daughter of—" The words caught in her throat. "I am the daughter of the king."

"Open the gates!" a desperate voice called out. *Callum.* Thea jumped from her horse as the gates creaked open. Callum raced into view. He stood frozen, eyes wide, mouth agape. "Thea?"

They ran for each other, colliding with a force that nearly knocked her back, but he lifted her from the ground, secured in his arms.

"Thank the Gods," he cried as he held her. "We've had little news since Highclere fell."

She clung to him. It had taken twelve agonizing days of travel, but she'd made it.

He moved to release her, but she gripped him tighter, fearful to let him go. A long moment passed before she could convince herself nothing would happen when she did.

When her feet touched the ground again, he looked her over, studying the fading bruises and nearly healed cut on her cheek. His eyes moved the length of her, and he nearly sobbed when he spoke. "You're so thin."

Over his shoulder, Cat appeared. She wore a nurse's apron, and her blonde hair was braided back. Her walk turned into a sprint as she kept her eyes fixed on Thea. She slowed as she grew closer, stopping a pace away. "You're really here?"

Thea nodded, and Cat closed the space. Thea reached for Callum again, pulling them both around her.

"Are you all right?" Cat asked, sobbing, her arms locked tight.

"No." Thea let go of them and stepped back to better see their faces. "But I am closer to it now that I am here."

"*What happened?*" Callum asked. Such a small question asked so much.

Our father is dead, she thought. *Our kingdom is lost.* "We need to go somewhere we can speak."

Callum nodded, and Cat reached for her hand. Thea turned back to Cerys and Nara, feeling something that gratitude would be a poor substitute for. "Thank you for everything. Cerys, I—"

"Go," Cerys said, waving her off. "Be with your family. We will speak on the morrow."

Thea nodded, inclining her head to Nara before she turned back to her siblings.

The courtyard was overrun. Tents and medical beds had been erected over the entirety of the space. People were cooking, washing clothing. More than she could count. Injured soldiers, women, children, the elderly, all those who had fled Highclere.

Thea had only been to Eastwatche once as a child. It was larger than she remembered. The stronghold was nearly half the size of Highclere Castle, rising four stories. Like the capital, it was crafted from limestone, but some of the smaller buildings were built from sea pebbles. The air was rich with salt. She gazed up at the cawing of seagulls high above.

She followed Callum past staff and soldiers, meeting eyes with Reginald Roth. The familiar face gave her hope that others may have escaped the siege. She feared asking.

Callum led them to a room on the third floor. It held a long table with twelve neatly arranged chairs. Carafes and bottles covered one end, maps and documents on the other. It reminded her of the days she'd spent with her father and the council before the city fell. Before her entire world changed.

Cat squeezed her hand. "I will go and fetch Conall."

The door opened, and Breeda appeared. They ran to one another, Breeda locking her arms around her. Thea melted into it, relief flooding through her. Breeda pulled back, quickly, her hands firm on Thea's shoulders. "I saw Cerys and came searching for you. When I arrived and you weren't here, I feared the worst." Breeda took Thea's face in her hands. "Were you traveling here this entire time?"

Thea shook her head.

The color drained from Breeda's cheeks. She took in the bruises on her face. Thea swallowed, determined not to break again. She had many things to tell, and she had spent the last twelve days steeling herself for the task.

Breeda stroked her hair. "You are here now, my girl. That is what matters."

"As are you," Thea said, "and I am glad for it."

Breeda offered to fetch Conall in Cat's stead. Thea took a seat at the end of the table, her brother and sister on each side. They sat quietly, waiting.

Callum's eyes flicked around the room, continually landing on her. He was working up the nerve to ask. "Where are Father and Evelynde?"

Thea's chest hollowed at the mention of him. "He is…"

Cat's lips trembled. "Thea, where is Father?"

"*Please.*" Thea looked down. "I will tell you everything when we are all together. There is much to say, and I do not think I can say it twice."

The door swung open, thumping against the wall. Thea jumped and turned to see Marten standing in the threshold. She sprang from her chair as he ran, stopping inches from her. She reached for him, and he wrapped his arms around her, lifting her from the ground.

"Thank the Gods," he cried.

She clung to him. She'd had no news of Aremore and had feared the worst. Relief washed over her in waves, and she pulled back to look at his face. She touched his cheek, unaffected by their audience. "When did you get here? How?"

"I've been here for well over a moon." The excitement fell from his manner. "It is quite a story and not a good one, I fear." He sighed against her, so close their lips nearly grazed. "They said you ran during the siege?"

"It is quite a story," she mirrored, knowing she could stop. She knew her face expressed that hers, too, was not a good one. She peered around his shoulder to see Conall standing in the doorway. She let go of Marten, stepping back. "And I have to tell you all now."

The six sat around the table as Thea told them everything. She recounted the battle in as much detail as she could recall. Not one said a word. All eyes were wide and attentive.

She told them of her capture in Dunclere. Cat covered her mouth and wept when she described how they'd hung Dianna and Williard on the bridge. She told them of her exchanges with Lorcan Dracos and the dinner, and about her cell and how they'd used their powers and gotten in her head.

Thea said nothing of the pit and gave them a tempered version of the beatings, withholding anything severe.

It felt wrong to lie, but these were things she was not ready to share and perhaps never would. Speaking of them would give them life. All she wanted was for the memories to die.

When Thea told them of their father's death—and the means of it—Callum raged. Cat sobbed uncontrollably, and Thea had to stop the story for a time while Conall consoled her, vowing justice. As awful as it had been, it was not as severe as she'd feared. It felt like telling someone something they already knew.

When she spoke of her power and of those she killed, Conall and Cat, though they tried to hide it, were horrified. Marten studied her as if he didn't believe it could be true. Breeda listened, eyes fixed on her with a mix of pride and intrigue. Callum said he hoped they'd suffered.

Thea withheld her jump from the window. She knew she wouldn't be able to withstand the looks when she told her family how she'd tried to take her own life. It had felt different, holding the blade to her chest in challenge to Neith. That had felt like fighting. Jumping from her window had felt like giving up, and she was never giving up again. Though, she told her family nothing of her encounter with Neith either, at Nara's request.

Her story ended with her arrival in Eastwatche.

Time passed while they sat in silence.

Conall stood, breaking the fugue. "I am sorry," he said, swallowing, "for all that you have endured." He looked everywhere but her eyes. His were swollen and red, like every other set in the room. He steadied himself on the back of his chair. Thea thought he would say more, but he turned and walked from the room.

Cat stood next. "Sweet sister, were I a better person, I would know what to say. I think you are the best among us." She was unsteady on her feet as she followed.

Callum's face was red and raw from wiping away his tears. He stood and knelt before her, taking her hands in his. "I will see their heads on spikes. I swear to you." He kissed her cheek before leaving.

It was a meaningful gesture, one born of love, and hate. But Thea could not help but pity the naivety in him. It had lived in her not long ago and had brought her nothing but suffering and regret.

They needed time to process all she had said, and she well understood.

Breeda was the last to leave. Only Thea and Marten remained. He moved to the chair beside hers.

"I am sorry," he said. "For it all, for your father."

"I do not even know what they did with his body." She waited for him to make a vow like Callum's, to threaten retribution. He simply gazed at her with sorrowful eyes. She looked around at the empty seats. It only then occurred to her one face remained unseen. She turned to him. "Where is Leanne?"

His brows creased, lips parting. "*Gods*, do you not know?"

"She left for Eastwatche with Callum a halfmoon before the siege." Thea shook her head. "We had no word in Highclere after."

Marten sighed, and his head fell into his hands.

"Marten, what do I not know?" Fear crowded her chest, taking up the space that should be reserved for air. "Did she have the baby?"

"She did."

"And are both well?"

"They are alive."

"Then for Godssake, please tell me what is amiss!" Thea smacked the table, and they both flinched. She pulled back a trembling hand.

"They stopped in Aremore with the orders for my father to march south," he said, eyes wide, startled by her manner. "Leanne fell into childbirth the day they were set to depart. It was difficult, but both mother and child, a boy, survived. Leanne was weak and stayed behind with the child while Callum and the rest of the party traveled to Eastwatche. She was meant to follow as soon as she recovered. I was going to escort her myself."

Thea listened intently, dread building, knowing the story was about to shift.

"My father readied his men with plans to march south, but a rider arrived from Highclere with news of the siege. They could only say that the city had fallen. They had no news of the king. Or you. My father called off the march." Marten looked down, shaking his head. "An envoy from Thrane arrived days later. I was not included in the audience. The following day, he told me of his intentions to travel to Highclere and offer surrender." Marten clenched his jaw. "I... disagreed, and he *confined* me, under guard," he said, like he still could not believe it true. "He took Leanne and the child with him."

Thea closed her eyes. Rage flared, red and hot behind them. When she spoke, it came out low and slow. "Leanne is in Highclere with her child?"

"As best we know." He reached for her, but she sat back.

Thea covered her mouth. Conall had listened as she recounted what they'd done to her and, in his mind, everything they could be doing to his wife. Her body recoiled at the notion. She couldn't think of it. "They will use her to bargain with Conall."

"Or Parthe," Marten suggested. "I assume that was my father's design. A sign of good faith. An offering of sorts." He looked at her timidly, and with apology, as if it were his fault.

Thea stood, pacing the room. "Where is your father's army now?"

"Many of his men did not have the stomach for his actions," he answered. "They released me, and over half marched here, pledging fealty to me as their lord."

Relief, affection, and gratitude overwhelmed her. She returned to her chair, hands resting over his. *"Thank you."*

"It was the right thing to do." He gave her a sad smile. "It is my army now. Conall was made regent when Highclere fell, until—"

Thea knew what he would say. Until they received the very news she brought.

"Conall declared my father a traitor. He was stripped of his title and I was made Duke of Aremore." Marten tried to hide the trepidation in his voice. He had never been close to his father, but she had no doubts his actions caused pain.

"I know you will serve the people well," she said, "but I am sorry for the means that put you here."

His face tightened. "He made his choice. I made mine."

Thea could see it weighed on him more than he wished. "Shall I call you *Your Grace*, now?" she asked, in a sort of jest, trying to bring air to the room.

"No." He grimaced, looking down. "Please, no." When his eyes returned to hers, they were tender and pleading. "Call me anything you wish. Call me fool if it pleases you. So long as you speak to me."

It pulled a sincere smile from her.

Her thoughts drifted to the night before the siege when she had spoken with her father, feeling she had made a mistake with Marten.

He laced his fingers through hers. She felt the cold metal of the re-straints, saw Dryden's dark eyes. She jerked her hand free, clutching it to her chest as she sat back in her chair.

Marten peered at her quizzically, but she spoke before he could ask.

"Your wife?" Thea swallowed. "Where is she?"

"Here," he said quickly. "By her choice."

"And she is well?"

"She is."

"I am glad," Thea said, nodding her head. She folded her arms over her belly, retreating inward. Marten looked at her like one might a wounded bird. She bit her cheek, turning away. Her foot tapped in frantic rhythms against the stone floor.

Marten stood, keeping a cautious pace. She looked up at him as his hand outstretched, beckoning her to take it. She hesitated, but reached for it, and he gently pulled her to her feet, their bodies grazing. His hands rose, his movements still slow, cradling her face, and brushed the hair from her cheek, tracing the fading remnants of the bruises and cuts. "I cannot fathom what you have endured. I—"

Thea covered his lips with her fingertips, shaking her head. She could speak no more of it.

He exhaled, leaning down so his head rested against hers. "You are safe now."

Safe. She nearly laughed. No one was safe. But she wanted to pretend. If only for a moment.

Her eyes closed as she breathed in the familiarity of him, resting her hands on his chest. Her fingertips curled into the soft fabric of his tunic, drawing him closer.

"I thought of you every day," he whispered against her lips. "Every moment, you have been on my mind. I could not allow myself to believe you were gone."

Thea thought herself a fool for how she'd pushed him away. Every reason, every justification now felt insignificant, trivial. But there was something new scratching below the surface. Something she could not quite comprehend.

His lips moved as if to kiss her, but the door opened, sending them both stepping back.

"I am sorry," Cat said, eyes cast down. She retreated and started to close the door, but Thea held up her hand, beckoning her forward.

"It is all right. Come in."

Marten dropped his gaze and stepped aside, not concealing his disappointment.

"I thought you might be hungry and wish to rest," Cat said. "I had a bath drawn for you and a plate of food brought up to one of the spare rooms. It is being prepared now."

Thea nodded and smiled. "Thank you. I would like that very much." She glanced at Marten before returning her eyes to her sister. "Will you give us a moment?"

"I'll be in the hall." Cat backed up, closing the door behind her.

Thea stepped forward, taking both of his hands in hers.

Marten looked down at their hands, then up, meeting her eyes. "It is too much, I know."

"I need some time."

"Of course."

Thea pressed up on her toes, placing a gentle kiss on the corner of his mouth. She pulled back to find a faint, sorrowful smile. She walked around him and opened the door, glancing back to find him still standing in the same spot, facing away, head hanging. He didn't turn around as she let it fall between them.

Cat took her to a washing room on the third floor. A large bath was waiting, full and still warm. She helped her undress. Her clothes were filthy and clung to her body. The last time she bathed with any significance was in the creek, the day after they'd escaped.

Cat tried to temper her reaction, but Thea felt her sister's shock. She stood in front of a tall mirror, looking over her naked form. She studied the dimming purple and yellow stains on her skin. Her fingers traced the pink scars on her wrists where she'd been shackled to the table. Her cheeks were gaunt, and her skin had a sickly gray cast. Cuts and scrapes in various states of healing covered her arms and legs.

Thea looked at her sister through the reflection.

"All wounds heal," Cat said, gently, resting her hands on Thea's shoulders. "Those we can see, and those we cannot."

Thea sank into the water, staying under until her lungs burned. She scrubbed her body furiously until she felt every inch of her was raw, and the skin would grow anew.

By the time she was clean and dressed, the sun had nearly set. She forced herself to eat, finishing half the plate of bread, cheese, and fruit

Cat prepared. Her sister tucked her into bed and crawled in behind her, holding her while she slept.

It was dark when she woke. Moonlight and a gentle breeze swept through the lone window in the room. She turned in the bed toward Cat, who slept beside her, chest slowly rising and receding. Thea watched her, still and peaceful, overwhelmed with gratitude Cat had not been at High- clere. She prayed to Cassia to look after Leanne and Evelynde. She hoped they slept warm in their beds and knew nothing of the cold pits below.

Thea rose quietly and walked to the window, peering out over the dark, endless sea. The moon was large and bright, half full.

Restless, she wandered the quiet halls, unsure where to go.

She made her way down to the ground level, finding access to the beach on the east side. She curled her toes in the sand, smiling at the sen- sation. It had been years since she'd traveled to the coast. Thea loved the sea, but it was as if she'd somehow forgotten. Putting eyes on it restored the affection.

She walked to a large, flat rock a few feet from the water. Climbing on top, she stretched out, limbs in all directions. Gentle waves climbed the shore, crashing gently against the stone. It sent the sea misting up on the soles of her feet. The stone was still warm, as if it had immersed itself with sunlight. Thea closed her eyes. Every time the sea retreated, it took a piece of her tension with it. She thought to herself to stay out there all night.

"If you fall asleep and drown, I'll have saved you for nothing."

Thea jumped, eyes snapping open. Nara stood over her. She hadn't heard her approach.

"*Godsdamn.*" Thea huffed, sitting up. "Did you need to frighten me so?"

Nara walked around the rock, leaning against it, gaze cast out on the sea. "You really don't sleep, do you? Even here, back with your family, you wake as you did every night on the road."

Thea sighed, trying to settle her still-thumping heart. "If you are so abreast of my sleeping habits, then yours must suffer in kind."

"It is a recent development," Nara admitted. She turned from the sea and climbed up onto the rock beside her. She was also barefoot, and her trousers were soaked to her knees. It appeared as if she had been out for some time, walking the tide.

"Where is Cerys?" Thea asked.

"Sleeping. I did not wish to disturb her with my discontent."

Thea nodded, familiar with the feeling. They sat together in silence, watching the waves. In the twelve days on the road, they'd shared much time in a similar state. It had not taken long for Thea to see the reasons Cerys admired her so. Nara was abrasive, and while Thea could think of no one she'd met as forthright, it was easy to see the decency in her. She thought of how Nara had fought to get them out of the city. Thea had never seen such a thing. Such a person. She wanted to be brave like her. Strong like her. Things Thea had never felt about herself. The past moons had done nothing but show her how helpless she was. "What will happen to me?"

Nara turned to look at her. "That is for you to decide."

"I'm scared," she admitted, though she thought *petrified* would be a better word. Thea had hoped she would feel some relief when they arrived in Eastwatche, but she was more fearful than ever.

Nara smiled, or the closest thing to a smile Thea ever saw her make. "Then you are not stupid." Nara held her gaze for a breath before she sighed and stood from the rock. "We will meet tomorrow. First, with your brother and whomever else he wishes to include. Then later, those of us from the Citadel and the other Etherborn here will hold an assembly."

Thea frowned. "You wish me to attend?"

"You are Etherborn, are you not?"

"Yes, but—"

"But what? Your power doesn't cease to exist simply because it is bound, Thea." She brushed sand from her trousers. "You are one of us."

One of us, Thea repeated in her mind. "But I cannot use it."

"You could learn to." Nara looked back out over the sea, and Thea followed her gaze. "You have many things to think on, but I fear little time to do so. I will leave you to it."

76

Nara

THE COST OF VALOR
AUTHOR UNKNOWN, 203 BQ
TRANSLATED FROM OLD ASARI BY MERIAH TURAN
HAIS Z'NOSIŠ, 1200 AQ

Nara watched from the rampart as Harker and a small party of soldiers approached the gate on horseback. She was told he arrived the sixday prior with an old man and woman in tow. He'd been riding out for days at a time since, searching for her.

He was dirty, and his usual shadow of a beard had grown since she'd seen him last.

Nara walked down the stairs, waiting a short distance as he dismounted. He wiped the sweat from his brow and passed the reins of his horse to a groom. He started in the direction of the keep.

"You look like shit," Nara called out as he passed by.

Harker stopped, pausing for a breath, before turning slowly. Relief washed over him as he took her in. "Godsdamn, woman."

"*What?*" she asked teasingly, shrugging a shoulder. "Were you worried about me?"

He pursed his lips, nose scrunching as he shook his head. "Nah." The shake turned into a nod, and he cleared his throat.

Nara stepped forward to embrace him, no desire to hide her happiness at finding him well. She reached for him, but he held up his hands.

"I'm filthy," he said, brushing dirt from his sleeves.

She scoffed and wrapped her arms around him. He did the same.

"It's bloody good to see you," Harker said, tightening his hold.

"It is good to see you, too." Nara feared this would become yet another time in her life that she would cry. She was determined not to make a habit of it.

Harker pulled back to look at her. "Cerys?"

Nara nodded.

He closed his eyes and exhaled.

"Calithea Ironne, too."

Harker shook his head again, chuckling. "You did it."

Nara tilted her head, frowning. "Did you doubt me?"

"Not for a second." He clapped her on the shoulder. "I reckon there's a story to tell?"

"Come," she said, reaching for his hand. "There is much to say."

Nara briefed him on everything that had happened, including her brother. She had decided back in Highclere to keep his presence a secret, not willing to risk the chance the information would somehow get back to Thrane. Only Cerys, Rowena Winstone, and now Harker knew, and that's how it would stay.

They went straight from their conversation to council with the new king. A brief ceremony had been held in the early-morning hours. It was a small, somber affair. Words were said, and a gold crown was placed upon his head. The rule of Conall II of Ire had begun.

"We need to send someone to the Citadel to request reinforcements. We have some time, but once Thrane stabilizes in Highclere, they'll come knocking on our door. We have to assume they are after the fleet." Nara looked around at the faces in the room. "We have a good position, and I think we can hold it with what we already have here." She looked down at the maps on the table. "For some time anyway." *Unless Lorcan sends the girl.*

"How fast can they get here?" Conall asked from his seat beside hers.

Nara had not yet been able to get a sense of his character. His father, though Nara had never met him, was widely known for his jovial spirit and charm. It was clear his eldest son was a different sort. He was quiet and thoughtful, perhaps a touch unsure. Only time would tell what kind of king he would become. "If I send someone tomorrow and the council agrees, fifty days. Possibly less."

"Word will reach field houses in the north," Cerys added. We can expect others to find their way here as well."

"Breeda," Nara said, eyes returning to the maps, "how many Etherborn are in Eastwatche now?"

"After your arrival, sixty and one—" She glanced at Thea. "Two," she corrected. "Sixty and two."

"Good," Nara said, nodding, "that's good." Her eyes moved back to the king. "What about your idleborn forces?"

Conall sat up at the question. "Seven thousand here in Eastwatche, two thousand reserves remain in Caern. As best we know, another five to seven throughout the kingdom. We're still working to establish a chain of information." He paused, flexing his jaw. "And which houses remain on our side."

Nara's attention moved back to Breeda. "What were the last estimates we had on Thrane's numbers?" She asked, but she already knew the answers. Sam had told her they had three hundred and fifty-two Etherborn, but she did not know how many died when she freed Cerys. Twenty?

"At least three hundred wielders and thirty thousand idleborn soldiers," Breeda answered. "Split between Highclere and Kingsport."

Nara was relieved their estimates weren't too far off. "Thrane is unlikely to attack us with a full assault in the time before we receive help from the Citadel. Lorcan won't risk losing Highclere or weakening his numbers. If I were him, I would be looking to make alliances. He knows the Esērii outnumber him many times over. I would be surprised if there weren't already emissaries on their way to everywhere from Parthe to Argal, as we speak. We should send some of our own to encourage them to drag their feet."

Nara turned to Conall. "They have your wife?"

He flinched but nodded. "And my son."

"Lorcan will want to take Eastwatche, but he's not a fool." Nara stood from her chair and started pacing the back of the room while she considered.

"You know him?" someone asked.

"My mother did," she answered. "Leanne Valois gives him leverage over Parthe. While he has her, he can force an alliance. Charles's love for his daughter is well known. Thrane will look to exploit it."

"I don't see Parthe aligning with Thrane. We've been allies for over a hundred years," Conall challenged.

Nara walked to him, leaning in. "If I had your wife here with a blade to her throat," she said in a low, controlled manner, "would you not yield this castle? What if it were your infant son?"

Conall lowered his eyes, fury washing over his face.

"If you go into war assuming the best of others, you're doomed before you've started. Betrayal is not always born from ill will." She returned to pacing.

"I think we need to slow down."

Nara stopped and turned. It was the other brother.

"We are grateful for what you've done, and what you're doing, but we do not know you," he added. Callum, she believed was his name.

Nara sat down, resting her feet on the table.

"You know Cerys," she said, pointing to her, pulling an apple from her pocket.

"Except we don't," Callum said, not accusatory, but hesitant, regretful. "We knew her as Sylvie."

Nara nodded. "True, true," she mused. "Who in the world picked out that dreadful name for you?"

Cerys's eyes narrowed. "You did."

Nara winked at her before turning back to Callum. "If you don't want our help, we can go. I do not find the north agrees with me." She leaned back in her chair, biting into the red flesh of the fruit. "But I do like these apples."

"*Nara*," Cerys said, brows drawn.

"No—that's not what I mean," Callum said, holding up his hands. "We're out of our depth. There is no denying that. It is only that it is not easy to—"

"This is your home. This is your family. I get it." Nara's tone was softer than she cared to be. "Should I continue?"

She watched the Ironne family, commanders, and nobles confer with each other around the table.

"Please," the king said, inclining his head.

"As I was saying, we need more Etherborn if we're going to hold Eastwatche long term. And this is likely to be a lengthy game. Everyone needs to settle in here. This is your new capital, and we will help you defend it as such. But, at the moment, that is not our biggest concern."

All looked at her expectantly.

"It is her," she said flatly, pointing at Thea.

Thea sank back in her chair as every face turned toward her.

"Do not feel badly," Nara said. "It is not your fault."

"What are you talking about?" Callum asked as his concerned gaze fell to his sister.

"It takes almost constant attention to keep her bindings up. Two wielders working together were struggling toward the end at Highclere. We cannot afford to put energy into that. Not while we are trying to hold Eastwatche. Even with additional forces, we cannot justify it. Not when the problem is growing." Nara addressed Thea directly. "Unless you desire to return to a prison of a different sort. I know you feel it getting worse."

Thea nodded, her gaze low.

"If you have a solution, let us hear it. She's our *sister*." The other Ironne girl, Catrianna, said.

"She needs to be trained at the Citadel," Nara said, taking a bite of her apple. "As soon as possible."

"What's the Citadel?" someone asked.

"Qalanēs. It is a city in Sibreen. Home to all Esērii."

"I have not heard of a city with that name in Sibreen," Catrianna questioned.

"You wouldn't have. It is hidden in the Aspar Mountains." Nara pondered whether she should be sharing such information. Not that the idleborn could find it.

"You can't train her here?" Callum asked.

"No. That is not what we," Nara answered and paused, gesturing to herself and the other Etherborn present, "do. And it wouldn't be safe here. She's been effectively shackled her entire life. The bindings have to be taken down slowly, in phases. It is a danger to her and everyone around her if it isn't done correctly. There are only a few that can do it, and they aren't here. Besides, if it works, she could be your greatest asset."

"Why do you think that?" the king asked, sitting up.

"She's the daughter of Sonia of Icena. She was one of the most powerful known Etherborn since the Great Quell. The name may mean nothing to you, but she's legendary amongst our kind." Nara shrugged. "It is worth trying. And if her cousin is anything by which to judge, Thea could share similar power, to some degree, at least."

The king looked at his brother. He was whispering with the Percy boy. "How long would she be gone?"

"Most Etherborn train from the time they are children well into adulthood. Given we have specific objectives, she might gain control over her power in two, perhaps three years."

"*Three years?*" Callum asked, his tone suggesting the idea preposterous.

"I don't want to go," Thea said, shaking her head, the tension in the room rising quickly.

"You don't really have a choice." Nara had not intended to say it so sternly, but they all needed to understand how dire the situation. She did not enjoy speaking of Thea as if she weren't present, but she had to be persuaded to go. Nara was not above using Thea's family to ensure it happened.

"Of course she has a choice!" someone yelled, and slammed their fist.

Nara's eyes connected with Marten Percy. He was on his feet, leaning over the table, eyes full of contempt. It flared her own temper.

"Marten Percy, do not raise your voice at me." She let her power flare out around her. "If you have not already, you soon will see I am short-tempered."

He had the good sense to look nervous. Nara had little patience for nobles like him. Like so many at the table before her. Favored from birth with good looks and unimaginable wealth. Privileged beyond their own understanding, always overvaluing their capabilities, overplaying their hand. Believing they could fight a war because they clank swords in a circle in front of a cheering crowd. It was naivety so profound the mere thought of it exhausted her. There he was, speaking for Thea, believing himself her defender. Probably getting off on the righteousness, well-intentioned or not. Nara tilted her head, feeling the need to strike. "Where is your wife?"

His eyes went wide, outrage washing over his face. Thea reached up for his arm, and he scowled, but sat down.

Cerys glared at her, the tight line of her mouth telling her that she was cross. Nara knew she would get an earful later. She took a deep breath and leaned across the table, eyes fixed on Thea's.

"I will tell you the hard truth that they will not. If you stay here, you are something else we have to take care of, a liability. We can't train you here and fight this war. If you want to help, then go. Come back when you add to the solution and not the problem."

Thea held her gaze, and Nara frowned when she could not get a read on her thoughts.

"That's enough." Callum stood, Marten right behind. "We'll speak no more of this. Come, Thea."

Thea looked up when she heard her name. Marten held out his hand. She hesitated, but took it, and the three walked out.

When the door clicked shut, the king sighed. "Let us reconvene on the morrow. We all need some time to think." He stood, and the rest followed him out. Only Nara, Cerys, Harker, and Breeda remained.

Nara sat back in her chair, arms folded across her chest. "These are children playing at war."

"They're frightened," Breeda said. "Give them time."

"We don't have time," Nara challenged.

Cerys rubbed at her eyes and sighed. "Let's speak openly. How long can we realistically hold Eastwatch? How many wielders do we truly need to put up a respectable fight?"

"With the girl, Lorcan's daughter, I honestly don't know," Nara said. "We're in uncharted territory. I could come up with a random figure, but I do not think it would serve us. Though, I would feel much better were we one hundred stronger."

"Will the council agree to send so many?" Breeda asked.

"We have to convince them." Nara rose from her chair, making for the bar cart in the corner. She returned with a bottle and four glasses, filling all. "In the meantime, we need to be clever."

Breeda nodded. "We have a better understanding of their capabilities now. We won't underestimate them again. What we need are numbers. Both Etherborn and idle. Every single body counts."

Nara, Breeda, and Harker tossed back their drinks. Cerys's sat untouched in front of her. They sat quietly for a time. The direness of the situation weighing heavy.

"We need to convince Thea to go to the Citadel. I need your help with that," Nara said to Breeda.

"She will not be forced," Cerys said, looking sternly between the two women.

"No," Nara agreed. "But some innocent persuasion won't hurt."

"I will speak with her," Breeda said, reaching for the bottle.

Harker looked at Nara. "She seems… I hate to say it, but a bit broken."

"She is *not*," Cerys said, not withholding her irritation. She leaned forward in her chair, eyes fixed on Harker. "She has been through more than most would not survive. You would do well not to underestimate her."

Harker held up his hands. "Apologies."

"Cerys has formed quite the attachment," Nara jested. She glanced at Cerys from the side of her eye and was met with another glare. The amusement fell from Nara's face, knowing she was only adding to the chastisement she would receive later. "But she is right. The girl is stronger than she seems."

"She is her mother's daughter." Breeda tossed back another whiskey.

When no one spoke further, Nara stood. "Very well," she said. "Let us find a meal before next we meet."

77

Thea

"Esērii belong not to themselves, but to each other, as a collective being. No one can rule without being ruled in return."

ESĒRII BIJRAH Z'OURA

ADE NYANTHI AND PHILOMENA TALIESIN, 805 AQ

Marten huffed, pacing around the room. "Don't worry. We're going to figure this out."

Callum was not far off his heels. They'd ranted and raved the entire walk from the council room to the sleeping quarters assigned to her.

Thea didn't speak. She sat in a chair at the table by the window, watching.

Marten paused, turning toward Callum. "We could take her somewhere."

"Where would be safe?" Callum asked. "You heard what they said about her *bindings*. She needs at least two of them with her."

Them, Thea repeated in her mind. She thought back to what Nara had said. *Problem. Liability.* That's what she was. She felt sick.

"Perhaps we could bargain with someone from the Citadel to bring the people they need to train her here," Marten suggested.

Callum's brows rose, and he tapped a finger to his lips. He looked at Marten as he considered.

"Though I do not understand what all of this training is about," Marten added. "It is not like we're going to put her on the front lines." An abrupt laugh bumped up against his closed lips.

Thea's mouth fell open. Callum glanced at her, eyes a bit uneasy as if he, too, felt the sting.

The two continued to make suggestions far outside their influence and control. She drowned them out, gazing out the window, looking at the sea. She didn't care to hear it. They were making plans on her behalf, right in front of her, as if she weren't even there.

Thea had become weary of sitting idly while others charted her course. She wanted to stand up and scream at them, but she didn't have the spirit for it. She'd instead let them exhaust themselves with possibilities that would never be.

"*Thea*, are you listening?" she heard Marten ask.

She looked up and blinked. "Yes." But she wasn't.

"Surely you're not considering this?"

"What?" she asked, shaking her head. "I don't know."

"Thea. You can't go to fucking *Sibreen*," Marten said.

Thea turned to look at her brother. "Callum, may I speak with Marten alone?"

Callum glanced between the two. "Of course," he said, with an awkward cadence. "Rest, and I'll see you later for supper. Do not worry." He kissed her cheek and left the room.

The moment the door clicked, Thea turned to Marten. "Why not?" she asked sincerely. "Why should I not go? What is here for me now?"

He recoiled as if she'd struck him. "You can't be serious."

"I'm sorry," she said, holding up her hand, "that is not what I mean." Her head ached. It fell into her hands, and she tried to rub some of the tension away.

Marten knelt before her, still as frantic as he'd been the last hour. "Listen to me," he said, taking her hands in his. "We need to stay together. Callum and I will find a solution. Conall can't force you to go any more than *they* can."

He said it with such disdain. *They*. Etherborn. But she was Etherborn.

Marten leaned closer to kiss her, but she pulled back and stood, walking across the room. "We cannot do that. Someone will see."

"I don't care if someone sees." He rose to face her. "Besides, *who*? My father? I left him behind when I marched half his army to Eastwatche."

"Your *wife*, Marten," Thea reminded, irritated it needed to be said.

He shrugged. "I doubt she cares. She is free to do as she pleases."

"That is not the point."

"The *only* thing that matters to me is you." His expression melted into one of sincerity, and it cooled her vexation. He walked the few steps to close the space between them. "When we didn't know where you were, I couldn't bear it. I rode out every day, hoping to find you on your way here."

Thea touched his cheek, and he leaned into it. She told herself he was only trying to help. He took the touch as a sign of encouragement.

Marten reached for her, drawing her body against his. His tender eyes implored her, and she stepped into the embrace, familiar and warm.

He leaned forward, brushing his lips against hers. It was soft, as if asking. When she didn't pull away, he deepened it, his tongue parting her lips. Thea returned the kiss, dismissing the feeling of wrongness. She wanted to feel something, *anything* but the grief that had been slowly eating away at her since Highclere fell. Her hands found his chest, then shoulders, moving up around his neck as she opened her mouth for him.

Thoughts tumbled through her mind, diverting from the moment. Random and elementary at first, they quickly turned dark. She saw the pit, Dryden's dreadful eyes. She went stiff. Heat rushed from her belly into her chest, causing her heart to flutter. But it was fear, not desire, that gripped her.

Marten pulled back and frowned. "Are you—"

She shook her head and stepped forward, crashing her mouth back onto his. He straightened, surprised, but groaned when she ran her hand along the length of him, growing firm.

Her pulse continued to climb. Her breath grew thin. She let her head fall back as his lips found her neck, feeling suddenly suffocated by his touch.

Thea pulled at the ties of his trousers as they walked backward to the bed. She stroked him as his mouth found hers again, waiting for desire to find her. The back of her legs hit the bed, and he fell on top of her, lifting the skirts of her dress until they were up around her waist. Marten reached between them, and she flinched, unready, as he plunged into her. He immediately started to move, picking up speed with each thrust.

It was desperate, clinging. But the pain of him was better than what ached within her. She clutched around his body, trying to find their connection. He continued until his face pressed into the pillow beside her, stifling the sounds of his release. She lay still beneath him while he panted.

For the first time in her life, she wanted him to leave.

✥

An hour passed before Cerys came to fetch her. The dining hall was loud and crowded. The sixty Etherborn stood in small groups, most faces unknown to her.

Cerys took her hand, leading her through the crowd. Many turned to watch as they walked past the rows of tables and chairs. She was met with warm smiles and nods of encouragement. A few regarded her with curious eyes.

They took seats in the front, next to Breeda. Nara, a man she now knew to be named Harker, and several others, all wearing a gold pin of some sort, sat at a single table facing the crowd. Thea's heart thumped, fearing she did not belong. Breeda glanced at her, as if sensing its wild pace, giving her a reassuring smile.

Nara wore a purple patterned dress, her hair twisted up in a high bun. Gold jewelry to match her pin adorned her ears and neck. She looked regal, Thea thought. In command. Nara held up her hand to silence the room.

"This is an open assembly. We aim to dispel rumors and provide clarity. We will read a statement outlining the events taking place since the attack in Godsreach, then open the floor for discussion." Nara gestured to a woman sitting at the end of the table.

The woman stood, holding a parchment open before her. "On the fifteenth day of the Blossom Moon, in the year 1204 AQ, Lorcan Dracos, under the banners of Thrane, attacked the Straethan village of Godsreach. The Esērii present were murdered or taken captive, the townspeople slaughtered, and the village razed."

No one interrupted or reacted as she spoke. All listened intently, including Thea, who paled when the woman described a mountain cut in half. She continually used the word *nether*, of which Thea had never heard. She continued recounting the estimates of Thrane, how they'd split into two forces. Most of which Thea already knew.

When the woman spoke of Sonia, and then of Thea, she felt eyes turn toward her. Cerys had given her warning, but it did little to prepare her for how utterly exposed she felt. She had to grip the bottom of her chair to keep herself from running.

As the woman told the events of their escape, Thea made note of a rather prominent exclusion. As Nara had asked of her, the report also made no mention of Neith Dracos letting them go. Thea looked at Nara, finding her eyes already on her. Nara had not given her reason when she'd made the request on the journey, nor had Thea pried for one.

The report ended with the stated intention to send messengers to all field houses in the north as well as the Citadel on the morrow. The woman rolled up the parchment and retook her seat. The room remained quiet, and Thea could not help but be impressed by the order of it all.

"Any who wish to speak may now queue," Nara said to the room as she gestured to the empty space between the tables.

Several in the crowd stood, forming a line down the hall.

"How can we be sure it was nether?" asked the man who stood first. "Nether is little more than myth."

"We cannot be sure, but I read the firsthand account of Rowena Winstone of the fight at the ruins in Straeth. I cannot imagine what else could be the cause of what was described."

The man seemed satisfied with Nara's answer. He nodded and returned to his seat. The woman behind him stepped up. She asked about the wards around the keep. The process continued for half an hour until all who stood asked and were answered. Nara called the assembly to a close, and conversations started as all moved about the room.

Men and women she did not know greeted her, expressing their condolences and prayers for her father. She was told several times how much she looked like her mother. She did her best to smile through it and nod, thanking them for their consideration. No one was treating her like a burden. No one was treating her like a bastard. If anything, she felt more an equal than she had ever before.

78

Nara

"Look for those upon whom the pin weighs heavy."

THE WAY OF ETHER
ASHERAH GALANIS, FIRST CONSUL, THE CITADEL, 808 AQ

"You were cruel today, Nara," Cerys said as she pulled off a boot.

"I know, but it is what she needs to hear. If she can't take a little heat from me, she has no chance at the Citadel." Nara pulled the heavy gold from her ears, tossing the hoops on the bedside table. "It is the truth, Cerys, you know it."

"Maybe it is," she said, as her second boot hit the floor, "but you don't know her like I do. If she's incapable, it is because they made her so. She's terrified and traumatized, and dealing with an entire other level of shite than the rest of them. I know what they did to her in Highclere. They made me listen to her screams. The fact that she is here is a testament to what she can endure. She is a good person, and she needs our support." Cerys pulled off her tunic, tossing it over a chair.

"Being 'a good person' is not going to get her through accelerated training," Nara said as she flipped the clasp on her necklace.

Cerys turned to glare at her.

Nara held up her hands. "All right, I get it. You care about these people. I'll... talk to her."

"*Thank you.*" Cerys tugged at the laces of her trousers until they fell. She stepped out, leaving them and her undergarments where they lay on the floor.

"I see some things don't change," Nara mused.

"What is that?" Cerys asked as she splashed water from the basin on her face.

"Your lack of tidiness nor your proclivity for existing in the nude," Nara teased. "Not that I'm complaining of the latter."

Cerys gave her a wry smile and climbed on the bed, pulling the silk sheet over her. The thin fabric clung to the curves of her body, and she looked ever the statuesque work of art burned in Nara's mind.

Nara poured a tall glass of wine, sipping it as she paced the room. She had done her best to be the face of reason, of order, as was expected of her. But it weighed heavy, as it always did. Anytime Sam came to mind, she pushed it away. She felt responsible for leaving him behind. If she had only tried harder. Said more, or something better, been smarter. He could be with her now. Her mind had been so fixed on getting Cerys at the time that everything else seemed secondary. She could not think of what they would do to him if they found him out. All the things they'd done to Cerys. To Thea. Nara dreaded the letter she would write tomorrow telling her mother of all that occurred. She would raise her mother's hopes only to crush them once more.

"Come to bed," Cerys beckoned. "I see your wheels spinning."

Nara sighed. "I do not think I can sleep."

"I do not have designs on sleep."

Nara paused her pacing. Getting lost in Cerys was likely the only distraction that could pull her from her thoughts. She cocked a brow. "This morning was not enough? If I recall, my name left your lips more than once."

"We have been apart a year." Cerys tugged on the sheet, exposing one of her long legs. "We have much to make up for."

Nara would not argue that. She thought back to each and every lonely night she spent thinking of her and what a poor substitute her own touch had made. Her eyes moved from the tip of Cerys's toe up the length of her leg to where it disappeared beneath the silk sheet. Nara's thoughts drifted to what was under. What she could touch, taste, revel in. But she could not shrug all that which hung heavy on her back. "I'm sorry."

"Do not be sorry." Cerys rose from the bed, walking to face her. "You're taking on too much, as you always do."

Nara huffed. "I made that choice when I asked the council to put this damned pin back on my chest." She looked down at the golden eagle and sneered.

Cerys shook her head. "Too much of the burden, I mean. It is who you are. Pin or not." She raised her hands to hold Nara's face. "There will be many times for us to worry, my love, but we must learn to live in the moments between."

Nara smiled, nodding. She looked at the bright-eyed woman before her. "You are right." She wrapped her arms around Cerys's waist, drawing her closer, fingertips caressing the smooth skin of her back. "But I don't know how to do that."

Cerys sighed. "Turn around."

Nara pulled back and eyed her quizzically. Cerys grabbed her shoulders, turning her away. She felt the clasps of her dress come undone, and it fell loose to the floor.

"Now, lie down on your belly."

Nara peered over her shoulder. "What—"

"I mean to rub your shoulders, woman." Cerys gave a swift smack to her backside.

Nara frowned but did as requested. She felt legs swing around her, straddling her back. Cerys's slick, wet warmth nestled into the small of it. The sensation sent heat rising from Nara's core. She sighed as Cerys worked her fingers deep into the flesh of her neck.

She would have to figure out what they were going to do if the Citadel did not send enough reinforcements. They would likely have to abandon Eastwatche. Ire altogether. Fall back to where? Ire still possessed one of the largest fleets in the world. They could sail it south.

"For *Godssake*, will you relax?"

"I'm trying!" Though she wasn't. *That girl is going to be a problem.* Nara had tried not to think of her, dealing with the things for which she could find answers. There was no answer for the girl. She wanted to believe Sam, that he could turn her, but there was too much at risk. An image of Cerys wrapped in the girl's blue ether, unable to draw breath, sprang to mind. It sent a spike of panic through her. "We don't have to stay here."

Cerys's hands stopped moving. "What do you mean?"

"We can leave. The two of us. We don't have to stay and fight for these people."

"You mean defect? *Go nomad?*" Cerys lifted, moving to sit beside her.

Nara pressed up on her forearms. "We can simply leave in the night."

Cerys was quiet for a breath as she considered. Her nose scrunched as it often did when she was deep in thought. "What about Sam?"

"As soon as they find out who he is, which they will, they will execute him, or worse." Nara swallowed. If she were not here to find out about it, then she could live her life pretending it never happened. She had mourned him once. She did not think she could do it twice. "He made his choice. You know this as well as I."

"I'm sorry," Cerys said, lying next to her. "It is cruel you had to say goodbye to him again. You know I will go if that is truly what you want."

Nara waited for the *but*, knowing it was coming.

"But I have seen what Thrane can do, Nara, and it is terrifying. If they are allowed to win this, I fear there will be no world for us to run to." Her round brown eyes took on a heaviness. "I would stay. I would do the right thing." Cerys reached across the bed and cupped Nara's cheek. "And I know that is what you would choose, too."

Nara wanted to fight. To change her mind. But changing her mind would be changing her, and Nara would never, could never, do that. Her selflessness was something Nara long admired and loved about her, but also feared it would one day be her undoing. Cerys believed staying was the right thing to do. And somewhere, however deep it resided, Nara knew it, too.

One side of Nara's mouth tugged up. "Then we stay."

Cerys nodded. "We stay."

They lay together, hands clasped between them.

"At least we are together," Cerys whispered.

"Yes," Nara said, tucking a curl behind Cerys's ear. "At least we are together."

79

Neith

"I grow wary, dear sister, of his influence on you. Do not yield your mind, nor your will, in favor of your heart."

UNOFFICIAL CORRESPONDENCE FROM SONIA THRONDSEN TO LIA
THRONDSEN, 1183 AQ
RECOVERED AFTER THE BLOODY DAY

"It is quite a different view from the palace in Necrium."

Neith grimaced. It was not a voice she desired to hear. Before morning council, she'd walked out onto the western balcony to be alone. The castle was quiet at such an early hour, and she found it a peaceful place, looking out over the endless green mountains and turquoise lake.

Dryden appeared next to her, leaning against the balcony wall.

She didn't bother to look at him. "Is there something you need? It was my aim to find peace before the hours to come."

His low laugh met with closed lips. "Perhaps I have come for conversation."

Neith turned, narrowing her eyes on him. "As I said, I sought peace." The amusement in his features flared her temper.

"How fares my daughter?"

Neith smirked, turning back to the view. "Very well indeed. The only bruises that mar her body now come from the training she endeavors—and excels—in."

He seemed unaffected by the accusation. "Yes, I have heard intriguing things of your unit. A young but eager lot. Loyal, too. Ayla has never defied me so." His dark eyes appraised her as if he might discover the secret why.

"I have found it comes easily when respect and appreciation are given."

Dryden dipped his head, brows raised. "Like the respect and appreciation you show Samad Hassan?"

Neith kept her body still, despite the spike in her pulse. "I do not appreciate disguised threats," she said, attempting to sound disinterested. "If you've formed some opinion, you've done so in vain." She could feel him staring at her, scrutinizing, from the corner of her eye.

"I find you much changed since Godsreach, but you still need to work on your bluff."

Neith sighed, long and drawn. "Say what you mean to say, General. If I desired to play games, I would seek out children."

Dryden laughed, and it was as unsettling as all his other manners. "Much changed indeed." He stepped closer, speaking lower. "Do you know what your father thinks about it?"

Alarm flared through her as she tried to understand if he was bluffing, too. She kept her gaze on the mountains, fearing his dark eyes would unravel her. "I do not think my father thinks anything of my relationships with my soldiers, as I have one with each."

"You can stop now," he said, some of the amusement in his tone giving way to irritation.

She finally looked at him again, letting her face reveal all the disdain she felt. "Even if there were something to know, it would be no concern of yours. Take care before you overstep."

"The actions and intentions of Thrane's Praxa are of concern to all."

She swallowed. "I don't know what you mean."

"Your father has made his intentions known to me." His dark eyes held a satisfaction that set her blood to boiling.

Neith turned her entire body to face his, stepping closer. "Who do you believe yourself to be to speak to me so?" Her power rumbled around her. It brought no fear to his eyes. Only intrigue.

"I believe myself your ally," he said, looking down at her.

It was her turn to laugh. She studied him, having never stood so close. He smelled of leather, soap, and spice.

"You dislike me and believe that a deterrent. It is not. You do not like my tactics." He shrugged. "It matters not. When you are queen, you will find quite quickly you have a need for someone like me. All kings and queens do."

Neith lifted her chin. "We shall see."

"Indeed." He spoke assuredly as if it were simply fact. One side of his mouth quirked, and he stepped back, breaking the tension between them, turning toward the lake.

Neith stood firm in place, glaring at him, trying to make sense of the exchange.

"Your father is acting rashly," he said. "It will pass, but we must contain the damage he might look to do. He is quick to strike at any threat."

His cavalier manner in speaking on such subjects irritated her, but she shrugged, doing her best to appear unconcerned. "Samad Hassan is a loyal soldier in our army. A valuable one. He is no threat to my father or to Thrane. It is a pastime."

Dryden glanced at her, sidelong. "If only that were true." His eyes moved to her chest. "Where is the moon necklace he carved for you? Hiding smartly under your tunic, I presume?"

Neith swallowed. Ayla told her Dryden had been watching. Now she knew to what degree.

"Your father has grown unpredictable. Something I do not care for," he said, vexation heavy in his tone.

Neith folded her arms. "What is stopping me from going to him this very moment, telling him all you have said?"

"Nothing," he answered. "But you will not. You are far too intelligent for that." Dryden turned to look at her again. "You know it will not end with the outcome you desire."

Neith could not believe her father would hurt someone she cared for. Even if he cared not for her feelings, which she did not believe true, the act would only drive her away. He may be her father, he may be the king, but he needed her. They *all* needed her. She thought perhaps it was time to lean into that. "If something were to happen to *anyone* that I care for, it would not encourage my participation in this war. Cares aside, my father is too clever to take such a risk."

"You are right to say so." Dryden paused, nodding slowly. "It is only that these things tend to have a way of working themselves out. People succumb to accidents," he said, shrugging. "Sometimes they simply disappear." He looked at her with a subtle but knowing smile. "I was told of such a tale not long ago. Three soldiers vanished." He snapped his fingers. "War is very precarious, Captain Dracos."

His words sent her spinning. She stared at him, more baffled by him than ever. While she would heed his words, they did nothing to temper her hate for him.

"So, you have what?" she asked. "Come to warn me? Forgive me if I find you suspicious."

He stood up straight. His taunting demeanor fell away. "Even when we fight for the same side, we need alliances within."

Neith closed the space between them, glaring up at him. "I will never align myself with someone like you."

Dryden peered down at her, seemingly unbothered by the insult. "We shall see," he said, repeating her words from earlier. He smiled one last time before turning and walking away.

All day, Neith's thoughts were of nothing but Dryden's warning. She considered the possibility it was all some sort of ploy. Perhaps it was. Her gut told her not.

Neith watched Sam across the campfire in a game of cards with Bellamy. She was fearful to take her eyes from him, but terrified of being too close.

It had been a quiet night in the gardens until some of the First stumbled out of the dining halls. They'd started sparring for sport, the raucous cheering spoiling the peace. Several from her own unit took part, returning with swollen eyes and split lips, calling it all good fun. Neith did not find she agreed.

Sam looked up from his game as it finished, frowning when he set eyes on her. He said something to Bellamy, and both stood, making their way around the fire. "Come," Sam said, holding his hand out to her, "let's go back to the barracks."

She nodded, and he lifted her up. Taking notice, Petra, Max, and Ayla followed.

They made their farewells, and the small group departed, walking past the makeshift fighting circle. A man Neith did not know kicked a woman, sending her flying backward. Neith looked away, no taste for the violence.

"Sister!" an animated and eager voice called out, cutting through the noise of the crowd.

Neith cursed. She turned to see her brother grinning impishly, his arm wrapped around Katya's shoulder, a mug in hand.

"Join us!" Roman gestured with his arm, spilling some of the ale.

She thought first to ignore him, but many in the gathering had taken notice of the interaction. "The hour is late, brother."

"Ah, yes, I forget the children must take early to bed." A few snickers echoed through the crowd. Petra and Max stepped up beside Neith, eyes asking for permission. She shook her head.

Neith bit back the insult she wanted to spit and instead simply said, "As you say. I bid you good night." She turned away, but he tossed his mug aside and marched straight toward her. She took a full, heavy breath and looked at her friends around her, urging restraint.

Roman stopped a few paces before her, a taunting smirk etched broad across his cheeks. "Too afraid to take part in our little game?" He gestured to the circle behind him.

Again, Neith swallowed the words she wished to use in favor of better sense. "You do not seem short of players. And why would you want to play with, as you say, *children*?"

"Very true," he said, lips pursing. It was a ridiculous notion. Roman was not even two winters her elder, and many in her unit were of his age. It was simply something he knew would rattle her. Roman's unit had soldiers as old as their father. He believed it made him superior. "If it were my unit on castle watch perhaps the Esērii would not have escaped."

Rage washed through her, sending a red haze over her eyes. She felt her muscles contract and twitch against it. His smug expression broadened, taking in with pleasure what pulsed through her. What he was able to do.

There were many from the Second present, and it was not only her that his words enraged. Angry whispers and curses spilled from the lips of more than one disgruntled face.

As much as she wished to quell the confrontation, she could not let such disrespect go unchallenged. It took all her self-control not to haul back her fist and send it flying toward his face. Just as Petra had taught her to.

"Perhaps you are right, brother," Neith said, nodding. "If your unit had not been dropping in numbers, then it might have been so." Her head took on a lean. "How many were you when we crossed the mountain?" She waved her hand. "That doesn't matter. What matters," she said, staring directly into his eyes, "is that it was more than it is now."

It struck the chord she desired.

"There were the three that ran in the night, never to be seen again." Neith shook her head in artificial concern. "And last I heard, it was five that left your unit to join another this past sixday." Roman's face twisted into a snarl, and she met it with her own. "Your soldiers are abandoning you, brother, and this behavior, right here, *this is why.*"

Roman stood staring at her, the insult beating against his composure. He looked down for a breath, and when his eyes returned to hers, so did his arrogance. "Oh, dear sister," he said, closing the space between them. "You are no one to lecture me on leadership." He looked at her people around her. "Did you not know the first four that joined you were commanded to?"

Neith straightened. He was playing on her fears, nothing more. "*Lies.*"

He shrugged, his eyes rich with satisfaction. "Ask them yourself."

Neith stood across from him, chest heaving. She glanced back, and as soon as she saw Bellamy's face, she knew it was true. His eyes were wide, startled by Roman's allegation. The desperation quickly gave way to a look of uncertainty, of hesitation, of guilt. A look on him she had seen before. He opened his mouth to speak, but she turned away, biting back the sting.

She should have known. Perhaps she had. Neith hadn't believed herself worthy of them, and it appeared a just judgment. Indignity and rage boiled within her, sending heat to her cheeks. Her brother had made her look a fool because she was one.

"How sweet you are." Roman smirked as he walked a circle around her, catching Sam's shoulder on his pass back. "You truly believed they came of their own volition."

Neith felt power flare beside her.

"Step away." Sam's voice was low and rippling with violence.

Roman ignored him.

"You have a unit of children. Ordered by their mothers to follow you around. To make you feel capable." Katya and several others laughed. "Did you really think men and women would join a little girl?"

The sting of his words struck her eyes, adding to her humiliation.

Roman clicked his tongue and gave her a feigned expression of concern. His knuckle grazed her cheek, catching a tear on its descent.

"I *said*, step away," Sam repeated, and this time, the threat in his voice was material. Neith felt his power flare. The air around them heated.

"And this one," Roman said, gesturing lazily at Sam, "this one just wants to bed you."

Shame whipped across her cheeks. It took all her resolve not to turn and run.

"And when the day comes he finally weasels his way between your legs, he'll be gone the next." Roman said it with so much loathing it quashed any anger still clinging to her. All she felt was grief. He had just put a blade through any hope she had of ever finding him as her brother again. Roman was lost to her forever.

He looked down at her trembling lips, and Neith thought she caught a hint of uncertainty on him, but it quickly fell away.

Neith took in the faces surrounding them. For each that joined her brother in his delight at her dishonor, there were two who did not. Some glared at him with scorn, others with disgust.

Roman's eyebrows perked. "Oh, I see. Perhaps he already has." He reached up, grabbing her face in his hand. "Tell me, sister, are you his whore?"

Before her heart took its next beat, Sam was between them, forcing Roman back with a shove. Max and Petra were at his flank in the same breath. Bellamy moved beside her.

Roman laughed, flipping his hands in a mocking gesture. "Look, Katya, the children want to fight."

Katya grinned. "Should we give them one, my lord?"

Roman glanced back at his unit gathered behind him. "What do you say, Ulf?"

The tall, brutish man stepped forward, a violence-laced grin on his face.

No. Neith's breath hitched as panic crowded her chest. This was exactly what Roman wanted. This was his design.

"Stop this now," Neith said, with pleading eyes. "You've made your point." She was ignored.

"We challenge you," Roman said, speaking directly to Sam. Ulf and Katya stepped forward.

Neith's heart sank. If they accepted, she could not interfere. Her brother had purposefully picked the biggest man in his unit. She remembered him from the altercation with Thora. He was half a foot taller than Sam and unnaturally broad. He looked as if he could crush a man's skull with his bare hands.

"Do you accept—"

"We accept," Sam said quickly.

The six began removing their weapons, and the crowd moved back to make a circle, cheers of excitement ringing out. Petra glanced back and winked, but it did nothing to quell Neith's fear. She turned around to a fearful Ayla. "Go and find Magnus, *fast.*"

Ayla nodded, eyes wide, and sprinted toward the castle.

"Neith," Bellamy said from his place beside her, but she ignored him, walking to the circle's edge, pushing people aside.

Sam spoke quietly to both Max and Petra before they nodded and spread out in the circle. Roman, Katya, and Ulf were already waiting. The six circled each other, waiting to see who would make the first strike. Neith could only watch on in horror.

Roman charged Sam, swinging wildly. Sam sidestepped, blocking the blows before landing a kick to Roman's chest that sent him sprawling on his back.

Ulf went for Max. Neith's heart thumped as she watched her friend evade the huge hands grasping for him. Max's fist made contact with Ulf's face, and it barely registered. None of them were going to be a match for the big man.

A swing of dark hair went flying as Katya landed a blow to Petra's belly. It brought her to her knees. Katya tried to take advantage, swinging at her face, but Petra rolled, swiping her legs at Katya's, who fell hard on her back.

The crowd cheered.

Roman and Sam were back to trading blows. Roman's nose was bloody, and Sam had a cut above his left eye.

A crack followed by a hair-raising wail cut through the commotion. Her head snapped to see Max, Ulf holding his arm back in an unnatural position.

Neith's stomach turned at the sight. Petra screamed, sending Katya to the ground with a swift kick to her face. She took off sprinting toward her brother, but Roman grabbed a fistful of her hair as she passed, pulling her back to the ground. Neith watched as the air was forced from her lungs. She well recognized the panicked look of one trying to take a breath that would not come.

Another crack and another scream. Ulf had hold of Max's other arm, which now bent in a place it should not. In an instant, Sam was on Ulf's back, arm wrapped around his neck. Ulf released Max, and Neith watched as he fell to his knees, then back, writhing on the ground. Ulf clawed and swiped at Sam, trying to peel him off. Petra was back on her feet, taking swings at Roman. She nearly had him down, but Katya tackled her from behind.

Ulf was slowing. He fell hard on his back, and Sam cried out but didn't let go. Sam's face twisted with effort as Ulf rolled, trying again and again to shake him off. Ulf's movements grew sluggish until finally he stilled, body going limp.

Sam released him, struggling to move beneath the weight of the giant man. Max was still on the ground. Both arms lay lifeless at his sides. Sam staggered to his feet, one hand clutching the left side of his chest. After a few paces, he took off, sprinting toward Petra, who was trying to fight off both Roman and Katya.

Fury radiated off of him as he ran. He moved so fast it was difficult for her eyes to keep pace. He slid in between the three, catching a blow meant for Petra's face. His elbow swung up toward Roman, making contact with his nose again. Roman shrieked as blood gushed and splattered through the air, landing on some of those closest in the crowd. Cheers erupted, incited by the violence.

With only one opponent to face, Petra went wild on Katya, knocking her back. She jumped on top of her, sending fist after fist until the venomous woman lay still, her white hair stained red. Petra fell back, panting, giving Katya one last angry kick with her heel.

Roman delivered a jab that grazed Sam's cheek. Sam responded with a fist to the gut that sent her brother to his knees, followed by a swift uppercut to the chin that hit with a hard crack, sending him flying.

Roman heaved, arching on the ground.

Sam took slow, fatigued steps to stand over him, glaring down, eyes wild with rage. "Yield to me."

Roman coughed and gagged, breath returning, shaking his head. "Never." He snarled, teeth stained red. He tried to climb to his feet but stumbled forward. Sam stepped back, watching him crawl.

Roman tried again to rise, and Neith closed her eyes. Relief settled over her as she realized her friends would win, but she derived no pleasure watching her brother further disgrace himself, despite his actions toward her. He should yield. He had lost. But he wouldn't give them that.

"Roman, yield!" she called out.

Sam reached down, grasping the collar of Roman's vest. He was clearly worn, somewhat unsteady on his feet, but leaned down so close their faces nearly touched. "Yield. To *me*." The threat in his words sent chills through her. Sam's power reverberated around him, sizzling and snapping in the night air. He pulled back his fist in warning of a final blow.

Several in the crowd repeated her call for a yield.

The air cracked, and the ground shook. "You will all yield!"

All eyes snapped toward Magnus, who stood at the edge of the circle, Ayla behind him, hands on her knees, panting.

"What is this?" Magnus stormed through the circle, looking each one down before stopping at Sam. Sam released Roman, stepping back. "What has occurred here?"

"A challenge," Sam answered, his eyes still fixed on Roman.

"Initiated by who?"

"By me," Roman said, spitting blood.

Katya stirred. Ulf had not woken.

Max no longer screamed, but his face twisted in pain as Ayla ran to him. Petra stumbled to stand next to Sam.

"This is over," Magnus said. "Everyone leave, *now*."

As the crowd dispersed, Neith met eyes with Bellamy, standing on his own. His eyes were fixed on her, heavy with regret.

"Was I not clear, Lieutenant Silva?"

Bellamy ignored Magnus, still staring at Neith. Her eyes swelled, but she turned away. She didn't watch him leave as she went to Max. His left humerus was split in two, and on the right his shoulder was dislocated and arm broken at the wrist. She looked down at her friend. "This will hurt."

"Do it," he said between desperate breaths.

She got to work.

"This infantile rivalry ends now," Magnus said, turning to address them all.

"This was a challenge," Roman said, still on his knees. "You can't interfere."

Magnus pulled him to shaky feet, face nearly pressed against his as he spoke. "You are lucky I did, or you would be lying on the ground like these other two. You lost, Roman."

He pulled free from Magnus's grip. An aid team arrived, and Ulf was loaded onto a stretcher and carted away. Katya climbed to her feet. She walked to Roman, and they stumbled off. Roman took one last sneering look at Neith.

When Neith put Max's shoulder back, he cried out between gritted teeth. Ayla clamped her eyes shut.

"I'm sorry," Neith whispered.

Max nodded, his jaw still clenched.

Petra stumbled to his other side next to Ayla as Sam collapsed by his head. Both were panting, utterly drained from the fight.

Neith finished repairing Max's breaks then sat back on her heels, brow heavy with sweat. "Be careful with them for a few days. Especially your shoulder."

Max sat up, bending and moving his newly healed arms. His eyes were heavy, but he smiled. "Thank you."

"Of course." Neith returned the gesture, but it was taut. Worry, fear, anger—all still pulsed through her.

Magnus approached, eyeing them. "I suspect news of this will travel among the ranks. It will make you the target of some and a champion to others. Many are growing tired of Roman and his antics, but he still has many friends. You should watch your backs."

Neith wanted to scream that they had been, and that she was tired of this. But she nodded instead.

Magnus extended his hand, pulling her to her feet. He beckoned her a short distance from the others. He avoided her eyes, gazing behind her. "What prompted this?"

"Roman approached us, unwarranted. He made insults toward me," she said, glancing back, "and to Sam… and the *nature* of our relationship."

Magnus's eyes grew tight, finally meeting hers. The anger in them nearly caused her to step back. He took in her face and sighed, then softened.

"You need to be careful." He reached up as if he would touch her, but paused, withdrawing his hand. Neith frowned. "Roman grows more bitter by the day, and losing here today will only fuel it. You need to be smarter."

She blinked. "What should I do?"

"You need to be sure you can trust those you keep around you."

Neith looked at the four on the ground. They were now talking and laughing. "I trust them."

"Then keep them close." He turned to leave. It was bizarrely abrupt.

"Magnus," she called after him. He turned back, nothing in his manner retaining its usual warmth. "As you said, many will speak of what happened this night. If my father hears the rumors, what will he do?" She needed to understand if Dryden spoke true. "I speak specifically about Sam and myself." Neith cast her eyes down, feeling sheepish.

Magnus inhaled, considering, his eyes unsure. "I cannot say."

Neith knew there were many words left unsaid. His hesitation sent her thoughts in wild directions. She could not help but feel she'd disappointed him somehow.

"Would Sam be in danger? Please answer me honestly. I know you care for him."

Magnus looked over her shoulder. "Perhaps," he said. "You see how… *temperamental* your father grows. It would not surprise me if he did not care at all, nor if he tossed Sam in a cell." His eyes narrowed on her as he leaned forward. "As I said before, you need to be smarter."

Smarter, not smart. His words confused her, but she nodded frantically, trying to swallow. "I understand."

He gave her a reluctant smile before turning and walking back toward the castle.

Neith stood for a moment, facing away from the others with her eyes closed, attempting to gather herself. When she turned back, Sam's eyes were on her. She gave him a look that said *later*.

Neith repaired a broken nose and several cuts on Petra before taking Sam back to her room. She was worried doing so would breathe life into the rumors, but she had to speak with him, and it had to be now.

She called for fresh water and towels and then sent the servants away. He sat on the edge of one of the tables, watching her intently as she cleaned the blood from his face, healing lacerations as she progressed. His gaze held an adoration that pained her, chipping away at the resolve for what she knew she had to do. He tucked a loose strand of hair behind her ear, letting his thumb trace her cheek. She couldn't help the soft smile that formed from it. He leaned in to kiss her, but she pulled back, walking to the washbasin. She filled it with fresh water and returned to continue her work. When she had the guts to look into his eyes, she found them confused and a little pained.

"What is wrong?" he asked.

"Did you know about Bellamy and the others? Did you know my father sent them?" Neith turned his face as she examined the cut above his eye.

Sam sighed. "No. But I suspected."

"I have to dismiss them."

"Do you?" He looked at her, considering. "Perhaps they joined because they were ordered to, but that does not mean that is why they stay."

"Magnus warned me to only keep people close that I can trust." The cut closed, now only a thin pink line. It wouldn't scar.

Sam shrugged. "Look them in the eye and ask. You'll know."

Neith exhaled as if the notion was ludicrous. She had little confidence in her judgment. She was questioning everything she had lived as truth for nineteen years.

"Why did you accept the challenge?" she asked, a touch irritated. "You could have refused."

"No, I could not have. Not after what he said to you." His arms wrapped around her waist, and she didn't have the heart to stop him.

She leaned her head against his, breathing him in. "He did it with intention. He knew it would get a rise from you. And now people will believe it true."

Sam didn't respond.

She stepped back, eyes rising to his. "Have you thought about what may happen if we were to be discovered?"

"Yes," he admitted.

Neith grabbed the hem of his tunic, gesturing for him to lift his arms. He released her, doing as she beckoned, wincing as she pulled it over his head. She ran her hands over his chest and sides, calling to his ether to discover his wounds. "Two of your ribs are fractured."

Sam didn't speak as she worked to heal them. He flinched when the bones snapped into place, but otherwise sat quietly, watching her. The more time that passed, the more sorrowful his eyes, as if he knew where she was going, what she was about to say. When she finished, she looked down, gathering courage.

When it didn't come, she sighed and touched his face. The sad, beautiful face of the man who fought for her. Who protected her. "We have to stop, Sam." Neith thought he would immediately protest, but he sat unmoving, eyes never leaving hers. She wished they weren't so beautiful, sparkling amber in the candlelight.

"Is that what you want?"

"No." She shook her head. "It is the farthest thing from what I want. But I cannot bear even the prospect of you getting hurt. What happened tonight was nothing. If my father finds out, I do not know what he will do. He may already know." Neith shivered at the thought. "And this feud with Roman isn't over. It will only escalate."

"We're fighting a war," he said, arms returning to her waist. "I could get hurt at any time. I could die any day."

Neith ran her fingers over the scar on his neck. She looked up at him with sad, but serious, eyes. "I will not be a contributing cause."

"I'm not afraid—"

"You should be," she said abruptly, grasping his face in her hand. Whether he was naive to the danger or simply being cavalier, both possibilities concerned her. "I'm serious, Sam."

He pulled her closer, resting his head against hers. "You are worth the risk."

Neith closed her eyes, fearing she was not strong enough to separate herself. "My father may have you killed."

"Neith, we do not know what he would do. He may not even care."

She shook her head, dismissing the notion. The temptation of it was too attractive to consider. "Perhaps not, but he grows further erratic by the day. You see how he has been since Calithea escaped. No one can predict what he will do." If he found out that she could have stopped them and chose not to… "He may hurt you to hurt me."

Sam frowned, drawing back. "Why would he hurt you? You are one of only two people he seems to truly care for."

"I do not know if I believe that anymore," she said, casting her eyes aside. "He needs me. That does not mean he cares for me." She tried to step back, but his arms tightened around her.

"Please don't pull away from me. Not again." His eyes darted between hers, the fervor in his voice growing. "Do not decide for me what I'm allowed to risk. You gave me a choice, and I chose."

"You don't understand—"

"No, Neith, it's *you* that doesn't understand." Sam released her, shaking his head. "You told Calithea Ironne you knew no one would risk themselves for you. But you are wrong."

"Don't say that." Neith closed her eyes. For nineteen years she thought she had purpose, belief… conviction. Told what to think, what to believe, how to feel. In less than two moons' time, so much had changed. Sam was a big part of it. The biggest part. "This world cannot afford to lose you." She reached up to touch his face, and he leaned into it. "Not over me."

He pulled back and stared at her, baffled, and for the first time she'd seen directed toward her, angry. "You speak about yourself as if you are nothing."

"I am nothing next to you."

"You are *everything!*" Sam stood and marched off, his hands on his head. He turned back to look at her from across the room. "You are everything beautiful, kind, and gentle in this world. You don't get to decide what I think or what I feel about you. I know who you are," he said, hand clamped to his chest. He exhaled, and it fell limp to his side. "Even if you do not."

"I am a *weapon*, Sam. A means for my father's ambition. I'm not a real person," she said, shaking her head. "I never have been. I wasn't raised to be. Not even born to be. I see that now."

Sam strode back, taking her face in his hands. "We are not what we are born to, Neith. If you are attempting to influence me away from you with accusations of your character, you will find it a useless tactic."

"I've killed people," she said. "I will kill many more before this is over."

He released her face, his hands trailing down her neck, gaze following. "So have I," he said, leaning down to kiss her. Neith could not find it in herself to pull away. It was soft and gentle. He whispered against her lips, "So will I."

"*Why?*" she asked, pulling back to find his eyes. "I try to make sense of it, but I cannot. I see you hesitate. I see what it does to you. You are not like the others, Sam. You have no family here. No ties. Why did you come?"

He stared at her for several breaths, then shrugged. "I thought I believed in it. In some ways, I do. I don't know. I don't know what I believe anymore." He looked down. "But everything is different now. Maybe I can't say why I came," he said, eyes returning to hers, "but I know why I stay."

Neith studied him, trying to read every sign on his face. "Why do you stay?"

"You know why." He edged closer, their bodies touching, gazing down at her. Looking into her. Through her.

"Tell me. *Please.*"

"Because I love you."

A sound escaped her. A sob, or gasp, she wasn't sure. He had said it without hesitation, and it stripped her of her defenses. As if it was and had always been.

"If you ask me to fight beside you, I will. If you ask me to stop fighting, I will. If you tell me you want to leave this place, I will take you." He reached for her hand, bringing the pink scar to his lips, then held it against his chest. "I am not Thrane's. I am yours."

Her lips parted with a sharp inhale. He stood before her, vulnerable and beautiful, and *hers.*

"You would... *leave* with me?"

"I would," he said, unmoving, unyielding.

She could have him executed for that admission alone. He knew this, and he was risking it all. On her. *For* her. "That is treason."

The word hung between them.

"So it is," he said. "Yet it is of little significance in all that I would do for you."

Neith closed her eyes, silent tears spilling down her cheeks.

"But, if you do not want me," he said, and released her hand, "I will find a way to let you go."

Her eyes snapped open, and she gaped at him. She nearly laughed at the absurdity of it. The vulnerability, the uncertainty in his eyes, made her feel like a villain. She reached forward, taking his face in her hands. She had to say it. Out loud. She had to meet him there.

"I wish that I could say beautiful things to you, as you say to me." She shook her head. "But I don't know how. I can tell you that I love you, because I do, but it does not feel adequate. It is not enough. What I feel, what you are to me, is so much more." The fear in his eyes eased. "You must know, surely you know, as you are mine, I am yours."

His lips crashed onto hers, feverish and desperate, and everything she needed to tell herself she would not leave his side. She had been a fool to even think it. Sam was the best person she'd ever known. Being loved by him was a gift. Not one she could believe she deserved, but not one she could refuse. She would never consider it again.

When the kiss stilled, he pulled back to look at her, holding her face. "We cannot be parted."

She was still afraid. Not of her father, or the war. Neith was afraid because she knew she was going to give herself to him. Completely, wholly, in every way she knew how. She feared what she would say next would strip him of the love he had only just professed.

"I let her go," she whispered. Her eyes went wide with the confession. It was as if she could not help herself. The words tumbled from her lips of their own accord.

Sam frowned. "What do you mean? *Let who go?*"

Neith didn't answer, only stared at him, stunned by what she'd confessed. Her shaking hand came up to cover her mouth, and she gasped, part in panic and part in relief that it no longer weighed on her.

Sam's hands moved to her shoulders. "Neith," he said, speaking slowly, "who did you let go?"

"*Calithea,*" she said, scarcely audible, carefully surveying his reaction.

His narrowed eyes studied her face at a frenzied pace. "Neith—"

"And two other women. Hawthorne and another I did not know. An Esērii woman who came for them. I chased them as they fled." She shook her head, shrugging her shoulders. "But I let them go." Neith said the last part with a wild laugh, as if she still did not believe her own actions.

"Gods..."

She watched as a flurry of thoughts spun behind his eyes. She feared the worst. "I betrayed my country."

Sam shook his head.

"I betrayed my father."

"*No*," he said. "What you did was make a decision not to betray yourself."

"I don't know what's happening to me," she cried, feeling her entire body shake. He pulled her against him, holding her tight. She fisted his tunic as she sobbed.

Sam pulled back, and his hands gripped her face. "You don't belong here. I've always known it. I know you," he said, almost strangely, as if confirming it for himself. He smiled, and the kindness in it, the admiration in it, had her leaning into his hands. She knew there was only one thing to be done.

"I want to leave this place," she said. "I want to leave this place with you."

80

Nara

"Look to the star of six that once was three."

AUTHOR UNKNOWN, C. 1500 BQ
TRANSLATED FROM SUMACIAN BY PARRY HAVERFORD
HAIS Z'NOSIŠ, 1204 AQ
RECOVERED 1203 AQ, SOMOS

Nara felt him before she heard his knock on her bedchamber's door. "Enter," she called.

It creaked open, and Harker stepped through. "Cerys asked me to come up."

She beckoned him to the desk where she sat, finishing a letter. She signed her name in ink, then held her right palm over it, burning the letters lightly with her ether. "This is for the council. I want you to go to the Citadel and bring back reinforcements. The girl is going with you. A ship is being crewed now."

"She agreed to go?" he asked, brows raised. "I'm surprised." He leaned back in his chair, hands clasped behind his head.

"Not yet," Nara answered, pouring wax onto the folded piece of parchment, "but she will." She pressed a stamp into the thick pool, leaving behind an impression of the eagle seal of the Citadel.

Harker frowned. "How do you know?"

Nara looked up from beneath heavy lashes, expression flat.

"Fair enough," he said, and chuckled. "Do you think she'll make it? If she does, it'll be interesting to see what she can do, being Sonia's daughter and all."

"If they can remove the bindings, and she survives it, then I think she has a chance." She sighed, a grimace forming. "Maybe not, I don't know. It's not going to be a pleasant experience." Nara pulled a fresh piece of parchment from the stack and started on another letter. This one to her mother.

"Aye," Harker said. "I feel for her. I think it's sad what they've done to her."

Nara's quill had yet to move from its starting position. She looked up at Harker. "Will you do something for me?"

"Of course."

"I cannot write this. Will you tell my mother and Sayeed of Sam? You are their friend. It would be best heard in person, from one who cares."

"Aye."

"And be sure to tell them to keep it quiet," she said, eyes imploring his. "We don't know who we can trust." He nodded, and she gave him a modest, grateful smile. She reached behind her for another sealed letter she'd completed the night before. "This one is for Meriah Turan. Place it in no hands other than her own. This is very important."

"Understood." Harker sat up, taking both letters in his hand. He tapped them on the table. "Do you ever ask yourself if we're doing the right thing? The Esērii, I mean. I'm not saying I believe what Lorcan believes, but maybe Sonia was right."

Nara inhaled, painfully deep, letting the air slowly escape. "I think about it every day. News of what happened here will eventually reach the southern continent. There is no way to contain it. I don't know what this means for us and what we do. The world is going to look very *different*."

Dread crept into his eyes, and Nara felt she likely looked the same. He slapped the table and stood. "Stay safe," he said, peering down at her. "Don't do anything stupid until I get back."

Nara chuckled and nodded, but both were ill at ease. "I wouldn't dream of letting you miss out on the fun."

He gave her a lopsided grin and turned, making for the door.

"Harker," Nara beckoned, and he looked back from the threshold. The brief jest fell from her face. "As fast as you can, yes?"

Nara found Thea on the beach. She was on her own, lying on the same large rock she'd found her on two nights before. "You're awfully fair-skinned to be sprawled out in the sun like that."

Thea sat up, squinting back toward her. "The sun brings me peace. If you've come to disrupt that, I beg you turn back and give me till midday."

Nara snorted and sat down next to her. Thea's eyes took her in.

"Why don't you wear shoes?" Thea asked.

"You're not wearing shoes," Nara said flatly, pointing to Thea's feet.

"I'm on the beach."

"So am I."

Thea sighed. "You know what I mean. You've scarcely worn them since we arrived in Eastwatche."

"Aren't you observant." Nara eyed her. "The way the sun brings you peace, I feel that way about the earth. Though it is not uncommon for wielders to go without shoes when practical. Especially the most powerful among us. Those able to tap into the ether around us, not only our own. It helps us channel."

"And that's you?" Thea asked, brow cocked.

Nara smirked, head tilting. "I saved you, didn't I?"

The ice melted a little from Thea's tone. "You did. Thank you." As if anticipating her, Thea added, "I still don't want to leave them."

Nara nodded. "I understand. It must be wonderful watching the man you love with his new wife."

Thea glared at her, not withholding her irritation. "Did you seek me out for a reason?"

"I was cruel the other day," Nara admitted.

"You were right." Thea looked to the opposite side of the beach. "You spoke the truth, and though you may be severely lacking tact, I would take it over the alternative."

Nara was not yet willing to admit she liked the girl, but would concede she was… interesting. "You need to go."

"I've already decided that I will."

A bark-like laugh tumbled from Nara's lips. "Just like that? Either I underestimate my ability to persuade, or you are dangerously fickle."

"I never said I wouldn't." Thea peered at her, sidelong, her tone a touch indignant. "I said I don't *want* to."

Nara huffed. "Days, you're an odd girl. You'll fit right in at the Citadel."

"Do not call me *girl*. You are, what," Thea asked, looking her up and down, "three years my elder?"

"Nearly six."

"Nearly six is not six. So five."

Nara couldn't stop her smile, and she caught Thea fighting one of her own.

Thea turned toward her, eyes narrowing. "Do you always converse as if you're playing a game?"

"Yes."

"*Why?*"

"I don't know." Nara leaned back on her elbows. "I suppose I enjoy when someone can give it back." Nara closed her eyes, lifting her face into the warmth of the sun. She found it far more tolerable than in the south. Perhaps, dare she say, pleasant.

"It reminds me of someone I met not long ago," Thea grumbled. "At least you actually say things. He was infuriatingly ambiguous."

Nara opened an eye to see Thea's face twisted into discontent, staring out at the sea. "Who was that?"

"His name was Alec Turan," she answered. "A cousin of Dorian of Sibreen."

Nara laughed from her belly, head falling back as it continued.

Thea turned to look at her, brows creased. "Do you know him?"

"I do," Nara said, still chuckling. "He is Etherborn, like us."

"Oh." A flurry of emotions flickered through Thea's features. "Yes, I suppose that seems obvious now."

"That's going to be interesting for you," Nara said, almost to herself. She rolled her eyes, remembering how he'd acted in Azmar.

Thea frowned. "What do you mean?"

"You'll find out soon enough."

Thea sighed, but didn't probe, only turned back to the sea. Her haunted eyes followed the waves crashing against the rocks. She had the unmistakable look one develops after insurmountable loss. The kind that never leaves. It pulled at a tiny thread in Nara's chest. Cerys had told her about what the Thraneans had put Thea through. About what she'd survived. Whatever Thea was thinking washed a subtle rage over her face. *Good,* Nara thought. She would need that, all of that, if she was going to survive mastering her gift, let alone the war.

Thea shifted forward on the rock, dipping her feet into the sand. "If I learn to use this *power*, as you call it. Will I be able to stop them?"

"You'll stand much more a chance than you do now." Nara moved forward to sit next to her. The sand was warm, and Nara watched Thea kick it about lazily. Whatever plagued her thoughts was still bouncing around.

"If I ask you a question, will you answer honestly?"

Nara considered for a breath. "I will."

"Will Eastwatche fall?"

Nara exhaled. "It is not a matter of if, but when."

Thea leaned forward, her head falling into her hands. Nara thought she was about to sob and considered retrieving Cerys, but no noise left her, nor did she shake.

"That is why we need every fighting person we can get. We must hold out long enough for your allies in the north to organize. The Citadel will send help, but it will take moons, maybe even a year before we can confidently hold Eastwatche, let alone think of an offensive countermove."

Thea stayed folded over for a time. The gentle crashing of waves was the only sound between them. Nara reached forward to pat her back, feeling painfully maladroit, but Thea sat up. Nara saw she had not been crying, quite the opposite. She looked resolute.

"Thank you for your candor. It is oddly comforting to receive truth for a change, even if it is not what one desires to hear." She turned toward Nara. "And thank you for what you did for me and everything you're doing here for my family. You have my gratitude. If, by chance, I am ever able to repay this debt, you will find me willing and able."

The sincerity with which Thea spoke made Nara uneasy. It was the second time she'd made such a claim. Nara wanted to make a jest or find some way to make light, but she found she cared not to hurt her. She gave her a reluctant smile. It felt awkward, and she groaned inside as she thought that perhaps Cerys was right about her. "Say your goodbyes, Thea Ironne, and then leave them all here. Put them, all of this," Nara said, gesturing around, "in the back of your mind. It is the only way you'll have a chance."

Thea looked down. A breeze came in from the water, catching her hair and concealing her face for a breath. When it receded, her eyes returned to Nara's. She nodded.

Nara clapped her on the back. "Come on, you're leaving now."

Thea stood, brushing sand from her skirts.

Nara was surprised she did not object to the rushed timetable. "Harker is going to take you to the Citadel. He has a letter explaining everything. When you're there, you'll meet a woman named Meriah. You can trust her." Nara intently did not share her family name.

"Meriah," Thea repeated.

"Harker is down at the dock waiting for you now. A ship is being prepared with a small crew and two Iren guards your brother is sending."

"You had them ready?" Thea asked. "How did you know I would agree?"

"I'm a convincing person."

Thea's brow creased. "Yes," she said. "I see that." Thea straightened her shoulders and held out her hand. "Until next we meet, Nara Nyanthi."

Nara reached forward, taking Thea's hand in her own, grasping it firmly. "Until next we meet." Nara watched her walk back to the keep, thinking for the first time that perhaps she might just have a chance.

81

Thea

"There is no one more free than one who has lost it all."

THE COST OF VALOR

AUTHOR UNKNOWN, 203 BQ

TRANSLATED FROM OLD ASARI BY MERIAH TURAN

HAIS Z'NOSIŠ, 1200 AQ

Thea didn't have much to pack. When she returned to her room, she found Marten sitting at the table by the window.

"You shouldn't be here, Marten," she said, closing the door behind her.

"I saw you on the beach with her. What did she say to you?"

"Nothing of concern," Thea lied. She walked to the trunk, pulling the two summer dresses gifted to her by her sister, tossing them onto the bed.

"She's awful," he said, turning toward her with a scowl.

"We need her. Without her, Cerys, and the others, we would all be prisoners of Thrane… or rotting in the earth." Thea moved to the dressing table, gathering a hairbrush and other articles of grooming.

"What are you doing?" he asked, watching her add to the pile on the bed.

Thea stopped, kneeling by his chair. She looked up at him, apprehensive for the words to come.

"Don't worry," he said, reaching for her hands, misunderstanding what plagued her. "We'll figure this out. Sending you to Sibreen for three years can't be the only option."

"I'm going, Marten."

He was still for a long moment until disbelief slowly twisted his features. He released her hands and sat back. "*No*, Thea."

Thea blinked. "*No?*"

"We don't know what's there. What if you're captured on the journey? What if it's not safe? There are far too many—"

She stood, staring down at him. "Marten, *stop*."

It was not quite shock on his face, but something like it. She could see he wanted to continue, but perhaps feared upsetting her.

Thea didn't have the drive to be offended over something so small. It only made her feel farther from him, firmer in her decision. "I have made up my mind."

Marten stood to face her. "*Why?*"

"I cannot stay here, not like this," she said, throwing her arms out to either side. "I feel like I'm tearing apart at the seams. I have no control over whatever this is, and it is scaring me."

"Thea," Marten said, eyes growing desperate as if finally believing she was serious, "*please.*"

"Please do not make this more difficult than it already is." This time she reached for his hands. "It is for the best."

He pulled free from her grip. "The best for whom? For you, for me? No, it is not."

"This is bigger than us. If there is any way I can help, I have to try."

"No," he said, shaking his head. "I don't want to be away from you. Everything has changed. We're at *war.*"

Thea sighed. It was time for her to accept there were parts of her Marten would never understand. She thought perhaps it had always been that way, only now it was unavoidable. "You're asking me to stay and be your whore, *again*. But what is worse, *so much worse*, is that you wish me to remain helpless. Dependent on those around me." She searched his eyes as they took on puzzlement. "And I do not think you even realize it." Thea thought over all the moments since the siege when she'd felt useless, like a burden. She would do anything not to feel that way again.

He scoffed. "You know I have never thought of you as a whore," he said, ignoring the second half of what she'd said. "Please do not insult me like that. Besides, you don't care what people think."

"Have you considered what it would be like for me? Waiting for you in my room at night, knowing the very next you'll spend with her." Thea shook her head. "I'm not doing that. I can't."

"I don't love her."

"You will in time," she said. "But it doesn't matter."

Pain washed over his face, and she could see he was fighting back tears. It injured her to be so cold, but she had to say goodbye. Nara had told her to leave it all there.

She tried again for his hand, and this time, he didn't pull away. "She'll be a good wife… a good mother to your children." Thea had no idea if that was true. It simply felt like the right thing to say.

He cast his gaze aside as the first tear fell. "That doesn't change my feelings for you."

She squeezed his hand, reaching up with her free one to hold his face. "It will. You'll see."

He looked at her like she was betraying him. "There's nothing I can say to make you stay, is there?"

She didn't answer, only shook her head.

Marten stepped back, gazing down. "When are you leaving?"

"Now."

"*Now?* What the fuck, Thea?" His hands covered his face, moving up and through his hair.

She grabbed her pack, tossing in her few belongings.

"I'll walk with you."

"No, I can't—I need you to stay here."

He looked hurt but didn't object. She wrapped her arms around him. He held on to her so tightly she struggled to breathe.

Letting go, he took her face in his hands and kissed her. It was desperate, but tender, and she didn't stop him. But she didn't feel it. That part of her was turned off.

Thea left her room knowing it was not the hardest goodbye she would make. She found Cerys and her brothers and sister waiting for her outside the hold. Cat had tears streaming down her cheeks, and Callum looked angry.

"Breeda is waiting by the boat," Cerys said. "When you're ready, I'll walk you down."

Thea nodded and turned to her sister.

Cat ran to her, wrapping her arms around her tight. "Please come back," she whispered.

"I will," Thea said, and meant it. She pulled back, holding Cat's shoulders. "You will say goodbye to the children for me? I do not think I can."

Cat nodded, chin trembling. Thea let go of her sister, knowing she could not linger.

Callum's face was red and full of fury. His right hand was busted and bleeding at the knuckles. "You don't have to do this."

"Yes, I do."

She knew he wanted to say more. He tugged her into a quick, but warm embrace. "You can change your mind at any time. I'll come and get you myself." He pulled back, glared at Conall, and stormed off.

Her eldest brother was difficult to read, as he always was. "Thank you," he said, and held out his hand. Thea could not remember a time they had ever touched. She clasped her hand in his, and he hesitated, but found her eyes and said, "Ire will grieve until her daughter has returned."

Thea nodded in quick succession, stunned by his display of affection. Conall released her hand, and she looked between her brother and sister several times before turning and walking away with haste. She didn't look back as she reached Cerys, and they continued the descent to the docks. Her hands were shaking, but she didn't cry. She only then realized she had not shed a tear since the day she jumped from her window. Not when they escaped, nor when she arrived in Eastwatche. She thought perhaps that part of her was broken. "I don't know what I'm walking into," she said to Cerys, her fear rising with every step. "I've never even been to Parthe."

Cerys stopped, turning to face her. "I wish I could go with you." She grabbed Thea's hands, giving them a squeeze. "I have no desire to lie to you, Thea. It won't be easy, but I *know* you can do this."

Thea wrapped her arms around her, holding her close. "In Highclere, we were true friends. It was real, yes?"

Cerys pulled back to look at her. "It was all real."

"Breeda told me she and my mother were sisters, not born of blood but forged by oath. If I return, then that is what we will be."

Cerys smiled, and her large brown eyes glistened under the bright sun. "*When* you return, that is what we shall be."

"You will look after my brothers and sisters?" The reality of where she was going, of what she was doing, threatened to overwhelm her. She felt at any moment she might break and take off running back to the keep.

"I will. Nara will as well. There is no one better to have here than her." Cerys leaned down to catch her gaze. "I swear it."

It gave her some small comfort.

They reached the dock where Breeda waited by the galleon. Crew members readied the ship, loading supplies.

Thea fell into her arms and stayed there for some time. Breeda stroked her hair as the dock swayed gently beneath them.

"The day your mother cast you into my arms was the hardest of my life," Breeda said. Thea felt her swallow. "I looked down at your little face as we sailed away, and knew I loved you then, as I love you now, and have every day between. I lost a sister, but gained a daughter."

Thea tightened her arms, feeling them shake.

"I know you are frightened. Allow yourself to be. Embrace it. Conquer it. So you know it cannot break you." Breeda pulled back and reached for Thea's face. "You have overcome so much, my brave girl. This is another part of your journey, and one day, when you are ready, it will bring you back here. To your home."

Harker took her pack and helped her onto the ship. They were drifting from the dock before she'd had a chance to gain her bearings.

She turned back to the keep. Marten was standing out on the parapet. Cat, Callum, and Conall watched from the beach below. She waved, and her brothers and sister returned it. Marten stood still, watching her sail away.

Thea walked to the front of the ship, looking out over the endless blue sea. Out toward the unknown. Nara's words replayed in her mind.

Leave them all here.

Epilogue

Neith looked up to a knock at her door. It was scarcely discernible against the sound of falling rain. She set her book on the desk beside her. "Come."

Expecting Maeve, she sat up straight when another emerged.

"*Magnus?*" Neith stood, but he raised his hand.

"Do not get up."

Neith noted the slight sway in his step as he closed the door and stalked toward her, taking hold of a spare chair on the way. He set it to face her a short distance before taking a seat. The scent of whiskey drifted in the air between them, thick and wet from the summer rain. He had not looked into her eyes. They were heavy in a way distinct from the drink. It fostered concern in her.

"Have you whiskey?" His deep, rumbling voice held the slightest of slurs.

Neith nodded and stood, walking charily across the room. Moonlight and gentle wind poured in from the open windows, setting a billow to the curtains. It caught the candles, flickering the dim light. She glanced back at him as she poured. His gaze was cast lazily into a dark corner of the room.

She returned with two full pony glasses. One for Magnus, and one for her that she had no intention to drink. He tossed the contents back before she returned to her chair.

The hair on her arms rose as she watched him sway in his seat. Thoughts of every kind took shape. As the silence grew, so did the anticipation, until it was heavy, crowding her chest. He struggled to speak. She looked away, feeling her gaze an exploitation.

She glanced toward the window as lightning struck. The crack of thunder caused her to jump.

"I had a daughter."

Neith's eyes flicked to his. Her mouth fell open, but no words escaped.

"She was still a little thing when I saw her last. I remember her face exactly as it was." There was grief in him, though muted by his indulgence. He stood and retrieved the bottle, bypassing the glass. He tossed it up, taking a large swig before setting it on the table between them.

Neith stared at him expectantly, struck by the confession and the strangeness of it, given their last interaction. A thousand questions tumbled through her mind.

"She is a woman grown now," he said. "I used to try to imagine what she looks like."

"*Magnus*," Neith said, low and mournful, but he held up his hand again.

"Do not pity me, Neith. I assure you, I do not deserve it." He took another drink. Neith feared he would fall from his chair should he continue.

"Where—"

"She is Esērii," he said, anticipating her query.

Neith nodded as an exasperated breath fell from her lips. "How have I not known this?"

He wiped the stream of whiskey trailing down his chin. "It is not something I often aspire to speak of." Regret, guilt, and something akin to misery washed over his face.

"Why are you telling me now? Why like this?" Neith felt strong in conflict of wanting to comfort him and understand his motivations. He had scarcely spoken to her the last moon, and when he did, he was short and reserved.

He ignored her questions. "I always knew I would see her again. Likely across a battlefield. Thousands of scenarios have plagued my thoughts over the years. All of them dreadful." Magnus set the bottle lazily on the ground beside him, and it toppled over, nothing inside to spill out. His face fell still. "I did not think it would be so soon."

Thunder cracked again.

Neith frowned. "You have seen her?"

"She was here," he said, his bloodshot eyes finally meeting hers, "in Highclere."

"During the battle?" Neith's breath quickened. Several Esērii had died during the siege.

He shook his head, and her frown deepened. His strange, indifferent expression stayed. The scrutiny in his gaze sent her shifting in her chair.

He leaned forward, resting his elbows on his knees, gaze returning to the shadows. "Your father is not an easy man. I know this," he said, almost to himself. "He values loyalty above all else. He demands it."

Neith retreated in her seat, puzzled by the swift change in subject.

"He cares for you in his way. The best way he can. But it is lost on no one it leaves many things to be desired." He glanced back with a reluctant tenderness. "I tried to be there for you in ways I knew he could not. I have loved you as my own daughter. Though I see now neither of us were truly up to the task."

Neith reached for the glass of whiskey she poured earlier and tipped it up. She let the empty cup fall clumsily back onto the table. "What is this?" she asked, trying to tame the anger building. "What are you doing?"

"You are grown now. As my daughter is. A woman making her own choices, deciding for herself her own beliefs." He gave her a taut smile. "I remember what it was like to be young. Driven by the ignorance and arrogance of it. How susceptible we are to dangerous thoughts. I know that all too well."

Her quickened heart was now thumping wildly in her chest. "If you've something to say, *say it.*"

"I, too, was a young person who made many mistakes. I worry for you, Neith," he said, his words turning to a plea. "You need to be smarter."

"Magnus," Neith said, laboring for patience. "What is—"

"The night of the escape," he interrupted.

Neith stiffened. "What about it?"

"That is when I saw her."

"I don't understand," she said, her irritation fading to alarm.

"Yes, you do," he said slowly, eyes settled on hers.

Neith looked down at the whiskey bottle, wishing it weren't empty. If this was a test, she was failing.

"I felt her," he said. "One does not forget their children, despite time and distance." His large, almond-shaped dark eyes grew angry in a way she'd not seen on him before. They turned wild with a meld of fury and frantic fear. It was a look she'd seen, but not on him. "I thought for a moment I would have to choose between you."

Neith felt her own eyes go painfully wide as realization crashed into her. The night of the escape, the alley. The woman with umber skin and large, defiant eyes. The same eyes she was looking into now. She remembered the fury, the desperation, in them. She remembered the familiarity she'd felt. It was mirrored before her now. A single panicked tear fell down her cheek. "You were there?"

Silence was his only answer. His anger faded as if the confession had relieved him of it.

"Does my father know?" The words came out far steadier than she'd expected.

He shook his head. "Our guilt is shared."

"Why?" she asked. "Why share yours?"

Magnus looked down for a moment, considering. When his eyes found hers again, they were steady, composed. "Secrets we bear alone eat away at us, Neith. They rot us from within."

Neith knew, far too well, precisely what he meant. What she did not know was if the concern was for her or for himself.

He stood, peering down as he towered above her. "So, you see, I have your secret, and you have mine," he said, low and with warning. "And we will never speak of them again."

ACKNOWLEDGMENTS

A Promise of Power lived in my head for years before it found its way to paper. It would have continued as such without the help of so many.

Thank you to my husband, Dan, for, well, literally everything. To Julie Tran for being the first person not married to me to read this beast of a book. To Courtney Kelley for your unwavering encouragement and belief in me. To Amanda Tucker for helping me piece together a blurb, which somehow felt more complicated than writing the 270k words. Thank you to all my friends, family, and community. Your support has meant everything.

Thank you to Kira Andrews and Maryssa Gammon. Your insights truly helped me shape the story. And to Timothy Repasky, thank you for your professionalism, patience, and kindness as you guided this first-time author.

And finally, to Shirl Atwell. Your belief in me from a young age built the foundation of my confidence, without which I would never have had the courage to write this story.

ABOUT THE AUTHOR

Rachel Enriquez is a former tech profes-
sional turned literary fantasy author driven
by a lifelong passion for immersive sto-
rytelling and imaginative world-building.
Based in Louisville, Kentucky, she lives
with her husband and their two sons. When
not writing, Rachel enjoys creating visual
art, diving into a great book or game, and
spending time with her family. Her work
explores identity, human connection, and
the consequences of power, blending layered plots, emotionally resonant characters,
and elements of the fantastic.

www.ingramcontent.com/pod-product-compliance
Lightning Source LLC
Chambersburg PA
CBHW060556300726

48975CB00005B/1348